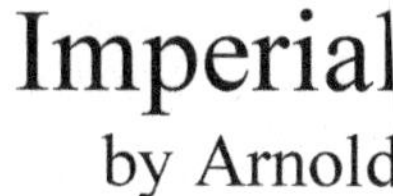

Imperial

by Arnold

Coming Soon
How I Stole 5.6 Million from Walmart
The Gods Return Loki's Trial
Zombie Squirrels

Loki's Publishing

Seattle, WA

Contents

Chapter 1 4 A.M.

Evelyn came down by the lift into the great front-hall. One of the clocks there showed seven minutes to four; the other showed six minutes to four. He thought: "I should have had time to shave. This punctuality business is getting to be a mania with me." He smiled sympathetically, forgivingly, at his own weakness, which the smile transformed into a strength. He had bathed; he had drunk tea; he was correctly dressed, in the informal style which was his--lounge-suit, soft collar, soft hat, light walking-stick, no gloves; but he had not shaved. No matter. There are dark men who must shave every twelve hours; their chins are blue. Evelyn was neither dark nor fair; he might let thirty hours pass without a shave, and nobody but an inquisitive observer would notice the negligence.

The great front-hall was well lighted; but the lamps were islands in the vast dusky spaces; at 2 a.m. the chandeliers--sixteen lamps apiece--which hung in the squares of the panelled ceiling ceased to shower down their spendthrift electricity on the rugs and the concrete floor impressively patterned in huge lozenges of black and white. Behind the long counters to the right of the double revolving doors at the main entrance shone the two illuminated signs, "Reception" and "Enquiries," always at the same strength day and night. The foyer down the steps, back beyond the hall, had one light. The restaurant down the steps beyond the foyer had one light. The reading-room, cut out of the hall by glass partitions, had no light. The grill-room, which gave on a broad corridor opposite the counters, had several lights; in theory it opened for breakfasts at 6 a.m., but in fact it was never closed, nor its kitchen closed.

Reyer, the young night-manager, in stiff shirt and dinner-jacket, was sitting at the Reception counter, his fair, pale, bored, wistful face bent over a little pile of documents. An Englishman of French extraction, he was turning night into day and day into night in order to learn a job and something about human nature. He would lament, mildly, that he never knew what to call his meals; for with him dinner was breakfast and breakfast dinner; as for lunch, he knew it no more. He had been night-manager for nearly a year; and Evelyn had an eye on him, had hopes of him--and he had hopes of Evelyn.

As Evelyn approached the counter Reyer respectfully rose.

"Morning, Reyer."

"Good morning, Mr. Orcham. You're up early."

"Anything on the night-report?" Evelyn asked, ignoring Reyer's remark.

"Nothing much, sir. A lady left suite 341 at three o'clock."

"Taxi or car?"

"Walked," said Reyer the laconic.

"Let me see the book."

Reyer opened a manuscript volume and pushed it across the counter. Evelyn read, without any comment except "Um!" At 10 a.m. the night-report would be placed before him, typewritten, in his private office. He moved away. Near the revolving doors stood Samuel Butcher (referred to, behind his back, as Long Sam), the head night-porter, and a couple of his janissaries, all in blue and gold.

"Well, Sam," Evelyn greeted the giant cheerfully.

"Morning, sir," Sam saluted.

The janissaries, not having been accosted, took care not to see Evelyn.

"I gather you haven't had to throw anyone out to-night?" Evelyn waved his cane.

"No, sir." Sam laughed, proud of the directorial attention. Evelyn pulled out a cigarette. Instantly both the janissaries leapt to different small tables on which were matches. The winner struck a match and held it to Evelyn's cigarette.

"Thanks," Evelyn murmured, and, puffing, strolled towards the back of the hall, where he glanced at himself in a mighty square column faced with mirror.

2.

No! The nascent beard was completely invisible. Suit correct, stylish. Handkerchief peeping correctly out of the pocket. Necktie--he adjusted the necktie ever so little. Shoes correct--not a crease in them. Well, perhaps the features lacked distinction; the angle of the nose was a bit too acute; the lower lip heavy, somewhat sensual. But what friendly keen brown eyes! What delicate ears! And the chin--how enigmatic! The chin would puzzle any reader of the human countenance. Forty-seven. Did he feel forty-seven? Could he even believe that he was forty-seven? He felt thirty--thirty-one. And the simpleton thought that he looked at most thirty-five. In two and a half years, however, he would be fifty. God! What a prospect! Well, he didn't care one damn how old he was, or looked, so long as he felt ... On the whole, quite a presentable creature. But nobody would glance twice at him in the street. Nobody could possibly guess that he was anyone out of the ordinary. A pity, possibly. Yet what is, is, and must be accepted with philosophy. Nevertheless, he was acquainted with idiots, asses, greenhorns and charlatans whose appearance was so distinguished that they could not enter a restaurant without arousing respectful curiosity. Funny world.

The séance at the mirror lasted three seconds--time to adjust the necktie, no more. He moved off. The clock over the counter showed five minutes to four. Clocks had their moods; they raced, they stood still, in discordance with the mood of the beholder, maliciously intent on exasperating him.

Within recent months Evelyn had hung the walls of the great hall with large, old coloured prints of antique, sunk or broken-up Atlantic liners, and underneath each a smaller photograph of a modern vessel. He glanced at an American print of a French liner of the sixties, paddle and sail. He read the quaint legend beneath: "Length 375 feet. Breadth of beam 46.Depth of hold 33. Burthen 3,500 tons. Horse-power, 1,250."*Burthen.* Comic! Yet in her time this ship had been a crack. Under the print was a photograph of the "Ile-de-France." Yes, this idea of his of marine prints in the hall had been extremely successful. It was aimed at American visitors, who constituted sixty per cent. of the clientele, and it hit them all day and every day. Difficult at certain hours to pass through the great hall without seeing an American gazing entranced at a marine print.

That contrarious clock still showed five minutes to four. Long Sam stood moveless; his janissaries stood moveless; young Reyer sat moveless. The electric lamps burned with the stoical endurance of organisms which have passed beyond time into eternity. The great hall seemed to lie under an enchantment. Its darkened extensions, the foyer and the immeasurable restaurant, seemed to lie under an enchantment. The brighter corridor and grill-room seemed to lie under an enchantment. Diminished men awaited with exhaustless patience the birth of day, as they might have awaited the birth of a child.

Chapter 2 ARRIVALS

Sound and lights of a big car, heard and seen through the glazed frontage of the hall! Revolution of the doors! Long Sam was already outside; his janissaries were outside; the doors were whizzing with the speed of the men's exit. Reyer came round the counter. The enchantment was smashed to bits: phenomenon as swift and unexpected as a street-accident. Evelyn wondered who could be arriving with such a grandiose pother at four o'clock in the morning. But his chief concern was the clock, which now showed three minutes to four. If Jack Cradock did not appear within three minutes the stout, faithful little man would be late for his rendezvous. And it was Jack's business to be not merely on time but before time. Evelyn was uneasy. Uneasily he glanced down the dim vista of the foyer and the restaurant, his back to the doors through which Jack ought to enter. He heard voices: Long Sam's, Reyer's and another's.

He turned, in spite of himself, at the tones of that third voice, polite, but curt, assured, authoritative. Between a felt hat and a huge overcoat he saw a face with which he was not unacquainted, Sir Henry Savott's (baronet). Then he remembered that Sir Henry, passenger by the "Caractacus"--45,000 tons--from New York, had reserved two suites overlooking the park. A small, spry, rather desiccated face, with small, searching eyes, a clipped, iron-grey military moustache, and a bony, imperious chin. Staring curiously about as he talked to Reyer, Sir Henry descried Evelyn, and, unceremoniously leaving Reyer, stepped spryly towards the Director, who advanced to meet him in the middle of the hall. False youthfulness, thought Evelyn, proud of his own comparative youthfulness. The fellow must be fifty-seven, and pretending to be forty-seven--unsuccessfully! The two shook hands with mutual smiles.

"Hope you haven't got up specially to meet us," said Sir Henry. "Too bad!"

"No," said Evelyn quietly and carelessly.

The infernal impudence of these spoilt millionaires! To imagine that he, Evelyn, would get up specially to meet anybody on earth!

"I'm glad," said Sir Henry, who was sorry, hiding all consciousness of a rebuff.

"See. You've come by the 'Caractacus'?"

"Yes. My daughter has driven me and her maid and some of the light stuff up from Southampton. She's the devil's own driver, Gracie is, particularly at night. There are two or three cars behind us. But most of the passengers preferred to have their sleep out on the ship and wait for the boat-train."

"You're three days late," said Evelyn.

"Yes," Sir Henry admitted.

"Funny rumours about that ship," said Evelyn.

"Yes," said Sir Henry darkly, in a manner definitely to close the subject of rumours. He was a large shareholder in the company which owned the line.

Evelyn perceived two girls in conversation with an assiduous and impressed Reyer. The young man's deportment was quite good, if a trifle too subservient. One of the girls wore a magnificent leather coat. Doubtless Gracie, celebrated in the illustrated press for her thrilling performances at the wheel at Brooklands. The other, less warmly clad, must be the maid.

Gracie looked suddenly round, and Evelyn saw her face, which however he hardly recognised from the photographs of it in illustrated papers. At a distance of twenty feet he felt the charm of it--vivacious, agreeable, aware of its own power. Perhaps very beautiful, but he could not be sure. Anyhow, the face--and the gestures--of an individuality. Evelyn at once imagined her as a mistress; and as he fenced amiably with the amiable Sir Henry, who he had some reason to believe would one day soon be trying to engage him in high finance, his mind dwelt upon the idea of her as a mistress. He was not an over-sensual man; he was certainly not lascivious. He was guilty of no bad taste in conceiving this girl, whom he now saw for the first time, as a mistress in the privacy of his heart. What goes on in a man's heart is his own affair. And similar thoughts, on meeting young and attractive women, wander in and out of the hearts of the most staid and serious persons, unsuspected by a world of beholders apt to reason too conventionally. Evelyn's was an entirely serious soul, but it had a mortal envelope. He was starved of women. For years women had been his secret preoccupation. He desired intimacy with some entrancing, perfect woman. Not the marital intimacy. No. Never again the marital intimacy. He would make sacrifices for the desired intimacy. But not the supreme sacrifice. Work first, career first, woman second, even were she another Helen.

For nearly twenty years Evelyn had been a widower. Six weeks after his marriage a daily series of inescapable facts had compelled him to admit to himself that his wife was a furiously self-centred neurotic who demanded as a natural right everything in exchange for nothing. An incurable. He had excused her on the ground that she was not to be blamed for her own mental constitution. He had tolerated her because he was of those who will chew whatever they may have bitten off. He had protected himself by the application of the theory that all that happens to a man happens in his own mind and nowhere else, and therefore that he who is master of his own mind is fortified against fate. A dogma; but it suited his case. At the end of three years Adela had died, an unwilling mother with a terrific grievance, in childbed; and the child had not survived her. The whole experience was horrible. Evelyn mourned. His sorrow was also a sigh of transcendent relief. Agonising relief, but relief. Not till the episode was finished did he confess to his mind how frightfully he had suffered and how imperfectly he had been master of his mind. He had never satisfactorily answered the great, humiliating question: "How could I have been such a colossal fool, so blind, so deaf, so utterly mistaken in my estimate of a woman?" He was left with a quiet but tremendous prejudice against marriage. I have had luck this time, he thought. Once is enough. Never again! Never again! He divided wives into those who were an asset and those who were a liability; and his strong inclination was to conclude, in the final judgment, that of all the wives he knew not one was an asset. One or two of them might have the appearance of an asset, yet if you could penetrate to essentials, if you could learn the inner conjugal secrets, was there one who was not a liability? He tried to stand away from himself and see that he was prejudiced, but he could never honestly convict himself of a prejudice in this matter.

He saw the maid and Reyer pass towards the lift like apparitions. He noticed that the pretty but tired maid was well-dressed, probably in clothes that a few months earlier her mistress had been wearing; but that nevertheless every nervous movement and glance of the girl divulged her station. He heard Sir Henry's voice and his own like faint echoes. He saw the janissaries pass towards the lift like apparitions carrying ghostly suit-cases. He saw Miss Savott herself go towards the doors like an apparition, then hesitate and glide towards her father like an apparition. And in those brief seconds the sole reality of his mind was the three years of marriage with Adela, years whose thousand days and a day swept in detail through his memory with the miraculous rapidity of a life re-lived by a drowning man.

"Gracie, this is my friend, Mr. Orcham, the king of his world--I've told you. My daughter."

And now Gracie was the reality. Instinctively he put one hand to his chin as he raised his hat with the other. Why had he not shaved? The hair on his enigmatic chin seemed half an inch long.

"I do hope you haven't got up specially to meet us," said Gracie.

Her father's words, but spoken differently! What a rich, low, emotional, sympathetic voice, full of modulations! A voice like shot silk, changing at every syllable!

"No, I didn't," he replied. "But if I'd known you'd be here so early I certainly might have done. The fact is, I've got up to go with my meat-buyer to Smithfield Market."

He looked and saw the faithful Cradock standing meekly expectant at the entrance. The dilatory clock at last showed four.

"I must just lock up the car," said Gracie. "Shan't be two minutes." She ran off.

"I'm going to bed," Sir Henry called after her.

"All right, daddy," she called back, not stopping.

"I'm fortunate enough to be able to sleep whenever I want to!" said Sir Henry to Evelyn. "Useful, eh?"

"Very," Evelyn agreed.

Wonderful with what naïve satisfaction these millionaires attributed to themselves the characteristics of Napoleon! He accompanied Napoleon to the lift, and stayed for a moment chatting about the hotel. It was as if they were manœuvring for places before crossing the line in a yacht race.

2.

When Evelyn returned to the hall Gracie Savott also was returning. She now carried the leather coat on her arm, revealing a beige frock.

"No, no," she said when he offered to take the coat. "But have you got a gasper?"

"I never smoke anything else," said Evelyn.

"Neither do I," said Gracie. "Thanks."

He thought: "What next?"

The next was that Gracie moved a few feet to a table, Evelyn following, and put the newly lighted cigarette on an ash-tray, opened her bag, and began to titivate her face. She was absorbed in this task, earnest over it; yet she could talk the while. He somehow could not examine her features in detail; but he could see that she had a beautiful figure. What slim ankles! What wrists! *Les attaches fines.* She had a serious expression, as one engaged on a matter of grave importance. She dabbed; she critically judged the effect of each dab, gazing closely at her face in the hand-mirror. And Evelyn unshaved!

"Has daddy really gone to bed?" she asked, not taking her eyes off the mirror.

"He has."

"He's a great sleeper before the Lord. I suppose he told you about our cockleshell the 'Caractacus.'"

"Not a word. What about it? We did hear she'd been rolling a bit."

"Rolling a bit! When we were a day out from New York, she rolled the dining-room windows under water. The fiddles were on the tables, but she threw all the crockery right over the fiddles. I was the only woman at dinner, and there wasn't absolutely a legion of men either. They said that roll smashed seventeen thousand pounds' worth of stuff. I thought she'd never come up again. The second officer told daddy next day that *he* never thought she'd come up again. It was perfectly thrilling. But she did come up. Everyone says she's the worst roller that ever sailed the seas."

During this narration Gracie's attention to the mirror did not relax.

"Well," said Evelyn calmly. "Of course it must have been pretty bad weather to make a big ship like that three days late."

"Weather!" said Gracie. "The weather was awful, perfectly dreadful. But it wasn't the weather that made her three days late. She split right across. Yes, split right across. The observation-deck. A three-inch split. Anyhow I could put my foot into it. Of course it was roped off. But they showed it to daddy. They had to. And I saw it with him."

"Do you mean to say--" Evelyn began, incredulous.

"Yes, I do mean to say," Gracie stopped him. "You ask daddy. Ask anyone who was on board. That's why she's going to be laid up for three months. They talk about 're-conditioning.' But it's the split."

"But how on earth--?" Evelyn was astounded more than he had ever been astounded.

"Oh! Strain, or something. They *said*it was something to do with them putting two new lifts in, and removing a steel cross-beam or whatever they call it. But daddy says don't you believe it. She's too long for her strength, and she won't stand it in any weather worth talking about. Of course she was German built, and the Germans can't build like us. Don't you agree?"

"No. I don't," said Evelyn, with a smile to soften the contradiction, slightly lifting his shoulders.

"Oh, you don't? That's interesting now."

Evelyn raised his cane a few inches to greet Jack Cradock, who replied by raising his greenish hard hat.

"Now," thought Evelyn, somewhere in the midst of the brain-disturbance due to Gracie's amazing news. "This is all very well, but what about Smithfield? She isn't quite a young girl. She must be twenty-five, and she knows that I haven't got up at four o'clock for small-talk with women. Yet she behaves as if I hadn't anything to do except listen to her. She may stay chattering here for half an hour."

He resented this egotistical thoughtlessness so characteristic of the very rich. At the same time he was keenly enjoying her presence. And he liked her expensive stylishness. The sight of a really smart woman always gave him pleasure. In his restaurant, when he occasionally inspected it as a spy from a corner behind a screen, he always looked first for the fashionable, costly frocks, and the more there were the better he was pleased. He relished, too, the piquancy of the contrast between Gracie's clothes and the rough masculinity of her achievements on Brooklands track in the monstrous cars which Sir Henry had had specially built for her, and her night-driving on the road from Southampton. Only half an hour ago she had probably been steering a big car at a mile a minute on a dark curving road. And here with delicate hands she was finishing the minute renewal of her delicate face. Her finger-nails were stained a bright red.

So the roll from which nobody hoped that the ship would recover, the roll which had broken seventeen thousand pounds' worth of stuff, was merely 'thrilling' to her. And she had put her little foot into the split across the deck. What a sensation that affair ought to cause! What unique copy for the press! Nevertheless, would it cause a sensation? Would the press exploit it? He fancied not. The press would give descriptive columns to the marvels and luxuries of a new giant liner. But did anybody ever read in any paper--even in any anti-capitalistic paper--that a famous vessel rolled, or vibrated, or shook? Never! Never a word in derogation! As for the incredible cross-split, result of incorrect calculations of the designer, no editor would dare to refer to it in print. To do so would damage Atlantic traffic for a whole season--and incidentally damage the hotel business. The four-million-pound crack was protected by the devoted adherence of the press to the dogma that transatlantic liners are perfect. And let no one breathe a word concerning the relation between editors and advertisement-managers.

Miss Savott had kept the leather coat on her arm while doing her face. The face done, and her bag shut again, she dropped the cloak on the small table by her side. Womanish! Proof of a disordered and inconsequent mind. She resumed the cigarette, which had been steadily sending up a vertical wavering wisp of smoke.

"Mr. Orcham," she said ingratiatingly, intimately, stepping near to him, "will you do something for me? . . .I simply daren't ask you."

"If I can," he smiled. (Had experience taught her that she was irresistible?)

"Oh, you *can!* I've been dying for years to see Smithfield Market in the middle of the night. Would you mind very much taking me with you? I would drive you there. The car's all ready. I didn't lock it up after all."

Here was his second amazement. These people were incredible--as incredible as the split in the 'Caractacus.' How did she suppose he could transact his business at Smithfield with a smart young woman hanging on to him?

She added, like an imploring child:

"I won't be in the way. I'd be as small as a mouse."

They read your thoughts.

Not 'as quiet as a mouse.' 'As small as a mouse.' Better. She had a gift for making her own phrases.

"But surely you must be terribly tired. I've had four and a half hours' sleep."

"Me! Tired! I'm like father--and you--I'm never tired. Besides, I slept my head off on the ship."

She looked appealingly up at him. Yes, irresistible! And she well knew it!

"Well, if you really aren't too tired, I shall be delighted. And the market is very interesting."

And in fact he was delighted. There were grave disadvantages, naturally; but he dismissed them from his mind, to make room for the anticipation of being driven by her through the night-streets of London. Sitting by her! He was curious to see one of these expert racing drivers, and especially the fastest woman-driver in the world, at the wheel.

"You're frightfully kind," said she. "I'll just--"

"How did you know I'm never tired?" he interrupted her.

"I could see it in your shoulders," she answered. "You aren't, are you?"

"Not often," he said, proud, thrilled, feverish.

"See it in my shoulders," he thought. "Odd little creature. Her brain's impish. That's what it is. Well, perhaps she can see it in my shoulders." Indeed he was proud.

"I'll just fly upstairs one moment. Shan't keep you. Where's the lift?" But she had descried the lift and was gone.

"Reyer," he called. "Just see Miss Savott to her suite."

Reyer ran. The lift-man judiciously waited for him.

And Evelyn, Nizam of the immense organism of the hotel, reflected like an ingenuous youth:

"I know everyone thinks I'm very reserved. And perhaps I am. But she's got right through that, *into* me. And she's the first. She must have taken a liking to me. Here I've only known her about six minutes and she's--" Somewhere within him a point of fire glowed. He advanced rather self-consciously towards the waiting Cradock. And, advancing, he remembered that, on her first disappearance, after saying she would be two minutes, Gracie Savott had been away only half a minute. She was not the sort of girl to keep a man waiting. No!. . . But barely half his own age.

Chapter 3 THE MEAT-BUYER

Jack Cradock's age was fifty-nine. He was short, stoutish, very honest, and very shrewd. His clothes were what is called 'good,' that is to say, of good everlasting cloth well sewed; but they had no style except Jack's style. His income nearly touched a thousand a year. With his savings he bought house-property. No stocks and shares for him. He had as fine an eye for small house-property as for a lamb's carcass. He had always been in the Smithfield trade. His father had been a drover when cattle strolled leisurely to London over roads otherwise empty. He went to bed at eight o'clock, and rose at three--save on Sundays. Daylight London seemed to him rather odd, unnatural.

He had been meat-buyer to the hotel in the years when it was merely a hotel among hotels, before Evelyn took control of it. In those years there existed in the buying departments abuses which irked Jack's honesty. He saw them completely abolished. He saw the hotel develop from a hotel among hotels into the unique hotel, whose sacred name was uttered in a tone different from the tone used for the names of all other hotels. He recognised in Evelyn a fellow-devotee of honesty in a world only passably honest; a man of scrupulous fairness, a man of terrific industry, a man of most various ability and most quiet authority, a real swell. Jack had heard that Evelyn gave lectures on wines to his own wine-waiters, that he tasted every wine before purchase, and chose every brand of cigar himself; and Jack marvelled thereat. He had heard, further, that Evelyn knew everything about vegetables; but Covent Garden, which he regarded as a den of thieves, had no interest for Jack. Apart from potatoes and occasional broad beans and spring onions, he never ate vegetables; salads he could not bear.

Of course Evelyn did not know as much about meat as Jack--who did?--but he knew a lot, and he did not pretend to more knowledge than he possessed. That was what Jack liked in Evelyn: absence of pretence. He adored Evelyn with a deep admiration and a humble, sturdy affection equally deep. Evelyn often asked after his wife, and the boy in the navy.

He was now waiting for his august governor with impatience well concealed. He saw Gracie run off to the lift. He himself had never been in any but the service-lifts. He had never seen the restaurant except when it was empty and the table-tops dark green instead of white, and the chairs packed; but he knew the restaurant-kitchen, and had frequent interviews with the gesticulatory and jolly French chef in the chef's office outside whose door two clerks worked. He had never been in any bedroom. He imagined all manner of strange and even unseemly happenings in the suites. He rarely had glimpses of the hotel's clientele, and his shrewd notion was that he would be antipathetic to it. Still, it wanted the best meat, and he provided the best meat; and that was something. He strove conscientiously to think well of the clientele.

He did not like the look of Miss Gracie Savott. She coincided too closely with what he would describe in his idiom as 'a bit too tasty.' He was aware that women, more correctly ladies, smoked, but he objected to their smoking, especially the young ones; his married daughter, nevertheless a fine and capricious piece, did not smoke, and had she attempted to do so would probably have been dissuaded from persevering by physical violence at the joint hands of her father and her husband. As a boy he had seen ancient hags smoking short clay pipes on the house-steps of large villages. A hag, however, was a hag, and a cutty pipe suited her indrawn lips. But that a fresh young girl, personable, virginal, should brazenly puff tobacco--that was different.

Nor could he approve of Gracie's general demeanour towards the governor. Too bold, too insinuating, too impudent. Hardly decent! Most shocking of all was the spectacle of Gracie daring--daring to paint and powder her saucy face in the presence of the governor. Shameless! And the governor tolerated it! If the governor had not been above all criticism Jack would have ventured in his heart to criticise the demeanour of the governor towards Gracie. Too boyish, too youthful; a hint of the swain about it! Well, the chit was gone now.

2.

The governor strolled slowly down the hall to the doors where Jack stood waiting. A little self-conscious, the governor was, in his walk. Seldom before had Jack seen the governor self-conscious. His confidence in the governor was a great solid rock. He felt a momentary tremor in the rock. It ceased; it was not a tremor; it was imperceptible: he had been mistaken. Yet...

"Morning, Jack. Sorry to keep you. Shan't be a minute."

"Morning, governor. No hurry, but we ought to be getting along. I have a taxi waiting." The customary tranquil benevolence of the governor's tone reassured him.

"Just tell me again about that Jebson young man. I want to know exactly before I see him. You said he's only recently come into the business."

"Yes, sir," Jack began. "And if you ask me, he thinks he's the emperor of Smithfield. His uncle's a tough 'un, but nothing to young Charlie Jebson. I get on pretty comfortably with everybody in the markets except him. Tries to make out he don't care whether he does business or not. But he can't put that across me. No! And everybody but him knows he can't. His uncle knows it. Ten shilling a stone's the right price for the best Scotch. And Charlie knows that too. But 'ten and six,' he says. 'Ten and two,' I say, wishing to meet him. 'Ten and two! You've got the b. ten and two fever, Cradock,' he says. 'And you've got the b. half-guinea fever.' I says. 'Don't ask me to come back,' I says. 'Because I shan't. I've got my best coat on,' I says. Then he turns on me and gives me a basinful, and I give him one. Nothing doing, governor. And his uncle's afraid of him. It was all over the Market."

"Well," said Evelyn, with a faint, mild smile. "We'll give him a miss in future."

"Yes, governor," said Jack anxiously. "But supposing he takes it, supposing he accepts of it! Jebsons have the finest Scotch beef in the market. It was Charlie's grandfather as started the Scotch beef trade in Smithfield. And the best Scotch--it's none so easy to come by. Sometimes three days and I don't see a side I fancy--not what you may call *the* best."

"Try him with ten and four."

"Yes, governor, and have all the rest of 'em jumping at me. Besides, I told him ten and two was my last word."

"That's enough," said Evelyn. "If you said it you said it, and we shan't go back on you, even if we have to buy Argentine!" He soothingly patted Jack's shoulder.

Jack was more than soothed--he was delighted. This was the rock, and never had it quivered.

"The fact is," said Jack in an easier tone, "Charlie's got it into his head that I'm making a bit on it. And that's why when you said you'd come up with me one morning and show yourself, I thought it 'ud be a good move. If that won't settle Master Charlie, I don't know what will."

To himself Jack was thinking: "Well then, why doesn't he come? I could have told him all this in the taxi. And this is the first time I've ever had to tell him anything twice. I'm going to be late."

"Listen!" said Evelyn, after some more unnecessary talk. "You go on. Take the taxi you've got. I'll follow. I'll ask for Jebsons', and you'll find me somewhere near it. Sir Henry Savott--very important customer and a very important man too, in the City--wants me to take his daughter and show her Smithfield. Bit awkward. Couldn't refuse though. They have a car here. I might get there before you, Jack." Evelyn laughed.

Jack mistrusted the laugh. He had no suspicion that the paragon of honesty had told him a lie; but he mistrusted the tone of voice as well as the laugh. Something a wee bit funny about it.

"Do you mean that young lady you were talking to, governor?" Jack asked in a voice that vibrated with apprehension.

"Yes, that's the one. Off you go now."

Jack passed quickly in silence through the revolving doors. He was thunderstruck. He could hardly have been more perturbed if the entire hotel had fallen about his ears. The entire hotel had indeed fallen about his ears. The governor, the pattern, the exemplar, the perfect serious man, taking that prancing hussy into Smithfield Market! Of all places! There was never a woman to be seen in Smithfield before nine o'clock, unless it might be a street-singer with her man going home after giving a show outside the Cock Tavern. The talk to-morrow morning! The jokes he'd have to hear afterwards--and answer with better jokes! Rock? The rock was wobbling from side to side, ready to crash, ready to crush him. He climbed heavily into the taxi, sighing.

Chapter 4 THE DRIVE

For the first ten minutes of waiting Evelyn forgave the girl. During the second ten minutes he grew resentful. It was just like these millionaires to assume that nothing really mattered except their own convenience. Did she suppose that he had risen at three-thirty for the delight of frittering away twelve, sixteen, nineteen irrecoverable minutes of eternity while she lolled around in her precious suite? Monstrous! Worse, he was becoming a marked man to Reyer, Long Sam, and the janissaries. They did not yet know that he was waiting for a girl; but they would know the moment she appeared and went off with him. Worse still, she was destroying the character with which he had privately endowed her. She arrived, smiling. And in an instant he had forgotten the twenty minutes, as one instantly forgets twenty days of bad weather when a fine day dawns.

"Sorry to keep you. Complications," said she, with composure.

He wondered whether the complications had been caused by a forbidding father.

She had changed her hat, and put on a thin, dark, inconspicuous cloak.

The car was Leviathan. A landaulette body, closed. She opened one of its front-doors, and picked up a pair of loose gloves from the driver's seat. An attendant janissary found himself forestalled, and had to stand unhelpful.

"Open?" she asked, in a tone expecting an affirmative answer.

"Rather."

"No. I'll do it. This is a one-girl hood. You might just wind down the window on your side."

In ten seconds the car was open.

"But I'm going to sit by you," said Evelyn.

She was lowering the glass partition behind the driver's seat.

"Of course," said she. "But I like it all open so that the wind can blow through."

By the manner in which she manœuvred Leviathan out of the courtyard, which an early cleaner had encumbered with a long gushing hose-pipe, Evelyn knew at once that she was an expert of experts. In a moment they were in Birdcage Walk. In another moment they were out of Birdcage Walk, and slipping into Whitehall. In yet another moment they were in the Strand. It was still night. The sun had not given the faintest announcement to the revolving earth's sombre eastern sky that he was mounting towards the horizon. There was an appreciable amount of traffic. She never hesitated, not for the fraction of a second. Her judgment was instantaneous and infallible. Her accelerations and decelerations, her brakings, could hardly be perceived. Formidable Leviathan was silent. Not a murmur beneath the bonnet. But what speed--in traffic! Evelyn saw the finger of the speedometer rise to forty--forty-two.

"Do you know the way?" he asked.

"I do," she replied.

Strange that she should know the way to Smithfield.

Suddenly she said:

"What brought *you* into the hotel business?"

He replied as suddenly:

"The same thing that brought you to motoring. Instinct. I was always fond of handling *people,* and organising."

"Always? Do you mean even when you were a boy?"

"Yes, when I was a boy. You know, clubs and things, and field-excursions. I managed the refreshment department at Earl's Court one year. Then through some wine-merchant I got the management of the Wey Hotel at Weybridge. I rebuilt that. Then I had to add two wings to it."

"But this present show of yours?"

"Oh! Well. They wanted a new manager here, and they sent for me. But I wouldn't leave the Wey. So to get me they bought the Wey."

"And what happened to the Wey?"

"Nothing. I'm still running it. Going down there this morning. Can't go every day. When you've got the largest luxury-hotel in the world on your hands--"

"The largest?"

"The largest."

"Have you been to America? I thought in America--"

"Yes. All over America. I expected to learn a bit in America, but I didn't. You mean those '2,000 bedrooms--2,000 bathrooms' affairs. Ever stayed in one? No, of course you haven't. Not your sort. Too wholesale and rough-and-ready. Not what *we* call luxury-hotels. Rather behind the times. They haven't got past 'period'-furnishing. Tudor style. Jacobean style. Louis Quinze room. And so on. And as for bathrooms--well, they have to come to my 'show' to see bathrooms."

He spoke as it were ruthlessly, but very simply and quietly. When she spoke she did not turn her head. She seemed to be speaking in a trance. He could examine her profile at his ease. Yes, she was beautiful.

2.

At Ludgate Circus, a white-armed policeman was directing traffic under electric lamps just as in daylight.

"How funny!" she said, swinging round to the left so acutely that Evelyn's shoulder touched hers.

In no time they would reach their destination. For this reason and no other he regretted the high speed. The fresh wind that precedes the dawn invigorated and sharpened all his senses. He recalled Dr. Johnson's remark that he would be content to spend his life driving in a postchaise with a pretty woman. But the pretty woman would not have been driving. This girl was driving. She profoundly knew the job. Evelyn always had a special admiration for anybody who profoundly knew the job. She even knew the streets of commercial and industrial London. Before he was aware of it, the oddest thoughts shot through his mind.

"Her father might object. But I could handle her father. Besides--what a girl! Lovely, and can do something! No one who drives like her could possibly *not* have the stuff in her. I've never met anybody like her. She likes me. No nonsense about her! What a voice! Her voice is enough. It's like a blooming orchestra, soft and soothing, but so. . . Here! What's this? What's all this. It isn't an hour since I met her. I'm the wildest idiot ever born. Marriage? Never. A mistress? Impossible. Neither she nor any other woman. The head of a 'show,' as she calls it, like mine with a mistress!"

He laughed inwardly, awaking out of a dream. And as he awoke he heard her beautiful voice saying, while her eyes stared straight ahead:

"What I admire in you is that you don't *act.* I know you must be a pretty biggish sort of a man. Well, father's pretty big--at least I'm always being told so--but father can't help acting the big man, acting what he *is.* He's always feeling what he is. You're big and so you must know you're big; but you just let it alone. It doesn't worry you into acting the part. I know. I've seen lots of big men."

"Oh!" murmured Evelyn, cautious, non-committal, and short of the right words. But he was thinking rapidly again:

"And *she* hadn't met *me* an hour ago! What a girl! No girl ever said anything as extraordinary as what she's just said. And it's true, what she says. Didn't I see it in her father? I was afraid I might have seemed boastful, the way I talked about me and my 'show.' But apparently she didn't misunderstand me. Most girls would have misunderstood. Really she is a bit out of the ordinary."

Smithfield Markets with their enclosed lighted avenues shone out twinkling in the near distance, on the other side of a large, dark, irregular open space of ground. Gracie glanced to right and left, decided where she would draw up, and, describing a long, evenly sustained curve, drew up in a quiet corner, slow, slower, slowest--motion expiring without a jar into immobility. She clicked the door and jumped down with not a trace of fatigue after a bedless night nearly ended. Her tongue said nothing, but her demeanour said: "And that's that! That's how I do it!"

"Well," remarked Evelyn, still in the car. "You said something about me. I'll say something about you. You can drive a car."

Gracie answered: "I don't drive any more."

"What do you mean--you don't drive any more?"

"I mean race-track driving. I've given it up. *This* isn't driving."

"Had an accident?"

"An accident? No! I've never touched a thing in my life. But I might have done. I thought it wasn't good enough--the risk. So I gave it up. I thought I might as well keep the slate clean." She smiled ingenuously, smoothing her cloak.

"And what a slate! What a nerve to retire like that!" Evelyn reflected, and said aloud: "You're amazing!" He had again the sensation of the romantic quality of life. He was uplifted high.

"So here we are," said Gracie, suddenly matter-of-fact.

A policeman strolled into the vicinity.

"Can I leave my car here, officer?" she questioned him briskly, authoritatively.

The policeman paused, peering at her in the dying night.

"Yes, miss."

"It'll be quite safe?"

"I'll keep an eye on it, miss."

"Thank you."

Evelyn, accustomed to take charge of all interviews, parleys, and pow-wows, had to be a silent spectator. As he led her into the Market, he trembled at the prospect of the excitement, secret and overt, which her appearance would cause there.

Chapter 5 GRACIE AT SMITHFIELD

Gracie, though for different reasons, felt perhaps just as nervous as Evelyn himself when they entered the meat-market; but within the first few moments her nervousness was utterly dissolved away in the strong sense of romance which surged into her mind and destroyed everything else therein.

The illimitable interior had four chief colours: bright blue of the painted constructional ironwork, all columns and arches; red-pink-ivories of meat; white of the salesmen's long coats; and yellow of electricity. Hundreds of bays, which might or might not be called shops, lined with thousands of great steel hooks from each of which hung a carcass, salesmen standing at the front of every bay, and far at the back of every bay a sort of shanty-office in which lurked, crouching and peering forth, clerks pen in hand, like devilish accountants of some glittering, chill inferno.

One long avenue of bays stretched endless in front, and others on either hand, producing in the stranger a feeling of infinity. Many people in the avenues, loitering, chatting, chaffing, bickering! And at frequent intervals market-porters bearing carcasses on their leather-protected shoulders, or porters pushing trucks full of carcasses, sped with bent heads feverishly through the avenues, careless of whom they might throw down or maim or kill. An impression of intense, cheerful vitality, contrasting dramatically with the dark somnolence of the streets around! A dream, a vast magic, set in the midst of the prosaic reality of industrial sleep! You were dead; you stepped at one step into the dream; you were alive.

Everything was incredibly clean. The blue paint was shining clean; the carcasses were clean; the white coats of the salesmen were clean; the chins of the salesmen were clean and smooth; many of them showed white, starched collars and fancy neckties under the white coats. Very many of them had magnificent figures, tall, burly, immense, healthy, jolly. None of them had any air of fatigue or drowsiness or unusualness. The hour was twenty minutes to five, and all was as customary as the pavements of Bond Street at twenty minutes to noon. And the badinage between acquaintances, between buyers and sellers, was more picturesque than that of Bond Street. Gracie caught fragments as she passed. "You dirty old tea-leaf." "Go *on,* you son of an unmarried woman."

Gracie was delighted. A world of males, of enormous and solid males. She was the only woman in the prodigious, jostling market. A million males, and one girl. She savoured the contrast between the one and the million, belittling neither. Of course Evelyn and she were marked for inquisition by curious, glinting eyes. They puzzled curiosity. They ought to have been revellers, out to see the night-life of London. But the sedate, reserved Evelyn looked no reveller, nor did she in her simple, dark cloak. But, she thought, they knew a thing or two, did those males! With satisfaction she imagined the free imaginings behind their eyes. She was proud to be the one against the million. Let them think! Let their imaginations work! She felt her power. And never, not even at 100 m.p.h. on the race-track, had she lived more exultantly. She was always demanding life, and seldom getting it. Now she was getting it--the full cup and overflowing.

2.

Withal, at a deeper level than these Dionysiac sensations, was a sensation nobler, which rose up through them. The desire for serious endeavour. At the wheel of a racing-car, built specially for her to her father's order, Gracie had been conscious of a purpose, of a justification. The track involved an austere rule of life; abstinence, regularity, early hours, the care of nerves, bodily fitness. Eight or ten months ago she had exhausted the moral potentialities of racing. Racing held nothing more for her. She had tired of it as a traveller tires of an island, once unknown, which he has explored from end to end. She had abandoned it. Her father had said: "You can't stick to anything." But her father did not understand.

She had fallen into sloth and self-indulgence, aimless, restless, unhappy. Her formidable engine-power was wasting itself. She had rejoined her smart friends, formed the habit of never wanting to go to bed and never wanting to get up, scattered her father's incalculable affluence with both hands, eaten, drunk, gambled, refused herself no fantastic luxury (Sir Henry being negligently, perhaps cynically, compliant), lived the life furiously. And the life was death. Against his inclination, her father had taken her with him to America. She had had hopes of the opportunities and the energy of America. They were frustrated. In New York she had lived the life still more furiously. And it was worse than death. While in New York Sir Henry had put through one of his favourite transactions: sold his splendid London house at a rich profit. He had a fondness for selling London homes over the heads of himself and Gracie. He had two country-houses; but the country meant little to Gracie, and less to him. Hence, this night, the hotel. The man would reside in hotels for months together.

Gracie had reached the hotel, in the middle of the night, without any clear purpose in mind. She had loved with violence more than once, but never wisely. She had now no attachment--and only one interest: reading. She had suddenly discovered reading. Shakspere had enthralled her. On the Atlantic voyage she had gulped down two plays of Shakspere a day. At present, for her, it was Shakspere or nothing. The phenomenon was beyond her father; but it flattered his paternal vanity, demonstrated to him that he had begotten no common child. First racing, now Shakspere! Something Homeric about Gracie, and she his daughter! Out of Shakspere and other special reading, a project was beginning to shape in the girl's soul, as nebulae coalesce into a star. But it was yet too vague to be formulated. Then the hotel. Then Evelyn Orcham, whose name Sir Henry had casually mentioned to her with candid respect. Then the prospect of fabled Smithfield before dawn. Evelyn had impressed her at the first glance: she did not know why. And she divined that she in turn had impressed him.

She admired him the more because he had not leapt at her suggestion of going with him to Smithfield, because for a few moments he had shown obvious reluctance to accept it. Not a man to be swept off his feet. A self-contained, reserved man. Shy. Quiet. Almost taciturn, with transient moods of being confidential, intimate. Mysterious. Dangerous, beneath a conventional deportment. You never knew what might be hidden in the depths of a man like that. Enigmatic. Diffident; but very sure of himself. In short. . . was he married? Had he a hinterland? Well, his eyes didn't look as if he had.

And now she was in Smithfield, and her prophetic vision of it, her hopes of it, had been right. Smithfield had not deceived her. A romantic microcosm of mighty males, with a redoubtable language of their own. A rude, primeval, clean, tonic microcosm, where work was fierce and impassioned. A microcosm where people *got up early and thought nothing of getting up early,* and strove and haggled and sweated, rejoicing in the purchase and sale of beef and mutton and pork. To get up early and strive, while the dull world was still asleep: this it was that appealed to Gracie. Freshness and sanity of earliest dark cool mornings! She wanted to bathe in Smithfield as in a bath, to drench herself in it, to yield utterly to it. Smithfield was paradise, and a glorious hell.

Chapter 6 BIRTH OF DAY

"Ah! There's Cradock," said Evelyn. "He's our buyer. I'll introduce him to you. The little man there. The one that's sticking a skewer into that lamb."

Gracie recognised the man who had been waiting in the great hall of the hotel. Having stuck the skewer into the carcass, Jack pulled it out and put it to his nose. Then, while Evelyn and Gracie watched, he stuck a skewer into the next lamb, and finally left a skewer in each lamb: sign that they were his chosen.

"Chines and ends," Gracie heard him say, as he scribbled in a note-book.

He saw Evelyn.

"Here we are, Cradock," said Evelyn. "This is Miss Savott. Knows all about motor-racing. Now she wants to know all about Smithfield."

Jack clasped her slim hand in his thick one.

"I do think your market is marvellous, Mr. Cradock!" Gracie greeted him, genuine enthusiasm in her emotional low voice. Her clasp tightened on the thick hand, and held it.

"Glad to meet you, miss."

"It's so big and so clean. I love this blue paint."

"Glad to hear that, miss. There's some of 'em would sooner have the old green. . . a bit of it over there." He pointed.

"That's nice too. But I prefer the blue, myself."

Jack was conquered at once, not by her views on blue and green paint, but by her honest manner, by her beauty, and by the warmth of her trifling, fragile, firm fingers. He thought, "Governor knows what's what. Trust him!" And since the relations of men and women are essentially the same in all classes, and his ideas concerning them had been made robust and magnanimous by many contacts with meat-salesmen of terrific physique, he began privately to wish the governor well in whatever the governor might be about. Anyhow it was none of his business, and the governor could indeed be trusted, had nothing to learn.

"You see those lambs, sir," he murmured. "I guarantee there isn't ten lambs like them in all London to-day!"

Evelyn nodded. The carcasses were already lifted off their hooks. Gracie saw them put on a huge carving block, and watched a carver in bloody blue divide them with a long razor-knife and a saw. In a moment the operation was performed, and so delicately and elegantly that it had no repulsiveness. The carvers were finished surgeons for Gracie, not butchers.

"That's got to be served, for lunch at the hotel this morning," said Jack to her. "We hang the beef for five or six days--used to hang it for twelve or fourteen. But you ladies and gentlemen alter your tastes, you see, miss, and we have to follow. You see all that calves' liver there. Not so many years ago, I could buy as much as I wanted at sixpence a pound. Would you believe me, it costs me two shillings these days! All because them Harley

Street doctors say it's good for anæmia." He turned to Evelyn: "That's Charlie Jebson, governor. Next door." He jerked his head.

"Let's go and talk to him," said Evelyn, easily.

Mr. Charles Jebson was a very tall man, with a good figure, and dandiacal in dress.

"This is my governor, Mr. Orcham, Charlie. And this is Miss Savott, come to see what we do up here. Mr. Charles Jebson."

Charles became exceedingly deferential. He shook hands with Gracie like a young peer in swallow-tails determined to ingratiate himself with a chorus-girl. Gracie smiled to herself, thinking: "What a dance I could lead him!"

"You do get up early here, Mr. Jebson," she said. "When do you sleep?"

"I don't, miss," he replied, smirking. "At least--well, three or four hours. Make it up Sundays. Perhaps you know the Shaftesbury, in Shaftesbury Avenue. Express lunch and supper counter. That's mine. They call me 'the governor' there, when I go in of a night to tackle the books and keep an eye on things. Not so much time for sleep, you'll freely admit." Gracie's notion of him was enlarged. White coat before dawn. Restaurateur in the centre of theatre-land at supper-time! A romantic world!

"It's all too marvellous!" she said admiringly.

Charlie showed pride. A procession of four laden porters charged blindly down the avenue, shouting. Gracie received a glancing blow on the shoulder. She spun round, laughing. Jack moved her paternally away to shelter. A nun, hands joined in front, eyes downcast, walked sedately along the avenue, a strange, exotic visitant from another sphere. The spectacle startled Gracie, shaking all her ideals, somehow shaming her.

"Why is she here?" she demanded of Jack with false casualness.

"I couldn't say, miss, for sure. Little Sister of the Poor, or something. Come for what she can get. Food for orphans, I shouldn't be surprised. They're very generous in the Market." He added discreetly, as Gracie made as if to return to Evelyn, "Governor's got a bit of business with Mr. Jebson."

"Oh yes." And she asked him some questions about what she saw.

"Refrigerators," he said. "Thirty years ago when I first came here there wasn't an ice-box in the place."

Gracie could overhear parts of the conversation between Charlie and Evelyn. Evelyn laughed faintly. Charlie laughed loudly. It went on.

"I hope we shall be able to continue to do business together, Mr. Jebson," Evelyn said at length.

"It won't be my fault if we don't, sir," Charlie deferentially replied.

"That's good," said Evelyn. "I know there's no beef better than yours. I didn't know you had a restaurant. I've often noticed the Shaftesbury. One night I shall come in. I'm rather interested in restaurants." He laughed.

"Thank *you,* sir. It'll be a great honour when you do."

General handshaking, which left Charlie Jebson well satisfied with the scheme of the universe. The three proceeded along the avenue.

2.

"That'll be all right now, I think," Gracie heard Evelyn murmur to Jack Cradock. And she recalled what Evelyn had said to her about an instinct for handling people. As it was extremely difficult to walk three abreast in the thronged avenues, Jack, now elated, walked ahead. But sometimes he lagged behind. Everybody knew him. Everybody addressed him as Jack. (The Smithfield world was as much a world of Christian names as Gracie's own.) Nevertheless the affectionate familiarity towards Jack was masked by the respect due to a man who was incapable of being deceived as to the quality of a carcass, who represented the swellest hotel in London, who had a clerk, who spent an average of a hundred pounds sterling a day, and who would take nothing but the best.

Cradock stopped dead, in the rear.

"Hello, Jim. I want a hundred pounds of fat."

"Two and four," was the reply.

"That's where you're wrong. Two shillings."

"And that's where *you're* wrong."

"Two and two," said Jack.

"Oh," said Jim, with feigned disgust. "I'll give it you for your birthday. I know how hard up you are."

Jack scribbled in his book and strode after the waiting pair. But a heavy hand was laid on his shoulder.

"Hello, Jack. Not seen you lately. Had a fair holiday?"

"Yes," said Cradock. "I have had a *fair* holiday. I'm not like some of you chaps. When I go for a holiday I take my wife." He hurried on.

"Excuse me, miss," he apologised to Gracie.

The trio arrived at a large fenced lift.

"Miss Savott might like to go down," Evelyn suggested.

Cradock spoke to the guardian, and the chains were unfastened.

"If you'll excuse me, governor. I'll see you afterwards." And to Gracie, with a grin: "I've got a bit to do, and time's getting on. If I don't keep two ton o' meat in stock down at the Imperial Palace the governor would pass me a remark." With a smile kindly and sardonic, benevolent and yet reserved, Jack Cradock stood at the edge of the deep well as the rough platform, slowly descending, carried the governor and young lady beyond his sight.

"What a lovely man!" said Gracie, appreciative.

"You heard that phrase in America!" was Evelyn's comment.

They smiled at one another. The hubbub and brightness of the vast market vanished away above their heads. The lift shuddered and stopped. They were in silence and gloom. They were in a crypt. And the crypt was a railway station, vaster even than the Market, and seeming still vaster than it was by reason of the lowness of its roof.

"As big?" said the lift-attendant disdainfully in response to an enquiry. "It's a lot bigger than Euston *or* St. Pancras *or* King's Cross. If you ask me, it's the longest station in London...No, the meat trains are all come and gone an hour ago." An engine puffed slowly in the further obscure twilight. "No, that's only some empties."

Vague, dull sounds echoed under the roof: waggons being hauled to and fro by power-winches, waggons swinging round on turn-tables. Men like pigmies dotted the endless slatternly expanse. The untidy platforms were littered with packages: a crate of live fowls, a case of dead rabbits, a pile of tarpaulins. The pair walked side by side along a platform until they were held up by a chasm through which a waggon was being dragged by a hawser. When the chasm was covered again they walked on, right to the Aldersgate end of the station, whence the Farringdon Road end was completely invisible in the gloom. Neither spoke. Both were self-conscious.

"What are you thinking about?" Gracie asked curtly.

"If you want to know, I was thinking about that split ship of yours. And you?"

Gracie's low, varied voice wavered as she replied:

"I was only thinking of those lambs, when they were in the fields, wagging their silly little tails while they sucked milk in."

Evelyn saw the gleam of tears in her eyes. He offered no remark. Nervously Gracie pulled her cloak off and put it on her arm.

"It's so hot. I mean I'm so hot," she said.

She had indeed for a moment thought of the lambs. But the abiding sensation in her mind, in her heart and soul, was the sensation of the forlorn sadness of the deserted dark crypt, called by the unimaginative a railway station, and of the bright, jostling back-chatting world of men suspended over it on a magical system of steel girders. All the accomplishment of adventurous and determined laborious men--men whom her smart girl friends would not look twice at, because of the cut of their coats, or their accent, or their social deportment! She wanted ardently to be a man among men; she felt that she was capable of being a man among men. Her ideals, shaken before, were thrown down and smashed. She liked Evelyn for his sympathetic silence. She persuaded herself that he knew all her thoughts. By a shameless secret act, she tried to strip her mind to him, tear off every rag of decency, expose it to him, nude. And not a word said.

"Ah!" she reflected with a yearning. "His instinct for handling people! Could he handle me? Could he handle me?"...

When they regained the surface, Jack Cradock was waiting for them. She was astounded to see by the market-clocks that the hour was after half-past six. Then something disturbingly went out. A whole row of electric lights in the broad arched roof of the central avenue! New shadows took the place of the old. She glanced at the roof. Grey light showed through its glass. Dawn had begun. Never in Gracie's experience was a dawn so mysterious, so disconcerting, so heartrending. Jack Cradock was very amiable, respectful, self-respecting, and matter-of-fact.

Outside she resumed her dark cloak, tipped the policeman before Evelyn could do so, and slowly climbed into the car. She drove to the hotel slowly, not because of the increased traffic in the lightening streets, but as it were meditatively.

"I might write down my impressions of all that," she murmured to Evelyn once, half-emerging for an instant from her meditation.

Chapter 7 THE HOTEL WAKING UP

In the courtyard of the hotel a lorry loaded with luggage was grinding and pulsating its way out. The courtyard had dried after its morning souse.

"That's the last of the big luggage for the 'Leviathan'," Evelyn explained, as Gracie brought the car to a standstill in front of the revolving doors and the two janissaries. "Special train leaves Waterloo at 8.20. Passengers hate to have to catch it, but they always do manage to catch it--somehow."

Gracie made no reply. A chauffeur, who had been leaning against the rail of the luggage-hoist in a corner of the yard, advanced towards the car.

"Good morning, Compton," Gracie greeted him, as she followed Evelyn out of the car. "How long have you been here?"

"About an hour, miss."

"Have you had the big stuff sent upstairs?"

"Oh yes, miss."

"There's the beginning of a rattle in the bonnet here. Have a look at it."

"Yes, miss. Certainly, miss. Any orders, miss?"

"Not to-day. But I don't know about Sir Henry."

"No, miss."

"Better put the car in the hotel garage, and tell them to clean her. If I want her I'll get her out myself. I'm going to bed. You ought to get some sleep, too."

"Very good, miss."

In her beautiful voice Evelyn noticed the nonchalance of fatigue. He was glad she was tired, just as earlier he was glad she had not been tired.

On the steps under the marquise she took off her cloak; then preceded Evelyn to the spinning doors.

"There's something at the back of your left shoulder," said Evelyn, in the doorway.

"What?" She did not turn round.

"A stain. Why! It's blood."

"Blood?"

"Yes. You must have got it after we came up into the Market again. You weren't wearing your cloak then. You were wearing it before. And you couldn't have got it down in the station."

"What a detective you are!" she said, still not turning round.

Evelyn saw a deep flush gradually suffuse her neck. How sensitive she was! No doubt she hated the thought of blood on her frock.

"The valet will take it out for you, if your maid can't. They're very good at that, our valets are."

"At getting out blood-stains?"

"Any stains." Evelyn gave one of his short laughs, though her tone had rather disturbed him. The blood-stain was obscene upon her. He hated it.

She glanced back, not at Evelyn, but at the janissaries, who, well-trained, averted their eyes. He wished that she would put on her cloak again, and in the same instant she put it on, while her bag slapped against her corsage. Then she entered. On the outer mahogany of the head-porter's desk hung a framed card: "s.s. Leviathan. The special boat-train will leave Waterloo at 8.20a.m.," followed by the date.

"How many departures by the 'Leviathan' this morning, Sam?" Evelyn asked. Long Sam was half-hidden within his lair.

"Eighteen, sir," said Sam, consulting a book that lay open on the desk.

"Hm!"

The great hall had much the same nocturnal aspect as when they had left it, but with a new touch of lugubriousness, and a more intense expectancy--expectancy of the day, impatient now and restless. Day had begun in the streets and roads and in St. James's Park, but not in the hall. The fireman was handing to Reyer his time-clock, which checked the performance of his duties more exactly and ruthlessly than any overseer could have done. Reyer, comatose and pale from endless hours of tedium, accepted it negligently.

A high pile of morning newspapers lay on the counter near the still-closed book-and-news shop. Evelyn strode eagerly towards it, and examined paper after paper.

"Not a word," he called to Gracie.

"Not a word about what?"

"Your split ship. I looked at the posters in Fleet Street. Nothing on them. Of course there wouldn't be. Terrific thing, and yet they can hush it up. And there isn't a newspaper office in London that doesn't know all about it by this time. And you'll see it won't be in the evening papers either."

Gracie, standing hesitant, said nothing. She was too weary, or too depressed, to be interested any more, even in her complexion. Reaction! But Evelyn felt no fatigue. His imagination was now no longer responsively awake to the fatigue of Gracie. On the contrary he felt extraordinarily alive.

"See," he said, pointing through glass walls to the grill-room, where a couple of men, attended by two waiters, were already breakfasting, "my hotel's waking up for the day. You're just in time to see my hotel waking up. It's a great moment."

He loved to watch his hotel waking up. Something dramatic, poignant, in the spectacle of the tremendous monster stirring out of its uneasy slumber.

A youngish woman in a short black frock approached through the dark vista of the restaurant and the foyer. She tripped vivaciously up the first flight of steps, then up the second. She entered the hall.

"Good morning, Miss Maclaren."

"Good morning, sir." Bright Scottish accent, but serious.

"Housekeeper," he murmured to Gracie. "That is to say, one of our housekeepers. We have eight, not counting the head-housekeeper, who's the mother of us all." Affection in his eager voice.

Gracie stared and said nothing.

"Isn't Miss Brury on duty to-day, Miss Maclaren?" he continued.

"She's unwell, sir."

"Sorry to hear that. Things are a bit late this morning."

"Yes, sir. Something wrong with the clocking apparatus. Turnstile wouldn't turn. Mr. Maxon couldn't explain it, but he got it put right."

"Everyone except heads of departments has to clock in," Evelyn explained to Gracie. "Thirteen hundred of 'em, not counting the Laundry and the works department--outside."

"What a swarm!" Gracie spoke at last; there was no answering enthusiasm in her tone, but Evelyn was not dashed. He had forgotten the split ship and the blood-stain. He was the creative artist surveying and displaying his creation--the hotel. He was like a youth.

A procession of girls and women followed Miss Maclaren through the vista of the restaurant and the foyer into the great hall. They wore a blue uniform with brown apron, and carried pails, brooms, brushes and dusters. Some of them swerved off into the corridor leading towards the grill-room. Others began to dust the Enquiries and Reception counters. Others were soon on their knees, in formation, cleaning the immense floor of the hall. Miss Maclaren spoke sharply, curtly, now and then to one or other of them.

"You always have to be at them, but they're a very decent lot," she murmured as it were apologetically to Evelyn, her hands folded in front of her, nun-like, while surreptitiously she summed up Gracie with hostility.

"Yes," thought Evelyn, enjoying the scene as though he had never witnessed it before. "The women-guests are fast asleep on their private embroidered pillows upstairs, all in silk pyjamas and nighties, and these women here have cleaned their homes and got breakfasts and washed children and been sworn at probably, some of them, and walked a mile or two through the streets, and put on their overalls, and here they are swilling and dusting like the devil!" And aloud he said to Gracie: "Come and see the restaurant. Won't take a moment."

They went down steps and down steps. (The earth's surface was level beneath, but the front part of the hotel had been built over a basement; the back part had not.) One lamp still kept watch over the main part of the dead restaurant; but in a far corner was another lamp, and beneath it a fat man was furiously cleaning about a thousand electroplated cruets. Rows of cruets. Trays of cruets. Beyond, a corridor leading to the ball-room in the West Wing.

"Yes," said Gracie feebly.

They returned.

"Here's the ladies' cloak-room," said Evelyn, even more animated, and turned aside.

He took her arm and led her in. Room after room. Table after table. Chair after chair. Mirror after mirror. Clock after fancy clock. In the dim twilight of rare lamps the long suite of highly decorated apartments looked larger even than it was. A woman was polishing a mirror.

"It's a wonderful place," said Gracie politely. "I think I must go to bed, though."

He escorted her to the lift. Leaving the liftman to wait, she stood back from the ornate cage--such a contrast with the shuddering wooden platform at Smithfield--and glancing up at Evelyn, her eyes and face suddenly as shining and vivacious as his, she said to him in her richest voice, low, emotional, teasing:

"Do you know what you are?"

"What am I?"

"You're a perfect child with a toy!"

What would his co-directors, the heads of departments, the head-housekeeper, Jack Cradock, have thought, to hear him thus familiarly and intimately addressed by a smart chit who was also a stranger?

"Am I? I do believe I am," he answered, enraptured.

2.

But when the lift had taken her up out of sight, he thought, though lightly: "Who does she think she is, cheeking me, after inviting herself to Smithfield and all that? Never saw her in my life until this morning, and she has the nerve to call me a child!" Nevertheless, her impudent remark did please him. He indeed admitted, proudly, that he was a child--one part of him, which part had carelessly forgotten to grow up.

The mishap with the turnstiles was prominent in his mind. The organisation of the hotel was divided into some thirty departments, and the head of each had a fixed conviction that his department was the corner-stone of the success of the hotel. Evelyn, Machiavellian, impartially supported every one of these convictions, just as he consistently refrained from discouraging the weed of interdepartmental jealousies inevitably sprouting from time to time in the soil of strenuous emulation which he was always fertilising. Thus the head Floors-waiter did not conceal his belief that the room-service was the basis of prosperity; the Restaurant-manager *knew* that the restaurant was the life-blood of the place; the manager of the grill-room was not less sure that the grill, where at lunch and at supper the number of celebrities and notorieties far surpassed that of the restaurant (though it cost the hotel not a penny for bands), was the chief factor of prosperity; the Audit-manager was aware that without his department the hotel would go to hell in six months; the Bills-manager had no need to emphasise his supremacy; the head of the Reception, who could draw from memory a plan of every room with every piece of furniture in it, and who knew by sight and name and number every guest, and had a file-record of every guest, including the dubious, with particulars of his sojourns, desires, eccentricities, rate of spending, payments--even to dishonoured cheques, who could be welcoming, non-committal, cool, cold and ever tactful in five languages--this marvel had never a doubt as to the identity of the one indispensable individual in the hierarchy of the hotel. And so on.

And there were others--especially those mightinesses the French, Italian and Viennese chefs. Evelyn always remembered the ingenuous, sincere remark of the chief engineer, who passed his existence in the lower entrails of our revolving planet, where daylight was utterly unknown. "You see those things," the chief engineer had said to a visitor. "If they shut up, the blessed hotel would have to shut right up." 'Those things' were the boilers, which made the steam, which actuated the engines, which drew the water from the artesian wells, made the electric light and the electric power, heated the halls, restaurants and rooms, froze or chilled perishable food, baked the bread, cooked the meat, boiled the vegetables, cleansed and dried the very air, did everything except roast the game over a wood fire.

Evelyn had admitted, to himself, the claim to pre-eminence of the chief engineer. But now he began to wonder whether the turnstile and clocking-in satrap was not entitled to precedence over even the chief engineer. For if the hotel depended on the engine-hall the engine-hall depended on the presence of its workmen. He smiled at the fanciful thought as he descended by tiled and concrete slopes and narrow iron staircases, glimpsing non-uniformed humble toilers of both sexes in soiled, airless rooms and enclosures, towards the cave of the Staff-manager's second-in-command who watched and permitted or forbade the entrances and exits of thirteen hundred employees.

The cave was a room of irregular shape, full of machines and pigeon-holes and cognate phenomena. The second-in-command, a dignified and authoritative specimen of the middleclass aged fifty or so, sat on one side of a counter. On the other side stood a young woman starting on her day out, dressed and hatted and shod and powdered and rouged for the undoing or delight of some young male: in her working-hours a chamber-maid. Between them, on the counter, lay a dispatch case, on which the girl kept a gloved hand.

"You can't leave with that thing until I've seen inside it," said authority.

"But why? It's mine."

"How long have you been here? Not long, eh?"

"A month."

"Well, when you've been here a month of Sundays you'll have got into your head that nobody can take anything out of here without me seeing what it is."

"I call it a wicked shame."

"It may be. But it's the rule of the hotel. Last year I caught a girl slipping out with a pair of sheets where they oughtn't to be."

"This despatch-case won't hold a pair of sheets," said the girl. "Anyone can see that."

Authority made no reply, but glanced inquisitively at a small group of men who were clocking in. The girl sulkily opened the despatch-case. Authority looked into it.

"That necklace yours?"

"Yes."

"Where did you get it from?"

"A lady gave it me."

"What floor? What number? What name? Is she still here?"

Question and answer; question and answer.

"Off you go," said authority, having written down the details on the slip-permit which the girl had handed to him:

"You'll know next time."

Off the girl went, haughtily. Evelyn felt sorry for her, as he emerged from the doorway where he had been listening to the encounter.

"Good *morning,* sir." Authority had suddenly changed to subservience.

"I hear you had some trouble with the turnstiles this morning, Maxon," said Evelyn benevolently.

"Trouble, sir? Turnstiles?" replied subservience, as if quite at a loss to understand the sinister allusion.

"Yes. Some charwomen were kept waiting."

"Oh! I see what you mean, sir. That wasn't turnstiles, sir. They've told you wrong. I'll show you what it was." Subservience sprang round the counter.

The two bent together over a steel contraption, and subservience explained.

"No turnstiles about that, sir. Clocking."

"Why didn't you let 'em through, for once?" Evelyn asked.

"Well, sir, I thought I should get it right every minute. Only a touch. And it wasn't long. It wasn't above five minutes. And it won't happen again. And if it does happen again, and it's your wish, sir--"

Evelyn changed the subject. After some general chat, whose sole object was to indicate to the excellent Maxon that Maxon enjoyed his special regard, he departed, having first jotted a reminding note for himself. The rule about outgoing packages irked his feeling for decency. But it was absolutely necessary. There was simply no end to the running of a hotel. How would Gracie Savott have behaved if confronted with the rule? A certain liveliness for authority! She was getting into bed now. Nothing had been said as to a further meeting.

3.

When Evelyn returned to the great hall Monsieur Adolphe, the perfectly attired, rosy-cheeked Reception-manager, who was an Alsatian but who had submerged the characteristics of his origin under a cosmopolitanism acquired during twenty-five years of activity in continental and London hotels, was hurrying busily about; for the "Leviathan" departures had begun.

American women, with the drawn, set faces of too-early rising, and great bouquets of flowers, were appearing, followed by placatory men who desired tranquillity even at the price of honour. If husbands and fathers suffered unjustly from wives and daughters, the injustice was at once passed on by husbands and fathers to baggage-porters and other officials. Adolphe's role was to establish an illusion of general loving-kindness. He fulfilled it: that was his life-work. But Evelyn stood always first in his mind, and for Evelyn's sake he cut short the oration of a Chicago millionaire.

"Sir Henry Savott has just telephoned down to enquire what time it would be convenient for you to see him to-day, sir. I've sent the message up to your room."

"Why did the message come to you, Adolphe?"

"I suppose because you'd been seen once or twice in the hall, and you weren't in your rooms. Excuse me, sir." Adolphe hastened away into the courtyard, half running.

Day had at length dawned in the great hall, which lived again, after the coma of the interminable night.

"If that fellow Savott really is Napoleon," Evelyn reflected, "he ought to be fast asleep now, instead of pursuing me with telephone-messages that take everything for granted. How does he know that I've not gone to bed same as he has?" He smiled in anticipation of protracted, fierce, and yet delicately manœuvred tussles with Savott. The fight for and against the rumoured hotel-merger was going to start sooner than he had expected. He smiled a second time, because he had firm hold of something that Sir Henry passionately wanted. Great fun! He reflected further: "It'll do that fellow no harm to cool his heels for a day or two."

Then he went to the counter, and wrote a reply to Sir Henry:

"Mr. Orcham is very sorry to say that he has outside appointments which will keep him away from the hotel all day." Nothing about to-morrow or the next day? No. More effective to say nothing about to-morrow or the next day. He had the goods, and delay and uncertainty would only inflame the desirer and so impair the desirer's skill in negotiation.

"What number--Sir Henry Savott?" he demanded, looking up across the counter at a clerk. "Page!" he called. "Telephone. Sir Henry Savott, 365."

Adolphe came in hurrying, explaining with a laugh: "I had to give Senator Gooden an extra shake of the hand because he came to us from another hotel, and I don't want him to go back there ever."

"Good," said Evelyn. "I've seen to Sir Henry Savott. You know nothing."

"Quite, sir," said Adolphe comprehendingly, and dashed off.

Car after car was now leaving the courtyard for Waterloo. Mowlem, the day head-porter, was at his grandest at the revolving doors. Evelyn ascended, and, looking at his watch, entered his private apartments. 7.45. At 7.45 he breakfasted. There, on the centre-table in the sitting-room, was his breakfast, with the newspapers arranged in what Evelyn had decided was the order of their importance to him. There, on the buffet, the spirit-lamp burned under a silver dish. There, near the door, stood his own man, with a smile of greeting. Evelyn shut the door on the whole world. He had half-an-hour to himself. No mail was ever brought to his rooms. Telephoning was harshly discouraged. Punctuality. Everything in its place. All the angles were right-angles. A logical orderliness. No will but his own functioned in those two rooms. He sat down, sipped at iced water, opened a newspaper, cleared his throat, stretched his legs, tore up the now answered telephone-message from Sir Henry Savott.

"All right, Oldham," he gave the signal. "Bit colder this morning, eh? Autumn." His voice was full of happy kindliness.

"Yes, sir," Oldham agreed, content, and with ceremonious gestures served the bacon and poured out the Costa Rica coffee.

Fresh rolls. Fresh toast. Piles of butter on ice. It was heaven, a heavenly retreat.

"I'll shave after breakfast, Oldham."

"Yes, sir. I have put out the things."

"Good."

Evelyn was secure and at ease. He had many matters on his mind: the clocking-in; the chambermaid--no insult intended; Sir Henry Savott; the relations between Jack Cradock and Charlie Jebson; a hundred others big and little. But they did not trouble him, because he knew he could deal with them all. He loved them. He needed them. They exhilarated him. They were his life. Without them he would have sunk into tedium. His life was perfect. Nobody could interfere with it, nobody disarrange it.

And then the tiny thought sneaked into his mind on tip-toe like a thief: was his life perfect? Yes! It was perfect. And it was full. Was it full? Was no corner of it empty? Did nothing lack? Yes! No! His life lacked nothing. It was balanced. Its equilibrium was stable. Supposing a woman, a beautiful woman, came into that sacrosanct room, as of right, flaunting her right, and began fussing about his health, commenting on his pallor, demanding to look at his tongue, fussing about the flowers and the exact disposition of the flowers, opening a newspaper and leaving it inside out on the floor, complaining of her loneliness in the world, complaining of her dressmaker, asking him whether he thought she looked five years younger than her real age, and, having been answered in the affirmative, asking him whether he *really* thought she looked five years younger than her real age; asking him whether he loved her, suggesting that he was disappointed in her! And so on and so on.

He knew it all. He had 'been there.' Intolerable! Delicious at rare moments, hell the rest of the time! His life was full. Another drop, and the glass would splash over. He had for years been lightly dreaming of a mistress. Silly! Boyish! A mistress would be a liability, not an asset. His career came first, with his usefulness to society, his duty to shareholders. He was a serious man with a conscience, not a gambler; commerce with women was the equivalent of gambling; it was staking tranquillity of conscience, staking his very soul, against a smile, a kiss, an embrace, the elegance of frocks and jewels. He opened a paper, gazed at the lines of type, and, engaged secretly in the controversy which beyond all others had agitated ambitious and powerful men for thousands of years and never been satisfactorily settled, he could make absolutely no sense of the news. Suddenly it occurred to him that Sir Henry might be wanting to see him, not about the scheme for a merger, but about his excursion with Gracie Savott into the wilds of London in the middle of the night. The girl might have wakened and told her father.

"Another slice, sir?"

"I think I will. I was up rather early. Remind me to shave."

Chapter 8 THE NEW LIFE

When Gracie entered the drawing-room of her suite, she went straight to the windows and opened them wide, looked at St. James's Park below, along whose avenues men and girls were already hurrying earnestly northward in the direction of the Green Park and Piccadilly; she thirstily drank in large draughts of the foliage-perfumed air, for it seemed to her that she could still smell Smithfield's meat. The flame-tinted new curtains waved their folds high into the room. Naturally Tessa the maid had forgotten the standing instruction to open windows on arrival. After a few cleansing moments Gracie passed into her bedroom. It was dark. She impatiently switched on the electricity. A suitcase, unfastened, lay on the floor, and a jewel-case, shut, on the bed. No other sign of habitation! The dressing-table was bare, save for the customary hotel pin-cushion and small china tray. The curtains had not been opened, nor the blinds raised.

"Tessa!" she called, after opening the window. No answer. She had a qualm of apprehension. She passed into the bathroom. Not a sign of habitation in the bathroom either. It might have been a dehumanised bathroom in a big furniture store. The next door, ajar, led to a smaller bedroom, Tessa's. Gracie pushed against it. Darkness there too. Gracie turned the switch. Tessa was stretched asleep on, not in, the bed. Gracie could see the left wrist which she herself had bandaged two or three hours earlier, and on the bandage was a very faint reddish discoloration. Gracie, who several years earlier after witnessing rather helplessly a motor-accident at Brooklands had qualified for a first-aid certificate, examined the bandage in silence. No danger. The wrist had bled since the bandaging, but was bleeding no longer. Tessa slept undisturbed. Her pretty face was so pale, tragic, and exhausted in sleep that Gracie crept out of the bedroom and softly closed the door in a sudden passion of quasi-maternal pity. The qualm of apprehension recurred.

In the bathroom she threw down her hat and cloak, and pulled off the beige frock. Yes, the blood on the shoulder was very plain. The swift, startling realisation of its origin had alone caused her to blush when Evelyn remarked on it. That blood came not from Smithfield, nor was it the blood of any slain animal. When Gracie had come up to the suite for two minutes before starting for Smithfield she had found Tessa in the maid's bedroom, a vague figure in the unlit gloom, and had summoned her very sharply--sharpness of excitement working above secret fatigue. A sudden alarmed cry from Tessa: "Oh! I've cut myself with the scissors!" A hand knocking against her shoulder in the gloom. How had the girl contrived to injure her wrist, and what was she doing with the scissors in the dark? Gracie, too hurried to pursue the enquiry, had dragged Tessa into the light of the bathroom, found the simple first-aid apparatus without which she never travelled, and bound up the wrist. The wound was somewhat sanguinary, but not at all serious. Tessa was an efficient maid, but apart from the performance of her duties lackadaisical, characterless, and slothful. She could sit idle for hours, not even reading, and when she read she read sentimental drivel. She was older by two years than Gracie, who always regarded her as a junior. A doctor had once pronounced her anæmic. The wrist duly nursed, Gracie had soothed and enheartened Tessa and told her to sit down for a bit; then, after changing hat and cloak, had run out. Thus in the suite had been spent the twenty minutes that Evelyn had spent waiting in the great hall.

Flickers of suspicious surmising had gleamed at intervals in Gracie's mind. She recalled having explained to Tessa, many months ago, a few picturesque details of anatomy learnt in the first-aid course--how there was a certain part of the wrist which, etc., etc.--how an incision upon that part would be just as effective, and assuredly less painful and messy, than an attack on the throat with a razor, etc. Playful teasing. Nothing more. Forgotten as soon as said. Remembered now. Had not Tessa's manner been sometimes strange on board the ship? Had not Gracie sometimes fancied that she might be victimised by an unrequited love--in the style of her novelettes? Absurd. Yet not wholly absurd. No one more capable of a desperate act when roused than your silly, taciturn, lackadaisical anæmic. Gracie was rendered solemn, was snatched momentarily away from self-contemplation, by the idea that she had perhaps for days been terribly close to a mortal tragedy without guessing it...However, Tessa was asleep. The peril of a tragedy, if peril there had been, was over. No wonder that, quitting the bedroom, Gracie had gazed on the maid as a mature mother on a senseless child.

2.

In her own bedroom Gracie knelt down and unpacked the suit-case; then arranged the toilet-table; then undressed completely, turned on the water in the bathroom and bathed. She opened the door of Tessa's room to make sure that the noise of the water had not wakened the girl. Not a sound there. She put on blue silk pyjamas, and surveyed herself, moving to and fro, in the wardrobe mirror. She laid her small, elaborately embroidered travelling pillow on the hotel pillow, lit the bed-lamp, drew the blinds, closed the curtains, got into bed, switched off the lamp. She shut her eyes.

She was intensely conscious of her body, of the silkiness of her pyjamas, of the soft ridges of embroidery in the pillow. Luxurious repose. Extreme exhaustion; not merely physical; emotional. Exhaustion induced by the violence of her sensations and her aspirations in Smithfield Central Market and in the crypt below it. Thoughts of Tessa had receded. Once again she was absorbed in self-contemplation. Despite fatigue, an impulse to initiate immediately her secret project grew in her. It became imperious. She fought it, was beaten. She lit the lamp, hesitated, arose, put on the rich dressing-gown from the foot of the bed, passed into the drawing-room, carrying with her the jewel-case. It was locked--of course. The key was probably in Tessa's bag. She was bound to go back to Tessa's room. Still no sound nor movement there. She found the bag; she found the key-chain. Now, she was no more interested in Tessa.

In the drawing-room she opened the jewel-case, and took from it a morocco manuscript-book, virginal, which she had bought in New York. It had a lock, and the tiny key hung from the lock by a silk thread coloured to match the binding of the gilt-edged book. She sat herself at the desk, with the book opened in front of her, and seized a pen. The moment, she judged, was critical in her life. It might, it should and would, mark the beginning of a new life.

Slowly had been forming in her the resolution to write--to write literature. She had written one or two poems, and torn them up. No doubt they were worthless. But she knew them by heart. And perhaps they were not worthless. She had determined to write a journal of her impressions. She wrote the word 'London,' with the date, and underlined it, her hand trembling slightly from excitement, her mind thrilled by the memory of acute sensations felt in Smithfield. Her sensations seemed marvellous, unique. If only she could put them on paper. Formidable enterprise!

Her eye fell on a three-signal bell-tablet on the desk, 'waiter, valet, maid.' She must have some tea. She pressed the little knob for the waiter. True, she needed tea, but what influenced her as much as the need was a wish to delay the effort of writing the first momentous sentence in the book, the inception of the new life.

When the waiter had received her order he said:

"If you please, miss, there is a telephone-message for Sir Henry; he does not answer the telephone and his bedroom door is locked."

"What next?" thought Gracie, startled; and asked the waiter in a casual tone:

"What is the message?"

The waiter gave her a telephone-slip. She read: "Mr. Orcham is very sorry to say that he has outside appointments which will keep him away from the hotel all day." She said to the waiter: "All right. I'll see that Sir Henry gets the message."

She was alarmed. She knew her father. If he had been suggesting an interview with Mr. Orcham, and this was the reply to the suggestion, there would certainly be an explosion, and trouble between the two men. The Napoleonic Henry Savott was just about the last man to tolerate such a curt message--especially from a hotel-manager! And somehow she could not bear the prospect of trouble between these two powerful individualities. ("Why can't I?" she asked herself.) After she had drunk the celestial tea, she rang up her father in the next suite. Fortunately Napoleon had wakened.

"I say, dad--yes, it's me--do you know you've been fast asleep and they've been trying to get a message to you, from Mr. Orcham. He says he'll let you know as soon as possible later in the day. He's frightfully sorry, but he's just had to go out on very urgent business." She rang off.

Well, there it was! She'd done it. She had ravelled the skein, and she would have to unravel it. How? She would face the problem later. Such was Gracie's method. Anyhow she would have to communicate with Mr. Orcham. But later. A rush of the most vivid impressions of Smithfield, sensations at Smithfield, swept from her brain down her right arm. She could actually feel their passage. She began to write. She wrote slowly, with difficulty, with erasures. Everything but Smithfield vanished from her mind. The concentration of her mind was positively awful; that is to say, it awed her. The new life had opened for her.

Chapter 9 CONFERENCE

That morning Evelyn called the ten o'clock daily conference of heads of departments in his own office. In the absence of instructions to the contrary, it was held in the office of Mr. Cousin. Emile Cousin, the hotel-manager (whose name was pronounced in the hotel in the English way), was a Frenchman, similar to Evelyn in build, and of about Evelyn's age, but entirely grown up, whereas bits of the boy remained obstinately embedded in Evelyn's adult constitution.

'Director' was Evelyn's official title, short for 'managing director'--the medium of communication between the organism of the hotel and the Board of Directors of the company which owned both the Palace and the Wey. The authority of the Board (of which Evelyn was vice-chairman) stood above Evelyn's in theory, though not in practice.

It was out of a sort of private bravado that Evelyn presided that morning at the conference, which had not seen him for over a week. He had been up extremely early; he had been to Smithfield; he had trotted about the place; he had accomplished all the directorial correspondence; and a full day's work lay before him. But his appointment at the Laundry was not till eleven o'clock. He had, as usual, time in hand, and he would not waste it; he would expend it remuneratively. He was tired. More correctly, he would have been tired if he had permitted himself to be tired. He did not permit. He exulted in the exercise of the function of management, and especially under difficulties. Could any private preoccupation, could any hidden fatigue, impair his activity? To ask was to answer. Nothing could disconcert, embarrass, hamper, frustrate his activity. "You understand," he would joyously, proudly, say to himself, "nothing!" It was in the moments which made the heaviest demand upon his varied faculties that he lived most keenly; and it was in those moments, too, that his demeanour was lightest.

The room was spacious; it had been enlarged some years earlier by the removal of a wall, and so changed from an oblong into the shape of an L. It had two vases of flowers, and there were plants in a box on the window-sill. (The spacious window framed a view of the picturesque back of a Queen Anne house and the garden thereof.) Evelyn did not particularly want the flowers and the plants. But Miss Cass did.

Miss Cass was Evelyn's personal secretary, aged an eternal thirty, well dressed, with earnest features and decided movements. She had a tremendous sense of Evelyn's importance. She was his mother, his amanuensis, and his slave. She could forge his signature to perfection. Among her seventy and seven duties, two of the chief, for her, were the provision of flowers, and the maintenance of a supply of mineral water on Evelyn's huge, flat desk. She had to make a living, and her salary was good; but the richest reward of her labours came on the infrequent occasions when Evelyn pulled a blossom from a vase and stuck it in his button-hole.

At conferences Evelyn sat behind the desk, with his back to the window; Miss Cass sat on his left at the desk, and Mr. Cousin on his right. The other members of the conference--being, principally, the Reception-manager, the Audit-manager, the Staff-manager, the Banqueting-manager, the chief engineer, the chief Stocktaker, the Bands-and-Cabaret-manager, the Publicity-manager, the Works-manager, and the white-haired head-housekeeper (only woman in the conference, for secretarial Miss Cass was not in the conference but at it)--sat about the room in odd chairs. Two of them were perched like twins each on the arm of an easy-chair. Neither the Restaurant-manager nor the Grill-room manager was in attendance, both having been at work very late. Their statistics, however, were in the hands of Miss Cass. The nationalities represented were Italian, French, Swiss and British, the last being in a minority. Evelyn and the sedate, reserved Mr. Cousin were smoking cigars. The rest--such as smoked--contented themselves with cigarettes. Subtle distinction between seraphim and cherubim in the hierarchy!

"Who's No. 341, 2 and 3?" asked Evelyn, glancing casually at a paper--the typed night-report.

"A Mr. Amersham--Australian," answered the Reception-manager instantly. "Why, sir?"

"Nothing. I only happened to notice that a lady couldn't persuade herself to leave his rooms till three o'clock this morning. Colonials are always so attractive," Evelyn continued without a pause, extinguishing several smiles: "Give me yesterday's figures for the restaurant, Miss Cass."

Miss Cass obeyed. "Ah! Nineteen pounds up on last year, but twenty-one more meals served. So it can't be that people aren't satisfied with the music or the cabaret. Average bill slightly less, and consumption of champagne per head distinctly less than last year. If we go on at this rate our £100,000 stock of wine will last for about fifty years. In fact Prohibition would serve no purpose. Might suggest to Maître Planquet that he ought to season his dishes with a view to inducing thirst."

Maître Planquet was the chef and grand vizier of the restaurant kitchens, and had been decorated by the French Government with the Academic Palms.

General deferential mirth. Everybody loved the Director's occasional facetiousness. Even Mr. Cousin, who never laughed, would smile his mysterious, scarcely perceptible smile. Everybody was relieved that the Director could joke about those statistics. A discussion broke out, for the most part in imperfect if very fluent English.

"I'd like to see the comparative graphs to-night, Miss Cass," Evelyn tried to end it, interrupting the wordy Banqueting-manager.

Evelyn knew, and they all knew, that the public tendency towards sobriety at meals could not be checked. The clientèle was a wind which blew where it listed. But there was good comfort in the fact that the clientèle, if increasingly austere, continued to grow in numbers. Evelyn, however, perceived that he could not end the discussion; at any rate he could not end it without a too violent use of his powers. It proceeded. He listened, watchful, and with satisfaction. Most of those men, and the woman, he had trained in their duties. And he had trained all of them in the great principle of loyalty to the hotel. They showed indeed more than loyalty; they showed devotion; they lived devotion.

The majority of them had homes, wives, children, in various parts of London; real enough, no doubt; cherished; perhaps loved. But seen from within the hotel these domestic backgrounds were far distant, dim, shadowy, insubstantial. When the interests of the hotel clashed with the interests of the backgrounds, the backgrounds gave way, eagerly, zealously. The departmental heads had their hours of daily service, but these hours were elastic; that is to say, they would stretch indefinitely--never contract. Urgently summoned back too soon from a holiday, the heads would appear, breathless--and smiling; eager for the unexpected task. One or other of them was continually being tempted to a new and more splendid post; but nobody ever yielded to the temptation unless Evelyn, frankly consulted, advised yielding. (He did occasionally so advise, and the hotels and restaurants of Europe, and some in America, were dotted with important men whose prestige sprang from their service at the Imperial Palace.) There were many posts, but there was only one Imperial Palace on earth. The Palace was their world and their religion; its pre-eminence their creed, its welfare their supreme aim. They respected and adored Evelyn. He was their god. Or, if the Palace was the god, Evelyn was the god-maker, above god.

There they sat, fiercely disputing, some in the correctness of morning-coats, others (who had no contacts with the clientèle), in undandiacal lounge-suits, smoking, gesticulating, wrangling, the Englishmen and Mr. Cousin taciturn, the other foreigners shooting new foreign lights on the enigma of the idiosyncrasies of the British and American clientèle: not one of them advancing a single constructive suggestion for fostering the appetites of the exasperating clientèle And there sat Evelyn, the creator of the modernised Palace, and of the religion of the Palace, and of the corporate spirit of its high-priests; a benevolent expression on his face, but an expression with a trace of affectionate derision in it. He let them rip, not because they were furthering the cult of the god by their noise, but because he enjoyed the grand spectacle of their passion. He deeply felt, then, that he had created something more marvellous than even the hotel. He knew that he was far their superior in brains, enterprise, ingenuity, tact; and this conviction lurked in his steady, good-humoured smile; but he knew also that in strenuous selfless loyalty he was not their superior. After all, the rewarding glory of success was his, not theirs.

2.

The altercation flagged, and, seeing her chance, Mrs. O'Riordan, the head-housekeeper, sixty-two years of age and as slim and natty as a girl in her black artificial silk, killed it with a question. Mrs. O'Riordan, who lived her whole life in two small rooms on the eighth floor, could only simulate an interest in the appetites of the incomprehensible clientele. What occupied her incessant attention was the upholstery of the chairs on which people sat, the carpets which they trod, the rooms in which they slept, the cloak-rooms to which the ladies retired, etc. She ate little, and somewhat despised cookery.

"I haven't got much time," said Mrs. O'Riordan. "What is going to be done about that mink-fur business?" And her glance said: "You are males. You ought to know. Answer me."

Mrs. O'Riordan, though she had no disinclination for the society of men, exhibited always a certain slight sex-bias, half-defensive, half-challenging. She was a widowed Yorkshire gentlewoman, had had two Irish military husbands, and still possessed three sons, one of whom regularly sent flowers to her with his best love on her birthday, while the other two, in India, only wrote to her in reply to her rare letters to them. In the solitude of her eyrie on the eighth floor, absorbed morning and night in the direction of her complex department, she sometimes found a minute to regret that neither of her husbands had given her a daughter. She would have liked a girl in those houses in County Meath. Together, she and a daughter would have formed a powerful opposition to the male ascendancy.

"Mink?" asked Evelyn, his tone conveying astonishment that he should be in ignorance of any happening within the hotel.

"I only heard of it myself an hour since," said Mr. Cousin.

"You were not in your office at half-past twelve last night, Mr. Cousin," Mrs. O'Riordan addressed the French manager, with a polite implication of reproach for slackness.

"No," said Mr. Cousin. "I went home at a quarter to twelve."

"Ah!" said Mrs. O'Riordan drily. "This happened at twelve-thirty."

She then related to Evelyn how a lady who had been dining with two other ladies had presented a ticket in the ladies' cloak-room, and on receiving a fur in exchange for it had asked for her 'other fur,' alleging positively that she had deposited two furs, the second one a priceless mink, given to her by a deceased friend in Chicago. The head of the cloak-room (who was better acquainted with the secret nature of women than the most experienced man in the universe), while admitting the deposit of several minks that evening by other guests (who had reclaimed them and departed), denied any knowledge of the fur from Chicago. Unfortunately, the ground-floor housekeeper, Miss Brury, was by chance in the cloak-room, and, being the head-attendant's official superior, she had taken charge of the dispute on behalf of the hotel. Unfortunately--because Miss Brury was very tired and nervous after an exhausting day of battle with the stupidity and obstinacy of subordinates and she had been over-candid to the guest, who had surpassed her in candour. The episode had finished with a shocking display of mutual recrimination. Both women had had hysterics. Guests of both sexes had paused at the open door of the cloak-room to listen to the language; and finally the owner of the alleged missing fur had burst through them, and rushed frantically across the hail crying aloud that the hotel was the resort of thieves, that the hotel-staff was in league with thieves, and that she would have the law on the lot of them.

Mrs. O'Riordan concluded:

"Long Sam told me that by the time she reached the doors she was demanding about a million pounds damages. No, she hadn't a car and she wouldn't have a taxi--said she wouldn't, not for a million pounds--another million pounds--be beholden to the hotel for anything...Oh yes, I came downstairs. I was reading. They fetched me--for Alice Brury...No, the two companions of the infuriated lady had left earlier. She'd stayed talking to someone...Miss Brury's in bed today."

Even Evelyn blenched at this terrible story, unique in the annals of the hotel. It was utterly incredible, but he had to believe it. And it was less incredible than the fact that he had been about, off and on, since four in the morning and yet no rumour of it had reached him. It was not on the night-report. Well, it could not have been on the night-report, whose records did not begin till one o'clock. But Reyer must have heard of the thing. Long Sam also. Suddenly the obvious explanation of the mystery occurred to him. Everybody had been assuming that he was already familiar with the details of the episode, he who always knew everything. And if *he* kept silence about the horror, what underling would care or dare to refer to it in his presence?

He saw shame on every face in the room. And well might there be shame on every face, for the pride of every person was profoundly humiliated.

"I've just been talking to O'Connor," said Mr. Cousin, impassible. "He's coming at once. He says he thinks he may have heard of the lady before. He's calling at the Yard."

O'Connor was the private detective of the hotel.

"I daresay he has," Evelyn observed. "The woman is almost certainly--well, doesn't matter what she is. She may get away with it. And if we have to pay her her million pounds or the National Debt, of course we shall pay it and look pleasant, and that will be that. It's that scene that matters. You're sure Miss Brury started it, Mrs. O'Riordan?"

"She admits it herself," answered the Irishwoman. "But when you think of the provocation--"

"There can't be any such thing as provocation in this hotel," Evelyn interrupted her blandly. "There never has been before, and there mustn't be again. If the customer is Judas Iscariot, he's still the customer till he's safely outside the hotel. That's a principle. The hotel turns the other cheek every time. I'm afraid we shall have to find another job for Miss Brury."

Murmurs of assent.

"The poor thing says she wouldn't stay on here for anything."

"Well then," said Evelyn. "We must struggle on as best we can without her."

"Yes," retorted Mrs. O'Riordan, rendered audacious and contrarious by nerves. "It's all very well for you men to talk like that. But if you knew the difficulties--" She glanced at Mr. Semple, the Staff-manager, as if for moral support. But the prudent Mr. Semple gave no response.

"We'll have a chat later," said Evelyn.

He was thinking that at least a year was required for the training of a housekeeper, and that Mrs. O'Riordan had referred not long ago to the dearth of really good candidates. Mrs. O'Riordan was in favour of engaging women of her own class, her theory being that gentlewomen could exercise better authority over chambermaids and valets, and also could deal more effectively with peevish and recalcitrant visitors; and Evelyn had agreed with her, had thought that he agreed with her; at any rate he had expressed agreement. Miss Brury was of a lower origin. She had failed to stand the racket. Her failure had seriously smirched the hotel. Would a gentlewoman have done better? Possibly, he thought. But he was by no means sure. Still, he would support Mrs. O'Riordan's desire for gentlewomen on the Floors. Mrs. O'Riordan, invaluable, irreplaceable (not quite, of course, but nearly), showed the independent attitude which comes from the possession of a small private income. He had known himself to accept her ideas against his own judgment. The fact was that she had a certain quality of formidableness...

Delicate situation, this, arising out of the scene and out of the dearth of good candidates. But he had complete confidence in his ability to resolve it. What a damned nuisance women were, gentlewomen as well as their social inferiors! He knew that the Banqueting-manager was boiling up for a commotion with the head-housekeeper about the use of a room near the ball-room. Tact--The telephone bell rang, and Miss Cass answered it.

"S O S from Weybridge, sir," said Miss Cass to Evelyn.

"Some difficulty with the contractors over the alterations to the restaurant. The work is at a standstill. Mr. Plott would be very much obliged if you could run down there at once, instead of this afternoon. But you can't. You are due at the Laundry at eleven. It's after half-past ten."

"Why can't I?" said Evelyn instantly. "I could go to the Laundry this afternoon. Tell them I'll be there at three--no, four. And tell Mr. Plott I'm coming to him now. And ask if my car is waiting."

"It's bound to be, sir. Brench is always early."

"I'll leave the rest to you, Cousin," Evelyn murmured to the hotel-manager.

In twenty seconds he was quitting the office, with gay nods and smiles, and a special smile for Mrs. O'Riordan. He was not gravely alarmed about the Wey restaurant. Nor was he flinching from problems at the Palace. Nor was his gaiety assumed. Problems were his meat and drink. He saw in the longish drive to Weybridge an opportunity for full happy reflection. He knew that he would return to the Palace, with detailed solutions whose ingenuity would impress everybody. His life was of enthralling interest to him. No other kind of life could be as interesting.

To-morrow, in addition to the General Meetings of the Company, there would be Sir Henry Savott to manipulate. Perhaps if he conferred with Sir Henry in the latter's suite, as he properly might, he would encounter Gracie again. But the figure of Gracie had slipped away, like a ship standing out to sea.

Chapter 10 LAUNDRY

The already famous Imperial Palace Hotel Laundry occupied part of a piece of freehold ground in a broad, tram-enlivened street in Kennington. The part unbuilt upon was a rather wild garden in which were many flowers. Evelyn foresaw the time when the Laundry would have to be enlarged, and the garden would cease to be. But at present the garden flourished and bloomed, and work-girls were taking their tea and bread-and-butter in it under the bright, warm September sun.

The spectacle of the garden and the lolling, lounging tea-spilling work-girls delighted Evelyn on his arrival that afternoon, as it always delighted him. He would point out to visitors the curving flagged paths, the scientifically designed benches, the pond with authentic gold-fish gliding to and fro therein, and the vine. The vine bore grapes, authentic grapes. True, they were small, hard, sour and quite uneatable, but they were grapes, growing in the open air of Kennington, within thirty feet of roaring, red trams. He was perhaps prouder of the garden as a pleasance for work-girls than of the Laundry itself. He had created the Laundry. He had not designed the buildings nor the machinery, nor laid brick on brick nor welded pipe to pipe, nor dug the Artesian wells nor paved the yards. But he had thought the whole place and its efficiency and its spirit into being--against some opposition from his Board of Directors.

It was a success. It drew over half a million gallons of water a week from the exhaustless wells; it often used six thousand gallons of water in an hour. It employed over two hundred immortal souls, chiefly the enigmatic young feminine. It fed these girls. It taught them to sing and to act and to dance and to sew and to make frocks. It kept a doctor and a dentist and a nurse for them. It washed all the linen of the Imperial Palace and the Wey hotels and all the linen that the hotel guests chose to entrust to it. It served also three hundred private customers, and its puce-tinted motor-vans were beginning to be recognised in the streets. It paid ten per cent. on its capital, and, with the aid of the latest ingenuities of American and English machinery, it was estimated to increase the life of linen by one-third. And considering the price of linen...Americans who inspected the Imperial Palace Hotel Laundry said that while there were far larger laundries in the United States, there was no laundry comparable with Evelyn's, either industrially or socially. Evelyn believed them. What he had difficulty in realising was that without his own creative thought and his perseverance in face of obstruction, the Laundry would never have existed. To him it always had the air of a miracle. Such as it was, it was his contribution towards the millennium, towards a heaven on earth.

As he entered the precincts a few of the uniformed girls smiled diffidently to greet him, and he smiled back and waved his stick, and passed into the building. He was a quarter of an hour late, but this lamentable fact did not disturb him. For he had done over four hours' concentrated hard work down at Weybridge. He had telephoned for the architect and for the principal partner of the contracting firm of builders, and they had both obeyed the summons. He and they and the manager of the Wey had measured, argued, eaten together, argued again and measured again, and finally by dint of compromises had satisfactorily emerged from a dilemma which, Evelyn softly maintained, common sense and foresight ought to have been able to avoid. Oh yes, he awarded part of the blame to himself! He had quitted the Wey in triumph. He had left the manager thereof in a state of worshipping relief, and the architect and the contractor in a state of very deferential admiration. He was content with Evelyn Orcham. A hefty fellow, Evelyn Orcham!

The one stain on the bright day was that he had settled nothing in his mind on the way down about the Miss Brury calamity; and on the way up to London he had been too excited by his achievement in the suburb to think about anything else. (Assuredly he was not completely grown up.) However, there was time enough yet to think constructively upon the Miss Brury calamity. He was conscious of endless reserves of energy, and as soon as he had dealt with the simmering trouble at the Laundry he would seize hold of the Palace problem and shake it like a rat!

And there stood Cyril Purkin, the manager of the Laundry, in the doorway leading to the staff dining-room. A short, fairly thin figure; a short but prominent pawky nose; small, cautious, 'downy,' even suspicious eyes; light ruffled hair; and a sturdy, half-defiant demeanour. A Midlander, aged thirty-eight, Evelyn sometimes wondered where the man bought his suits. They were good and well-fitting suits, but they had nothing whatever of a West End cut. The origin of his very neat neckties was similarly a mystery to Evelyn. His foot was small and almost elegant.

Mr. Purkin had begun life as a chemical engineer; he had gone on to soap-making, then laundry management, then soap-making again, then laundry management again. One day, when the foundations of the Imperial Palace Hotel Laundry had hardly been laid, Evelyn had received a letter which began: "Sir--Having been apprised that you are about to inaugurate a laundry on modern lines, I beg respectfully to offer my services as manager. I am at present..." The phrasing of the letter was succinct, the calligraphy very precise, regular and clear, and the signature just as formal as the rest of the writing. The letter attracted Evelyn. How had the man been clever enough to get himself 'apprised' of the advent of a new laundry on modern lines? And how came he to have the wit to write to Evelyn personally? Evelyn's name was never given out as the manager of the Imperial Palace. Mr. Purkin's qualifications proved to be ample; his testimonials were beyond cavil. His talk in conversation was intelligent, independent, very knowledgeable; and he had strong notions concerning the 'welfare' side of laundries, which notions specially appealed to Evelyn. He was engaged. He gave immense satisfaction. His one weakness was that he was the perfect man, utterly expert, utterly reliable, superhuman.

He was still the chemical engineer. He seldom mentioned sheets, chemises, collars, towels, stockings, and such-like common concrete phenomena. He would discourse upon the 'surface tension' of water 'breaking down,' albumen, 'Base Exchange,' centrifugal cleansing, the sequence of waters, 'residual alkalis,' chlorine, warps and woofs, 'efflorescence,' etc., etc. He had established a research department, in which he was the sole worker.

As he deferentially shook hands with the great man his attitude said:

"Of course you are my emperor, but between ourselves I am as good as you, and you know it, and you know also that I have always delivered the goods."

And yet somewhere behind Mr. Purkin's shrewd little eyes there was something of the defensive as well as of the sturdy defiant, together with a glimmering of an uneasy consciousness that he had not always delivered the goods and that he too was imperfect--though no fault of his own.

"I must really show you this, sir," said he, introducing Evelyn into the small managerial room where on the desk lay a pile of examination papers. "Question," he read out, picking up a paper, "Why are white fabrics blued in order to procure a general appearance of whiteness?' Answer: 'White fabrics are blued because there are more yellow rays in the spectrum, and we use blue to counteract the yellow rays.' Wouldn't you say, sir, that that's rather well and tersely put for a girl of sixteen and a half? These exam. papers are useful as an index to character as well as to attainments."

Evelyn heartily agreed, and for courtesy's sake glanced at the paper.

"I see you've got all the painting finished," said he. "Looks much better."

"Ah!" replied Mr. Purkin. "Ah! I must show you one thing that I thought of. An idea I had, and I've carried it out."

He drew Evelyn into the Laundry itself, walking with short, decided steps. They passed though two large and lofty interiors filled with machines and with uniformed girls (the girls did not all have their tea simultaneously), girls ironing, girls folding, girls carrying, girls sorting, amid steel in movement, beat, moisture, and a general gleaming whiteness. He halted, directing Evelyn's attention to a row of pipes near the ceiling, painted in different colours.

"Red for hot water, blue for cold water, yellow for steam. The three primary colours. When a minor repair is necessary it isn't always easy to tell at a glance everywhere which pipe is which. By this system you can't make a mistake. Costs no more. I thought you'd approve."

"Brilliant," said Evelyn. "Brilliant. I congratulate you." Possibly a trace of derision in Evelyn's benevolent laudatory tone.

"And there's the new drier," Mr. Purkin continued, and led his chief to a room where two women, one mature, overblown and beautiful, and the other young but as plain as a suet pudding, were working in a temperature of 119 degrees. Evelyn had to admire and marvel again. Nor was that the end of the tour of novelties. Mr. Purkin's ingenuity and his passion for improvements were endless. And as Evelyn went from table to table and from machine to machine and from group to group of girls, busy either individually or in concert, and from pile to growing or lessening pile of linen, and as he sought for the private lives and the characters of girls in the lowered, intent faces of girls, he sardonically thought: "This chap is putting off the fatal moment on purpose. And doing it very well too. Creating all this atmosphere of approval. Damn clever fellow! Pity he isn't clever enough to see that I can see though him."

But, back in Mr. Purkin's prim, stuffy, excessively neat little office, the Midlander boldly summoned the moment.

"I'm glad you were able to come to-day, sir, because I was getting anxious for you to see for yourself we aren't standing still here. I know you're always interested, very interested, but we like to see you here, all of 'em like to see you. It makes us all feel that we kind of 'belong'...Oh! Upon my word, I was forgetting to tell you that the number of pieces from private customers passed the twenty thousand mark last week--at last. You'll receive the figures to-morrow."

"Good! Good! You always said it would."

"But there was another thing I wanted to see you about."

"Oh!" Evelyn exclaimed, feigning ignorance.

"Yes. About those frilled dress-shirts last Thursday."

"Oh! That!"

"Yes," continued Mr. Purkin. "Yes, sir. You may have forgotten, but I can assure that I haven't."

Now the affair of the frilled shirts was one of those molehills which are really mountains. In a few hours it had swollen itself into a Mont Blanc. A guest who was a public character and who had been staying at the Palace for weeks and spending quite a lot of money, had complained about the ironing of his frilled evening shirts. Mrs. O'Riordan herself had taken the matter up. Mrs. O'Riordan had given her word that the frilled shirts should be ironed to the owner's satisfaction, and at the end of ten days Mrs. O'Riordan had redeemed her word. Triumph for the hotel. Smiles from the guest. And for Mr. Immerson, the hotel's Publicity-manager, material for one or two piquant newspaper paragraphs. On the last day of his sojourn the guest had reached the state of being convinced that his celebrated frilled shirts had never been so perfectly done before. No laundry like the Imperial Palace Hotel Laundry! His desire was to leave the Palace with the largest possible stock of frilled shirts ironed by its Laundry. "Can I rely on having these three shirts back to-night?" he had asked. *Of course!*Could he doubt it? Was it not a basic principle of the Laundry that all linen consigned in the morning was delivered absolutely without fail the same evening? It was.

But the unique shirts had not been delivered, and the next morning the guest, disillusioned, wounded, inconsolable, had had to depart without them. A child disappointed of a promised toy, a religionist whose faith has been suddenly struck from under him, could not have exhibited more woe than the deceived guest. True, the shirts were sent after him by airmail to Paris and got there first. But inefficiency remained inefficiency and the

Laundry's lapse had shocked every housekeeper at the Palace. The foundations of the Palace had for an instant trembled. The unimaginative individuals who snorted that three shirts ought not to be enough to shake the foundations of a nine-storey building simply did not understand that such edifices as the Imperial Palace were not built with hands.

Evelyn had by no means forgotten the affair. A minor purpose of his visit to Kennington had indeed been to get to the bottom of it. He knew that Mr. Purkin guessed this, and that Mr. Purkin knew that Evelyn knew that he guessed. Nevertheless the two men continued to pretend.

"I was under the impression that it had been explained," said Evelyn. "You had only one girl who specialised in these preposterous shirts, and she was taken ill or something at the very moment when your need of her was most desperate."

"No, sir," said Mr. Purkin with brave candour, "the matter has not been explained--to *you;* at least not satisfactorily. The girl, Rose, was not taken ill. She merely walked out and left us in the lurch. We have the best class of girls here. I remember when laundry staffs had to be recruited from riff-raff. We've altered all that, by improving the conditions. I knew Rose; I thought highly of her; I knew her father, a house-painter, most respectable. And yet she walks out! She'll never walk in again, I may say, not as long as I'm manager here. Naturally I got the shirts done, in a way, next morning. But that's not the point."

The drama of Mr. Purkin's deep but restrained indignation genuinely affected Evelyn. It seemed to produce vibrations in the physical atmosphere of the office.

"What a man!" thought Evelyn appreciatively. "Such loyalty to the I.P.H.L. is priceless. Of course his sense of proportion's a bit askew; but you can't have everything." He said aloud, gently: "Why did this Rose walk out?"

"Ah!" replied Mr. Purkin. "I will tell you, sir." He went to a file-cabinet, and chose a card from two or three hundred cards, and offered it to Evelyn. *"That's* why she walked out."

On the card was a chart of the wicked girl's mouth, of her upper jaw and her lower jaw. "Look at it, Mr. Orcham.You see the number of bad teeth on it. I ordered her the dentist. She made an excuse twice--something about her mother's wishes, I'm certain it wasn't the father. As you know better than anyone, every girl who's engaged by me here has to promise she'll allow us to keep her in good health, mother or no mother. On that afternoon I told her I'd made an appointment for her with the dentist for the next morning, and that she positively must keep it. I spoke very quietly. Well, as soon as my back is turned out of this Laundry she walks! Without notice! Of course it was the staff-manageress's business to see to it. But as she had failed twice, I had to take the matter up myself. No alternative. Discipline is discipline. And just *look* at the charts of that mouth!"

"Quite!" said Evelyn. He was laughing, but not visibly. "Quite!"

"The truth is," Mr. Purkin continued, "there would have been no bother--I'm sure of it--if only I'd had a little more moral support."

At this point Mr. Purkin pulled out his cigarette-case and actually offered it to the panjandrum. Probably no other member of the Palace staff, no matter how exalted, with the possible exception of Mr. Cousin, would have ventured upon such a familiarity with Evelyn. But Mr. Purkin was exceedingly if secretly perturbed, and the offering of a cigarette to the great man was his way of trying to conceal his perturbation; it was also a way of demonstrating the Purkinian conviction that he was as good as anybody--even Evelyn.

"Thanks," said Evelyn, taking a cigarette, not because he did not fear Mr. Purkin's cigarettes, but because he sympathetically understood the manager's motive--or the first part of it. "You mean support from the staff-manageress?"

"I mean Miss--er," muttered Mr. Purkin, and he blushed. He would have given a vast sum not to blush; but he blushed, this pawky, self-confident, disciplinary Midlander. He had opened his mouth with the intention of boldly saying Miss Violet Powler, the staff-manageress's name; but his organs of speech, basely betraying him, refused their office. A few seconds of restraint ensued.

"Sex!" thought Evelyn. "Sex! Here it is again."

He did not object to sex as a factor in the problems of a great organism. He rather liked it. And he knew that anyhow it was and must be a factor ever recurring in those problems. He had heard, several months earlier, that an 'affair' was afoot between Mr. Purkin and Violet Powler. How did these rumours get abroad? He could not say. Nobody could say. In the present case a laundry-girl might have seen a gesture or a glance, or caught a tone--nothing, less than nothing--as the manager and the staff-manageress passed together though the busy rooms. The laundry-girl might have mentioned it slily to another laundry-girl. The rumour is born. The rumour spreads with the rapidity of fire, or of an odour, or of influenza. It rises from stratum to stratum of the social structure. Finally it reaches the august ear of Evelyn himself. For it could not be lost; it could not die; and it could not cease to rise till it could rise no higher.

Evelyn had gathered that the affair was a subject for merriment, that people regarded as comic the idea of amorous tenderness between the manager and the staff-manageress of the Laundry. In his own mind he did not accept this view. To him there was something formidable, marvellous, and indeed beautiful in the mystic spectacle of Aphrodite springing from the hot dampness of the Laundry and lodging herself in the disciplinary soul of Cyril Purkin. Nor did be foresee harm to the organism in the marriage of Cyril and Violet.

"I wouldn't say one word against her," said Mr. Purkin, exerting all his considerable powers of self-control. "I chose her out of scores, and probably a better woman for the job of staff-manageress couldn't be found. But in this matter--and in one or two others similar--I'm bound to admit

I've been a bit disappointed. Discipline is the foundation of everything here, and if it isn't enforced, where are you? I'm bound to say I don't quite see...She's inclined to be very set in her views." He lifted his eyebrows, implying imminent calamity.

"Curse this sex!" thought Evelyn. "She's refused him. Or they've had a row. Or something else has happened. He wants her to go. He'll make her go. He can't bear her here. She's on his nerves. But he's still in love with her, even if he doesn't know it. What a complication! How the devil *can* you handle it? Curse this sex!"

But he was moved by the sudden disclosure of Mr. Purkin's emotion, and he admired Mr. Purkin's mastery of it. He had never felt more esteem for the man than just then.

Mr. Purkin lit both cigarettes, and the pair talked, without too closely gripping the thorns of the situation.

"Well," said Evelyn at length gently. "We'd better leave things for a while. If I do get a chance perhaps I might have a chat with Miss Powler--"

"Well, Mr. Orcham, if anybody can do anything you can." But Mr. Purkin's accents gave a clue to his private opinion that not even Mr. Orcham could do anything.

Soon afterwards Evelyn left, saying that he would 'see.' For the moment he could not 'see.' As he walked away, the last batch of girls was quitting the garden. He got into his car.

"Home."

Brench touched his hat.

"Wait," said Evelyn suddenly, and descended from the car.

2.

He had changed his mind. Why postpone the interview with Violet Powler? Was he afraid of bringing the trouble to the stage of a crisis? He was not.

He re-entered the buildings by the 'A' gates, which admitted vans loaded with soiled linen. The linen, having passed through the Laundry and become clean, was basketed and piled into vans which drove out through the 'B' gates. He wandered alone, apparently aimless, in the warm, humid, pale departments, until he recognised the door lettered "Staffmanageress." It was half open.

Without touching it he glanced in. Miss Violet Powler sat facing the window, her back to the door. She was talking to a young tall woman. A small table separated them, and on this table lay a finished shirt and some coloured threads.

"But Lilian," Miss Powler was saying. "You know well enough that a red thread means starched; you know that no articles from No. 291 have to be starched, and yet you put a red thread into this one. Why? There must be some explanation, and I want you to tell me what it is." Her tone was soothing, persuasive.

"But, miss," said the woman, holding up a red thread, "this isn't a red thread--it's green--not starched."

"That's a green thread?"

"Yes, miss."

"Take it to the window and look at it." The woman obeyed. "Yes, miss. It's green all right," said she, turning her head and confidently smiling.

Miss Powler paused, and then she began to laugh.

"Very well. Never mind, Lilian. You come and see me before you start work to-morrow, will you?"

Lilian, puzzled, left the room, and Evelyn stood aside for her to pass out.

"Colour-blind, eh?" Evelyn walked straight into the small office laughing. "I happened to hear. Door open. Didn't want to break in. So I waited."

"Yes, Mr. Orcham. Please excuse me. I hadn't the slightest idea you were at the door. Yes, colour-blind."

Evelyn put his hat on the small table and sat down. Miss Powler shut the door.

"As a funny coincidence I really think that ought to have the first prize." Evelyn laughed again, and Miss Powler smiled. "I suppose she's the one woman in the place who ought to be able to be relied on to tell green from red, and she's colour-blind! No, not first prize. No. It deserves a gold medal." His stick joined in the laughter by tapping on the floor. "Sort of thing you can't possibly foresee, therefore can't guard against, eh? Unless Mr. Purkin decides to institute eye-tests for the staff. But of course those delightful coincidences never happen twice. How's the Dramatic Society getting along?"

Miss Powler sat down at her desk.

It was her way of smiling, her way--at once dignified and modest--of sitting down, and her way of answering his question about the Laundry A.D.S., that suggested to him a wild, absurd, fantastical scheme for killing two birds with one stone.

Miss Powler wore a plain, straight blue frock, quite short. (The hotel rule prescribing black for heads of departments did not obtain in the Laundry.) As she sat down her knees had been visible for an instant. Her brown hair was laid flat, but glossy. Without being pretty, her features were agreeable, and her habitual expression was very agreeable. Her eyes, dark brown, were sedate, with some humour somewhere behind them, waiting a chance to get out. No powder, no paint. An appearance which mingled attractiveness with austerity.

Evelyn had in his office a private card-index of all the Company's principal employees. He rarely forgot anything once learnt, and now he had no difficulty in recalling that Miss Powler lived in Battersea, the daughter of a town-traveller in tinned comestibles--certainly a humble town-traveller. But there are women who when they leave the home lose their origin, just as a woman's hat loses its price when it leaves the shop. Only an expert could say with assurance of a hat on a woman's head in the street whether it cost five guineas or two. Miss Powler might have been the daughter of a humble town-traveller, or of a successful dentist, or even of a solicitor.

"Well," Evelyn began, "you're the staff-manageress, according to the label on your door, and I must tell you that I think you managed the Lilian member of the staff very nicely. Very nicely." Miss Powler smiled. "But all cases aren't so simple, are they?"

"They aren't, sir."

"I've been asking Mr. Purkin about the Rose member. Mrs. O'Riordan, our head-housekeeper at the Palace, was particularly anxious for me to enquire into Rose's case. In fact, between ourselves, that was one of the reasons why I came down here to-day." Two fibs and a semi-fib! He had not asked Mr. Purkin. Mr. Purkin had started the subject and volunteered all information. Mrs. O'Riordan had shown no anxiety whatever for him to investigate the affair. And the affair was not strictly one of the reasons for his visit, seeing that he had not heard of it until after the visit had been definitely arranged. But the two and a half fibs did not irk Evelyn's conscience. They were diplomatically righteous fibs, good and convincing fibs, designed to prevent possible friction. On a busy day he might tell as many as fifty such fibs: and he had never been found out. Miss Powler gave no sign of constraint or self-consciousness. To all appearance she had no nerves.

"I was sorry to lose Rose," said Miss Powler. "She was a first-rate fancy ironer. But of course if she hadn't gone of her own accord she'd have had to go all the same. Because she'd never have let the dentist attend to her. She's too fond of her mother for that. She adores her. The mother's rather pretty and really very young. When she was Rose's age she was a chorus-girl in a touring company for six months. She ought to have kept on being a chorus-girl. She certainly wasn't fit to be a mother. Her head's full of the silliest ideas, poor thing! One of her ideas is that dentists pull teeth out for the sake of doing it. Makes them feel proud, she thinks. No use arguing with that sort of a woman. They *really* believe whatever they want to believe."

"I know what you mean."

"She made Rose promise not to see the dentist, said it was slave-driving for an employer to force a girl to see a dentist. And all that. She'll go on the stage, Rose will, and her father won't be able to stop her. I'm very sorry for the girl. Naturally, if Mr. Purkin makes a rule and gives an order, there's nothing more to be said. I quite see his point of view. Yes. I agree with him--I mean about discipline. But I do think you can't improve silly people when they get obstinate. If they can't understand, they can't, and you can't make them. It couldn't be helped, but I always sympathise with the girl in Rose's position. I wish you could have heard her talk about her mother. She never mentioned her father. Always her mother. She worshipped her mother. And yet she gave you the idea too that she was mother to her mother, not her mother's daughter."

Evelyn had several times before had casual chats with Miss Powler, on Laundry affairs. But now he felt as if he were meeting her for the first time. The interview had all the freshness of a completely new revelation: like the rising of a curtain on a scene whose nature had been almost completely unsuspected. She had said not a word against the disciplinary Mr. Purkin. She had on the contrary supported his authority without reserve. Withal she had somehow left Mr. Purkin stripped of every shred of his moral prestige. She had been responding to the humanity of the Rose problem, while for Mr. Purkin the humanity had had no existence. She had faced the fact of the silliness of Rose's mother, and yet had warmed to the passion of Rose for the foolish creature.

Further, Evelyn now had knowledge in two cases, of her attitude towards women under her control and direction, and there was in it no least evidence of that harsh, almost resentful inflexibility which nearly always characterised such a relation. And her attitude towards himself was either distinguished by a tact approaching the miraculous, or was the natural, unstudied results of a disposition both wise and kindly in an exceptional degree; perhaps she had no need for the use of tact, did not know, practically, what tact was. Evelyn began to think that he had been under-estimating the physical qualities of her face and form. Five minutes earlier he would have described her as comely. But now he was ready to say that she was beautiful--because she must be beautiful, because, being what she was, she could not be other than beautiful. He had to enlarge his definition of feminine beauty in order to make room for her in it. Then her foot. Perhaps large or largeish. But a girl like her ought surely to have something to stand on! And were not small feet absurd, a witness of decadence? Then her ankles. Not slim. Sturdy. Suddenly be remembered the museum at Naples. An excursion which had not revisited his memory for a dozen years. He saw the classical sculptures. Not one of the ideal female figures in those sculptures had been given slim ankles. Every ankle was robust, sturdy; the fashionable darlings of to-day would call them thick. Yes, Miss Powler had classical ankles.

But he would not argue about her ankles, or her feet, or her figure, or her face. In his reckoning of her he could afford to neglect their values. What principally counted was her expression, her demeanour, her tone, the gentle play of her features, and the aura of tranquil benevolence and commonsense which radiated from her individuality. Mr. Purkin was a clumsy simpleton. He had not known how to make her love him. She did not love him. He did not deserve that she should love him. Why in God's name should such a girl love a Mr. Purkin?

Then her accent; a detail, but he considered it. Miss Brury had acquired a West End accent, with all the transmogrified vowel sounds of the West End accent. Miss Powler's accent was not West End. Neither was it East End, nor South. One might properly say that she had no accent. Was she educated? Not possibly in the sense in which Miss Brury was educated. But she was educated in human nature. Her imagination had been educated. And she possessed accomplishments assuredly not possessed by Miss Brury. Could she not dance, act, sing, direct a stage? Was not hers the energy which had vitalised the Imperial Palace Hotel Laundry Amateur Dramatic (and Operatic) Society? It was no exaggeration to say that she was better educated than Miss Brury. Anyhow she would be incapable of Miss Brury's fatal hysteria.

Evelyn rose. Miss Powler rose. He moved. He stopped moving.

"I had another reason for calling to-day," he said, yielding happily to a strong impulse. (Fourth fib.) "We may soon be needing someone rather like you at the Palace." He smiled. "I can't say anything more just now. But perhaps it wouldn't be a bad thing if you considered whether you would care for a change. Don't answer. Good-bye."

But her face answered, discreetly, in the affirmative. He departed. He flattered himself that he had discovered the solution of two entirely unrelated problems.

Chapter 11 SHADES

Evelyn's car had not moved three hundred yards from the Laundry before it was stopped by an oncoming car which sinfully swerved across the street, threatening a bonnet-to-bonnet collision. Fortunately this amazing and inexcusable assault took place in a fairly empty space of road. Evelyn did not at first realise what had happened. His chauffeur, grandly conscious of being in the right, and with a strong sex-bias which had persuaded him that women-drivers were capable of any enormity, sat impassive and even silent, prepared to await developments and a policeman.

Evelyn put his head out of his saloon window. The driver of the other car smiled and waved a hand freely. It was Gracie Savott. Gracie backed her car a few feet and then swerved forward again to her proper side and drew up at the kerb. Evelyn, fully sharing for the moment Brench's sex-bias, got down and walked across the street between approaching trams to Gracie's car.

"I've written all my impressions of Smithfield," she gaily called out to him as he passed in front of her and gained the security of the pavement.

Evelyn was startled by her astonishing performance with the car, and so resentful, that he could hardly bring himself to raise his hat.

"Was it to tell me that that you stopped me?" he asked stiffly. (By heaven, what next?)

"Don't crush me." She pouted.

"How did you know it was my car?" The second question was softer than the first.

"That's nicer," she said, smiling.

He thought that her tone was damned intimate. But fairness made him immediately admit to himself that his own brusque tone had set the example of precocious intimacy.

Gracie said:

"I asked the number of your car before I left the hotel. How else? And I was about five minutes in getting it. They told me you'd probably be at the Laundry, and they gave me the address. I had an instinct I might meet you on the way; that was why I asked the number. And a good thing I did!"

Evelyn's resentment was now submerged by a complete bewilderment. Was the girl pursuing him, and if so to what end? His bewilderment in turn was lost in dismay, in alarm for the demi-god Orcham's reputation. What would his staff think of this young woman demanding his whereabouts and the number of his car? What *could*the staff think? He had been first seen with her at 4 a.m. All the upper grades of the staff must have heard that he had escorted her to Smithfield, brought her back, shown her the ground-floor of the hotel at early morn. And now she had been recklessly betraying an urgent desire to chase him, run him to earth, and capture him! She, a girl, a notorious racing-motorist! Him, the sedate, staid panjandrum of the Palace! It was incredible, unthinkable, inconceivable. The whole hotel must be humming like telegraph-wires with the scandalous tidings. Could he re-enter the hotel without self-consciousness?

Clever of her to think of obtaining the number of the car before starting!...Had she really intended to enquire for him at the Laundry? And why? What was her business? And if her business was so cursedly urgent, hadn't she enough ordinary gumption to telephone? She was evidently an adventuress--in the sense that she loved adventure for its own sake. She was a wild girl. Had she not positively invited him, a stranger, to take her to Smithfield?

"Is anything the matter?" he asked.

"Not yet. But I must talk to you."

"Well?"

"Not here. We can't talk here," she said. "And not at the hotel either."

"Certainly not at the hotel," he silently agreed. And aloud--"Where, then?"

"If you'll get in--"

"But what about my car?"

"Send it home. I'd come with you in your car, but I can't leave mine here in the street, can I?"

Mist was gathering in South London. Dusk was falling. Trams with their ear-shattering roar swept by, looming larger than life in the vagueness of the mist.

Evelyn crossed the road again.

"I shan't want you any more to-night," he said with an exaggerated nonchalance to Brench.

The imperturbable man touched his cap, and glided away.

"She looks a bit better now. I've had her cleaned," said Gracie as she curved her own car into a side street in order to turn back eastwards.

She was wearing the leather coat, and loose gloves to match it. She pushed the car along at great speed among the traffic, driving with all the assured skill of which Evelyn had had experience twelve hours earlier in the day. Once again he was at her side. A few minutes ago he had been in the prosaic industrial environment of the hotel Laundry. And now he was under the adventurous hands of this incalculable girl on another earth. He felt as helpless as a piece of flotsam in some swift shadowy tideway of that other earth. His masculinity rebelled, asserted itself. He must somehow get control of the situation.

"Well?" he repeated, uncompromisingly.

"Not yet." Second time she had used those mysterious words. "I know a place." Still more mysterious! And there was nothing the matter 'yet'!

Evelyn's thought was: "What has to be will be."

Philosophical? Worthy of a man? No! Only a pretence of the philosophical. As for Gracie, she uttered not a syllable more. She drove and drove.

In Westminster Bridge Road a large public-house gleamed in the twilight. It had just opened to customers, and Labour was passing through its swing-doors. And through the doors, and through the windows, frosted into a pattern, could be seen glimpses of mahogany and glazed interiors, with counters and bottles and beer-handles and shabby tipplers of both sexes, and barmen in shirt-sleeves rolled up. The public-house stood on a corner. Gracie twisted the car round the corner and stopped it, opposite a protruding sign which said "Shades."

"Here it is," said Gracie, with a slight movement towards him which indicated that he was expected to get out of the car.

"Here?" he questioned.

"Yes."

"Do you know the place?" he questioned further.

"No. But I happened to notice it as I drove down. It calls itself the Prince of Wales's Feathers."

"Do you mean you want to go in here?"

"Yes. To talk. Why not? *We couldn't have a safer place."* Evelyn had never entered a London public-house. He shrugged his shoulders--those shoulders which she had admired. His faculty of amazement was worn out. He descended. Gracie locked the steering. Then she glanced into the body of the car. Nothing there to tempt thieves.

"That ought to be all right," she murmured.

2.

She stood at the heavy, narrow double doors, expectant that he should open them for her. He pushed hard against one of them. As soon as Gracie had squeezed through the door banged back on Evelyn. Then he had to push it a second time. He too squeezed through, and the door gave a short series of quick bangs, diminuendo.

A small room. A counter in front of them. Shelves full of bottles behind the counter. No barman at the counter. To the left a glazed mahogany partition, very elaborate. A panelled mahogany wall opposite the partition, and another opposite the counter, and advertisements of alcohol across the panels. A very heavily sculptured ceiling. A sanded floor. Along the two panelled walls ran two mahogany benches, with a small round barrel, its top stained in circles, at the angle. A powerful odour of ale. Sound of rough voices, strident or muttering, over the curved summit of the partition.

"Oh! What a horrible lovely place!" said Gracie, sitting down on a bench near the barrel. "But it's exactly what I thought it would be."

A barman appeared at the counter.

"This is mine," said Gracie to Evelyn, and to the barman:

"Two light sherries, please." And to Evelyn: "That right?"

"Right you are, miss," said the barman with cheerful heartiness, and reached down a bottle from one of the shelves.

Evelyn had been afraid that she might order beer; but she had ordered the only correct, the only possible, thing; sherry had at least an air of decorum; also it was the only wholesome aperitif. The girl knew her way about; he supposed that all these girls did; he supposed it was proper that they should, and although he did not quite like it he strove to broaden his views concerning girls in order to like it. "A bit too much of the oriental attitude about me about young women!" he thought.

"Here you are, sir," said the barman, addressing Evelyn this time. And Evelyn had to fetch the two full glasses from the counter.

"One and four, sir."

Evelyn paid.

The counter was wet with sherry. The barman rubbed it hard with a towel that had once been clean. The hearty, hail-fellow-well-met barman in his shirt-sleeves, to say nothing of the dirty towel, made a rude contrast with the manners which obtained at the celebrated Imperial Palace American bar, where the celebrated head-barman was a strict teetotaller with a head like that of a Presbyterian minister and a dispensing knowledge in the head of a hundred and thirteen different cocktails. At the Palace drinks were ceremoniously brought to seated customers by young men in immaculate white jackets--and Evelyn knew the exact sum per dozen debited by the Laundry to the hotel for the washing and getting-up of the white jackets. And no waiter there would venture to name the price of a drink until asked.

"You give me that twopence," said Gracie, fumbling in her bag, as Evelyn sat down with his change in his hand. "And I'll give you eighteenpence."

He accepted the suggestion without argument. Why should not girls pay if they chose? As for the particular case of Gracie, she probably spent on herself the equivalent of Evelyn's entire income, which nevertheless yielded a considerable super-tax to the State. Evidently her big baggage had arrived at the Palace, for she was wearing another frock and still another hat. Beneath and above the stern chic of the leather coat was visible the frivolous chic of the frock and the hat.

"Yours!" said Gracie, raising her glass. "You aren't cross, are you?"

"No. Why should I be?"

"I don't know," said Gracie. "But you look so severe I'm frightened."

"Take more than that to frighten you," Evelyn retorted, forcing a grim smile.

"Not a bad sherry this," he added, enquiring with his brain into the precise sensations of his palate. He was proud that he and no other selected the wines for the Palace. He recalled some good phrases from his formal lectures to the wine-waiters upon their own subject.

"But it is rather a jolly place, isn't it?" said Gracie. "Do come down off the roof to the ground-floor."

He smiled less grimly. Why not be honest? It was indeed rather a jolly place: strange, exotic, romantic. And he did like the freedoms of the barman, after the retired, artificial, costive politenesses of the Palace service. He saw charm even in the dirty towel. (And she had discovered the place, and had had the enterprise to enter it.) He was seeing London, indigenous London. The Palace was no part of London. Why not for a change yield to the attraction of the moment? Of course if he were caught sitting with a smart young woman in a corner of the Prince of Wales's Feathers in Westminster Bridge Road, his friends or his customers or his heads of departments might lift an eye-brow. But he could not be caught. Moreover the Feathers would be the height of respectability to ninety-nine decent Londoners out of a hundred. And even if it were not respectable--well, Gracie was above respectability. Violet Powler would not be. But Gracie was. She had robust ideas about things. He was bound to admire her robust taste, and her adventurous enterprise. Violet Powler would shrink from the invitation of the Feathers. He himself had shrunk from it. He suffered from masculine timidity and conventionality. Gracie and her sort had something to teach him.

"You know the telephone-message you sent to daddy this morning." Gracie began her business. "Well, daddy was fast asleep, and it came to me." She told him quite frankly what she had done. "That's why I wanted to see you." Here she lit a cigarette, and Evelyn, determined to surpass her, lit a cigar. She explained to him her father's Napoleonic sensitiveness. "I'd like you to do something. I couldn't bear any trouble between you and daddy," she finished, with eagerness. Her rich, changing voice fell enchantingly on his ear.

What did that mean: couldn't bear any trouble between him and Sir Henry? Did it mean that any such trouble might compromise the relations between her and himself, and that was what she couldn't bear? Odd, flattering, insidious, specious implication! He leaned closer to her:

"What would you like me to do?"

Intimacy was suddenly increased. How was it that they had become so intimate in a dozen hours of spasmodic intercourse? He knew. It was because they had gone off together on a romantic excursion in what was for her the middle of the night. One visit to strange Smithfield before dawn would create more familiarity, demolish more barriers between soul and soul, than ten exquisite dinners exquisitely served within the trammels of a polite code.Never again could they be mere acquaintances.

"Couldn't you ask daddy to dinner to-night--and me? He'd appreciate it frightfully."

Evelyn was astounded afresh. What on earth would the incredible girl say next? He could not phrase a reply.

Fortunately at this juncture four men entered the bar. They were clad somewhat in the style of Mr. Cyril Purkin, but more flashily. They had glittering watch-chains, jewelled rings, rakish hats and neckties and tie-pins, and assurance. If not prosperous, they looked prosperous. They glanced casually at Evelyn and Gracie, and glanced away. Men of the world, whom vast experience of the world had carried far beyond the narrow curiosity of hard-working persons--persons who had to look twice at sixpence. Evelyn was decidedly more interested in them than they were interested in him and Gracie. They leaned against the counter, called,

"Jock," "Jock," and when Jock came they ordered four double whiskies. They were discussing the day's racing. Then they talked about the secret significance of 'acceptances.' They sipped the whiskies.

One of them, the fattest, having sipped, and gazed at his glass, said in a meditative hoarse voice:

"When I've had a drop over night, do you know what I do? I get up early and I go down to my cellar in my nighty, and I draw myself a port-glass of gin, and I drink that and it puts me right. Yes. That puts me right."

"Well, give me Eno every time," said another gravely. At length in a murmur Evelyn answered Gracie's suggestion:

"No."

"No?"

"No. That wouldn't suit my book at all. Your father would misunderstand it."

A pause.

"He'd think I'd mean what I shouldn't mean," Evelyn added.

"I see," said Gracie. "I hadn't thought of that." She did see. "Well, if daddy asks *you* to dinner to-night, will you come?" Gracie demanded.

Why shouldn't he? If anybody's pitch was likely to be queered by the invitation and the acceptance thereof, it would be Sir Henry's, not Evelyn's. But what a girl! What an incomprehensible feminine, unfeminine creature!

"Yes," said Evelyn. "With pleasure. But in the restaurant, not upstairs But he won't ask me?"

"Oh! Won't he? You leave that to me."

A horn tooted outside.

"That's children playing with the car!" Gracie exclaimed , jumping up and draining her sherry.

Evelyn rose quietly also. He laughed. Gracie laughed. Yes, how thrillingly exotic she seemed in the heavy, frowsy, smoke-laden, fume-poisoned interior! They hurried out like children merrily excited by the prospect of a new escapade. The real children round the car ran off, bounding and shrieking with mischief.

"We may as well go," Gracie suggested.

"Yes, I ought to be going."

Near the junction of Bridge Street and Whitehall Evelyn asked Gracie to stop.

"Why?"

"Because I want to get out," said Evelyn.

"But I'll drive you to the hotel."

"No, thanks!" Evelyn answered very drily and firmly. And got out. He had no intention of being seen by his door-porters driving up to the Imperial Palace in Gracie's car with Gracie at the wheel. It simply would not do. And Gracie yielded with a sweet, acquiescent, almost humble smile. That was the only way to treat young women. Firmness. Let them be as capricious and arbitrary as they chose; what they really liked was to be compelled to obey.

Having moved forward a couple of score yards, Gracie halted the car again and waited for Evelyn to come up with it

"You're afraid of being seen with me in my car," she said, smiling not humbly but mischievously, half-resentfully.

"I am." Evelyn was blunt and careless, but secretly a trifle surprised by the accuracy of her thought-reading.

Gracie drove on. This curt exchange seemed to Evelyn to be further startling proof of intimacy.

He took deep breaths. He was conscious of a much-increased sense of being alive.

Chapter 12 DAUGHTER AND FATHER

Gracie had no sooner entered her sitting-room at the Imperial Palace, leaving the door ajar as she left most doors ajar, than her father pushed open the door and peeped in. She was just dropping her leather coat on to a chair, which was already encumbered with a rug. Sir Henry inferred from the coat that his daughter had been out in the car. He wondered why, but asked no question. The relations between these two were peculiar, yet logical enough, considering their characters. Before he got his title his wife had divorced him, and obtained the custody of the child, then aged seventeen. She obtained also an alimony of five thousand a year. She had tried for ten thousand, and failed. Five thousand or ten thousand: the figure had no practical interest for Henry Savott, but he had fought her ruthlessly.

After three weeks of living with her mother, Gracie had walked into her father's office one day, and said: "Daddy, I understand now." "Understand what?" "You know." Henry Savott had looked harshly at her and growled: "Better late than never." Gracie had then announced that she had not the least intention of living any longer with her mother. "I'm not going to be in anybody's 'custody'! What a word!" Henry Savott had reminded her that she was a minor, and that the decree of the High Court of Justice explicitly put her in her mother's power. Gracie, frequently a realist, had merely laughed. "I'd love to see the Court that could make me live with anybody I don't want to live with. I'm coming to live with you, daddy."

Henry Savott had been tremendously flattered. His daughter's unsolicited testimonial was the finest gift ever bestowed upon him, and he instantly saw that it would do much to restore his damaged prestige in the social world. He offered objections to Gracie's plan, but not convincingly. His maiden sister, who hated his wife, was induced to take theoretical charge over his household.

Gracie had enjoyed freedom from the very beginning of her new life; for her father was absorbed in his vast financial schemes, and her aunt, a hypochondriac with a magnificent constitution, was absorbed in the complex ritual of the treatment of her imagined diseases. As a rule hypochondriacs live for ever. But Miss Savott proved not to be immortal. She died suddenly, untimely, of a malady whose existence had concealed itself even from the hypochondriac's ferreting morbidness. Attired in black on the evening of the funeral, father and daughter had had one of their short, clear, monosyllabic conversations, the result of which was that Gracie at twenty became the head of Sir Henry's household. The unspoken but perfectly understood undertaking on Sir Henry's part was:

"Don't make a fool of yourself, and I won't make a fool of myself or of you. You leave me alone and I'll leave you alone." Twenty years earlier such an arrangement would have been regarded as immoral, but the Savotts were of those rather rare persons who look often at the calendar, not to know the day of the month, but to remind themselves of the Annus Domini. And the arrangement, being between two realists, worked. It suited both of them. Both possessed the faculty of not seeing what it might be inconvenient to see. Sir Henry in his old-fashioned way sometimes felt transient qualms; Gracie never.

Sir Henry had an immense admiration for his daughter, and especially for her worldly common sense. He was proud of her racing achievements, which had cost him a lot of money in the building of monstrously engined cars. In every department of expenditure she was an extremely costly child. But he was free; she was free; she was a capable hostess; and domestic extravagance never disturbed him; for he had a sense of proportion.

The miscarriage of a financial operation in the City might well in a day reduce his resources by more than Gracie could possibly squander in twenty years.

Such was their situation, and it explains why Sir Henry hid whatever curiosity he might have felt about the leather coat.

Two books lay on the floor of the littered, luxurious room. Sir Henry picked them up; for though he had learnt that his daughter's enormous untidiness was incurable, his own instinct for order would out.

"The Bible and Shakspere," he murmured. "Still?"

"The Bible and Shakspere still. And I don't know which is best," said Gracie.

"Why this surprising passion for the classics?" he twitted her.

"I only like them--that's all," said Gracie negligently. "I'm just reading the Psalms."

"Why the Psalms?" he continued to twit the girl, "I should have thought the biography of David would be more in your line--as a contemporary young woman."

"The Psalms *are* David's biography," Gracie replied.

He reflected:

"How does the kid think of these remarks of hers. Something in that. I never thought of it." He was not an ardent reader.

"Oh!" he said.

"Yes. The finest thing in all the Bible is in the Psalms."

"Oh!" he repeated, smiling. "What's that? I'd like to hear."

Gracie quoted with a certain solemnity:

"Be still, and know that I am God.' *Be still.*"Sombrely contemplative, she gazed at her parent, so dapper, so physically fresh in his age, so earthly, so active in his unending material schemes, so deaf and blind to the spiritual, so regardless of all that was incalculable by an adding machine. He fancied that her eyes were fixed upon his magnificent, regular white teeth, which she had once called cruel, and instinctively he closed his lips on them, thus ceasing to smile.

"Shall I ever get to the bottom of this kid's mind?" he asked himself, puzzled, uneasy, as it were intimidated; but still admiring. He dropped the books on to a table.

2.

Then there was a second swift disconcerting change in Gracie's mood.

"What are you going to do to-night, daddy?"

"I'm going to bed. You know I never do anything the first day, anywhere."

She seemed not to be listening to him.

"Because," she continued, "I've just seen Mr. Orcham."

"I'm waiting to hear from him," said Sir Henry drily.

"He's only this minute come back into the hotel. Been out all day."

"How do you know?"

"Don't I say I've just seen him?"

"You seem to be very friendly with him?" Sir Henry quizzed her.

"Oh! I am! He took me to Smithfield Market this morning."

"He asked you to go to Smithfield with him!"

"No. I asked him to take me."

"When?"

"After you went off to bed."

"I hope he didn't think I'd put you up to it," said Sir Henry, disturbed.

"How could he have thought that? I didn't know he was going to Smithfield until a minute before you went off. I'm glad I asked him. It was most frightfully amusing. And if I'd gone to bed I shouldn't have been able to sleep. It filled in the time perfectly. I was thinking you might invite him to dinner tonight."

"I invite him to dinner! And in his own hotel! No fear! The last thing I want is for him to think I'm running after him. You can understand that. If he doesn't suggest anything, after my message to him, *I* shan't suggest anything."

Gracie said with absolute tranquillity:

"Then you go to bed, and I'll ask him. I like him." Sir Henry exercised the self-restraint which experience of Gracie had taught him.

"He won't accept."

"I'll bet ten to one he will."

"In the restaurant? He won't."

"Well, we'll see."

Sir Henry reconsidered the position. If Orcham accepted an invitation from Gracie alone, it would mean that he might be getting wrong notions into his head. If he declined, undesirable complications might ensue. Sir Henry went to the door.

"You ask him for both of us. Nine o'clock. Send a note down. Let me know the reply." Sir Henry departed without waiting for Gracie to speak.

"Father," she ran to the door and called out after him in the corridor:

"What's his Christian name?"

She wrote, in her large hand: "Dear Mr. Evelyn Orcham. Father and I would be so glad if you would dine with us tonight in the restaurant. Nine o'clock. Please don't disappoint us. Yours sincerely, G. S."

She rang for the waiter.

Mrs. O'Riordan, the head-housekeeper, brightly sustaining the cares of her kingdom, entered, in front of the waiter, to pay one of those state-visits which she vouchsafed only to very important guests or very angry guests. She enquired whether Gracie's comfort and satisfaction were complete and without flaw. Gracie, recognising at once a superior member of the hotel-hierarchy, invited Mrs. O'Riordan to sit down. The two had quite a long chat. Then Gracie lavished more than an hour and a half upon her evening toilette, melancholy Tessa helping her as well as a bandaged wrist permitted.

Chapter 13 GREEN PARROT

Evelyn entered the foyer at one minute to nine. Certainly one of his gods was Punctuality, though there were greater gods in his pantheon. When master of his movements he was never late, nor early; his knowledge of the hour, and of the minute of the hour, was almost continuous.

A thin stream of guests was passing from the great hall through the foyer into the restaurant. Other guests were sipping cocktails at the small tables in the foyer; and still others were seated on the sofas, contributing naught to the night's receipts of the foyer, but safeguarding their stomachs. Not a single guest recognised Evelyn; Mr. Cousin would have been recognised and saluted by several of them; Evelyn's personality was more recondite. Only the knowing ones knew that Mr. Cousin, the manager, had a superior.

In the lounge were two cloak-room attendants, knee-breeched and gorgeous, who looked as if they had escaped from the Court of the Prince Regent, two cocktail pages in white and gold, a foyer-waiter dressed as a waiter, and two head-waiters of the restaurant, who stood on the lower stairs to receive diners; for every arriving party was personally conducted to its table and not abandoned by the conductor until the head-waiter of the table had received it into his hands. All these employees were immediately and acutely aware of the unusual presence of Evelyn, but, under standing orders, they ignored it: not an easy feat.

At nine o'clock Sir Henry Savott appeared; he glanced at his watch, and his austere face betrayed a high consciousness that punctuality was the politeness of emperors. He descried Evelyn. The two smiled, mutually approached, shook hands, and as it were took positions for a duel.

"I was just going to telephone up to you, and suggest an appointment for to-morrow," said Evelyn genially, "when I got your daughter's most kind invitation."

"Very good of you to accept at such short notice," said Sir Henry. "Have a cocktail?"

"Yes, thanks," said Evelyn simply, and indicated an empty table.

"What's the matter with the bar?" asked Sir Henry. "Ihear you've had it redecorated."

"But Miss--er--Gracie?"

"Gracie has never been known to be less than a quarter of an hour late for lunch or dinner," said Sir Henry. "Like most women she has a disorderly mind. Not disordered," he added.

The two males exchanged a complacent, condescending look which relegated the entire female sex to its proper place, and strolled side by side up the stairs, along the broad corridor which led past the grill-room into the American bar.

The cocktail department comprised two large rooms: the first was permitted to ladies; the second, containing the majestic bar, was forbidden to them. By a common impulse Sir Henry and his guest for the evening walked without hesitation into the second room and sat down in a corner. Each waited for the other to open. Neither knew that the mind of the other was preoccupied with one sole image: that of Gracie. Evelyn was thinking: "She said she'd fix it, and she's fixed it." Sir Henry was thinking: "What's the meaning of this whim for getting this fellow to dinner?...'Be still, and know that I am God.' Good God!" (But naïve pride was mingled with his non-comprehension.)

Sir Henry glanced around with feigned curiosity at the floodlighting, the silvern ceiling, the Joseph's-coat walls decorated in rhomboidal shapes which bar-frequenters described as cubistic or futuristic or both. He did not like it.

"Very original," he commented. "Charming. I expect it was good for a bit of useful publicity, this was."

"It was," said Evelyn. "Change from the traditional British bar, eh?" He saw himself and Gracie incredibly hobnobbing in the Prince of Wales's Feathers in Westminster Bridge Road.

A white-jacketed, black-trousered youth ceremoniously approached.

"Maddix," Evelyn murmured to him before Sir Henry could speak.

The youth hurried away.

There were four solemn revellers at the bar, and a priest and an acolyte behind it. The ascetic priest was a thin, short, middle-aged man with a semi-bald cranium, a few close-cropped grey hairs, and an enormous dome of a forehead above grey eyes. Leaving the bar and his customers to the care of the acolyte, the priest came tripping with dignity across the room and halted in silence at Evelyn's elbow.

"Well, Maddix, what's your latest? Apollo?" Evelyn asked, hardly smiling.

"The Apollo is quite new, sir. But my latest I've christened Green Parrot. I only really finished it last night."

"Not on the market yet?"

"Not as you might say, sir."

"Well, Sir Henry, will you try a Green Parrot?"

"Good evening, Sir Henry," said Maddix, his tone a mixture of deference and self-respect.

"Why of course it's Maddix!" Sir Henry exclaimed, holding out his hand. "How are you, Maddix? Haven't seen you since God knows when--at the Plaza in New York. You were a very famous figure there."

Maddix took the offered hand with reserve.

"Yes, sir," he agreed placidly. "I suppose I was. I suppose I was the best-known barman in New York for twenty years. Prohibition and Mr. Orcham brought me back home."

"And how are the boys?" Sir Henry enquired.

"Which boys, Sir Henry? The general bar population?"

"No. Your two sons of course." A swift change transformed the impassive countenance of the legendary world-figure, the formidable man whose demeanour divided the general bar population of the two greatest capitals in history into two groups, the group which ventured to address him as 'Maddix,' with or without familiar additions, and the group which did not venture. The countenance relaxed and showed human emotion.

"Thank you for remembering them, Sir Henry. The eldest is still over there. Fur trade. Seems to be dollars in it. The other one's with me and his mother, here."

"And what's he doing?"

"Well, Sir Henry, you may think it queer. But I've got a tennis court back of my little house at Fulham, and the boy's gone mad on tennis. He means to be a professional player. His mother isn't very pleased. But *I* say, 'What can you do--if he's made up his mind?' Between parents and children things aren't what they used to be, are they, Sir Henry?"

"They are not," the millionaire concurred, thinking of Gracie.

"A Green Parrot then, Sir Henry?"

"I'll risk it."

"And you, sir?"

Evelyn said:

"Soft."

"Excuse me, gentlemen," said Maddix. "I should prefer to mix that Green Parrot myself." He went away.

"A character!" observed Sir Henry. "How did you manage to get him away from New York?"

"I saw him once or twice when I was over there," Evelyn answered placidly. "He said he'd like to come home. I believed him. Considering Prohibition! A man who can live for twenty years behind a New York bar and never pick up an American accent--and never use a word of American slang--well, there must be something incurably English about him. I told him I had the finest American bar in the world, and I wanted the finest barman in the world to take charge of it. He came. Of course he gets the salary of an Under-Secretary of State. So he ought to."

"Not quite the cocktail hour here, is it?" said Sir Henry, again glancing around at the large, half-empty room.

"No. It's too late and too early. But it'll soon be the liqueur hour. Extraordinary how many men prefer to come in here for a drink at the end of a meal. They feel more at home near a bar, even if they don't stand at it."

2.

Two fat men in lounge-suits wandered in. The first word that Evelyn caught in their self-conscious conversation was the word 'Acceptances.' He knew and cared absolutely nothing about racing; but he had the wit to gather that Acceptances were one of the few human phenomena capable of making all men kin. The talk among the leaners against the bar suddenly rose to loudness. "And *I* say that gin is the--" he heard, from an affected and disputatious voice. (He would have liked to hear a profound remark concerning women from some other quarter of the room; but he was disappointed.) He thought:

"There was a quality about that wigwam in the Westminster Bridge Road that this place hasn't got. The free-and-easy! This place is too stiff." And he began to wonder how the Prince of Wales's Feathers' quality could be added to the qualities of the Imperial Palace American bar. "No!" he decided. "Couldn't be done. Wouldn't do, either." But he regretted its absence from the too correct and august atmosphere of the place.

Then a procession moved from the bar in the direction of Evelyn and Sir Henry: an acolyte solemnly bearing a tray upon which were two small glasses, one green, one yellow, followed by the priestly Maddix. Evelyn took the yellow glass, Sir Henry the green. The acolyte bowed and retired. Maddix stood awaiting in silence the verdict of Sir Henry. Evelyn absurdly wished that Maddix, with rolled-up shirt-sleeves exposing hairy forearms, might have exclaimed freely: "Well, what abaht it, guv'nor?"

Observing that Sir Henry's eyes were on Evelyn's glass, not on his own, Maddix allowed himself to remark:

"Mr. Orcham is not much for cocktails."

"I'm much more for cocktails than you are, Maddix," Evelyn said. And to Sir Henry: "Maddix is a strict teetotaller."

"Then how do you manage to invent these things?" asked Sir Henry, gazing now at the green glass.

"I taste. I never swallow."

Sir Henry both tasted and swallowed, and putting on the air of a connoisseur, amiably delivered judgment: "Very original. Very good."

Maddix bowed his gratitude--a bow hardly perceptible; he had divined that to the millionaire all cocktails were more or less the same cocktail. The experience of decades, the inventive imagination of a genuine creator, and some good luck had gone into the conceiving of the Green Parrot cocktail, and the millionaire recked not, sympathised not, understood not! He had been friendly enough about the human offspring of the cocktail genus, but to the miracles of cocktail art God had decreed that he should be insensible. As a fact Maddix did not know more than ten men in London who truly comprehended the great classical principles of the cocktail. Evelyn was one of the ten.

Sir Henry began to talk to Evelyn. Maddix sedately walked away, the artist sardonic because unappreciated by a barbaric public.

Presently Evelyn glanced at his watch.

"Perhaps we ought to go back to the foyer.'

"Lots of time," said Sir Henry soothingly.

At that moment the whole room, from the bar to the furthest corner, became agitated with a unique agitation, and every masculine face seemed to be saying: "Strange things have happened, but this is the strangest." Oblivious of the printed notice prominently displayed at the entrance, a woman was intruding. And not merely a woman, but a young woman, a beautiful woman, proud of bearing, clad in a magnificent frock of mauve and pink, and glinting with jewels. And neither apology nor challenge in her mien. Maddix started instinctively into protest at this desecration; then stopped, thinking: "A greater than me is here. Let him deal with the unparalleled outrage." And yet the outrage was delicious to every beholding male, even to Maddix himself. The woman went straight to Evelyn and Sir Henry, who both rose quickly. Sir Henry at any rate felt that she must be removed at once. Evelyn did not care whether she was removed or not: in the Palace he was above all laws; the one law was his own approval.

"I got tired of waiting for you in the foyer," the smiling woman greeted them with entirely unresentful charm. "So I asked where you were."

The two men were like sixth-form boys convicted of an impropriety.

"Been waiting long?" asked Sir Henry.

"Oh no! Not more than an hour. This place is more old-fashioned than I thought it was." Such was her indication of awareness that she was where she knew she had no right to be. "I think a public-house would be more up-to-date than this. I know I should adore public-houses. Don't you adore them, Mr. Orcham?"

"I'm not very well acquainted with public-houses," said Evelyn.

"Never been in one?"

"Oh yes. Once."

"How long ago?"

"Oh! Not very long ago."

Evelyn saw in her something of the woman who at the banked corners of the Brooklands track had many times staked her life on the accuracy of an instantaneous appraisal of positions, speeds and distances. He perceived that she liked his replies. He admired her tremendously. He was dazzled by her. He knew that she knew he was dazzled by her. Sir Henry also was somewhat overset, and quite incapable of reproaching her for the wilful audacity of her invasion. She had put him in the wrong. She triumphantly led out the two men as though they had been captives to an Amazon. She vanished from the view of the room, and to all the seated, entranced males the room seemed to be suddenly darkened.

Chapter 14 VOLIVIA

In the American bar the hour for cocktails had nearly finished, but guests were still drinking them, though perhaps with more refined gestures, in the foyer; and people were still passing down through the foyer into the restaurant.

Dinner-time at the Imperial Palace, if still not as late as in Venice, Paris, Madrid, was getting later, and nearer and nearer to supper-time. A crowded, confused scene of smart frocks, dowdy frocks, jewels genuine and sham, black coats, white shirts, white table-cloths, silver, steel, glass, coloured chairs, coloured carpets, parquet in the midst, mirrors, melody, and light glinting through the crystal of chandeliers.

A tall and graceful youngish man, with an expression of gentle smiling melancholy on his dark face, greeted Gracie, Sir Henry and Evelyn on the lower steps, and led them to a table on the edge of the empty parquet. Having seated them, he stood with bent, attentive head at Sir Henry's elbow.

"You're doing some business here to-night, Cappone," said Evelyn, losing the self-consciousness which usually afflicted him on the rare occasions when as a diner he descended those broad steps into the restaurant. Cappone's response was a soft triumphant smile. Sir Henry, always self-conscious at first in a public place, concealed his constraint as well as he could under a Napoleonic brusquerie. Gracie, stared at by a hundred eyes until she sat down, was just as much at her ease as a bride at a wedding. Created by heaven to be a cynosure, rightly convinced that she was the best-dressed woman in the great, glittering, humming room, her spirit floated on waves of admiration as naturally as a goldfish in water. Evelyn, impressed, watched her surreptitiously as she dropped on to the table an inlaid vanity-case which had cost her father a couple of hundred pounds.

"Same girl," thought Evelyn, "who was hobnobbing with me in a leather coat about two minutes since in the Prince of Wales's Feathers!"

Surely in the wide world that night there could not be anything to beat her! Idle, luxurious rich, but a masterpiece! Maintained in splendour by the highly skilled and expensive labour of others, materially useless to society, she yet justified herself by her mere appearance. And she knew it, and her conscience was clear.

Mr. Cappone having accepted three menus from a man who stood behind him with a tablet in his hand, distributed them among his guests.

"Well now, let's see," said Sir Henry, applying eye-glasses to his nose, and paused. "Oh! Look here, Cappone, I think we'll leave it all to you."

"Very well, Sir Henry. Thank you," said Mr. Cappone, gathering up the menus, and departing with his subaltern.

"That's right, isn't it, Orcham?" Sir Henry questioned.

"You couldn't have done better, Savott," said Evelyn, curt and confident.

"I suppose he's the head-waiter," said Gracie, indicating Mr. Cappone.

"Head-waiter!" Evelyn exclaimed, with an intonation somewhat sardonic, laughing drily. "I'm glad he didn't hear you. There are thirty head-waiters in this room. No. Cappone is the manager of the restaurant." The more Gracie dazzled him, the more was he determined to keep these Savotts in their place. After all, was he not old enough to be the girl's father? It was as if he resented her dominion equally with her ignorance of hotel terminology.

"And all he has to do is to look romantic and be exquisitely polite?" Gracie went on, quite wilfully unaware of her place.

"Yes. That's all," Evelyn agreed, and paused. "Well, there may be one or two other things he has to do. Settle the menus with the chef. Attend conferences. Watch the graph curves of the average bill every day. Explain satisfactorily the occasional presence of a worm in a lettuce--not so simple, that! Know the names and private histories and weaknesses and vanities and doings of every regular customer. Talk four languages. Keep the peace among his staff over the distribution of the tips. Know exactly how every dish is cooked. Persuade every customer that he has got the best table in the place. Prevent customers who prefer the *prix fixe* from choosing more expensive things than the price will stand. Find new waiters, because even waiters die and quarrel and so on. That's one of his worries, the waiter question. You can't bring foreigners into the country, and English lads simply refuse to go abroad to finish their education. Cappone says that English waiters would be as good as any, and better in some ways; only there's one thing they can't learn, and it's the most important thing."

"Ha! What's that?" Sir Henry demanded.

"That the customer is always right, of course. It's that terrible British sense of justice! Well, those are a few of the odd trifles that our graceful friend has to think about, besides looking romantic," Evelyn ended with a faint sneer. He thought:

"Why am I talking like this? Why have I got the note wrong?"

"It's perfectly thrilling," said Gracie, with an enchanting, excited, modest smile.

Evelyn said to himself:

"She understands. She has imagination. More than daddy has."

"Yes, yes," Sir Henry grunted absently, his inquisitive small eyes prying into the far corners of the restaurant.

"Do tell us some more," Gracie pleaded, leaning eagerly towards Evelyn across the table, her beautiful face all lighted up.

"About waiters?"

"About anything. Yes, about waiters." Evelyn's tone had apparently not in the least ruffled her. She was admiring him. She was kissing the rod.

"Well," said Evelyn. "Cappone says that English waiters look very smart in the street, off duty, but in the restaurant they don't care how they look, whereas his precious Italians look very smart on duty, and don't look like anything on earth in the street. I mean the *commis* of course, the youths in the long aprons. Not the *chefs de rang.* English or not, they *have* to look smart on duty."

He forced Sir Henry to meet his gaze. These people had got to know the sort of man they'd asked to dinner, and he would teach them. If daddy fancied he was going to buy the Imperial Palace for nineteen and eleven--

Mr. Cappone reappeared, to lay an orchid on the table in front of Gracie, who glanced up at him, and without a spoken word gave the Restaurant-manager such a smile as Evelyn had never before seen. And Mr. Cappone gave her a smile, respectful and yet adoringly masculine, that made Evelyn say to himself: "I couldn't smile like that to save my life."

"He's a dear," Gracie murmured, picking up the exotic flower. And to Evelyn: "Go on. Go on."

But at that moment a waiter arrived with a dish of caviare on a carriage, and another with three tiny glasses on a tray.

"Hello! What's this?" asked Sir Henry, suddenly attentive. "Vodka," said Evelyn. "I hope it's vodka." And his tone said: "No doubt you thought it was gin."

The repast began. They were all hungry. The unique caviare, the invaluable vodka, rapidly worked a miracle in the immortal spirit of Sir Henry. Gracie ate and drank with exclamatory delight. As for Evelyn, his testy mood faded away in fifteen seconds. The table now participated in the festivity of the great room. God reigned. The earth was perfect. No stain upon it, no sorrow, no injustice, no death! And life was worth living. Beauty abounded. Civilisation was at its fullest bloom. There was no yesterday, and there would be no to-morrow. And all because the pickled ovarian parts of a fish, and a liquid distilled from plain rye, were smoothly passing into the alimentary tracts of the three ravenous diners.

2.

Then in the orchestra a drum rolled solemnly, warningly, even menacingly; and everyone looked towards the orchestra, expectant. The orchestra, having for more than an hour drawn out of a series of Hungarian melodies the last wild, melancholy sweetness, began to play Russian dance music. The high curtains at the end of the room moved mysteriously apart, revealing a blaze of light behind. In the midst of this amber radiance stood a dark woman, half-clad or quarter-clad in black and white: costume of an athlete, ceasing abruptly at the arm-pits and the top of the thighs. She was neither beautiful nor slim nor elegant as she stood there, nor was her performer's smile better than good-natured.

"So you've fallen for it," said Gracie, under the loud applause which welcomed the apparition.

"Fallen for what?" asked Evelyn.

"Cabaret."

"We've had a cabaret here for two years," said Evelyn.

It was true, however, that for a very long time the Imperial Palace had set its face against cabaret. The Palace had been above cabaret, was too refined and dignified for cabaret, needed no cabaret, flourishing as it did on its prestige, its food, and the distinction of its clientele. But Evelyn had recognised that the Time-Spirit was irresistible, and cabaret had come to the Palace. Of course not the ordinary run of cabaret. Inconceivable that the Palace cabaret should be that!

Soup and hock were unobtrusively delivered at Sir Henry's table. Waiters on the edges of the room were unobtrusively inserting new tables between tables.

The woman stepped into the centre of the dancing-floor with all the mien of a victor; for, although this was only her third evening; she knew that she was a success. Everybody knew that she was a success. Waiters glanced aside at her as they did their work. In the distances guests were standing up to watch. In two days the tale of Volivia's exhibition of herself had spread like a conflagration through what is called the town--without the help of the press. When she opened Volivia had been nobody. Now, because she had so unmistakably succeeded at the Palace, she could get contracts throughout the entire western world of luxury. Her muscles knew it as they contracted and expanded, making ripples on her olive skin.

She flowed into a dance, which soon developed into a succession of abrupt, short, violent motions. Ugly! Evelyn was witnessing the turn for the first time. He was puzzled. "The public is an enigma," he thought. "They like it; but what do they like in it? I wouldn't look twice at it myself." Nevertheless the woman held his gaze. He snatched a glance at Gracie, who was completely absorbed in the spectacle, her vermilion lips apart; at Sir Henry, whose eyes were humid. Then his gaze was dragged back to the dancer. She was now beginning to circle round the floor; faster and faster, in gyrations of the body, stoopings, risings, whirlings: arms uplifted, disclosing the secrets of the arm-pits. In her course, she came close to the tables, so close to Sir Henry's table that Evelyn could have touched her. He saw her rapt face close; he heard her breathing. The sexual, sinister quality of her body frightened and enchanted him. She passed along. His desirous thought was:

"She will be round again in a moment." He understood then why she was a success, why the rumour of her ran from mouth to mouth through the town. Faster and faster. Someone applauded. Applause everywhere, louder and louder. Waiters stood still. Faster and faster. Her face was seen alternately with her bare back: swift alternations that sight could hardly follow. Louder and louder applause. A kind of trial of endurance between Volivia and the applause. At last she manœuvred herself into the centre of the floor, and suddenly dropped on to the hard floor in a violent *entrechat.* And kept the pose, smiling, her bosom heaving in rapid respirations, her tremendous legs stretched out at right-angles to her torso. And, keeping the pose, ugly as in itself it was, she now appeared graceful, elegant, beautiful and young. The applause roared about the great room, wave of it responding to every invisible wave of conquering sensual sexuality which effused powerfully from her accomplished body.

Sir Henry applauded loudly; Gracie applauded without any reserve. Evelyn wanted to applaud, but he restrained himself; he did not want to be seen applauding--not that anyone would have noticed him in the excited din.

Volivia rose, bowed and retired: Aphrodite, Ariadne, Astarte. The applause persisted. Volivia returned, and, with her, two male dancers, boyish, said by the learned to be her brothers, and by the more learned to be her nephews, or even her sons. They came into the category of the grotesque, dancing on their ankles, on the outer sides of their calves, with their knees seldom unbent. They had a reception whose enthusiasm was little less warm than that of Volivia's. Then Volivia, whose departure from the floor had hardly been observed, returned again, for a final trio or ensemble with the youths. This conclusion was the apogee of the number. Nothing whatever of the anti-climax about it. Call it a tumult, a typhoon, a tangled dervish confusion, so sensational in its mingling of two sexes that diners neglected to dine and forgot to breathe.

"The roof'll be off in a minute," shouted Sir Henry, furiously clapping, in the deafening clamour. Again Evelyn did not applaud. After the three had retired, Volivia reappeared alone, to accept that which was hers. The curtains joined their folds and hid her. The diners breathed, but did not yet eat. They were sorry that the number was over, but also relieved that it was over.

The next and last number was a clown, who translated the classical tradition of the English music-hall droll into French. He was an artist in the comic, and the diners laughed, but with more amiability than sincerity. And they ate.

Evelyn thought:

"What on earth has Jones Wyatt been thinking about? This clown fellow has been set an impossible task. It's not fair to him. He must come before Volivia, not after. I'll have it altered for the midnight performance."

"You know, really," said Sir Henry, while the clown was clowning. "Those boys were better than the girl." Evelyn nodded carelessly, reflecting: "Does he mean it? Or is he just pretending to be judicial, saving his face for us and for himself too? After the exhibition he's been making of himself!" If Sir Henry was trying to save his face there were others in the restaurant making a similar attempt.

"Where did you pick her up?" Sir Henry continued, as if indifferently curious.

"Prague, I believe. Praha's its new name, isn't it? I have a man always running about the Continent after really good turns. They're not so easy to find."

"Cost you a lot?"

Evelyn hesitated. He was on the point of saying "Oh! A goodish bit. I don't remember the exact figure." Just to keep Sir Henry in his place! Then he changed his mind. There was a more effective way of keeping Sir Henry in his place. The way of the facts. "Yes. Volivia and Co. stand us in for eighty pounds a week. The other turn forty or fifty. Bands and cabaret come to not a penny less than twelve hundred a week." And he added to himself: "Get that into your head, my friend."

"Bands so much?" Sir Henry gave an excellent imitation of imperturbability.

"Yes."

"How many bands?"

"Three."

"One's American?"

"Yes. Here they are." Evelyn waved towards the bustle and the glitter of new instruments on the bandstand.

"I knew they got biggish money in New York," said Sir Henry.

"They get biggish money in London," Evelyn retorted. "Why! I happened to be going out by the Queen Anne entrance the other day, and the whole alley was blocked with cars. I asked the porter about it--he's a waggish sort of a chap. He told me they were the cars of 'the gentlemen of the orchestra'!"

"By Jove!" Sir Henry exclaimed, glancing round. "There's Harry Matcham. The very man I want to see. That big round table."

"Lord Watlington?"

"Yes. Gracie, I think I'd better step over to him now and fix a date. Excuse me, Orcham--one second."

Mahomets go to mountains.

During this interlude of chat, Gracie had not uttered one word. Nor had she eaten. She was playing, meditative, with the chain of her vanity-case.

"Step over, daddy," she said.

"Lord Watlington hasn't had a dinner-party here for quite a long time," said Evelyn. "Cappone was beginning to think he'd deserted us." Gracie did not speak. Evelyn went on: "I see Mrs. Penkethman with him, and Lady Devizes and the two Cheddars. Rather Renaissance young men, those Cheddars, don't you think?" Gracie still did not speak. Evelyn went on:

"I don't recognise any of the others."

"You know," said Gracie suddenly, looking up into Evelyn's eyes with a soft smile, "that wouldn't do in a drawing-room."

"What wouldn't do?"

"That Volivia show."

"No. Scarcely," Evelyn agreed. "A drawing-room would be a bit too intimate for it. But if it pleases people in a restaurant--well, there you are; it pleases them. Volivia's the biggest cabaret success we've ever had here. Now before the war that turn wouldn't have been respectable. I do believe it would have emptied any restaurant--or filled it with exactly the sort of person *we* don't want. But we give it now, and the Palace is just as respectable as ever it was. More, even. Look at the people here!"

"It was shameless," said Gracie.

"Perhaps too shameless," Evelyn replied. "I admit I should have had my doubts about it if I'd seen it on the first night. But the proof of the pudding is in the eating. It's audiences that make a show respectable--or not. I've heard our Cabaret-manager say it takes two to settle that point--the show and the audience. But I don't think so. The audience settles it. I'm sure some of these variety artists start out to be--well, questionable." He was choosing his words so as to avoid abrading Gracie's girlish susceptibilities. He meant 'indecent.' "But sufficient applause, frank, unreserved applause, will make them feel absolutely virtuous with the very same show."

He was defending his Imperial Palace against the delicious girl who had used the adjective 'shameless.' She had changed now from the invader of the cocktail bar.

"I'm sorry you think it was shameless," he said.

Gracie smiled at him still more exquisitely and more softly. "I loved it for being shameless," she said, not with any protest in her rich, dark voice, but persuasively. "Why shouldn't it be shameless? We aren't shameless enough. What's the matter with the flesh anyway? Don't we all know what we are? If I could give a performance like Volivia's, wouldn't I just go on the stage! Nobody should stop me, I tell you that." Some emphasis in the voice. Then she restrained the emphasis, murmuring: "I'm rather like Volivia. Only she was born to perform, and I wasn't."

Evelyn was very seriously taken aback, partly by the realisation that he had completely misjudged her attitude, and partly by the extraordinary candour with which she had revealed herself. If she had averted her gaze, if her voice had been uncertain, he would have been less disconcerted. But she had continued to face him boldly, and her tones, though low, had given no sign of any inward tremor. And she had not made a confession, she had made a statement. She was indeed as shameless as Volivia. But how virginally, and how unanswerably!

Evelyn thought:

"I suppose this is the modern girl. I mustn't lose my presence of mind." He said, trying to copy her serenity: "And yet you say Volivia wouldn't do in a drawing-room! Why not?"

"Simply because in a drawing-room she'd make me feel uncomfortable. If I feel uncomfortable I always know something's wrong. But here I didn't feel a bit uncomfortable. *You* did, and so did daddy. But not me. Besides, you wouldn't agree that what can't be done in a drawing-room oughtn't to be done at all. A big restaurant's much the same as a bedroom. You see what I mean?"

"Not quite."

"Well, you will," said Gracie with gentle assurance. "Aren't you going to ask me to dance?"

"In the middle of dinner?"

"Why not? What a question, from you!"

3.

The Californian "Big Oak Band," with its self-complacent leader Eleazer Schenk at a green and yellow grand piano, was just emitting its first wild woodland notes; the first professional dancing couple was just taking the floor beneath the patronising glances of the dandiacal, tight-waisted bandsmen; and Sir Henry's wine-waiter was just pouring forth champagne from a magnum bottle. The general gay noise of chatter had increased. For not only at Sir Henry's table, but everywhere up and down the room, great wines after elaborate years of preparation were reaching their final, glorious, secret goal, quickening hearts as well as tickling palates. And under the influence of these superfine golden and ruby and amber liquids, valued at as much as five shillings a glassful, quaffed sometimes in a moment, the immortal tendency to confuse indulgence with happiness was splendidly maintained. The graph-curves of alcohol consumption per head might be downwards, to the grief of the hierarchs of the Imperial Palace; but on this Volivia night the sad decline was certainly arrested for a space. Mr. Cappone and his cohort of head-waiters and humbler aproned *commis* knew all about that.

"I don't dance," said Evelyn shortly.

He rarely did dance, and never on his own floor. For him, there would have been something improper in him, Director of the Imperial Palace, deity of thirteen hundred employees, disporting himself on the Palace floor. And further, he had not yet in the least recovered from the shock of Gracie's shattering remarks upon the moral excellence of shamelessness. 'We all know what we are,' etc. There she sat, to the left of him, lovely, radiant, elegant, fabulously expensive, with her soft smile, her gentle, thrilling tone, her clear, candid gaze, her modest demeanour--likening restaurants to bedrooms, and--'we all know what we are'! And he, Evelyn, monarch of the supreme luxury hotel of the world, had ingenuously been thinking that in his vast and varied experience he had nothing to learn about human nature!

"Oh! So you don't dance!" said she most sweetly.

She might, Evelyn reflected, be a bewildering mixture of contradictions, but she was the most enchanting creature he had ever met. She had bowed her glory in instant acquiescence.

"Why do you have American bands here?" she enquired in a new tone, as if conversationally to set him at ease after his curt refusal to dance. Yes, she was the ideal companion. He recalled the obstinacies of his dead wife.

"Because they're the best," he replied, in relieved, brighter accents. "We're miles behind them in this country. You see, the dance craze started earlier over there than here. They're better disciplined, and they have a better rhythm. They've taught us a lot. An English player who takes his work seriously will give his head to play next to an American for a month. Rather! Of course we get the best even of the Americans, because we give the best treatment, to say nothing of the best advertisement--not direct advertisement. Oh no! Never! The tall fellow with the saxophone--he earns fifty pounds a week. We give them a sitting-room and dressing-rooms, and a valet, and two porters to carry their instruments about. We even press their clothes for them free of charge. They behave like dukes, and we behave to them as if they *were* dukes. But we wouldn't look at 'em if we could find any English band as good, or nearly as good."

He had spoken with earnestness, for he was very sensitive on the subject of engaging American bands in a London hotel. Italian and French and Swiss managers, chefs, waiters--yes! They needed no defence. But American bands had to be defended.

"Well, I never knew that," said Gracie, her voice full of understanding and sympathy. "I thought it was a question of fashion, and pleasing American customers."

"Not in the least!" said Evelyn with fire. "We make fashions here. We don't follow fashions. And we don't kowtow to Americans or anybody else. The Palace is the Palace." He laughed. "Excuse me," he added, lightly apologetic.

"I like to hear you," said Gracie, and Evelyn felt that she did like to hear his vehemence. She was a girl of quick comprehension.

Sir Henry returned to his table. Gracie immediately rose.

"Mr. Orcham and I are going to have just one dance, daddy," she said calmly. "You get on with your trout. Then we shall be level again." And she looked down at seated Evelyn with an expectant, beseeching, marvelously smiling glance.

"But--"

Evelyn checked himself, mastering his amazement at her wanton duplicity. As for shamelessness!...He might have resisted, but for the half-timid supplication in her smile. No! He knew that he could not anyhow have resisted. He was caught. Mixture of contradictions! She was utterly incalculable! He rose in silence, forced a smile in response to hers, and took the hand of the baffling enigma. And no sooner had he taken her hand than he thought: "After all, why shouldn't I dance on my own floor? It isn't as if her father wasn't here." They embarked upon the sea of the floor, which was very rapidly filled with craft. From time to time in their circumnavigation they passed close by Mr. Eleazar Schenk, who, neglecting his fingers in a tune which they had been playing twice nightly for six or seven months, looked at Evelyn with a glance of condescending and naughty recognition. "I wish that fellow's contract was over," thought Evelyn, ignoring the glance.

At first neither he nor Gracie spoke. Then Gracie said:

"Are you doing it on purpose?"

"What?"

"Holding me off?" She put the question with a cordial, delicately appealing upturned smile. No criticism in it. A mere half-diffident suggestion.

"Sorry," said Evelyn, and drew her body nearer to his, so that they were touching, so that in the steps his foot was between her feet.

"You are a fibster," she said, with the same upturned smile. "You dance beautifully."

"I don't know any steps except this one," Evelyn muttered. "It's too monotonous for you."

"I'm loving it," said she, and for a moment shut her eyes, as if to exclude all sensations save those of the music and of being in motion with him, enclosed in his arm.

He could feel her legs against his, her body against his, her back against his right hand, and the clasp of her fingers upon his left hand. But there was nothing of Volivia in her contacts, only a delectable, yielding innocence. Or so it appeared to him. He desired not to enjoy the dance, but he was enjoying it. He would have been resentful of her trickery, but he could not summon resentment. He thought: "Is it possible that she has taken a fancy to me? If not, what can be the explanation of her game?" Then he privately withdrew the word 'game.' She was not a flirt, or, if a flirt, she had lifted flirtation to the plane of genius. He was intensely flattered, for, though she had trapped and annoyed him, he admired her tremendously. He admitted to himself that she was the most surprising, wondrous creature he had ever encountered. She was unique. A man cannot be more flattered than by the confiding, devotional acquiescence of a beautiful and stylish younger woman. Yes, her mien was devotional. And all the while he could feel the firmness of her legs under the filmy frock. His emotion was well hidden, but it surpassed anything in his experience.

A voice said behind him:

"Hello, darling!"

"Hello, Nancy darling," said Gracie.

The much-pictured Nancy Penkethman, dancing with one of the Cheddar brothers. The two couples sailed almost side by side.

"When am I going to see you, darling?" asked Nancy. "I'm perishing to hear all about New York."

Evelyn could feel upon him the inquisitive peerings of Nancy and one of the Cheddar brothers.

"What's wrong with to-night, darling?" said Gracie. "Up in my rooms. I'm staying here. So's father. Eleven-thirty, say. Bring the others along. We'll have a time."

"The Lord Harry won't come. He's got a political date with the P.M."

"Never mind. Bring whoever'll come."

The two couples separated in diverging curves. (Evelyn's manœuvre.)

The Big Oak Band ceased. Dancers clapped, Gracie hesitated. Evelyn loosed his partner. He had been chilled by the fact that Gracie was capable of being wakened out of the ecstasy of the dance by the sight of a friend, and of being at once sufficiently prosaic to arrange a meeting.

"Thank you very much," he said conventionally.

"I loved it," Gracie repeated.

"Good band, eh?" Sir Henry greeted them loudly. He had disposed of his trout, and grouse was being served.

"The best," said Evelyn.

"I say, daddy. Did you order a sweet?"

"No," Sir Henry replied. "I ordered nothing, and I never do order a sweet."

"But I want one," said Gracie.

"Well, have one. The Imperial Palace is yours."

"What about a soufflé?"

"That will take twenty to twenty-five minutes," Evelyn put in.

"What does that matter, sweetie?" ('Sweetie'! However, Evelyn knew that in Gracie's universe the word had no more significance than 'darling'; and he let it slip away.) "And while we're waiting couldn't we just go and see the kitchens? I've never seen a hotel kitchen, and I'm crazy about hotels now. 'Crazy'! Pardon!" Gracie laughed, placing her hand on her mouth. "Reminiscence of New York, of course."

"Crazy about hotels *now!*" Evelyn repeated in his mind. "That's not a bad notion," said Sir Henry, obviously attracted by the notion.

Evelyn said that he would have the greatest pleasure in showing them the kitchens. One of his fibs.

Chapter 15 CUISINE

The kitchens of the Imperial Palace restaurant were on the same floor as the restaurant itself, and immediately adjoining it. You passed through an open door, hidden like a guilty secret from all the dining-tables, then up a very short corridor, and at one step you were in another and a different world: a super-heated world of steel glistening and dull, and bare wood, and food in mass raw and cooked, and bustle, and hurrying to and fro, and running to and fro, and calling and even raucous shouting in French and Italian: a world of frenzied industry, whose denizens had leisure and inclination for neither the measured eloquence nor the discreet deferential murmuring nor the correct and starched apparelling of the priests and acolytes of the restaurant. A world of racket, which racket, reverberating among metals and earthenware, rose to the low ceilings and was bounced down again on to the low tables and up again and down again. A world without end, a vista of kitchens one behind the other, beyond the range of vision. The denizens were all clad in white, or what had been white that morning, and wore high white caps, with sometimes a soiled towel for kerchief loosely folded round the neck; professional attire, of which none would have permitted himself to be deprived.

The shock of the introduction into the Dantesque Latin microcosm, of the transition from indolent luxury to feverish labour, was shown in Gracie's features.

"You'll soon get used to it," said Evelyn, thinking with admiration how sensitive was the puzzling creature. "See here!" He examined a board studded with hooks, near the entrance, and pulled from one of them an oblong of flimsy pink paper. "See?" He pointed to the scrawled word 'soufflé.' "'37.' That's your table."

"And what's that?" asked Gracie, putting her finger on certain perforated figures.

"'10.12.' That's the time of the order. We stamp it. There's the machine that does it."

"Good! Good!" ejaculated Sir Henry, tersely.

Evelyn restored the paper to its hook.

"Oh!" cried Gracie, suddenly childlike. "Do let's see the soufflé made."

"We will!" answered Evelyn eagerly, also childlike in sympathy. But he thought: "Has she come here because she is really interested, or because she wants to persuade me that she is interested?" His mind was peopled with sinister suspicions which, previously squatting in dark corners, had on a sudden sprung upright and into the open. "But what a marvellous figure she makes here in her finery!" he thought.

"Oh!" Gracie cried again, perceiving a tank into which fresh water was spurting. "What's this?"

A cook sprang forward and, seizing a long handle with a net at the end, plunged it into the water and lifted out the net full of struggling fish.

"Des truites," said he proudly.

"They little know the recent fate of three of their brothers!" said Sir Henry with gaiety.

"How horrible! How can you, father? Put them back, please do." Gracie had laid a protesting hand on Sir Henry's arm.

The trout were dropped into the water.

Two waiters at the delivery-counter snatched up two loaded trays which had mysteriously been placed there, and hastened off into the other world.

"You're pretty busy here!" said Sir Henry, surveying the noisy scene.

"This is nothing," Evelyn replied negligently. "You should see the place at a quarter to two when everyone wants lunch at the same moment, and watch the battle at that counter. There'd be sixty cooks here then. This is comparatively a slack time."

Then approached down the vista a youngish, plump, jolly man, not to be distinguished by his attire from anybody else.

He had heard by the inexplicable telegraph which functions in workshops that the Director was in the kitchen, with guests; and he was hurrying.

"Ah!" said Evelyn. "Here's Planquet, the chef of chefs."

The man arrived, bowing.

"Let me introduce Maître Planquet," Evelyn began the ceremonial of presentation.

The master-cook protected himself against the hazards of contact with the extraneous world by a triple system of defence. Outermost came the cushion of his amiable jollity. Next, a cushion of punctilious decorum--obeisances, deferential smiles, handshakings, which expressed his formal sense of a great honour received; for he needed no one to tell him that only visitors of the highest importance would be introduced by the Director himself. Third, and innermost, a steel breastplate forged from the tremendous conviction that the kitchens of the Imperial Palace restaurant were the finest kitchens in the universe, and that he, Planquet, a Frenchman, was the head of the finest kitchens in the universe, and therefore the head of his ancient profession.

When he genially admitted, in response to a suggestion in French from alert Gracie, that he was a Frenchman from the South of France, his tone had in it a note of interrogation, implying: "Surely you did not imagine that any but a Frenchman of the Midi could possibly be the head of my profession?" His tone also indicated a full appreciation of the fact that Gracie was an exceeding pretty woman. Behind the steel breastplate dwelt unseen the inviolable vital spark of that fragment of the divine which was the master's soul.

While Sir Henry vouchsafed to him in the way of preliminary small-talk that he and his daughter and Mr. Orcham were in the middle of dinner in the restaurant, his unregarding, twinkling gaze seemed negligently to recognise that a restaurant, and perhaps many floors of a hotel, might conceivably be existing somewhere beyond the frontier of the kitchens, and that these phenomena were a corollary of the kitchens--but merely a corollary.

"Ah!" said Gracie, over a dishful of many uncooked cutlets, meek and uniform among various dishfuls of the raw material of art. "They have not yet acquired their individualities."

The master gave her a sudden surprised glance of sympathetic approbation; and Evelyn knew that the master was saying to himself, as Evelyn was saying to himself: "She is no ordinary woman, this!" And for an instant the Director felt jealous of the master, as though none but the Director had the right to perceive that Gracie was no ordinary woman. The master's demeanour changed, and henceforth he spoke to Gracie as to one to whom God had granted understanding. He escorted her to the enormous open fire of wood in front of which a row of once-feathered vertebrates were slowly revolving on a horizontal rod.

"We return always to the old methods, mademoiselle," said he. "Here in this kitchen we cook by electricity, by gas, by everything you wish, but for the *volaille* we return always to the old methods. Wood fire."

The intense heat halted Gracie. The master, however, august showman, walked right into it, seized an iron spoon fit for supping with the devil, and, having scooped up an immense spoonful of the fat which had dripped drop by drop from the roasting birds, poured it tenderly over them, and so again and again. Then he came back with his jolly smile to Gracie, as cool as an explorer returning from the arctic zone.

"Nothing else is worth the old methods," said he, and made a polite indifferent remark to Sir Henry.

But the next minute he was displaying, further up the vista, a modern machine for whipping cream. And later, ice-making by hand.

"The good method of a hundred years since." Then, further, far from the frontier, in the very hinterland of the kitchens, was heard a roar of orders. Two loud-speakers suspended from a ceiling over a table!

"Yes," the master admitted to Gracie's questioning, ironic look. "It is bizarre, it is a little bizarre, this mixture. But what would you, mademoiselle?"

Two shabby young men were working like beavers beneath the loud-speakers and round about, occasionally bawling acknowledgments of receipt of orders to colleagues in some distant county of the master's kingdom.

The party went in and out of rooms hot and rooms cold, rooms large and rooms small, rooms crowded with industry and rooms where one man toiled delicately alone. And the master explained his cuisine to Gracie, as one artist explains an art to another artist who is ignorant but who has instinctive comprehension. Down by a spiral staircase into the bakery and the cakery. Up into an office with intent clerks and typewriters. And everywhere white employees raised eyes for a second to the Director and his wandering charges and the master, and dropped them again to their tasks.

2.

Evelyn, with Sir Henry, was behind the other two. He watched the changing expressions on Gracie's face as she turned, and tried to read them, and could not. Then Sir Henry left him and with an authoritative query drew the master from Gracie's side. Evelyn joined her. They had mysteriously got back to the kitchen of the wood fire and the revolving game--but not the same game was revolving. Gracie approached the huge hearth, beckoning, and he stood close to her.

"What is she going to say?" he thought. He half-expected, after the exposure of the realities of cookery which she had been witnessing, that she would say that never again could she enjoy a meal. She confronted him with a swift movement; then paused, her lips apart. He saw Sir Henry cross-examining the master across the busy, reverberating kitchen. And on the edge of his field of vision be saw Gracie's beauty, and the dazzling smartness of her frock.

"I must work!" she exclaimed, in a rich, passionate whisper. "I must *work!* This place makes me ashamed. Ashamed. I wish I could put a pinafore on, and work here, with all these men, instead of going back to that awful restaurant full of greedy rotters. Why can't I work? I must begin my life all over again." Then, more quietly: "Well, I did start some work this morning, after Smithfield. Oh! I told you, didn't I? I swear I will keep it up. Don't you believe me?" Her tone was now wistfully appealing for confidence and encouragement.

"Yes, I believe you. Of course you will keep it up," said Evelyn, staggered by the astonishing outburst. He recalled that in the morning she had made a vague brief reference to writing. Was writing, then, to be her work?

"There's no 'of course' about it," she said sadly.

A man strode through the kitchen carrying a pale dish on a tray.

"Oh! My soufflé!" cried Gracie. "It is. I know it is. I'd forgotten all about it, and you never reminded me!"

She almost ran to the master.

"Good-bye, *maître!* Au revoir. You have been all that is most amiable to us. Thank you. Thank you."

"But--"

"Thank you again."

Her tone was definite, imperative.

The master, puzzled, took the proffered highly manicured hand. She was reducing him to his proper social level, after all this pretence about *maîtrise.* But the master brought his defences into action.

"Too honoured!" he said, with geniality, with deference; and yet the steel breastplate glinted through. The touch of his hand round hers indicated the proud reserve which as the prince of his great world he was entitled to show to no matter whom. And the master consoled his pride further by a Gallic reflection upon the nature of beautiful girls. Toys! Still, Gracie had very much impressed him.

Gracie scurried off towards the frontier, Evelyn following.

"My soufflé! It's gone!"

And indeed a waiter was now disappearing with it over the frontier. The tail of Gracie's brilliant skirt disappeared after him. The whole kitchen was momentarily agitated by the flying spectacle.

When Evelyn and Gracie reached table No. 37, having traversed the staring restaurant in a scarcely dignified dash, the soufflé was already magically deposited on the side-table from which No.37 was served.

Sir Henry did not arrive till quite five minutes later. What remained of the soufflé was then cold. But Sir Henry did not fancy souffles.

"That fellow has a nerve!" thought Evelyn, "pumping the ingenuous Planquet before my face, and behind my back too!"

Chapter 16 ESCAPE

At ten minutes to eleven Evelyn said that urgent work compelled him to leave them. He had not asked Gracie to dance again, and she had given not the slightest sign that she wished him to do so. Time had passed quickly. Evelyn had been relating the somewhat melodramatic professional history of Maître Planquet. Also quite a number of minutes had gone to the business, suddenly undertaken by Gracie, of writing a note and sending it across to Nancy Penkethman and obtaining a reply.

"But you're coming upstairs to my little party later," she said to Evelyn with a confident inviting smile. "You coming, daddy?" she added negligently to Sir Henry.

"No," said Sir Henry, promptly, positively and curtly.

Gracie kept her smile waiting for Evelyn's answer. A smile which could not reasonably have been described otherwise than as irresistible. Since the visit to the kitchens her demeanour to the guest had been even more exquisitely agreeable than before. Forgotten, apparently, was the short passionate outburst concerning work!

"I'm afraid I mustn't," Evelyn said quietly. He had no intention whatever of going to her party, to meet people whom he did not personally know, and of the frivolous, notorious sort, which he had no desire to know. Indeed he had been wondering how a unique girl such as Gracie, and a public power such as Lord Watlington, could have arrived at intimacy with smart, merely ornamental futilities such as Nancy Penkethman, Lady Devizes and the two tall Cheddars. Further, his sense of proportion, of the general plan of a day and of a life, made him hostile to the very idea of these suddenly, capriciously arranged festivities. Still further, he was tired, and he thought that Gracie ought to be tired too.

But he had a far stronger motive for refusing. He emphatically did not want to placard himself too strikingly with a famous girl like Gracie. Already (he recalled again and again) the entire upper-staff of his hotel was certainly aware that he had taken her to Smithfield at an ungodly hour that morning, and that immediately on their return to the Palace he had shown her over parts of the hotel. Also that she had been enquiring for him in the afternoon and had asked for the number of his car. And had he not dined with her that night? Was he not still, in fullest publicity, sitting at her father's table? Had she not danced with him? Had he not exhibited to her the kitchens of Maître Planquet? Impossible that he should add fatuity to indiscretion, and increase tittle-tattle, by going to her infantile party, which probably he would not be permitted to leave till 2 or 3 a.m.! And why should he imperil his next day's work by turning night into day? He was a serious man, admired, loved and feared by other serious men. He hated any form of notoriety for himself. And he would not yield to this bewildering, lovely chit.

"Oh! But you can't say 'No,'" Gracie protested sweetly.

"Afraid I must," Evelyn insisted, and rose to depart. "So many thanks for your hospitality," he said in a formal tone, addressed equally to father and daughter.

"But I've told them you're coming!" said Gracie.

"Whom?"

"Nancy Penkethman. In my note. I've promised you to them."

Evelyn laughed a little, saying: "A young woman as beautiful as you are is entitled to break any promise. I'm so sorry. Good night. I'm fearfully sorry."

"I say, Orcham," Sir Henry stopped him.

"Yes?"

"You aren't forgetting my message to you this morning?"

Evelyn acted shame and alarm.

"Upon my soul I was!" he exclaimed. "Old age! Old age. Do forgive me. You wanted to see me--wasn't it?"

"I'd like to have five minutes some time."

"You and your five minutes!" thought Evelyn. "Do you imagine I can't see through you?" And aloud: "I'll be delighted if I can be of any use."

"I'm busy to-morrow morning," said Sir Henry.

"And my afternoon's full up," Evelyn instantly retorted; and added, in a tone intentionally sardonic: "Our Annual Meeting."

"Oh, really! Well, there's no frantic hurry," said Sir Henry, very calm. "Shall we say day after to-morrow, or the day after that. I shall be here for a few days, might be here for a few weeks." Evelyn drew out his pocket engagement-book and they fixed a rendezvous.

"It's coming at last," said Evelyn to himself as he walked away. "As if the man didn't know I knew he knew all about the shareholders' meeting!" He was only sardonic, not apprehensive.

As for Gracie, the girl's smile, at parting, had lost none of its delicious, acquiescent sweetness. She might be erratic, wayward, unpredictable; but she had manners.

Evelyn went straight to his private office, satisfied with his own fortitude, but uncomfortable. He saw a thin line of light under the shut door. Miss Cass, hatted and coated, bag in one hand, was tidying his great desk. He was not expected in his office that night, and in the morning he liked the desk to be absolutely clear, save for a bottle of mineral water and a glass and some flowers.

"Anything urgent?" he demanded.

"No, sir. Nothing."

The next moment Miss Cass was gone, having shown her usual reluctance to quit work. Three days a week she enjoyed evening-duty till 11 p.m.--for the hidden life of the Palace, never dreamt of by visitors, extended daily over a period of sixteen hours, and more--but Miss Cass would willingly have served every night till eleven o'clock, or even twelve; indeed, she hated to leave her subaltern in command of the Director's sacred welfare.

2.

Evelyn took a cigar out of a box of Partagas in the middle drawer of the desk. Having lit it, he telephoned to the manager's room, and instructed the assistant-manager, M. Cousin not being there, to see what could be done about changing the order of the two turns in the midnight cabaret. Then for some minutes he devoted himself to a cigar worthy of devotion. Then there was a knock at the door, and, without waiting for permission, entered--Gracie. Evelyn was really disturbed, by the thought not of a danger to come, but of a danger past. If Miss Cass had been present at this astounding incursion! If Miss Cass had met Gracie even near the door in the corridor! A beautiful, stylish girl, unannounced, without an appointment, a girl with whom he was already far too closely associated in the minds of the upper-staff, invading the holy of holies after eleven o'clock at night! And to find the secret retreat, she must have made an enquiry. Therefore some member of the staff knew of her visit! Therefore many others of the staff would soon know! Monstrous! Incredible! He had lived dangerously in his time; but among men of business, not in this fashion.

"May I come in?"

"But you are in!" Evelyn smiled humorously.

"Then you don't want to see me?"

"I'm delighted to see you."

Evelyn was standing. Gracie approached the desk, and sat down opposite to him. Evelyn sat down.

"Now why won't you come to my tiny party?" she began at once. "You aren't working. You're only smoking."

"Yes, I'm working," he said. "You know, there's quite a lot of work goes on in this head of mine."

He was rapidly recovering from the shock of her unlawful irruption. She made an enchanting picture in front of him. Before speaking again she opened her bag, and critically beheld her face in the mirror thereof.

"Do you know--I must tell you," she said, "I'm sure you would prefer me to be straight with you. I must tell you you're misjudging me."

"Misjudging you?"

"Yes. Or you wouldn't have said what you did about me being so beautiful I was entitled to break *any* promise. If I am rather good-looking, I can't help it. And I loathe the idea that good looks 'entitled' a girl to behave in a way that a plain girl wouldn't dare to behave in. I say I loathe it, and I do. I'm not that sort. I do hope you understand." She was imploring comprehension.

"Yes," Evelyn admitted sedately. "Quite. I oughtn't to have said it. But I was only joking. I never once thought you were that sort." He would have preferred that their intimacy should not grow. But there it was, growing like the bean-stalk. And in spite of himself he was helping it to grow. "But I've got something to say, too," he proceeded. "Why did you make that promise to your friends without asking me? I was there while you were writing the note. You might just as easily have asked me."

"I might," she murmured, as it were absently. She was now busy at her face, acting upon her own criticism of it. "I ought. But I didn't. I'm frightfully sorry. It was cheek. But as I've got myself into a hole, you won't leave me in it. You'll just lift me out of it like a perfect dear. Don't be a spoiled darling. It wouldn't suit you."

Evelyn shook his head, smiling.

"I can't make out why you want me to come," he said.

"No, of course you can't. That's why you're such a dear. I want you to come because you're wonderful." Her eyes left the mirror and gazed at him.

"I'm not a bit wonderful," he said.

"I know you mean that. But you aren't a judge. I'm a judge, and I tell you you're wonderful. And I'm dying to have you at my party."

"Well," he thought, "she's an enchantress all right. But not for me. And she can't come it over me. Why the devil should I go to her party if I don't want to? I'm not a friend of hers, and it's no use her pretending I am. I won't go. And I won't and I won't."

But also he was thinking again, obscurely, that he must in some strange way have made an impression on her. And that she was bringing something new into his life. He was an extremely successful man. He had achieved his ambition. He had a passion for his work. He was at the very top of his world, secure. He had scaled Mount Everest, and there was no higher peak on earth. What else had he to live for, he, still under fifty? But she was bringing something new into his life. He had glimpses of vistas hitherto unnoticed. Was it conceivable that she was in love with him? Or was he a fatuous ass? If the former, what then? No, he was a mere hotel-keeper. True, her father had risen, and he had been an early riser, like Evelyn. But her father, though he had risen from a lower level than Evelyn, was a financier, immensely wealthy--if only on paper. And her father had begotten a daughter who in the last few years had raised him higher even than he was before. Through the magic of his daughter, he consorted on equal terms with the--well, with the smartest individuals in London. Evelyn tried to disdain smartness, but be did not completely succeed in disdaining it. Smartness had prestige for him. And he was a mere hotel-keeper. What absurd nonsense! Yes, absurd nonsense, but there it was! She was a marvellous girl. In two seconds he lived again through the whole of his day with her. Marvellous! He was free to marry. But as a wife, what a hades of a nuisance would the marvellous girl be! Liability; not asset.

"And I've been thinking these ridiculous thoughts for hours!" he said to himself, admitting that his mind was as disorderly as any girl's.

He said lightly to her:

"I hope you aren't really dying. I hope you won't die: because I honestly can't come. I've got an appointment in ten minutes from now. I should love to come, but--" He broke off. "You do believe me, don't you?"

"I'm not sure," she replied quietly, sadly. "I'm terribly suspicious, I can't help it, but I've a feeling you're treating me the same as you did when we began to dance."

"Oh! How?"

"Holding me off. I'm more frank than you like, and it makes you afraid."

Here indeed was candour--candour either brazen or magnificently courageous! He was shaken by the strong, sudden force of a temptation to yield, to go to her party. Why not? He had no appointment; he had nothing to do; and the sense of fatigue had left him. Her candour had expressed the exact truth about him, whether she knew it was the truth or not. He now desired to go to the party, to throw up his hands and say comically: "Come along. Upstairs. The lift! The lift! I can't wait." It was not that he was the least bit in love with her. If she attracted him, he did not know why. She had beauty, but he was not a man to over-estimate the value of feminine beauty; he had held beauty in his arms. She had brains, or what in a woman passed for brains; but he was alive enough to the defects of her brilliant mental apparatus, and he esteemed that her brain was much inferior to his own. He had, in fact, a certain sex-bias.

Nevertheless he desired to go to her impromptu party. That is to say, he desired to stay in her company, hated to let her out of his sight, feared that if he did he would regret having done so. She intrigued him considerably; and he admired her manners, and keenly savoured her admiration: that was all. But was it not sufficient? The party would assuredly be amusing, and if it was not amusing he could leave it. As for the gossip of the staff, to think twice about such a trifle was childish. Every one of his reasons for refusing her was either false or utterly silly. The trouble perhaps was that he was too proud to go, too proud to withdraw his word and surrender. He had said he could not go, and he would not go--not if he should have to regret his obstinacy for evermore. Why the devil could she not take 'No' for an answer?...Forcing herself into his private office as she had done!

"I must ask you to forgive me," he said, with a smile as sad as her smile.

"You've been very patient with me," she sighed, and snapped her bag to, and rose. "Good night."

"Good night." He followed her to the door and opened it.

"I'll see you to the lift," he said. She turned on him, transformed.

"No, *please!* I couldn't bear that!"

Fury, resentment, anger were in her rich voice. She banged the door, wrenching the handle out of his hand.

What an escape--for him, not for her! But an iron weight seemed to have settled in his stomach. And he was blanketed in a heavy melancholy. He said aloud in the empty, desolated office: "Have I ruined my life? Was this the turning-point?"

Chapter 17 2 A.M. TO 3 A.M.

Evelyn woke up in a state of some bewilderment. His feet felt cramped. He looked at them and saw that he was still wearing his evening shoes; also his dress-suit; also that many lights were burning; and finally, that instead of being in bed, as he had assumed, he lay on the sofa in the sitting-room of his private suite. Then, gradually passing into full wakefulness, he remembered that he had sunk on the sofa, not to sleep, but to reflect, to clear his thoughts, before getting to bed. He glanced at the clock, which announced twenty minutes to two, and at first he was sceptical as to its reliability; but his watch confirmed the clock. Characteristic of the man of order that he at once wound up his watch!

He rose uncertainly to his cramped feet, and lit a cigarette. He had slept without a dream for nearly two hours and a half; surprising consequence of extreme fatigue! His body appeared to him to be as refreshed and restored as though he had slept the usual six hours. He must now really get to bed.

But his brain was furiously active, engaged in an unending round of thought:

"That damned party is still going on. There were pros and cons, but I ought to have accepted the invitation. I was a fool to refuse. It was nothing after all. Only a little improvised party. Surely I was entitled to refuse. Surely she might have taken No for an answer. Her outburst was inexcusable, and it showed what she's capable of. The damned party is still going on. There were pros and cons, but I ought--"

And so on without end. Revolutions of an enormous fly-wheel in his brain, dangerously too big for his brain, leaving no space therein for such matters large and small as the substitution of Miss Powler for Miss Brury and vice versa, the changing about of the two cabaret turns, the vague Machiavellian menace of Sir Henry Savott, the everlasting problem of the downward curve in expenditure per head of customers in the restaurant, etc.

He glanced around the sitting-room, where everything exactly fitted his personality and everything was in its place; home of tranquillising peace; but now disturbed by a mysterious influence. No peace in the room now. He had held the room to be inviolable; but it had been violated--and by no physical presence. And Evelyn was no longer, as formerly, in accord with the infinite scheme of the universe, with the supreme creative spirit. He had never consciously felt that he had been in such accord. Only now that he was in disaccord did he realise that till then he had been in accord. Disconcerting perceptions! Curse and curse and curse the girl! She carried hell and heaven about with her, portable! She was just not good enough. She continually flouted heaven's first law...No hope of sleep. To get to bed would be absurd and futile. He would go downstairs. To do so might stop the fly-wheel.

He opened the door, extinguished all the lights, shut the door, opened it to be sure that he had extinguished all the lights. The dark room seemed to be full of minatory intimidations: a microcosm of invisible forces hitherto unsuspected. He shut the door on them; but soon he would have to open it again.

Descending a short flight of stairs, he walked along the main corridor of the floor below his own, under the regularly recurring lamps in the ceiling, past the numbered doors, each with a bunch of electric signal bulbs over its lintel. Inhabited rooms, many of them--not all, for it was the slack season--transient homes, nests, retreats of solitaries or of couples. Shut away in darkness, or in darkness mitigated by a bed-lamp. Some sleeping: some lying awake. Pathos behind the closed, blind doors. Not only on that floor, but on all the Floors. Floor below floor. He always felt it on his nocturnal perambulations of the Imperial Palace. And he could never decide whether the solitaries or the couples, the sleepers or the sleepless, were the more pathetic. The unconsciousness of undefended sleep was pathetic. The involuntary vigil was pathetic. Salt of the earth these wealthy residents in the largest and most luxurious luxury hotel on earth, deferentially served by bowing waiters, valets, maids! They pressed magic buttons, and their caprices were instantly gratified. But to Evelyn they were as touching as the piteous figures crouching and shivering in the lamp-lit night on the benches of the Thames Embankment.

He rang for the lift. Up it promptly came, and a pale, sprightly, young uniformed human being in it, who not long since had been a page-boy and was now promoted to the distinguished status of liftman. Night was common day to him; for, as hair grows night and day, so did the service of the Palace function night and day, heedless of sun and moon.

"Evening, Ted."

"Good evening, sir."

"Let me see, how many years have you been with us?"

"Six, sir."

"Excellent! Excellent!...Ground-floor, please." Evelyn noticed the No. 3 on the lift-well as the cage fell from floor to floor. The third floor was the floor of the party. Renewed disturbance in his brain! "When do you come on day-work?"

"I hope in five weeks, sir."

"Ah!"

The mirrored lift stopped. The grille slid backwards. Evelyn stepped out.

"Thank you, sir," said Ted, sat down, and resumed the perusal of thrilling fiction.

The great hall was empty of guests; the scintillating foyer too. The entrance to the ladies' cloak-room glowed with brilliant light. A footman stood at the entrance to the darker gentlemen's cloakroom, and within, at the counter, the head-attendant there was counting out money from a box. And in the still glittering restaurant only one table was effectively occupied--by two men and a woman. All the other tables were oblong or round expanses of bare white cloth. Eight or nine waiters shifted restlessly to and fro. A gigolo and his female colleague--the last remaining on duty of a corps of six--sat at a tiny table apart.

The orchestra, which Evelyn could not see from his peeping place, began to play a waltz, which reverberated somehow mournfully in the vast, nearly deserted interior. The professional dancers rose, attendant, then advanced. The gigolo took the woman from the table of three, his companion took one of the men. The second man stayed at the table and passed the time in paying the bill. The waiter bowed, ceremoniously grateful, as he received back the plate with a note and a pile of silver on it. To Evelyn the waltz seemed interminable, and the two lone couples on the floor the very images of pleasure struggling against fatigue and the burden of the night. The female gigolo was young and elegant; she must get some handsome tips, Evelyn thought. "Tips! My God!" he murmured to himself, recalling that in one week in June the waiters' tips in the restaurant had totalled more than eight hundred pounds. The waiters kept their own accounts, but they were submitted to Cousin, who submitted them now and then to Evelyn.

The orchestra, after threatening never to cease, most startlingly ceased. But at once it burst vivaciously and majestically into "God Save the King." The three males stood to attention; the women stood still. Then the three guests sat down again at their table, and Evelyn could hear the murmurs of their talk; he could hear also the movements of the departing band. The professional dancers had vanished. The waiters waited. At length the trio of guests left the sick scene of revelry, and came up the steps into the foyer. Evelyn turned his back on them. In a moment the table was emptied. In three more moments every cloth had been snatched off the rows of tables, and every table changed from white to dark green. The two male guests continued to talk in the gentlemen's cloak-room. The woman had disappeared into the ladies' cloak-room apparently for ever. But she came forth. The trio renewed conversation. Never would they go. They went, slowly, reluctantly, up the stairs into the great hall. The restaurant and the foyer were dark now, save for one light in each. The head-attendant of the vestiaire was manipulating switches. The entrance to the ladies' cloak-room was black.

"Ludovico!" Evelyn called to the last black-coated man, taunting the gloom of the restaurant. Ludovico span round, espied, and came hastening.

"Sir?"

"Did Volivia perform first or second in the second cabaret?"

"First, sir. The other turn--clown, I forget his name, sir--refused to appear first."

"Why?"

Ludovico raised his shoulders.

"All right, thanks. Good night."

And Ludovico ran down the steps again, and he too vanished. The gentlemen's cloak-room was black and empty. The great hall was silent, the foyer deserted except by Evelyn. The public night-life of the Imperial Palace had finished. But not the private night-life.

Refusing the lift, with a wave of the hand to the liftman, Evelyn began to climb the stairs; but he was arrested by the sight of the gigolo (coat-collar turned up, and a grey muffler wrapped thickly round his neck) and the girl-dancer (with a thin cloak hanging loosely over her frail evening frock). The pair were walking about two yards apart, the woman a little in front of the man: bored, fatigued, weary. For the purpose of symbolising the graceful joy of life he had held her in his arm a dozen times during the long spell of work; but now each displayed candidly a complete indifference to the other; each had had a surfeit of the other. They passed through the melancholy gloom of the foyer, up into the great hall, and at the revolving doors thereof Long Sam negligently saluted them--too negligently, thought captious Evelyn. He followed, aimless, but feeling a sickly interest in them.

Approaching the doors, he acknowledged Long Sam's impressive salute with rather more than the negligence which Long Sam had dispensed to the working dancers--just to punish him! Through the glass Evelyn saw the pair standing under the gigantic marquise, reputed to weigh several tons. They exchanged infrequent monosyllables. The gigolo shivered; not the girl. Then a taxi drove up, with a porter perched on the driver's step. The gigolo opened the taxi and the girl got in. Bang! The taxi curved away and was lost in the darkness.

The gigolo departed on foot. His feet traced a path as devious as a field-path. Fatigue? And he also receded into invisibility. Where did he live? Why did he not drive home, like the girl? What was his private life? And what the girl's? After all, they were not dancing marionettes; they were human beings, with ties of sentiment or duty. What was the old age of a gigolo? There was something desolate in that slow, listless, meandering departure.

2.

"Morbid is the word for me to-night," thought Evelyn, as he turned towards the hall and nodded amiably to Reyer, the night-manager, who stood behind the Reception-counter as listless as the dancers. His mind was not specially engaged with Gracie; he was afflicted by the conception of all mankind, of the whole mournful earthly adventure. He began a second time to climb the stairs. It was his practice to make at intervals a nocturnal tour of inspection of the hotel; so that the night-staff saw nothing very unusual in his presence and movements.

He walked eastwards the length of the first-floor main corridor all lighted and silent, and observed nothing that was abnormal. Then up one flight of the east staircase, and westwards the length of the second-floor main corridor. At the end of it, he looked into the waiters' service-room. It was lighted but empty. By day it would be manned by two waiters. From midnight till 8 a.m. only two waiters with one valet and one chambermaid were on duty for all the hotel, and they ranged from floor to floor according to demand. Among them they contrived to make good the quiet boast of the Palace that hot and cold dishes and cold and hot drinks could be served in any apartment at any hour of the night; for the grill-room kitchens, unlike the restaurant kitchens, were open all night as well as all day. The sole difference between night and day on the Floors was that in the night, instead of ringing for a waiter, guests had to telephone their orders to the central telephone office, which transmitted them.

Evelyn minutely inspected and tested the impeccably tidy service-room: the telephone to the central switchboard, the telephone phone direct to the bill-office, the gravity-tubes which carried order-checks to the kitchen and bills and cash to the bill-office, the geyser, the double lift with a hot shelf and a cold shelf; the books of bill-forms and order-checks, the ice, the machine for shaving ice to put round oysters, the dry tea, the milk, the mineral waters, the fruit, the bread, the biscuits, the condiments, the crockery, the cocktail jugs, the iced-water jugs, the silver and cutlery all stamped with the number of the floor, the stock-lists hung on the wall, and the electrically controlled clock which also hung on the yellow wall. Nothing wrong. (Once he had memorably discovered fourth-floor silver in the fifth-floor service-room: mystery which disconcerted all the floor-waiters, and which was never solved!) Everything waiting as in a trance for a life-giving summons. He went out of the room content with the organisation every main detail of which he had invented or co-ordinated years ago, and which he was continually watchful to improve.

Back again along the corridor, up another flight of stairs to the third-floor corridor lighted and silent. Room No. 359. Rooms Nos. 360-1. Rooms Nos. 362-3-4. Rooms Nos.365-6-7-8 Not a sound through that door: which was hardly surprising, in view of another quiet boast of the Palace that no noise from a corridor could be heard in a room, and no noise from a room in a corridor. Was she asleep, and in what kind of a night-dress--or would it be pyjamas? Or was her party still drinking, chattering, laughing, smoking, card-playing?

Then in the distance of the interminable corridor he descried two white tables drawn apart from the herd of tables that stood at the door of every service-room. And then both night-waiters emerged from the service-room with dishes, bottles and glasses which they began to dispose on the two tables. Evelyn turned swiftly back, and concealed himself in the bay of a linen-closet. After a few moments he heard the trundling of indiarubber-tyred castors on the carpet of the corridor, the fitting of a pass-key into a door, the opening of a door, more trundling. Then he looked forth. Corridor empty. Door of Nos. 365-6-7-8 half open. Both waiters were doubtless within the suite. He came out of the bay, and walked steadily down the corridor. Blaze of light in the lobby of the suite. Hats and coats on the hat-stand. Animated murmur of voices through the open door between the lobby and the drawing-room. Impossible to distinguish her voice. He went on, and into the service-room, which was in all the disorder of use. The pink order-check book lay on the little desk near the telephone. He examined the last two carbons in it. Suite 365. Time, 1.51. Two bottles 43. (He knew that 43 was Bollinger 1917.) One Mattoni. One China tea. One kummel. One consommé. Six haddock Côte d'Azur. Quite a little banquet before dawn: stirrup cups, no doubt! What a crew of wastrels! What untriumphant, repentant mornings they must have! But he felt excluded by his own act from paradise. He gazed and gazed. A telephone tinkled. He took up the receiver. "421--four, two, one--"

A waiter returned into the cubicle, maintaining at sight of the Director an admirable impassivity.

"Here, Armand. Telephone," said Evelyn, with equal impassivity. He handed over the receiver and left. The other waiter was disappearing at the other end of the corridor, on his way back to his permanent post on the fourth floor.

Evelyn marched as it were defiantly, but on feet apparently not his own, past No. 365. Door shut. No sound of revelry by night...He would not continue his tour of inspection. He could not go to bed. He descended, flight after flight of the lighted, silent staircase; glimpse after glimpse of lighted and silent corridors, all so subtly alive with mysterious, dubious implications. The great hall had not changed. Reyer leaned patient on his counter, staring at a book. Long Sam and one of his janissaries stood mute and still near the doors. The other janissary was examining the marine prints on the walls. As soon as he saw Evelyn he moved from the wall as though caught in flagrant sin.

"What's it like outside, Sam?" Evelyn called out loudly from the back of the hall.

"Fine, sir. A bit sharp;

Evelyn would have gone for a tranquillising walk, but he hesitated to travel back to the eighth floor for hat and overcoat, and he would not send for them. He spoke to Reyer:

"I suppose there are no overcoats not working around here anywhere?"

"I'm afraid not, sir."

"All right. Never mind. I only thought I'd go out for a minute or two."

"Have mine, sir. May be on the small side, *mais à la rigueur*--" He smiled.

While Evelyn was hesitating, Reyer dashed through a door far behind the counter, and returned with an overcoat and a hat. Long Sam helped Evelyn into the difficult overcoat.

"Not too bad," said Reyer, flattered, proud, and above all exhilarated by this extraordinary and astonishing break in the terrible monotony of the night.

"Splendid!" said Evelyn, nodding thanks.

A showy, but cheap and flimsy overcoat. No warmth in it. Very different from Evelyn's overcoats. (Unfamiliar things in the pockets.) Well,

Reyer was only a young night-manager. Fair salary. But not a sixteen-guinea-overcoat salary. A narrow, strictly economical existence, Reyer's. The hat was too large, at least it was too broad, for Evelyn. Now Evelyn had a broad head, and he believed in the theory that unusual width between the ears indicates sagacity and good judgment. Strange he had not previously noticed the shape of modest Reyer's head! He would keep an eye on Reyer. A janissary span the doors for his exit.

3.

The thoroughfare which separated the Imperial Palace from St. James's Park was ill-lit. Evelyn had tried to persuade Authority to improve the lighting; in vain. But his efforts to establish a cab-rank opposite the hotel had succeeded, after prodigious delays. Two taxis were now on the rank; and there were two motor-cars in the courtyard. The chauffeurs dozed; the taxi-drivers talked and smoked pipes. He crossed the road and leaned his back against the railings of the Park, and looked up at the flood-lit white tower over the centre of the Palace façade.

By that device of the gleaming tower at any rate he had out-flanked the defensive reaction of Authority. The tower was a landmark even from Piccadilly, across two parks; and simple provincials were constantly asking, "What's that thing?" and knowing Londoners replying: "That? That's the Imperial Palace Hotel." But nowhere on any façade of the hotel did the words 'Imperial Palace' appear. Evelyn would never permit them to appear. He believed deeply in advertising, but not in direct advertising. Direct advertising was not suited to the unique prestige of the Imperial Palace.

In the façade a few windows burned here and there, somehow mournfully. He knew the exact number of guests staying in the hotel that night; but their secrets, misfortunes, anxieties, hopes, despairs, tragedies, he did not know. And he would have liked to know every one of them, to drench himself in the invisible fluid of mortal things. He was depressed. He wanted sympathy, and to be sympathetic, to merge into humanity. But he was alone. He had no close friend, no lovely mistress--save the Imperial Palace. The Palace was his life. And what was the Palace, the majestic and brilliant offspring of his creative imagination and of his organising brain? It had been everything. Now, for the moment, it was naught.

"What a damned fool I am!" he reflected. "Why the devil am I so down? I don't care twopence about the confounded girl. Am *I,* the hotel-world-famous Evelyn Orcham, to go running around like a boy after a girl? It's undignified. And I don't mind *who* she is, or what she is! Anyway I've taught her a lesson!"

He withdrew his body from the support of the Park railings, and walked briskly westwards. Restlessness of the trees in the chill wind! Large rectilinear dim shapes of the enormous Barracks (whose piercing early bugles made the sole flaw, in the marvellous tranquillity of the hotel). Then the looming front of Buckingham Palace, the other Palace! And even there, high up, a solitary window burned. Why? What secret did that illuminated square conceal? He felt a sudden constriction of the throat, and after a long pause turned back. Three motor-cars in quick succession hummed and drummed eastwards. Eternal restlessness of trees beyond the railings! He thought he could detect the watery odour of the lake in the Park. The seagulls had revisited it in scores that day. He had seen them circling in flocks over the lake. Very romantic. What a situation for a hotel in the midst of a vast city! He walked as far as Whitehall, too melancholy and dissatisfied even to think connectedly. And at last he re-entered the Palace. One of the taxis had gone, and both the motor-cars. Everything as usual in the great hall. Reyer behind his counter.

"Much obliged," he said, smiling with factitious cheerfulness, as he gave up the overcoat and the large soft hat.

"Not at all, sir," answered Reyer, pleased.

"That the night-book?"

Reyer handed the book to him. He read, among other entries:

"Three ladies and two gentlemen left No. 365 at 3.5. One of them was Lady Devizes."

Evelyn thought: "She's by herself now. Perhaps her maid is undressing her. She must be terribly exhausted, poor little thing." She was pathetic to him.

"My floor, please," he said to the liftman, and went to bed. Next morning among the early departures he saw the name of Miss Savott.

Chapter 18 THE VACANT SITUATION

Just before noon, on the morning of Gracie's most unexpected departure, Evelyn was entering the Palace after a business interview in Whitehall. He felt tired, but he had slept, and none but a close student of eyes and of the facial muscles which surround them would have guessed that he was tired. Evelyn could successfully ignore fatigue. Indeed he now took pride in the fact that after two very short nights and one very long and emotionally exhausting day, and with a critical day still in front of him, he had deliberately intensified the critical quality of the latter by adding to his anxieties the inception of a new and delicate task: which task concerned the future of Miss Violet Powler.

As for Gracie, he had learnt that she had left for the Continent by the 9 a.m. train--not the more fashionable 11 a.m train--with the whole of her luggage and a maid whose arm was in a sling. Sir Henry had not seen her off, and was remaining in the hotel. Evelyn surmised that the impulsive girl had chosen the earlier train because in the circumstances it was just as easy for her as the other, if not easier. Doubtless she had said to herself: "I'm up late. I'll stay up, and catch the first train. That will give me two hours less in his ghastly hotel, and two hours more in Paris." For Paris was certainly her destination. Where else should she go? He surmised further that, if her maid was disabled, Gracie had done her own packing, and the maid's too. He was sure that she was 'that sort.' Also she was the sort that could take pride in ignoring fatigue. A point of resemblance between them! He liked to think of the resemblance. Of course her departure was the result of pique. Well, let it be! He found a sardonic pleasure in her pique. Do her good! His emotions about her were evaporating with extreme rapidity in the fresh air and the common sense of morning. He needed nobody to tell him, for he could tell himself, that no young woman, however enchanting, could make a lasting impression upon the susceptibilities of a wise man old enough to be her father in an acquaintanceship of sixteen or seventeen hours. She had been calmly but firmly ejected from his mind. Nothing of the astounding episode stayed in his mind except inevitable masculine self-satisfaction at a sentimental conquest, and shame for the absurd feelings which had disturbed his soul after her resentful outburst until he finally settled for the night. One might call him a fish, not a warm-blooded man; but such now was his mental condition, pleasing or the reverse.

Passing through the ever-spinning doors into the great hall he gave a benevolent nod to Mowlem, the day hall-porter, who rendered back the salute with equal benevolence and more grandeur.

Mowlem was one of about a dozen members of the staff each of whom considered himself the most important member of the staff--after Evelyn. He was quite as tall as Sam, and broader, but he pretended to no physical prowess. On the very rare occasions when law and order seemed to be in danger in the great hall he had methods subtler than Long Sam's of meeting the situation. American citizens nearly always became his friends. Once, an ex-President of the United States, suffering from the English climate and insomnia, had caused Mowlem to be roused from bed, and the two coevals had spent a large part of a night in intimate converse. Mowlem was understood to be writing, with expert assistance, a book of reminiscences of the Imperial Palace entrance-hall, for a comfortable sum of money.

While crossing the hall, Evelyn heard his own name spoken in a discreet feminine voice behind him.

"Can you give me one minute?" asked Mrs. O'Riordan, who also had been out on an errand.

The head-housekeeper in her street attire looked as smart and as spry as any visitor, and she was modestly but confidently conscious of this momentous fact.

"Two," said Evelyn, having glanced at the clock.

He moved towards a corner at the end of the Reception counter, and the Irish 'mother' of the Palace followed him.

"I *think* I've found someone to take Miss Brury's place," said Mrs. O'Riordan, confidentially murmuring. "She's young, but she's had experience, and--she's a gentlewoman."

"That's good," said Evelyn, cautiously, recalling the head housekeeper's theory about the advantage of engaging gentlewomen as floor-housekeepers.

He divined at once that Mrs. O'Riordan was specially anxious to be persuasive. Her grey hair never prevented her from exercising a varied charm, of which charm she was very well aware. As she stood before him, he could plainly see in her, not the widow aged sixty-two, but a vivacious Irish maiden of twenty-five or so. The maiden peeped out of Mrs. O'Riordan's bright eyes, was heard in her lively though subdued voice, and apparent in the slight quick gestures of her gloved hands. At her best, and when she chose, Mrs. O'Riordan had no age. The accent which she had put on the word 'think' was a diplomatic trick, to hide the fact that she had decided positively on the successor to Miss Brury. And the successor was no doubt a protégée of the head-housekeeper's, a favoured aspirant. Assuredly Mrs. O'Riordan had not discovered the exactly right girl by chance in the last twenty-four hours. He foresaw complications, a new situation to be handled; the tentacles of his brain stretched out to seize the situation.

2.

Then he noticed a young woman in converse with Mowlem. A young woman dignified, self-possessed, neat, carefully and pleasingly clad; but at a glance obviously not a gentlewoman. Withal, Mowlem was treating her as a gentlewoman; for the old man had the same demeanour towards everybody. Never would Mowlem have been guilty of the half-disdainful demeanour which on the previous night Long Sam had adopted to the professional dancers. The young woman was Violet Powler, certainly telling Mowlem that she had an appointment with the Director for noon, and enquiring the way to his office.

Evelyn, because he was tired and had a full day's work before him, had boyishly determined to straighten out the Brury affair without any delay, and Miss Cass had received early instructions to get Miss Powler on the telephone at the Laundry. He averted his face from the doors so that Violet should not see him.

"Perhaps you would like to have just a look at her?" Mrs. O'Riordan suggested.

"Yes, I should," he smiled. "But you can take her references and have everything ready in the meantime. Only don't clinch it. I have someone in mind myself for the job."

Mrs. O'Riordan did not blench, but that she was somewhat dashed was clear to Evelyn. Inevitably she was dashed.

"Oh, of course," she said with sweet deference. "If that's it--"

"Not at all!" Evelyn smiled again, and more lightly. "You go on with yours, and we'll see. I shouldn't be a bit surprised if yours is far more suitable than mine."

"Is she a gentlewoman, may I ask?" Mrs. O'Riordan asked.

Evelyn's eyes quizzed her.

"That depends on what you call a gentlewoman. She's had what *I* should call a very good education."

"But her people?"

"Her father's a great traveller." Evelyn wanted to laugh outright and boldly add: "A town-traveller." But prudence stayed him.

"Oh!" murmured Mrs. O'Riordan, indicating that she did not feel quite sure about the social status of great travellers, and indeed that there were great travellers and great travellers.

At this moment Evelyn was excusably startled by a most unexpected and strange sight: Sir Henry Savott talking to Violet Powler, three or four yards down the hall, away from the doors. Sir Henry was smiling; Violet Powler was not; but the two had an air of some intimacy. What next? Evelyn kept his nerve.

"Well, I shall be hearing from you," he said to Mrs. O'Riordan, and departed quietly in the direction of his office.

Naturally he could appoint whomever he liked to a floor-housekeepership in the Palace. And none would cavil. But peace, real peace, had to be maintained, and immense experience had taught him the difficulty of eliminating friction from the relations between women, even gentlewomen! There was nothing he feared more in the organism of the Imperial Palace than secret friction. Moreover he knew what he owed, of respect and fair dealing, to the faithful and brilliant Mrs. O'Riordan. But he was absolutely set on appointing Violet Powler. The idea of doing so was his, and he had an intuition--he who derided intuitions in other people--that it would prove satisfactory. He admitted to himself that he had his work cut out.

Chapter 19 POWDER AND ROUGE

"This interview is unofficial," said Evelyn.

Violet Powler was sitting opposite to him on the other side of the big desk in the Director's private office. She had loosened her black cloak, and Evelyn saw under it the same blue frock which she had been wearing on the previous afternoon. Her hat was a plain felt. He could see nothing of her below the waist. He remembered that her feet were not small, nor her ankles slim; but he could not recall whether she had high-heeled shoes. As a housekeeper at the Imperial Palace she would have to wear black, and high heels, and he rather thought that the force of public opinion among the housekeepers would corrupt her to make up her face. Those pale pink lips would never do on the Floors of the Palace. If she kept them untinted every floor-housekeeper would say on the quiet to every other floor-housekeeper that poor Violet--what a Christian name! Battersea or Peckham Rye all over!--had been imported from the Laundry, and what could you expect?...No!

He had been inclined yesterday to regard her as beautiful; but now, detached, rendered a little cynical by recent events, he decided that she was not beautiful. Her features were regular. She was personable. It was her facial expression--sensible, sober, calm, kindly, contented--that pleased him. She would have no moods, no caprices. She was certainly not one of your yearners after impossible dreams, your chronic dissatisfied, all ups and downs. Even Mrs. O'Riordan had moods, despite her mature age.

"The matter is in the hands of Mrs. O'Riordan, our head-housekeeper," Evelyn said further. "I've really nothing to do with it. But I thought I'd better find out first whether you thought the job would suit you. We want a new floor-housekeeper here. There are eight Floors and eight floor-housekeepers."

He then told Miss Powler what were the duties of a floor-housekeeper. He told her with an occasional faint glint of humour. Her serious face did not once relax; but he fancied that he could detect a faint answering glint in her brown eyes. He was determined to see the glint in her eyes, because he had discovered her as a candidate for floor-housekeepership; as such she was his creation; therefore she simply had to be perfect, and without humour she could not be perfect. (Not that many of the floor-housekeepers had humour. Mrs. O'Riordan generally had, but sometimes hadn't.) Still, he was obliged to admit that Miss Powler's eyes were less promising to-day than yesterday. Yesterday, however, she was at home in her own office. To-day she was in the formidable office of the Director, and might be nervous. Yesterday he had acquitted her of all nerves.

"It really all comes down to a question of human relations," he finished. "I'm quite sure you could manage the chambermaids excellently. They're the same class as our laundry-maids, and you know them. But the visitors are a very different proposition, and quite as difficult. And partly for the same reason. The supply of chambermaids is not equal to the demand. Neither is the supply of guests." He almost laughed.

Miss Powler's lips relaxed at the corners into a cautious momentary smile.

"You mean, sir," said she, gravely, straightening her already straight back, "I've been used to being given in to, and with guests I should have to give in."

A crude phrase, but it showed that she had got down to essentials.

"Not give in, only *seem* to give in," he corrected her. "Say a bedroom's cold because the visitor hasn't had the sense to turn on the radiator. Well you turn it on, and fiddle about with it, and then admit that there was something wrong with it, but you've put it right, and if it isn't right you'll send a man up to see to it. Then just before you leave you say: 'These radiators are rather peculiar'--they aren't--'may I show you how they turn on?' You've won, but the guest thinks she's won. It's always a she. No. That's not fair. It isn't always a she. Mrs. O'Riordan says there's nobody more exasperating than a New York stockbroker all strung up after five days' strenuous business life at sea in a liner." Violet did smile. "It appears that American men are super-sensitive to the bugle-calls in the mornings. Wellington Barracks next door, you know. Those bugles can't be explained away. They'd wake Pharaoh in his pyramid. I've thought of keeping a graph to show the curve of explosions of temper due to those bugles. Probably about half a dozen a week. Well, you always say that the bugles were unusually loud that morning; you've never heard them so loud before; and that I'm negotiating with the War Office to get them done away with. I'm not of course. But it soothes the awakened, especially if you admit that the bugles are absolutely inexcusable. As they are. Put them in the right, and they'll eat out of your hand, visitors will. If you argue you're lost. So's the hotel. Now I've given you a sort of general idea. What about it?"

"I should like to try," said Violet with composure. "I often have to do much the same with my laundry-maids."

Evelyn laughed.

"If I may say so," Violet added.

"I think you may," said Evelyn. And to himself: "She's all right. But I'd better not be too funny." He said in a formal tone: "Then I'll mention you to Mrs. O'Riordan."

"Thank you, sir. I'm very much obliged to you for thinking of me," said Violet, with dignified gratitude.

"Of course there would have to be a period of training."

"Yes, sir. I understand that."

"But in your case it oughtn't to be long...In your place I wouldn't say a word at the Laundry. Mrs. O'Riordan might have somebody else she prefers."

"No, sir. Of course." Violet spoke here without conviction. Her steady face seemed to say: "You aren't going to tell me that this Mrs. O'Riordan will refuse anyone that's been mentioned to her by you."

Sbe rose to leave, for Evelyn's manner amiably indicated that the interview was over. Evelyn did not move from his chair. Suddenly he decided that he would just touch on a detail which had been intriguing him throughout the interview, but which he had hesitated to bring into the conversation.

"I happened to see you talking to Sir Henry Savott in the hall. Then you know the great man?" He spoke with bright friendliness, socially, as one human being to another, not as a prospective employer to a prospective employee.

"Well, sir. I know him, if you call it knowing. He came up to me--in the hall. My sister was his housekeeper, at a house he had at Claygate--he sold it afterwards. My sister was ill in the house, and as I happened to be free, I was engaged to do her work, for a month. Of course I could see my sister every day, and she kept me right. I could always ask her." Violet's demeanour was perfectly natural and tranquil, but reserved. She added: "It's a small world; but I've heard it said you meet everyone in the hall of this hotel, sooner or later." She smiled, looking Evelyn straight in the face.

"But this is very interesting," said Evelyn, animated. He was intrigued still more; for, like many other people, he had heard all sorts of stories about Sir Henry's domestic life. "Then you do know something of housekeeping?"

"A little, sir. I think I managed it all right. But of course, as I say, I had my sister to tell me things."

"A large staff?"

"About forty, sir--indoor and outdoor. My sister had charge of everything, indoor *and* outdoor."

"Then *you* had charge of everything?"

"Yes, sir. But my sister was there."

"Sir Henry entertained a lot?"

"Yes, sir. A very great deal, and often without warning us." Evelyn opened Miss Powler's dossier, which contained, among other things, her references and testimonials.

"You didn't say anything about this, I see, when you came to us."

"Oh no, sir."

"I suppose you didn't count it as a regular engagement."

"No, sir. And it was so short. But if I had asked him I think Sir Henry would have given me a testimonial."

"Was Lady Savott there?"

"Oh no, sir." Just a slight betraying emphasis on the 'no.' "I've never seen her ladyship."

"Then you left, and your sister took on the work again."

"Yes, sir, for a bit."

"She left. No?"

"My sister is dead, sir."

"Oh!" Evelyn's face showed sympathy. "She was older than you?"

"Yes, sir. Five years. Nearly six."

"Did she die in the house?"

"No, sir. After she'd left. Sir Henry asked me to go back. But I was very comfortable at the Laundry then. So I didn't go. I don't believe much in chopping and changing."

"Quite. You know Miss Gracie?"

"Yes, sir."

"She was living in the house?"

"Oh yes, sir."

"An extraordinary young lady, isn't she?"

"Yes, sir," Violet replied with imperturbable blandness; but their eyes somehow exchanged a transient glance of implications--or Evelyn thought so.

2.

Perhaps, he thought, she should not have put any implications into her glance. On the other hand perhaps he himself should not have used the inviting word 'extraordinary' about Miss Gracie. The fact was, that when he liked the person to whom he was talking, he had a tendency to speak too freely. He had often observed this in himself. He admitted that Violet had taken little or no advantage of his friendly social tone. No expansiveness in her short, guarded answers to his inquisition! Discretion itself!

He felt inclined to try to break down her discretion. Not in order to get at secrets, though he divined that there were secrets, but simply for the pleasure of breaking down her discretion. A slight, impish wantonness in him. He checked it. The disclosure about Miss Powler's professional sojourn at Sir Henry's house was very agreeable to him. It would help him in his handling of Mrs. O'Riordan. In his mind he instantly composed the tale which he would relate to Mrs. O'Riordan. She could never withstand its allurement. Large house. House of a millionaire. Staff of forty. Everything managed by Violet, who had taken control at a moment's notice, and had given entire satisfaction. And had said nothing about her success to anyone. He would say nothing about the sister giving counsel in the background. Or he would only casually allude to the sister. He could make an irresistible story, and the more irresistible because of his now-strengthened conviction that Violet was a real 'find,' and would soon prove herself a pearl among Palace floor-housekeepers. Strange glance she had given him in accepting his suggestion that Miss Gracie was an extraordinary young lady!

He rose, gaily. Yes, she had high heels. Excellent. No need to say anything about the heels. And she had her own smartness. She was smart in her world; she evidently gave attention to her clothes. And if she could be smart in her world, why not in the world of the Palace? She would be capable of anything. Later, he would be able gently to tease the beloved Mrs. O'Riordan: "My discovery, Miss Powler! Not yours, mother. Mine!"

Miss Powler went towards the door. Her hand was on the knob.

"You know," he said, on an impulse, "there'd be one thing, rather important, if you don't mind my mentioning it--"

"Please."

"If you do come here--powder and rouge." He waved a hand. The lightness of his tone was meant to soothe her

She flushed ever so little. He had got under her guard at last. The flush amused and pleased him. She had no caprices, no moods, no nerves. Yet the flush!

She was equally different from the girl that Mrs. O'Riordan had once been, and from Gracie Savott. These two had feminine charm. They were designed by heaven to tantalise and puzzle a man, to keep him for ever and ever alert in self-defence, alert against attack. Whereas Miss Powler, sedate, cheerful, kindly, tactful, equable, serious, reserved...But what was feminine charm? It might have a wider definition than he had hitherto imagined. He had read somewhere that every woman without exception had charm. He liked Miss Powler's muscular shoulders, and the way she held them; and her sturdy ankles. "And that Gracie girl liked *my* shoulders," he thought. Considered as an enigma, Miss Powler, with her impregnable reserve, was at least on a level with the Gracie girl. Nothing on earth so interesting as the reactions of sex on sex. It was as if Gracie had pulled a veil from his eyes so that he was perceiving the interestingness of all women, for the first time. Revelation.

"Yes, of course, sir," said Miss Powler. "To tell the truth, I'd thought of that. It would be part of the business."

"They'd put you up to all that here."

"Yes, sir. If necessary. But I know something about make-up."

"Oh?" Evelyn was surprised.

"Well, sir. You see. Our amateur dramatic society. I've had to make up plenty of girls. They love it. And I've had to make up myself too." The flush disappeared.

"Of course!" Evelyn exclaimed. "I was forgetting that." And indeed he had totally forgotten it. She had caught him out there. He felt humbled. She might well know a bit more about make-up than any of the housekeepers.

She opened the door.

"It would hardly do at the Laundry," she said. "I shouldn't like it there. Not but what a lot of the laundry-maids themselves do make up. But here I might like it."

She smiled. For one second she was a girl at large, not a laundry staff-manageress seeking to improve her position. Evelyn did not shake hands with her. Why not? he asked himself. Well, there was an etiquette in these ceremonials. A Director did not shake hands with a floor-housekeeper. He stood still near the closed door, thinking.

Chapter 20 THE BOARD

The Imperial Palace had a number of private rooms in the neighbourhood of the restaurant, used chiefly for lunches, dinners and suppers, and each named after an English or British sovereign. At twenty minutes past two on the day of Evelyn's interview with Miss Powler, six men sat smoking in the Queen Elizabeth room round a table at which they had lunched--after a Board meeting.

At one end of the table was the West End celebrity and wit, old Dennis Dover; at the other Evelyn. At the sides were two youngish, exceedingly well-groomed men, a much older man, and a middle-aged man. The last was Mr. Levinsohn, unmistakably a Jew, solicitor to the Imperial Palace Hotel Company Limited, and senior partner in the great 'company' firm of Levinsohn and Levinsohn. The other three were Messrs. Lingmell (old), and Dacker and Smiss (the youngish dandiacal pair). Except for Mr. Levinsohn, the company consisted of Directors of the Imperial Palace Hotel Company Limited. The celebrated Dennis Dover was chairman of the Board, Evelyn being vice-chairman and managing-director of the Company. Youngish Dacker in addition to being on the Board worked daily in the Company's offices as Evelyn's representative and buffer. Youngish Smiss also worked daily in the Company's offices, his special charges being the business side of the Wey Hotel and the Works Department in Craven Street off Northumberland Avenue. ("Outpost in the enemy country!" Mr. Dover had once called the Works Department.) Mr. Lingmell did little but attend Board meetings. He was a director because he had always been a director. Twenty-five years earlier he had retired from hard labour with a sufficient fortune gained in the wholesale brandy trade, and he still had the facial characteristics which one would conventionally expect to find in a man who had dealt on a vast scale in brandy because he liked it.

As for Dennis Dover, now past seventy, of huge frame, with a large pallid face, his renown in the West End was due partly to his historic connection with the management of grand opera, partly from his dry and not unkind wit, and partly from his peculiar voice: which was not a voice but only about one-tenth of a voice; it issued from a permanently damaged throat through his fine lips in a hoarse thin murmur. Strangers thought that he was suffering from a bad cold, and that his voice would become normal in a day or two. It had not been normal for several decades. Youngish Dacker, when he first joined the Palace Board and appeared somewhat nervously at his first Board meeting, had happened to have a very sore throat. "Morning, Dacker. Fine December fog to-day, eh?" Dover had greeted him in the hoarse thin murmur. And dandiacal Dacker had replied in a hoarse thin murmur unavoidably just like Dover's: "Good morning, Mr. Dover. Yes, a fine December fog." Mr. Dover, whose infirmity no one had ever dared to ridicule to his face, had leaned forward to Dacker and murmured with a grim smile: "Young man, men have been shot at dawn for less than that."

Glancing at his watch and at Evelyn, Mr. Dover benevolently and encouragingly thus addressed Mr. Dacker and Mr. Smiss:

"Now, you lily-livered, have some brandy, for your hour is at hand."

At half-past two, in the larger banqueting-room, the Board had to confront its judges, the shareholders, at the Annual General Meeting, which meeting was to be followed on this occasion by a Special General Meeting. The youngish men smiled as easily as they could; for indeed they had betrayed apprehensions concerning the special meeting, at which was to be proposed a resolution limiting the voting powers of shareholders Everybody at the table felt apprehensive about the fate of that resolution, but Mr. Dacker and Mr. Smiss alone had failed to conceal anxiety. The fate of the resolution might well involve the fate of the Imperial Palace Hotel itself.

"Obey your venerable chairman, gentlemen," murmured Dennis Dover, and raised his mighty bulk and filled the glasses of Messrs. Dacker and Smiss with Waterloo brandy (which Mr. Lingmell said was so old as to be indistinguishable from water). "Your alarm does you credit, seeing that you won't have to speechify at the meeting and that you hold no shares worth mentioning, and that if the Palace goes to pot the ancient prestige of the Palace will set forty hotels fighting for your services...To the Resolution! To the Resolution!"

The toast was drunk, but by Evelyn and Mr. Levinsohn in Malvern water; and the Chairman descended cautiously back into his chair.

Mr. Dover had a good right to the position he held in the Company. Not merely was he the largest shareholder. His father, aged fifty odd when Dennis was begotten in the hotel itself, had built the original Palace. He had first called it the Royal Palace, because of its proximity to Buckingham Palace; but in 1876, when Disraeli made Queen Victoria Empress of India, Mr. Dover had loyally changed 'Royal' to 'Imperial.' The name Palace had been copied all over the world. Dennis always maintained that the French use of the word *palace* as a generic term for large luxury hotels had derived from the reputation of the original Palace for luxury, and was not due to the prevalence of imitative Palace Hotels throughout Europe.

In the late 'fifties the Palace luxury had made it the wonder of the earth. It was then reputed to have a bathroom on every floor; and some people stayed in it in order to see what a bathroom was really like. Then a Crown Prince stayed in it, then a monarch, and Queen Victoria would recommend it to some of her foreign distant cousins. Soon the Palace had established two royal suites. Soon, despite the fact that every hotel-expert in London had condemned it as being too impossibly big, it became too small, and the elder Dover had enlarged it. More than once it had been enlarged, altered, replanned, reconstructed; but the Queen Anne character of its charming façade had always been preserved. The last and greatest and most ruthless of the enlargers was Evelyn. When Evelyn had finished--but he had never finished--all that had survived of the original Palace was the Queen Anne character of the façade; not the façade, only the character.

2.

As a child Dennis Dover had lived under the roof of the Palace, in its most majestic days. The elder Dover had amassed incalculable money under that roof. But he had made a common mistake. He had forgotten that the earth revolves. He had assumed that luxury could go no farther than his luxury had gone. When he died, rich, though not as rich as in the grandest days, the Imperial Palace, with all its unique prestige, was beginning to be a back number. Trustees under the will of the founder had done no better than trustees usually do. Then Dennis Dover had taken command, and the public had been invited to buy the Imperial Palace. The public, ingenuous as ever, and blinded by the glitter of prestige, had bought. The Palace recovered a little, lost ground a little, recovered a little, paid a dividend, passed its dividend, and was on the very edge of being transmogrified into a block of superlative flats, when Dennis Dover had chanced to sojourn at the Wey Hotel and to find Evelyn, then in his thirties.

In ten years Evelyn, starting as an invalided A.S.C. officer towards the end of the war, and spending three-quarters of a million borrowed in instalments with much difficulty on debentures, had, after the formation of a new company, made the Palace for the second time in its career the wonder of the wide world. Twice in its career the prestige of the Palace had thus shot up like a rocket; but Evelyn had no intention that it should ever fall like a rocket.

Such, perhaps too briefly stated, was the history of the Imperial Palace Hotel, whose royal suites, owing to a dearth of royalty, were now occupied by cinema-kings, presidents of republics and similar highnesses.

As the six passed in irregular formation through corridors and downstairs towards the larger banqueting-room (called the Imperial--the smaller banqueting-room was called the Royal) Dennis Dover stepped between Dacker and Smiss, and putting a hand paternally on the nearest shoulder of each of them, and looking down from his superior height at their upturned young faces, squeakily murmured:

"You don't mind me referring to the colour of your livers, boys? Sign of affection."

They smiled. They knew their own worth; and they hoped that the Chairman knew it and knew also that their interest in the Palace was fanatical, and that they were intensely proud of having been elevated to the Board at a cost to themselves of only a hundred qualifying shares each. What they did not know was that father Dennis Dover loved them the more for their apprehensiveness concerning the Resolution.

The Chairman himself was apprehensive, but he was old enough to be a fatalist; and the risks attending a resolution to be proposed at a meeting of a limited liability company could arouse no emotion in one who would soon be crossing the supreme frontier. Old Lingmell was equally unmoved, but not for the same reasons as father Dennis. He never spent time in thinking about the supreme frontier. His investments were secure, and the earth and the fruits thereof were good enough for him. Mr. Levinsohn felt no emotion either; for him the matter was strictly professional, one among a hundred such matters. As for Evelyn, he felt a certain anxiety; but he was built on a rock, the rock of his creative, organising brain, which the foolishness of no shareholders could damage, which was more valuable than any investments, and which had a world-market waiting to compete for it.

Chapter 21 SHAREHOLDERS

The six men sat in a row behind a long green-topped table at one side of the square-shaped Royal banqueting-hall; and ageing Mr. John Crump, secretary of the Imperial Palace Hotel Company and a member of Evelyn's directorial staff, sat at one end of the table, with minute-books, balance-sheets, the register of shareholders, and--most important of all--a pile of proxies, under his hand. The Chairman and Evelyn were in the middle of the six, who had no documents beyond a sheet or two of rough notes or blank paper. Evelyn discouraged the exhibition of documents in business, and father Dennis, with whom his understanding was always sympathetically perfect, regarded documents as a symptom of a fussy mind.

In front were the shareholders, two or three hundred of them, including a few women, ranged in rows on the brilliant parti-coloured and gilded banqueting chairs, and each holding a copy of the white annual report and accounts.

Those chairs, with the rich pendant chandeliers, were the sole reminder of the original purpose of the spacious chamber. At night, and sometimes at the lunch hour, tables were joined together in lengths, in the shape of an E, or a rake, or a Greek letter, or a horse-shoe; they were white, then, covered with china, plate, cutlery and glass, flower-decked, gleaming, brilliantly convivial; and the people sitting round them, ceremonially clad, grew more and more jolly under the influence of the expensive succulence provided by Maître Planquet, until by the time the speeches had begun and the cohort of waiters, marshalled by Amadeo Ruffo the Banqueting-manager, had vanished away through the service-doors, every banqueter had become the most lovable and righteous person of his or her sex, in every breast all food and drink had been transformed by a magical change into the milk of human kindness, and the world had developed into the best of all possible worlds: with the final result that the attendants in the cloak-room received tips far exceeding the ordinary.

Now, the scene was dramatically different. The rows of shareholders, some stylish some dowdy, some harsh some gentle, some sagacious some silly, some experienced some ingenuous, some greedy some easily satisfied, some avaricious some generous, were all absorbed in the great affair of getting money--the money which paid for banquets. A nondescript, unpicturesque, and infestive lot, thought Evelyn, who knew a number of them by sight and a few by name. Some faces were obviously new, and Evelyn looked at these with suspicion.

Without rising, father Dennis said in his hardly audible hoarse murmur:

"The secretary will kindly read the notice convening the meeting."

And Mr. John Crump, nervous as always on august occasions, got up and read the notice in a voice rendered loud and defiant by his nervousness.

Then three unpunctual shareholders crept in on guilty tiptoes, and sat down, and chairs scraped on the parquet.

Then father Dennis cumbrously rose.

"Ladies and gentlemen," he began in his murmurous squeak.

"We're off!" thought Evelyn, humorously agog.

Yes, they were off, and there would be no surcease until the Resolution was carried or lost by the votes at the special meeting.

Father Dennis never wasted words on shareholders, partly on account of his throat, and partly because he delighted to starve them of words--at the end of a good year--and also to shock them by his casual brevity.

He said, while some shareholders put hands to ears:

"Figures speak louder than loud-speakers. I am sure that you have all studied our figures with that impartial conscientiousness which distinguishes all good shareholders. I need not therefore weary you with information of which you are already in full possession. I will merely remark, as much for my own satisfaction as for yours, that last year was a record year in the Company's history, that our net trading profit after deducting fixed dividend on preference shares, debenture interest and sinking-fund charges, was equivalent to twenty and a half per cent. on our ordinary capital, and that we propose to declare a final dividend making fourteen per cent. per annum, for the year, instead of last year's eleven per cent., and incidentally I will point out that we are allotting £75,000 to our reserve fund, instead of last year's £60,000. I move the adoption of the accounts and the payment of the dividend as recommended, and I call upon Mr. Evelyn Orcham, our managing director and orator, who will be less summary than myself, to second the motion." With that he subsided into his chair, and glanced sardonically around as if to say: "You can put that in your pipes and smoke it; and go to hell."

No applause greeted the statement of good tidings. The shareholders had been in possession of the tidings for days. At a banquet they would have loudly applauded a silly and insincere speech which was not worth twopence to their pockets. But to-day their stomachs had not been warmed. And they were shareholders--who take as a right all they can get and whose highest praise is forbearance from criticism.

Evelyn rose. He was not an orator, and speechifying made him nervous. But he always knew just what he wanted to say and he would say it plainly, if too slowly. Now and then he would employ an unusual adjective which tickled him. The sheet of notes which he held in his hand was merely something to hold. He was not positively inimical to shareholders, for they were necessary to his life-work. But he disdained them as a greedy, grasping and soulless crew whose heads were swollen by an utterly false notion of their own moral importance. Nevertheless he used a tone different from the Chairman's. The Chairman was a London figure, and could carry off any tone; and there was a pacifying glint in the Chairman's old eye. Evelyn loved the Chairman's brief pronouncements, which father Dennis called his 'turn.' But part of Evelyn's job as a hotel-manager was to flatter shareholders. Bad might come again, and then shareholders who had been flattered would be easier to handle than shareholders who been treated year after year with cynical curtness. Therefore Evelyn flattered, but with a hidden private cynicism which even exceeded the Chairman's.

2.

"Ladies and gentlemen," he began. "Your hotels"--and his thought was "*Your* hotels? Good God! They aren't your hotels. You couldn't have started them. You couldn't run them. You don't understand them. You've no idea what wonderful, romantic things they are. You know nothing about them, except a few arithmetical symbols which I choose to offer you and which are beyond your comprehension. You didn't buy shares because you are interested in hotels; only because you believed that you could squeeze a bit of money out of them. Whereas 'your' hotels are my creation. I live for them. I have a passion for them. Without me they would be hotels, common hotels, not *the* hotels. If I left them, as I could, your precious dividends would diminish and might disappear. 'Your' hotels are mine, and if you denied this I could prove it to you quick enough. Ignoramuses! Is any one of you aware, for instance, that at this moment I am wondering how the devil I can entice *my* customers in *my* restaurant and *my* grill-room to consume more than a dozen and a half champagne per hundred covers? Does any one of you guess that in my opinion an average of one-sixth of a bottle of champagne per person dining or lunching is a shockingly low average--especially considering the qualities of *my* champagne? Not one of you! Barbarians! Benighted savages! Unworthy of respect! *'Your'* hotels!"

In the midst of these lightning reflections he went on aloud to the audience:

"Your hotels, thanks entirely to the willing and generous co-operation which the Board has received from you in supporting us in a policy of large annual expenditure in order to keep your establishments abreast or in front of the times"--("This sentence is getting out of hand," he thought. "I'd better kill it.")--"your hotels, I say, have passed through an extremely difficult year not without credit. I will first of all refer to the difficulties."

And he did refer to the difficulties: the poorness of the previous London season, the obstinately high price of commodities; the dearth of good service; the austerity of customers; the rapacity of customers, who once asked only for food and drink at meals, then demanded music, then demanded dancing-floors, and now were demanding cabarets; the unwillingness of Americans to come to Europe in the anticipated numbers; the monstrous and crushing absurdity of the licensing laws; the specious attractions of continental resorts; the curse of the motor-car, which had pretty well strangled week-end business to death; and forty other difficulties...until you might have been excused for wondering why the Imperial Palace Hotel had not been forced into so-called 'voluntary' liquidation. The brighter side of the enterprise he glossed over. The arithmetical symbols he touched upon lightly, using the plea that they were self-explanatory to shareholders so intelligent as the shareholders of the Imperial Palace Hotel Company Limited.

"In conclusion," said he, "I should like to refer to one point. Your hotels, and particularly the Imperial Palace, have been called dear--in their charges. I resent the word, and I think that you will resent it. They are expensive; but dear they are not. We try to give, and I claim that we do give, better value for money than any other hotel in this country. And the proof that the public shares this opinion lies in the undoubted fact that the public is patronising your hotels more and more. The public cannot be deceived for long. Many hotels have attempted to deceive it, and they have failed to do so. We--I mean everybody present when I say 'we'--have not attempted to deceive it. I am sure that you, the shareholders, would never agree to a policy of pretending to the public that your hotels are what they are not. We maintain that they are the most luxurious and efficient in the world, and that their charges are as low as is consistent with the desire for perfection which animates us all. Ladies and gentlemen, I thank you for the patience with which you have listened to my halting remarks--our ironic Chairman ought not to have dubbed me 'orator'--and I have great pleasure in seconding the motion."

One or two shareholders clapped, but, finding themselves unsupported, ceased abruptly.

3.

"Good old platitudes!" thought Evelyn, as he sat down, relieved at having safely accomplished his speech, and he surreptitiously winked at smiling father Dennis. The meeting was finished, save for questions and formalities. "And these people in front will go home feeling that they've done thing important!" thought Evelyn.

The Chairman asked drily:

"Any questions, ladies and gentlemen?"

A mature lady rose and with a self-possession unusual and perhaps indecorous in a shareholder of her sex asked why in the Profit and Loss account all payments--wages, salaries, washing, licences, advertising, bands, fees, liveries, insurance, stationery, electric light, repairs, renewals, etc., etc., etc., etc.--were lumped together in one huge item. To which the Chairman responded that such was the universal custom in Profit and Loss accounts of limited companies.

The lady's question was a very justifiable one; it jabbed a hole in the beautiful convention which regulates the pacific union between shareholders and Board. Many shareholders would have liked further illumination of the subject. Some knew the right answer. But as the lady wore an eyeglass, a starched white collar and a sailor's-knot tie, she got no help; the subject was not further illuminated, and feminine curiosity, which had thus flouted the sacred immemorial customs of company practice, went unsatisfied.

Then a gentleman apologetically enquired whether Atlantic telephone had had any 'repercussions' upon the business of the hotels. The Chairman answered that so far as he knew the Atlantic telephone had had no 'repercussions'--he mischievously gave the faintest emphasis to the splendid word--but that the managing director might have something to say. Evelyn said that the Atlantic telephone had had no repercussions, but that the shareholders might be interested to learn that in the past year visitors at the Imperial Palace had spent £6,123 in using the Atlantic telephone; that was appreciably more than £100 a week.

There were no other questions from shareholders. What questions indeed could shareholders ask, after a record year, a fourteen per cent. dividend, and an allocation of £75,000 to reserve? The resolution was carried unanimously. Two directors who had to retire were re-elected unanimously. The auditors were reappointed unanimously. And what the official report described next day as a 'hearty' vote of thanks to chairman, directors and staff was carried unanimously. Evelyn's heart lightened, prematurely--a mechanical repercussion. It grew heavy again as the Chairman rose and said:

"The proceedings of the Ordinary General Meeting being now terminated, the Secretary will kindly read the notice convening the Special General Meeting."

"Now we really *are* off!" thought Evelyn.

Chapter 22 THE RESOLUTION

In calling upon Evelyn to move the Resolution which was the sole reason for the Special General Meeting, father Dennis hoarsely and squeakily murmured:

"The meeting will I hope pardon me if I refer to a purely personal matter. I am suffering to-day from rather serious throat-trouble, and my medical adviser, in whom I have as much confidence as a sane man can have in a medical adviser insisted that I should make only one speech--and that as short as possible," he added with a roguish old smile.

Titters of laughter, which were, however, sympathetic. Every year the Chairman thus mentioned his throat, as though the malady had but quite recently supervened.

Evelyn did not wholly regret the sad state of the Chairman's throat, because in practice it raised himself from second-fiddle to first-fiddle at the annual gatherings. Also the nervousness which had beset him in his speech at the Ordinary Meeting was now completely dissipated in exciting emotion. Let none imagine that the moving of a Resolution at a Special General Meeting of the shareholders of a limited liability company cannot be emotional. Liability may be limited by Act of Parliament, but not emotion--neither drama.

The shareholders were fully acquainted with the terms of the startling Resolution, but Evelyn began by reading it in tones which almost justified the Chairman's description of him as an orator. The Resolution provided that instead of having one vote per share, each shareholder should have only one vote per five shares. And further that no shareholder, no matter how large his holding of shares, should have a total of more than ten votes. He pointed out that obviously the Resolution gave an advantage to the small shareholder, since a holder of fifty shares would wield the same voting power as a holder of fifty thousand shares. And he pointed out that, as the Chairman of the Board happened to be the largest shareholder in the Company, the Board could not be accused of an attempt to favour its own individual interests at the expense of any other shareholders.

Then he spoke very vaguely of the possibility of foreign interference in the destinies of the Company. He made no accusation. Oh no! He spoke of a mere possibility--but a possibility against which, if the shareholders in their wisdom agreed, it might be advisable to protect the Company. Were the shareholders prepared to allow the control of a British company to pass out of British hands? If so, well and good. If not, the Resolution was the surest safeguard, the only real safeguard, against such a contingency--a contingency which, he ventured to think, was of a most sinister nature. The shareholders, who were doubtless thoroughly acquainted with all the phenomena of industry and finance, had of course noticed in past months that foreign interests had been ousting British interests in various very important British undertakings. He would not assert that any scheme was definitely afoot for getting control of the Imperial Palace Hotel Company.

He would be content to say that in the last couple of years, and especially in the last few months, blocks of shares had changed hands, and transfers had been registered, in a manner calculated to arouse the suspicions, but no more than the suspicions, of a watchful Board. The Board had desired the attendance of their good friend Mr. Levinsohn, who had acted with signal success for many years as solicitor to the Company. He, the speaker, could not pretend to Mr. Levinsohn's unique authority in Company affairs, and Mr. Levinsohn would give the shareholders his valuable views on the subject before them. Confessing that his own feelings as to the proper course to be followed for the welfare of the Company were both clear and deep, and then formally moving the Resolution, Evelyn sat down.

Certainly he had shown some emotion, some sense of the drama of the occasion. But his clear and deep feelings, though he might not have admitted the fact even to himself, were due less to a regard for the welfare of the Imperial Palace Hotel Company than to the risk of his life-work and his career being imperilled by the substitution of any other Board for the Board which while nominally his master was really his tool.

Evelyn's heart knocked against his waistcoat, but its beat was strong and regular. He was nervous again; his glance flitted nervously about the banqueting chamber, in which the sobriety of the green-topped table contrasted so strangely with the glory of the chandeliers, the brightness of the decorated walls and the gaiety of the chairs.

Ruffo peeped cautiously in through the double service-doors and the doors slowly and silently shut him out of sight

Father Dennis's face had an expression of bland, negligent cynicism. Lingmell's bloated, wise features were calm and absorbed in his everlasting dream of fleshly satisfactions. The two old men were still incapable of excitement. The two younger directors were employed in subduing their fever into an imitation of tranquillity. Evelyn understood them, but he doubted whether they understood him. He was too far above them in attainments and position to be fully understood by them. They might work hard; they might display a heroical loyalty; but never could they reach his height, for they had not his qualities. He felt sorry for them; for either their ambitions were humble or their ambitions would be disappointed. The future king of the world of hotels was not on the Imperial Palace Board; perhaps he was hidden somewhere in the upper staff.

The shareholders, stiff on their festive chairs, were grim, unresponsive, waiting, flinty-souled.

2.

Then Mr. Levinsohn stood on his feet. He was impassive, absolutely at ease. Noticeably, unmistakably a Jew, he reeked as little of anti-Semitism as of a few drops of rain. He was above race. He had been elected to the Carlton Club. He knew half the secrets of the City. The demand for his counsel exceeded the supply. The lowest fee charged by his firm for permitting the appearance of its august name on a company prospectus was seven hundred and fifty guineas. The universal City opinion was that he had a subtler and profounder comprehension of the mentality of shareholders than any other man in England. He surveyed the body of Imperial Palace shareholders as an alienist might survey a ward of lunatics in an asylum; his handsome, hard, semi-oriental face was as mysterious as the placid surface of a bottomless ocean.

Mr. Levinsohn said:

"Ladies and gentlemen, I shall not detain you long. Need I say that I share the sentiments expressed by your Vice-chairman. At the same time I think that--patriot as he is, and a man of imagination, something of the artist in him, no one can be the great organiser Mr. Orcham is without having a large amount of imagination--he has perhaps not quite sufficiently stressed the strictly practical business side of this proposal."

Mr. Levinsohn paused, rubbing his blue chin. The attention of the shareholders had been seized instantly. They were wondering what would come next. What! The Company's solicitor criticising the Vice-chairman! But nothing mattered, not even that; for they, the shareholders, were judges and jury; and naught but horse-sense could sway them; and from their verdict there could be no appeal. Evelyn was slightly puzzled; but he said to himself that Mr. Levinsohn was anyhow the first man who publicly at a Company meeting had shown a real understanding of him. Curious, how this middle-aged Jew, speaking in a gentle conversational tone, as careless about the form of his sentences as one individual to others in a lounge, could without any apparent effort or art, put a spell upon those tough shareholders!

Having placated his chin, Mr. Levinsohn proceeded:

"We are all men and women of business here, and we are all patriots, and anxious if possible and fair to ourselves to keep British commercial enterprises in British hands. But patriotism is a burden, and in common justice the burden ought to be equally shared among the citizens. Your shares stand on the Stock Exchange round about thirty-five shillings--in my opinion decidedly below their real value. Supposing a group of foreign interests--say American, purely as an illustration--came along and offered you fifty-five shillings a share, as might well happen. Patriotism might urge you to refuse, but in refusing you would be throwing away something like two and a half million pounds, you, a comparatively small body of citizens. The loss in actual cash would not be shared equally by the electorate, it would fall exclusively on *you.* Would this be fair? It would not, and I should be rather surprised if your Vice-chairman did not say the same. The suggestion would be monstrous. No reasonable person could make such a demand on you. Let us look facts in the face. You would accept the offer, and you would be right." (Murmurs of assent from the gilt chairs.) "And another thing. True, the magnificent Imperial Palace and Wey hotels would be lost to British control. But the wealth of Great Britain would have been increased by two and a half million pounds and *you* would have at your absolute disposal the total purchase money, between six and seven million pounds, for reinvestment in British industry and commerce under British control. It seems to me clear that if the--purely hypothetical--offer were actually made, the truest patriotism and the most far-seeing business sagacity would accept the offer. Your Company might cease to exist, but it is necessary to take a broad view, and in the broad view British industry and commerce as a whole would gain a considerable advantage. Bad business is never good patriotism."

The first genuine applause of the meeting greeted this aphorism.

"I have nearly finished," Mr. Levinsohn continued. "But not quite. I have spoken of an offer, purely hypothetical as I say. Can an offer so handsome ever materialise? It never could materialise if the prospective buyers of your undertaking first obtained control of the Imperial Palace Company by quietly getting hold of a majority of the shares, which as things stand would mean a majority vote at a General Meeting. If by this means any prospective buyers first obtained control they would be sellers as well as buyers, and they would sell to themselves at any price they chose to name, and those of you who had kept your shares would find yourselves between the upper and nether millstones. You would get left. The Resolution before the meeting will, if you pass it, prevent this quite possible ramp. For these reasons, if you ask my advice--not otherwise--I should advise you to vote for the Resolution. Let me say that I am entirely disinterested. I hold no shares in your Company, or in any of the many companies which do me the honour to employ my professional services."

Mr. Levinsohn, having finished in the same conversational tone as he had used at the start, quietly sat down.

No applause. A number of shareholders were whispering to each other in small groups.

"Talk about an artist!" thought Evelyn. "This fellow is a finished artist. I can manage a hotel. But this fellow has shown me that I don't know the first thing about handling shareholders. Makes a good effect first by pretending to disagree with me. Then simply rolls them all up. Damned clever of him not to tell the Board beforehand exactly what line he was going to take!" He would have liked warmly to shake Mr. Levinsohn's hand, which he felt sure was always quite cold.

Mr. Smiss timidly seconded the Resolution.

"Any observations?" asked father Dennis quietly. "The Board will be glad to have the views of shareholders, and to answer any questions."

3.

A pause. Then a little, scrubby man rose from the front row and, looking round at his fellow shareholders behind him, said ina rasping voice:

"With great respect for the wisdom of the Board, and giving full weight to the opinions which have been so ably expressed by the Vice-chairman and my friend the Company's solicitor, I venture to differ from them as to the advisability of passing this most drastic and even revolutionary Resolution. I may say that I am not without experience in the management of public companies, as my friend Mr. Levinsohn knows. My experience has taught me that ownership ought never to be divorced from control--"

At this point father Dennis pushed a scribbled note along the table to Mr. Levinsohn. "Who is your friend? How many shares does he hold? D.D." Mr. Levinsohn wrote on the paper and pushed it along to Mr. Crump, the secretary. In a moment father Dennis had the reply: "Dickingham, a solicitor. Probably one of Savott's nominees and speaking for all of them," in Levinsohn's handwriting; and at the bottom, in Mr. Crump's: "1,500. Bought six months ago."

Dickingham was continuing: "This Resolution, if carried, would obviously divorce ownership from control." He turned again to the people behind him: "If you pass the Resolution, you will be entirely in the hands of the Board. Large shareholders will have no power. And it is well known that the average small shareholder always supports his Board. I make no reflection upon the small shareholder. I am one myself, and I make no doubt that there are many here. As a rule the small shareholder is right to support his Board. But the result will be the same, whatever his motives: an autocracy of the Board, an autocracy which will last as long as the Board chooses it shall last. If a similar Resolution to this could be translated into politics--which happily for our national welfare it cannot--and put before the House of Commons as a measure of electoral reform, it would be laughed out of the House by every political party. In fact no political party would dare to introduce such a measure, were such a measure conceivable. I admit that it is not. The principle which has made the Empire what it is is the principle of control going hand in hand with ownership. The Resolution would abolish control by ownership."

The speaker amplified his arguments at length, and ended: "There is a proverb: 'Where your treasure is, there is your heart also.' I beg you, ladies and gentlemen, to think of all that that wisdom means. I feel that at this moment the fortunes of the Imperial Palace Hotel Company are trembling in the balance."

Mr. Dickingham was applauded in several parts of the room. Then three other men rose in succession, and, with much less suavity of phrasing than Mr. Dickingham, spoke against the Resolution. Then silence.

Father Dennis lifted himself, and hoarsely squeaked:

"I have the pleasure to put the Resolution. Those in favour--" Many bands were raised. "The Resolution appears to be carried. But of course, if any of you would prefer a poll to be taken--"

"Poll! Poll! Poll!" cried a number of voices, fiercely, savagely. "Poll! Poll!"

Mr. Crump began to finger the pile of proxies by which some dozens or scores of absent shareholders had delegated their voting powers to the Board.

Mr. Dickingham was on his feet:

"Mr. Chairman, if you will permit me to suggest it, I should like to examine the proxies--of course in collaboration with my friend the Company's solicitor."

"I have not the smallest objection," squeaked father Dennis magnanimously.

The battle was now joined.

Evelyn drew symmetrical patterns on a piece of paper, continually enlarging them and making them more elaborate and shading them. His absurd heart was still more insistently beating. Mr. Dickingham had said truth: the fortunes of the Imperial Palace Hotel Company were indeed trembling in the balance. Perhaps also Evelyn's own fortunes. The autocrats of a big merger of hotels might or might not invite him to manage the whole lot. But the Palace was the Palace, unique. Anyhow he would not accept a subordinate position, as manager of one hotel, not even were that hotel the Imperial Palace itself. Either he would be autocrat or he would be nothing--he would start life again. He could not bear to look at the group of the two lawyers and the secretary, examining the proxies, comparing them with the share-register. He could not judge the total strength of the opposition. Nor could anybody else on the Board or off it.

Presently he heard father Dennis say: "Shareholders now kindly substantiate their claims to vote."

Shareholders approached the table, some diffidently, some defiantly. The assembly was in disorder. Noise of voices, explanatory and argumentative. Mr. Crump had rather more than he could do, but the two lawyers in their professional calm and patience helped him both practically and morally. One by one the shareholders returned to their seats. Then Mr. Dickingham sat down, his face illegible.

Mr. Crump rose and ceremoniously delivered a paper to the Chairman, who showed it to Evelyn and lifted himself again:

"The Resolution is carried, by a majority of 22,111 votes," he squeaked, and then added with characteristic gratuitousnaughtiness: "Ownership has exercised control."

"For the last time," shouted Mr. Dickingham in his rasping tone, springing up.

"An improper observation," said the Chairman, smiling.

"I am sorry you should think so, sir," said Mr. Dickingham, pale and furious. "And I will point out to those shareholders who do not know it that you closed the Transfer books a month ago, and I understand will keep them closed until after the confirmatory meeting a fortnight hence. You have thus prevented new genuine holders of shares from voting at this meeting or the next. If it had not been for this piece of sharp practice, probably illegal, your Resolution would have been lost to-day, and well you know it!"

Some uproar. Father Dennis replied with extraordinary mildness:

"The Board followed a perfectly normal procedure in closing the Transfer books. They acted within their rights. And they certainly did their duty. This gentleman"--he indicated Mr. Dickingham to the other shareholders--"is a lawyer. He is therefore aware that this is not the proper place to raise a legal question. There are the Law Courts. May I remind you, ladies and gentlemen, of the statutory Special General Meeting a fortnight hence for the purpose of formally confirming the Resolution which you have been good enough to pass to-day. The proceedings are now terminated."

4.

Before the room had begun to empty, Mr. Levinsohn came up to the Chairman.

"Good afternoon, Dover," he said briefly and evenly. "I have another meeting at four o'clock." He shook hands with father Dennis and with Evelyn, and left, hurrying.

Everybody left. Shareholders could be heard in lively but hushed conversation beyond the open doors at the end of the banqueting-room. Evelyn had glimpses of them taking their hats and coats at the special vestiaire outside. Lingmell departed, with one nod which served for both father Dennis and Evelyn, the thought in his mind being that he had done his duty by the Imperial Palace Hotel Company and was free for a time to devote himself completely to himself. Dacker and Smiss went off at speed, conscientiously to resume at once the round of their important daily work. Mr. Crump gathered together his paraphernalia and, piling it all on the large Register, carried the whole away like a laden tea-tray. Ruffo entered through the service-doors, anxiety on his face. He was responsible for the arrangement of the room for a banquet that evening, and wanted the place to himself and his waiting minions at the earliest possible moment. Nevertheless, seeing Evelyn and father Dennis still together, he disappeared yet again. Evelyn, however, had noticed him and his impatience. Father Dennis and Evelyn had sat side by side without speech. Evelyn slowly tore up his patterned paper into smaller and smaller pieces.

"Rather a lark!" hoarsely murmured Dennis Dover, with a grim, benevolent humorous smile at Evelyn.

"What?"

"Savott wandering about the hotel while all this has been going on. Eh?" He spluttered laughter and touched Evelyn on the arm.

'He knows by this time," said Evelyn.

"You may bet your shirt he does!" said the old man, giving another shaking laugh.

Evelyn smiled. He reflected that he had been wrong about old Dennis. Old Dennis was not old. And he was not always cynical in his cheerfulness. There was still a free, impulsive, warm youth in that body so aged, so cumbrous, so unwieldy, and so dilapidated. His bleared eyes gazed into Evelyn's eyes with quick sympathy. What could it matter to old father Dennis whether or not the Imperial Palace changed ownership? Nothing. Father Dennis had lived beyond such trifles. But it mattered tremendously to Evelyn, and father Dennis's delight was for Evelyn. He was fondly attached to Evelyn. And Evelyn, realising this exquisite fact anew, felt tears spring to his eyes. He wanted to be by himself--he was so happy, so overcome by the spirit of loving-kindness pouring into him and permeating him from its magic source in the secret and divine place hidden somewhere in father Dennis's coarse mortal envelope.

They rose and left the room together, and before they had reached the vestiaire, Ruffo and his shirt-sleeved corps had rushingly invaded it, carrying tables. Evelyn put the old gentleman into his vast overcoat, walked down the steps with him to the Queen Anne entrance, and helped him into his car.

"We must have that Board meeting to-morrow to elect our chairman," said Evelyn as he was closing the door of the car.

"I reminded Lingmell," squeaked father Dennis. "Noon, isn't it? But he won't come. Doesn't matter. There'll be a quorum without the old ruffian." The car moved.

Evelyn strolled to his private office. Dacker, his *alter ego* in the affairs of the Palace, was standing at the big desk.

"I was just waiting for you, sir."

"Want anything?"

"No, sir. I thought you might."

An even increased devotion in his tone. His features were all joyous exhilaration.

"No. Nothing," said Evelyn. "I'm going to have my tea upstairs. I'll be down at five again."

"Yes, sir." Dacker's smooth face said: "You are entitled to your retreat on this magnificent occasion. In your absence I shall watch over your interests."

Evelyn went up in the lift to his home, and telephoned:

"Get hold of Oldham, will you, please, and ask him to bring me my tea here. The Darjeeling, tell him. Thanks."

He dropped into the easiest chair that the Works Department of the Palace could devise and make. A masterpiece of comfort. He picked up the current number of *The Economist,* his favourite weekly, and began to read it. A pretence! He did not read it. He was too happy to read, or even to think. He yielded his mind utterly to the sensation of happiness, saying to himself that he had never been so happy, never at any previous moment of all his life. The vista of his life in the future stretched beautifully before him. This kind of happiness had no complications. Nobody had the right to violate his retreat, man or woman. His monarchy was as absolute as that of a sultan--sultan without a purdah.

Oldham softly entered with the tea-tray, which he set on a table by Evelyn's side.

"I've brought you some hot ry-vita in case you should fancy it, sir."

"Thanks, I shall."

"Thank you, sir."

Oldham glanced about the ordered room to see that its orderliness was perfect. It was perfect. Then he glanced at his master. Happiness was on Oldham's face too. Proud happiness, not for himself, but for Evelyn. Oldham knew. They all knew. Probably Oldham did not understand just what had occurred. But he knew that something supremely good for Evelyn had occurred. And his devotion was exalted. Evelyn thought:

"What have I done to win all this loyalty? I don't deserve it."

Chapter 23 SUSAN

The reason why Evelyn altered his rendezvous with Sir Henry Savott, Bart., from a mere encounter in the Directorial private office to a super-intimate dinner in his own living-rooms upstairs was simple. He had chanced, on the morning after the meetings of shareholders, to sit side by side with Savott in the barber's shop of the Imperial Palace. Here, white-robed, in the most modern operating-theatre in London, ensconced in arm-chairs (from Chicago) which by a turn of a handle could be transformed into sofas or beds or stretchers fixed at any desired angle from the perpendicular to the horizontal, cropped, lathered, shaved, laved, anointed, trimmed, rubbed, combed and brushed by forty instruments and decoctions and oily perfumed compounds actuated or administered by electricity or caressing human hands, the two men had simultaneously submitted themselves to similar experiences.

They had begun together; they talked amiably from chair to chair; they heard a fellow-patient enquiring from an operator how in an electric scalp-massage the current passed from the throbbing machine into the skull; they exchanged confidential smiles at such naïveté; they heard the candour of unwitting customers concerning the characteristics of the Imperial Palace and the peculiarities of other visitors; and they exchanged more smiles; they overheard bits of extraordinary feminine conversations through partitions which imperfectly separated the male department from the female, and out of discretion forbore to glance at one another; they discovered that neither of them had ever in his life accepted the services of a manicure, and further that in nearly every detail they had the same tonsorial tastes; they chatted freely about neckties, collars, handkerchiefs and evening waistcoats. And, finishing simultaneously, they had stood up together, recreated, shining, and scented, and beheld themselves in mirrors and seen that they were marvellously fine. The sole difference between them was that whereas Sir Henry paid cash Evelyn only scribbled his initials on a check.

They left the luxurious marble apartment, cronies. There is nothing like a barber's shop for producing rapid intimacy. Yet they had not bared their souls. In the entrance-hall Sir Henry had praised the operators and the installation. And in return Evelyn had said: "I say, supposing we alter our date? Come and dine with me to-night in my secret castle upstairs, if you're free. We shall be more at home there," And Sir Henry had said: "I'm not free. But I'll get free. Eight-thirty? Would that suit you?"

And Maître Planquet had received special orders; the guardian of the wine-cellars too. And Miss Cass, learning the new arrangement, had of her own accord intimated that it would be a pleasure to instruct the florist about just a few choice flowers.

Thus the two met again in Evelyn's sitting-room at precisely eight-thirty. No uneasy waiting about for women. They were too intimate to feel the need for shaking hands.

"Very nice of you to have me escorted up here," said Sir Henry, who had found a white-gloved page-boy waiting outside the door of his suite.

"Well," said Evelyn, "it's a little withdrawn, my castle. Have a glass of sherry?"

"If I might have one of your 'soft' cocktails," Sir Henry suggested.

"Two," Evelyn murmured to Oldham, who was in attendance

None but Oldham himself ever served at a meal in that room. A waiter assisted, but he was forbidden by law from appearing in front of the screen which hid the door.

"I see I'm behind the times," said Evelyn, observing that Sir Henry wore a flower in his smoking-jacket, and he took a flower from a vase and inserted its stalk into his buttonhole. "That's better."

Sir Henry laughed deprecatingly. Evelyn poked the fire, whose function was exclusively to cheer, not to supplement the radiators. As they stood before the fire, sipping orange-juice, smoking cigarettes, and talking of nothing in particular Evelyn thought:

"After all, why shouldn't I have him up here? Shows him who I am, and that I'm not suspicious of him, don't want to hold him off, as I held off his strange daughter--so she said! Fact is I can handle him better up here than down in my office. He's thinking already I'm going to fall for him. I don't like his teeth, but he's a lot more agreeable to-day than he was yesterday. He's damned civil. Is it all put on for my benefit? No. Couldn't be. There's something about him that rather appeals to me. His tone. His eye. A shade too small, his eye, but--He may be quite all right. And I don't care a curse *what* his reputation is. Don't I always say you ought to take people as you find them? He may be a thoroughly decent fellow. Well, then! After all, it isn't a sin to want to buy the Imperial Palace. Anybody's entitled to try. And anybody's entitled to lay hold of all the shares he can before he starts to bargain. Childish to bear him a grudge. And if he imagines he can get the better of me--well, we shall see."

Oldham took the emptied glasses, and Evelyn and his guest sat down to the small round table.

"I really must congratulate you on your castle," said Sir Henry, glancing round.

"Well," said Evelyn, "one does what one can to be comfortable. No reason, is there, why I should make any visitor more comfortable than I make myself?"

"You're right."

It was a man's menu. No caviare. No oysters. No hors d'œuvre. Turtle soup. Sole *Palace.* Pré-salé with two vegetables. No sweet. A savoury. Oldham offered a 1921hock. Sir Henry accepted, but Evelyn noticed that he drank only a mouthful. The same thing happened to the champagne.

"They understand food and drink in your castle," said Sir Henry.

"As to that," said Evelyn, "I'll tell you my motto: Plain, and as perfect as you can get it. I hope it hasn't been too plain."

"Couldn't be," said Sir Henry tersely. No trace in him of the gourmand whom Evelyn had observed at the dinner in the restaurant.

The meal was finished in less than half an hour--before they had passed beyond small-talk about such trifles as the Stock Exchange, international politics, protection; on all of which, as it seemed to Evelyn, Sir Henry spoke sound, impartial, unsentimental sense. In short, they agreed. Sir Henry tasted port, refused cognac, and drank coffee. Oldham handed Partaga cigars, and, the table having been cleared of all but finger-bowls, ash-trays, and cigars, bowed interrogatively, got a nod from Evelyn, and disappeared, closing the door without a sound.

2.

"Shall we sit by the fire?" Evelyn suggested, after a pause, and said to himself: "It's getting time he began."

They sat in easy-chairs on opposite sides of the hearth, with a smoker's table between them.

"This is very pleasant," thought Evelyn; but he felt like an infantryman five minutes before zero-hour. He was of course firmly decided that Sir Henry, and not himself, should be the first to mention business. Sir Henry seemed to be absorbed in the delight of his cigar. He puffed it vigorously, gazed at it as if in ecstasy, and puffed it again. "Tranquillity, the hush before wild weather," thought Evelyn.

"I saw from the departure list that Miss Gracie has left us," said Evelyn, feeling the host's duty to keep conversation alive.

"Yes," said Sir Henry, suddenly vivacious. "Yesterday morning. Gone to Paris with Lady Devizes and one of the Cheddars. Decided it all in a minute, as they do." He gave a short, dry laugh. "Woke me up to tell me she was off. Girls are a problem," he added confidentially. "Only thing to do is to leave them alone. At least that's my conclusion. Most of them are fools, if you ask me. But Gracie isn't. How did she strike you, Orcham?"

"Well," said Evelyn, careful to appear detached and judicial. "I hardly know her. But I should say she's about as far from being a fool as any young woman I ever met. I certainly never met one more intelligent."

Sir Henry leaned forward: "Quite. But do we want a lot of intelligence in a woman?"

"Yes."

"I suppose we do. Yes, you're right, we do...We do." Sir Henry looked at the fire.

"And as for beauty--" Evelyn stopped.

"You know," said Sir Henry eagerly. "I'm her father and all that. But Gracie really *is* extraordinary."

"I can believe it."

"She's given up motor-racing. Perhaps she was right. But it would have been just the same if she hadn't been right. She's taken to literature now. Writes. Naturally she wouldn't show me anything. Reads nothing but Shakspere and the Bible. Very strong on the Psalms. You'd never guess what she thinks is the finest thing in the Bible. She quotes it to me. 'Be still, and know that I am God.' Forty-sixth Psalm." Sir Henry laughed nervously. "I'm dashed if I understand just what it means, but you know, it sticks in your mind. Mystical, I reckon." He sniggered. "I've been thinking about it ever since. What does it mean? It means something to her. I expect you think I'm making a noise like a father."

The Biblical phrase fell into Evelyn's mind like a lighted torch into a heap of resinous wood. Flames burst forth. The whole heap was on fire. He knew, or rather fancied he knew, what the phrase meant. And whatever it meant, it was the most remarkable sign of Gracie's extraordinariness that had yet been disclosed to him.

"Perhaps," he said, meditative. "Perhaps, we aren't *still* enough. Never occurred to me before, but perhaps we aren't." He was astonished at the effect of the phrase on him. He too, after all, did not surely know what the phrase meant, but he felt what it meant, and the spiritual emotion which it aroused in him put the whole of his mind--his ideals, his aims, his principles, his prejudices--into a strange and frightening disorder. Saul, smitten on the way to Damascus! The talk had taken an odd, a disconcerting turn. And through that extraordinary girl with her visits to Smithfield before dawn and her 2 a.m. parties and her flight to Paris--all equally impulsive, improvised and unforeseeable even by herself!

"Well, well!" Sir Henry murmured, as if to indicate that that was that, and no use worrying your head about it! And Evelyn saw that the subject could not profitably be pursued further. Moreover he had a strong instinctive desire not to discuss it. He preferred to let the phrase burn undisturbed in his mind. But, he thought, how could even a Sir Henry switch off from it abruptly to business? Business--after that mighty and menacing command!

In a new, casual tone Sir Henry said: "I met a friend of mine here yesterday morning."

"Oh?"

"When I say 'friend' I mean I know her. A girl named Violet Powler."

"Yes," said Evelyn. "I noticed you talking to her in the hall. She's staff-manageress in my Laundry."

"So she told me."

"I'm thinking of taking her on here. What about her?"

"Oh! Nothing. Only she's a first-rater, Violet is."

"She said she'd been acting for a time as your housekeeper at--I forget where. Claygate, did she say?"

"Yes. It was while her sister was ill. Those two sisters were wonderful. It's a positive fact that inside twenty-four hours Violet had picked up the entire job. I never saw anything like it. Never! I tried to get her back again; but she wouldn't come. I gave up trying."

"Why wouldn't she? I should have thought it was a much better situation than anything I could offer her."

"Perhaps it was. But of course I don't know how good your situations are. I know I'd have given her practically any salary she cared to ask. I wouldn't like to say whether Violet or Susan was the best of the two. Susan was the eldest."

"Died, didn't she?"

"She did," said Sir Henry quietly. And still in a very quiet pathetic voice, and with gaze averted, he went on: "When I tell you I very nearly married Susan--" He ceased.

"Well!" thought Evelyn, with more than the notorious swiftness of thought: "If Susan actually *was* anything like Violet, that's the best thing I ever heard about you!"

He was indeed astounded. He saw Violet Powler in a new light, as the sister of an exceedingly opulent Lady Savott; but he could not imagine Susan as stepmother to a Gracie. And yet, why not? If she was anything like Violet, she would have been adequate for that or any other role. He was flatteringly confirmed in his opinion of himself as a judge of individualities.

More ammunition for him in his imminent contest with Mrs. O'Riordan about the selection of Violet Powler as a Palace floor-housekeeper!

"Really!" he breathed sympathetically. He truly felt sympathetic.

As Sir Henry was looking at the hearthrug Evelyn could scrutinise his face at leisure, without rudeness. He saw the Savott reputation in those features. The small eyes with their perforating and yet far-away gaze, the hard jaw, the inhuman regular teeth! (Evelyn's teeth were somewhat irregular, and he thanked God for it.) But there must be, there was, another facet, unnoticed by the world of affairs, to Henry Savott's individuality. He could see it now, in the attitude humble and soft. And even, if under the influence of Savott's confession, he only imagined he saw it, it must still be there: for not merely must Savott have responded to the fineness of Violet's sister, but she in turn must have found fineness in Savott.

"My private affairs," said Sir Henry, "used to fill a lot of space in the newspapers. So I daresay you know more about them than I do myself." He glanced up, with a terrible sardonic smile, then lowered his eyes again. "It was before I got free of Lady Savott that I wanted to come to an understanding with Susan. But she was so afraid she'd be mixed up in the divorce proceedings, and I couldn't make her see she wouldn't be, couldn't possibly be. You know if a woman doesn't see a thing for herself you can't reason her into seeing it. No. She wouldn't give even a provisional consent. Didn't like the idea of it. And when I was free it was just too late. I did everything I could to save her life. Everything...She was on my side right enough against Lady Savott. She knew the facts. She'd seen 'em. It was seeing Violet yesterday that brought it all back to me. Funny, I don't know to this day whether Violet knew how things were between her sister and me! I doubt whether Susan ever said a word to a soul. Tremendously reserved; and as for discretion!...Excuse me boring you. It came over me, all of a sudden. Well, well!" Sir Henry gave renewed attention to the Partaga.

Evelyn was flattered once more by the confidence. He was saddened; but his sadness was not unpleasant; it had a quality of beauty. Strange, startling encounter, there in the handsome and comfortable room, after the perfect meal, the perfect wines, and in the middle of the perfect cigar! And flowers in their button-holes! Strange encounter with this dictatorial and ruthless specimen of the top-dog; prince of practitioners of company-mongering, whose schemes might and did imperil the happiness of thousands of under-dogs, and also many middle-dogs! All his wealth and all his power had not sufficed to save him from the fate of being himself, in a different sense, an under-dog too. Well might the man's heart echo with the Psalmist's intimidating 'Be still and know that I am God!' Genuine and affecting sympathy for the survivor of the tragedy drew Evelyn towards Sir Henry. And yet in the very moment of his compassion, he was thinking: "I bet it hasn't prevented him from amusing himself since."

"Now look here!" said Sir Henry in a voice suddenly strong and perhaps more domineering than he meant it to be. "I've not come here to make a nuisance of myself."

"Not at all," Evelyn mildly interjected.

"Yes, yes. A damned nuisance!" Sir Henry stood up and stood straight. "I've come here to try to do a bit of business, anyhow to begin it. You know what it is of course."

"What I do know," thought Evelyn, "is that whether you intended it or not, you and I'll never be on a purely business footing again." He kept silence and waited, merely waving his cigar as a sign of concurrence.

Chapter 24 DOGS

"Now," said Sir Henry, still standing, with his back to the fire, and perhaps somewhat masterfully, looking down upon Evelyn, who lounged in the easy-chair. "I want you to believe that I have nothing whatever to conceal from you. If I tried to conceal anything from a man like you, I know I shouldn't succeed--for long. You know too much about your business, and you're far too clever. Don't think I'm flattering you. I'm not. And what's more, you must know I'm not. You must know very well that in your own line you're the first man in the world. Now don't you? Honest to God!"

"There are one or two pretty fine men in Germany," said Evelyn.

"Do you think they are equal to you? Do you?"

Evelyn leaned forward, and with his elbows on his knees let his forearms droop towards the floor.

"Do you wish to make me talk like a conceited ass?" he asked, cigar between teeth.

"No. I wish you to answer a question. Yes, or no?"

All Evelyn's intense natural reserve rose up to prevent him from giving a direct answer.

"How can I tell? How do I know whether the German fellows aren't equal to me? I'm an interested party."

"Of course you're an interested party. But I'm not asking you what you *know.* I'm asking you what you *think.* You have an opinion. What is it?"

"Well, I don't think they are equal to me."

"Confession is good for the soul," said Sir Henry, smiling, and making a brilliant display of his teeth.

"I'm not so sure about that," Evelyn thought. "And why does he use these worn-out phrases? 'Confession is good for the soul!' Good God!"

"Thanks" said Sir Henry. "May I have another cigar?"

Evelyn negligently pointed to the box on the table. Sir Henry picked one, bit the end off--his sharp teeth made a matchless cigar-cutter--and lit the new cigar from the old, violently puffing forth clouds of blue smoke.

"He doesn't know a lot about cigar-smoking," Evelyn thought. "He's got that cigar too hot right at the start. And he's finished one already, and mine's only half through."

"Well," resumed Sir Henry, carefully dropping the end of the old cigar into the fire and turning to Evelyn again, with a benevolent expression. "So far so good. Well, as I say, I'm going to be perfectly open with you. That isn't always my way in big negotiations. But it's my way this time, because I feel it'll be the best way with you. No other reason. No question of moral principle and so on. Candour isn't necessarily the best policy. It often isn't, by Jove. But in this case it is. I reckon myself a very good judge of character. You can appreciate frankness, because you aren't sentimental."

"That's true," thought Evelyn, really flattered again. "He *is* a bit of a judge of character. And he's devilish different tonight from the man who stood me a dinner the night before last." Evelyn was impressed, and he admitted to himself that his first estimate of Sir Henry had been inadequate. He said nothing; just waited.

"I'll tell you something possibly you don't know. Let me mention a few hotels. For instance, the Majestic in London, your only serious rival, and the Duncannon in London. The Concorde and the Montaigne in Paris. The Minerva at Cannes. The Escurial in Madrid. The Bottecini at San Remo. The Albergo Umberto in Rome."

"That's eight."

"Yes. What do you think of them?"

"Not a bad selection," said Evelyn coldly. "Fairly representative Very fairly."

His mind passed with extreme rapidity through the list. He was well acquainted with every one of the eight, either from personal knowledge or from reliable report; with its good and its bad characteristics, the nature of its clientele, its efficiencies and inefficiencies, its past, its present and its prospects; also with the percentages of its dividends earned, its dividends actually paid out, or in the alternative its trading loss. And in his mind, assessing all the eight simultaneously and instantaneously, he considered and decided--by no means for the first time--how each of them could be improved. An imposing lot truly; but less imposing to Evelyn than to a layman; as a first-rate virtuoso's piano-playing is less *imposing* to another first-rate piano virtuoso than to a layman.

And what he would have called 'the conceited ass' in himself reflected upon the immense fuss which would be made of him if he walked into any one of them and presented his card: "Mr. Evelyn Orcham, Managing Director, Imperial Palace Hotel, London." Of which immense fuss he had on various occasions had experience. For he was a retiring man, though he would never coddle his shyness to the extent of hiding his identity from fellow-managers.

"I now have control of all the eight," said Sir Henry with lightness, ineffectually trying to pretend that to have obtained the control of eight such hotels was to a person built on his scale a mere trifle of an achievement. "I don't say I've bought them. I've actually bought one--and no doubt you can guess which one--but I have options which will give me control of the other seven at any moment I choose."

"The Majestic?" said Evelyn, naming the establishment which Sir Henry had bought.

Sir Henry nodded, smiling.

"Not a vast amount of profit-earning there," said Evelyn.

"On the hotel itself, no. But think of the real estate owned by the company, my friend. Its value has appreciated by a good sixty per cent. in the last fifteen years. And the figure they put it at in their Balance Sheet is grotesquely below the value to-day."

"Quite. I agree. But you spoke of it as a serious rival to the Palace. It isn't. They haven't even the sense to spend fifteen thousand pounds on replacing their worn-out carpets and curtains. To say nothing of the furniture."

"I haven't particularly noticed the carpets and curtains," Sir Henry rather haltingly admitted.

"You will next time you go in there," Evelyn answered drily. But less drily than he felt. For Savott's announcement had excited in him sensations of admiring wonder. Though the man might show the foibles of a Napoleon he had, too, a true Napoleonic grandeur of conception, and, if he in fact held the boasted options, which he probably did, he certainly had in addition a Napoleonic power to realise his conception. As he stood there on the hearthrug in the comfortable modest room, insulting a fine cigar by smoking it too quickly, he was tossing millions about. And he had had the courage and the originality to love and fight for the daughter of a small town-traveller; and the misfortune to lose her. A few minutes earlier he had been a wistful emblem of tragedy. He was still that emblem, for Evelyn; but he was a great deal more now: he was an emblem of confident, imaginative might.

Evelyn marvelled at him, and pitied him. He wanted to say to him eagerly, "You're a bigger chap than I thought." And he wanted magically to raise Susan Powler from the dead, so that he might see a cherished woman fold the ruthless giant in her honest arms and kiss away calamity from those ferreting eyes, and by her homeliness reduce a colossus to the human dimensions of a lover. Evelyn was thrilled.

"You've got eight," said he with feigned cold indifference; and paused. "But you want nine."

2.

"I want the Imperial Palace," Sir Henry exclaimed, and could not refrain from a grandiose Napoleonic gesture. "If I can't bring the Imperial Palace into my merger, I'll drop it. I could sell the Majestic at a profit already. I would sell it. And I'd get rid of my options too. I'd clear out of hotels and try something else. I haven't the least desire to mess about with an affair if it's going to be only second-class. Second-class isn't a bit my line. But I'll admit I don't want to clear out of hotels. The luxury hotel, as you've made it, my dear Orcham, seems to me to be the most characteristic of all modem creations. It stands for the age, just as much as the Pyramids did for Egypt. Our age can be proud of it--I mean as an organism. It's marvellous, and there never was anything like it before. The luxury hotel--"

"What about the department-store?" Evelyn interjected.

"I agree," said Sir Henry quickly. "The department-store is just as characteristic, *and* original, as the luxury hotel. But as you probably know, I've handled the department-store--both here and in Australia. My department-store merger is a proved success--and half the City prophesied failure for it. Well, that's done. And now I'm in for a hotel-merger. Only, it must be first-class. Splendid! Gorgeous! Something to sing about and write home about! Otherwise I wouldn't give tuppence for it. Of course there've been hotel-mergers already. I expect you know a lot more about my friend Hoster's merger than I do. It's pretty big. I've no dependable information as to how it's doing. But however well it's doing it wouldn't be good enough for me. To my nose it smells of the suburban street and the provincial up from the country and the conducted tour and God knows what else! No, no! The Imperial Palace is the standard for me. And that's why I'm so keen on interesting you in my proposition. Orcham, I'm damnably keen."

Evelyn was moved by the surprising lyricism of the City man. He was beginning to glimpse the qualities which had lifted up Sir Henry to be a figure in the world of high finance. His imagination was impressed--by the revealed fact that Sir Henry had imagination. He beheld Sir Henry with a satisfaction that was aesthetic. He was even ever so little scared. But he showed none of his emotion.

"I can't quite understand this mania for mergers. It seems to me to mean the destroying of individuality," he said. Nobody could be more misleading, more mystifying, than Evelyn when his mind was fluid and he had to play for time.

"Destroying of individuality!" cried Sir Henry. "Oh, hang it! I've let the thing out." He seized the match-box.

"No, Savott!" Evelyn stopped him. "You can do most things in this room, but you aren't allowed to re-light a good cigar." He stretched his arm, plucked the extinct cigar from his guest's fingers, and threw it into the fire. "Oblige me by taking a fresh one."

Sir Henry shrugged his shoulders humorously, and obliged, and resumed his talk while lighting the fresh cigar.

"Destroying of individuality!" he repeated, muttering at first with the cigar between his teeth. "You of all people to say that! Look at the present case. It would mean the extension of *your* individuality. It would give your individuality a scope--a scope--well, you see my idea? I won't say anything about your greatest abilities. But take your efficiency. A merger means the spread of your efficiency; it means the spread of the Imperial Palace standard. Is that nothing? Destruction of individuality! Why! On the contrary! A merger always means increased power and influence for the top-dog. And why is the top-dog the top-dog? Why are you a top-dog?"

"Yes. But what about the under-dog?" Evelyn asked, thinking again the thoughts which had stirred in his mind earlier about top-dogs and under-dogs and middle-dogs.

"It's no use talking about under-dogs," said Sir Henry, with a transient impatience. "Nothing can stop mergers. They've come, everywhere, in everything. They're still coming, and they'll keep on coming more and more. They're bound to. All big enterprises will get bigger, and small enterprises will be swallowed up or go to hell. Bound to. I'm not a scientist, and I couldn't make a very clear story of evolution. But I've got the hang of it. And what I say is, the merger is evolution. Anyhow, part of it. There it *is!* It may be a bit rough on a lot of people. But what are you going to do about it? Pull it up with a jerk? You can't. You might as well try to tie a rope to the moon and pull that up. Evolution will go on. Where to? We don't know. At least I don't. Nor care either. All I know is I feel in my bones I've got to go on. Do you suppose I'm taking on this job for money? I've made money. I'm a rich man, very rich. And I want money--want it all the time. I'm interested in money, but I'm much more interested in my instincts. And I'm sure my instincts are right. If they lead me to money, I can't help that. Money's a side-issue. Pleasant enough, of course--but only a side-issue. I'm pushing evolution forward. Somebody has to push it forward, and I'm somebody. What will happen next, after mergers have had a fair show? Who can tell? Not me. It doesn't concern me. Something--call it God or Nature or what you please--something's put certain instincts into my *bones,* I tell you. I'm not a religionist, but I have a conscience. Yes, I'm conscientious. Sense of duty, somewhere down inside me! And the duty is to use my instincts. Or let them use me. I shouldn't like to say which it is. There might be some bad consequences. Well, let there be! My conscience will be clear. And I know jolly well there'd be some good consequences. And soon!"

"Does he think he's a besom and going to sweep me into a corner?" thought Evelyn, sardonic. But Evelyn was bluffing to himself; for he could feel that he was being swept up by the vigorous besom and already on his way to the corner. The power of the City Napoleon loomed formidably over him. "This fellow's situation precarious?" he thought, recalling sinister rumours concerning the reality of Sir Henry's position. "Rot! His position could never be precarious. And if one situation went to smithereens he'd build another and a better one in about half a minute. Still, that Resolution was a pretty wise precaution." He had to fight against the impulse to enrol himself as a partisan of Henry Savott.

He said aloud, in a voice that made Sir Henry's seem coarse and rhetorical:

"As we seem to be talking, I may as well tell you that my sentiments about the plight of the under-dog in this evolution of yours are rather strong. In a place like this you get some very melodramatic contrasts, and they make you think. And when I think for instance of you in your suite, or me here, and then of some of the fellows and girls down in the basements, I get a sort of a notion that there must be something wrong somewhere. And your mergers aren't likely to do such a devil of a lot to put it right. The reverse."

3.

Sir Henry dropped smoothly into an easy-chair opposite Evelyn and when he spoke his restrained tone showed that he had accepted the reproof of Evelyn's quietude.

"And hasn't there always been something wrong? And won't there always be?" he enquired, almost insinuatingly. "When there are no under-dogs the world will have to come to an end, because there won't be anything to improve. Perfection's another name for death, isn't it? And I must just ask you again: What are you going to do about it? About these under-dogs? Mergers mean mass-production and lower prices. What's the matter with this country is that there isn't enough mass-production. Mass-production is the only chance for the under-dog, as far as I can see."

Sir Henry had spoken slowly and more slowly. He paused. Then began again, very low and very deliberate.

"I'm continually hearing about the soul-destroying monotony of organised labour in these days. One man doing one tiny fraction of a job all day every day. Well, that's part of the penalty of cheap prices. But people forget that cheap prices aren't all penalty. They do have the advantage of raising the purchasing power of the under-dog; therefore raising his standard of life. Do you want to go back to the old methods? Even if you could, you'd only raise prices and lower the standard of life. But you couldn't go back. Because we simply don't go back. And do you want to stand still? Everyone knows you can't stand still. Then you must go forward. More mass-production! And--more machinery! I seem to see that machinery may at last put an end to the under-dog. It may wipe him off the earth by throwing him out of work. Well, somebody has to suffer. Anyhow when he's dead he isn't an under-dog. See here! On the voyage over, this last week, I thought I'd have a look at the innards of the ship. I thought they must be rather like a hotel, and I wanted to pick up all I could in the hotel line. I did pick up some trifles. Of course you know, but I didn't know, that there are no bottle-washers in those big ships. All the washing-up's done by machinery and the drying and everything, and better done than any bottle-washer ever did it or ever could do it."

"Oh yes!" said Evelyn. "All the big hotels have that machinery. Been in use for years."

"Wait a minute. Wait a minute." Sir Henry spoke more loudly, and with some excitement. "There are no miserable bottle-washers any more in the big shows. They're gone. They may have died of starvation, and their families with them. But they're gone. No more monotonous, dirty, greasy, soul-destroying labour for bottle-washers. Now that's all to the good. That's what I call an advance. And lots of other underdogs will follow the bottle-washers. Frightful martyrdoms no doubt for a generation or two. But it can't be helped. There is a chance that mass-production and machinery will abolish the under-dog. There's no other chance. So in the sacred cause of social progress I am determined to bear with fortitude the present and future misfortunes of your under-dogs." Sir Henry laughed grimly.

"You may be right," said Evelyn reluctantly. Then, a little ashamed of this assumed reluctance, he added in a more sympathetic tone: "You probably are right. Anyhow it's soothing to the mind to think you are...But I'm afraid I've been leading you off the point."

"No, no!" Sir Henry amiably smiled. "I led myself. It was I who began about dogs. However, I'll get back. I've nearly finished. I told you I'd be perfectly open with you, and I will. It's a bit unusual for a buyer to be enthusiastic about what he wants to buy. Doesn't help him in bargaining, does it? I can't help that. I'm after the Imperial Palace, and you know why. No one knows better. But the Imperial Palace would be no earthly use to me without Mr. Evelyn Orcham. Without him I wouldn't have it at any price. He *is* the Imperial Palace. He brought it from ruin to the most brilliant success in the shortest time on record. Of course there are hotels that have started from nothing and succeeded terrifically from the very day they opened. There are at least two in London. And even Mr. Evelyn Orcham couldn't teach much to the fellows that run them. Only they're cheap hotels. Even under-dogs--some under-dogs--stay in them for a day or two without being broke. They aren't luxury hotels, and it's the luxury hotel and nothing else that interests me. I want something I can look at, with women walking around that I can look at, and money flowing out of pockets like water. There's no fun in running a cheap hotel."

"Oh yes, there is," Evelyn contradicted.

"Well, naturally there is. I mean not my sort of fun, and your sort of fun. I couldn't bear anything that I had a hand in to be spoken slightingly of. I couldn't bear it! 'Must be funny kind of places,' I've heard people--some of your visitors--say of those cheap hotels; and if I'd been in control of the funny kind of places I should have knocked the people down. Simply that. Because I couldn't have borne it. You don't know me if you think I shouldn't. You understand me--what I mean?"

"Perfectly," said Evelyn. "I daresay I should feel the same. But I'm not a prize-fighter."

"Well, I am," said Sir Henry with emphasis. "Off the point again!" He sniggered; then suddenly became serious: "Now Mr. Evelyn Orcham isn't merely the king of the hotel world. He's boss of the market in hotel-managers. And there aren't any under-bosses. There's nobody but him--for a buyer like me, who won't have anything but the best. He owns the finest article in the market--himself--and he can put his own price on it, without arguing. He's in the strongest position that any seller could be in. You see, I realise all that, and I wouldn't pretend I don't. I want to buy Mr. Evelyn Orcham. Damn it! Of *course* I want to buy him. He's the foundation-stone and the keystone and everything of my blooming arch. And I'm ready to pay for him. And when I've got him safe, I want to make him the head-god of the greatest hotel-combine that ever was. Nine big luxury hotels! And I want him to put his stamp on all of them, so that everybody can see the brand at a glance. I want everybody in the luxury world to know that every one of those nine belongs to the Orcham group--and nothing more need be said, no questions asked, no doubts raised, no qualms, no fears, apprehensions. 'It's an Orcham hotel. It's dear, but it's worth the money. You know where you are in his shows.' That's how the luxury crew have got to talk among themselves. And that's how they would talk, by God! Why! In London and Madrid and Paris and San Remo and Cannes and Rome we should put every other swell hotel out of business. Right out. We should divide the luxury crew into two sections--those who had the sense and the money to stay in an Orcham, and those who hadn't... Now, Orcham, is it worth your while to take the thing on? Or am I a ranting idiot?"

Evelyn answered at once:

"If you want my candid opinion, I should say that you don't coincide very closely with my idea of a ranting idiot. But it isn't worth my while to take the thing on. You see, I'm very fond of the Imperial Palace. There's a genuine attachment between us. I'm happy here. I'm content. I don't want anything else."

4.

Sir Henry jumped up from his chair, and began to eat his cigar instead of smoking it.

"Then you will excuse me," he burst forth, stressing nearly every syllable. "But what I say is you've no right to be happy and content here. How old are you? You can't be fifty. Fancy any man under fifty being happy and content! I'm a long sight older than you; but I'm not happy and I'm not content. And I don't want to be, either. When I'm happy and content I shall be so near to being dead that you wouldn't notice the difference. Why man, if you're happy and content you might as well say you haven't got anything else to live for! And what *would* you have to live for? You've made this place once, complete. You've exercised your genius on it. You can't go on making it. It's made. All you have to do is to keep it where it is. A touch here and a touch there. No more. And your genius going to waste! Waste! You've realised one ambition, and a jolly good ambition. You've created the finest luxury hotel in the world. Haven't you got any more ambitions? Or are you at the end? Under fifty! Shall you be satisfied to sit down and fold your arms?" He spread out his arms, and then folded them. But folding his arms did nothing to tranquilise his almost fierce excitement.

With a casual air Evelyn remarked:

"There isn't much sitting down and folding of arms about this place."

Dropping his arms, Sir Henry, cigar between teeth, went back to his chair once again, sat down, and folded his arms anew, but with a comic, apologetic gesture. He stared at Evelyn, faintly smiling.

"Excuse me!" he said, as it were ruefully, and pleadingly. "I really do beg you to excuse me. When I get keen I'm apt to--well, you know. So do I know--curse it!" He showed considerable charm. Indeed for the moment he was irresistible.

"Not at all!" said Evelyn, making no effort to resist, and with a smile quite as charming as his guest's. "Not at all. You're very interesting. A talk is a talk. Do go on." As a fact he found Sir Henry more than interesting--acutely disturbing. But his reserve was a shield to him. And although upon occasion he could, like Sir Henry, put all his cards on the table, he chose not to do so on this occasion.

"Let me say just one thing more," Sir Henry said, ingratiating, appealing, astonishingly placid after his fevered eloquence. "Your talents *are* being wasted here--in my opinion, that is. Are you justified in wasting them? Perhaps you are. I'm merely asking the question. There's still quite a great deal to do in the world. Perhaps luxury hotels aren't the be-all and end-all of life. But they're a factor. And they happen to be your field. And what we want more and more to-day is efficiency. Efficiency is a speciality of yours. Why shouldn't nine luxury hotels set an example of absolutely tiptop efficiency? Any efficiency, particularly when it's spectacular, stimulates all other efficiencies."

Sir Henry's voice died away. He rose slowly, and held out his hand.

"You aren't going?"

"Yes," said Sir Henry. "Thanks immensely for a perfect evening. I couldn't have enjoyed an evening more."

"But--"

"Seems to me I ought to give you a chance to think it over. That's all I ask. For you to think it over. No hurry. I should hate to hurry you. You'll ring me up, or I'll ring you up. I'm not leaving the Palace yet. I don't vanish out of hotels like Gracie. *Au revoir.* Your hospitality is the sort I can appreciate. Of course being in the Imperial Palace it would be."

Evelyn shook bands unwillingly. At the door Sir Henry turned.

"And I say," he murmured with another rueful smile, "I rely on you to forgive all the noise I've made."

He departed. The door banged.

Evelyn gently threw the last inch of his first evening cigar into the fire.

"A masterly exit," he thought.

Chapter 25 EARLY MORN

Evelyn had luck that night. He did not possess the Napoleonic gift of sleeping at will and for any willed length of time. Indeed he seldom slept uninterruptedly for more than three hours together, and he praised God when God granted him a total of five and a half hours' sleep in three instalments. He probably did not sleep well because he was not very interested in sleep. What really interested him was waking up, getting up, and satisfying himself by contemplation of the dawn that the ancient earth was revolving as usual. But on just that night it mysteriously happened to him to receive from heaven five hours' unbroken sleep. So that he arose with full mental vigour in the morning twilight and drew the curtains and raised the blinds and beheld glistening roofs and clouds gliding above them from the eternal south-west; and began to reflect upon a new problem, as eagerly curious about it as a child about a new toy.

It was in these earliest morning hours, after a fair night, that Evelyn most pleasantly savoured life. He had leisure then, more time than was necessary for the due performance of what he called his 'chores.' He possessed three dressing-gowns of different thicknesses. Oldham always laid them side by side in an unvarying order on the back of his easy-chair. He chose the one which seemed to him to suit the temperature of the morning. He turned on the electric radiator. Steam-heating was good enough for the visitors to the Palace, but not for its Director. He turned on all the lights, for he liked the fullest illumination, Saying that whatever he was doing he preferred to see clearly what it was.He beheld the room, and the tidiness of the room provided fresh satisfaction every morning. Every morning was the beginning of the world and of his existence. No clothes and no linen were ever left lying in the room. Nothing was out of place: neither the books on the large bed-table, nor the glasses and bottle and weekly papers and cigarette-box on the square table behind the bed, nor the appointments on the dressing-table, nor the pumps and slippers on the floor.

Now, he lit the finest cigarette of the day, and opened windows wide, and, warm in his camel-hair gown, defied the tang of the air of sunrise. He glanced at the clock on the mantelpiece and the encased watch on the bed-table, and noted with relief and pride that they announced precisely the same minute of the same hour. He considered what suit he would wear, what shirt, what necktie, what handkerchief, what socks, what shoes. He hated anew the prospect of shaving. He drank the celestial juice of two oranges carefully distilled for him overnight by Oldham. He ate half a handful of seedless raisins, also prepared for him by Oldham.

Among the books on the bed-table was an India-paper Bible. He scarcely ever read it, but he liked to feel that in case he wanted to read it the Bible was handy. On this morning he picked up the Bible, found the Psalms, found the Forty-sixth Psalm. Yes. There it was, the memorable sentence: "Be still and know that I am God." The sentence awed him. It seemed to contain the whole wisdom of thirty centuries of human experience. And he had lived for nearly fifty years in ignorance of it. He repeated and repeated the sentence. But no better than on the previous night could he have defined its significance, even to himself. He strolled into the bathroom, strolled back, leaving the door ajar, took off his dressing-gown, and, with customary conscientiousness, performed blood-stimulating physical exercises on the floor and upright in front of an open window. Then he shut the windows, resumed the dressing gown, and luxuriously, voluptuously, and a little breathlessly reclined in the easy-chair. One chore done!

As a rule at this stage of the day he read periodicals. But now he had no desire to read. He wished to enjoy his mind. He was not given to self-analysis. He would think out his plans, but the originating cause of all his plans had little interest for him. He lived his life by deep impulses into which he never enquired. He rather despised the individuals who were always worrying themselves about themselves. His attitude was God's: I am that I am. To wonder why he was what he was hardly occurred to him. And whither he was going did not trouble him more than whence he had come. He constructed no chart, wrote out no annual balance-sheet. He merely knew, felt, that he had work to do and that he was doing it pretty well and was thereby kept continually busy.

2.

But to-day, in the freshness of the morning and the cherished order of the room, he entered upon some sort of an examination of that unexplored strange creature, Evelyn Orcham. At leisure, and secure from any invasion, he began to reflect, not without mild excitement. He was happy. Henry Savott had feverishly informed him that at his age he had no right to be happy. Nevertheless he was happy. He damned Henry Savott. Still, the man had impressed him. In his daily life Evelyn was more used to bestow wisdom than to receive it. And to have positively explosive instruction flung in his face with violence was to say the least disconcerting.

The younger son of the Chief Customs Inspector of an important East Coast port, Evelyn had been brought up with two extremely taciturn men--his widowed father and his brother. The two men and the boy seldom talked and never argued, even at meals. The two men showed no curiosity about anything, and apparently thought that nothing was worth talking about. Each was an individual island entirely surrounded by spiritual solitude; and the boy became an island. The elder brother entered the Customs service, married a girl who chattered incessantly, and reached in course of time the chief inspectorship of another East Coast port. His children were growing up. He asked no more from life. He never wrote to Evelyn, nor Evelyn to him. Immediately on leaving school Evelyn heard casually of a catering job at a provincial Exhibition, and on the strength of a school reputation as organiser of field-excursions, casually wandered off to get the job, and got it. Nobody either encouraged or discouraged his enterprise of leaving home. He just departed with an exchange of "Ta-ta, ta-ta." And he never saw his home again. His father died while away on holiday, and at the funeral Evelyn spoke about forty words to his brother, and his brother about twenty words to Evelyn. "Ta-ta, ta-ta," once more. Withal, the pair were conscious of mutual esteem. Evelyn rose by step and step to the top of his profession. When he arrived at the panjandrumship of the Imperial Palace Hotel he sat down to write the news to his brother. But he desisted and cast the sheet into the waste-paper basket, because he was afraid that his grave and silent brother might reply on a post-card and despise him for breaking the grand family tradition of taciturnity. All he could be sure of about his brother was that he was not dead; for tradition would assuredly have summoned him to a brother's funeral.

Once fairly established in the hotel world, Evelyn of course had to learn the art, and especially the craft, of conversation. He learned it as he might have learned mathematics or juggling or conjuring. He talked, but he remained reserved. He had always been, and he still was, reserved even with the person whom be least mistrusted--himself. At no period of his wonderful ascent had he made many friends.

The career of hotel-management was as absorbing as that of ship-captaincy. There were, in practice, no fixed, regular hours of work for the chief and his immediate subordinates. During twenty hours daily, from 6.30 a.m. to 2 a.m., the big hotel was as it were in full navigation of the high seas; and during the poor brief remnant of the twenty-four the vessel was not in port; she was only hove to. A critical situation was as likely to supervene by night as by day. Evelyn's most intimate friend was old Dennis Dover, and it was he who had late one evening likened a big cosmopolitan hotel to a baby. "You *never* dare leave it," father Dennis had said. "The darned thing's always liable to wake up before dawn and cry itself into convulsions if you aren't there." The Imperial Palace Hotel tolerated no rival interests. Everybody who served it became enslaved to it. The hotel took the place of wife, children, friends, hobbies, sports. Apparent exceptions occurred now and then; not, however, real exceptions. Thus the sardonic middle-aged grill-room chef, Rocco, had begun recently to flirt with golf; but his colleagues prophesied that the affair would be flirtation and no more.

As for Evelyn, he had forsaken sports and pastimes many years ago. And why should Evelyn embarrass himself with a pack of friends when he was happy without them?

But on this particular morning he saw his present as well as his future in the new searchlight directed upon them by Henry Savott. He was the celebrated panjandrum of the Imperial Palace Hotel. He had 'got there.' Good! And in ten years, in twenty? When he was approaching three score and ten, would be have retired-unthinkable--or would he still be the panjandrum of the Imperial Palace Hotel? Would not the livelier of his acquaintances and colleagues then be saying behind his back: "Yes, terrific fellow! Made the place! Perhaps he's been there a bit too long. Thirty years. In a groove. You can't teach him anything now"? Possibly he was already fairly deep in a groove of habit and self-complacency. Was it not true what Savott had said, that a touch here and a touch there should suffice to keep the vast organism of the Imperial Palace in the path of prosperity? Could he, Evelyn, deny that his talent for imaginative efficiency was being to some extent wasted? He sat quiet, and waited for inspiration. Without at all realising it, he was fulfilling the behest of the Psalmist's deity: "Be still and know that I am God."

He heard a faint whine. It was the sound of the vacuum cleaner which twice a week a chambermaid and a valet between them employed upon his sitting-room. The day had started. The humble were abroad and active. But how came it that he could hear the sound across the bathroom, in a bedroom theoretically impervious to all noise? Ah! He had left the bedroom door ajar. He rose and shut the door. The whine ceased to be audible.

Could he successfully inspire the managers of eight hotels in four different countries with his own spirit, energy, enthusiasm, tact, tireless ingenuity in organisation? He might be able to teach Rome and Madrid. But could he teach Paris and the Riviera; he an Englishman, handicapped, despite his renown, by the fact of being a native of the land which had the worst hotels in Europe? Well, he thought he could. He knew he could. Already he could see how he would have to set about the mighty task: stay in each of the hotels, say nothing, watch, praise, study local conditions, allow for local standards; a touch here and a touch there at first; cautious suggestions; then bolder strokes; a few abrupt dismissals; exchanges of important members of staffs between one hotel and another; promotions, degradations; soft answers; the iron hand; encouragement of the larger harmony through transient violent discords; flittings from city to city; rapid and frequent returns to London to maintain the peace of the Imperial Palace, and to galvanise and electrify the Majestic and the Duncannon into a more and more active reforming energy.

There was the language difficulty. Absurd! He was inventing difficulties. The entire hotel-world was polyglot. And he could speak French admirably. He had learned French as he had learned conversation, and for the same reason. And if he felt any apprehensions about Madrid, which he had seen only once, he could take with him once or twice Adolphe, the *chef de reception* of the Palace, and the supreme linguist of all the Palace staff.

The projected enterprise of modernising hotels made a fascinating panorama in his mind. It was an enterprise perfectly suited to his faculties. Had he not already conducted two similar enterprises to triumph, in his beloved first-born, the Wey, and then in the Imperial Palace? In both cases had he not performed the miracle of raising the dead; and to what glorious life? In the privacy of his self-esteem he doubted whether there existed on earth another man as fortunately qualified as himself for the realisation of Savott's dream. By the way, it was Savott's dream; not his own. And Savott might well be an excellent man to work with. Savott would understand without too much argument, because he had imagination.

Nevertheless Evelyn hated the visionary project. He shrank from the sight of it, averting his eyes. Why shoulder the weight of ten thousand new anxieties? Why wander homeless? Why leave the adorable habitual comfort of his everlasting home? He feared, tremblingly hesitant. Ha! The groove! Dramatic proof, this hesitation, that he was indeed already sunk in a groove, that in his shelter he shivered at the mere thought of the winds of the world. But supposing that he declined Savott's offer--how would he feel afterwards for the rest of his life? Shamed, remorseful, disappointed, stultified, lethargised? Would he not. know in his heart that he was a coward? Then he perceived a flaw in Savott's grandiose scheme. It was not sufficiently grandiose. The fellow did not know enough. He was missing the finest, the most glaring opportunity in Europe. Deauville! There were only two authentic luxury hotels in Deauville. Savott should have bought options on both of them. The trouble in Deauville was the shortness of the season. But the season ought to be lengthened, could be lengthened. That bright young man Immerson, author and controller of the unique indirect publicity of the Imperial Palace, had once in Evelyn's presence sighed for the chance to do in Deauville what he had done in London and Weybridge. The Deauville people had amazingly succeeded with their hotels, but they had not succeeded in stretching their season. Their imagination lacked breadth and sweep.

3.

A quiet knock. Evelyn got up and walked to the right-hand window. Oldham entered.

"Morning, Oldham," Evelyn greeted him, but without turning round.

"Morning, sir."

These two understood each other perfectly--not almost perfectly, but perfectly. Evelyn's attitude towards Oldham was one of affection and appreciation. Oldham's to Evelyn one of affection and devotion. Because of his aversion for physical exercise and his inexhaustible interest in eating, Oldham, who was five years younger than Evelyn, looked five years older, and Evelyn always thought of him as older.

Once, a long time since, they had had a skirmish which might have developed into a calamitous shindy if Evelyn had not the presence of mind to shut his own mouth. Oldham valued that forbearance. It had been reported to Evelyn through the floor-housekeeper, that in a quarrel with a chambermaid about their respective duties Oldham had remarked: "If you think I'm a bloody chambermaid--" Evelyn had been infuriated at such behaviour; less at the language used to a girl by a respectable man of an age to be her father, than at the respectable man's evident unfairness in presuming on the immense advantage of his position as Evelyn's private and confidential servant. Evelyn was very seldom infuriated; one might say never. But he happened to be himself extreme punctilious in his demeanour to all his employees; he had a special detestation of masters who were rude to their servants and Oldham's iniquity had taken him by surprise. Also, Evelyn's fury had taken Oldham by surprise; and Oldham had retorted too soon, before he had recovered from the surprise. The next day Oldham had briefly expressed contrition, and the quarrel was over. They had never had another. The first and last quarrel had seemed to draw them more closely together; both had realised that a rupture would be desolating.

Evelyn had tried for years to put sense into Oldham about eating, outdoor exercise, and personal tidiness. He had failed and had abandoned the efforts. He might have succeeded as regards personal tidiness, if Oldham's *gourmandise* had not made him too stout to get into Evelyn's cast-off suits. Instead of wearing these perquisites Oldham sold them. As in all other matters Oldham was meticulously tidy, Evelyn had accepted the situation.

"Striped," said Evelyn, still not turning round. (Each of Evelyn's suits was christened with a short epithet.) "Black-and-white shirt, black tie, black French shoes." He said nothing about socks because socks had to match the tie.

"Yes, sir...Excuse me, sir," said Oldham. "Mrs. O'Riordan is unwell and thinks she ought to stay in bed. She would very much obliged if you could go and see her after breakfast. That was the message, sir." His shocked tone said: "Yes, that's the message, and I give it you, but it's the biggest piece of cheek I ever heard of in this hotel, and I beg to take no responsibility for it. *You* going to see the housekeeper because she's 'unwell,' as she calls it!"

"All right," said Evelyn, absently. "Remind me."

"Yes, sir."

Evelyn himself perceived not the enormity of the message, but at the back of his brain, behind the circling thoughts concerning his presence and his future, he was somewhat disturbed. He guessed: "It must be about the new floor-housekeeper. She wants to settle that business at once, and I may have some trouble with the old girl." At last he turned to go into the bathroom. Oldham had switched on the light in the huge wardrobe-cubicle which gave on to the bedroom and which held the whole of Evelyn's attire. The man was handling a pair of trousers.

"Here! Steady!" Evelyn enjoined him. "I told you the striped, not the broad stripe." When Evelyn had bought a second striped suit the new one had been dubbed 'broad-stripe' to distinguish it from the old one.

"Sorry, sir," Oldham apologised, after a brief pause for cerebration, in the thick, obscure tone which always indicated that he was secretly worried. Indeed the audacity of Mrs. O'Riordan was still abrading his sensitive nerves so loyal to Evelyn.

Evelyn passed into the bathroom, where Oldham had already made every minute customary preparation for the morning rites. The spectacle of the sacred traditional disposition of the bathroom appealed pleasurably every day to Evelyn's passionate sense of order. Razor, razor-towel, chair, bath-towels, mat, mirror, soaps, height and temperature of water in the bath--each item was arranged strictly in accordance with the changeless daily formula. And he enjoyed the spectacle this morning, but absently.

He was not thinking of Mrs. O'Riordan. He was thinking: "What am I alive for? What is my justification for being alive and working? I cannot keep on creating the Palace. I have created it. The thing is done. I can't do it again."

For the first time he was addressing to his soul the terrible comprehensive question, which corrodes the very root of content in the existence of millions of less fortunate people, but which had never even presented itself to Evelyn until the previous night:

"Why?"

If Henry Savott's proposition could not furnish the answer to the question, what could? As late as within the last twenty four hours--nay, twelve hours--he had been condemning Savott's scheme as a dastardly and hateful conspiracy to be countered at any cost. Only a minute ago he had been hating it. But now the visionary project was changing its appearance: and in spite of himself he saw in it the chance of salvation--he who but a little earlier would have derided any hypothesis that he needed salvation.

He shaved with cautious tranquillity. He lay long in the warm water; and as he lay a lamp seemed to be ignited in his brain, and it burned up slowly into a steady flame which illuminated the whole of his brain. And it was the figure and symbol of Savott's scheme, and the one veritable answer to that dread conundrum: why was he alive, and why should he go on living? And though he tried to pretend that his brain was dark, he could not, because of the convincing brightness of the lamp. And even when, reluctantly, he withdrew himself from the warm water and with a towel violently rubbed his skin as if he would rub out the flame itself, it still burned unwaveringly. And Evelyn had to carry the lamp into the bedroom. In the bedroom he beheld all his clothes laid out according to formula and with the zealous accuracy of a man who knew why he was alive and had found the reason completely satisfactory.

Then, while he was seated at the mirror tying his cravat, there was a tap on the door and the door opened, and Oldham entered, consternation on his pale, flabby face.

"Mrs. O'Riordan is in the sitting-room, sir," said Oldham, ashamed, shocked by his own tidings.

"What?"

With admirable presence of mind Evelyn neither turned his gaze from the mirror nor ceased to tie the cravat.

"She wants to see you at once, sir."

"Who let her into the room?"

"She came in, sir."

"But I thought she was ill."

"Yes, sir."

"What time is it?"

"Twenty minutes to eight, sir."

"Now, look here, Oldham." Evelyn swung round on the chair. "Get her out. Use your famous tact. Say I'm late. Say I'm not dressed. Tell her I'll come along and see her in her own room as quickly as possible."

"Yes, sir," Oldham agreed, doubtfully, and departed.

Evelyn had not been able to extinguish the lamp, but this unparalleled occurrence extinguished it. Scarcely could he believe what he had heard. What! A member of the staff invade his sacred castle, and before breakfast! Such an act was unheard of in all the history of Evelyn's panjandrumship. Nobody dared to come into his castle, save upon special request and as a favour--and never on hotel business. Mrs. O'Riordan must have had one of her rare nerve-storms. But even so--! He was all spruce and ready to leave the bedroom before Oldham returned.

"Well?" he asked, showing anxiety despite an effort to hide it.

"She's gone, sir."

"Was she dressed?"

"Well, sir, she was *dressed,* as you might call it."

"What do you mean?"

"A neg*lee*jay, sir." Oldham departed once more.

Evelyn passed through the now disordered and sloppy-floored bathroom into the sitting-room, which was as clean and bright as a new pin. He rang the bell, sat down to the breakfast table, and opened "The Times." First he looked at the City page and noted that Imperial Palace shares had risen one-eighth. Good! Then he turned to the obituaries and to the announcements of betrothals, weddings, births, deaths, dinner-parties, receptions; for it was part of his work, as of Cousin's and Adolphe's and Cappone's and Ruffo's, to maintain close familiarity with the daily annals of the great self-advertising world. Then on the sports page his eye caught a paragraph about Woolwich Arsenal Football Club. Then Oldham brought in breakfast.

"I say, Oldham," he enquired with seeming vivacious interest, "what's this about the Arsenal this season?"

He hoped to get one up on Oldham in the matter of football news, but as usual his hope was disappointed. Oldham had seen the news in another paper, his own, where it was a front-page item. The man's sole distraction was Association Football. As a slim youth he had played centre-half. He seldom attended a match; in fact he attended a match no oftener than he attended his wife, who lived in a Berkshire village. But he always knew all about all teams, players, matches. The desire of his life was to win a £1,000 prize offered by a Sunday paper for twenty-two correct results. He had never got beyond eighteen; and Evelyn prayed that he would stick eternally at eighteen, lest £1,000 in cash might ruin him both as a man and as a valet. Evelyn had no curiosity whatever about Association Football or about Rugby either; he kept a careless attention on Association news solely in order to be able to discuss it intelligently with Oldham, who loved to display his vast knowledge. This morning they talked at some length. But the conversation was a piece of bravado, a horrible and unconvincing make-believe. Both were humiliatingly aware of its false character. Each knew that the other was obsessed, worried, appalled, overset by Mrs. O'Riordan's shocking, incredible invasion in a *negligé.* Both had been unmanned thereby. But each nevertheless was nobly determined to play the intrepid man in face of insulting behaviour and oncoming trouble.

Oldham left. In five minutes he came back, freighted with still worse news.

"Mr. Plimsing is outside, sir," said he, having carefully shut the doors. "Wishes to see you, sir."

"What next?" cried Evelyn, pushing away his plate with a gesture betraying serious agitation. Oldham intensified the woe in his visage. "What did you tell him?"

"Nothing, sir."

Evelyn raised his voice slightly: "Well, tell him this. Tell him I can't see him here. Tell him I'll see him in my office at nine o'clock. No. I'll see him here at nine o'clock. And not before. I don't care how urgent his business is. I wonder what's come over the place this morning!"

Mr. Plimsing was the hotel detective; formerly in the C.I.D. department of Scotland Yard.

Chapter 26 NERVE-STORM

"How sweet of you to come!" murmured Mrs. O'Riordan sweetly, as Evelyn entered her sitting-room.

She reclined on a sofa which had been drawn up near the hearth, where a small fire burned. Her slim body was enveloped in a rosy *negligé,* a magnificent garment. Her head rested on a small white embroidered pillow, under which were three variegated and ribboned cushions. She smiled with a coquettish consciousness of grace, of the exceeding neatness of her grey-white coiffure, of the rouged and powdered finish of her lips and complexion, and of the elegance of her wrists and manicured hands emerging from the lacy sleeves. But the most elegant thing on the sofa was a black cat, curled up on the eiderdown covering her feet. Mrs. O'Riordan's attitude and demeanour combined those of a Madame Récamier and an Olympia, inviting, refusing, teasing, voluptuous, intelligent.

The room was over-full of furniture and knickknacks and flowers. Portraits of men, women and mansions thronged the walls. The room was a boudoir. But in one hand Mrs. O'Riordan held some letters, and at her side, on a pouf, sat a young, pink-faced, short-frocked secretary, notebook open on knees. The Récamier, the Olympia, the odalisque, had been dictating answers to correspondence.

Evelyn's apprehensions momentarily vanished at the warm spectacle of the domestic interior. He thought: "I can deal with this all right." And he thought what a shame it was that such a woman, such a cunning piece of femininity, should be compelled by fate to knit her brows over business when she ought to be occupied solely with her ageless charm, the attractions of her boudoir, and the responsiveness of men to her fine arts. Monstrous it was that she, whose function in life was obviously to scatter money, should have to earn it, and in order to earn it should be dictating letters at 8.30 a.m. The whole situation was against nature. He had always known, or at any rate guessed, that Mrs. O'Riordan was somewhat ardently feminine; but never before had he had such evidence of her temperament. The sight amounted to a sudden revelation; for he had not been in her sitting-room for years, and not once had he seen her in aught but the strict shining head-housekeeper's black.

He said nothing, waved his hand vaguely as though it held his stick, waited.

"Shoo! Run!" said Mrs. O'Riordan to the little secretary, frowning, rather crossly. In an instant her face had assumed its smile.

"She's wound up; all nerves; a bit hysterical," thought Evelyn.

The little secretary jumped to her feet, and, with a shy, pleasant glance at Evelyn, obediently hurried out of the room.

"You don't look ill," said Evelyn. "What's this I hear about you being ill?"

"Pleurisy," said Mrs. O'Riordan

"Pleurisy?" he exclaimed.

"Oh! If you don't believe me, just look." She raised her head and shoulders, and with one hand pulled down the *negligé* at the back, exposing one shoulder-blade and the edge of a white undergarment. "Come nearer and look." It was a command that she uttered. Evelyn saw the ends of a series of strips of plaster.

"You see how he's plastered me all up."

"Who?"

"Dr. Constam of course." Dr. Constam was the young hotel-doctor. "So that when I move, the pleura won't rub. I sent for him before seven o'clock. I had such a sharp pain. It's only a very slight attack, but it *is* pleurisy." She lowered her head on to the pillow. "And that's not all. He says there's something funny about my liver. Well, I always knew there was. The gallbladder isn't working properly. But otherwise I feel very well. Only he's told me I must keep as quiet as I can. As if I could!"

"And your idea of keeping quiet is to come down to see me before I'm dressed!" said Evelyn, with a gentle, sardonic smile

"You aren't very sympathetic. Pleurisy's pleurisy, you know. It's nothing yet; but it might be very serious if it wasn't taken in hand at once. I've had it before."

"Well, you ought to be in bed, then."

"I am in bed, practically. I'm only lying here while my bed's being made. He says I mustn't eat any fats--that's because of the gall-bladder, or drink any alcohol--or as little as I can. I shall certainly drink *some.* I came down to see you because I just couldn't wait. I know it was very naughty of me. I know you're God. Mr. Cousin thinks he's God too, but he isn't. Do sit down. I want to talk to you."

"Very well. But oughtn't you to leave everything till you're better?"

"No, I oughtn't," said Mrs. O'Riordan. Evelyn was moving about the room, carelessly examining the portraits. "And please do sit down. You fidget me. Please!"

Evelyn sat, at some distance from the sofa, on a chair by the sideboard. Yes, he thought, Mrs. O'Riordan was in a strange, sensitive mood, a mood surprising to him. She had ceased to be an employee. He had ceased to be the Director of the Imperial Palace. He was a man, and she was a woman, and she knew her power and was using it, with a grand impetuous disregard of their relative positions. Despite her alleged maladies, she seemed to be uplifted, and responsive; Evelyn felt uplifted also. He enjoyed his plight. The cat stood up on Mrs. O'Riordan's hidden ankles, yawned, arched its back, and gazed at Evelyn with real contempt.

"Well?" Evelyn calmly encouraged the invalid, folding his hands and crossing one knee over the other. He said to himself that Mrs. O'Riordan would have to look much more like a sick woman than she did before he could behave to her as one. He had, however, quite forgiven her scandalous and untimely invasion of his castle.

"It's about Miss Brury," said Mrs. O'Riordan, stroking the cat, which had strolled up to her shoulders. "Darling!" (This to the cat.) "She came to see me last night. She wants to be taken back. She cried and I cried, and any woman with any heart would have cried. This notion that men have that women are hard on one another is ridiculous. It's men that are hard on women, and don't we know it! Alice says she hasn't got a penny--gives all she has to her married sister, who has about a thousand children--what a husband!--and she simply daren't ask for another place because everyone will know what happened here. And why shouldn't she come back? Tired to death, and she has to deal with a drunken thief in the cloak-room--"

"Drunken?"

"Yes."

"You never said that before."

"Because I didn't think of it. And Miss Brury didn't either. Good-natured women don't think these horrid things of one another. But it occurred to me all of a sudden. And so I sent down to Cappone to find out what that precious party had had to drink. Hock. A bottle and a half of champagne. Three ports, and three Armagnacs. She must have been drunk--or halfdrunk. But some of them hide it so cleverly. So I went to see Cousin immediately. This was last night. He was just leaving, and I kept him over three-quarters of an hour, and glad I am I did too! What annoys me in Mr. Cousin is he's always so calm. It's unnatural--especially in a Frenchman. A Frenchman ought to know that a woman with something on her mind hardly likes talking to a stone wall. Well, Mr. Cousin doesn't seem to know that. He just said Alice couldn't be taken back, and she couldn't and she couldn't and she couldn't. The pain I had got worse and worse. I told him I was very unwell, but do you suppose he cared? No more than you do, Mr. Orcham!"

"I'm very sorry," said Evelyn.

"Yes. You look as if you are! You wouldn't see me before because you were in your braces, and now you're twiddling yourthumbs and you're 'very sorry.'" Mrs. O'Riordan laughed with a surprising attractiveness which her remarks belied.

Evelyn, fearing that her gaiety might at any moment turn to hysterical sobbing, smiled with prudence. But he remained in a conditionsecretly uplifted.

2.

"I'm afraid we can't have Miss Brury back at the Palace," he said.

"Of course you men always agree."

"But I'll find her another place, if you really want me to."

"Where?"

"Well, at the Laundry."

"At the *Laundry!"*

"Why not?"

"Oh, nothing! Only it's an insult. I haven't trained Alice to iron shirts and pants."

"She might be staff-manageress. It's an excellent job."

"Glad to hear it!" said Mrs. O'Riordan, with charming scorn. But in spite of herself she was a little bit dashed by the splendour of the offer. She went on: "Of course when a girl's in a hole, through no fault of her own, and hasn't a penny, you can safely humiliate her, and she's obliged to thank you for humiliating her. Don't I know! I daresay you think I'm being impudent."

"Not at all," Evelyn replied blandly. "I like you when you're very ill--like this."

And he did. Instead of resenting her present lack of self-control, he admired, as never before, the extraordinary self-control which almost continuously for years and years she had managed to maintain in the past. He appreciated, now, the tremendous effort which it must have entailed for her: keeping the peace among a pack of women and girls; mollifying and kowtowing to a pack of hypercritical visitors; trying to prevent the unscrupulous visitors from stealing coat-hangers and ashtrays and even electroplate--for the Palace, like all hotels, was no better than a den of well-dressed thieves; watching over the sewing-repairs; placating the Works Department, especially when trouble arose between the Works carpenters and her own private carpenters who carpentered exclusively within the hotel; pestering and being pestered by the electricians, dictating her wordy letters; passing on complaints about room meals to the grill-room chef; clashing herself against the insensate rock which was Mr. Cousin; getting up early and going to bed late; always, always, being sweetly diplomatic with the panjandrum; and always, always pretending that she allowed nothing to worry her or ever would! She, the Olympia-Récamier on the couch! She was marvellous. Let her break out. Let her be impudent. Let her be as womanish as she chose. She had earned the right to be so. The truth indeed was that brief intercourse with Gracie Savott had somehow given Evelyn a new insight into women and quickened his sympathy for them. Strange, considering the way Gracie had behaved! But it was so.

"Oh! So you like impudence!" She raised her eyebrows seductively, and her clear voice was seductive.

"Yes, when it's yours, mother."

"Please don't call me mother," she snapped, in quite another voice, frowning suddenly.

"You darling!" he nearly said as he cajolingly smiled, as to a petulant young beauty. What was wrong with her? Was it merely liver and a touch of pleurisy? Everyone referred to her as mother. She frequently, with pride in her tone, referred to herself as mother. He himself, and several others in the hierarchy, often addressed her as mother. "Sister," he corrected aloud, while sustaining the smile.

"I hate to be called mother, and if you're so hard on poor Alice Brury I can't understand why you should make such a fuss about chambermaids having to open their bags and things to that brute Maxon. Yes, I got your note. I didn't answer it because I was so angry. Of course it's not nice for girls to have to open their bags. Did you imagine we hadn't thought of it? As a matter of fact I long since started a system of them showing their bags to their housekeeper. But housekeepers can't always be on the spot to O.K. the bags with a bit of chalk. And even if they are, what's to prevent the girls from getting a friend to hand them something on the stairs as they go down? It all seems easy and simple to you; but you're a man and you don't know. Any chambermaid could get the better of you. Chambermaids are awful. They'd leave as soon as look at you. And you have to be after them the whole damn time. Just ask Miss Maclaren. She could tell you a few things. Chambermaids, oh yes! But when it comes to Alice Brury, who's been *perfect,* you're absolutely flinty, you and your Mr. Cousin!"

Evelyn said:

"But it mustn't be forgotten that the unhappy Alice left us at a moment's notice. I mean without any notice at all."

"Yes," cried Mrs. O'Riordan. "And that's what I'm going to do! I'm too young for this place. That's what's the matter with me!"

Her voice had risen sharply. She had been lying on her back. Now she twisted her body a little, laid one cheek on the embroidered pillow, and threw her right arm over her face. The letters slipped from her right hand and floated down to the carpet. The cat jumped after them and they rustled beneath its paws. A strange sound was heard--Mrs. O'Riordan sobbing. Evelyn, in accordance with his habit when he could not decide what to do, did nothing. He was startled.

"She'll get over this," he thought. "It's the beginning of the end of the nerve-storm. She'll be through in about a minute now. Then she'll be sorry. They're always like that."

He had never conceived the Imperial Palace without its mother. Probably nobody had. But to his own surprise the conception of the Imperial Palace without its mother at once attracted him. She was charming, efficient, conscientious. Still, she was undeniably sixty-two; and who could go on for ever? Already several times it had occurred to Evelyn that 'if anything happened'--and who *could* go on for ever?--there was always Miss Maclaren, who was Scottish--better than being English, Welsh or Irish!--had worked on every floor of the hotel in turn, and had carried on quite smoothly in the stead of Mrs. O'Riordan during the mother's last summer holiday. If mother had died, the Imperial Palace would have survived, and if mother chose to retire the Imperial Palace would survive. Emile Cousin at any rate would support the blow with fortitude. The slowly developing antipathy between those two had been causing some mild concern to Evelyn. Nevertheless the retirement of mother, if indeed she really meant to retire, would be a mighty and reverberating event in the domestic life and politics of the Palace.

3.

Mrs. O'Riordan, having ceased to sob, was softly weeping, but she had presence of mind enough to draw a handkerchief from a pocket inside her *negligé* and dab her eyes. Evelyn saw her gazing at him from under her arm. The eyes were glinting and gleaming at him.

"You might rescue those letters from the cat," Mrs. O'Riordan murmured.

Evelyn obeyed.

"You're better now, aren't you?" he said, bending over her. "Perhaps you could sleep a little."

"Better!" she said, with amazing swift brightness and lightness. "I couldn't be better. I was only crying because I'm so happy. I'm much too happy to sleep. Sleep! I wouldn't sleep for anything! I'm going to be married. That was *really* why I came down to see you this morning--to tell you! I wanted you to be the first to hear about it. But when you walked in here I didn't know just how to begin. You frighten me. You frighten everybody."

Evelyn moved away, laughing.

"Well, I don't see anything to laugh at," the mother protested.

"I was only laughing because I'm so happy--in your happiness," Evelyn retorted. "May one ask who is the favourite of fortune?"

Mrs. O'Riordan sat up and faced her employer.

"Colonel Sir Brian Milligan, Bart.--age sixty-eight, if you don't mind." She gazed at Evelyn in splendid triumph. "Look at me," her gaze seemed to say to him. "I'm the future Lady Milligan. And I *am* too young to be the mother of this hotel. I'm young enough to catch a man and hold him even if I am only a hotel-housekeeper. Any man, except cold-blooded fishes like you and your Frenchman!"

Evelyn's eyes glistened with pleasure. He was proud of mother, enraptured with her conquest. He knew something about Milligan, who was an irregular diner and luncher in the grill-room and had once spent a few nights in the hotel. How clever of her to entrance and enchant this not-unknown figure of a Colonel! And the future Lady Milligan would conscientiously and brilliantly play her part in the affair. She had presided in drawing-rooms before, and she would preside in drawing-rooms again. No more early mornings for her, no business correspondence, organisings, diplomacies, repressions, unnatural deprivations! She would be able to be fully her natural self. She would be petted, spoilt--she would see to that! She would lead the fine old fellow a dance; but so delicately, so deliciously! Do him good too! She who was 'too young' at sixty-two, she who would never be old, would rejuvenate him in spite of himself. Had she not been young enough to invade even Evelyn's castle in her girlish anxiety to announce the tidings? And Evelyn was the first to know!

He secretly chuckled at the thought of the liveliness of the married life of those two, and of the surprises that awaited Sir Brian. Some of the surprises would be exquisite, some not. No! They would all be exquisite, but some would be disturbing. Her nerve-storms would test his masculine calm and authority. She would never go too far. She would always win, while often appearing to lose. She was infernally clever. Had she not been clever enough to hide the growth of the extraordinary idyll from all the world? How she had managed that, Evelyn neither knew nor cared. She had managed it.

"He's rich, isn't he?" he asked.

Mrs. O'Riordan's demure reply was:

"We are very fond of one another. Very fond. I adore him--but don't tell him that when you meet him--and I shall try my hardest to make him happy."

Evelyn accepted the rebuke.

"You'll succeed," he said. "It's a certainty."

"Of course," she said. "At my age I don't want to be silly and talk about passion. And yet--" She stopped, and smiled innumerable implications. "You know, his father lived to be ninety-eight, and got himself into frightful trouble with a housemaid three years before he died. And Brian's exactly like a boy. D'you know, he writes poetry! Nobody sees it but me and he makes me tear it up. At least he thinks he does. Naturally I keep it. I wouldn't destroy it for anything. I mean of course I do tear up the paper, but I learn it off first. He'd be furious if he knew. He's very passionate, by temperament. I've told you his age. But what's that? Sixty-eight--and a boy!"

"And you're twenty-two," said Evelyn. "The six is a misprint for a two."

"You are nice," she said, with sudden tenderness.

"I feel nice," said Evelyn. He did. He thought he had never been so happy, never beheld a spectacle so ravishing as the spectacle of the feminine half of this idyll. "When are you going to get married?"

"Ah!" said Mrs. O'Riordan, mother and head-housekeeper of the Imperial Palace Hotel. "That will depend on you. I won't leave you in the lurch."

Evelyn had an impulse to say:

"You can leave now. You can get married to-morrow. You can begin your honeymoon to-morrow night." But he checked himself. He would not wound her by implying that a personage so important could be dispensed with as easily as an Alice Brury, could depart and leave no trace of difficulty behind.

He said:

"Now listen to me, bride. This hotel will not be allowed to interfere with your happiness. You make your plans, and this hotel will fit in with them. I know you're the impatient sort."

"I'm not."

"Yes, you are. You do all you can to hide it, but if you imagine you've hidden it from me you're wrong."

"But what shall you do?"

"Oh! Never mind. Something."

"But I do mind," she objected plaintively, touchily. "I'm very interested."

"Of course you are...Well, what about raising Miss Maclaren to the throne?"

"She's rather Scotch and stolid."

"She may be. But she's a rock."

"Yes. But she's rather young for the post."

Evelyn laughed.

"I like that," said he. "I like that from you, of all people. Here I've been entrusting the entire place to a girl of twenty-two for years and years, and now I'm told Miss Maclaren's too young!" Mrs. O'Riordan gave a pouting, delighted smile. "However, we'll talk it over." He decided that he would not ask her approval of Violet Powler. Why should he? New appointments were no longer any concern of hers. He would only formally submit the girl to her. "I must go now. Remember what I said, please. The hotel shall fit into your plans. By the way, I suppose I can tell the staff?"

"About me? I wish you would. I'm rather nervous about telling them myself."

"I'll tell them. And I'll come in and see you later in the day when I'm somewhat calmer, and wish you every happiness. And you do as you're ordered and go to bed." He went to the door; then paused. "We shall give you a dinner. I mean the heads of departments. Not more than thirty. Quite informal. I shall ask Mr. Dover too."

"My dear sir," said Mrs. O'Riordan. "You mustn't. I couldn't bear it. I should feel so--"

"We shall give you a dinner," Evelyn repeated. "And you'll bear it magnificently. Of course you'll cry. But they'll all love to see you cry. I expect I'm the only person who *has* seen you cry--and me only this once...I must run."

Mrs. O'Riordan shook her head.

"Not a dinner," she weakly murmured.

"Yes, a dinner. I suppose you expect a wedding-present. What would Sir Brian think if we let you go without giving you a wedding-present? Well, there'll be a dinner. No dinner, no present."

He kissed his hand to her and left. The next instant he returned, into the room, mischievous.

"I say," he smiled, "it seems you can't keep off your Irish Colonels. Getting quite a habit with you."

She was fondling the cat, whose purring was clearly audible. She said, with dignity:

"Not at all. Sir Brian was a friend of both my husbands."

"And no doubt he has a house in County Meath," Evelyn pursued, not to be dashed.

"And what if he has?" She laughed self-consciously, frowning as well as laughing.

"I knew it," said Evelyn.

He walked back to his room with the studied sedateness proper to a panjandrum. But he was in the highest spirits.

Chapter 27 CRIME

"Good morning, sir," said Plimsing, who was waiting outside the gates of Evelyn's castle.

"Morning, Plimsing," said Evelyn, looking at his watch. "One minute late. Sorry to keep you. Come in. What is it?"

Plimsing raised his left arm. He never lost a fair chance to consult his wrist-watch, which was ornamented with diamonds and the Spanish royal insignia.

"If the trains on the Southern Railway were only a minute late, sir, life would be much simpler for some of us," said Plimsing, with a courtly Foreign Office air. He lived beyond the Crystal Palace.

Evelyn smiled almost ingratiatingly. Like all respectable people, he was conscious of a desire to stand well with policemen, and when he met them would instinctively suit his demeanour to the occasion.

Not that the hotel-detective was a policeman; nor ever had been. Tall, burly and fair, rosy-cheeked, with a large fair moustache, he had the appearance of a beef-fed British farmer, except that his black suit, including a morning coat, and his gleaming tie-pin showed a little more smartness of style than the agricultural. But he did also resemble a policeman, and in mackintosh overalls and white armlet he would not have seemed out of place conducting the orchestral traffic of Piccadilly Circus on a wet day.

He was still appreciably under fifty. As an officer (detective inspector) of the Criminal Investigation Department at Scotland Yard he had been allowed, thanks to his fluency in a language which he imagined to be French, to specialise in the protective surveillance of distinguished foreign official visitors to London. Also on similar duty he had accompanied British princes abroad. It was soon after the vicissitudes of the war that Evelyn had put a spell upon him, to the detriment of Scotland Yard, with which, however, Plimsing's relations had remained intimate and very cordial. Outside the hotel Plimsing usually referred to the Imperial Palace as 'my hotel.' He used in professional conversation such words and phrases as 'police-circles,' 'we' (meaning 'we police'), 'subtle individual,' 'one of your super-prostitutes,' 'energetic action,' and 'H.R.H.' How his vigilance for potentates, politicians and princes specially fitted him for the preservation of order and common honesty in a large hotel neither he nor anybody else could have said: certainly not Evelyn; but it gave him a tremendous prestige with visitors, and a lot of prestige even with Evelyn, who had chosen him partly on that account, but more because of his quiet, composed manner and voice, and his twinkling, rather naïve expression. Despite his expression he talked of the worst turpitudes and immoralities of hotel-thieves, men and women, with the bland casualness of a clergyman discussing the weather. Apparently no infamous vagary of human nature could surprise him or in the least degree trouble his calm of a virtuous householder residing in an impeccable suburb somewhere beyond the Crystal Palace. In short, he was as entirely benign as a policeman holding up a hundred motor-cars for the passage of a perambulator.

"What is it?" Evelyn repeated, within the room. They both stood. -

"Rather a busy morning, sir," Plimsing began, fingering his tie-pin, which carried the British royal insignia. "I happened to be here early on another matter when I received information to the effect that the second-floor valet being called to roomwent in and left his pass-key in the door. This procedure was of course quite contrary to regulations, and I have told him so. When he came out the pass-key was gone. As I said to him, I take a very serious view of this culpable negligence; for, as I need not point out to you, sir, even if the pass-key came back a duplicate of it could have been made in the meantime. I regarded it as so serious that I took the liberty of calling here to tell you at once, as Mr. Cousin was not yet on duty. However, it's all right, sir. Since I saw Oldham I made enquiries, and on the strength of certain information received I telephoned to Scotland Yard, having two individuals in my mind's eye, and they sent an officer in an express car to the Majestic, where both individuals were arrested, and on being searched one man was found to have the pass-key in his left-hand hip-pocket. Smart work, sir, if I may say so, having taken no part in the identification."

"Very. Most satisfactory," said Evelyn.

"I may add that I should have gone to the Majestic myself, sir, to take observations; but I was prevented by an Amsterdam diamond merchant, also fifth floor, who was just leaving and could not find a pair of trousers, which he alleged must have been stolen during the night. After some search and a little cross-examination I convinced him that he was wearing them. He was so apologetic that I ventured to ask him if he would let me drive with him to Victoria, as he was going to Paris by the 8.20 Newhaven-Dieppe. He did so, and gave me valuable information about diamonds, of which he had a large quantity on his person, in a receptacle stitched to the back of his necktie, sir. I was glad to know this. He invited me to feel them, which I did."

2.

"I congratulate you," said Evelyn, somewhat impatiently. "I'm rather pressed for time. Mrs. O'Riordan is leaving us, and I have to make arrangements." He gave the enormous news with an intonation as casual as he could assume. He could no longer keep it to himself.

"Ah!" said Plimsing, twinkling. "Going to marry Sir Brian Milligan at last, I presume, sir."

"Yes," said Evelyn shortly, with a casualness which did even greater credit to his histrionic powers than his statement of the news. For he was astounded and ashamed by this demonstration of recondite knowledge on the part of the detective. How came it that Plimsing had known so much and he, Evelyn, nothing at all? He wanted to question Plimsing, but from pride he would not. Also Plimsing had completely taken the wind out of his sails.

"I will not detain you, sir," the detective smoothly proceeded with a diplomatic movement towards the door. "But you will be relieved to know that the matter of the so-called Mrs. de Rassiter is now settled. I shall submit a formal report in due course."

"Mrs. de Rassiter?"

"The mink-fur lady, sir. She has been identified as a female who was fined for being drunk and disorderly in Soho in the early hours of the day before yesterday morning. I called on Messrs. Murkett and Co., formerly Murkett and Mostlethwaite, the solicitors who sent you that lawyer's letter by messenger about the alleged missing fur. They had also sent in a claim to an insurance company, as I ascertained by enquiry, acting on a hint from my friends at the Yard. Must have got the drink at a night-club in Greek Street, but she probably had had a good deal before leaving here. So I surmised from what I heard of her behaviour before she left. A very shady firm, Murketts, sir. Mostlethwaite's already inside, and Murkett will soon be there too if he isn't careful."

"'Inside'?"

"Yes, sir. In prison. No one can understand why Murkett hasn't been struck off the rolls. I insisted on seeing Mr. Murkett. I said to him, I said: 'Perhaps you aren't aware that your client's real name is Ebag.' I said no more. Mrs. Ebag left by the 8.20Newhaven-Dieppe this morning, sir. That was why I was so anxious to be there. I wanted to be quite sure. Sorry I couldn't have her arrested, but there had been no time to assemble my evidence. She will come back to London. They always do. They can't keep off, no more than rooks off a cornfield. I didn't want to tell you anything until I could tell you everything. I know how busy you are. But as I was here...Good morning, sir. And I hope I've not detained you."

"Not at all, Plimsing. You've done excellently."

"Thank you, sir." Plimsing raised his left wrist again.

"Then you think the woman was a bit 'on' when she made the row m the cloakroom."

"I should say so, sir. If she hadn't been she'd never have begun the thing. I soon made up my mind that the coup had not been prepared. Good morning, sir. You won't hear another word from Murketts."

Plimsing departed, with thoughts of asking for an increase of salary.

Chapter 28 COUSIN

After a minute Evelyn left his castle. On the surface of his mind floated light thoughts about the efficient and stately detective. Had he a wife? Evelyn had learnt less about him than about any of the other principal members of the upper-staff, Plimsing being somehow in a class by himself. If he had a wife, did he address formal speeches to her in the style of his speeches to Evelyn? "Having written and duly delivered my report for the day to Mr. Cousin, Maria, I proceeded, by motor-bus, to Victoria and caught the 6.5., in which I occupied a compartment with three gentlemen, one of whom I knew slightly and exchanged with him a few words about the financial situation in the City," etc. Or was he a different kind of man at home, who fondled and tousled his fat wife, who told him not to be a silly old fool, and upon request gave him a glass of beer as a preliminary to supper? And was his brain aware that his eyes were humorous and his professional deportment enough to make a cat laugh?

Beneath the light thoughts, graver thoughts. Mystery of an immortal soul! Evelyn was environed by mysteries. Friendly with all his colleagues and subordinates, he *knew* none of them, except Dennis Dover. He was more like a man on a desert island than the vitalising centre of a vast organisation. Something ought to be done about it. Yes, since the encounters with Gracie Savott, and the great encounter with her father, new perceptions had awakened in him. And beneath these graver thoughts, a thought, one thought, one burning mass of a thought: the thought of Fate's injustice to Miss Alice Brury. He pictured to himself the young woman, full-bosomed, with full lips and large eyes that belied her trained, stiff, formal demeanour and her excellent, earnest, conscientious intentions. There were two Miss Brurys, as there were two Mrs. O'Riordans. Of the latter he had seen both. Of the former he had seen only one, but now he was divining the other.

From sheer devotion to duty Alice Brury had taken a very delicate social situation out of the hands of her inferior, the cloak-room attendant. Why should she be blamed for not guessing that her opponent was semi-intoxicated? To distinguish between the half-drunk and the sober was notoriously a matter of excessive difficulty; experts continually came to quite opposite conclusions in it. Miss Brury had failed in the affair. She had lost her head under the strain, shown signs of hysteria, and--worst sin of all against the steely code of the hotel--raised her voice! Then she had run away, deserted her post, in desperation and despair. In other words, from an inhuman housekeeper she had descended--or was it ascended?--to be a human woman. She was certainly somebody's daughter; she might be somebody's sweetheart. Five minutes' lack of self-control, and her career was in the way to be ruined! Cousin had been adamantine against her readmission into the cosmos of inhumanity. And Cousin was right. Rules were rules. He, Evelyn, could not possibly gainsay Cousin in Cousin's own kingdom. Nevertheless the thing was monstrous, utterly and absolutely monstrous. Evelyn uneasily wondered how many similar affairs, less spectacular, had happened unknown to his almightiness in the secret annals of the hotel...And yet, for personal reasons, he would prefer that Miss Brury should not come back. He had discovered Miss Powler. Miss Powler was his invention, his pet aspirant. He saw in her unlimited potentialities. If Miss Brury came back, Miss Powler could not be admitted; and therefore the problem at the Laundry would remain unsolved. He must talk to Cousin, and, to be fair to Cousin, he must take heed not to have any air of authority in the discussion.

He went downstairs, nodding absently here and there to employees of various grades, and opened the withdrawn door over which gleamed in light the formidable words: "Manager's Office." An alert, bright, smiling secretary was at her desk in the ante-room, doing something with the mouth of one of the pneumatic tubes through which repair-slips and other notifications were despatched to subterranean dens.

"Good *morning,* Mr. Orcham." The secretarial face mystically beamed the tidings that 'mother' was engaged to be married.

With an answering smile, but silently, Evelyn passed her and walked straight into Cousin's private room--an apartment worthy of Cousin's high position. A startled young man sprang up from the managerial chair at the managerial desk, like a jack-in-the-box.

This was Monsieur Pozzi, the assistant-manager of the hotel, a Frenchman, a protégé of Cousin's, with both continental and London experience, and a perfect command of the English language. He had been in the service of the Imperial Palace for about six months, but Evelyn had had little or nothing to do with him. It was understood that he gave plenary satisfaction to his immediate chief. Some notion of his importance was conveyed by the fact that he had received permission to send out his own Christmas cards to the clientele. At that moment he was making a rough sketch of the greeting. Not more than seven or eight of the upper staff had the right to distribute their personal good wishes to the clientele. Pozzi was more than French; he was Parisian, though with some admixture of Italian blood. He was indeed startled by Evelyn's abrupt and unexpected entry, but not a bit perturbed. He smiled; he bowed gracefully; he was grace itself--slim, sinuous, elegant, correct, charming, easy without sauciness, self-respecting without rigidity.

"Mr. Cousin will be here in one minute, sir. He's just having a word with Ruffo."

"Oh!" said Evelyn, sitting down on the sofa. "What about? Ruffo's here early this morning."

"Yes, sir. There was no big banquet last night. It's about some little difficulty over extra waiters for to-night."

"I see," said Evelyn, rather drily, as one who was aware of occasional slight frictions between Ruffo and the Restaurant-manager over the transfer of first-flight head-waiters from the restaurant to Ruffo's department for very special banquets.

"I wonder, sir," said Pozzi, at his most attractive, standing dutifully in front of Evelyn on the sofa, "whether I might ask you a great favour."

"You can *ask,* my boy," Evelyn answered, with a sardonic benignity.

"It's this, sir. You probably know that a few of us, Adolphe, Dr. Constam, Major Linklater, and myself, have a little lunch-mess of our own in 156. Rocco has taken to golf, and we are giving him a club, or a set of clubs. There will be a lunch. Mr. Cousin has promised to come, and if *you*would kindly come and preside, we should all be very delighted. And I needn't say how flattered Rocco would be."

"But it would mean that I should have to subscribe towards the clubs."

"Oh no, sir! We shouldn't dream of such a thing. Mr. Cousin is not subscribing."

"No," said Evelyn. "But I am. Here!" He pulled a ten shilling note from his waistcoat pocket.

"Really, sir?"

"Take it," Evelyn commanded.

Young Pozzi obeyed, blushing. Yes, a blush clearly visible on his olive skin!

"You are a sport, sir," he exclaimed, almost dancing, with the effusiveness of youth--for he was a mere thirty-one, and young at that. "Thank you ever so much."

No formalism. No constraint. But freshness, naturalness, youthful vivacity. Evelyn suddenly realised that he lived in a world of constraint. Only sometimes at the daily conference, when a serious question was on the carpet, did even the foreigners drop their subdued formalism--among themselves, never to Evelyn nor to Cousin. The handling of visitors, every one of whom had to be treated as a sultan, had made hushed formalism a habit with them. Evelyn longed for oaths, wild words, exorbitant gestures, even impudence to himself, such as he had had that morning from the future Lady Milligan. He thought:

"This boy is alive. I am not. He is a breath of air in all the stuffiness."

"What's the date of this orgy?" he asked.

"The eighteenth, sir. Twelve forty-five. Rocco will make a special effort with the menu."

"Write it down for me, will you?"

Pozzi jumped to the desk, wrote, and handed the slip to the panjandrum, who crushed it into a trouser-pocket, where he could not possibly overlook it.

"That's agreed then," said Evelyn.

"Bravo! Bravo!" cried Pozzi.

2.

Mr. Cousin walked in, sedate, smiling, reserved. The secretary had warned him of Evelyn's arrival. Pozzi, bowing, walked mercurially out, but not before snatching up his Christmas card sketch from the desk.

"Shall we have the pleasure of seeing you at the Conference this morning?" Cousin asked, with his matchless but implacable courtesy.

"Not unless there's anything urgent."

"Nothing urgent for the Conference, but I did want to get your instructions about Miss Brury. Mrs. O'Riordan had a long talk with me here last night."

"Of course," said Evelyn, "the whole situation is altered now that she's leaving."

"Leaving? Who?"

"Mrs. O'Riordan. Haven't you heard about her?"

"No," said Cousin, sitting down on the sofa by Evelyn's side. "She was very amiable last night."

Inspirited by the discovery of at any rate one person who knew less than himself, Evelyn communicated the news of the engagement. Naïvely he expected signs of commotion in the manager's demeanour, but in an instant be realised his own naïveté.

"Tiens! Tiens!" Cousin murmured calmly, and continued in French: "Well, since six months I have had a little idea that something bizarre was going on in that dear lady. She has had a little air...of another world...I don't know what. Indescribable. Certainly she has temperament...At her age! It is not natural. But what would you? Englishwomen are always incomprehensible. A mixture so curious." He half closed his eyes. "It is bizarre. But nothing could surprise me. For Sir Brian Milligan--there are men to whom it is necessary that they should complicate their lives. The excellent baronet is perhaps offering himself in this case a complication more serious than he imagines. But what do I know? Between ourselves, my dear director, I avow frankly that I comprehend nothing, but nothing, of the affairs of the heart in this city of London otherwise so sympathetic to me. That is to say, I comprehend as an observer detached, with the brain, but I feel--nothing, but nothing. All that says nothing to me. Madame O'Riordan has indubitably had some luck, and I felicitate her."

Evelyn was aware of the birth of a sense of intimacy with Mr. Cousin. Nevertheless he was somewhat dashed, in spite of himself.

"As regards her successor, what do you think of Maclaren--as a provisional appointment?" he suggested, abruptly turning the conversation.

"Ah! The Maclaren! Yes. That is quite another thing. She is not English. The Maclaren--one can come to an understanding with her. Yes, yes. It is an idea, that. Happily she is not a *femme du monde.* Madame O'Riordan has lately had a rage for *femmes du monde.* True, she is one of them herself. But I do not share her views in the matter. To me it is unnatural that a *femme du monde* should hold a servile situation. It is against nature. It demands that she should play a role. Artificial. She must think more about her role than about her work. Perhaps among the numerous Russian princesses that one sees now in Paris there are a few capable of persuading themselves to be born again into a state of servitude. But Russians are Russians. An Englishwoman can never be born again. It is the aristocratic race, above all. Madame O'Riordan brought to me a candidate for the position of the poor Brury. Very *femme du monde.* Oh, very! Niece of a knight who blew his brains out. I did not encourage her."

"I agree with you," said Evelyn warmly, changing all his views on the subject in a moment. Not with his brain, but with his heart.

He saw daylight. Everything would be easy. Cousin would begin with a prejudice favourable to Violet Powler because she was not a gentlewoman. There could be no friction. He at once told Cousin about Miss Powler, emphasising her origin, about the delicate position at the Laundry, and about his plans for making an exchange between Miss Brury and Miss Powler. Cousin nodded several times.

"I am glad," said Cousin, in English, "that you support me against this extraordinary proposal for taking Miss Brury back again. It must happen sometimes that someone must suffer. And Miss Brury has been unfortunate. But to take her back would be impossible unless we were to ignore the interests of the hotel. And your ingenious suggestion would solve the problem. Of course I accept it, without reserve. If you are satisfied--"

"You had better have a look at Miss Powler for yourself."

"Of course. If you wish it. But I am sure--"

"I will send for her."

Cousin then seemed to resume his habitual mood of taciturnity, after the astonishing exhibition of communicativeness.

Evelyn hurried away to his office and to Miss Cass. He was uplifted anew, but differently now. He felt that be was somehow climbing out of his groove. Dangerous to put an inexperienced woman into a post so important as that relinquished under stress of emotion by Miss Brury. But danger now attracted him. And Violet. Powler had all the talents. She would succeed. Miss Brury would be saved. Miss Maclaren was acceptable to the Frenchman. Mrs. O'Riordan could not interfere. All things were working together for good. Of course he must see Cyril Purkin and explain. Everything must be done quickly, instantly. Miss Cass had a busy time telephoning to the Laundry-manager to come at one hour, and to Miss Powler to come at another, and telegraphing to Miss Brury to come at still another hour. She reported that all was in order, and that she had so reported to Mr. Cousin. The new heaven and the new earth were in train.

Chapter 29 VIOLET'S ARRIVAL

Another lamp was burning in another brain, Violet Powler's: which with Evelyn's lamp in Evelyn's brain, made two. Violet, all unconscious of what she was doing, had brought her bright but materially invisible lamp into the hotel one morning at five minutes to ten. According to instructions she reported at Mr. Cousin's office. But she saw only the manager's secretary, Mr. Cousin being engaged at a conference. The secretary, name unknown, was an agreeable and vivacious young woman. She shook hands with Violet, seemed to know all about her, and sharply ordered a page-boy, who had come with a cablegram, to escort Violet to her quarters on the eighth floor. Violet, she explained, was first to install herself and then to report for orders to Mrs. O'Riordan, also an inhabitant of the eighth floor.

Violet, despite her common sense, thought that the secretarial demeanour was somewhat casual, having regard to the importance (for Violet) of the occasion. Surely the arrival of a new floor-housekeeper could not be a daily event in the life even of a great hotel!

The secretary, on the other hand, thought that Violet's demeanour was astounding casual, though cordial enough, having regard to the importance of the occasion. Surely it could not be a daily event in any girl's life to walk out of a South London laundry straight to a fine situation in the greatest hotel on earth! But the secretary could not see Violet's lamp.

Violet and the tiny page-boy went up in the lift; the lift-man was very respectful to Violet; the page-boy found her room and having opened the door made as if to leave.

"One moment," said she. "Which is Mrs. O'Riordan's room?"

The page-boy gave the indication and pointed a white-gloved hand.

"And what's *your* name?" she asked.

"John Croom, miss." And he added, grinning, "Jack."

She smiled, patted his shoulder; he left; and Violet shut and bolted the door of her new home.

It was a smallish room, looking on a courtyard. And the courtyard was a deep well (of which Violet could not see the bottom) whose sides were white tiles inset with tiers of windows. Still, the room was larger than the one she had that morning quitted in her father's little house in Battersea, and it was more elegantly furnished: a sort of bed-sitting-room, with a sofa and a desk and a business-like nest of drawers in the sitting portion of it.

Her simple and recently fretful and pessimistic mother would have deemed it a magnificent apartment. Mrs. Powler had cried at parting, and amid her tears had deplored Violet's facial make-up and expressed the hope that Violet would not be allotted to an attic whose only window was a skylight. Her father, having a rendezvous in Vauxhall, had accompanied Violet a certain distance in a tram. They had said good-bye in the tram, and shabby passengers in the huge squalid vehicle had beheld with inquisitive wonder the kissing of the shabby old man by the rouged and powdered young lady whose smartness cast doubt upon her virtue. But when moisture showed in Violet's eyes the judgment of the passengers was softened and Violet received the benefit of the doubt.

Now she dropped her bag and her gloves and her hat and her thin cloak on the bed. Her luggage had been despatched in advance by the simple device of sticking a card bearing famous initials in the protruding square window of the front room in Renshaw Street. Because she apprehended that the luggage might be delayed, Violet had decided to leave home in what she informed a suspicious mother was to be her working dress and face. But the luggage had reached its destination. It lay in a pile at the foot of the bed.

First she examined critically the interior of the wardrobe, giving it ninety marks out of a possible hundred. Then she examined herself critically in the wardrobe mirror, and gave herself ninety marks out of a hundred. Yes, she would pass. Brown hair, permanently waved. Finger-nails curved in a crescent. Black dress bought ready made at a mighty store in Clapham and altered to fit by Violet herself. Quite stylish. A thin girdle (for keys). New shoes; new stockings. As for her make-up, it made her feel as if she was in the wings waiting to "go on" in Gilbert and Sullivan comic opera--except that the skin under the eyes had not been darkened. She hoped, she was convinced, that her face would successfully stand the scrutiny of seven floor-housekeepers and a head-housekeeper. She was hardly at ease, yet, in her new face; but at any rate it had so far provoked no slightest sign of astonishment or dismay on the faces of the members of the hotel staff. She unfastened the bag and retouched her features here and there. Then she examined the room more closely. Well, it was good in her sight. Wash-basin, h. and c. She turned a tap. The h. was tremendously hot. She sat on the bed, springing up and down. Soft. On the desk was quite a large vase of fresh flowers.

Instantly, as she patted the flowers, the Imperial Palace rose in her esteem to the full height of its reputation. Somebody with imagination had thought of those flowers and of their effect on the arriving, intimidated stranger. Vast as the organisation was, it had not been too vast to think of a trifle of flowers for her comfort. She said to herself that she would be happy in the Imperial Palace.

She had an impulse to unpack her possessions. No! That would not be right. Her duty was to report for duty at once. At the Laundry she would already have done two hours' work. Still, she dawdled hesitant about the room. She would hardly admit to herself that she was afraid, positively afraid, to go forth into the corridor. But she was. The corridor was the corridor to the new life. She went forth into the corridor, and as she did so the lamp in her head suddenly burned with a brighter flame. From the end of the corridor, where her room was, she saw the apparently endless vista of a kingdom. She saw herself the vicereine of the kingdom. And in five seconds she was seeing herself as the head-housekeeper of the Imperial Palace Hotel. Why not? There would be no Cyril Purkin in the Imperial Palace to disquiet and harass her.

Nevertheless she felt really frightened. It seemed impossible to her that she, she, straight out of a laundry, could manage a floor of the Imperial Palace. Pooh! Why not? The job might well be easier than that of managing a couple of hundred or more girls all in one way or another temperamental. And she firmly believed in herself: which fact did nothing to mitigate her fright--stage-fright.

She walked steadily down the deserted corridor, passing number after number until she reached Mrs. O'Riordan's room (unnumbered). The door was ajar. She knocked. No answer. Cautiously she stepped in.

The spectacle of the sitting-room made a most sinister impression upon Violet. The walls were bare. A large number of nails, and a large number of small rectangular patches, showed where pictures had been. The mantelpiece was empty. There were no cushions and no knickknacks anywhere. There was the carpet, the rather plentiful furniture, and nothing else, not even a book. Feeling like a trespasser, she passed into the bedroom, the door to which was wide open. Similar phenomena. The bed had been slept in, but she could see no nightgown nor slippers. The interior of the large wardrobe was exposed, and quite empty. Three trunks of various sorts and sizes, and a wooden packing-case and a shapeless bundle, encumbered the floor. They were labelled: "Mrs. O'Riordan, Cloak-room, Euston Station." The melancholy of an abandoned home, of a semi-spiritual death, of something that was and is not, pervaded the rooms deprived of their individuality.

Mrs. O'Riordan had gone, and she would not return. Violet had been told that the head-housekeeper would remain for at least another week, during which she was personally to instruct the newcomer in her work. At the beginning of the negotiations for Violet's entry into the Imperial Palace, she had understood that a period of six months, soon afterwards diminished to three months, would be necessary for proper tuition in her duties. Then it had been intimated to her that a young woman with experience such as hers would easily learn the duties in a week of intensive training under Mrs. O'Riordan herself. She had successfully survived the ordeals of a personal catechism by Mrs. O'Riordan and another by Mr. Cousin. Salary and conditions of notice had been arranged, and the contract signed. Everything had marched smoothly according to plan. And now--this! She returned to the sitting-room and sat down on the sofa, uneasy, desolated! Then, as there was a bell handy, she rang it. A plump chambermaid, in early middle-age, appeared.

2.

"Good morning."

"Good morning, miss." The chambermaid's attitude, while reserved, was not at all unfriendly. The woman had a fat, good-natured face. Her blue print morning dress showed a stain, and one shoulder-strap of the apron was twisted.

"Do you look after this room--these rooms?"

"Yes, miss."

"I'm the new floor-housekeeper. My name's Powler, Violet Powler. Will you tell me what yours is?"

"Beatrice, miss."

"Beatrice what?"

"Mrs. Beatrice Noakes."

"Been here long?"

"Oh yes, miss. Ever since me poor husband died, 1917."

"In the war?" Beatrice nodded. "I'm sorry to hear that--I mean about your husband."

"Yes, miss," Beatrice said casually. The fact was that her husband had long ceased to have any reality in her memory. Not even his shade haunted it.

"Any children, Mrs. Noakes?"

"Oh *no,* miss. If I had I shouldn't be here, should I, seeing we sleep in. I've worked on every floor of this hotel, miss," she went on more vivaciously. "Same as Miss Maclaren. Miss Maclaren used to take me with her whenever she moved."

"Well that shows she trusted you."

"Yes, miss. My word! And now she's going to be head-housekeeper--"

"Yes, yes. And you'll still be on this floor."

"Yes, miss."

"I think we shall get on."

"You and Miss Maclaren, miss?"

"Miss Maclaren of course. But I meant you and me. I'm sure you'll be able to tell me all sorts of things I've got to know."

"Well, miss, I always like to help--when I'm asked. I never put myself forward, if you know what I mean. But when I'm asked, I'm *there."* Beatrice smiled helpfully.

"Do you know where Miss Maclaren is?"

"No, miss. She ain't been up here this morning."

"Is Mrs. O'Riordan coming back?"

"That I couldn't say, miss," said Beatrice, caution in her voice.

"You've seen her this morning?"

"Mrs. O'Riordan? Oh yes, miss."

"She didn't say?"

"No, miss." Still caution.

"Has she asked you to her wedding?"

"Well, miss, no. But I do believe she would have done--just to the church. Just to come in and see her go off like. But it's a great secret, I hear. Nobody knows anything. They want a *quiet* wedding. I hope it won't be at a Registry Office. But it won't. Because Mrs. O'Riordan's a Roman Catholic. Every Sunday morning she went to Mass, as they call it."

"I see her luggage is all packed."

"Yes, miss. Some of it's gone. And I did hear the rest is being sent for to-day some time. You could have knocked me down with a feather when she told me this morning when I brought her tea she had to leave at once. How she packed them trunks between last night and to-day *I* don't know. I'm quite free to tell you, miss. She only said to me I wasn't to say a word till she'd gone. Well, as she has gone--well, I didn't say a word."

"Everyone seems to trust you, Beatrice." Beatrice smiled happily. "I'm very much obliged." Violet rose from the sofa.

"Anything I *can* do, miss--"

"Thank you, Beatrice."

The room was less desolate, its melancholy diminished. As soon as Beatrice had shut the door, Violet took up the telephone and, composing her voice, asked to be put on to Mr. Cousin's secretary. She heard an answering enquiry within ten seconds, and said:

"I thought I ought to report that Mrs. O'Riordan had left before I got up here. Violet Powler speaking, in Mrs. Riordan's room. She's gone away."

"Gone?" Serious astonishment in her tone. "But she can't have gone. She must have just gone out for something. She'll be back again soon."

"I don't think so," said Violet, and described in detail the state of Mrs. O'Riordan's late home. She finished: "There's nobody up here for me to refer to. Miss Maclaren isn't anywhere about. Will you please tell Mr. Cousin?"

"It's all frightfully queer," said the thin secretarial voice. "I can't disturb Mr. Cousin just now. Listen. If you'll wait where you are I'll give you a ring in a minute or two." A note of sympathetic intimacy in the voice.

"Thanks very much. I say. Do you mind telling me your name? I shan't feel so strange when I've got to know a few names."

An amiable comprehending laugh in the telephone. "Yes, of course. Tilton." The voice spelt the name. "Christian name same as yours."

"What? Violet? Really!" Violet's tone seemed to indicate a pleased surprise that there should be another Violet in the whole world.

"No!" The voice laughed. "I knew I should catch you, Miss Powler. Marian."

And Violet laughed saying: "How nice!" Violet's full name was Violet Marian Powler. Miss Marian Tilton had seen it in the formal contract.

"When you have a moment, come down here and see me. Any time. And I'll show you the upper-staff file and go over some of the names with you. *Au revoir,* Miss Powler."

Violet thought that she might be making a friend. Already she was beginning to relish her social environment. But with caution. At their previous brief encounters she had suspected that the second Marian might conceivably be a little too dashing and worldly for her personal taste. Still, she felt capable of being dashing and worldly too, if necessary. She was absorbing, as through the pores of her skin, the atoms of the Imperial Palace atmosphere. Every moment she learnt something, and every moment she grew more at ease. Marian Tilton. Beatrice Noakes. Beings that belonged to two different orders; but both friendly and both ready to be helpful and to assume that she Violet, was all right. And there was no more Cyril Purkin, who couldn't keep away from her and couldn't bear her. Intense relief in that thought! Cyril's one kiss had cured her of him for ever and ever; though it had been a kiss sober and respectful enough.

The mysterious vanishing of Mrs. O'Riordan was shaping into a first-class sensation. And she was the discoverer of the vanishing. And what of it? Mrs. O'Riordan was leaving, anyhow. Well, she had left. And Violet was glad that she had left. Why? Because there must be something rather queer about a lady who in such a high position could play such a trick in such a place as the Imperial Palace. Mrs. O'Riordan gone, they could all as it were make a fresh start on a clean page. And further, Mrs. O'Riordan's flight seemed somehow to humanise the formidable, frightening, inhuman organism of the Imperial Palace. Funny, human things happened there, as they happened in laundries. One touch of nature...etc. Trite! But how true!

She glanced round the room. And the room had now almost entirely lost its melancholy of a home deserted by a mistress whom it would never see again. She wondered what Miss Maclaren would make of it, and what Miss Maclaren was like; for she had not yet met Miss Maclaren. The tinkle of the telephone bell gave her a shock.

"That Miss Powler? Miss Cass speaking." A voice drier than that of Marian. Voice of one higher than Marian Tilton in the company of cherubim and seraphim. "Mr. Orcham says please will you come down and see him immediately." Authority in the voice.

So Marian had telephoned to Miss Cass. And Miss Cass had imparted the strange news to her master, and her master had deemed it stupendous enough to justify him in sending for Violet to come to him immediately!

"Thank you, Miss Cass. I'll come at once."

And now, as she quitted the room, Violet was really all in a flutter. She had not seen Mr. Orcham since the interview at which he had so oddly hinted about rouge and powder. She remembered her blush at that interview. She felt as though she would never forget it. Everything had moved very harmoniously, step by step, since the interview. Cyril Purkin had quietly and urbanely told her that Mr. Orcham wanted her at the Palace, and that therefore he, Mr. Purkin, could of course offer no objection to her leaving the Laundry. For one week she had given instruction in the management of laundry-girls to her successor, Miss Brury, who had begun with condescension and ended with gratitude almost meek. And no sign from Mr. Orcham. But she surmised, felt, knew, was absolutely sure, that the unseen hand of Mr. Orcham had guided events. And now she had arrived in her new situation, and within half an hour the great invisible Mr. Orcham had summoned her, because of her astounding discovery! A very different place, this, from the homely Laundry!

She walked along the corridor and saw the lift. Ought she, now a member of the staff, to dare to use the lift? Or was there a staff-lift? She had heard of such things. Yes, she chid herself for being all in a flutter. She rang the lift-bell and waited, and up came the lift out of immeasurable depth, as promptly as though she were the Marchioness of Renshaw and staying in the hotel. The bony-faced, sallow lift-man gave her a decorous smile of recognition as he slid back the grille; He knew who she was and what she was.

"Ground-floor, please."

"Yes, miss," the man compliantly answered, feeling in his heart, so acutely sensitised to the varying influences of individualities, that here was a polite, self-possessed, firm young lady who would certainly stand no kind of familiarity.

Chapter 30 OFFICIAL INTERVIEW

"Good morning, Miss Powler. Welcome to the Imperial Palace."

This was Evelyn's greeting to Violet when she entered Evelyn's outer office, where apparently he was just finishing a conversation with the authoritative Miss Cass, who sat at her desk and beheld the incomer with a firm impartial glance. He offered his hand, not to a floor-housekeeper, but merely to a new and possibly nervous member of the great Palace commonwealth of which he was president.

"Good morning, sir. Thank you, I'm sure. You sent for me, sir." Violet had expected to be nervous, but she was nervous beyond her fears; so much so that quite involuntarily she averted her face as she shook hands. "Good morning, Miss Cass," she murmured, as quite involuntarily she caught Miss Cass's glance.

"Good morning, Miss Powler," Miss Cass responded, in a strong, almost peremptory voice, but nevertheless with a cheerful and not unfriendly smile, and bent at once over her desk, as one who had in train mighty matters which must not suffer delay. Violet had encountered Miss Cass only once before.

"Come in, will you," said Evelyn, and when they were in his room and the door shut, and he was pulling a cigarette out of his case, he said curtly: "Sit down," and smiled at her.

Curious that she should feel more diffident now than at any of their previous meetings. She was ashamed of herself. Evelyn, his back turned to Violet for a moment, dropped a match into an ash-tray on his desk and puffed smoke, as it were meditatively. By all his movements Violet realised afresh and more clearly that he was a gentleman. So different from Cyril Purkin, whose every gesture and tone demonstrated continuously a total lack of distinction. And she thought: "And I'm not a lady, either, and could I ever be?" Distinction could not be acquired.

"Funny about Mrs. O'Riordan," he said, suddenly facing Violet, and laughing easily. "You don't know the explanation, but I do. And I may as well tell you. We were going to give her a staff-dinner to-morrow night. She always said she could never go through with a dinner and hear her health proposed, and wedded happiness--you know she's going to be married. I didn't believe her, and I insisted on the dinner. Well, I was wrong. She left a note for me this morning. Here it is." He touched a letter which lay on the desk. "She's run away from the dinner. That's all. I'm sorry. But these brides--! It doesn't matter of course in the least, dinner or no dinner. Still, I'm sorry. Miss Maclaren gets her job--Mrs. O'Riordan's--and she'll take over at once, anyhow this afternoon. I've telephoned her and I've told her something about you, and I think you'll like her. And of course she'll be on your floor. You'll pick up your work in a couple of days. Miss Brury was doing ground-floor when she left us, but Mr. Cousin is starting you on Eighth--easier for you to learn there. But of course we do move our housekeepers up and down. You'll know how to handle customers--I think

I told you--and you know all about linen and how to deal with maids. It's all much simpler than it sounds. Some sense is all that's required. You trust yourself to Miss Maclaren, and if she isn't about, just act on your own. You're bound to be all right. Only don't worry Mr. Cousin. Ever heard of the chain of responsibility? Well, we're all links in the chain. Miss Maclaren is the next link above you, and Mr. Cousin's above her, and I'm above Mr. Cousin, and the Board's above me. But remember, you can't skip links. Mr. Cousin can go to the Board only through me, and you can go to Mr. Cousin only through Miss Maclaren. It's a necessary arrangement in a big place like this. Is that clear?"

"Quite, sir."

"How do you feel--on your first morning?"

"Well, sir, I'm rather nervous."

"You don't look it a bit, and so long as you don't look it, it doesn't matter. In fact it's rather a good thing to be nervous."

Violet thought that there was wisdom in this last remark. But otherwise she was somewhat critical of the panjandrum. He seemed to her to be taking things very lightly. How could she learn her job--the job of housekeeping for an entire floor of the immense Imperial Palace--in a couple of days? The notion was frivolous. (And yet simultaneously, as she criticised, she had a conviction that she indeed could learn the job in a couple of days. All housekeeping was in essence alike. And of luxurious housekeeping she had had some experience at Sir Henry Savott's, where the figures of the housekeeping-books had so startled her in the first week that she could never forget them.)

The panjandrum seemed, too, to assume that his domestic machine worked and would work by itself. He probably knew nothing about the detail of housekeeping. In fine, he was a man, and a man inclined to be prematurely airy and gay. Perhaps superficial! Her nervousness did not in the least hamper her strongly developed critical faculty, which faculty however she always hid away from view, like a possession semi-sacred, occult, too precious for any exposure to the public gaze. Few of her equals or her superiors had even guessed the existence of that sharp, acid faculty.

2.

"Is there anything you want to ask me?" Evelyn suggested. Violet reflected. "No, sir...No, sir. I only hope I--er--my dress and so on--I hope it will do." She looked younger, girlish, confused, quite charming in her sudden constraint. There was a hardly perceptible change of bodily pose, nothing more than the disclosure of an impulse towards a change of pose, to the end that he might see her more completely. .

It was naught. Evelyn glanced at her anew.

"I'll tell you more about that when you stand up," he said.

She faintly smiled, dropped her eyes, maidenly, modest; hating herself for her attitude, her feelings. Staff-manageress of a laundry, floor-housekeeper in a large fashionable hotel--and lacked the wit not to be girlish and silly! She scorned herself ferociously. Where was her self-reliance, to say nothing of her self-esteem? Weak as water: that was what she was. She would have given a lot to be back at the Laundry, nicely firm with the girls there, nicely untouchable to Mr. Purkin.

"I hope you'll succeed here," Evelyn went on. "Because I'm responsible for your coming here. I think you will succeed. I'm sure you will. Not my business to engage floor-housekeepers, you know. I never interfere. But when I was down at the Laundry that day, you remember, we were rather in a quandary, and it occurred to me you might be the very person we needed. Yes, and I think you are."

"I shall try to be, sir," she answered conventionally, uncertainly, searing herself with invisible, inaudible criticism.

He must be taking her for a ninny. How could he take her for the same girl who had favourably impressed him at the Laundry? He couldn't.

Evelyn said:

"There's a woman up on your floor who might be rather useful to you if you get on the right side of her. Bertha--Bertha something. Noakes, is it? I'll find out. Quite a friend of mine. Used to be on my floor. We shift her about whenever we're in difficulties. She's up there now because Mrs. O'Riordan was doing head-housekeeper and floor-housekeeper as well; and not in the best health either."

"Do you mean Beatrice Noakes, sir?"

"Beatrice. Beatrice. Of course. I simply can't remember names. So you've come across her already?"

Violet related the Beatrice episode, and in doing so scraped together some self-confidence.

"I can see that Heaven is watching over you," said Evelyn. *"You* won't let me down."

"Let you down, sir?"

"Nothing, nothing. Mrs. O'Riordan told me she wouldn't leave me in the lurch. Only she did. However, all things work together for good."

"It's absolutely certain that I shan't leave you in the lurch, sir," said a new Violet Powler.

"No, you won't. I say, I should be glad if you'd just see this afternoon to Miss Maclaren being fixed up nice and cosy in her rooms. She'll never do it for herself, anyhow until there's nothing else wants doing anywhere on the floor. And she'll object to you bothering about it. Say it's an instruction from me. That'll settle it. Have some flowers put in the room, in both rooms."

"Yes, sir," said Violet eagerly, warmly.

A pause. Violet stood up.

"Yes," said Evelyn, examining her appearance as though she was a mannequin. "I should think you'd do very well. But ask Miss Maclaren. I shall be surprised if, before you're much older, one of 'em doesn't ask you what lipstick you use." He was sardonic, teasing.

"Thank you, sir." Violet moved to leave him.

"Here. One moment." He stopped her. "I have to go down into the engine-room. You'd better come with me. You ought to see the *real* part of the place. Besides, it makes conversation with customers. It's an idea I had only yesterday. For the floor-housekeepers. What can they know of Floors who only the Floors know? There's a great deal more in this hotel than meets the eye. And it ought to meet the eye of important young women like you."

Chapter 31 BOWELS OF THE HOTEL

Violet went down with Evelyn into the unknown, first through a door to a staircase of bare stone, then along a narrow corridor, then down a slope which was ridged to prevent slipping, then by turns and twists until she had quite lost the sense of direction. The two walked side by side when space permitted; sometimes Evelyn without hesitation stepped in front of her, sometimes he pressed himself against a wall courteously to let her precede him as a woman should precede a man. Once or twice a graceless menial employee passed them unrecognised and unrecognising.

They were in the Imperial Palace, but it was another Imperial Palace: no bright paint, no gilt, no decorations, no attempt to please the eye, little or no daylight, electric lamps but no lamp-shades; another world in which appearances had no importance and were indeed neglected.

She glimpsed a large open space, a room lacking a fourth wall, in which a number of girls in overalls were bending over big wicker-baskets of soiled linen, separating, transferring, sorting. In semi-obscurity they had something of an air of dimly-tinted phantoms; they were absorbed; they did not look up or away. The spectacle vaguely recalled the Laundry; but the Laundry had no basement; everything was light in the Laundry. Here she had the sensation of being underground, though in fact she was hardly yet underground. Of course she had a feeling for the romantic; the word itself, however, was hardly in her vocabulary--at any rate for use.

She was still rather awed by the strangeness of her sudden magic removal from the environment of the lowly, commonplace Laundry to the enormous and majestic environment of the Imperial Palace. Here she was, walking with the supreme ruler of the bewildering hotel, almost as an equal--did he not make way for her?--the man who was above everybody, the man who could say even to Mr. Cousin "Come," and he would come. Hardly credible! And the change had arisen out of the supreme ruler happening to overhear her talking to a colourblind girl! She was awed, yes, but she was proud.

"I can't be *quite* ordinary," she thought, with that false humility which people assume even to themselves. For she knew very well that she was far from ordinary. She had a fairly accurate idea of her unusual worth, being as free from conceit as from any form of inferiority complex.

"Here!" said Evelyn, stopping. "We may as well look in here." She saw, painted in black on a brownish yellow wall the words, "Audit Department. Mr. Exshaw," and a pointing arrow. They entered a very large low room divided by glass partitions into various enclosures, with a long passage and doors into each enclosure. Numbers of male clerks at desks strewn with prodigious account-books. All the clerks absorbed, bent, like the linen-girls.

"Mr. Exshaw in?" Evelyn called out loud.

"Yes, sir," said someone.

They walked to the end of the corridor. Violet thought that she would have been frightened to death to venture alone into this new world. She needed protection. And she had it, the mightiest possible protection. She was as safe as a child in its cot. A transient, pleasant surmise: was it Mr. Orcham who had ordered flowers for her bedroom? Absurd. And yet--had he not told her to put flowers in Miss Maclaren's rooms? He might--he just might have.

Evelyn strode into the final enclosure--more spacious than the others. A big, high desk, at which stood a short, spectacled, grey-haired man, a pen behind his ear, the biggest account-book she had ever seen in front of him, minutely ruled horizontally and vertically.

"Morning, Exshaw."

The man seemed to wake out of a trance (pretence, thought Violet critically), and as he gazed at the visitors his eyes hardened

"Ah! Good morning, Mr. Orcham." It was as if the man had said: "On careful inspection I realise that you are a gentleman named Orcham and my chief."

"Got a moment?"

"As many as you wish, sir." With a dignity that threw doubt on the statement.

"This is Miss Powler, one of our housekeepers," said Evelyn lightly.

Violet bowed. Mr. Exshaw gave a start, then curtly nodded. "I've come to the conclusion that it will be a good thing for the floor-housekeepers to get some kind of a notion of the more or less secret *works* of this place." Evelyn went on. "Miss Powler is the first to come. You may expect a few more visits. Don't you think it's rather a scheme? Widen their horizons, eh?" Evelyn laughed; more correctly, he sniggered.

"Well, sir," Mr. Exshaw answered, having judicially pondered, "we do think now and then that if the Floors knew about the way we straighten things out for them down here it might be good for their souls. Which floor?" he demanded of Violet.

"Eighth," said Violet, low.

Mr. Exshaw peered at her through his spectacles, apparently saying to himself: "So this specimen is a floor-housekeeper. Interesting to see. What next I wonder!" And the Floors seemed to be a very long way off--phenomena heard of, written about, checked, reprimanded, but invisible and materially non-existent.

"Ah! Eighth!" said Mr. Exshaw at length, aloud. "Eighth is a wonderful floor for breakages. There must be somebody up there who plays hockey with tumblers. Breakages in the restaurant cost us a hundred pounds a week, but the percentage on Eighth I should say is higher. I don't mean they cost the hotel a hundred a week, because we only pay a quarter, but the waste's there. You got the special memo day before yesterday, Miss--er?"

"This is Miss Powler's first day here," Evelyn put in, before Violet could speak.

"Ah!" said Mr. Exshaw, more benevolently, for he was a just man. He rapped on the glass behind him, and a youth rushed in. "Bring me N here," said Mr. Exshaw to the youth.

N proved to be a heavy, red-bound book of account.

"You might like to see, Miss--er. Restaurant. Grill." He turned pages over. "Floors. First. Sixth. Eighth, yes. Here you are. Here's the analysis of breakages on Eighth, week by week. Here's last week."

Violet obediently looked, but she could see nothing save a dance of numerals. She had a ridiculous sense of shame on behalf of the eighth floor. Her wandering gaze saw that the window offered a fine view of a white-tiled blank wall about six feet off, and that Mr. Exshaw's spectacles were steel-rimmed.

"Yes," said the ninny in her. Yet she was not unused to vast statistical volumes at the Laundry, nor to male clerks bending over the same. But at the Imperial Palace the scale of things was more grandiose.

"You'd be very clever if you grasped all this in a month of Sundays, Miss--er," said Mr. Exshaw kindly.

She thought he was perhaps a nice man, if a trifle self-important in the presence of the panjandrum whom he ignored. The next minute he shut the book with a slam.

"I suppose she can see everything, sir?" he surprisingly addressed the panjandrum.

"Certainly," said Evelyn, "so far as I'm concerned. It's up to you."

"She might like to see how the floor order-slips are analysed."

"Oh, I should!" said the ninny.

Thereafter, as the accountancy mechanism not only of order-slips, but bills, of estimates (estimate of £41,000 for next year's linen renewals), wages (Mr. Exshaw skimmed rapidly over the wages), staff-meals, graphs, and forty other categories, passed before her, Violet felt herself in a daze, a maze and a nightmare. And she marvelled at the brain of Mr. Exshaw, head-demon of the unparalleled cave.

"I think you can't carry any more, young lady," he said triumphantly.

Violet, weak, smiled. "Thank you very much, Mr. Exshaw," she said, beholden.

"Not at all," said Mr. Exshaw brightly.

Violet and her protector were hardly out of the room before Mr. Exshaw resumed the huge book on which be was engaged when they had disturbed him. Evelyn stuck his head back into the enclosure.

"Mrs. O'Riordan has left us," said he, delivering a tit-bit of hotel news.

"So I hear, sir," said Mr. Exshaw casually, without looking up.

When they were safely out of the cave, Violet said:

"It *is* wonderful. I should call it exciting."

"It is, isn't it?" said Evelyn.

She thought he liked her nervous animation. He glanced at her quite appreciatively, humanly. Very different from Cyril Purkin! She felt happy, if agitated.

"I'd no idea--" she softly exclaimed.

"No, you hadn't,' he said, quite ruthlessly. "But you'll soon be getting an idea. That's what you're down here for. Exshaw was in this place before I came on the scene. Nobody in the hotel knows his job better."

Some hardness in his voice. One moment he was smiling at her appreciatively; the next moment his tone seemed to be warning her: "We may as well look the fact in the face--you are an ignorant simpleton here. You'll learn, but you don't realise how much you have to learn, and I don't expect you to realise it."

Where now was the admired shepherdess of laundry-hoydens; and where the composed, quietly imperative daughter of Renshaw Street from whom two parents drew solace, harmony and moral strength? Still, Mr. Orcham was protecting her. There was more beneath his lightness than she had imagined. And yet had she not always, since the career-turning interview, divined everything of force that there was beneath his lightness? She said to herself that she would not mind being admonished, corrected by him, because he was a just man. She could look up to him.

She could never have looked up to Cyril Purkin, though she admitted Cyril's excellence--his conscientiousness, his devotion to duty, his industry, his clear head. If she had married Cyril, what a secret disaster! A narrow man. Never laughed, or, if he did, always at something silly. He exhibited more self-confidence than he felt. Married to her, he would have appeared to rule her, whereas in reality she would have ruled him, and they would both have known it, and Cyril would have resented it as though the fault was hers, and she would always have had the sensation of not being supported. For many years at home she had been the supporter, and she desired relief. With Cyril she would have had no relief.

Now Mr. Orcham, on the contrary, exhibited less self-confidence than he felt. In thought she was beginning to make a hero of Mr. Orcham. She needed a hero, had never had one. Probably she would not run across him once a month, if at all. But that would not interfere with the gradual process of hero-creation. His image would be set within her brain in the full light of the lamp of passionate ardour, assiduity and endeavour which burned there.

2.

"Might look in at the printing-shop," Evelyn suggested as they resumed the pilgrimage together. It was close by. More males, but of the artisan type, not the clerkly. All absorbed. Several machines, worked by hand. Piles of cards and sheets. Evelyn took off a card as it emerged from a machine.

"Breakfast menu for the grill to-morrow morning. For the Floors too."

"Oh yes," Violet said. She could think of nothing else to say. She was tremendously anxious to seem intelligent. But how could she seem intelligent?

"Here's a notice to the floor-waiters," said Evelyn, picking up a sheet from a small pile. "It will be stuck on the walls of the service rooms to-night. Isn't striking enough, perhaps."

Only one old man, a compositor setting up a special programme for a banquet, saluted Evelyn, who spoke to nobody. Violet surprised one or two male glances at herself. She would have preferred that Mr. Orcham should explain her in the printing-shop as he had done in the audit-office. But Mr. Orcham didn't. They left the printing-shop.

"Does the hotel do all its own printing?" Violet questioned "Rather!" said Evelyn. "And it manufactures its own beds; and its own silversmiths repair its own silver and electroplate and so on. Here! You'd better just glance at the Stocks Department."

Much of the Stocks Department had no daylight, but the darker chambers were illuminated, irradiated, by the energy of the enthusiasm and loquacity of the manager, Mr. Stairforth, to whom Evelyn carefully presented his eighth-floor housekeeper. Mr. Stairforth, like Mr. Exshaw, was grey in the service of the Palace. Withal he had remained a boy. So intense was his pride in Stocks that he delighted to receive callers. And he delighted to send subordinates to and fro to fetch things for the practical illustration of his remarks to callers. He talked incessantly, and with extreme clarity and rapidity. He could not stand still. He could not refrain from imparting knowledge. He was eager with Violet, seeing in her a virgin subject. He drew the pair urgently from room to room, pouring out statistics in a quenchless stream. He never hesitated for a figure.

"Here's the stationery. £3,250's worth. Specially made paper. Our own water mark. Look! Here's a time-sheet." He held it up against an electric lamp. "See? Time-sheets are the most indispensable things in the hotel. Every five minutes has to be accounted for here. Now fancy goods. We give away twenty thousand fans a year. That's only one item. So on and so on. Now the glass."

He was leading them into a huge and horrid cavern. He administered to Violet colossal figures about glass. Also he explained in detail how glass was transported. Cocktail glasses Yes. Cocktails were the most profitable trade in the hotel. Mr. Orcham would agree. Nineteen bars in the hotel, but of course mainly service-bars. Still, bars. Mr. Stairforth knew everything, everything. He had a million compartments in his head, and could open any one of them and expose its contents in the tenth of a second. On! On! China, now. The Palace carried that day £21,150's worth of china and glass. Electroplate. Countless shelves of it. Innumerable repetitions of one article. Cruets, for instance. Coffee spoons, for instance. 297 coffee spoons missing in four months. £161's worth of silver lost in four months.

On! On Yes, here was the silversmiths' repair shop. You saw how they bent them back into shape. Very ingenious. And the re-plating. Yes, yes. Now the linen. 40,000 serviettes, 24,000 chamber-towels. 24,000 table-cloths. 5,730 sheets. Varied from week to week of course. Pity she couldn't see the wine stocks; but they were chiefly at Craven Street. £322,000's worth of wines, including £50,000's worth reserves in France. £5,000's worth of cigars. Curious that cigars matured best in a room with a south-east aspect. A big cigar took eighteen months to mature, a little one only six months. On! On!

Evelyn looked at his watch.

"You must go. You must go. I quite understand, Mr. Orcham. Quite. You haven't *begun* to see things, Miss Powler. But any time you can come down, I shall be at your disposal. I think that all housekeepers, *and* others, ought to visit the Stocks Department. Valuable knowledge. Yes. Valuable. Good-bye. So glad you came. Not at all. Not at all. Delighted. I love people to be interested as you've been."

"That man," said Evelyn in the corridor, "that man has seventeen children and seventeen grandchildren. At least seventeen was the last I heard. It may be eighteen by this time. He must be getting on."

3.

He conducted her through more corridors and then down a very steep, narrow, steel staircase. Increasing warmth. An odour of warm oil. Rumblings of machinery in motion. Violet saw from above an interior that recalled a glimpse which she had once had of the engine-room of a Margate steamer; but this interior was very much larger. A broad man came to meet the visitors at the foot of the steel staircase.

"Good morning, sir. I was beginning to think something had turned up to stop you from coming."

"No!" said Evelyn. "I should have telephoned you in that case. This is Miss Powler." He explained Violet and her presence there. "Mr. Ickeringway," he said to Violet. "Our chief engineer. We robbed the Navy of him."

Mr. Ickeringway cordially pressed Violet's hand in a hand broad to match his body. A man of fifty, neat in navy blue, with grey hair, a loud voice, a calm pale face, and an expression on it of authoritative and slightly humorous fortitude.

"If you could see the new well now, sir. It's just the moment." He turned to Violet: "Yes, miss, I'm a naval man. We've a staff down here of sixty-eight, and all but three of 'em are naval men too."

He led them across the great engine-hall to an enclosure where were three frightening steel-rimmed and brick-lined holes, with thin shafts running down them into Australia.

"Five hundred feet deep, miss," said Mr. Ickeringway, and then suddenly began a discussion with the panjandrum, who bent his head towards the chief engineer's. Violet gazed around, and saw clumps of machinery here and there, some moveless, some whizzing, clicking, sizzling; also a few of the sixty-eight visibly wandering around on inspections, or stationary at some job.

By this time the ex-staff-manageress of the Laundry (whose small engine-room Cyril Purkin had never encouraged her to see) was incapable of receiving any but vague impressions of semi-stupefied amazement. She had ceased to try to follow intelligently the procession of wonders, or even to try to seem intelligent. She did not listen to the conversation between the two men. She heard Mr. Orcham finish it with the words:

"That's understood then. You can go right ahead."

"Better look at this, miss," Mr. Ickeringway woke her. "It's the new artesian well. Electric pump. It blows the water from the bottom straight up on to the roof. You wouldn't think we use 22,000 gallons of water an hour in the Palace. But that's it. 22,000. And soft water. This is about the only hotel in London that has soft water. Because we don't depend on public supply."

"Of course," said Evelyn. "We couldn't have had all this--" he waved an imaginary cane in the direction of the open hall--"if we hadn't built our new wings. All this is under the new last wing. Wouldn't have been room for it under the old part of the building." .

"Now you'd better begin with the boilers, miss," said the chief engineer, and drew the party out towards the mammoth row of boilers, from which ran a series of thick serpentine hosepipes. "If anything happened to these, miss--well! Nine fires. Oil-fed. Twenty-five tons of oil a day. Equal to fifty of coal. Yes. And here's the turbine. 4,500 revs., miss, and you can hardly hear it. It's bedded in springs so it won't vibrate the hotel down."

Suddenly there was a terrific roar. Violet started violently. She thought that the entire hall was about to blow up and blow the hotel into the air. Evelyn's hand was strongly on her arm.

"It's all right. It's all right!" he protectively soothed

And she was in fact tranquillised instantly. So that she felt safe amid mysterious perils and called herself a baby and an idiot.

"They're only testing the new semi-Diesel," said the chief engineer casually, and pointed to where two pigmy men in beige overalls were perched on a huge dark active mass of a machine. The roar died away. Violet was led on from machine to machine, comprehending the purpose of none.

She heard the chief engineer say:

"There isn't much of a load on now. There'll be more at one o'clock, and a lot more in the evening. We get through a lot of current. Well, there are twenty-nine electric lifts. And a thousand horse-power of electric motors. And about six thousand light-units a day we get through. Come and see where we wash all the air for the public rooms and corridors, and ozonise it, and warm it in winter and cool it in summer."

On, on! The brine-bath, twenty-eight tons of brine. The icemaking apparatus (reached by a slope upwards). Seven tons of ice a day. Violet gazed.

"You'd better not stay in here," Evelyn cautioned her. He was benevolently protecting her again. "So liable to catch cold in these sudden changes of temperature. I shouldn't like you to be laid up the first day." He smiled. She smiled weakly, unintelligently.

Back into the engine-hall.

"And you do all your own repairs here, don't you, Ickeringway?" said Evelyn, as if prompting the chief engineer in the recital of the catalogue of marvels.

"We do, miss. All. I think we may say that this is a self-containing unit, same as a ship, but a bit more." Violet addressed another glance of flabbergasted admiration to Mr. Orcham and Mr. Ickeringway. She saw that Mr. Orcham was passionately proud of his establishment, and she thought it was nice of him, and so man-like and so child-like, to be so innocent in his glorious pride.

4.

A few minutes later Evelyn looked at his watch. The chief engineer, in common with all the other heads of departments, knew the proper response to that gesture.

"A wonderful fellow, that," said Evelyn, at the top of the steel staircase. "I've never seen him excited. Never. And his men would do anything for him. They simply worship him. I don't quite know why."

"Yes," thought Violet. "And *you* simply worship all your heads of departments. You're so proud of them you can't keep it to yourself. And of course they wouldn't do anything for you! Oh no! Naturally they wouldn't!"

Silence in the long, narrow, squalid corridor. No rumour or vibration of any machinery. A workman passed, halting close against the wall to leave room for the two visitors from the luxury world. Then another. In the silence Violet soon regained her poise. She was touched as much by Mr. Orcham's simple pride in his heads of departments as by his calm protectiveness over her. There were tears of emotional sympathy in the eyes of her soul, if not a trace of feeling in the eyes of her serene face.

"It makes you think," she murmured.

"What? All that? You haven't seen half. Not half...yes. You could understand anyone wanting to buy this place," he said.

"Oh yes!" she agreed eagerly. "I suppose you get lots of offers."

"I don't get lots, but I get one now and then." He spoke carelessly, as if such matters had no importance.

"I remember somebody thinking of trying to buy it a long time ago."

"Oh!" Evelyn's tone sharpened into astonishment and curiosity. "Who was that?"

"Sir Henry Savott. He told my sister once, and she told me. She said to me: 'He hasn't finished with his department-stores business, but he's thinking about something else--hotels. Imperial Palace and so on.' I remember the very words." Instantly Violet had an idea that she might be breaking a confidence. But she did not care. She exulted in her wrongdoing, if wrongdoing it was. She wanted to interest him, and he would certainly be interested. The information might even in some unguessable way be useful to him. And her sister was dead.

"Oh!" said Evelyn very lightly. *"Indeed!"* As if he considered that Sir Henry had a nerve to think of buying the Imperial Palace.

"But I expect he gave up the idea," Violet added.

"And when was this?" Evelyn asked.

"I couldn't say, sir, now. Years since." Evelyn said no more.

When by the swinging-door marked "Private" they had re-entered the decorated and gaudy world of mirrors and gilt and luxury and uniformed attendants, Violet stopped resolutely at the lift, which she recognised as her lift by the features of the attendant.

"Thank you very much, sir. About those flowers for Miss Maclaren's rooms, sir, that you said I was to see to. Can you tell me how I get them? Where? I oughtn't to ask Miss Maclaren, ought I?" She half smiled.

"No," Evelyn replied, with an almost snubbing frigidity. "You'd better not ask me things like that. You go upstairs and find out. You'll have far more important things than that to find out. I count on you to fall on your feet. The Floors are in a bit of a mess, I mean as regards supervising. So I count on you."

"Sorry, sir," said Violet, meekly accepting the rebuke.

She pressed the rebuke to her bosom, like a saint an arrow. He was right. She had been wrong. Imagine a floor-housekeeper worrying the Director with a silly question about flowers! Obviously it was her *business* to fall on her feet--part of her duty. She had been presuming upon his benevolence towards her. He waved a hand negligently.

"Good-morning, sir. Thank you again."

As the lift ascended she reflected: "I'd better keep as quiet as possible about all this sightseeing this morning. I don't want to start with a lot of jealousies. I'd better pretend it was nothing, but he just told me to come and I went, and they'll all have to go. It's a pity I was the first to go. That'll make them jealous--without anything else."

Still, at the bottom of her soul she was not displeased that her yet unknown colleagues should be jealous of her relations with Mr. Orcham. Relations! The thought recurred: Would she ever see him again? What about the chain of authority? Now she had to learn her job in a couple of days or so. She decided that she could. She resolved that she would. The lamp blazed up in her brain with fresh ardour. And she felt joyously inspired to terrific deeds.

Chapter 32 INITIATION

On the eighth floor, her own, Violet saw a fairly young woman in black talking to Beatrice Noakes in the doorway of the head-housekeeper's room. The fairly young woman in black, catching sight of Violet, immediately stepped out into the corridor, at the same time dismissing Beatrice.

"You're Miss Powler?" she called, while Violet was still twenty feet away.

"Yes."

"My name's Maclaren, and I suppose I'm head-housekeeper now. I've been asking for you everywhere." The accent was Scottish, the voice bright, but obviously that of a woman both fatigued and harassed.

"Sorry," said Violet. "Mr. Orcham sent for me."

"Just come in here a moment, will you? I've only got five minutes. I must go back to Fourth." Miss Maclaren shut the door, and the two stood close together in the half-dismantled room.

"What did Mr. Orcham want?"

Violet explained that she was the discoverer of Mrs. O'Riordan's flight, and related the circumstances preceding the telephonic summons to the Director's office. She finished: "He said as I was down there he'd show me some things in the basement, so I should know."

"Oh!" murmured Miss Maclaren negligently.

Looking at her closely, Violet at once put eight or ten years on to her first estimate of Miss Maclaren's age; the new head-housekeeper had wrinkles and a rather worn expression. Her powder was not very well distributed.

She seems inclined to be decent," thought Violet. "But she's disturbed. As she's my boss I'd better be a bit careful.' And aloud, with pleasant animation: "I should be so glad if you'd just tell me what I have to do."

"You have to inspect all the rooms that are unoccupied or empty for the time being. First of all you turn on all the lights, whether it's daylight or not, to see they're in order. Try the curtains. See all the taps are right and don't drip. And the locks right everywhere, and everything clean. Bed-linen has to be changed every two days. But some visitors want it changed every day. And you have to watch the chambermaids and--"

"I've talked to one, as I said."

"Beatrice, I expect. She's good. But she thinks she's Mr. Cousin." Miss Maclaren's tone hardened. "She'll want to run you, instead of you running her."

"I think I can see to that," Violet put in with a smile.

"Never give them an inch--I mean the maids. Not an inch. And don't give them half a minute in the mornings. They have to sign on at half-past six. And every second morning you have to be on duty at half-past six to see them sign on, on both Eighth and Seventh. Miss Prentiss--she's Seventh--does it on the other morning. In turns, you see. I may as well tell you the hours now. You have half a day a week off, and every second week-end--from Saturday at three, about, till Monday morning. You have four hours off every day--if you're lucky. When you have early morning duty, 6.30, you finish at nine at night. On the other days you begin at nine in the morning and finish at midnight. Of course they're long hours."

"Oh! That's all right," Violet responded, with an enthusiasm which she did not quite feel.

She had not known the hours. Mr. Cousin had said nothing about them. Nor had Mrs. O'Riordan. Miss Brury might have given her information during the week they had spent together at the Laundry; but Miss Brury had plainly indicated an unwillingness to talk about the Imperial Palace. She even affected not to know that Violet had been engaged for the hotel. Violet now calculated that her hours would be between sixty and seventy a week, whereas at the Laundry they had been fifty-five a week. Also at the hotel she would have only three clear evenings off in a fortnight. No more evening rehearsals of the Dramatic Society, and other fun! She feared for the future of the Dramatic Society, whose members she had left in a state of forlorn depression. In spite of this, the lamp still burned brightly in her brain.

"And then," Miss Maclaren proceeded, "you have to be ready to go into any room instantly, if any visitor asks for the housekeeper, to settle any trouble."

"Yes," said Violet. "I remember Mr. Orcham telling me about that when he first sent for me. I daresay I can manage it. I've had to do it before." She related her sojourn as temporary housekeeper at a large place in the country. "Do I have any keys?" she enquired.

"You have a pass-key to the rooms and duplicate keys of the linen-closets. That's all. Now you'd better begin now with--let me see--my head's all in a whirl." Miss Maclaren put her hands over her eyes. "Mrs. O'Riordan leaving like this. I'd no idea of it, Miss Powler. Not a *notion.*"

"It must be frightfully trying. Mr. Orcham told me that I must first of all see to your rooms here."

"Oh! That doesn't matter," snapped Miss Maclaren. "There's lots of things more important than that."

"But if he finds out I haven't done it," Violet smiled. "I might be in trouble--right at the start. He seemed very anxious for it to be done. But of course I know I take my orders from you."

"Oh! Very well!" Miss Maclaren impatiently yielded. "But I do wish Mr. Orcham wouldn't try to run everything himself. He always does." She smiled with a sort of dismal comic resignation. "Let him have his own way. I'm on Fourth now. I'll give instructions for all my things to be sent up immediately. And you do what you like with them. I've no time. There's been an oak and wicker bedstead simply broken to bits on Fifth. Some actress. She must have done it herself in one of her tantrums. But of course nobody's done it! Mr. Cousin's secretary just tells me in her casual way Mrs. O'Riordan's gone, and Mr. Orcham telephones me himself and says

I'm to take charge as quick as I can, and the first thing I have is this bedstead affair. It's worth £40at least. If I was Mr. Cousin I should ask her royal highness to leave to-day, but he won't, I know he won't, because she's supposed to be a great actress and good publicity. You'd hardly believe it, but she's making a fuss because a new bedstead hasn't been brought in at once! That'll just show you the kind of thing a housekeeper has to face. Has your luggage come?"

"Yes. It's here."

"Have you unpacked?"

"Not yet."

"Well, while you're waiting for my things you go and get straight yourself."

Violet gave three little nods of obedient assent. The two had not even shaken hands, but Violet was already feeling sympathetic towards her superior. She thought: "I'll let her see she can depend on me." She had the sensation of having been in the hotel for days.

Miss Maclaren hurried off. Not a word about her return. Not a word about meals. Not a word as to whether that night Violet would be on duty till nine o'clock or till midnight. As soon as she was gone Violet went to her own room and rang the bell, and then, having pulled open all the drawers and cupboard-doors, instantly began to unpack; she had found in the top middle drawer of the desk a lot of empty forms for hotel linen and for laundry.

2.

"Oh! Can I help you to unpack, miss?" said an eager voice, Beatrice's.

Violet was bending over a trunk on the bed. Beatrice seemed fatter than before. Plump was a slightly inadequate description of her. And she was certainly more eager. The tidings of the definite departure of the head-housekeeper had spread through the entire hotel, exciting its life, and giving to everybody a quite unaccustomed zest.

"No thank you, Beatrice. But I'll tell you what you can do."

"Yes, miss."

"And at once. Go and do out Miss Maclaren's rooms, as quick as you can."

"Miss Maclaren is on Fourth, miss."

"She's coming up here. I meant Mrs. O'Riordan's rooms. What's the number of them?"

"Oh, I see, miss. They've no number."

"Well, go and do them out now. And put Mrs. O'Riordan's trunks and things out into the corridor."

"I misdoubt if I can move the big one by myself, miss. And chambermaids aren't supposed--"

"Well, then, get someone to help you. Get a waiter."

"Oh, miss, not a waiter. I daren't. Us and the valets are about equal as you may say. But a waiter. If I got giving order-messages to the waiters I should have old Mr. Perosi down on me like half-a-ton of coal."

"Who's Mr. Perosi?"

"He's the head-waiter for all the Floors, miss. And he's terrible particular. Mrs. O'Riordan and him once had some words, an' it was just like the hotel being on fire. Mr. Orcham had to settle that, he had. Of course

"Then get a valet to help you."

"Well, miss--"

"How many valets are there on this floor?"

"Two, miss. What I was going to say, miss, one's pressing a suit urgent at this very moment, and the other's off."

"And the other maids? How many are there of you up here?"

"Four, miss. And forty rooms. Besides all the bits of sewing we have to do for visitors. Of course there's more rooms on the other floors. But here you see there's more store-rooms and the carpenter's shop, besides the head-housekeeper's rooms, and the lampshade room. There's more maids on the lower floor, but forty bedrooms among three of us!..And things are a bit messed up to-day. Miss Prentiss didn't see us sign on this morning, and you know what young girls is, miss. I've been telling 'em. They were fearful late this morning. But of course, miss, if you--"

"Come along, Beatrice. Come along," said Violet, stopping the spate once more, and preceded her down the corridor to Mrs. O'Riordan's late home, and into the bedroom thereof.

She thought, reflecting on what Miss Maclaren had said:

'This Beatrice just isn't going to run me, anyway." And aloud, gaily: "Now take that outside, and take *that* outside. And I'll take this." Three of the lighter articles of baggage were thus deposited in the corridor. "Now come back. Take that end of this trunk. I'll take the other."

"Yes, miss."

When all the baggage was in the corridor Violet said, a little breathless, but very happy:

"Now you get your brushes and things and do these rooms out, and come and tell me as soon as they're finished."

"Yes, miss."

"You'll easily do them before your dinner. When *is* your dinner-time?"

"Twelve o'clock, miss. And if we're late--"

"But you won't be late."

"No, miss. I was only saying if we are late we're likely to lose on it. There's two relays. I'm in the first this week. When I first came here the food--well, you couldn't eat it. But it's better now. Though they do say it only costs the management one-and-six a day a head of us. You see our dining-room's down in the upper basement. Same as yours, miss. The floor-housekeepers have a table in the room next to ours. The page-boys eat in there too. It's just been redecorated. It ain't very easy to find, miss. But they'll tell you at the lift."

"I daresay they will," Violet agreed, departing, and Beatrice waddled away in search of utensils.

To Violet, the woman was now rather a different creature from the relatively cautious, reconnoitring Beatrice whom she had talked to at their previous interview. Decent still, and inclined to be obliging, and assuredly cheerful; but too desirous of imposing herself. Violet knew the type well. No means of silencing that type. It would chatter even if it was drowning at sea in a gale of wind. Violet leaned now to Miss Maclaren's general estimate of chambermaids. Give them an inch...Still, there was an expression on the florid face of Beatrice that pleased her. She divined that the key to the handling of Beatrice was a resolute and unfluctuating cheerfulness. In regard to Miss Maclaren, she hesitated as to method. She suspected that Miss Maclaren was a worrier, whose bright voice was intended to indicate that she was for ever bearing up in great and unfair ordeals; a fixed believer in the injustice of destiny towards herself. Here Miss Maclaren had been promoted to the sublime situation of head-housekeeper at the Imperial Palace Hotel, and yet she was finding sorrow and grievance in good fortune! Violet surmised that the plant of Miss Maclaren's existence would best flourish in an atmosphere of brave gloom, watered occasionally with tears. But Violet could seldom weep. Arid she despised tearfulness in others. Her instinct was nearly always to be bland and smiling. Withal she decided that Miss Maclaren was able, conscientious, industrious, and to be relied upon, which was something, if not everything.

"I've got to be damn careful," said Violet to herself in warning. Nobody had ever heard her use an improper word, except the late Susan. (The sisters would now and then luxuriate in frightful swearing matches, for fun, to give colour to grey life.) Now Violet had no one to swear with; so, infrequently, she indulged in solitary, silent swearing, to the same end.

As, with rapid judgment of the suitability of particular drawers and cupboards for particular articles, she made continual dashes from the bedside to the wardrobe, dressing-table or desk, distributing her attire and possessions, none could have guessed that her mind was dwelling upon the imagined figure of Mr. Orcham. It was. Sometimes she could see his face quite plainly. She liked his funny teeth, and his warm eyes, and the way he held his head up and walked more on his toes than on his heels. (A bit stealthy, somehow.) But his chin puzzled her, and his nose stuck out too much. He was always changing. Now stiff and curt, now flexible and acquiescent. There were moments when you'd think he was going to be positively intimate; and then no, he was as straight as a poker again. Fearfully well dressed, but quietly. She was sure that he preferred girls to look smart. He must be mildly interested in women. She knew nothing about him, in that department, save that he was a widower. He was one of your mysterious bland persons. (She liked blandness, and practised it naturally, without effort.) Something of the child in him. And something of the woman in him. Not what you'd call so frightfully masculine. Yet he was.

And you couldn't guess from the way he behaved that he was a terrific swell. Yet you could. Of course she didn't know very much about terrific swells. Perhaps they were all like that. No, it couldn't be so. Because Sir Henry Savott wasn't like that, and he was a terrific swell, and some of his friends who came to Claygate were swells too, and they weren't like Mr. Orcham, either. Well, perhaps one or two of them might have been. But not like Mr. Orcham after all. She'd never met anyone like Mr. Orcham. Yes, she judged for the second time that day, he was a gentleman. Here was the thought that brightened her lamp. She would never see him, because you couldn't miss links in the chain of responsibility. But a large part of her inspiration to work was the desire to be worthy of his choice. He had chosen her--he said so. *He* had chosen her; he, the head of the whole hotel. Difficult not to forget that he was as high up as he certainly was--there was something *equal* about him. He might be stiff, but he never looked down on you. The way he would stand aside for you, and open doors for you--not always, but sometimes--it made you almost think you were a lady. Of course she *was* a lady, but she knew what she meant.

3.

She had purposely left her door open. She heard a trundling, squeaking sound in the corridor, and peeped out. A valet in sleeves of shiny black pushing a luggage-carrier.

"These Miss Maclaren's things?"

"Yes, miss."

"All right. You know the rooms?"

"Yes, miss."

"You're from Fourth?" She enjoyed saying 'Fourth.'

"Yes, miss."

Little more than three-quarters of an hour had passed. Evidently Miss Maclaren had the gift of getting things done with speed. Violet continued her unpacking until she heard the trundling sound again. Then she hurried to the head-housekeeper's rooms. They were finished. Praise was due, thought Violet.

"You've been pretty quick, Beatrice."

"Thank you, miss. I think you'll find everything's clean. Of course when we--"

"What are these keys?"

Four keys, one large and three small, lay prominent on an arm of the sofa.

"Miss Maclaren's sent them up, miss. They're your pass-key and the keys of the linen-closets."

"Good." Violet at once attached them to the key-chain on her girdle.

"I suppose I'd better undo some of these things, miss. It doesn't matter about my dinner." Beatrice pointed to a couple of trunks and some small bags and an umbrella and a lot of cloaks and oddments reposing right in the middle of the doorway leading towards the bedroom.

Violet looked at the clock near the ceiling over the fireplace. "It does matter about your dinner, Beatrice. I shan't be late for mine and I won't have you being late for yours. Off you go! You'll just be in time."

"Oh! If it's like that, miss!" Beatrice smiled richly. "I was only going to tell you--"

"Tell me afterwards, when you come up."

"But *you* won't be up, miss."

"Well, when I do come up then."

Beatrice went out, smiling still against rebuff. And the moment Beatrice was gone Violet seized on the cloaks. Poor garments. No style. A shabby pinkish transparent mackintosh. A shabby umbrella. A good, warm, heavy rug, which Violet immediately laid on the sofa. Two large photographs of two serried bands of young men--one band in football kit--with wide white margins in black frames. Two smaller photographs, an old man and an old woman, similarly framed. And another photograph of a tiny country cottage with low hills behind, framed in straw with bows. Miss Maclaren's relatives? Miss Maclaren's birthplace? One cushion. Two vases. Ten books. Violet hung the two large photographs on either side of the hearth, and the portraits on either side of the door; and she put the vases and the cottage with hills on the mantelpiece, and the cushion on the easy-chair. The room became inhabited, took on some faint similitude of a home.

Then she dragged the trunks and the bags into the bedroom. She opened the smallest of the bags. Toilet. Brushes, toothbrush, sponge in a bag, pin-cushion, etc. She disposed the articles on the dressing-table and the lavatory basin. One of the trunks was not completely shut. She opened it--and closed it. No! Sacrilege! She would have been glad to empty the trunks and the other bags; but she dared not. Prying! She must be damn careful. However, she hung up the cloaks and the mackintosh in the enormous wardrobe, and propped up the umbrella in a corner. Well, Miss Maclaren probably wouldn't mind her things being unpacked for her. She wasn't that sort. But Miss Maclaren just *might* mind. You never knew!

"My God! The flowers!"

She had forgotten them. She had meant to enquire from Beatrice about the machinery for getting flowers. "It slipped my memory, miss": a phrase familiar to her in the Laundry. She hated it. How did you get flowers? She might telephone down to the other Marian. No. That would be a sign of weakness. Stocks Department? She might telephone down to Mr. Stairforth, the breathless talker. No. She daren't. Besides, though there must be a stock of flowers somewhere, she had noticed no stock of flowers in Mr. Stairforth's dark realm. She felt helpless. She felt alone on the floor. She looked around. There were two glass vases of flowers, one on the window-sill: but the blossoms were obviously faded and forlorn beyond revival. She ran into her own room and returned thence with the large vase of flowers. Quite enough in it for two vases. She threw the dead flowers into the waste-paper basket, emptied the vases at the lavatory-basin, refilled them, and divided the flowers and arranged them in the vases, one in each room. They made a most respectable display. She ran back towards her own room with the empty vases, her keys swinging and rattling very cheerfully, and was accosted by a pale waiter emerging from one of the rooms.

"You are asked for here, miss," said the waiter briefly, in a foreign accent, without enquiring who or what she was.

"Me? I'm the new floor-housekeeper."

"Yes."

"Who is it?"

"I do not know quite. I have been three days away ill."

"Is it a lady?"

"No. A gentleman."

"Very well. I'm coming."

She went on to her bedroom with the vase. She was rather frightened. Her major duties were commencing. She fingered her pass-key. Supposing she couldn't fit it into the door...An angry or a dissatisfied customer? Tact, tact!

Chapter 33 A FRIEND

The door, she saw as soon as she stood close to it, bore three numbers, and she assumed therefore that it opened into a suite of three rooms and that the single occupant was a person of wealth. One of her unformulated definitions of a person of wealth was a traveller who could afford a private sitting-room in a hotel--any hotel, not merely an expensive hotel such as the Imperial Palace. A hotel private sitting-room seemed to her to be the very symbol and illustration of fabulous luxury. As for three rooms, what could a visitor want with three rooms. "How silly of me!" she thought suddenly. "Of course! The bathroom is one of the rooms!"

Happily the key fitted itself without any fuss into the lock. She was extremely nervous as she turned the key, pushed open the door, and withdrew the key. Never in her life had she seen a visitor's bedroom in any hotel. Her summit of luxury had been a bedroom in a rather good boarding-house at Ramsgate. She had witnessed various wonders of the Imperial Palace, but its guest-rooms were absolutely unknown to her. And yet she was floor-housekeeper on Eighth. Uncanny situation! 'Uncanny' was the only word for it. The visitor might expose her ignorance by his first question, his first demand. And the customer might be a very strange type of man, might even be a foreigner. She guessed that these big cosmopolitan luxury hotels were inhabited by all sorts of strange, haughty individuals. For a moment again she almost wished herself back in the homely vaporous security of the Laundry, ordering girls about and keeping an invisible wall between herself and Mr. Cyril Purkin.

In front of her was a tiny lobby or hall. Hats and coats clustered on a hatstand--sufficient of them for several men. A half -opened door ahead showed a bathroom. There were doors on either side, both shut. She tapped on one. No answer. She opened it. Bedroom. Then she tapped on the other one.

"Come in!" An authoritative male voice, muffled by the thickness of the door.

Her heart announced an increased activity. Yes, she was frightened. As she opened the door she might have been a soldier going over the top in the Great War. A gentleman was standing expectant in the middle of the room, hands in pockets. For one second, in her perturbation, Violet did not recognise him. Then the figure and the rather wizened face with its small eyes resolved themselves for her into those of Sir Henry Savott. She had a feeling of thankfulness. At any rate this was no overbearing stranger. She knew Sir Henry and a lot about him and his idiosyncrasies. Had she not served him for a month and seen him both bland and stern? Also he had been remarkably polite to her in the entrance-hall of the Imperial Palace not long since. She was indeed relieved.

Sir Henry's features relaxed into a smile astonished and welcoming. He had ceased to be the consciously great man which he had always been in the big house at Claygate during her stay there. He moved towards her with hand outstretched; the hand clasped hers with warmth; and at the same time he exclaimed:

"Now what--what in the name of coincidence is the meaning of this? How are you? I'm delighted to see a familiar face." All in one breath.

Violet explained what she was.

"This is my first day here," she said. Somewhat excited by the encounter, she had an impulse to add: "And this is the first room I've seen, and you're the first visitor who has sent for me, and I hardly know where I am yet." But a natural prudence silenced her. Instead, she added: "What can I do for you, Sir Henry?" in a rather formal tone. An instinctive sense of propriety always prompted her to keep herplace and to encourage other people to keep theirs. Sir Henry, however, in his cordiality, apparently desired not to be formal. He sat down.

"Do sit down," he said.

"I'm all right, thank you, Sir Henry," Violet answered firmly, but very nicely. She was not going to be caught by any waiter or other chance entrant sitting down in the room of a male visitor, and especially on her first day. No! Moreover, if such a freedom was not forbidden by the hotel code, well, it ought to be!

She had never been aware of much sympathy with Sir Henry. He had characteristics which she disliked. His quick, sharp gestures and movements, designed--she often thought--to deceive people as to his age. His bristly moustache, which in her opinion ought either to be allowed to grow a little more or to be completely suppressed. His chin, which was ugly and sinister. His teeth, which seemed always hungry. And his glance, inquisitive and suspicious. If she trusted him, it was not without reluctance.

Still, her sister Susan, while reserved about him--even to Violet--had certainly both trusted and liked him. He had meant a deal to Susan; and he had invariably treated Susan well. As indeed he had treated Violet herself. Violet had nothing definable against him; and, further, she had followed Susan in sympathising with him in his conjugal difficulties. And now, as she stood primly before him, she felt sorry for him. And neither he nor anybody else could have guessed why.

It was because the sitting-room was so small. (The bedroom too was small.) After the immense spacious interiors of the house at Claygate, it seemed a perfect shame to Violet that the great opulent man should have to content himself, or should content himself, with rooms relatively so tiny. As a fact, neither of his rooms here was much larger than her own. She was disappointed in the size of the rooms at the amazing Imperial Palace.

"Well, Miss Powler," said Sir Henry. "I'm genuinely glad to see you here. I seem to remember Mr. Orcham mentioning to me that there was some idea of your coming here. I'm glad because I'm quite sure you were thrown away at that Laundry. This is just the place for you."

('Miss Powler.' At Claygate he had always called Susan 'Susan' and Violet 'Violet,' except in the presence of the servants.)

"You're very kind, Sir Henry," Violet responded. "But I've a great deal to learn."

"Not you. You were first-rate at my house. You know all about maids and valets and so on. And you know exactly how to treat guests. You've got nothing to learn, really, except--what shall I say?--the geography of the hotel. And a few tuppenny-halfpenny rules."

"It's understood it takes six months or more to train a housekeeper here, Sir Henry," said Violet. But she was impressed by his instant grasp of essentials, and, flattered, she felt inclined to agree with his estimate of the situation.

"Not for a woman like you," said he, positive and slightly impatient. "A fool couldn't be trained in six months or six years. But you have intelligence, and you know it. You're bound to have a successful career. Of course"--he raised a finger--"accidents *do* happen. I don't think for a moment they will, but you can't be sure. I'm convinced you'll rise high in this place. But if anything should happen, I want you to know that in some other hotels, anyhow one--and there may be more--what I say goes. And if ever you want a change, you just send me one line, one line, and I'll fix it. Oh yes! I'll do it for my own sake, and glad to!"

"It's very kind of you, Sir Henry. Very kind. But I hope I shan't--I don't think--"

"Neither do I. I'm only saying 'if.' And there's something else--you don't mind me giving you a tip, do you?"

Violet shook her head and smiled. Assuredly Sir Henry was strengthening her belief in herself. And he was indeed kind. Assuredly she felt uplifted once more.

"I suppose you don't know any French?" Sir Henry resumed. "No. I know you don't, because I remember once when I had Monsieur Messein down at Claygate and there was some mix-up in his bedroom, Miss Gracie had to interpret."

"No, Sir Henry. I did begin to learn French at the South-West London Polytechnic, but I forgot it all as soon as I left there."

"Well, take my tip and learn French. In this new business of yours here it'll be of the greatest use to you. Wouldn't be much good in an ordinary English hotel, of course. But this is a cosmopolitan show where you get all sorts of clients. It would give you a sort of a standing, you see. In France and so on housekeepers and cashiers and reception-clerks--they're often women--can speak English, have to; but in England, even in London, how often do you see a housekeeper who can talk anything but English? Scarcely ever. I undertake to say there isn't one housekeeper in the I.P. can speak French. Of course you always hear that English is the international language. It may be. It is. But not in the luxury world, and the luxury world's your world, you know. Think it over, will you?"

"Oh, I will, Sir Henry," Violet replied, enthusiastic, but--as it were--dreamily enthusiastic.

She was dreamy in the suddenly induced marvellous vision of herself as a young woman able to gabble away in French to foreigners who could not speak English. "Give her a sort of standing!" It would. In her vision she could hear Miss Maclaren saying on other floors in her lowland-Scottish accent: "Better send for Miss Powler. Where's Miss Powler? Miss Powler can talk French. Miss Powler will see the lady--or the gentleman." It would be wonderful. Too wonderful to be true! She wanted to begin to learn French the next minute. The lamp burned still brighter in her brain. Mr. Orcham could talk French, she was sure. He would be impressed if he knew that she could talk French too. Mr. Cousin *was* French. What fun it would be if, one day when she had to go down and, see Mr. Cousin, she started the interview right off in French! What a difference between the old Violet in the Laundry, and the new French-chattering Violet in Sir Henry's luxury world!

But she was a practical girl, and she emerged from her dream into realisation.

"It might be rather hard for me to do it here, Sir Henry,"she said. "The hours are pretty long, and perhaps I couldn't get out."

"Hard? Here? Couldn't get out? What do you want to get out for? Why, there must be scores of people in this place who talk French better than they talk English! And some of them would be glad to teach you. You could easily come to an arrangement. Simplest thing in the world. A little enterprise needed; that's all."

"I shall," said Violet positively, her brown eyes lighted up. "I'm very much obliged, Sir Henry."

2.

He had spoken benevolently, persuasively, even coaxingly. She felt more sympathetic towards him than she had ever felt. Why was he so good-natured? Possibly because she happened to be Susan's sister. Surely he would not have shown the same interest in any other housekeeper! He couldn't. Of course she had served in his house, run his house. But ages ago, and not for long. The reason for his interest must be Susan. Anyhow he was full of common sense. And he certainly did grasp a situation. Violet admired common sense and grasp more than anything else. He had opened her eyes, that he had!

In her admiration she grew nearly at ease with him. Her association with him in the past helped her to forget now that he was a millionaire, a big public figure, whose name and whose photograph were constantly in the newspapers. She saw in front of her not a legend but a human being, who wanted a floor-housekeeper to look after some ordinary matter for him in his rooms. It might be the starching of his shirts. (Though it was the effect of life in the Laundry that turned her thoughts first to shirts, she did recall that he used to be a bit particular about his shirts.) And in advising her he had not tried to come the bigwig over her. Not a trace of 'side.' No indication whatever of the difference in class which separated them. He was just friendly and decent, in a nice kind of fatherly style. And yet not quite fatherly. No. Just as a friendly decent man to a decent self-respecting woman much younger than himself.

In her heart she apologised to him for her reservations concerning him. The small, intimate sitting-room had a very agreeable, reassuring atmosphere. Her simple father and mother would have been proud to overhear that interview. And Mr. Orcham would have admitted that she was falling on her feet.

"I'd like something done about this desk," said Sir Henry, suddenly rising and going to the window, beneath which was a small knee-hole desk, painted green to match the general tint of the room.

"Yes, Sir Henry." Violet braced herself to receive orders. Even her voice was braced.

"It's too small for me."

"Yes, Sir Henry."

"I want a larger one."

"Yes, Sir Henry."

"And I want it changed as quick as you can."

"Yes, Sir Henry."

The benevolent paternal human being was transformed into the millionaire autocrat; but there was still some benevolence in his tone, abrupt and commanding as it had become.

He continued:

"I *was* down on the third floor. I had a larger desk there. I've been out of London for a bit since I met you in the hall that day. I got back yesterday, and I moved up here yesterday evening...Pretty view from here, isn't there?" He stared out of the window across St. James's Park and the Green Park towards Piccadilly, all lying under a mist-veiled autumn sun. "It was really because of the view I decided to come up to this floor. You see, on the third floor you're just level with the tops of the trees, and you can't see a thing. I like a view. Space. I can't do with being shut in. See the new Devonshire House there? Then there's another thing. Say what you like about sound-proof rooms, it's always quietest on the top floor. Now about this desk. You see, my secretary, or one of 'em, has to be able to work at it sometimes. There were two desks in my room downstairs."

"I expect it was a larger room, Sir Henry."

"It certainly was. These rooms are too narrow for their length. Still, I prefer this room of the two. Only I want a larger desk. Understand?"

"Yes, Sir Henry. I'll get it as quickly as I can. But the head-housekeeper's had some trouble downstairs, and as I told you, I don't know a thing here yet. This is a question of geography." She faintly smiled.

"Quite, quite," Sir Henry amiably concurred. "But I want a larger desk and the sooner the better." His voice hardened. It was as if he took away with one hand what he had given with the other; as if he had said: "I don't care about your head-housekeeper and her troubles, and it's no affair of mine that you don't know a thing. I want my desk."

"I'll go right now."

"That's a good girl."

This appellation startled Violet ever so little. She moved towards the door.

"Just a minute. You remember Jim?"

"Jim, Sir Henry? I'm afraid I don't."

"Yes, you do. He was second footman at Claygate."

"Oh yes!" But she did not remember Jim. Even in her one month at Claygate she had witnessed several changes of footmen.

"Well, I made him my valet. He's here with me now. He was taken ill in the night on the journey, and I've sent him to bed. I wish you'd go and see for yourself what's the matter with him. And then report to me. If he's going to be really ill I must get a temporary. I only want to know how I stand."

"Yes, Sir Henry." She was somewhat cooled, critical. At first she had thought that the great man was anxious for his valet. Then she thought that the great man was concerned only for himself.

"I'll stay here and wait," said the great man, warningly.

"Yes, Sir Henry."

Violet hurried out. How to procure the larger desk? Having procured it, how to get the change effected? How to discover where this Jim was lodged? She would not ask. Sir Henry would not know. He would probably retort: "Oh! Don't ask me." Yet on the whole, for a first encounter with a visitor in her capacity of floor-housekeeper, the meeting had passed off very well. And Violet was happy, and still uplifted, and still held a higher opinion than before of Sir Henry Savott. What a world was this Imperial Palace world of rich, bewildering novelty and romantic surprises! And she was on her mettle.

Chapter 34 VIOLET AND MAC

"What's this?" Miss Maclaren demanded, with chill civility, of the waiter who brought into her newly acquired sitting-room a small tray containing a pot of tea, a jug of hot water, milk, sugar, and two cups and saucers.

"Two teas," answered the waiter. It was the same man who had given to Violet the message from Sir Henry Savott.

"I didn't say two 'dry' teas," said Miss Maclaren in a hard, uncompromising tone, drier than the driest tea could be. "Please take this away, and let me have it all on a larger tray, the one Mrs. O'Riordan always had, and her tea-pot, and plenty of bread-and-butter, and cakes, and some black-currant jam. And I'm in a hurry, please."

In silence the waiter withdrew with the tray.

"That's just like them," Miss Maclaren explained her grievance to Violet, whom she had invited to take tea with her. "However, I believe in beginning as you mean to go on. He knew perfectly well. The floor-housekeepers have their tea downstairs where they have their other meals. Only if they want tea upstairs they can have it in their bedrooms. But it's what we call a 'dry' tea. Nothing to eat with it, you know. But the head-housekeeper is at liberty to have whatever she wants, and she's served by a floor-waiter, same as a visitor. Mrs. O'Riordan always had that, and I shall. He was only trying it on. He hasn't been here very long, and he's ill half the time, or pretends to be. Still, he ought surely to have seen enough of me to know I'm not the sort of person to try things on with. He soon will know--I'll attend to that! Don't you think I'm right?"

"Rather!" Violet agreed.

She saw in Miss Maclaren a person who loved authority, who was very jealous of her authority, newly acquired with the room, but who felt the need at first of a little moral support in the exercise of the same. As one who had until the previous day exercised a great deal of authority over more than two hundred women and girls, Violet regarded herself as nearly the moral equal of Miss Maclaren, and she felt that Miss Maclaren so regarded her. But she was privately critical of Miss Maclaren's method. Stony was the word to apply to it. No allowances made. Violet usually managed to put herself in the place of a wrong-doer; which enabled her often to read the wrong-doer's thoughts and thus gave her a considerable advantage in handing the wrong-doer. It was because she was reading Miss Maclaren's thoughts that she had replied with such sympathy, "Rather!"

"You must have had some lively times down at the Laundry now and then," said Miss Maclaren.

"You may depend I had!" said Violet, with a troubled expression feigning dark memories of the lively times. She added:

"But of course it must be much more difficult here--especially for you, with eight floors to keep an eye on and so many different sorts of people too. We'd no foreigners at the Laundry anyhow." The benevolent, deceitful little piece had here said exactly the right thing to the brave martyr of the Floors. Miss Maclaren despised and mistrusted all the foreigners on the staff, except perhaps Mr. Cousin, whose impregnable blandness appealed much more to her than to the somewhat temperamental Mrs. O'Riordan.

The sun was low in the sky. Not a ray of it came through the window. The flame of the small autumn fire showed brighter in the first onset of the dusk. The sofa was drawn close at an angle across the hearth. Miss Maclaren sat in a corner of it, without leaning back. Violet sat on the pouf. The two black-robed creatures, prim with office, soon lost some of their primness in a chiefly physical sensation of nascent intimacy. Violet opened her bag and boldly employed her lipstick.

"What lipstick do *you* fancy, dear?" asked Miss Maclaren.

(Mr. Orcham was uncanny.)

"Michel," said Violet, pausing in her work. "It's a kind of an imitation of Tanger, you know. But I think it's better. Not what you'd call cheap, but it lasts for ages. If you ask me, I think the most expensive is the cheapest."

"Yes?" said Miss Maclaren doubtfully. "I don't know what mine is, really. But I know it's about finished. Mrs. O'Riordan always had Chanel."

"Yes. That's one that lasts for ages, too."

Then the waiter arrived with another and a superior tray, laden apparently with the whole contents of a Bond Street tea-shop and a superior tea-service and superior china. He hesitated.

"Shall he put it on here?" Violet suggested, rising from the pouf.

"Yes."

Violet sat down by Miss Maclaren's side. Intimacy was increasing.

"Thank you," said Miss Maclaren, less harshly, to the waiter, who stood expectant with a pad of order-slips in his hand.

"Will you sign, please, miss?" The waiter spoke with marked deference.

"Oh!" Miss Maclaren exclaimed, caught. She had forgotten that only 'dry' teas required no signature. She signed the check, having first scrutinised it. Glancing over the tray, she added to the waiter in the most friendly manner, "Yes, this will be all I want. Thank you very much."

"Thank you, miss." The waiter left.

"He's learnt his lesson," said Miss Maclaren, but with no bitterness; rather with a smile. The magnificent spectacle of the tray had mollified her. She picked up a *petit four* and ate it at once. Then another. Her mouth half-full, she mumbled to Violet: "Milk? Sugar?"

Violet had one lump, Miss Maclaren three. Miss Maclaren was of those who enjoy their tea. Further, she had a sweet tooth--when sweets were gratis. This immense and crushing weight of the Imperial Palace seemed to slip from her responsible shoulders The look on her worn, well-shaped face gradually changed; the wrinkles were smoothed out; even Violet's demeanour changed in sympathy with Miss Maclaren's.

"It must be rather fun, being head-housekeeper," she ventured.

"Well, I suppose it is, dear," said Miss Maclaren, who at that moment was defining a head-housekeeper as a personage who could have what she chose for tea. "I mean--it is and it isn't. Now Mr. Cousin asked me down for lunch to-day, and Mr. Orcham was there too. Naturally, I couldn't refuse, though really I hadn't a minute and they must have known it. Wasn't as if they had much to tell me that was useful. No. Just talk. It's extraordinary the amount of time men waste. I could have had my lunch in five minutes. Do you know, I was there over an hour. It was in Mr. Cousin's room. I suppose they just wanted to be friendly."

"And so they ought!" Violet put in. "But it was nice of them." She wondered if she would ever be invited to lunch with the swells. Never.

"Oh, it was," said Miss Maclaren, who scarcely tried to conceal a justifiable pride in the event. "And my word they do have meals, those two." The greedy woman was speaking. "Mr. Cousin didn't say a lot, but Mr. Orcham did, and they were both full of Mrs. O'Riordan. Mr. Orcham's made up his mind she shan't have her wedding-present. He said he told her if she didn't come to the dinner she wouldn't get any present. And she did say she would come. So he's sending the plate back to the silversmith's, and he says he's going to return all the subscriptions. That means ten shillings I never expected to see again. Oh! He was very light and jolly about it. But he meant it. You could see that. And when he means a thing he does mean it, Mr. Orcham does. She oughtn't to have run off like that. No! I must say I was very surprised. I should never I have thought it of her."

"I should think not indeed!" said Violet. "But I think just before weddings women do get into a state. I've noticed it."

"Really?" Miss Maclaren casually murmured. "Still, she shouldn't have done it." She lifted her shoulders censoriously, poured out more tea, ate bread-and-butter, ate jam, ate more cakes.

2.

There was a tap on the door. Mrs. O'Riordan's fluffy little school-gir1ish secretary entered, notebook in hand.

"In half an hour, Agatha," said Miss Maclaren, turning her head, grandly. The secretary nodded and vanished.

"Have another of these little cakes--petty fours as they call them," Miss Maclaren hospitably suggested.

"No, thanks. I can't eat any more."

"You haven't had any jam. Do have some."

Violet smiled and moved her head slowly from side to side.

"Another cup of tea?"

Violet nodded her head.

Having poured out two more cups, Miss Maclaren took for herself more bread-and-butter, more jam, and more little cakes. She ate very quickly.

"No use leaving anything for *them,"* said she, seizing as it were sadly the last bit of food on the tray. "The cakes that are no more!" her glance at the empty plates seemed to say. But her demeanour had become quite animated, even gay. She was a completely changed woman: happy in the satiating of her passion. She liked eating; she had authority to order what she wanted; she had got it; and she had consumed it. She leaned back.

"Very nice of you to arrange these rooms for me, Violet," she said; and added: "They christened me 'Mac' in this place. But I'm not going to have any 'Macs' now--except of course when I'm alone with someone, like this."

"No," said Violet. "It wouldn't do, would it? I should have unpacked your trunks too; but I thought perhaps I'd better not. People prefer to do that themselves."

"I've done it," said Miss Maclaren.

'You *are* quick," said Violet, who was really impressed by this despatch.

"Oh! That doesn't take me long!" said Miss Maclaren. "I've done it too often. But hanging pictures and so on. No. I never seem to have a moment for that. Downstairs my pictures never were hung. And if you hadn't hung them here, I don't know when they would have been done." Her gaze was apparently set on one of the vases of flowers. But she said no word about Violet's flowers. Evidently she was a woman, rare, who could look at flowers without seeing them.

"And what have you been doing on your first day? I've had to leave you to yourself." Miss Maclaren laughed.

Violet answered:

"I'd better make my report, hadn't I?"

She told about Sir Henry Savott's urgent demand for a new desk.

"Savott? What number?" Violet gave the number of the suite. "But that was occupied by a Mr.--I forget his name, only it wasn't Savott; a Canadian."

"Sir Henry came in last night, he told me."

"I'm sure he isn't on the floor-list," said Miss Maclaren.

"That must be her ladyship again. She must have had the slip from the Reception Office--and forgotten it. Other things tooccupy her mind!" Miss Maclaren both sardonically enjoyed and severely disapproved Mrs. O'Riordan's negligence. "You see, she was doing floor-housekeeper up here as well as head-housekeeper. You'd have thought she could manage it, wouldn't you? Well, what about the desk?" Violet related that a valet had advised her to go to the carpenter's shop.

"And did you go?"

"No, I sent for the head-carpenter. The valet said there was some spare furniture in his shop."

"Now that's right," said Miss Maclaren. "Send for them. Never go to them unless you can't possibly help it."

"Well, there wasn't a desk--at least not one large enough. And Sir Henry wanted it green. I went to the shop myself to see."

"So you didn't get one?"

"Yes, I did. I don't know whether I did right or not, but I looked in all the empty rooms and I found a large desk in 847. So I exchanged that one for the one in Sir Henry's room. Was that right?"

"Yes, it was," said Miss Maclaren. "But the desk in 847 isn't green."

"It has some green lines picked out on it."

"So it has," Miss Maclaren agreed, after reflection. "How did you get the desks shifted?"

"I just asked the valet if he'd get it done for me, and he did."

"Which valet was it?"

"Don't know his name. Red hair."

"Oh! He *did?"*

"Yes. I think the carpenters helped. I left them to do it and went away. When I came up from lunch it was done. I was very late for lunch. It took me about ten minutes to find where the place was. The housekeepers' table was empty. But there were two page-boys eating in the same room."

"Well, dear, that wasn't so bad for a first day. I don't believe in page-boys having their meals in the same room as the floor-housekeepers. I've often thought of it. It's not nice. And I mean to get that altered if I can. What else? Anything?"

The conversation, vivacious enough, and deeply interesting to both women, burrowed down into recondite details of administration. Violet absorbed new knowledge through her pores. She mentioned the illness of Sir Henry's servant, Jim.

"I went to see him. He said he knew he'd got bronchitis, and I thought he had too. So I sent for Dr. Constam."

"Who told you about Dr. Constam?"

"Marian Tilton. That's her name, isn't it? Mr. Cousin's secretary. I telephoned down to her. She's very obliging."

"Yes. I suppose she is," Miss Maclaren concurred. "But don't you go and say too much to her. She's the worst gossip in the hotel. I'm always very careful with *her.* What did the doctor say?"

"Oh! It was bronchitis. But only a touch."

"He wouldn't have said it was only a touch if it had been a visitor on any of the floors," observed Miss Maclaren.

"Wouldn't he? But I really think it *was* only a touch this time. I've been to see the man since. I knew him, you see, before. I knew Sir Henry Savott too."

Violet hesitated for a moment, but the hesitation ended by her telling pretty fully the story of her brief connection with the Savott household at Claygate. Miss Maclaren listened with both ears, and did not cease to question until she had learnt more of Susan Powler's illness and death than anybody outside the Powler family. Intimacy was still further increased.

The very room was warm with intimacy. Tones of voice sank lower. Inflections and glances and gestures acquired a new freedom and variety.

"Then you must know a lot about our business," said Miss Maclaren, at the close of the talk. "I wish I'd known this morning. I shouldn't have been so nervous for you. Mr. Cousin or Mr. Orcham might have told me, I think." The head-housekeeper's respect for her subordinate had increased as much as the intimacy. After all there was a glamour about managing a large country mansion for a celebrity that even the Imperial Palace could not offer. Silence fell for a moment.

Violet was thinking:

"I'm glad I told her. She might have heard one day and it wouldn't have done for her to think I hadn't been open with her. She's a nice old sort. No trouble about keeping in with her if you go about it right. She's fussy, but she's a great worker, and she knows her job and she'll see that I do mine."

Then the telephone-bell tinkled in the room. Miss Maclaren jumped with a nervous start to answer it.

"Oh, dear!" she murmured, with resignation. "Can't people leave me alone while I'm having my tea?"

3.

In the telephone dialogue, Miss Maclaren said little, listening much more than she talked. Violet heard only such phrases as:

"Oh! Quite satisfactory, sir. She's...Very well, sir...To-night? Yes, to-morrow morning *would* be better. Certainly, sir. I'll arrange it...Oh yes, sir. I can manage." Miss Maclaren hung up the receiver, sighed, and returned to the sofa.

"I'm sorry, Violet, but the orders are that you are to go down to Third to-morrow morning, and take over there. It was Mr. Cousin speaking. I do think it would have been better for you to stay up here with me for a bit, while you're getting into it. But that's the order. He didn't give any reason. But I should like to know whether I'm head-housekeeper or not. It ought to be my business to decide what housekeeper is to be on what door. Miss Venables is doing Third and Fourth at present, and she might just as well go on doing them both, until you're settled down. I thought we'd settled it all at that lunch of theirs. I told them there was no need to have eight housekeepers. Waste of money, I told them. I can easily do Eighth myself, same as Mrs. O'Riordan had to do for a week and more. But I do wish you could have stayed with me. I'm so sorry, dear."

"So am I--Mac," Violet replied, using the diminutive with a certain constraint for the first time.

And she was rather more than sorry. She was upset. These mysterious powers downstairs! They said go, and you went. No reason given. They ordered, and you obeyed, blindly. You weren't a human being. You were a robot. You had to exercise judgment, tact, take responsibilities, be smart, powder your face. But you were a robot. Supposing she'd been doing wrong over the desk, as she might have been doing! What trouble! Taking on herself to change furniture without authority! But she was a robot nevertheless. Nothing like this could have happened at the Laundry. Cyril Purkin had been above her, technically, but he was always a bit timid, apologetic, and full of explanations whenever he encroached on her territory. Third floor! It was a foreign land to her. It was like Canada. Fancy having to emigrate to Canada at less than a day's notice. And she was unpacked and fixed on Eighth! And she felt at home there. To her, Eighth was the nicest and the cosiest floor in the hotel. No other floor could be half as nice.

She felt helplessly involved in a terrific and ruthless machine. And why was she being moved? Why? Miss Maclaren thought there was no sense in it, and so there couldn't be any sense in it.With Miss Maclaren the interests of the hotel would have come first. She would have sacrificed herself and Violet and anybody to the interests of the hotel. That was certain. You could feel in Miss Maclaren a tremendous loyalty and devotion to the hotel. Well, if Miss Maclaren couldn't see the point of the move there just wasn't a point. Surely Mr. Orcham had had nothing to do with the order. No, it was just a whim of that strange Frenchman. Already Violet was beginning to catch the head-housekeeper's prejudice against foreigners.

"Agatha will be here in a minute," said Miss Maclaren, glancing at the clock. "I must dictate some letters. I'm not very good at it. Did you have to do any dictating at the Laundry, dear?"

"Oh no! Mr. Purkin did all that."

"He was a bit curt in his letters to Mrs. O'Riordan," said Miss Maclaren.

"Yes, I daresay," said Violet. "But I don't think he means to be," she smiled.

And Mac smiled quite suddenly.

"No. I'm sure he doesn't," said she, as if suddenly persuaded to revise her opinion of Mr. Purkin as a business correspondent. "And talking of the Laundry," she went on, "the linen will be coming in about seven--you know when it leaves the Laundry--I wish you'd see that it's checked *carefully,* and I want you to look right through the linen-closets, and see if everything's arranged for the best and report to me, will you?"

"I will," said Violet, with enthusiastic, consciously comforting willingness, conveying the idea that her special delight would be to do what was asked of her.

"Let me see now," said Miss Maclaren. "This will be your late night. Midnight, you go off. Have you had any time off to-day?"

"I've had plenty of time when there wasn't anything to do."

"You ought to have gone out," said Miss Maclaren, who seldom took the trouble to go out herself. "I'd like us to have another quiet chat to-night. Come along here about half-past eleven. I'll expect you. But be sure to tell the night-waiter and the valet and the maid where you're to be found. In case. You never know."

Agatha tapped and entered. Miss Maclaren frowned instinctively, preparing herself to shoulder again the full burden of the Imperial Palace.

"You've brought that correspondence I asked you for with the Works Department?"

"Yes, Miss Maclaren."

Violet dined in the society of Miss Prentiss and Miss Venables. There were no page-boys. Later she went through the linen-closets. She was humorously surprised to discover herself highly critical of the laundry work. She admitted defects which, if they had been brought to her notice by the hotel staff, she would never have admitted in the Laundry. By eleven-thirty she was almost reconciled to the emigration order. Mac and she gossiped till nearly one o'clock in the morning, hedonistically heedless of the clock. At parting they kissed: a prim kiss. Mac said that Violet must come up for tea again the next day--not for mere pleasure, certainly not, but to receive any advice or information which she might need for the proper conduct of Third.

"Have you packed at all, you poor dear?" Mac enquired.

"No. I shan't think of it till morning."

"That's right. And don't you go down a minute before nine o'clock. That's your time on Third."

Violet walked slowly through the long narrow corridor, in which all the lights save three had been extinguished. No sound. No sign of human existence, except a pair of shoes on doormats here and there. Ghostly. Weird. Light showed through the half-open door of the waiters' service-room. A man in a dressing-gown emerged from a room nearly opposite Violet's, dropped a letter into the letter-shoot, and disappeared back into his room. And in the strange solitude of her home-for-one-night, Violet undressed slowly and meditatively. She smiled to herself. On the whole she was very well pleased with her debut.

"What a hell of an exciting day!" she remarked aloud.

Chapter 35 RETURN TO EIGHTH

The next morning Violet, already installed and at work on Third, went into one of the principal suites there. It was empty, and her business was to inspect. Third was a territory very different from Eighth. Its main corridor was broader, more deeply carpeted, more richly decorated, its ceiling loftier. The corridor alone sufficed to establish in every heart the conviction that wealth abounded and that no price could be too high for tranquillity and the perfection of silent and luxurious service. Even a vacuum-cleaner, at work on the crimson carpet, seem to purr like a tiger tamed and domesticated to the uses of the lords of the earth. And the menials of the staff moving upon humble tasks seemed to apologise to the invisible lords for their own miserable existence.

The suite was planned similarly to that of Sir Henry Savott on Eighth, but on a vaster scale: a large entrance-hall, a large bathroom full of gadgets unknown on Eighth, a huge bedroom on one side and a huge sitting-room on the other. Brocaded upholstery everywhere, multiplicity of lamps, multiplicity of cushions, multiplicity of occasional tables; everywhere a yielding, acquiescent softness.

Everything that the caprice of infinite power might demand, and yet emptiness, a total absence of individuality, of humanity. A feeling in the rooms of expectancy, awaiting with everlasting patience the arrival of life-giving, imperious, exacting lords of the earth. In the bedroom, twin-beds covered with silk till the lords should come, destined to receive upon their resilient springs and their pillows the delicate sensitive bodies of lord and lady fresh perfumed from the bath. Thereon they would deign to recline, repose, slumber, perhaps snore. Strange thought!

The blinds were up, the heavy double curtains drawn apart. Violet looked out of the windows, opened them, saw the trees which obstructed Sir Henry Savott's view, tested every lamp--there were thirty-seven--tested every tap, every gadget, pulled down the blinds, pulled the curtains together, opened every drawer and every cupboard, tried every key and knob and bolt, passed a hand along ledges to discover dust, bending down in order to descry dust on glass-tops of tables. And made notes.

A tap in the bathroom which obstinately dripped. In the sitting-room a lamp whose filament had 'gone.' A curtain-hook which had escaped from its ring. Flowers required. Small stain on a white linen cover of one of the pedestals in the bedroom. And a large dark stain on the bedroom carpet, very noticeable and ugly. Also a drawer unlined with paper in the chief wardrobe, and only eight coat-hangers in the wardrobe--not enough. Quite a list! She knew the machinery for remedying every defect except the stain on the immense carpet in the bedroom. Neither lord nor lady could hope to be able to sleep peacefully in a bedroom with a stained carpet. The physical side of the complex enterprise of living which these lords and ladies had invented was indeed extremely difficult for themselves and extremely arduous for their attendants. From the bedroom Violet heard voices in the entrance-hall. An arriving visitor. She saw through the open door a dapper and diplomatic reception clerk, and Sir Henry Savott.

"Yes," Sir Henry was saying. "I'll come back at once to my old rooms. I've nothing to complain of upstairs, and the outlook is much finer there; but it's all too small. I find I can't manage. So if you don't mind I'll come back here this afternoon. About five. Not before."

"Certainly, Sir Henry. Certainly."

"I shall have to leave all the moving to your people, without superintendence. My man's ill." The two went into the sitting-room, and Violet heard further the voice of Sir Henry: "Now as regards this desk. There's a desk in my sitting-room upstairs that I should prefer to this one. Can it be brought down?"

"Certainly, Sir Henry. Certainly."

Then the two came to the bedroom. Violet was a little nervous. She prepared a discreet smile for Sir Henry. But Sir Henry did not smile. He merely nodded perfunctorily.

"I want one of these beds taken out. It's only in the way. I had it removed before, but of course it's been brought back again"

"Certainly, Sir Henry. Naturally."

"Thank you."

The two retreated.

"That will do, thanks. I'll just look round," Violet heard Sir Henry say to the clerk. After which the entrance-door closed and Sir Henry reappeared in the bedroom, smiling and friendly.

"So you're down here now, Violet," he said, offering no explanation of his previous stiff formality.

"Yes, Sir Henry."

"Well, I'm glad I've seen you. I didn't come across you again yesterday, and I did want to thank you for looking after Jim so well. He's better. And he was very pleased to see you, very pleased. I went along to have a look at him this morning."

"Oh yes!" Violet murmured.

"And there was another thing. You succeeded brilliantly in the affair of the desk, and I was much obliged. Have you got charge here to-day?"

"Yes, Sir Henry."

"Well, that relieves my mind. I know I shall be safe. Goodbye for the present." And off he hurried.

To Violet it was all very odd. And the stained carpet troubled her. She went to the corridor service-telephone and was lucky to get Miss Maclaren in her own room. She wanted counsel from Mac, who at once reassured her as to the carpet.

"It's a really bad stain?" asked Mac.

"Frightful."

"People *are* careless. How big is it?"

"About a foot square at least."

"All right. Don't bother. I'll see to it."

"But can it be done before five?"

"Of course. Look under one of the corners of the carpet. Doesn't matter which. You'll see a tab with a number on it. Give me the number."

Whereupon the neophyte of the Imperial Palace learnt that every carpet in the Palace had its exact duplicate, in size and shape, at the Works Department in Craven Street, and that an exchange could be effected in a couple of hours at most. Violet was impressed by the reckless grandeur of the domestic machine.

"And I say, Violet," continued Mac. "There's just come up another order. You are to come back to Eighth this afternoon. I don't know why. But I expect it's struck them at last that what I said to them about your being up here with me for a bit was only common sense. I'm so glad."

"So am I," Violet replied, too astonished and disturbed to respond adequately to Mac's gladness. Those mysterious powers down below were more mysterious than ever. To them you were no better than chessmen on a chessboard. And you had no better right to question them than the chessmen the chess-players.

2.

The tone of sincerity which Miss Maclaren had used in the phrase "I'm so glad" remained warmly in Violet's mind. It was clear that the head-housekeeper really did want to make a friend of her. Apparently Mac had few friends or none on the staff. Miss Venables and Miss Prentiss had shown reserve in their references to her at lunch on the previous day. Violet guessed that while they neither liked nor disliked their new superior they were perhaps preparing themselves to be restive under what they feared might prove to be a too strict and exacting régime. Why has she taken to me?" Violet thought. "There's no contrast between us. We're much the same." Yet she well knew that they differed in at least one important aspect. Both of them conscientious and industrious, Mac was victimised by a tendency to harassed gloom, but Violet was animated by a tendency to cheerfulness. Violet had a desire always to lift Mac out of a pit of depression, and she was aware that the satisfaction of the desire would demand a slightly wearisome continuous moral effort on her part. She felt sorry for Mac, more sorry for her than fond of her. And in some strange way she felt sorry also for Sir Henry Savott; felt as though she ought to remain on Third until he was entirely comfortable there, until she had assured herself that all his requirements, whatever they might be, had been fulfilled. She had a personal relation to Sir Henry, and nobody on the staff could understand his temperament as she understood it. At bottom, beneath all his imperious demeanour, he was a bit helpless, was Sir Henry.

Coming out of Sir Henry's suite, she met Mr. Perosi, the head of all the floor-waiters, the jealous commander of twenty-five or thirty men. A tall, broad, heavy, grey-haired fellow (French despite his name), whose weight pressed too hard on his feet, which were generally tired and sore.

"Excuse me, Mr. Perosi--you are Mr. Perosi, aren't you?" The middle-aged functionary, stopping, slowly nodded his head and gave Violet the faintest fatigued sardonic smile. "I don't know a thing yet about flowers here. And I want some for this suite. What do I do?"

"You telephone down to the flower-shop. You know the flower-shop?"

"Never heard of it."

"It's on the right in the corridor between the hall and the grill-room. They always have carnations and roses. And if you want any special flowers for a visitor at any time, you can always get them. A visitor orders a bouquet of orchids at midnight--well any time after eight o'clock you telephone to the manager's office. They have a key of the shop there when it's closed, and whoever is on duty opens the shop and sends you up orchids--or anything else. Of course in the ordinary way all flowers are taken out of the sitting-rooms at seven in the morning every morning, and the vases put into the corridor and they go down to the flower-shop to be examined. They're back again before nine, changed or freshened, you see. Bedroom flowers are changed when the visitors have left their rooms. It is very simple, Miss Powler."

"Oh!" Violet exclaimed eagerly. "You are kind. I was wondering how it was all arranged. Thanks very much. Sorry to trouble you." She thought, pleased: "He knows my name." Mr. Perosi's glance became benevolent, paternal.

"If you want to know anything else, come and ask me. Fourth is the floor to find me. End of the corridor." He pointed.

"There was something else, but I oughtn't--"

"What?" Perosi was suddenly harsh.

"I hardly like to ask you. But I've decided to try to learn French. I suppose there are plenty of Frenchmen on your staff, Mr. Perosi. I only thought--"

"I'm French," said Perosi in his perfect colloquial English. "My father was born in Milan, but I'm French. So you wish to learn French? That is good. I will see. Come to me to-night. I will see."

"You *are* kind. But I'm returning to Eighth this afternoon."

"And then? What does that matter? Telephone to me." He passed on his way.

"Why don't they like him?" Violet thought, meaning the other housekeepers. "He's a dear."

A sensation of happiness flowed into her, but it did not quite destroy the vague unease which had been set up by the incomprehensible order to go back to Eighth.

Chapter 36 MESS LUNCH

A very small room, so small that the telephone had to be precariously perched on the window-sill. Photographs of seductive, acquiescent, provocative and lightly clad girls on the walls; also two photographs in a different style, on either side of the long, low window--portraits respectively of Maître Planquet, chef of the restaurant kitchens, and of Commendatore Rocco, chef of the grill kitchens. The latter was a new addition to the walls. An oval table, relatively large, occupied most of the room. Indeed there was no other furniture except chairs and a small sideboard well stocked with bottles.

Seated at the table were Adolphe, the rosy-cheeked Reception-manager; Major Linklater, a tall, thin, retired army-officer whose business it was to fly about in aeroplanes and meet customers on liners at Southampton, Cherbourg and Plymouth, and know them and all concerning them; Immerson, the young, slim publicity-manager, whose dandyism of attire rivalled even that of Mr. Dacker and Mr. Smiss (the youthful members of the Board); Pozzi, the assistant-manager; and Commendatore Rocco.

The Commendatore, sole member of the staff with an honorific title, dominated the table. A big man and a grim man, he was dressed professionally in gleaming stainless white, and had a white cap on his mighty head. The Commendatore, chief guest of the mess on this great occasion, spoke little or not at all. When he did speak he used Italian to Adolphe (who could chatter colloquially in most civilised languages) and French to the others. His voice was deep, nearly a growl; and his soul was deeper. Perhaps even he himself had never plumbed his soul quite to the bottom. He had a sardonic, observant eye. He noticed his portrait hung on an equality with Maître Planquet's, and made no remark thereon. But he thought: "And not too soon!" Not that the Commendatore was jealous of the wider reputation of Maître Planquet! No. He merely desired due recognition of the fact that Maître Planquet was not the only chef in the Imperial Palace. The Commendatore was much older than the Maître. He was a relative of the once-famous Rocco of the Grand Babylon Hotel, but never mentioned the fact. His career had included several of the supreme restaurants, and the kitchen of a deceased Rothschild. He had refused a startlingly munificent offer from New York, with a memorable aside to a friend: *"Ce sont des barbares, les New-Yorkais."* He had been a known chef when Maître Planquet was an infant, and in the privacy of his mind he regarded the Maître as a promising youngster to whom he could teach a thing or two if he chose and if the youngster would learn. He had never done anything save cook or superintend cooking and play "manila," called by the Commendatore "maniglia," a card-game which he preferred because it could be played by any number of gamblers from two to five; his principal subordinates took care to learn it. But now he had yielded to golf while the world wondered. A new and very special club in a pliant case was propped against the wall in a corner of the room, ready for presentation to the Commendatore.

Such was the mess (a mess without a name) and its guest. Two other guests had yet to arrive. Mr. Orcham and Mr. Cousin, and two empty chairs seemed to be growing impatient for their arrival. A couple of waiters circled restlessly around the table, showing their expertise by not getting in each other's way. From time to time the Commendatore growled to them an imperious enquiry, which they respectfully answered. The Commendatore, beneath his sardonic calm, was somewhat nervous for the plenary success of the repast which he had composed and supervised with the nicest captious attention down below. Cocktails were being sipped.

At half-past twelve Evelyn entered, smiling. Everybody stood.

"I'm not late," said he. "But I'm not used to these early hours."

The mess lunch was always at twelve-thirty, partly because that was the continental hour for lunch, and partly because it fitted in with the duties of the staff better than the English hour. Evelyn took his seat at the head of the table, and the others resumed their chairs.

"Where's my friend Cousin?" he asked.

"Coming, sir--we hope," said Major Linklater.

"Damn that hammering," said Evelyn. "I must stop it." He rose.

"That's what we all say," said the Major.

The Imperial Palace was in a continuous state of structural improvement, and a band of workmen were busy on a roof just below the level of the window. But before Evelyn could reach the window, the noise ceased as by magic. Workmen's dinner hour.

"You have only to rise, sir," laughed Adolphe.

"I'm sure Mr. Cousin won't mind if we start--will he, Pozzi?"

"Certainly not, sir."

The meal began at once.

"Ah!" said Evelyn. "Hot hors d'œuvre! So you're going on with that idea of yours, Commendatore. I've not had this one before."

The Commendatore replied:

"My director, no one has had this before. I invent six new ones every day. Another two days, and it will be a month since I began. That will make one hundred and eighty-six new combinations. That is work, if I may dare to say so. I have been reserving this one expressly for to-day." He ate reflectively, critically, appreciatively, as though listening with attention to a new poem or piece of concerted music. "Yes, truly it is not bad. The mushrooms, prepared like this...It is necessary to drink sherry with it. As for me, I never touch sherry; but sherry should go with it."

All the lunchers eagerly lauded the novel dish. Sherry was served. Evelyn forbade the wine-waiter with a gesture.

"Vittel," he murmured. And aloud to the Commendatore:

'We don't get these in the restaurant."

The glance of the Commendatore signified: "Of course you do not. The restaurant is only the restaurant, but the grill is the grill." His growling tongue said: "My director, if once you would come to the grill--"

"I will. *Demain, sans faute,"* Evelyn answered.

"I shall be too honoured, my director. Lunch?"

"Lunch."

"I shall give myself the pleasure of occupying myself with it specially."

On the rare occasions when he did not lunch privately, Evelyn lunched in a corner of the restaurant. He realised that he would be well advised to divide his patronage less unequally.

2.

The Commendatore had the same thought, and his tone, though formally submissive, did not hide the thought and was not meant to hide it. He glanced as it were stealthily about him. Publicity men, managerial men, reception men, even the Director himself: what were they? Naught! He, Rocco, was the sole artist and creator in the room. He alone really understood. The others, kindly, and clever enough in their way, were savages. *La haute cuisine.* He dreamed. Golf--not serious, a game, a diversion. *La haute cuisine.* Not fifty people in the world were equipped by education and natural taste to comprehend it. Planquet might comprehend that hors d'œuvre. Yes, possibly the youngster would comprehend it. Yes, he must admit that the youngster would. The Director comprehended wines, cigars. That he knew, though it was almost incredible that an Englishman should comprehend any wine but champagne. And even champagne...With their mania for *extra sec!* It was time the Director patronised the grill. Not to do so amounted to an insult. But he, Rocco, was truly too benevolent. He might retire, for in Italy he would be a rich man. Or he could choose between a dozen high situations. But after all, the Imperial Palace--there were not two of *them!* And Rocco was extremely flattered that day. The artist despised, but the man admired, the *chic* of his hosts; he in white, they in black. And golf! Very smart, golf. The entry into society, into the *beau monde.* He, son of a small rice-grower!

The telephone-bell rang. Pozzi jumped to it and listened; then sat down.

"Mr. Cousin is detained," said he, and after a moment added: "Sir Henry Savott."

"What about Savott?" Evelyn questioned.

"It is he who is detaining Mr. Cousin."

Evelyn rose and stepped across to the telephone himself.

"Manager's office, please...that you, Cousin? Orcham speaking. You have Sir Henry Savott with you. I only wanted to tell you this. There is no accommodation on Eighth. You understand?...Yes. Right."

Nobody understood what the instruction implied. It made them all think, uneasily, but agreeably too; the suggestion of a skirmish between the

Director and an important visitor was always exciting. Even Adolphe, who knew everything about visitors, was at a loss to understand the instruction. Evelyn sat down again, and in a gay tone immediately addressed Adolphe:

"Well, Adolphe, how are you getting on with that novel I lent you?" Evelyn read a large number of books--nobody knew when--and he talked of what he read. The novel was the latest example of the fashionable, brilliant, daring variety, which had been recommended for suppression by the godly and which not to have read amounted to a social solecism.

"I finished it last night, sir," said Adolphe. "I should call it mild. The chapter in the underground bakehouse between the girl and the baker nude down to the waist is not bad, but I'm afraid they wouldn't think much of its realism in Czecho-Slovakia." Everybody laughed, for Czecho-Slovakia was one of Adolphe's weaknesses.

"Now don't boast, Adolphe," said Major Linklater. "You aren't a Czecho-Slovakian. You wish to heaven you were."

"I very nearly was," Adolphe innocently retorted.

"Yes, we've heard that story about a million times," said Major Linklater. "So spare us, my beamish boy."

"I wish somebody would tell me the meaning of that word 'beamish'," Adolphe retorted. "It isn't in the dictionary."

"And it never will be," said the Major. "It would set any dictionary on fire, and there'd be a smell of sulphur. You have to be English and you have to have your name put down for it when you're eight years old, and then perhaps the high-priest will vouchsafe to you its meaning when you're eighteen. Otherwise you haven't an earthly. Tell us about the bakehouse scene."

After Adolphe had picturesquely and boldly described the bakehouse scene, which had been discussed at hundreds of dinner-tables, in and out of the Imperial Palace, Major Linklater went on, to Evelyn:

"May I have that book, sir, after Adolphe? I should love to know what Adolphe thinks would be thought mild in Czecho-Slovakia."

"I'll make a present of it to the mess," said Evelyn. "Then you can talk bawdy and everyone can join in."

"Dr. Johnson," murmured young Dr. Constam.

"Noble sir!" exclaimed Major Linklater. "Gentlemen! The health of the noble Director."

There was some applause, actual clapping of hands, amid which the next dish was introduced into the room--a John Dory fish, cooked and sauced from an absolutely original recipe of the only creative artist present.

"Serve me first," the Commendatore gruffly told the waiter.

"I am not very sure of this dish." He tasted.

"That goes," he growled with relief, and glanced at the Director, who tasted.

"This is quite new to me," said the Director.

"Yes, my director," said the Commendatore, grimly triumphant. "And to the world."

"First time on any stage!" said Major Linklater. "Gentlemen, we drink to the success of the Commendatore's novelty."

Suddenly, after a lot more benevolent badinage, young Dr. Constam said in his quiet, cheerful, modest voice:

"I have a piece of really stupendous news."

"Don't hesitate," Evelyn encouraged him.

"Perosi has at last fallen."

"Down the lift-well?" Adolphe surmised.

"For a woman." Dr. Constam looked round as if to say:

"Beat that if you can!"

"What! Old flatfoot?"

"The same. I think his relations with our glittering bevy of housekeepers have always been very correct. But distant. Oh yes, distant. Well, I happened to meet him this morning, and it's a positive fact that he began all on his own talking about the new housekeeper--I forget her name."

"Didn't know there was a new housekeeper," Major Linklater said.

"No. You're always a month or so behind the times," said Adolphe. "If the Palace was burnt down you wouldn't hear of it till it'd been rebuilt. Well, who is she?"

"Her name is Powler," said Evelyn.

"Well," Dr. Constam continued. "As I say, he began talking about her. Said she was very agreeable and serious. And she wants to learn French, and he's going to give her lessons himself."

"No bakehouse scenes, I hope." Adolphe laughed.

Young Immerson, sitting next to him, pressed his foot hard on Adolphe's toe.

"He used to be a schoolmaster," said Evelyn calmly. "Commendatore, tell me something about this most distinguished sauce, will you?"

All were subtly aware of a certain constraint. And the conversation faltered and lost its gaiety until after the fish had been removed. Not a word more as to Perosi, or as to Violet Powler. Then young Pozzi looked at his watch.

"Your chief doesn't seem to be coming," said Evelyn.

"Doesn't look like it...Will you make the presentation, sir?"

"Most assuredly not," said Evelyn. "This is a hotel-staff affair. If Mr. Cousin isn't here, you're his second-in-command, and you must perform the ceremony."

At which Pozzi, with a graceful timidity which delighted Evelyn, went to the corner, seized the golf-club and handed it in its case to the Commendatore with ten halting words in Italian. The Commendatore had to pretend to be surprised, and the company had to pretend that the great golfer of the immediate future would be Commendatore Rocco and that the sequel would play hell with the grill-kitchens and ruin the whole hotel.

"I think I may add one thing," said Evelyn. "Rocco has the ideal temperament for a good golfer. It's like a rock. Gentlemen, fill your glasses." They all stood. Even Rocco, disproving Evelyn's statement as to the rockiness of his temperament, stood, from sheer nervousness.

The ceremony was finished, and the meal finished very quietly afterwards. Mr. Cousin had failed to appear. Men looked at their watches. Staff-lunches had to be rapid at the Imperial Palace. Soon all, except Evelyn and Immerson, had gone--Rocco first, with his magnificent club, his pride as a creative artist, and his dream of triumph over eighteen holes.

The two laggards were standing, while Immerson held a gold lighter to Evelyn's cigarette.

"Can you spare me a minute, sir?" Immerson suggested with his customary deference.

3.

Evelyn nodded. The senior of the waiters had already departed; the other was in the tiny service-room which adjoined the mess-room. Immerson happened to be one of Evelyn's young pets, perhaps the chief among them. He was a quiet fellow who spoke, when he did speak, in a low, restrained voice. At the luncheon he had said hardly a word. He had been at the Imperial Palace only three years, and was still a few months under thirty. He had come out of the blue to see Evelyn. When Evelyn had enquired what had decided him to leave general advertising in order to specialise in hotel advertising, he had answered: "My Christian names, sir. An omen. A signpost." His Christian names by chance were "Frederick Gordon"--name of one of the pioneers of the modern British hotel world. When Evelyn had asked him what were his leading ideas about the hotel business from his point of view he had answered: "It's no use waiting for business to come in You have to go out and get it. And you won't get it by display-ads of the kind you're putting now in London dailies. Londoners don't use London hotels, except their restaurants, and even if your restaurant is full your hotel won't pay if your bedrooms are empty."

Immerson was engaged, on salary plus commission. He stopped all the Palace's newspaper advertising in London, and was running campaigns in the provinces and abroad for the inculcation of a theory that London, the world's centre, was a jolly and bright city, and for depreciating the attractions of the Riviera and other resorts. He ran also columns of gossip in many provincial papers, and in these columns the words "Imperial Palace" constantly appeared, as though by accident. He never paid for space in a newspaper.

He had seized with enthusiasm upon Evelyn's scheme for establishing an "Imperial Palace" bureau in New York, and had improved on it by persuading non-competing luxury hotels throughout Europe and in Egypt to co-operate in sharing the advantages and the expense thereof. His recent visit to the United States had been a very brilliant success. Incidentally, one of its results was to multiply the functions of Major Linklater, the hotel's official welcomer to England's shores. Evelyn's final verdict on Immerson was that the young man had more, and more original and more audacious, imagination than any other person on the staff. "This boy," Evelyn had said to himself, "must be co-opted to the Board as soon as Lingmell has the grace to retire--if not sooner."

"Forgive me," Immerson began, leaning against the mess-table. "No doubt you have noticed the drop in North Atlantic shares these last few days."

North Atlantic was the illustrious company which owned the fleet of liners all of whose names ended in "us."

"I have not," Evelyn answered. "Why should I? Because transatlantic liners are called 'floating hotels'?"

"They fell several shillings yesterday, and they're falling still more to-day. And to-morrow they'll probably go down with a bump."

"Why?"

"The 'Daily Mercury' is coming out to-morrow with a terrific stunt about that splitting of one of the decks on the 'Caractacus'. They've been collecting all the details, and they've found a woman who had her thigh broken in a lurch of the ship during the voyage. The Company has paid her handsomely to hold her tongue, but some women can't rely on themselves to do that." Immerson gave a faint smile. "The 'Daily Mercury' is bound to lose some steamer advertising, but it doesn't carry much, and it reckons that what it loses on the swings it will make on the roundabouts. Anyhow the story'll be a great story. It's quite possible that traffic will be affected."

"Not for long."

"No. But even a month is too long for us. If traffic's affected we shall be affected. You see--forgive me for reminding you, sir--the 'Caractacus' is German built, and there are several other German-built ships on the New York services. They'll all be affected, especially as the 'Caractacus' is laid up for what's called reconditioning. The 'Mercury' will go on the anti-German lay. I've been to the North Atlantic people this morning and offered them a few hints on how to react. And I'm going again this afternoon, if you approve, sir. I think I can get something in one of to-morrow's papers, the 'Echo'--it has a bigger circulation than even the 'Mercury'."

"You go right on," said Evelyn. "I leave it to you."

"Thank you, sir. But I haven't come to the point yet."

"Oh?"

"No, sir. From what I hear, our friend Sir Henry Savott is at the bottom of all this. He's a very large shareholder in North Atlantic, and my private information is that one reason for the fall in the shares is that he's been unloading heavily. He'll buy in again when the fall has reached its limit, and he might make a couple of hundred thousand over the thing in the end...No, not that much; but quite a lot."

"Is he a director of North Atlantic?"

"Oh no, sir. If he had been he daren't have done it. No! He's far too clever to be a director. But I daresay he has a director or two in his pocket."

"Well," said Evelyn, masking an excusable agitation. "It's all very interesting--very interesting indeed. When you say that Savott is at the bottom of it, do you mean he's at the bottom of the 'Mercury' stunt as well?"

"Nothing would surprise me less, sir," Immerson replied with characteristic caution.

"I must go now," said Evelyn, not because he was due for another appointment, but because he wanted to be alone.

"Pardon me for detaining you, sir," Immerson deferentially apologised.

The other waiter returned, and the next moment the two waiters, busy clearing the table in the room now deserted by their betters, were freely discussing in French the alluring details of the bakehouse chapter.

Chapter 37 THE NEW MILLIONAIRE

The next night Evelyn, with time to spare after a busy forenoon and afternoon of varied diplomatic and administrative toil, was putting on a dinner-jacket at leisure in his bedroom. He had in his mind a surfeit of matter for meditation.

Having returned to the Imperial Palace from an excursion as to which Evelyn knew nothing except that it had included Paris, Sir Henry Savott had suggested a second interview and had invited him to dinner. Evelyn had found an excuse for insisting that the meeting should occur in the same place as the first one, his own dunghill or castle. He would not give up the advantage of the ground which he had chosen.

Sir Henry's proposal had occupied his thoughts for days. He had pretended to himself that he had come to no decision, even a tentative decision, about it. But the pretence was a failure. He had tried, in vain, to discover good reasons for declining the proposal without any further discussion. He had talked it over with Dennis Dover, and the throaty old man had obviously felt the attraction of the offer. It was an offer which appealed to his imagination, as to Evelyn's. It was a grandiose, glittering offer. It might have drawbacks, pitfalls, snares; acceptance of it would necessarily be preceded by a terrific battle of terms and conditions; but father Dennis had made plain his view that it ought not to be turned down out of hand. Evelyn agreed; impossible for him to disagree. The temptations of the offer, to Evelyn, were tremendous, and the more he reflected upon them, the more tremendous they seemed and were. Evelyn was like a man who hesitates and fears to admit that he is in love with a beautiful, dangerous woman; yet well knows that he is in her power.

Also father Dennis had said: "I can't live for ever. What will happen to my shares if I die? My grand-nephew will happen to them, because nobody else can happen to them."

Of course, by the Resolution passed at the Special Meeting and very soon to be formally ratified, the Board of Directors would still have control of the Imperial Palace Hotel Company, and could in theory ride over any shareholder, however large. But in practice it might be difficult to do so. The moral factor in the situation would count. At best, that notorious grand-nephew, old Dennis being dead, could not be refused a seat on the Board; and a director who is the largest shareholder in a concern can hardly be ignored. Anything might occur; trouble would assuredly occur. Whereas if the Imperial Palace became merely the leading item in a vast merger, the incalculable grand-nephew would be deprived of his paramount importance. There were other pointers to an acceptance of Sir Henry's proposal, and not the least of them was Evelyn's secret instinct and inclination growing daily within him.

And then had come young Immerson's tidings, followed by the highly sensational stunt article in the "Daily Mercury," which had reverberated throughout London, and was a chief topic of conversation; and North

Atlantic shares had had a fall as sensational as the article, though later in the day they had risen again somewhat. Could Evelyn bring himself to have dealings with the man who, he was convinced, was primarily responsible for the stunt and the fall? The notion revolted him. Accustomed to rapid and definitive judgments, he was for once embarrassed by genuine irresolution. In twenty minutes he would be face to face with Sir Henry, and he had not decided what attitude to adopt. His mental discomfort was extreme.

And there was something else, more strange. The affair of Violet Powler. He had heard--and not by chance--that Savott had moved from the Third to the Eighth floor. Cousin had told him of the change as a phenomenon quite extraordinary, inexplicable. Why should a millionaire leave the rich spaciousness of Third for the small rooms of Eighth? Savott's specified reasons--the better view and the greater tranquility--had appeared to Cousin remarkably insufficient. Evelyn had feigned to regard them as sufficient and had dismissed the caprice as trifling. But in fact he had been perturbed by it. Savott had spoken with appreciation of Violet. Violet had the excellences of her sister. Savott had nearly married the sister, on his own admission. He knew that Violet was entering the service of the Imperial Palace. Evelyn had the absurd suspicion that Savott, having somehow learnt on his arrival that Violet was to be stationed on Eighth, had gone up there with the intention of renewing relations with her, of reconsidering her. Yes, an absurd suspicion. But, entertaining it, Evelyn had deviously arranged that Violet should descend to Third. Then Savott had returned to Third. The suspicion ceased to be absurd, and grew into a positive certainty...And why should not Savott seek to renew relations with Violet? Violet was well able to take care of herself. Beyond any doubt she was not at all the sort of young woman to be deceived by even the cleverest speciousness. As old Perosi had said, she was 'serious.' But Evelyn did not like the look of the thing. Violet was safe. Savott might be perfectly honest. He, Evelyn, had no interest in Violet except as, in a sense, a protégée. He simply did not like the look of the thing. It annoyed him. It outraged him. He would not allow Savott to play any games in his hotel. Never! He had control of the situation, and he would exercise his control.

So he had restored Violet to Eighth, and had instructed Cousin to inform Savott that there was now no accommodation on Eighth. Not that he knew that Savott had been suggesting to Cousin a return to Eighth. Cousin had volunteered nothing about the nature of the interview with Savott. And Evelyn had not questioned Cousin. Either he was too proud to question his manager, or he feared to receive an answer which might entirely demolish his theory of the inwardness of Savott's odd peregrinations. He would not have Violet on the same floor as her former employer, and he had no wish to argue the point. The point was decided. Funny! It was all extremely funny, a lark, a regular game. Evelyn laughed aloud: a harsh, sinister laugh. He had had an impulse to ask Oldham whether Oldham was acquainted with Savott's valet. But, again, pride had stopped him.

2.

At this very moment Oldham entered the bedroom. The flabby face of the stoutish, unkempt man was transfigured by some mighty emotion. Evelyn noticed this, but he ignored it in a sudden determination to let pride go and question Oldham.

"Do you know Sir Henry Savott's valet?" he demanded at once.

Oldham was dashed, as by an unexpected obstacle.

"Well, sir, I *know* him. He's been ill."

"Yes, so I heard."

"I don't really know him. As you may see, sir, when I tell you he's never told me his surname. But we've had one or two chats. He being a valet, and me too."

"Ever talked to him about our housekeepers?"

"Well, sir, we may have mentioned it."

"He asked you?"

"Now I come to think of it, I believe he did speak about the new one--Miss Powler. Just in the way of talk."

"Did you tell him anything?"

"No, sir. I couldn't. I didn't know anything, except she'd come from the Laundry. Seems she used to be with Sir Henry, sir. *He* told me that. Else I doubt if I should have remembered it. Yes, and he asked me what floor she was on, and I told him. Then when I saw him day before yesterday--was it?--and he was up and about, and Miss Powler had been moved to Third, he happened to ask me what floor she'd been moved to."

"And you told him?"

"Yes, sir."

"Well," said Evelyn stiffly, in a tone somewhat censorious. "I wish you wouldn't gossip about hotel affairs to visitors' servants." He knew that the reproach was unfair, but he would not admit to himself that it was unfair.

"Sorry, sir," Oldham apologised, but with a strange, surprising, defiant stiffness far surpassing Evelyn's stiffness.

"That's all. What do you want? I didn't ring."

"No, sir. The fact is I've just heard something, and I thought you might like to know. Sorry if it's inconvenient." Oldham was wounded. He made a move to retire.

"What is it?"

"Well, sir. It's like this. I've won that thousand pounds. I've had a letter this minute."

"What thousand pounds?"

"Football Results Competition, sir. It'll be in next Sunday's paper. I have to call and see them myself to get the cheque. And they want me to be photographed."

"I congratulate you," said Evelyn with a charming sympathetic smile. "It's the best piece of news I've heard for a long time."

"Thank you, sir," said Oldham, quickly mollified, but still sturdily--man to man, not as valet to master.

Evelyn had lied. It was not the best piece of news he had heard for a long time; it was the worst. He divined instantly that he would lose Oldham. He was overset by a feeling that Oldham was necessary to him, that existence without Oldham would be impossible. A marvellous, an incredible thing had happened in the life of Oldham. The man was vibrating with heavenly joy. Evelyn, as his friend, ought to have shared the joy. He did not. He hardly made an attempt to enter into Oldham's unique sensations. He even resented Oldham's astounding luck, simply because one consequence of the luck meant that he, Evelyn, would be for a period incommoded.

"So I expect you'll be leaving?" he said, and waited for the reply as for the death-sentence from a judge.

"I won't leave you till it suits you, sir," Oldham replied. "Certainly not. You've always been very kind to me, sir, and I'd like to be--" He stopped, realising that for a valet, even a wealthy valet, to offer to be very kind to his employer would be a too daring sin against established convention.

Yes, the fellow would leave. He had evidently decided to leave. It would be nothing to him to break the lien that had bound him and his master together in daily, intimate habit and intercourse. Servants were all alike, incapable of gratitude. And they were all children. Now you would have taken Oldham for a sensible man. But was he? How could he be, if a thousand pounds was enough to induce him to abandon a secure livelihood? The truth was that when a sum of money passed a certain figure servants ceased to be able to estimate its value. As Central African natives could not count beyond ten, so 'they' could not count beyond, say, a hundred or a couple of hundred. To Oldham a thousand pounds was as good as a million, as good as ten millions; it was infinity--and therefore inexhaustible. And Oldham was drunk with bliss.

"That's very good of you, Oldham," said Evelyn. "But of course you must tell me when. Got any plans?"

"Well, sir, I was thinking I might do worse than buy a little tobacconist's business. You see them advertised. I saw one the other day on sale for two hundred pounds cash. Camberwell. Camberwell's a very nice part, don't you think so, sir?"

"Yes, I think it is."

The usual thing. Tobacconist's business! Why a tobacconist's business? Did Oldham know anything about tobacco, and buying and selling, and dealing with customers, and so on and so on? He did not. He just pictured himself standing behind a counter and smoking a cigarette or a pipe or even a cigar, and handing out packets of cigarettes and matches and pipes and an occasional cigar, and raking in money all the time and chatting in a worldly, benevolent, easy fashion with customers. The ideal life for the Oldhams of the earth! Simpletons! Fools! Blasted fools! Within a year the man's capital would be halved. Within two years he wouldn't have a cent. He would be on the streets, seeking a situation in the cushiony sort of job that he was now so idiotically preparing to quit! Could you believe it of a man such as Oldham? Well, you could. It was exactly what you ought to expect.

"Excellent!" said Evelyn, amiably and without conviction. "But be careful how you buy. You'd better consult me before you do anything. Or better still, talk to someone down in the audit office. You'd need an expert to go into the figures. I've heard some funny tales about this business-buying business. There are swindlers who make a regular trade of it."

"Oh!" said Oldham, magnificently self-confident in his opulence. "I shall be careful. I think I may say you know me, sir. But I'm much obliged to you, sir, and when the time comes I shall ask your advice."

Nincompoop! Noodle! *Folie des grandeurs!*

Then Evelyn softened, little by little. The man was entitled to his own life. He was entitled to leave if it suited him to leave. And as for the gratitude which masters are continually expecting, and not receiving, from their servants--what about Evelyn's gratitude due to Oldham for efficient and faithful service during years and years? Did Evelyn feel it? He did not. He felt resentment. He strove to conquer his resentment, and to some small extent he succeeded. After all, Oldham was not a thief, nor a slacker, nor incompetent. He was a fortunate man, thanks to his encyclopædic knowledge of form in Association Football. Evelyn dismissed him with a gentle pat on the shoulder, which delighted Oldham and confirmed him in his new creed that all men are equal. Evelyn smiled, but far down beneath the smile he was extremely perturbed and pessimistic. He cursed these newspapers which would increase their already vast circulations by appealing to the gambling instincts of the populace.

Chapter 38 FALSE REPRIEVE

"You taught me something that honestly I didn't know about cigars," said Sir Henry at a quarter to ten that evening, as he lit one of Evelyn's cigars after the second dinner in Evelyn's fortress. He added, looking meditatively at the bright end of the cigar: "But I'm certain to forget. I always light a cigar about five times. It's a habit, and I shall never get over it." He laughed carelessly.

"You didn't forget last time, once I'd made my protest," said Evelyn.

"Didn't I?" Sir Henry's tone indicated that really he couldn't recall what he had done or not done, and that anyhow the matter, to him, had no importance.

Gracie had remarked to Evelyn that while her father was a great man, he had the weakness of acting the great man. But during the dinner the great man had indulged in no histrionics. He had talked simply, unaffectedly, about the lighter side of his short stay in Paris, spoken of Gracie, and of the two Cheddar brothers, one of whom was also in Paris, of the big spectacular revues there specialising in naked women, and of his own inability to 'follow' a French play.

But now Evelyn's critical faculty pounced upon Sir Henry's demeanour in the cigar incident as probably a proof that Gracie had been right. He decided that what Sir Henry had really said was: "I am a great man, a unique man, and if I choose to relight a cigar, it's correct because I do it. I can afford to treat a cigar as I please, and I shan't risk any prestige by my oddness. I'm Sir Henry Savott, I am." And Evelyn in his heart rather condescended towards the conscious performer in Sir Henry.

Still, the millionaire had again proved himself an agreeable and diverting companion, sometimes charmingly ingenuous, and rarely coarse. He had said not a single word as to the proposed hotel-merger: to Evelyn's relief. For until the end of the meal the coveted panjandrum of the coveted Imperial Palace had not fully regained his self-possession. But now the would-be retail tobacconist had quitted the sitting-room for the last time, and with such a perfect affectionate deference in his final murmur to the master that Evelyn had reinstated him in esteem and liking, and the waking nightmare was dissolved, its obsession vanished away, and Evelyn's sense of proportion restored. He was in a proper condition to face the great man with assurance, and use wile against wile. As before, the great man would have to begin.

The great man did begin, on a topic which both he and his host had so far avoided. The first phenomenon was a smile, followed by a hardly audible laugh. Evelyn glanced at him interrogatively.

"I was just thinking about the 'Caractacus' fireworks in the 'Mercury' this morning. I suppose you saw it?"

"Yes," said Evelyn drily. "It was what they call 'brought to my notice.' I also saw the North Atlantic reply this afternoon in the 'Echo.' What they said about the split being caused by structural alterations of their own to make room for extra lifts was rather effective, I thought. It gives their architect away, but it sounds true, and if it's true it does save the reputation of the ship as originally built."

"The reply was very clever," said Sir Henry.

"Yes," thought Evelyn, "and if I told you it had been put together by one of the fellows on my staff here you might be a bit startled."

"Only," Sir Henry went on, "it came out about two hours too late. The North Atlantic market had gone to pieces before noon. The shares recovered a trifle this afternoon, but not much. They've had a tousling."

He rose, and walked slowly to and fro in the warm, curtained room; then stood with his back against the damask draperies of the window, and at that distance from Evelyn grew confidential:

"The 'Mercury' people came to see me about the thing last week. They wanted my evidence. I refused to tell them anything, naturally. But of course I had to be careful. If I'd shut my mouth absolutely they'd have used that to support their story, me being a very large holder of North Atlantics. So I pretended to be very open--and didn't give away anything that isn't known to at least five hundred people. You know, the comfort of those crack hell-for-leather liners is one of the most ridiculous legends ever invented by our reptile press. When I say 'reptile' I'm saying it in a Parliamentary sense. The papers aren't bribed. They don't keep the legend alive for money. The biggest steamer advertisement is nothing to a big daily. No. They keep it alive because it sounds so nice. Good copy. Symbol of luxury, and everybody wants to read about luxury. But even in good weather those rushers positively *shake* half the time. It isn't a mere vibration. It's like having electric massage all day, including at meals. And in bad weather they're no better than 12,000 tonners. Not as good. Some of 'em roll till sometimes the only way to keep yourself upright is to lie flat on the deck. They're liable to throw piles of plates across the dining-saloon, and chuck you all over your cabin. They drop from under you until you think your stomach's above your head. I mean in bad weather. The food isn't too awful, considering they have to serve five or six hundred people at once. But nobody can feed five or six hundred at once on *really* good food. It can't be done. And the prices are insane. I paid £1,000 for my suite last time I came over. And there was a bigger ass than me on board. He paid thirteen hundred. And the tips! All for 27knots! Well, I prefer 18 or 19 knots. I'll never do it again."

A pause. Evelyn said:

"On New Year's Eve here I shall serve a thousand people at once, and the food will not be too awful. It'll be the best there is."

"Ah!" murmured Sir Henry. "But you are you."

"You try it--on New Year's Eve."

"I will," said Sir Henry. "I'll make a pointof trying it."

He returned to his chair, smoking his cigar with conscious restraint.

"I don't mind telling you," he continued in a lower tone, dreamy, "as soon as the 'Mercury' people had been to see me I began to sell my North Atlantics. I sold a big packet, and I kept on selling 'em."

"And now you'll buy back," said Evelyn sardonically.

"And now I shall buy back," Sir Henry agreed. "I bought a lot this morning at rock bottom, and a lot more this afternoon a bit higher, and I'm ready for more to-morrow. I shall clear quite a lump of money on the 'Mercury' stunt. Well, one must live...And why not?"

Evelyn repeated in his mind: "And why not?"

The fact was that Savott had 'dropped from under' Evelyn's feet. The great man had been perfectly open. He had frankly confessed. No! 'Confess' was the wrong word. There had been nothing to confess. Confession implied sin. The great man had not sinned. He had behaved as any speculative investor would behave. He had not broken the code. The code was intact. It might be, as Immerson had suggested, that he was at the bottom of the 'Mercury' stunt. But that was a supposition and could never be proved. And even if he had been at the bottom of it, what then? He had not departed from the truth. The details were indisputable. The deck had split. Indeed, by smashing the age-long Fleet Street sentimental conspiracy of hush-hush about Atlantic liners, the great man, assuming what might be termed his guilt, had done good. Evelyn hated any policy of hush-hush in anything. And yet he was of pure English blood: that is to say, he had in him, so far as he knew, no tincture of Scottish, Irish, Welsh, French, German, Italian, American nor Jewish.

2.

"By the way," said Sir Henry. "I had a long talk with your man Cousin yesterday. In the end I asked him to lunch."

"What's he going to say now?" Evelyn thought. Having been twice down to Weybridge and once to the Laundry and attended a long Board meeting, he had not seen Cousin for more than a couple of minutes in the two days, and he knew nothing of the nature of the interview which had prevented Cousin from attending the luncheon given to the Commendatore.

Sir Henry proceeded:

"I heard by accident that Cousin had been connected with the Concorde in Paris and the Minerva at Cannes--"

"Yes, he was manager of the Minerva for a time," Evelyn interjected.

"So he said. Well, as both the Concorde and the Minerva are included in my proposed team, it struck me it might be useful to get some independent views about them. So I did."

"I hope you were satisfied," said Evelyn, and thought:

"Here I go again! Wrong again! I imagined he was manœuvring with Cousin to get back to Eighth. And he wasn't at all. This suspiciousness is growing on me. If I let it, I shall soon be as suspicious as a millionaire."

"On the whole," Sir Henry replied, "I was very well satisfied with the look of things. You don't mind me talking to him, do you?"

"Certainly not," said Evelyn. "Why shouldn't you?"

"I needn't tell you I didn't ask him anything about *this* place. No."

Evelyn thought: "It would have been just the same if you had." He said nothing.

Sir Henry was restless. He sat back; then demanded suddenly:

"Well, what's your decision about my proposal, Orcham?" There it was at last! The question, unexpected at that moment, hit him like a stone.

"Decision?" He repeated the word hesitatingly. "Why! I don't even know what the proposal is yet. You don't expect me to say Yes or No to a mere idea, do you?" He gazed fairly at the father of Gracie classing him as a wild, impulsive creature, for all his astuteness. Was that the way the princes of finance allowed their minds to skip from hilltop to hilltop across the landscape? Something the matter with him! He peered more boldly into Sir Henry's little, shrewd eyes, striving as it were to pierce through them into the crafty brain behind; but striving vainly. He could not even define the general expression on the man's face. It seemed a candid expression. But was it? The ruthless teeth were hidden as Sir Henry pursed his lips.

"You misunderstand me," said the financier with a smile quite gentle. "All I meant was: Have you decided to examine my proposition? Or not. If not, I won't trouble you any further. If yes, I'll put the entire scheme before you within the next day or two. All the figures and calculations. And a definite offer as to price for Imperial Palace shares, and also of course as to the terms of the contract with you personally."

Having said this, he faintly hummed a fragment of Auld Lang Syne, evidently inspired by Evelyn's reference to the New Year's Eve banquet, and inspected the burning stump of his cigar.

Evelyn had the sensation of having been reprieved; from a sentence passed not by the financier but by himself. But he knew that the sensation was false. There was no real reprieve. He knew that a decision to examine the proposition was the equivalent of a decision to sell the Imperial Palace to Savott's merger. Once the two parties began to bargain, an agreement would be ultimately certain. Nothing could stop it. Savott had a powerful supporter; that supporter was Evelyn himself. Evelyn could not seriously resist the glittering temptation which Savott dangled in front of him. One Evelyn did indeed resist, but another Evelyn was entranced by the resplendency of the promise of the future, and the first Evelyn could not for long resist unaided. It seemed to the composite Evelyn that he shut his eyes and jumped from a great height.

"Of course," he said, in an even tone. "Of course we shall be charmed to *examine* the proposal. Let us know when you're ready." He felt relieved now: a man who knows the worst.

"Good! I will," said Sir Henry cheerfully, showing his perfect teeth.

And Evelyn was whispering to himself: "My God! My God! If anyone had foretold this to me a month ago I should have--My God! My God!" A fuse had been lighted before dinner and it had gone on slowly and silently burning during dinner and after dinner, and now--the sudden explosion!

"I say," said Sir Henry. "There was one thing I wanted to mention to you. Nothing to do with this. About that girl Violet Powler."

"Yes?" Evelyn muttered, alert and hostile.

"You've only got to say no, and you can forget I've spoken. I'll forget too. I'm buying a new house. I shall want a housekeeper. Don't shoot me, I know she's in your employ, and to lose her might be rather inconvenient for you. I admit she's one in a thousand. But I knew her first. And she knows me. Now would you mind if I made her an offer of the job of housekeeper at my new house? I won't breathe it if you object. And in any case I wouldn't try to over-persuade her. No! I'd say: 'There it is, miss. Take it or leave it.' You see I'm being quite open. Perhaps I'm asking too much. Perhaps it isn't fair. I just mention it--that's all." Savott's face was the very mirror of candour and goodwill. This Savott could surely not be the cunning coarse Savott with whom and his daughter Evelyn had dined one night in the restaurant.

"My dear fellow," Evelyn exclaimed. "Naturally you must ask her. I wouldn't dream of standing in the girl's way."

A little later the two men parted, all smiles and handclasps and cordial friendliness. They might have been sworn brothers.

"Delightful castle!" said Sir Henry, quietly enthusiastic, glancing round the room. "I love it. And once more--you're really very kind. I appreciate it. Good night."

3.

Evelyn put out the lamps in the castle; and in the light of the low fire and of the corridor lamp through the wide-open doors two glasses on the table glinted mysteriously. He shut the inner door on the hot interior wherein as it seemed to him a decisive and intimidating event had occurred. This event filled his mind, but the ether of the thought of it was suffused with the ether of the thought of Savott's intentions towards Violet Powler. Evelyn had to descend to his office, and in doing so he made one of his periodical peregrinations of the hotel, walking slowly along corridors and down flights of stairs, eschewing lifts.

He saw his hotel now with a different vision, as though he had left it and come back and found it a strange land and himself a stranger in it. If he had not laughed at his own feeling he might have fallen from sentiment into sentimentality.

He had covered about a quarter of a mile of carpet, and glanced at scores of baffling numbered doors, and seen no sign of life in the nocturnal coma of the place except the swift ascent of an illuminated lift behind a steel grille, and had reached the fourth floor, when a trifling event happened such as can happen only in the multiple existence of a large hotel. He heard a door open behind him and a low shriek. He turned and saw a young, dark woman, a white bath-towel wrapped round her body, which was dripping with water.

"Fire!" she breathed, scarcely audible, hoarse in her terror. He stepped very quickly in front of her through the doorway. Instantly he had passed from out of the vast, vague anonymity of the hotel into an inhabited, circumscribed home. Garments flung and hung on a hat-stand; a short umbrella on the floor. Before him, the open door of a bathroom full of steam, and bright in the steam a great blaze arising from the glass-topped table which stood in the same spot in every bathroom. The flame, a couple of feet high, waved in a draught set up between the open window of the bathroom and the open door of the suite. The origin of the conflagration was a spirit-lamp, and its fuel a newspaper or several newspapers.

He seized the spirit-lamp, very hot to the touch, and flung itwith a single movement into the bath, which was half full of steaming soapy water. It sizzled for a fraction of a second and sank into the depths. Then he snatched at a face-towel and crushed the burning newspaper to extinction. A moment, and the danger was over. There never had been any danger, for the paper would have burnt itself out harmlessly on the glass of the table.

"All right now," he said with the calm of a consciously superior being, to the young woman who was cowering in the lobby as if to hide her bodily shame.

But Evelyn had no mercy on her bodily shame. Young women careless enough to let spirit-lamps ignite newspapers must accept all the consequences of their silly acts. This one was a beautiful thing, scarcely emerged from girlhood. (He must find out about her.) The ample bath-towel hung precariously on her, reminding him of the tantalising cover-designs of certain French, German and American illustrated weeklies in which the pose of a woman in an entirely inadequate garment has been caught at the very instant when the flimsy attire is giving way under strain to reveal that which ought not to be revealed. An instant later, and the last poor remnant of decency would be gone.

In a few seconds this very young woman had somewhat accustomed herself to the immodesty of her predicament.

"I was having a hot bath," she weakly murmured.

"So I see."

"And I got out to open the window because I was afraid I might faint--"

"You aren't all alone in here?" Evelyn questioned.

"No. My husband is there. But he's asleep and nothing would ever waken him."

Her husband! What was she doing with a husband at her age? Something shocking about it. Some fat man old enough to be her father, no doubt. Always in the Imperial Palace there were such couples, respectable and disgusting.

"Well, don't take cold," Evelyn advised the wife curtly, and quitted the excessive intimacy of the lobby for the somnolent desert of the corridor, shutting the door behind him She had offered no thanks. He had given her no chance to express gratitude.

Perosi was padding as fast as he could towards him.

"I thought I heard a scream, sir," said the ageing big man, alarmed and rather breathless.

"You did. But you've got very good ears. It's all over. Spirit-lamp in the bathroom in 415. I've put it right. Hysterical woman. The usual thing. Who are they?"

"I can't remember the name exactly. It's a queer name. The lady seems to be English. But the gentleman is a Roumanian."

"He would be," thought Evelyn, and said aloud: "Well, you needn't trouble any more. I've seen to it."

"Thank you, sir." Perosi, tranquillised, faced about to return to his cubicle-office at the end of the corridor. Then Evelyn saw Violet Powler standing hesitant at the door of Perosi's cubicle. She saw Evelyn, but did not move. Perosi faced about again.

"I wish to tell you, sir," said he to Evelyn. "I'm giving lessons in French to Miss Powler. She is very anxious to learn. I told Dr. Constam yesterday morning and Mr. Pozzi this afternoon. There's no secret about it. I hope you approve, sir."

"Of course, Perosi. By the way, I want a word with Miss Powler. Miss Powler!"...He called aloud. And to Perosi:

"Thank you, Perosi."

The old stickler for propriety, the upholder of the full strictness of the hotel code, the watcher of reputations and prerogatives, especially his own, having put himself right with the panjandrum, bowed and shuffled away towards his little room, while Violet Powler obediently came forward, and Evelyn waited for her in the deep silence of the long corridor bordered on both sides by withdrawn homes of a night.

In the light falling on her from above Evelyn noticed for the first time that her cheek-bones were set just a trifle higher than the average. Her head was certainly broader than the average. Her eyes, far apart, almost exactly matched her hair in colour. True, her lips were rather thin, but then her mouth was wide--a sign of benevolence. She walked well; no trace of anxiety, diffidence, self-consciousness in her gait. Was she distinguished, or did he imagine it? He had once by chance seen her mother, an ordinary, somewhat plaintive woman of the lower middle-class. Could the daughter of such a woman have distinction? Improbable. She was a puzzle to him...She showed no curiosity as to the cause of Perosi's alarm. For her evidently, that affair was finished and therefore had no further interest. Confident, yet modest. Reserved, yet curiously candid. Anyhow, though she was a newcomer in the world of the Imperial Palace, two important men were already competing for her, fighting for her: Savott and himself. He realised that, and in one part of his mind was amused at the thought.

"Yes, sir?"

An expression on her face of impartial but benevolent consideration--ready to deal with whatever question he might confront her with.

"I hear you're learning French," he said. "It's a very good idea. And you haven't lost time over beginning."

If she was taking her lesson, this must be her evening off--from nine o'clock. Therefore she must have been on duty at 6.30a.m. The hour was now getting late, but she seemed quite fresh, and her make-up could not have been more than an hour old. He observed the nice finish of her finger-nails, for she had clasped her hands in front of her at the level of her waist.

She smiled faintly, and said nothing, only lifting her head half an inch or so.

"This will save me the trouble of sending for you. I had something I wanted to tell you." The benevolence of his tone equalled the benevolence of her look.

"Yes, sir?"

"I've been seeing Sir Henry Savott to-night. Sir Henry has bought or is just buying a new house, and he asked me whether I should object if he offered you the post of housekeeper. He said of course you'd worked for him already--before you worked for us. I said I shouldn't dream of standing in your way. You're absolutely free. Under your contract we can give you notice and you can give us notice. A month, isn't it?"

"Yes, sir."

"Yes. A month. Well, that's how it stands. I thought I would let you know--in fact *ought* to let you know--what you may expect, and that you're under no sort of obligation to me, to us, beyond the terms of your contract. If we thought we ought to dismiss you, naturally we should dismiss you. Not that we've the least notion of doing that. Far from it. But we should feel ourselves at liberty to do it. And just the same you're at liberty to dismiss us." He smiled broadly at the last words, and Violet smiled too.

She answered:

"Thank you, sir. It's a thing that will need a lot of thinking over.

"Yes. Good night." Evelyn turned briskly to go back along the corridor the way he had come.

"Good night, sir."

"And no doubt now she'll proceed with her French lesson, as if nothing had happened!" he thought.

4.

He was shocked. He was hurt. Had he not been behaving to her in a style marvelously magnanimous? Had he not been exhibiting the very ideal and perfection of human justice? Had he not been pluming himself on a superfine and needless generosity? Most employers, if not all other employers, though some of them might have accorded the formal permission to Savott to approach the employee, would have sung a different tune to the employee herself. They would have said: "We don't expect you to leave us like this. You've just come. We've taken you into the first hotel in the world. You ought to regard yourself as extremely fortunate. We can't have our staff playing fast and loose. Sir Henry Savott ought never to have made such an extraordinary suggestion. Now he has made it we look to you to realise that you have a moral duty to us, and we hope--" etc., etc. But he, Evelyn, had been incredibly benign. And what does the girl say in reply to his benignity? "It's a thing that will need a lot of thinking over." And walks off. Yes, he was hurt. He was very disappointed in his pet housekeeper, his discovery, his protégée.

But there was the other man in Evelyn, the man who gloried in the godlike judicial quality of his mind. This man said: "I must be fair. She had something to hire out, and I hired it. In hiring her I didn't confer a favour on her. I hired her, not for her advantage, but for the advantage of the Palace. If I hadn't thought she would be a splendid asset to the Palace I should have left her where she was at the Laundry. The change may be a grand thing for her, but that wasn't why I engaged her. The notion of a moral duty on her part is simply preposterous. It makes me think of the sickening attitude people take up to their servants in private houses. The girl's absolutely entitled to give the question 'a lot of thinking over,' and to decide solely in her own interests, and to ignore my interests. Savott could certainly pay her a much better salary than we could, and in his house she wouldn't have anybody over her--except him. And he wouldn't worry her. No chain of responsibility there. The truth is she'd be an idiot not to jump at Savott's offer."

Nevertheless, he was hurt. And would the affair end with housekeepership? Might it not...She was Susan's sister.

Well, and why should it end with housekeepership?

Evelyn descended to his office depressed. He lit a cigar and tried to find his whereabouts in the confusing darkness of circumstance. If the hotel-merger came to fruition, he would be in the plight of a man with one darling child who marries into a numerous family of very miscellaneous children. He was about to lose his domestic prop, Oldham. And probably he was about to lose the pearl of housekeepers. Of course it didn't matter, really. Yet it mattered, somehow. Still, there was one gleam: she had refused Savott once when she was at the Laundry.

Chapter 39 HOUSEKEEPERS

When Violet returned to her room on Eighth she found an unstamped letter conspicuously placed on the desk. The envelope bore at the back the words "Imperial Palace." Hence the missive must be from somebody within the hotel. The handwriting of the address seemed not unfamiliar. Thus she reflected before opening the letter. It was quite a long letter: both sides of a large single sheet of notepaper. Of course she looked first at the signature: "Hy. Savott." The letter began:

"Dear Miss Powler," and contained an offer of a situation as housekeeper of a shortly-to-be-acquired house in Mayfair. The salary suggested was large. The writer said that he had obtained the permission of Mr. Evelyn Orcham to approach her about the matter. The tone of the letter was urbane, friendly, faultless: tone of an equal, not of a superior.

She felt flattered. Mr. Orcham's original statement had extremely surprised her, and the letter intensified her surprise. Yet within her was a sensation of calm self-confidence which diminished her surprise. After all was she not, with her proved and admitted efficiency (which no false modesty inclined her to doubt), a fine proposition for any wealthy householder? She had done the job satisfactorily years ago, and she knew herself capable of doing it again satisfactorily.

As for leaving the Imperial Palace so soon after entering it, Mr. Orcham's own fair words had reassured her on that point. The hotel had the right to safeguard its interests, and similarly she had the right to safeguard hers. Moreover, she was hardly satisfied with the post of floor-housekeeper. Though the hours were very long, and Violet missed the old freedom of her evenings, there was not enough work to do, and the work lacked responsibility, made insufficient demands on her powers. And she had been somewhat offended by the apparently causeless shifting from floor to floor. She could not take exception to it; nevertheless it had offended her. On the whole Sir Henry's offer tempted her. And how quiet he had been in making it! Just like him! Deliberately she withheld herself from coming to a decision, even to a provisional decision. She glanced at her watch, slipped the letter into a drawer and locked the drawer, and left the room. She had a rendezvous with Mac.

The moment she put her head into Mac's room she became aware of some disturbance in the social atmosphere--unseen lightning which played under the ceiling, unheard thunder in the distance of the corners. Three prim, tense, constrained black-frocked figures were there: Miss Maclaren sitting on the sofa; Miss Venables and Miss Prentiss standing, one on the hearthrug, the other near the desk.

"Oh, sorry! I didn't--" Violet murmured, and was withdrawing when Miss Maclaren stopped her.

"Come in, dear. Come in, *please!"* Mac implored her, and Mac's Scotch accent was much more marked than usual.

Violet obeyed that and shut the door. Now there were four black-frocked figures in the room, figures of women who seemed to be up and about at all hours of the late night and of the early morning, who existed in and solely for the Imperial Palace, breathed the Palace, ate and drank the Palace, and who had learnt the art of dispensing with sleep. Violet thought she was different from the other three, but already she was less different from them than she thought.

"Venables thinks she's overworked here," said Mac.

"Yes, I do," said Miss Venables.

She was a woman of thirty-six or seven, dark, plump, of average height; neat enough, but a bit careless about her complexion. She had a thin gold chain round her thick neck. Her hair was plastered down, rather like a young man's. Her body, while not actually trembling, appeared to be mysteriously moving beneath her dress. Her large hands were clasped in front of her, her head was slightly raised, thrown back, and turned to one side: a characteristic attitude with her when in a state of emotion. Violet had a habit of clasping her hands. They were clasped now; but as soon as she noticed Miss Venables' hands she unclasped her own, saying to herself that she must lose that housekeeper's trick.

"What do you think, Violet?" asked Mac. "What's your opinion?"

But before Violet could reply Miss Venables went on in her carefully cultivated voice:

"At least I don't say I'm overworked--so long as I'm left alone to do my work as I've always done it. I don't even mind doing both Third and Fourth for a time, to oblige the *management.* I always gave satisfaction to Mrs. O'Riordan, and she wasn't easy to please either."

Violet kept quiet. She had come to a conclusion about Miss Venables in the first three days. Miss Venables hid a fundamental commonness beneath that tone of fine manners which she had deliberately acquired and which ruffled Violet by its pretence. She was a worker; she was conscientious; but she happened to be afflicted by a sense of her perfection so strong that any criticism, even an implied criticism, offended her. And she was continuously on the watch for the slightest implication of the slightest criticism.

"Well," said Miss Prentiss. *"I* think we're overworked, and I don't care who knows it."

Older than her companion in revolt, Miss Prentiss, tall, erect, gaunt as a telegraph-pole, and with as much human juice in her as a telegraph-pole, was capable of being very sweet in response to sweetness, but she was never more than aridly sweet. Violet had come to a conclusion about Miss Prentiss also. Miss Prentiss, not a bad worker if in the vein, was a secretive woman with a taste for scandal arising from suppressed sex-instinct. An accomplished mistress of the dark hint, she could talk faster than any woman in Violet's experience (which was considerable). On the other hand she had a sustained power of taciturnity when silence suited her. Violet thought that both she and Miss Venables were quite decent creatures. Of the two Miss Prentiss had the better style, a style better also than Mac's.

"Well, what do you say, Violet?"

"I think our hours are long," Violet at last answered. "But I shouldn't say we were overworked."

"Oh! Wouldn't you!" Miss Venables exclaimed. "Well, wait till you've been here a bit longer. You forget that we've all been trying to help you, Miss Powler--Mac particularly. You're such *great* friends. But you wait till you've been here a bit longer."

"Yes." Miss Prentiss turned on Violet. "You've got friends here. Mr. Orcham brought you. Don't think we don't know all about it."

"Mr. Orcham isn't a friend of mine," said Violet warmly. "I scarcely know him. He asked me to come here and I came."

"Yes," said Miss Prentiss. "And I suppose he didn't take you down to the basement and show you everything there himself."

"But *I* told you that," said Violet.

"It doesn't matter who told us."

"But he's going to take all of you down to the basement."

"Well, he hasn't begun yet, anyhow. And I suppose you weren't hobnobbing with him in the corridor down on Fourth ten minutes ago either."

Violet was certainly shocked by this revelation of the speed at which interesting news could travel from floor to floor in the vastness of the Palace. And she was very much more severely shocked as Miss Prentiss proceeded:

"And then Sir Henry Savott. Who was it who was carrying on with *him* up here on Eighth? They sent you down to Third to stop it. And he follows you down to Third! And they have to send you back to Eighth, to stop it again."

Violet was angry, as well as astounded. At first she could not speak. Then she began to speak, but controlling herself, ceased on the first syllable.

"Miss Prentiss," said Mac with protesting dignity, "you ought to be ashamed!"

"Well, I'm not then," said Miss Prentiss, facing Mac. "It's the talk of the hotel...And I wish to say again that I shall give in my notice to-morrow morning." She spoke with a soft, fierce, mincing disdain.

"And so shall I," added Miss Venables, in her loftiest Mayfair accents. "That's what we came to tell you. We told you when we came in. And we tell you again. There's plenty of places waiting for girls like us. So you needn't think, Miss Maclaren! Good night."

"Good night," said Miss Prentiss.

The farewells were directed solely to Miss Maclaren. Miss Prentiss closed the door in the same manner as--Violet had noticed--she deposited her knife and fork on her plate in the restaurant, soundlessly.

2.

Violet was being very brave, when she saw that Mac had begun to cry, whereupon she began to cry herself, at first against her will and sparingly, then plenteously and with abandonment. It was that phrase 'carrying on with *him'* that had perturbed Violet. Monstrous, utterly unfounded slur! And then the odious insinuation that she had been sent down to Third by a watchful all-knowing management in order to separate her from Sir Henry, and sent back to Eighth with the same intent! She was revolted. She felt as though a pail of slops had been thrown at her, as though she could never be clean again. Mac's sobbing sympathy for her in the frightful slander was very touching, and it alone would have sufficed to undo her self-control.

She sat down on the sofa close by Mac. There were two sleepless black-frocked creatures in the room now, and they were united in a close embrace, Mac's arms flung passionately round Violet's neck. No longer were they key-rattling housekeepers, sternly devoted to duty, but weak girls martyrised by hard destiny and the injustice of fate.

"What am I to do? Tell me what I am to do?" Mac sniffed uncertainly. "Here I'm appointed head-housekeeper, and the first thing is two of my staff give notice! What will Mr. Cousin say?"

Violet stopped crying, almost with a jerk, as she realised that Mac's grief was not for her, Violet, but for herself. She gently freed her neck from the encircling arms, and stood up.

"Where are the tea-things?" she asked. "In the bedroom?"

Mac nodded, being unable now to articulate.

"I'll make some."

Violet went straight into the bedroom, switched on the electricity, and lit the spirit-lamp which was on the glass shelf above the lavatory-basin. After a moment Mac appeared all wet in the doorway.

"I've got that indigestion again," said she.

"Nerves," said Violet soothingly. "Some tea will put it right. You don't have to do anything, my dear." She filled the flat saucepan and ledged it over the blue flame. "Where's the tea-canister? They're only jealous of you. Mr. Cousin will understand. And I'm quite sure Mr. Orcham will."

"I only told those women about some things they hadn't done, this afternoon. I was very careful with them, but I had to tell them off a bit, hadn't I? They've been against me ever since I was appointed. Dead against me. I've felt it all the time."

"Well of course! They're jealous!"

"Have they said anything to you about their being jealous, either of them?"

"Not they!" Violet exclaimed. "They knew what they'd get if they did."

"D'ye mean they thought one of them ought to have been given the post, instead of me?"

"I shouldn't be surprised," said Violet. "And if one of 'em had got the job, wouldn't the other one have been jealous all the same! Wouldn't she just! I think Prentiss was the worst. Do you remember what you said to me the other day?" Violet had now covered the saucepan and put the teapot on the lid to get warm.

"What?"

"You said there were too many housekeepers in this hotel. So there are. If you tell Mr. Cousin you think one housekeeper ought to be enough for every two floors, and that anyhow you'd like to try it, and you don't want any fresh ones to take the place of that pair--if you tell him that he'll see the point quick enough. And so will Mr. Orcham. You take it from me, Mac."

"D'ye really think so?"

"Of course I do. *They* know how jealous girls are! Blast the canister! Why the hell won't it open?"

Never before had Mac heard bad language from the lips of her Violet. But she did not flinch.

"And how nasty they were to you!" said Mac, at last perceiving, in her relief at the suggested policy, that Violet too had something of a grievance against Miss Venables and Miss Prentiss. "Such nonsense! Disgusting, that's what it is! Makes you feel perfectly sick! At least it does me--I don't know how you feel."

"Oh! That's nothing, all that," said Violet with a stiff smile. "But I *should* like to know what put the idea into their heads."

"They just made it up. I mean Prentiss did."

Violet, however, surmised that Prentiss had indeed heard some murmur descended from on high, and that she had given the true, humiliating explanation of the tactics of the management in jumping her from floor to floor. And she was staggered. The real explanation she did not suspect for one moment. She acquitted Mr. Orcham of any share in the shifting, and attributed it entirely to the foreignness of Mr. Cousin. But on what conceivable ground could even Mr. Cousin have accused her in his French mind of 'carrying on'?

"Of course I shall leave," she said calmly. "What else is there to do?"

And then Mac, losing the last fragment of her Lowland phlegm, dropped on her knees at the feet of Violet and convulsively clasped her legs.

"Don't leave me!" she implored, pressing her face against Violet's skirt "That would be three. And where should I be then? I never liked anyone as much as I like you. You simply can't leave me. I'll see you through all right. Violet! Violet!"

The appeal was irresistible. Strange that, as Violet yielded emotionally to its power, in the same instant she saw clearly that for her own sake she must not leave, could not leave. If she left and went to Sir Henry Savott as his housekeeper--sinister word--the Imperial Palace would hum from top to bottom with the scandal of her shame. Everybody would say that the correctness of the suspicion against her of 'carrying on' had been only too horribly proved. She would not herself hear those mischievous tongues, but she would know that they were at work. And she could not tolerate the knowledge. Whereas if she stayed, the scandal would die away. She resolved to write a refusal to Sir Henry.

"Very well, dear," she said quietly to Mac, and lifted Mac up.

The water boiled. The tea was borne into the sitting-room. They drank side by side, and were tranquillised.

"That's a clever idea of yours about what I ought to say to Mr. Cousin, dear," said Mac. "You're awfully clever. You are a dear." Her Scotch accent had somewhat subsided.

The clock showed past midnight.

Chapter 40 NEGOTIATION

The scene of the supreme encounter concerning the merger had been laid by Evelyn in his private office. Old Dennis Dover and Evelyn himself sat side by side at the large desk, their backs to the window. Sir Henry Savott, also at the desk, faced them. There was nobody else in the room. These three alone were fighting over the terms upon which the Imperial Palace (with the satellite Wey Hotel) should add its indispensable prestige and power to Sir Henry's projected group. The desk was littered with papers--statistics, balance-sheets, valuations, estimates, reports, and mere jottings, scribbled by one or other of the three as the discussion proceeded. Ashtrays were laden with cigarette and cigar ends; the air was full of smoke.

The conference had begun at eleven-thirty, and now the small clock on the mantelpiece apologetically showed three minutes to two. In the two hours and a half nobody had entered, no telephone bell had rung; Evelyn had taken his precautions for absolute tranquillity. At intervals each of the three men had glanced covertly at the relentless clock. It never stopped, and sometimes it had seemed to move its hands with a most unnatural speed. The three, especially Dennis Dover, had hoped that agreement on the main point at issue would surely be reached by half-past one; then surely at twenty to two; then surely at ten to two. Disappointment followed disappointment. But every instant of the grand altercation appeared to be crucial. No one, therefore, dared to suggest a break for lunch. All three feared that to adjourn might be to lose valuable ground won at such expenditure of finesse, cunning diplomacy, and sheer brainwork.

Savott was tirelessly energetic, vivacious, good-humoured. Evelyn was tirelessly wary, watchful and bland. But in the old man fatigue had engendered both taciturnity and obstinacy. Father Dennis, exhausted, would die rather than be the first to propose a dangerous armistice. Not much more than a decade between him and Savott, and yet they seemed to belong to different generations, not only physically, but in outlook and in mental methods.

"Listen!" said Savott brightly, in a new tone, as though he were starting the third and last movement, the allegro, of a sonata. He lit a new cigarette. "Listen! I quite admit you're trying to meet me on minor but not unimportant points. I'll make it £2 10s a share, to be paid in either cash, Orcham shares, or Orcham debentures convertible into Orcham shares."

The altercation was as to the price at which the Merger was to buy or otherwise take over the ordinary shares of the Imperial Palace Hotel Company. Savott had already christened the Merger the "Orcham Company," and he insistently repeated the magical word so flattering to Evelyn. One of his subtle devices in negotiation.

Father Dennis shook his grim head.

"No! Not quite good enough!" Father Dennis murmured hoarsely in his invalid throat.

"I'm afraid not," said Evelyn blandly in support of his Chairman.

Savott raised his arms, not in surrender, but as a sign that futile stalemate had been achieved in the great game. Then the door slowly opened, with no warning knock. Two waiters entered, one after the other, each pushing a wheeled table loaded with food and drink and the apparatus of a meal.

"Aha!" Savott exclaimed, jumping up.

The aged eyes of Dennis Dover gleamed hungrily and thirstily. Evelyn smiled the smile of a master of tactics. Foreseeing the possibility of a protracted sitting, he had ordained that, if the secret conference was still in session at two o'clock, at two o'clock precisely refreshments should be brought in without any preliminaries of permission asked and granted. He had chosen in detail the food and the drink, including Dennis Dover's favourite cocktail, caviare, Derby Round, and Russian salad. There the refreshments were, alluring, irresistible; a magnificent fact to be faced, and faced immediately.

"Fall to!" said Evelyn.

"Fall to!" said father Dennis.

"You are unique, Orcham!" said Savott, candidly admiring.

"He is unique!" growled and squeaked father Dennis.

"Open one of those windows--wide," said Evelyn to a waiter. And when the window was wide open he said to the waiters: "You can both go. We will help ourselves."

The trio were alone again together.

"Aha!" Savott repeated himself, drinking a cocktail after he had passed one deferentially to father Dennis, who, grumbling as often before at the discomfort of the Palace chairs, rose to take the glass.

All three men were now standing up, stretching their arms and legs, walking to and fro in the freshness of the new air from the window, glancing at Miss Cass's horticultural window-boxes, pecking here and pecking there with forks, offering plates to one another, drinking, munching not without noise. Documents were hidden under plates and glasses. In three minutes father Dennis was beginning to be rejuvenated and also mellowed. With his immense, unwieldy and yet noble bulk, his age, his experience of the world, he unconsciously assumed dominion over his companions. Evelyn saw Savott transformed swiftly from the canny, astute negotiator into the avid gourmand of the dinner-table in the restaurant weeks earlier. As for Evelyn himself, he could not hide his satisfaction, and he made no effort to do so.

"If you think I can stand that hurricane in the small of my back, you've been misinformed," croaked father Dennis, his mouth full, after a few minutes.

Evelyn closed the window.

"Now let's see how far we've got?" said Savott, dropping into an easy-chair, crossing his legs, and lighting a cigar before he had quite finished with a peach.

"Yes," Evelyn agreed. "Let's see how far we've got."

"Yes," said father Dennis, "let's look on the bright side for a change."

The will to reach agreement by compromise was stirring.

"Your salary as Managing Director is settled," Savott addressed Evelyn.

"My salary is settled," said Evelyn.

"I think you have reason to be satisfied with it," said Savott, smiling.

"Quite," said Evelyn.

The salary was indeed very high. Evelyn's earnings would be nearly doubled.

"And the term? You still insist on a twelve years' contract? Ten is more usual, you know. I should prefer ten, as a matter of form. Of course I expect your contract to run for twenty years, thirty. But as a--"

Evelyn interrupted the sentence with a shake of the bead and a lifting of the broad shoulders.

"Twelve," said he, smiling very amiably.

"All right. All right!" Savott laughed.

Evelyn's private reason for demanding a twelve-year contract was that it would carry him in security past the age of sixty. He had an idea of retiring at sixty; or, if his vitality forbade such a step, then of buying a smallish hotel in an English seaside resort and proving to the world that the existence of a truly first-class hotel in an English seaside resort was not an impossibility.

"And the constitution of the first Orcham Board of Directors is agreed?" Savott proceeded.

"It is," said father Dennis. "But it's understood that after serving as Chairman of this fabulous Merger for one year I shall step down and leave the throne to be fought for by rival pretenders."

"That's a detail, Mr. Dover," said Savott.

"It isn't a detail at all," said father Dennis. "For me it's the most important point in the whole damned conspiracy to bleed innocent travellers. Even now, instead of presiding over mergers, I ought to be in bed surrounded by my devoted grandchildren." He added with a squeak: "Only I haven't any grandchildren."

The other two laughed.

"Next," Savott went on, "I agree that my valuations of the Majestic and the Duncannon and the continental hotels are to be approved by your valuers. Orcham agrees to make a tour at once of all the hotels, and the entire arrangement is to be subject to his being satisfied. I've shown you my scheme for raising capital and underwriting it, and I agree to produce to you as soon as possible my contracts for this purpose with the three City houses I've told you of."

Savott continued from item to item. Father Dennis and Evelyn listened and nodded when necessary. There was no discord.

"I fancy that's all," Savott finished, content with the orderly clearness of his résumé of the plan, with his strong grasp of all the statistics, and with his accomplishment as a negotiator and deviser.

Mind alone is creative. Sir Henry Savott had now all but thought his Merger into existence. One more touch, and the vast design would magically appear, visible, concrete, complete, the wonder of the world.

2.

"It isn't all," growled father Dennis.

"No. It isn't *all,"* said Savott. "Naturally. Let's come back to the price of Imperial Palace shares. I've quoted you £2 10s. Now seriously, what about it?"

Father Dennis shook his ancient head, and glanced at Evelyn, who also gave a negative sign.

"You really mustn't make it too difficult for the Orcham Company to pay a dividend," smiled Henry Savott.

"We have to think of our shareholders," said father Dennis. "And we haven't got to think of anything else. If you consider our price too high--"

"I do," said Savott.

"Then it's for you to say so plainly and definitely, and the scheme's on the scrap-heap."

"But your own valuations of your own property don't justify--"

"Valuations! Valuations! And our reserves, in cash and gilt-edged?"

"I'm not forgetting them."

"But you're forgetting that we're selling you something that can't *be* valued," father Dennis squeakily continued. "If you weren't forgetting that you surely wouldn't talk about valuations. We're selling you the very *sine qua non* of your scheme. What is the scheme without the Imperial Palace and Orcham? You'd never have thought of it without them. What the Merger must have is our prestige. Take that away and it's worth exactly elevenpence three farthings."

"I quite agree," said Savott lightly, even submissively. "And wasn't I the first to say so? But I should like you to remember this. If I'd got hold of a majority or anywhere near a majority of Palace shares, as I meant to do, only you scotched me by altering the voting power of your shares while my head was turned the other way--what would have happened? I should have been able to name my own price for your shares, and what I'd lost on the shares I should have made on the Merger, and more."

"Certainly," father Dennis hoarsely whispered. "There's no argument about that. But we did alter the voting power, thereby putting you gently into the soup, my friend. *If* this and *if* that, you would have been able to name your own price. But as there don't happen to be any ifs, we can name our price. And it's a price the Merger can well afford to pay. It isn't as if we hadn't come down a bit. Our price is £2 15s."

"That's your lowest?"

"Our lowest."

"Well, I'm sorry. My last word is £2 10s." said Sir Henry genially, and as he spoke he began to collect his papers together on the desk. A deciding gesture.

Evelyn gazed at him, met his hard, steely eyes. There was no compromise in them; nor in his teeth. The gourmand had quitted the body of Sir Henry Savott. His tiny eyes were two brass tacks, and the Imperial Palace had at last come down to those brass tacks. The battle was finished. The opposing armies would both have to retire.

"I'm sorry," Sir Henry repeated meditatively. "Yes, I'm very sorry. I'm more disappointed than I can say. I must apologise to you for putting you to so much trouble for nothing. I don't complain, mind you. Not in the least. You know your own business best. Only I've got a sort of a notion of my business too. We differ, and there's no more to be said. But you'll find yourselves wrong about one thing. I shall go on with my Merger. Nothing is indispensable, not even the Imperial Palace. I've set my heart on a merger. I've never set my heart on anything and failed to get it. I'll carry the Merger through, and I'll give you the fight of your life, whatever it costs me. There must be another Orcham lying about somewhere in the world. I'll find him."

"Bravo!" Evelyn exclaimed, touched to admiration for the man's passionate, exalted demeanour. Savott was once more the poet who had divulged himself at the opening dinner in Evelyn's castle.

But Evelyn was very deeply depressed, realising now fully for the first time how powerfully the great scheme of the Merger had appealed to his instincts. And in his disappointment he felt that he had nothing to live for. And he was desolated by the thought that all their work, all Savott's creative faculty, all father Dennis's broadminded caution, all his own watchful mastery of detail, had come to naught. Naught! He sympathised with Savott as much as with father Dennis and himself. And he questioned the wisdom of father Dennis's rather abrupt handling of the climax of the fray. Still, he was rigidly loyal to father Dennis. They were intimate friends. They understood one another. They trusted one another absolutely. And after all the Merger would have been at best a dangerous and chancy enterprise!

Sir Henry Savott at this depressing juncture behaved with an infinite discreet propriety. Many men would have dawdled, would have exasperated affliction by futile remarks. Sir Henry, having pulled his papers from beneath plates, stowed them all into a despatch-case, said "Good afternoon" very simply and amicably, and moved briskly to the door. He was indeed a man, thought Evelyn. And the rumours of his precarious position as a high financier were indeed silly. Somehow Evelyn felt ashamed, for all three of them.

Having opened the door, Sir Henry startlingly halted and faced the enemy.

"Split the difference," he snapped harshly.

Evelyn's heart jumped. Father Dennis looked at Evelyn, and Evelyn at father Dennis. Evelyn saw a look of persistent obstinacy in the old man's furrowed face. He withstood the look and smiled. A mighty demon had rushingly entered into him and assumed control of all his faculties.

"It's a deal," said the demon, with quiet assurance.

"Oh, very well!" father Dennis whispered pleasantly, having yielded to Evelyn's astonishing sudden domination.

The Imperial Palace was sold.

Evelyn and father Dennis were the masters of the Imperial Palace Board, and the Board was the autocrat of the Company; and all minor outstanding difficulties between the Company and the Merger were easily capable of settlement. In six words the Imperial Palace had been sold.

3.

Dropping his despatch-case conveniently near the door, Sir Henry Savott returned to the desk. The three shook hands, not unsentimentally. Conscious of the sentimentality, and determined to correct it, father Dennis stood up and growled, "Damn it all!" and went to one of the wheeled tables and poured out three liqueur brandies with his infirm hand, spilling some priceless liquid. And Evelyn, who never in any circumstances took either spirits or liqueurs, said, "Damn it all!" and gazed at the brandy and slowly drank. They all three drank together. Having committed this sublime folly, Evelyn smacked his lips. Old Dover and he were more occupied with one another than with Sir Henry Savott. Had they been attentive they would have noticed moisture in his little eyes. Sir Henry had not staked millions, but millions somehow had been staked. He had staked the value of years of mole-tunnelling, and of a week of the delicatest diplomacy and bargaining. He had staged a rupture, and acted it with convincing realism. He had acted to the last second. He knew that if he had not gone to the door and given his opponents time for regret, he would not have managed to squeeze out of them the concession of half the difference; and he had decided that beyond half the difference he would not and could not yield. Further, he had staked his belief in himself. Still further, he had secured the five hundred thousand pounds which was the least personal profit that he expected to make out of the whole transaction. Sir Henry had lived through intolerable years in a quarter of an hour. Old Dover was indifferent to the scheme's success or failure. Evelyn would very quickly have reconciled himself to its failure. But to Sir Henry the fruition of the scheme was necessary, both morally and financially. None save himself knew, and few genuinely suspected, that his career had arrived at a point when a failure might ruin it--at any rate temporarily. Well, he had succeeded. Multitudinous risks and perils yet lay before him. But he had triumphed so far, and for the future he had an equal confidence in himself and in Evelyn Orcham. He had won, and he would win. Hence the emotional moisture in his tiny eyes: phenomenon which his late opponents, now his allies, had been too self-absorbed to observe. The moisture quickly vanished.

"My car's been waiting two hours, and even chauffeurs have to eat," squeaked father Dennis. "Good-bye. Seems to me I look like being the biggest shareholder even in your new Company, Savott." He gave a sardonic, masterful grin as he strode cumbrously from the scene of battle.

"By the way," said Sir Henry to Evelyn, with an affectation of nonchalance concerning the upshot of the mighty encounter. "That Powler girl declined my offer."

"Oh yes!" Evelyn answered. "So I heard."

"Did she tell you then?"

"No. But she told my head-housekeeper she should stay here, and the thing got about. Things do, you know. This place is a regular whispering-gallery." He laughed easily. But he was uneasily thinking of a phrase used by Savott at the height of the battle: "I've never set my heart on anything and failed to get it."

A little later Sir Henry quietly departed, and Evelyn was alone in his office amid a disorder of dirty crockery, electroplate and glass. After a crisis he always liked solitude. He walked slowly about the room, smoking one of the non-nicotine cigarettes which he kept specially for use when he had indulged unduly in cigars. He smiled to himself. The deed was done. Nothing but some incredible mischance of destiny could prevent him from becoming in a few months the absolute autocrat of the most grandiose chain of luxury hotels in the world. The Imperial Palace Company would be wound up. Hence the Board of Directors of the Imperial Palace would cease to be. Either the youthful Dacker or the youthful Smiss would be elected to the Board of the new big Company.

There would not be room for both of them: continental interests must be considered. But which of them: Dacker or Smiss? He was inclined to nominate Dacker, with whom he was in closer personal relations. Smiss, however, would be invaluable on the Board when it had to deal with the works' departments of its hotels: and he spoke more foreign languages than Dacker. What did it matter? These young men must take the rough with the smooth; and anyhow the one who lost a directorship could be compensated in forty ways. He, Evelyn, would henceforth have the distribution of an enormous patronage!

Suddenly he thought, with a qualm:

"Am I equal to the job? I wonder. Everybody believes in me. But do I believe in myself?" Yes, a qualm; a momentary sensation of all-gone-ness beneath the heart!

Suddenly he thought:

"That fellow Savott's been a bit obscure about his underwriting after all. I suppose it'll be all right. I bet anything Harry Matcham Lord Watlington's really at the back of it. Those City houses don't often stand by themselves."

Suddenly he thought:

"Why did the fellow choose that moment to tell me he'd missed fire with the Powler woman? I expect it was just a subconscious nervous reaction from the strain. He's been working hard, the fellow has, these days. So have I."

As a fact Evelyn, absorbed in the complex skirmishing preliminary to the great battle over the price to be paid for Imperial Palace shares, had almost forgotten the existence of his protégée from the Laundry. He had heard that she was not going to desert the hotel, but he had heard as in a dream. And for him Violet was a shade. What difference could it make to the huge "Orcham" Company whether a mere floor-housekeeper of *one* of its hotels, be she never so admirable, stayed or departed? A detail! A trifling detail! The entire perspective of life was altered now. Evelyn dropped the cigarette-end, and impulsively left the room, passing through Miss Cass's secretarial office.

4.

"Anything urgent for me?" he demanded.

"No, sir. There's only the--"

"Is it urgent?"

"No, sir."

"Then we'll let it simmer."

Did she look at him in a strange way, or was he imagining the strangeness? In either case she *knew.* She was necessarily aware of the negotiations, and she would have guessed the result from Savott's demeanour as be went out, if not from father Dennis's, if not from his own. Astonishing, the faculty of that brisk, self-possessed woman for divination! Often her knowledge of secrets had surprised him. In displaying her knowledge she always skilfully assumed that he must know that she knew. But he trusted her. She was a tomb for secrets. But was she a tomb? Was he justified in trusting her?

Why had he grown suspicious? Beyond the outer door a waiter was waiting.

"May I take away the things, sir?"

"You may."

He would stroll round his hotel--one of his hotels! He always enjoyed these strolls, and sometimes they were rather useful. But a few yards down the side-corridor he met Ceria, the Grill-room-manager, emerging from Cousin's managerial office.

"Well, Ceria," he greeted the young man. "What are you doing here at this hour? I always understood you spent the afternoon in the bosom of your family at Hampstead."

Ceria smiled. He was a little younger than Cappone, the Restaurant-manager, and his smile, wistful, innocent, appealing, was judged to be more enchanting than even that of Cappone. Ceria counted among Evelyn's finest selections. He had made the grill-room the regular resort of the newspaper-magnates, the film-kings and the theatrical stars of London. At lunch the place was now crowded. At dinner it was fairly full. At supper it was very full. No self-respecting actress could dispense with two or three appearances a week for supper in the Palace Grill. To be seen frequently there, to be on terms of intimacy with Ceria, was the final proof of success. The one trouble about Ceria was the pronunciation of his name. The film-kings unanimously pronounced it "Seeria." The more learned and cosmopolitan pronounced it "Cheeria," save a few daring wags among them who called him "Cheerio." Only the highest highbrows pronounced it in the Italian way. Ceria had the same wonder-working smile for all of them: the smile of perfect health and almost perfect happiness. Ignoring Evelyn's question, Ceria said, excited:

"My Feras have arrived, sir."

"Your what?"

"The fish from the Lake of Geneva. By aeroplane. Caught this morning. On my dinner menu to-night."

Evelyn remembered hearing of the Fera enterprise.

"Have you told Immerson?"

"Oh yes, sir."

Immerson would make something of the Feras in his weekly gossip paragraphs.

"I congratulate you," said Evelyn. "It's a great stunt."

"Mr. Immerson calls them my 'flying fish,' sir."

Ceria laughed with joy. He would have talked at length on the piquant subject of the day; but Evelyn left him with a nod. What the devil did fish matter? One dish, one night, in one restaurant, in one of his hotels. Still, he had his eye on Ceria. The grill-room was very firmly established in renown, and under Ceria was an older man, a Frenchman, who could well carry on the great work. Whereas Ceria, shifted to the Majestic, might marvellously vitalise the semi-comatose Majestic restaurant.

Evelyn strolled on into the great entrance-hall. There were the mirrored columns, the ceiling lights, the coloured prints of old steamships and the photographs of modern steamships underneath them, the sofas, the easy-chairs, the little tables, an underling at the Reception counter, another at the Enquiries counter, with their eternally illuminated signs, pageboy entering in a book the times of the tell-tale signal board which told the story of every ring of every visitor's bell on the Floors above, the newspaper-stand deserted, large old Mowlem, the hall-porter, splendid and dignified in his cubicle between the revolving doors! Odd: the Palace existed exactly as usual, not witting that it had been sold, that the old order had changed into the new!

He turned to the right, down into the foyer, which was empty. The last of the dilatory lunchers had gone. The bands-men were carrying away from the restaurant their lighter instruments and their music. Waiters were setting the tables for the afternoon *thé dansant.* The gentlemen's cloak-room was empty and had only one attendant. The glass-walled reading-room was quite empty. The hotel was at its deadest. Evelyn stayed a few moments, humming to himself the extraordinary fact that nobody guessed at the tremendous revolution. He strolled back to the entrance-hall. And there was Sir Henry Savott conversing earnestly with the portly Mowlem! Evelyn watched the interview. What chicane now? It was curious that on the very slightest evidence he would instantly begin to suspect Savott of chicane, plots, manœuvres. Yet he liked and sincerely admired the man. He had learnt to like him, and had been compelled to admire him. Never had Evelyn been presented with so clear a statement of involved facts and figures as Savott had laid before him and old Dover concerning the proposed merger. And Savott had prepared the array of statistics himself. Savott said that he had done it with his own brain and hand, and Evelyn believed him.

Evelyn thought:

"Supposing in a year or two's time the fellow starts hankypankying with the 'Orcham' shares, in the vein of his performance with North Atlantic!"

And then he thought with affection and pleasure of Dennis Dover, who had so "decently" followed his perhaps too arbitrary lead in closing the share bargain. Moreover, father Dennis might have got cash or debentures for his huge holding of shares in the Imperial Palace Company. But, because he loved Evelyn, he had decided from the first to stand by Evelyn, and to exchange his Palace shares for shares in the new Merger Company, the Orcham Company. Loyalty! Evelyn was touched. Evelyn would make the new Company a success, if only for the sake of father Dennis.

He saw Sir Henry nod to old Mowlem and then push his way, with the aid of a janissary outside, through the revolving doors. Evelyn strolled to the hall-porter's cubicle.

"Sir Henry in any difficulty, Mowlem?" he enquired.

"No, sir. Mr. Adolphe didn't happen to be at the Reception, so Sir Henry came to me. He's leaving us later in the afternoon."

Evelyn saw Sir Henry's automobile curve away into Birdcage Walk.

"Oh! Where is he going to?" Evelyn asked. And said to himself: "What's the meaning of this? He didn't tell me anything about leaving."

"Sir Henry didn't say, sir. Only told me to have his luggage down at five.'

"Well, Mowlem, I shall be leaving myself for a while in a day or two."

"For long, sir?"

"No, not for long. It depends."

"Continent, sir?"

"Yes."

"When you come back, sir, I should like a chat with you, if you can spare me a moment."

"Oh?"

"Yes, sir. Of course you know I always said I should retire at sixty. And I'm sixty next month."

"Now, Mowlem, Mowlem!" Evelyn protested, with a sadness which he really felt. *"You* may have said you were going to retire. But *I* never said you were. What does Mr. Cousin say?"

"To tell you the truth, sir, I haven't mentioned the matter to Mr. Cousin." Evelyn heard in the important functionary's patriarchal, stately tone a reminder that he, Mowlem, had been in the service of the Palace years and years before Mr. Cousin had ever been heard of, that compared to himself Mr. Cousin was a mushroom, and that Mowlem judged himself entitled to deal direct with Mr. Cousin's superior.

"Mr. Cousin won't let you go. He thinks too highly of you," said Evelyn benevolently.

"Well, sir," Mowlem replied with dignity, "we shall see. Sixty is sixty. Times change." He gazed at Evelyn steadily.

Then Jim Savott's valet, pale after his illness, appeared in the hall, questing for the hall-porter. Evelyn walked away.

"Mowlem knows," thought Evelyn.

Somehow he felt guilty. And he still felt guilty, self-conscious, when, half a minute afterwards, he entered Cousin's office and said, with a painful effort to be casual:

"Well, Cousin. *C'est fait"*

Chapter 41 AN ATTACK

One night, a week or two later, Violet was taking her French lesson from old Perosi, but in the waiters' service-room on Eighth. Miss Maclaren had gone downstairs to talk direct with Ceria, the Grill-room-manager, about certain questions which had arisen concerning the Floors night-menus. Violet was on late duty that evening. Miss Maclaren seemed to dislike giving permission even to her dear friend and prop, Vi, to leave Eighth during her own absence; and Miss Maclaren being again dyspeptically indisposed, was hardly in a condition to be argued with. Hence Perosi, who now treated Violet very paternally and benevolently indeed, had with unique and august condescension offered to desert Fourth, his proper home, and come up to Eighth for the purpose of the lesson. He knew that the lesson might at any moment be interrupted by some trifling emergency on Sixth, Seventh or Eighth; but he was majestically ready to accept the risk; the fact was that the ponderous man enjoyed his role of tutor.

In the still warmth of the little service-room, from which the floor-waiter had been ejected before his evening spell of duty was over, both Perosi and Violet--but Violet first--heard an unusual stir at the steel gates of the neighbouring lift. The door of the service-room was kept always ajar. They both went into the corridor. An excited page-boy had stepped out of the lift. Within the lift were Ted, the liftman, who had just 'come on,' and Ceria himself. Also Miss Maclaren. Pale, perspiring, agonised, Miss Maclaren sat on the cushioned bench of the lift, and Ceria was supporting her in his arms.

"Qu'est-ce qu'elle a? Qu'est-ce qu'elle a?" Perosi demanded.

"Elle a eu une attaque," Ceria replied, in his Italian accent.

Despite her tuition, Violet understood only the last word.

"She must be carried to her bedroom," said Violet quickly. It was obvious that Miss Maclaren suffered acute pain.

The bell in the lift rang several times impatiently, and a tiny light glowed yellow on the signal-box: 'Ground-floor.' The bell continued to ring. At a gesture from Ceria, Ted took the moaning woman round her knees, and Ceria took her under the arms, and between them they moved her out of the lift. Ceria was already somewhat breathless, for alone without aid he had carried her from his little office to the lift.

"Keep her head lower, Mr. Ceria," Violet suggested.

"Take the lift down, kid," said Ted to the page-boy, glancing back. Thrilled by his responsibility, the white-gloved dwarf obeyed.

The procession of Mac's body passed along the corridor, Violet in front, Perosi muttering behind. Violet ran into Mac's room, left the entrance-door open, left the bedroom-door open, turned down the bed-clothes with two rapid movements. In half a minute Mac lay panting and writhing in pain on the bed; the liftman had reluctantly departed.

"I'll telephone for Dr. Constam," said Violet. "Where does he live? I suppose he doesn't happen to be in the hotel?"

"The doctor is coming," Ceria answered with a sad, sympathetic and yet proud smile. "I said to them to telephone for him before I came up. He is in the hotel. Santa Maria!" His wistful eyes said: "I had forgotten nothing. This is Imperial Palace staffwork." He added aloud: "I think it was the doctor who was ringing for the lift."

It was. Going to the door, Violet met Dr. Constam entering. The young man nodded.

"In here?" he asked quietly, and strode into the bedroom. He nodded to Ceria.

"Right, Ceria."

Ceria left, also reluctantly. Violet and Dr. Constam were alone together in the bedroom. The doctor was now the expert in charge. He bent over the bed to examine.

"Shall I sponge her face for her?" Violet asked.

"No. Wait a minute."

Violet discreetly moved away from the bedside, and thoughts scurried through her mind. Miss Maclaren was very ill. Climax of her dyspepsia. Why were dyspeptics always greedy? The hotel had ceased to exist. Hotel duties had lost all their importance. The martyr to hotel duties was very ill. How startlingly rapid were changes! Mrs. O'Riordan was married--Lady Milligan. She had forfeited her wedding-present. She was gone, without trace, and for ever. Alice Brury was at the Laundry. Violet had left the Laundry. Venables and Prentiss were soon to leave the Palace. Violet felt as though she had lived in the hotel for many months, instead of merely a few weeks. She was learning French. The interrupted French lesson had passed clean out of her head. Mr. Orcham was away on the Continent. The hotel was functioning as smoothly as usual. Nevertheless his absence was mysteriously felt. Mac herself had remarked that very morning on the strange effect produced upon the mind by Mr. Orcham's absence. Violet had felt it, though she had not been accustomed to seeing him. Mac was very ill. Violet wanted to do something for the sufferer, but she was helpless. Where was Perosi? He had vanished.

"Get me some water, only a sip, will you?" said Dr. Constam.

Violet was quick. He poured the sip down Mac's throat.

"Where's the telephone?"

"In the sitting-room. Can I 'phone for you, doctor?"

"No." The doctor was brusque but quite courteous.

Violet, gently caressing Mac's brow, heard him telephoning. She gathered that he was calling up a hospital. His tone at the telephone was authoritative. He seemed to hold the hospital, all the hospitals in London, under his sway.

"It's extremely urgent," she heard him say. "You'd better send an ambulance. No. The motor-ambulance. Yes, at once. I'll be ready." He came back into the bedroom, and said to Violet: "There's a nurse in 538.

She can't be very busy. Go and fetch her--yourself. Tell her I sent you. And bring her along."

"Yes, doctor. Is this something serious?" she whispered from the door.

"It's serious. But exactly what it is I'm not sure yet. Colon anyhow. Run. And then get a stretcher." He spoke in a scarcely audible murmur.

Violet ran. Perosi was standing outside.

2.

"Mr. Perosi," she threw at him. "The doctor wants a stretcher." No more than that. She left him to procure the stretcher.

When she returned with the nurse, who was much too deliberate and detached for Violet's taste, Perosi was manœuvring a stretcher through the door into the sitting-room.

"Come on, nurse," said Dr. Constam, in the doorway between the rooms. "We've got to get this young woman here downstairs. An ambulance is coming. You," he addressed Violet, "go and ring for the lift. And keep it. Don't bring the stretcher in," he addressed Perosi. "We should never get it out again with the patient in it."

Violet hurried to the lift-well, and rang, rang. She waited, waited. At last she heard the lift crawling upward. Then a new procession. The laden stretcher, its burden well covered, Dr. Constam at the foot, Perosi at the head, the nurse by the side. At the lift, Ted took a hand. The lift had just space for the stretcher. Ted closed the steel gates. Doctor and nurse were within. The lift sank away. With it, Mac sank away out of the life of the hotel. The swiftness of the transformation of the service life of Eighth was positively frightening. Mac had disappeared. It was almost as if she had been erased, deleted. Violet and old Perosi exchanged a long, solemn look.

More than once, Violet, who had returned to Miss Maclaren's rooms--for no purpose that she could define, was rung up by various departments of the hotel for definite, authentic information as to the sick woman. Clearly Mac had anxious friends in the organism of the Palace. Clearly news of the disaster had spread through the vast building with the usual extreme rapidity of evil tidings. Violet answered every enquiry with a quiet reassurance. She never did and never could luxuriate in a calamity. Her instinct was invariably to minimise trouble. Nevertheless she was very troubled. The telephone calls in themselves had the effect of making her think that she had under-estimated the gravity of the event.

She was not aware that the spectacular passage of the stretcher through the great hall had created a tremendous impression. In the Imperial Palace, as in all hotels, cases of serious illness or death were whenever possible smothered up. Visitors in hotels object strongly to any reminder that disease exists and that death happens. Therefore sick bodies and dead bodies are removed surreptitiously, by secret exits. But the urgency of that night's case had permitted no compliance with the customary etiquette. At the revolving doors the stretcher with its bearers, compelled to wait for the dilatory ambulance, had even got itself entangled with departing and arriving revellers from and to the restaurant and grill-room. Nothing to wonder at, then, in the enormity of the sensation.

Violet was deeply disturbed in two ways: in her grief for Mac's perilous misfortune, and in her anxieties about the housekeeping of the hotel. Mac would at best be absent for weeks; she might never return; at any moment during the night or next day or the day after the telephone might announce the decease of poor old Mac. In the meantime, who would temporarily be charged with the control of the housekeeping? Assuredly Venables or Prentiss; for the other floor-housekeepers had neither the experience nor the moral weight necessary to sustain them in the arduous job. And Violet was alarmed at the prospect of being subjected to the rule of either of these ladies who were now her foes and whom no ideal of magnanimity would prevent from being tyrannical and absurd. She longed for the soft, masterful presence of Mr. Orcham, who was equal to every occasion.

Quite apart from Mac's tragic disappearance, the vanishing of Mr. Orcham had disquieted Violet; it had disquieted all the staff except the lowest menials. Official information as to its cause had not been vouchsafed, or at any rate had not percolated down to the stratum of floor-housekeepers. But the newspapers had given immense front-page prominence to rumours of a great hotel-merger; so much so that the foundations of the Palace seemed to tremble under the feet of the staff, and even floor-housekeepers had taken to scanning the financial columns of their favourite dailies. Mr. Orcham's name had suddenly become familiar to citizens, astonished by the abrupt revelation of the importance of someone whom they had never heard of. But not his photograph, for despite pressing demands from journalists nobody in the hotel could furnish a portrait of the panjandrum--the reason being that no portrait existed. Then one morning the staff had been thrilled by the appearance of a lifelike photograph in a picture-paper. It had been obtained in Cannes, by a long-distance lens, unknown to the victim, and it had been transmitted by telegraph: proof enough of the news-value of the panjandrum's face. And surely the rumour that the august and unique Imperial Palace might deign to merge into anything whatever was sufficient to give an inestimable news-value to the likeness of its Director.

3.

Violet had a desire to talk to somebody. She was arguing with herself whether she might seek out old Perosi, when there was a tap at Mac's door. Instantaneously the door opened, and Mr. Cousin imperturbably entered. Violet jumped up from her chair. And well she might, for not once hitherto had she seen Mr. Cousin on Eighth, or heard of him being there! The truth was that, unlike Evelyn, Cousin was not fond of perambulating the Floors. He preferred to exercise the function of management from his office, to be the Mahomet to whom mountains came. Even when he did visit the Floors he would not ascend higher than Seventh. The former Mrs. O'Riordan had been subtly antipathetic to him, and because of this he had lost the habit of Eighth, habit which he had not yet resumed.

Mr. Cousin smiled blandly.

"I am glad you are here, Miss Powler," he said. "I wanted to see you."

"Yes, sir."

He sat down. The hour was close on midnight, but Mr. Cousin's perfect dress-suit, shirt, collar and cravat were as fresh as though he had just put them on. In the daytime he had sartorial equals, perhaps superiors; but at night he was unrivalled.

"Please sit down," said he. Violet obeyed. "It is very sad, this. I hear that you were present."

"When Miss Maclaren was brought up? Yes, sir."

"Tell me about it."

Violet told. She thought that he listened with negligence.

"Everything is in order on the Floors?"

"So far as I know, sir," Violet replied. "But of course I don't know about all the Floors."

"For the future, at least until Miss Maclaren has recovered, it will be your business to know everything about all the Floors. I must have someone in control, someone who is responsible. And you will be good enough to take Miss Maclaren's place for the present. Provisional, of course." Violet was extremely surprised, and yet the realistic core of her mind was not surprised. She knew her capacity, but would admit it with reluctance, and only in a crisis.

"But surely," she said, excited. "Miss Venables or Miss Prentiss. They...I...All of them have been here longer than I have, much longer."

"That is possible," said Mr. Cousin with tranquillity. "But Miss Venables and Miss Prentiss are leaving. And having regard to their conduct, I do not wish to add to their responsibilities. As for the others...No." He waved a hand and benevolently smiled. "It is you alone who are indicated."

He did not say that from several visitors he had heard praise of Miss Powler's cheerfulness, obligingness, tactfulness, helpfulness, efficiency.

"Very well. Thank you, sir," said Violet quietly. What else was there to say? If you refused the responsibility you said "No" at once. If you accepted it you said "Very well" and "Thank you," and the matter was ended. Certainly you did not indulge in any silly, insincere self-depreciation.

"In case you need help or advice, come to me. Naturally you will have difficulties, but--" He waved his hand again.

"But about allotting the Floors, sir? I expect that Miss Maclaren has spoken to you about her new plan--"

"That will be as you decide," Mr. Cousin interrupted her.

He rose. She rose. Then he amazed her by holding out his hand. She took it. They both smiled.

"What hospital is Miss Maclaren in, sir?"

"St. James's," said Mr. Cousin. "You see, we have endowed more than one bed there with the surplus from our Breakages Fund. They were very crowded, but of course they wished to oblige us. Good night, Miss Powler."

He bowed, just perceptibly. Gallic chivalry! Then he said, leaving: "It may interest you to know that Mr. Orcham has just been telephoning to me from Cannes. So I told him about Miss Maclaren, and that I had decided to put you in temporary charge. He approved. Good night again."

Violet wondered what might be the tremendously important business which could draw these two great personages together on the telephone wire so late in the evening. She was not aware that every evening Evelyn enquired by telephone after the health of the Palace, as a man enquires nightly after the health of a mistress from whom he has been compelled to absent himself.

For some minutes the fact that Miss Maclaren was very ill was entirely submerged in her mind by the fact of her incredible, frightening, almost stupefying appointment as temporary head-housekeeper in the finest luxury hotel in the world. The post had been Lady Milligan's. It was now hers. Her parents would be amazed and delighted. No! They would be delighted, but not amazed. They would say: "Of course! Quite natural. Just what was to be expected!" Because their belief in her gifts and her character was a religion with them. It was utterly complete, so complete that it seemed silly, touching. Poor things!

Then the light wastefully burning in Mac's bedroom caught her attention. She passed into the bedroom. The bed lay in disorder The eiderdown had slid to the floor. She tidied the bed, shook the pillow into shape, and covered everything, including the eiderdown, with the counterpane. And having arranged the bed, she arranged the room. Mac, though a fanatic for tidiness in the rooms of visitors, was strangely negligent of her own room. She would even leave her flowers to wither up in their vases.

Melancholy martyr, the victim of fate. She had occupied the highest post of its kind over the whole earth, and probably the best paid in Europe. She had climbed till she could climb no further. And had her happiness been thereby increased? It had been diminished, considerably. The change had destroyed her peace of mind, her sleep, her self-confidence; and intensified her already exaggerated conscientiousness. Nature had not meant her for supreme authority. And now in a moment she had been swept away. And doubtless in the hospital ward her last thoughts before submitting to the anæsthetic, and her first thoughts on awaking from it, would take the form of foolish worrying anxiety as to the housekeeping of the Palace. Violet felt heavy with sympathetic woe.

She heard movements in the sitting-room. Venables appeared in the doorway between the rooms, and Venables too was charged with woe.

4.

"I did knock," said Venables, as usual defending herself before she had been attacked, "but nobody answered. Mac's gone?"

Violet reflected: "As if she didn't know perfectly well Mac's gone!" She said: "Oh! An hour ago at least."

"I thought I'd better come up and see. I didn't really know what had happened. I suppose it's appendicitis?"

"Can't say."

"But it must be."

"Perhaps it is. Only Dr. Constam told me he didn't know. He's gone with her to the hospital."

"You were here all the time?"

"Yes."

The colloquy showed constraint on both sides; for these words were the first to be exchanged between the two floor-housekeepers since the fearsome scene in Mac's sitting-room days and days earlier.

"Gwen and I have been wondering how this place is to be carried on."

Violet reflected: "Yes; and that's what you've come up to find out." She said: "I think you had better take over Sixth and Fifth. I'll see to this floor and Seventh. I'll speak to Prentiss tomorrow."

"Oh, indeed!" Venables sniffed, and her dark head began to tremble.

"Yes."

"But who'll be in charge?"

"Mr. Cousin says I am to be."

"So you've been down to see him already?" Fierce but restrained resentment in Venables' tone.

"No, I haven't. He came up here to see me about it."

A long pause.

Venables said, with a ferocious sarcasm, but carefully ladylike:

"May I use the telephone, please?"

"Of course. Why do you ask such a question?" Violet managed to smile.

Venables stepped back into the sitting-room. Violet heard her say:

"I want you to get up then, dear. Slip something on. I want you to come here at once, as quick as you can, dear." Her voice trembled, as her head had been trembling, with terrible emotion.

Violet sat down at the foot of the bed; and the waves of Venables' excitement seemed to rush in a continuous torrential, invisible stream through the door and break against Violet's resisting temper. An awful silence. Violet felt as if she were awaiting the explosive thunder of the crack of doom.

Then, after an immeasurable period, Prentiss appeared.

"I thought you were never coming, dear!" Violet heard Venables say. The exalted, trustful, vibrating emphasis that Venables laid on that word "dear"! The two housekeepers came just within the bedroom and stood together, allies defensive and offensive. Prentiss wore a purple dressing-gown pinned at the neck, and bedroom slippers on her bare feet. Her greying thin hair was in disarray. By contrast with the other two in their primly correct housekeeper frocks she had an abandoned, indecent air.

"Do sit down," suggested the alert, watchful Violet.

They did not sit down.

"Now, Powler," said Venables, "will you please tell Prentiss what you've told me." Then turning to Prentiss: "I want you to hear from her what she told me, dear."

"About Mr. Cousin?"

"If you don't mind."

Violet complied.

"Well!" the tall, telegraph-pole woman murmured horrified, outraged, under her breath.

"I can't help it," Violet mildly protested. "Mr. Cousin came up himself and gave me my orders. I don't give orders. I take them."

"You soon started giving orders to me!" Venables exclaimed. She clasped her hands and, lifting her head, turned it to one side, shaking.

"But I didn't give you any order," Violet pleaded, as pleasantly and persuasively as she could. "I only said I thought you'd better take over Fifth and Sixth. If you've anything against that, let me hear it for goodness' sake!"

"Is it an order or isn't it?" Venables persisted, apparently determined to drink the bitterness of her cup to the last drop.

"Have you got any other suggestion?"

"Is it an order or isn't it?" Venables demanded a second time.

"I don't call it an order," said Violet. "But of course if you prefer to call it an order I can't stop you, can I?"

"Well!" Prentiss muttered. "Venables has been here six years and I've been here seven, and have you been here seven *weeks?"* Her voice rose a little, but only a little.

In all the annals of the Imperial Palace, and of the Royal Palace before it, there had never been a conflict so acute as this one. The conflicts between Sir Henry Savott on one side and father Dennis and Evelyn on the other, conflicts involving immense sums of money, were social trifles to it. The mortally injured pair had lost the freshness of their youth in the service of the Palace; and Miss Prentiss had seen the oncoming of middle-age declare itself in that service. The Imperial Palace was their home, their landscape, their climate, their atmosphere, their habit. They knew the Palace through and through, though they had never seen its deep foundations as Violet had disgracefully been privileged to see them. On Mrs. O'Riordan's desertion each of them had expected to be raised to her throne. Why not? Had they not the seniority of years, if not of service? Were they not efficient? Had a black mark ever been notched against them, until their defence of dignity under the monstrous assault of Maclaren? Maclaren was not a lady, couldn't be if she tried. Whereas Prentiss was admittedly a lady, and Venables, by the mere power of thought, had created herself a lady.

And who was Powler? A laundry-woman! Introduced into the hotel by Mr. Orcham, and soon caught trying to captivate Sir Henry Savott! And the laundry-woman, an inexperienced neophyte, ignorant of the A B C of hotels, was raised over their heads by the foreigner Mr. Cousin! And there on the bed sat the laundry-woman triumphant, with her energetic youth, with her unwrinkled complexion, with her damnable complacency! The situation was intolerably unfair. It was more than human nature could stand. Justice had ceased from the earth. God was no more in heaven. If holy hatred could have killed, Violet would have died on the spot.

As for Violet, she did worse than hate; she disdained. She could have informed the rebels why they had been passed over. It was because, with all their experience and their efficiency, they lacked charm in the handling of visitors and in their relations with the staff. Mrs. O'Riordan could assume charm like a new frock. And because they lacked tact. And because they were for ever conveying to others their sense of their own importance and breeding and sinless perfection. And because, in the end, in the encounter with Mac, they had tried to break the chain of authority, than which, to Mr. Orcham, nothing was more sacred. They had committed the supreme crime. Violet had an obscure feeling that she ought to sympathise with them, to be sorry for them. But she could not be sorry for them. No! She disdained them. And she didn't care. She was in no way to blame. In her inexperience she had imagined that in the sublime and august Imperial Palace, synonym of Paradise, the horrors of warfare were impossible, inconceivable. Innocent! She now comprehended that there was as much human nature in the Imperial Palace as anywhere else, even more than in the Laundry. She saw in the flesh before her the great fact that human nature will out. She was intimidated, but no one should guess that she was intimidated. "I won't speak. I won't give them a chance," she said to herself.

"I should like to know what Mr. Orcham would say to this," Prentiss remarked coldly.

Violet explained that Mr. Orcham had approved by telephone.

Suddenly Prentiss flared:

"Then it isn't Mr. Cousin! It isn't Mr. Cousin after all. Mr. Orcham brought you here and you're his pet. Yes, he brings you here and he pushes you up all the time. And why? Why, I should like to know." Prentiss nearly forgot that she was a lady and had had a governess all to herself once.

"I shan't speak," Violet repeated privately, feeling as if she were holding back a tiger by a bit of thin string.

Prentiss had started, and Prentiss continued, and in five minutes of destructive, eloquent diatribe, she had torn Violet's character to pieces and thrown the pieces on the floor by the bedside.

"I shan't speak," Violet still said to herself. She pitied Prentiss and Venables; but her pity was contemptuous.

"I don't know what *you* mean to do, my dear," said Prentiss lovingly to Venables. "But tomorrow morning I shall walk out of this place."

"So shall I, dear," Venables responded in her society tone; and took the thin, veined hand of her companion.

"Well," said Violet with detachment. "You can settle that with Mr. Cousin."

The outraged pair, exemplars of dignity both of them, drew away. The entrance-door closed on them. They deserved what Violet was incapable of bestowing--compassion. In an ideal world Violet would have cast herself down at their feet, kissed Prentiss's bedroom slippers. But she only smiled. She only said to herself, pleased with her self-control: "I didn't speak. I didn't give them a chance." But a moment later she began to use the most dreadful language, and in the sitting-room she lit one of Mac's cigarettes.

Chapter 42 CERIA AND SIR HENRY

"Who is he, that one?" murmured the boyish-faced Ceria, in French, to his second-in-command. He had been chatting with two regular guests who always sat at a table in a far corner of the Imperial Palace grill-room; and when he returned towards the middle of his kingdom he saw that table No. 33 was occupied by three men, only two of whom he recognised. One of the two was chairman of a British film company, the other an owner of eight or ten minor but large cinema theatres in the suburbs. Ceria was aware that 33 had been booked for the film chairman. The second-in-command was aware that Ceria, though the scarcely perceptible indicative jerk of his head had been very vague, could be directing attention to nobody but the stranger who sat between the pair of habitués at 33. The second-in-command, shrugging his shoulders to signify that he could not answer the question, beckoned to a headwaiter and repeated to him Ceria's enquiry.

"That one? He ought to be Sir Henry Savott," said the head-waiter, proud of his knowledge, and pretending to be astonished at such ignorance on the part of his superiors.

Ceria lifted his eyebrows. He knew everything about Sir Henry Savott except the gentleman's physical appearance. Everybody on the upper staff had learnt the surpassing importance of Sir Henry in the recent secret history of the Imperial Palace.

In the restaurant of course he was a fairly familiar if infrequent figure, and received sedulous personal service from Cappone himself. But herein was no reason why he should be famous in the grill-room. The grill-room and the restaurant were two different worlds. Just as there were patrons of the restaurant to whom it never occurred to enter the grill-room, so there were patrons of the grill-room who would not dream of entering the restaurant--partly because of the band, which in artistically performing high-class music interfered with conversation, partly because the general atmosphere of the grill-room was less prim than that of the restaurant, and partly because they met their friends in the grill-room and would not be likely to meet them in the restaurant.

The restaurant catered for a few truly smart people and a crowd of well-dressed and well-behaved nonentities to whom smartness was an ideal. The grill-room catered for active leaders of commercial, industrial, theatrical, cinematographic and journalistic society. In the clientèle of the grill-room there was a much larger proportion of names and faces known to newspaper-readers than in the clientèle of the restaurant. And quite probably the wealth in the grill-room, per man, exceeded the wealth in the restaurant. (One regular luncher in the former was reputed to have made twenty millions in thirty years of ordering the labours of other individuals.) The restaurant was the haunt of persons who existed as beautifully as they knew how. The grill-room was the haunt of persons accustomed to command, who *did* things or got them done, who specialised in neither manners nor attire (except a star-actress and a fashionable chorus-girl or so), who dared the Atlantic six or seven times a year, who greeted one another with broad gestures across half-a-dozen tables, and who began to look at their watches about a quarter-past two.

Ceria moved towards 33 in the execution of his social duties, but on the way thither he was stopped twice by visitors, and once by a head-waiter who needed guidance in a delicate situation.

The hour was 1.30 and the grill-room, which Ceria conducted as well as an orchestra consisting mainly of soloists can be conducted, had scarcely one empty table. The company had arrived from various parts of London, in many cases at some cost of time and convenience, for the site of the Imperial Palace was better suited to butterflies than to bees; but fashion and Ceria had made it popular with bees, who have their own snobbishness, who will pay for it, and who had persuaded themselves that they could not afford to lunch elsewhere than under Ceria. The noise of chatter was at least as loud as might have been the sound of music; but happily it was chatter and not music, it was evenly distributed, and as it proceeded from the lunchers it did not dominate them. A strange and exciting spectacle, the grill-room. The restaurant was a mile off, the Floors ten miles off.

2.

At length Ceria reached 33. Youthful, with a modest smile and a most misleading air of diffidence (like others on the staff he had formed his deportment on that of Mr. Orcham), he gave the greeting of welcome to his two acquaintances, and bowed deferentially to Sir Henry Savott.

"If you don't know Sir Henry Savott, Ceria, you soon will do," said the chairman of the film company, with a Scotch accent. He laughed significantly, as one who had nothing to learn about the intimate connection between Sir Henry and the Imperial Palace.

"Glad to know you, Ceria," said Sir Henry, and benevolently offered his hand.

"I've never had the pleasure of seeing you here before, Sir Henry. But I know you well by sight." Thus spoke the charming and diplomatic liar. "I hope you like your new house. One hears that it is very wonderful."

While he felt flattered, Sir Henry reflected: "This fellow knows his job." He said aloud that his new house might be worse. Then, in the ensuing pause, he added: "How are the New Year's Eve arrangements getting on? We shall be in next year before we know where we are."

Ceria replied, with a show of proud enthusiasm:

"I believe that nearly every table in the restaurant has been booked already. Mr. Cousin told me yesterday that before Christmas comes he will be refusing very many applications. Mr. Cappone said several hundreds. It will be a record New Year's Eve for the Imperial Palace. Last year was a record too."

"That's fine. I haven't reserved a table yet, but I shall do. You might tell Cappone, if you don't mind," said Sir Henry, who had not forgotten Evelyn's boast.

"Certainly, sir," agreed Ceria, with a new kind of a smile which said to Sir Henry: "This will help you to understand that there is only one Imperial Palace."

"But surely you aren't going to turn people away," Sir Henry went on with bright, friendly astonishment and deprecation.

"What are we to do, sir? There was some suggestion of using the ball-room as another restaurant, and clearing the tables at half-past twelve; but of course it could not be done. People will want to eat and drink till two o'clock at least, and people will want to begin to dance at midnight."

"But there is this room," said Sir Henry. "Tables here for three hundred and more. But perhaps this room *is* to be used."

"Good idea!" the Scottish chairman interjected. "Have a separate function here, and I'll give you the first showing of my new forty-minute film." The notion excited him. First film ever exhibited in the Imperial Palace! Unique publicity! Etc.

Ceria shook his head sorrowfully, for he envied Cappone on New Year's Eve and on no other night. "We must keep this room for those who do not like New Year's Eve dinners and suppers. And then, our visitors who are staying in the hotel! Impossible! Quite impossible!"

"Yes, yes," Sir Henry concurred.

The chairman was dashed, and began to fidget his very solid body.

"My maxim," said the owner of cinemas, "is the greatest pleasure for the greatest number. You could fill this room with a special festivity. Could you fill it with your old fogeys, and if you could, would they spend as much money?"

"No, sir, I hardly expect to fill it, and they would not spend half as much. *You,*" he glanced at Sir Henry, with forlorn hopefulness, "you would perhaps speak to Mr. Cousin, sir."

Sir Henry said nothing in reply.

A moment later Ceria left the table, somewhat meditative. Always he felt himself an exile from the renowned Palace New Year's Eve celebrations, during which the grill-room lived desolate hours enlivened by merely sedate "souvenirs." He would have given a very great deal to be the autocrat of a New Year festivity of his own, complete with orchestra, cinema, balloons, streamers, missiles, caps, toy-instruments, incandescent puddings and all.

Chapter 43 SABBATH

Violet was occupying Miss Maclaren's sitting-room, partly as a sign of authority, but much more because in her position of acting head-housekeeper, she had frequent need of a room for interviews. That she did not use the bedroom also was a tactful admission of the temporary nature of her seat on the high throne of the former Mrs. O'Riordan. Her rule had so far been marked by no untoward incident. Miss Prentiss and Miss Venables, while working out their notice under Violet's general instruction, kept themselves to themselves and as invisible as might be. Their desperate resolve to depart instantly and leave the Palace in a fix had been abandoned without a word said on the morning after Miss Maclaren's seizure and Violet's outrageous rise to power.

Violet had refrained from any direct criticism of their performances, preferring tranquillity to an ideal perfection. Agatha, the head-housekeeper's pink-faced, fluffy little secretary, had acted as go-between; Agatha had a very convenient faculty of being passionately loyal to the occupant of the throne, no matter who the occupant was. Miss Cass, Evelyn's grand secretary, had been fairly sympathetic to Violet, though the absence of her master had given her too much freedom and a somewhat extravagant sense of her own importance in the world of the hotel. Miss Tilton, Mr. Cousin's secretary, had been very helpful, in her dashing way; the friendship between her and Violet, based on identity of one Christian name, was progressing. Beatrice Noakes, the fat chambermaid on Eighth, had been extremely helpful, if extremely loquacious. Peace had been achieved and maintained.

It was Sunday. Sunday is more acutely Sabbatical in fashionable hotel than anywhere else in London, save a few homes which still keep their islet-heads bravely raised above a flowing tide of irreligion. Visitors to the Imperial Palace considered it incorrect to be seen in London on Sunday--at any rate until the evening. Many left on Saturday for the weekend, but kept their rooms, with a noble disregard of expense. Many slipped inconspicuously away early on Sunday morning for a day's golf or perilous motoring. Some stayed in bed. Ceria's grill-room was a melancholy desert at the lunch hour. The restaurant was scarcely a third full--of apologetic persons or persons who had no shame. The entrance-hall and the foyer had a thick moral atmosphere which seemed to deaden footfalls and reduce pace. The mere aspect of the reading-room rendered it inviolate. The staff was more than decimated. Apparently none of the visitors, and none of the staff except a few Latins who attended early Mass, had any preoccupation concerning the infinite, the mystery of the grave, the dread consequence of sin, the menace of a flouted deity. Self-righteousness was notably diminished, almost swallowed up in tedium. The afternoon was terrible. But in the evening, in the vast restaurant, with jazz, Hungarian rhapsodies, jugglers, dancers, and caviare, bisque, and multi-coloured alcohol, the

Palace did appreciably recover its weekday animation and geniality. Monday indeed began on Sunday night.

In the head-housekeeper's sitting-room sat Violet, wearing not her raven duty-frock, but a frock of bright hues and a hat that suited. She was less a head-housekeeper than a prosperous daughter about to go forth and dazzle her simple parents' home. She might have gone earlier; but the imponderable weight of housekeeping responsibility had hugged her down. And she was also a student of conversational French. The lesson was just finished; the benevolent and fatherly Perosi had stood up to leave. He was leaving with regret. His pupil's progress flattered him, and he enjoyed her calm, sensible, matter-of-fact and smiling society. The two were genuinely attached to one another. Perosi had two satisfactions in his heart. Though in such condition of health as might have excused him from the office, he had been to Mass at 8 a.m. And this lesson had been the first lesson to be conducted entirely in French. The time of the next lesson was being arranged when a knock at the door disturbed the seclusion.

"Come in," Violet called instantly in a loud, clear voice. For, though Perosi was old and Violet young and both of them were reputable beyond slur, it was well that the appearances of respectability should fully corroborate the fact thereof, and a moment's delay might have damaged the appearances.

2.

Ceria came in, boyish, diffident, gentle. He began:

"Bon jour, mademoiselle, comment allez-vous?" (For he had heard of the French lessons, and his brain worked very swiftly.)

And Violet, despite her amazement at seeing him, answered in a sort of dream, very nervously, but correctly:

"Trés bien, monsieur, je vous remercie. Et vous-même?"

Perosi was enchanted. It was nothing to him that the lesson had happened to contain those very phrases. The girl had understood French from an unexpected visitor (what a dreadful Italian accent the young man had!), and, keeping her presence of mind admirably, had replied in French!

But Perosi concealed his enchantment, and easily. He had a grievance against the innocent Ceria. His greeting of the Grill-room manager was stiff, reserved and plainly inimical. The grievance had arisen thus. Two visitors on Eighth had complained to Miss Maclaren about breakfast-dishes theoretically hot being in practice cold. Miss Maclaren had passed on the complaint to Perosi, perhaps rather clumsily. Perosi knew the cause of the trouble: a defect in the electric hot-plate in the service-lift, which defect an electrician had not contrived at once to cure. Ceria was known to be ultimately responsible for the floor-meals, and one of the visitors had spoken to Ceria. Perosi was convinced that, on the evening of her seizure, Ceria had sent for Miss Maclaren in order to discuss the matter with her. Perosi could not tolerate such a proceeding, which was a blow to his cherished prestige and a sin against the cardinal principle of the chain of authority. The service of meals on the Floors was his affair, and no other person's affair. His notorious passive antipathy to all the housekeepers (with the sole exception of Violet) sprang from, and was fed by, real or fancied interference by housekeepers in his exclusive domain. He held that Ceria's going behind his back to criticise him in private confabulation with Miss Maclaren was a monstrous act. Therefore was his demeanour towards Ceria hostile. One result was that the gloomy air of Sunday seemed to have penetrated into the room with the entrance of Ceria.

But no sooner had Perosi's face declared hostility to Ceria than he saw a disturbed expression on Violet's face. He thought, alarmed: "I have represented myself to this most sympathetic young woman as a man full of general kindliness. I must on no account destroy the character which I have created for myself in her eyes. More than anything I wish to stand well with her." And he began with much Latin subtlety to change his attitude. And as he changed it, so did his hidden feelings change towards Ceria, and so was Violet reassured. The air of Sunday was gradually dissipated.

"I came to enquire the latest news about Miss Maclaren," Ceria was saying.

"Do sit down," said Violet. "I called yesterday at the hospital to leave some flowers, but I was not allowed to see her. But Dr. Constam telephoned me this morning that if they could do without a second operation she would very likely pull through. If they *must* have another operation he wouldn't prophesy. Anyhow, the poor thing is holding her own for the present."

"Did he tell you exactly what it is?" Ceria asked.

"He didn't. They hardly ever do, you know." Violet smiled sadly. "I think she will pull through. People generally pull through, don't they? Do sit down, Mr. Ceria. Won't you sit down again, Mr. Perosi?" She felt as if she was presiding at a reception.

"But you are going out," said Ceria, sitting down.

"Not the slightest hurry."

Perosi looked at his watch.

"I must go down to Fourth," said he. "Thank you." On his way to the door he stopped and addressed Ceria very blandly. "You were the first to see Miss Maclaren. *Comment ça est-il arrivé? Personne n'en satl rien--à ce qu'il parait."*

Ceria out of politeness to Violet answered in English, shaking his head:

"She telephoned that she wanted to see me. I asked her to come down to my office. She had the attack as she came in. Very severe pain, I should say. I helped her to sit on a chair. She would have fallen off if I had not held her. Then I carried her to the lift. That was all. I know no more than anybody else."

"She didn't speak?"

"She could not."

"She did not say why she came to see you?" Perosi daringly probed.

Ceria shook his head again: "Nothing. I cannot guess what she wanted."

Impossible for even Perosi not to credit the young man's sincerity. The old man was perfectly satisfied, and once more in the full bloom of his benevolence. He said, in a new tone suddenly and quite dramatically warm:

"Ceria, my friend, I hear you are thinking of organising a New Year's Eve celebration in the grill-room to accommodate visitors who have not succeeded in obtaining tables in the restaurant. It is a fine idea, that! At New Year's Eve there is little to do on the Floors. If I can help you in the service, dispose of me."

Violet was thrilled by this startling announcement, which after the rather laboured and melancholy exchanges on the subject of Miss Maclaren's illness sounded a sort of trumpet-note of inspiring enthusiasm. Not often did the old man show enthusiasm concerning anything. Violet had heard the widespread news of the unprecedented demand for tables in the restaurant on the great night; but not a word had reached her of the scheme for bringing the grill-room into the geography of the mighty feast. She knew nothing of the grill-room, had never seen it.

As for Ceria, he was still more startled than his hostess. He had not mentioned Sir Henry Savott's casual suggestion to any member of the staff, nor at a daily conference, for the reason that he had regarded it as too impossible to be worth discussion. Sir Henry Savott had apparently not been ready to stand sponsor for it. And assuredly, Mr. Cousin would not for a moment consider it. And now Ceria amazingly learnt that somehow the scheme had got abroad in the hotel. And the scheme blossomed magnificently afresh from the shrivelled seed in his mind. He pictured in a flash the entire splendid fête in his grill-room, and himself in charge of it, and his very friendly rival Cappone outshone, not in size, but by sheer force of *chic* and inventive novelty; and paragraphs about it in Mr. Immerson's weekly gossip columns. His eye shone; his cheeks flamed.

"Have you heard of it then?" he hesitatingly asked.

"I heard," said Perosi.

"How?"

Perosi gave a shrug. "I seem to have heard," he said vaguely.

He enjoyed being mysterious. The truth was that the cinema-owner, present at the lunch two days earlier, had mentioned it, with ornamental additions and exaggerations, to Perosi on the previous night during the service of an intimate dinner in the suite which he was occupying in the Palace for a week of some secret negotiation. Perosi had mistakenly understood that the thing was as good as settled; whereas the fact was that Mr. Cousin himself was in complete ignorance of Sir Henry Savott's fanciful notion. Sir Henry, when in the creative mood, was capable of throwing off half-a-dozen such coruscating sparks in half a day.

Now Ceria, the centre of the scheme, could not possibly appear to be less well informed about it than Perosi, who had only 'heard' of it.

"It will be discussed at the conference to-morrow morning," he said, as one who was at the heart of the matter, deciding on the instant to introduce it at the conference himself. He took Perosi's offer as a significant omen. Perosi, though a minor deity in the pantheon of the Palace, had a prestige beyond his rank. He was accepted by his superiors as a serious and sagacious person. Both Mr. Orcham and Mr. Cousin listened with respect to his opinion, whether they had sought it or not. He had had great experience of hotel work; and before Ceria had dawned on the Palace, Perosi had been a valued head-waiter in the grill-room. But for lack of ambition, lack of personal style, and a certain superficial surliness of manner, he might have risen very high in the Palace.

What puzzled Ceria was that Mr. Cousin, the scheme having as it seemed been on the carpet for two days, had not summoned him into the managerial office. He guessed that it must be Sir Henry who had mentioned the wonderful idea, his own, to Mr. Cousin. And an idea of Sir Henry's was not one to be lightly cast aside.

Perosi departed, in full lustre.

3.

Violet wondered why Ceria outstayed Perosi. He had received the information about Mac which he had come for. And Mr. and Mrs. Powler, at home in Renshaw Street on the south side of the Thames, would grow impatient for the arrival of their marvellous daughter. Still, Violet, if she had had a magic power to choose between sending Ceria away and keeping him, would have kept him yet awhile. She liked him. She liked his presence, the innocent, diffident, unworldly look on his face. She was attracted to him, not as a male, but as a human being. So sensible, so ingenuous, so agreeable to behold! Similarly she liked old Perosi. So grim, so benign. She liked *people.* She liked to know about them and to understand them. This was only her second meeting with Ceria. At the first, she had immediately appreciated his concern for the stricken Mac (though there was something nonchalant in it), and the discretion of his disappearance from Mac's room when he could no longer be useful. She liked to hear him talk his very correct and fluent English, in which every sound was subtly foreign: so that he could not have said even 'knife' without betraying his foreign birth.

Of course his foreignness was a vague barrier dividing them. Foreign, full of mystery, he would always be. But she did not object to the barrier, because she had no wish for intimacy with him. To enjoy his acquaintance was sufficient for her. What did not present itself to her mind was the fact that, just as Ceria was foreign to her, so was she foreign to him. Exotic, elusive. They chatted about nothing, Sundayishly. Their talk was simple, and it was cheerful. But for Violet, beneath the flow of the conversation, there was an undercurrent of sadness for the tragic plight of Mac. She fancied that she could detect the same sadness beneath the social tone of Ceria's sentences.

She was wrong. Ceria was certainly preoccupied, but not with the fate of Miss Maclaren. His mind was busy upon the dream of the possibilities of a New Year's Eve fête in his grill-room. Violet had a very imperfect conception of the importance of New Year's Eve in the corporate life of the Imperial Palace. She had never seen a fashionable, luxurious New Year's Eve fête, and never imagined one. She was perhaps aware, from rumours and glimpses, that tremendous preparations were afoot, and that the entire hotel was slowly gathering its energies together for a grand climacteric of display designed orgiastically to receive the New Year into the infinite succession of years. But as regards the esoteric spirit of the effort, she belonged to an ignorant and uninitiated laity.

"You are going out," said Ceria suddenly, without rising, and as though he had not made this surprising discovery before.

"Not yet," she replied. "Are you generally here on Sunday afternoons? I thought that--"

"I am never here on Sunday afternoons, and not often on Sunday evenings. But my mother and my sisters went away this morning to the Riviera. They would have gone to Italy, our home, but there might have been complications for the return. They are not naturalised British subjects like I am. My eldest sister has been unwell."

"I'm sorry to hear that."

"Not ill. Unwell. It is the damp climate. They have gone for a month. My house is empty. You understand--the sadness of an empty home. I could not tolerate it alone. After lunch I stayed here. *Laisser aller!*" He smiled plaintively, as it were appealing for sympathetic comprehension.

"What a pity you did not call earlier then!" Violet smiled. "I might have given you some tea."

He thanked her deprecatingly. Mac's illness was the pretext for his call; no more. He had called because he had lost three women endeared to him by habit of life; he was accustomed to the companionship of women, this deferential functionary of whom his patrons thought that the grill-room was his sole and everlasting world; and in the arid desert of the hotel on Sunday afternoon he had sought an oasis--a woman's room. He had liked Violet for the calm efficiency of her reception of Miss Maclaren's tortured body. He had liked her soothing presence. Her expression and her gestures had remained in his memory. And now he liked a new expression on her face, an expression--which he did not know was characteristic--of kindly alacrity to observe and consider sympathetically any phenomenon that might offer itself to her cognisance. He was offering himself to her cognisance. And her smile was responsive.

"Do you live near here?" she asked. "I suppose you do, because of getting home at nights."

He told her exactly where his home lay: a little beyond Hampstead. With an increasing naïve eagerness he described his home, his mother, his elder sister and his younger sister, his garden, the tennis-court--with not enough space at the ends for truly scientific back-line play. He was so graphic in his mild fervour that Violet *saw* his home and the old lady and the two girls. Did the ladies feel exiled in North London? Did they not long for Italy? Not a bit. They were devoted to London. They loved the English and the English character and ways. There was no tedium in London. Both Emilia and Daria spoke English better than himself, Ceria. The old lady spoke a little English. But at home they spoke nothing but Italian. They had an Italian maid-cook, and the cuisine was strictly Italian. The English were wonderful. The English domestic cuisine, however...Well, they had experienced it in a boarding house at Brixton for a few weeks. The stream of home-detail slackened, trickled. Ceria rose.

"I must go. May I telephone you for news of Miss Maclaren to-morrow?"

Violet nodded.

"I do hope your New Year's Eve dinner will be arranged," she said politely, not quite realising how much the fête meant to him.

"Ah yes!" he sighed, with Latin pessimism. Then brightly:

"I was so glad that Perosi favoured it. Perosi is listened to here in the Palace. He is a historical monument. If when he sees Mr. Cousin he should chance to say a word--it would have influence."

"Really?"

"Yes, yes. I have noticed before."

"I shall tell him he must. I shall tell him." Violet's tone was confident, almost imperious, the tone of a woman who knows her feminine power. She rose. She seemed to be suddenly inspired with enthusiasm for Ceria's scheme. "I shall tell him to-night when I come back."

"How nice of you!" Ceria's eyes shone. So did Violet's.

A quarter of a minute after his departure she was following him down the lighted corridor. She ran into her bedroom at the end, switched on the electricity, put on her coat, snatched her bag, examined her face, switched off the electricity. She was out of the hotel. She walked quickly, past the dim groves and water of St. James's Park, past Queen Anne houses, the Abbey, hospitals, grandiose Government offices, to the corner of the Embankment and Westminster Bridge, and sprang on to a tram with the right illuminated sign on its forehead. Buildings were smaller, roads wider and straighter, motorcars fewer, costumes and suits less smart. The tram slid roaring by the Laundry, and the Laundry touchingly recalled to her what seemed like her distant youth. Cyril Purkin was no doubt in his little house there. South London was another world, the world, again, of her far-distant youth. Condescending to it, she yet loved it, because she knew every yard of it and it was her home.

The tram stopped. She jumped down. Tiny houses on the broad thoroughfare. She walked a little under the recurrent glare of the street-lamps; then turned to the left, then to the right. Tiniest houses, some lit, some dark, some with names, some without. She halted at a low wooden gate opening into a front-garden as big as a counterpane. One projecting window; slits of light at the edges of the three blinds. A light over the door.

The moon is not farther from the earth than Violet was then from the Imperial Palace. She rang the tinkling old bell briskly. She tapped on the door. Her father would as usual say something faintly sardonic about her artificial complexion. Her mother would remark on her new gloves. How slow were these parents! The door opened. Her mother! Her mother kissed her as she stood on the doorstep, looking with strange enquiry at this new daughter. How narrow and stuffy and old was the lobby! Her father in his old creased housejacket appeared at the door of the sitting-room.

"I must positively be back at the old Pally by ten o'clock, children," she exclaimed.

It was her father who had somewhat derisively attached the diminutive "Pally" to the greatest luxury hotel in the world. South London had to maintain its self-respect.

Chapter 44 THE VAMP

Violet found a mild and soothing satisfaction in the short Sunday evening visit to her home; but as she waved a good night to her parents standing side by side in the front doorway, her father puffing at his pipe, the thought in her dutiful daughterly mind was:

"Well, that's done!"

Her father and mother were not really interested in the Palace, and her father's comments on the things she told him showed no comprehension of either their importance or their significance. Her mother was inquisitive about the details of Miss Maclaren's seizure, but to Violet her curiosity seemed morbid and her prejudice against hospitals almost childish. Both parents had been much more interested in the life of the Laundry, probably because they saw it from the street several times a week. What really did interest them was the daily functioning of the little home: the enormities of the charwoman who 'came in' for half a day on alternate days, the caprices of the kitchen range, the inexplicable peeling of paint on the back-door, the new wireless in the next house, the kittening of the cat. They assumed that Violet would be eager for every tiniest morsel of house-gossip.

Her father had of course never been inside the Palace, had never dreamed of going inside, could not conceive of any circumstances which might lead to his going inside. Her mother had never even seen the hotel, or, if she had long ago seen it, had not noticed it. She spoke of making a trip to look at it, as she might have spoken of a trip to New York. The hotel was far beyond their range. Violet was miraculously rising in the hotel. The hotel, for them, was a place existing solely in order that Violet might rise in it.

As for Violet, this excursion into South London--she had made several before--was the first to awaken her fully to the quick growth of her affection for the Palace. As she journeyed eastward in the tram she was positively impatient to be back on the Floors with all their endless small surprises and anxieties; quite ready to be immersed again in a sea of trouble--what some people would call trouble but she wouldn't. And in particular she was impatient to talk to Mr. Perosi. She had convinced herself that by talking to Perosi she might help to help the Palace towards a greater glory on New Year's Eve. Her sole reason for returning to the hotel not later than ten o'clock was information received from Perosi himself that he would be leaving the hotel at that hour on a visit to a friend at the Majestic. Strictly, she had been entitled to a week-end off, but a truly earnest temporary head-housekeeper could not think of absenting herself for so long a period from the supervision of the huge organism--especially as she had had word from Mr. Cousin that her salary would be raised during the term of her high office. But for the desire to have an interview with Perosi, however, she would not have returned till midnight.

Mr. Maxon, the Staff-manager's second-in-command, was fussing about restlessly in the dark staff-entrance, though nobody was clocking-in and nobody was clocking-out. Naturally Mr. Maxon did not expect a head-housekeeper to clock-in. On the contrary he very amiably opened the wicket for her and expressed his view that the night was fine, with which Violet very amiably agreed. It occurred to her that her father would have made an excellent assistant Staff-manager. She enquired of Mr. Maxon whether Mr. Perosi had left the hotel. He had not. But she met Perosi, strangely clad in a fawn-coloured lounge-suit and a brown overcoat and softhat to match, in the main basement-corridor, he having descended in a service-lift. She stopped him. They were alone in the stony corridor.

"I'm so glad I've caught you," she said, with a calm, gentle smile. She had intended that smile to be captivating, but at the moment of composing the smile she was too proud, or too honest, to use the wile which she had contemplated. She was disappointed with herself. She thought: "Why can't I do it? Why am I so stiff?"

For she had set her mind on 'vamping'--there was no other word--the benevolent grim old gentleman, on demonstrating the influence over him which she believed she possessed. According to Ceria, Perosi's opinions about hotel-policy had weight. Ceria desired that the weight of Perosi's opinions should turn the scale in favour of a special New Year's Eve fête in the grill-room, and had she not said to Ceria, of Perosi:

"I shall tell him he must"? Her instinct was to help Ceria. Ceria was a child, and she wanted to give him a toy. Ceria was so charming, so innocent, so diffident, so pathetic, so bereft of his womenkind. Ceria would have to sleep through Christmas and the New Year in his desolate home. He deserved compensation, and Violet was determined that if she could bring it about he should have the dazzling compensation of a fête in his grill-room.

"Qu'est-ce que c'est? Vous me le direz en français," said the French master, quizzically, rather alarmingly. His experience of housekeepers had endowed him with a sort of second-sight; and by nature he was suspicious.

Violet shook her head to the command to say her say in French. Perosi knew that he was ordering the impossible of his pupil.

"You remember what you said to Mr. Ceria this afternoon in my room about that scheme for a New Year's Eve dinner in the grill-room?" Perosi nodded cautiously. "Well, after you left he talked about it. He seems frightfully keen on it, but he's afraid they'll turn it down. Now I was just thinking--everybody in this place knows what influence you have here, and I was just thinking that if you did get a chance to put in a word to Mr. Cousin, perhaps you might...You see what I mean. It's only an idea that crossed my mind. And everybody *does* know your influence. I've often heard of it."

Not a very clever speech, she thought. Lame! And the last sentence was a gross and deliberate exaggeration. But she smiled again, looking up at the man with an appeal in her eyes.

2.

Perosi's gaunt face softened. She thought: "After all I'm doing this fairly well."

Perosi had feared some request for a favour the granting of which might upset the strictness of the ritual of his branch of the Floors-service. You never knew with these women, even the most sensible of them! Instead, Violet had flattered him. It was true that he had influence. He was nobody. He was only the head-floors-waiter. But he had influence with the mighty--and incidentally his post of head-floors-waiter was an exceedingly important one, if you looked at it properly! Perhaps none more important under Mr. Cousin!

"No!" he said gently, hardening his face again. "I shall not speak to Mr. Cousin."

"Oh!" Violet exclaimed timidly. She really did feel like a sweet young girl at the mercy of a stern and powerful male.

"But," Perosi went on, relenting with grim roguishness. "I shall speak to Mr. Orcham."

"Mr. Orcham! But--"

"Mr. Orcham has telegraphed from Boulogne that he will be here to-night. Victoria 10.47. I've only heard this minute. If they'd let me know early, I should not have changed my clothes. Now I must change back again, because when Mr. Orcham returns after an absence I take his orders myself. So I shall not go to the Majestic. I take just a little walk to the river and back, to breathe. That is why I go out earlier than I said. I shall see Mr. Orcham in his room, and if I can I shall say a word. He likes me to take his orders myself--I mean for a meal, if he is hungry. I shall certainly see him."

"That's splendid!" said Violet. "And it's very nice of you." She smiled gratefully, admiringly: final gesture of the vamp successful.

Perosi went off, buttoning his overcoat and turning up the collar.

But Violet was vaguely disturbed by the news of Mr. Orcham's imminent arrival. Mr. Orcham was great and terrible. He had been terrible about Venables and Prentiss. Still, he had confirmed her astonishing appointment as temporary head-housekeeper. He was a man about whom nothing could be prophesied. Violet had a notion that the mice might have played more harmoniously if the cat had not returned so soon.

Chapter 45 THE PANJANDRUM'S RETURN

Evelyn, at a quarter before midnight, had been in his castle for thirty-five minutes. His mood was that of a returned traveller for whom work and anxieties have been accumulating during his absence. He was relieved and even glad to be back, but he shrank from the consequences of being back; he shirked the burden awaiting his broad shoulders. Also he was self-conscious as a supreme ruler re-entering a kingdom which has been left in charge of inferior beings. He had desired to meet nobody of importance until Monday morning. The prospect of effusive, deferential greetings from this person and from that as he came through the revolving doors into the great hall, answering enquiries about his health and his journey, responding suitably to expressions of pleasure at the sight of him, listening to hints of urgent matters which would immediately demand his notice, making polite enquiries about the health and the doings and the happiness of other people--the prospect of all this was more than he felt himself able to bear.

Call it weakness, cowardice, what you please, the panjandrum had chosen to re-enter his kingdom by the staff-entrance, to the intense astonishment of Mr. Maxon, who of course had attributed the caprice to every motive except the right foolish one. He had driven to the hotel quite alone, impatiently abandoning Oldham and baggage at Victoria. He had ascended to Seventh partly by a service-lift and partly by walking.

But even so, sneaking into his own house like a thief, he had not been able to avoid being somehow enveloped in the intangible blanket-folds of the hotel atmosphere. On the way up he had caught two or three bars of the orchestra far distant in the restaurant. Same old routine, hackneyed, desolating: so it seemed to him. People would be dancing and guzzling in the restaurant on the night of judgment and doom. But that must be the new Paris-American band which Jones-Wyatt, the Bands-and-Cabaret-manager, had engaged. Well, he did not very much like it. He could not possibly judge it with fairness, but his inclination was not to approve it, not to approve anything. He was in a hypercritical state of mind. Certain phenomena at the staff-entrance and in the basement-corridor had ruffled him, though he had said nothing about them to Maxon. He had passed unseen along the main corridor of Seventh, opened his door, slipped inside his castle, shut the door. He was safe. None would dare to disturb him. Yes, Perosi would dare to disturb. He knew the ritual on these rare occasions. Perosi regarded himself as a privileged person. And Perosi had dared to disturb him. He had to be pleasant and chatty with Perosi. He would not eat. No, not even the least snack. He had dined on the train from Folkestone. To placate Perosi, to save Perosi's gnarled face, he had asked for a liqueur brandy and hot water.

Serving the beverage with marvellous quickness, Perosi had shown an exasperating tendency to fall into hotel-gossip. Evelyn had bravely and nobly smiled, while attempting to check the tendency. Perosi had remarked that he had been very interested to hear of the project of a separate New

Year's Eve festivity in the grill-room. Then it was that Evelyn had performed a miracle of self-control and deceitfulness. One of his fibs without words. Neither by telephone nor by letter on his journeyings had he been vouchsafed one single syllable about this astounding project of a separate New Year's Eve festivity in the grill-room. Nevertheless he had replied mildly and casually to Perosi:

"Yes, yes," as if he had been familiar with the project for weeks, as if he himself had invented the project. And Perosi, hoodwinked, and perceiving that the moment was inopportune for a friendly discussion, had left the room. "I'm a bit tired, Perosi," Evelyn had said. "Good night. Thank you."

Then Evelyn had heard baggage being thudded into his bedroom through the bedroom door. By now every member of the staff would be apprised of his advent. There was Maxon. Before he had reached Seventh everybody would have learnt that the panjandrum had come--and by what strange entrance! He had sat awhile lounging in his soft travelling-suit, thinking of all his hotel-inspections, on the whole satisfactory, in various cities, and of the suddenly decided tiresome journey and the rough Channel voyage. He had meant to sleep one night in Boulogne, a sympathetic port, just for change and rest. But when the train stopped at the harbour station he had felt that after all he could not tolerate a night in Boulogne, and his consequent counter-orders and orders had considerably overset the exhausted Oldham. And it was not true that he had dined in the Pullman crowded with peevish passengers. He had only pretended to dine. The Channel, following many days of fatigue, had somewhat seriously deranged him, and indeed was partly responsible for his captious, sensitive temper.

Having finished the soothing brandy and water, he bent down and unlaced his brown boots, which for hours had been slightly incommoding him. Then, restless, he went into the bathroom. The bedroom door was open. He stared at Oldham stooping, straightening himself, sorting clothes, handling them gently, almost lovingly. Oldham knew well that there would be no respite for a valet until every garment and belonging was in its proper place and the trunk and the two suit-cases hidden away. A valet was not entitled to be fatigued by journeys, deranged by the Channel. A valet had to be superhuman. And Oldham really did seem to be superhuman in those moments. The truth was that on the journey he had made a tranquillising decision, a decision not uninfluenced by the loss of sixty pounds odd, all unknown to Evelyn, in a Paris *tripot.*

"I suppose, sir," he said, as it were dreamily, with his back to Evelyn. "I suppose you wouldn't care for me to withdraw my notice?"

Suggestion startling to Evelyn, among whose chief worries was the horrid thought of having to replace Oldham and train his successor...Silence...Oldham secretly trembled at his own boldness. Evelyn ought to have felt comforted. But he did not. Instead, he reflected bitterly: "Inconstant ass! Coward! He's afraid. And he doesn't know his own mind.

Why the devil should I let him withdraw his notice? Fancies himself as a retail tobacconist, and then funks it! But I might have guessed he'd give in when it came to the point!"

When the silence had continued for a few minutes, he said very drily:

"We'll talk about that to-morrow. I shall have to think it over." He added, commandingly: "Be as quick as you can. I want to go to bed."

"Yes, sir."

2.

Evelyn returned to the sitting-room, wearing pumps, and murmuring inaudibly to himself. A breath-taking sight confronted him: two letters lying on the centre-table. He was outraged by the sight, which strained to the snapping point his already exacerbated nerves. It was a rigid rule of the Palace that no correspondence should in any circumstances be delivered in his private rooms, which were held by him to be sacred. His office was the only proper place for correspondence, and for any documents relating to business. Also, he had determined not to touch business until the next day. He desired, and would positively have, nothing but peace. He impulsively opened the door and called out:

"Oldham!"

"Yes, sir." In response the man came as far as the bathroom.

"Who has put these letters here?" Evelyn's tone was very curt and imperious. Yet he admitted to himself that obviously Oldham was not in a position to answer the question.

"I really couldn't say, sir," said Oldham, placatory because he now wanted more and more to keep his situation.

"They have been put here since I went into the bedroom to speak to you. Someone must have brought them here." Evelyn knew even as he made it that this was a silly remark.

"Yes, sir."

"You don't know who did it?"

"No, sir."

"Well go, and find out--at once."

"Very good, sir," said Oldham, thinking to himself: "He's just told me to hurry up with the unpacking and here he pushes me off to do something else! What a life!" But he still wanted to keep his situation.

Evelyn firmly decided that he would not read the letters. No! He would send them downstairs to his office unopened and deal with them in the ordinary course the next morning. Then, glancing at one of the envelopes, he recognised the handwriting of Sir Henry Savott, and had a qualm. What could be wrong? He rather violently tore at the envelope. "My dear Orcham. This is to tell you that my friend Mr. Oliver Oxford, managing director of the Carlyle Oxford British Films Company, has an idea to suggest to you for the proposed New Year's Eve affair in your grill-room. Please listen to him. I think it was I who first thought of a special affair in the grill-room for New Year's Eve. Oxford is a friend of mine. Yours."

Curse the fellow! Trying to interfere with the management of the Palace! And all because, the hotel-merger being practically arranged, he was now turning to film-mergers. Evidently for reasons of his own the fellow was anxious to oblige this Oxford person. Of all the impudence! He, Evelyn, would show Savott what was what! The other envelope was large and of an ornamental nature. It bore on its face the words:

"Carlyle Oxford British." Extraordinary, despicable, how these English film companies would imitate American companies, even in their titles! But Carlyle, Evelyn knew, was an American. He read the second letter. What a signature of self-conscious flourishes! The letter afforded to Evelyn the virginity of an absolutely new kind of silent film, of which Carlyle Oxford British had the highest hopes, and in which they had an unparalleled confidence, for use in the Palace Grillroom on New Year's Eve, if Evelyn cared to avail himself of it. And would Evelyn come and see the film in the private theatre of Carlyle Oxford British in Lisle Street, at any time convenient to himself?

What *was* this grill-room scheme? It appeared to be very much in the air. First old Perosi. Then Savott. Then this Oxford--no doubt a Hebrew. Evelyn was clearly the only person in the world who knew nothing about it. He lit a cigarette. Why did not Oldham come back? What was the nincompoop up to? Surely it was a simple enough thing to find out who had introduced correspondence into the sitting-room! Evelyn went to the telephone, and demanded Mr. Cousin. He had no wish to speak to Mr. Cousin. He wanted to know whether Mr. Cousin was on duty. Mr. Cousin was not supposed to be on duty on Sunday nights; but Evelyn thought that the Manager, aware that his Director was returning, might have had the grace to be available. The telephone answer was that Mr. Cousin was away till Monday. Naturally! There was always something subtly independent about Cousin. Evelyn had been in search of a grievance. He found it. Then he telephoned to his secretary, Miss Cass. He knew that Miss Cass was on holiday for the week-end, but still he thought that the girl might by some magic have contrived to be present to welcome him. The reply from the hotel-exchange was that the Director's office was closed. Another grievance.

At last Oldham came back, flurried. He had failed in his mission. Perosi, a waiter, a valet, the liftman, several pages, a chambermaid: he had carried out a thorough investigation, and all these people denied any complicity in the mysterious delivery of letters into the castle. Evelyn had a gleam of light.

"Find out if a Mr. Oliver Oxford is staying here."

"Very good, sir." In a quarter of a minute Oldham conveyed the answer. Mr. Oliver Oxford was staying in the Palace. Suite 743. Quite near to Evelyn's castle. He guessed the solution of the enigma. Mr. O.O., having heard of Evelyn's arrival, had written the letter and delivered both letters himself. No doubt he had knocked, received no answer, and stepped impudently into the room. Evelyn noticed that Savott's letter was dated several days earlier, and had probably been waiting to be used in the presumptuous Hebrew's own good time.

The image of Violet Powler swam into his mind, possibly drawn there by a subconscious yearning to be tranquillised. He was accustomed to think of Miss Powler as a tranquillising creature; he had never forgotten, and he never recalled without pleasure, the scene at the Laundry when she had handled so gently the colour-blind woman. All the floors were now in charge of the inexperienced Miss Powler, with his approval. An audacious experiment. But during his absence had he received from Cousin any criticisms, any complaints, of her performance? Not one. Had Cousin shown the least misgiving as to her capacity? No. Cousin's letters and his nightly telephoning had been salted with hints of the inadequacy of other members of the upper staff; but Miss Powler's efficiency had not once been arraigned. He looked at the clock. Three minutes to twelve. He picked up the telephone, then hesitated. If this was an early night for her she would be gone to bed, but if not there were still three minutes before, according to rules, she was entitled to leave duty. He asked the Exchange for her. In a moment he heard her voice.

"Mr. Orcham?"

"Speaking. I've just returned, Miss Powler. I didn't want to trouble you at this time of the night, but I was rather anxious to have the latest news about Miss Maclaren. How is she to-day?"

"Not out of danger yet, sir."

"Oh! Sorry to hear that! I was hoping--" He stopped.

"It's rather a long story, sir."

"I say," said Evelyn in a tone more colloquial, "I wonder if you'd mind very much coming down now and telling me. I'm in my room--not my office."

"Certainly, sir."

Why had he invited her to come down to him, especially as he really had little to learn about Miss Maclaren's illness? Well, her voice had soothed him. It was like a balm to his sore nerves. It was the most soothing (yet firm) voice within his memory of women's voices. His wife; Mrs. O'Riordan, a wonderful old girl, extremely capable, but no consoler for a weary man; Miss Maclaren, always consciously bearing a weight of responsibility; Miss Cass, devoted enough and pleasant enough, but steely; Venables, Prentiss and others, nobodies who invariably by their prim voices raised a barrier between themselves and him. Ah! Cousin might stick to his lawful rights; Miss Cass might gad away for the week-end; but his favourite, Miss Powler, his discovery, his candidate--she was at her post! He might have known it. Miss Powler was not an employee to be fussy and exacting about hours. Not she! A tap at the door.

3.

She came into the room, quietly smiling. Her appearance startled him; for instead of the regulation housekeeper's black, she was wearing a bright-coloured frock. The psychological effect on Evelyn of this simple frock was considerable. It pulled him from his chair, impelled him a few steps across the room and thrust forward his right arm.

"Excuse my dress, please. I've just been home to see mother and father," she said as they shook hands.

"It's a very nice dress," he said, and pointed to a chair. "Do sit down. It's you who must excuse *me,* sending for you like this. Now tell me the whole story."

She sat. He said to himself that she was surprisingly changed--for the better. Her expression had the same placid benevolence, but she had gained tremendously in ease of manner, in worldliness. She must have been continuously learning from visitors. He had thought before that she might be anybody's daughter. He thought now that she might be anybody's daughter-except a small town-traveller's; she might be a peer's daughter, or an artist's, or a stockbroker's. Of course she had not quite Lady Milligan's style; but a quality was hers which the Yorkshire gentlewoman lacked: poise. At a heavy expense of nervous energy, Lady Milligan gallantly kept a semblance of poise--not the real thing; and at intervals she lost even the semblance. Whereas Miss Powler could be genuinely calm for ever and ever at no expense of spirit.

Violet related briefly the tragic tale of Mac from beginning to end.

"Um!" was Evelyn's only comment, but he put a lot of sympathy into it. He took a cigarette. Then it struck him that he ought to offer Miss Powler a cigarette. But he offered the cigarette to the bright frock. At any rate, if Violet had been in official black he would not have dreamt of such an approach. He made it solely for the sake of his own good opinion of himself as a polite man. He was sure that she would refuse the cigarette, and that she did not smoke. She was not the sort of girl who smokes; nor the sort of girl who, if she smokes, would care to smoke in the presence of her employer.

"Won't you have a cigarette?"

"Thank you," said Violet.

He was startled, for the second time. He had to hold a match for her. The interview modulated into a new key.

"What's *your* idea about this scheme for a special New Year's Eve dinner in the grill-room?" he asked, rather impulsively: partly because the scheme was like a bluebottle in his mind, and partly to cover a slight self-consciousness, concerning the cigarette. He thought, and he was bound to think:

"Supposing anyone came in and saw her and me smoking together, and her in that frock, and the time after midnight, especially as I sneaked into the hotel. Of course no one will come in, but supposing--"

Violet made no reply.

"You've heard of it?" he said.

"Yes, I have heard of it." She looked at him through the smoke and gave a smile.

"Who told you?" he was on the point of saying; but he did not utter the words. No decent employer ought to put such an ambiguous question to an employee; it would have had the air of an invitation to tell tales.

"I don't know anything about those things," Violet went on cautiously. To her there seemed to be a faint note of hostility to the scheme in Mr. Orcham's voice. *"This scheme!"* Had his tone been different she might have hinted at Mr. Ceria's passionate eagerness for the scheme, might have shown some sympathy for Mr. Ceria's cause. "I'm quite a beginner here. I don't know half enough about the Floors yet, and as for anything else--" She smiled again, lightly, as one who is confident of being fully understood. Then she said: "I expect they're waiting for you to settle it. I'm sure everybody's glad you've come back. We've all been rather lost without you. Mr. Cousin was saying only the day before yesterday he hoped you'd be back soon."

"You've been seeing Mr. Cousin pretty often?"

"Not seeing him. On the telephone. I've had to ask him about dozens of things. He's been very kind to me. No one could have been nicer."

"Well," said Evelyn. "Mr. Cousin's the man you have to deal with, not me, you know."

"Yes, I do know."

Evelyn reflected that never before had any housekeeper spoken as Miss Powler spoke of Cousin. All the other house-keepers had been wrong. Cousin was a good fellow, and he had been quite justified in not upsetting his own arrangements for the sake of being available on the chance of Evelyn wanting to see him. Evelyn was a fine judge of tact. His opinion that Miss Powler had an unusual measure of tact was confirmed. So they had all of them missed the presence of the panjandrum! The panjandrum was soothed--either by the cigarette or by the tact.

He threw the cigarette into the fire, two-thirds smoked. Violet was smoking hers very slowly. He was impatient for her to finish. He had a desire to make some enquiries about her experiences as head-housekeeper. But he thought that to talk professional shop with her when he had invited her down to get news of Miss Maclaren would be taking an improper advantage of the occasion. Still, conversation had to be maintained, and his social duty was to maintain it.

"Heard anything about your old home?" he asked.

"My old home? Oh! You mean the Laundry?" She laughed outright. "No. Except that Miss Brury is getting on splendidly. Mr. Purkin came up to see Mr. Cousin, and I happened to meet him. He told me so himself."

"Excellent! Excellent! I had an idea she would. That change we made is working out very well." A pleasant appreciative innuendo in his voice that she, Violet, was giving satisfaction.

"I'm so glad you think so, sir."

The first time she had said 'sir' in the interview.

There was another lull in the talk; he began to feel agreeably sleepy; but he could not dismiss her until her cigarette was consumed. Fortunately he happened to hit on a new topic.

"How is the French getting on?"

"Very slowly," she replied. "But Mr. Perosi is a very good teacher."

"And does the very good teacher think that progress is slow, or is that only your own idea?"

"He says it's pretty quick, considering. But to me it does seem terribly slow. Really!"

"I know the trouble I had," Evelyn mused aloud. "And even now, when I'm said to be mighty fluent, I often think I've done no more than scratch the surface of the infernal language. If you ask me, French is the most difficult language in the world--except English."

They went on talking. Evelyn reflected. Beneath the current of conversation he had been thinking that whatever might occur on the Floors he would keep this girl in her present post, for she was a born lubricator, the enemy of all friction. He had a mazy dream, if the dangerously sick woman ever came back, of allotting a pension to Miss Maclaren so that she should not stand in the way of Miss Powler. But the mention of French started another dream. He had found a lot of friction at the Minerva Hotel at Cannes, even in the slack, wet pre-Christmas season. Why not transfer Miss Powler to Cannes as soon as her French grew to be practically serviceable? She would go, if asked. She was not one to jib at a new experience. Another hazardous experiment; but wherein lay the advantage of being supreme autocrat of a luxury hotel merger if you could not try hazardous experiments? He would be told that nobody had ever heard of an English house-keeper in a French hotel, that she could not possibly "shake down" with a French staff, etc. Nonsense! And anyhow, she would shake down with the clientèle, which was ninety-five per cent. British and American. To the clientèle she would be balm, a rock of refuge, an oasis, an all-comprehending angel, everything that was sympathetic.

And yet--no! The Imperial Palace had first call, and it could not spare her.

She rose, and carefully dropped the cigarette-end into the fire. As she gave him an interrogative glance he rose too.

"Well," be said. "It's late. I mustn't keep you."

"Well," she said, with urbanity but also with sturdy affirmation of a hard fact. "Our hours are very long."

Her eyes met his. "Stomach that, my boy!" he said to himself. He nodded, as it were casually, but he was somewhat dashed by the direct blow. He said to himself: "I admire her for that."

"Thank you so much," she said.

He took her hand nonchalantly, but with a fake nonchalance.

"You're very kind and I do appreciate it," she added.

There was such an undeferential sincerity of goodwill and gratitude in her voice and smile that he was secretly overcome. No housekeeper, no member of the female staff, had ever used that tone to him. None, except Mrs. O'Riordan, had thrown down the barrier of status, of official rank, as Violet did then. And though there had been no barrier between him and Mrs. O'Riordan, though Mrs. O'Riordan could charm and blandish with the best, there had always been something formidable, daunting, in her social demeanour towards him, even at its sweetest and most alluring. He privately glowed with pleasure at Violet's unstudied humanity. He felt that he could look happily and confidently at the future. The manipulation of a chain of vast hotels seemed easier than before. He was enheartened.

Oldham stepped into the sitting-room through the bathroom door.

"I beg pardon, sir," said Oldham clumsily, though he had done nothing which needed to be pardoned.

"Just in time," Evelyn reflected, thinking of the cigarette. A near shave! His attitude to Oldham in the bedroom had been unreasonable, if not unjust. Hence he felt a grudge against Oldham, and had an impulse to continue in unreason and injustice. But the simple goodwill of Violet had aroused and enlivened his own goodwill. Also he would not for worlds have displayed himself to Violet as less than the perfect employer and man. The truth was that he was affected precisely as old Perosi had been affected in the afternoon.

"What is it, Oldham? Come in," he said benevolently.

"I've finished all the unpacking, sir. Is there anything else, sir?"

"No, thanks," said Evelyn. "Thanks very much. Sorry to have kept you up."

"Thank you, sir. Good night, sir. Good night, miss."

Oldham departed. Violet departed. Evelyn went to bed joyous. Miss Powler must certainly have approved his demeanour to Oldham.

Chapter 46 ANOTHER CONFERENCE

The next morning Evelyn reigned afresh in the directorial office; and Reggie Dacker, his dandiacal fellow-director (usually referred to as the 'alter ego' of the panjandrum), and Miss Cass, his authoritative secretary, were with him and under his law. Despite untimely wintry weather, he was cheerful, brisk, and quite in the mood for reigning. Before going to bed he had told the night floor-waiter not to call him. He had had a very good night, and within two minutes of waking up he felt equal to running a hundred luxury hotels.

Towards Oldham he had been benevolent, telling him that of course he could withdraw his notice if he chose, and that indeed in the panjandrum's opinion he would be wise to choose. The relation between the two was at once restored to its former perfection, and both of them were relieved and delighted, and both of them tried, without complete success, to hide their feelings. He had breakfasted with deliberate sloth, dawdling, chatting to Oldham, wasting time.

He had telephoned an amiable greeting to Cousin, saying that he, Evelyn, must see to his own business first, but would put in an appearance at the daily conference if possible. In his heart he had no expectation of attending. Why should he attend? If he had not hastened his arrival by three days the Conference would have proceeded that Monday morning satisfactorily without him. Cousin had mentioned in his characteristically aloof tone that the project for a special New Year's Eve fête in the grill-room would be brought forward, as Ceria had asked for its discussion. To which Evelyn had replied with detachment that he knew nothing about it. To which Cousin had brightly retorted that he knew nothing about it either, but that it seemed to be somehow in the air. Whereupon receivers were hung up.

There were two piles of documents and letters for the panjandrum's august notice: Reggie Dacker's and Miss Cass's. Dacker's of course had precedence. But Miss Cass had a robust notion of the importance of her pile. In a pause due to Dacker's failure to find a paper, she pushed a letter under Evelyn's eyes.

"This is urgent, sir," said she firmly, in a low voice.

Evelyn did not read the letter. He glanced up at her as she stood over him.

"It depends what you call urgent," said he. "Seeing that I wasn't expected back till Wednesday night, nothing can be urgent tillThursday morning. Supposing I hadn't been here to-day?" One of his theories about women was that they lacked the sense of proportion and were incapable of distinguishing between one urgency and another. One of Miss Cass's theories about men was that they lacked the sense of actuality and were incapable of seeing things as they were. What was the point (thought Miss Cass) of supposing that he wasn't there? He *was*there. He might as usefully have supposed that the hotel had been burnt down. She took back the paper, but she had no resentment, because the panjandrum was in a heavenly temper after all (not that his temper was ever bad--she admitted), and most men, even panjandrums, were children and queer in the head.

Dacker discovered his document and passed it across the desk. Evelyn studied it very attentively. It concerned a matter which in Evelyn's opinion far transcended all other matters in urgency and intrinsic importance. Compared to that matter, projects for fêtes, disturbing graphs showing the curves of individual consumption by visitors, estimates for alterations and decorations, even the merging of luxury hotels into one grand homogeneous enterprise, were trifles. Evelyn had begun a very elaborate fighting campaign for the reform of the licensing laws of his country. For months he had been engaged on the preliminary organisation of the campaign. He was just returned, now, from a continental tour of towns whose citizens bought and drank in the way of alcohol what they pleased, when they pleased, where they pleased. The contrast between the Continent and Britain was utterly exasperating to a British publican. And Evelyn, if not a publican, but the manager of the greatest luxury hotel on earth, was treated by the licensing laws exactly as if he was the landlord of the lowest drinking den in Limehouse. He could not allow to be served, in the public rooms, the most ordinary and respectable beverages before a certain hour or after a certain hour, and both hours were preposterous. Not five times in a year was there a case of offensive inebriation at the Imperial Palace. And yet his head-waiters were forced to walk round his restaurant and his grill-room at a given moment and submit themselves and him to the indignity of telling visitors of irreproachable manners and social standing that they must order their alcohol then or never. The situation was monstrous, and would have been incredible did it not exist. The wonder was that any high-class hotel could keep its doors open. The wonder was that a revolution, with glass-breaking, arson, and the overthrow of Governments, had not occurred. :

Why had Britain fought and won the war if the sequel was to be the abolition of natural liberties which obtained in Britain before the said war, and which still obtained throughout the Continent? Etc., etc. It was laughable. But it was also ruinous, humiliating and intolerable. Admittedly the head of the hotel world, he held it to be his duty--and many other hotel-keepers held it to be his duty--to lead the movement for reform. And he was leading it, with all the subterranean, subtle ingenuities of which he was capable.

Members of Parliament, journalists, publicists, powers in the City were being regimented for the campaign. And he talked to them! By God! He talked to them! Perhaps too vehemently, with an excessive exaggeration. He loved to set side by side those two phrases, 'lowest drinking den' and 'greatest luxury hotel.' He enjoyed the melodrama of their contrast. His excuse was that he felt very deeply on the subject. Nobody had convincingly answered his arguments, the arguments of the hotel world, and nobody could. On all other subjects Evelyn could be as detached, as judicial, as Cousin himself. But on the subject of the licensing laws--well, his business acquaintances and his principal subordinates would say to one another that if you wanted to have fun and witness a real firework display you had only to start Mr. Orcham on the licensing laws. The movement which he was leading had had a lot to do with the appointment of a Governmental Licensing Commission. The Commission marked a forward step. Evelyn, however, was extremely dissatisfied with the choice of its members.

On this Monday morning he was busy with Reggie Dacker on some details of the campaign, and the document which Dacker had ultimately produced related to it. And yet suddenly, worried by a teasing thought, and possibly amazed by tiny pricks of his directorial conscience, he broke off the discussion with Dacker and said:

"Excuse me for three minutes, will you, my boy? I must just--" And, demanding a leaf of foolscap from the assiduous Miss Cass, he wrote out in his clear hand a short memorandum.

"Put this in an envelope and take it to Mr. Cousin yourself--at once, please," he said, as he folded the leaf in four.

"But the Conference won't be finished," Miss Cass demurred.

"I hope it won't," said Evelyn with a genuinely cheerful laugh.

2.

And so Miss Cass, bearing the foolscap envelope, passed down the corridor, and opened the door (in a rather dark corner) over which burned night and day the electric sign "Manager's Office," and went in. Miss Tilton, Mr. Cousin's secretary, was not at her desk, at which sat idly a page-boy ready to answer the telephone. He smiled timidly at Miss Cass, who gave him a nod.

Even before she opened the inner door into Mr. Cousin's private room she heard the sound of vivacious, argumentative conversation The room was full of men and smoke. Mr. Cousin presided at his desk, a desk large but not as large as Evelyn's; and by his side sat young Pozzi, his second-in-command. At the end of the table was Marian Tilton, with notebook, just as Miss Cass sat with notebook at the end of *her* principal's desk. Indeed, in various ways the disposition of Mr. Cousin's room showed the influence of Evelyn. A dozen or fifteen men, and Violet Powler (serene and receptive), all heads of departments, constituted the Conference: an attendance somewhat fuller than usual. Evidently the chief protagonists were Ceria, Immerson, the publicity head, Ruffo, the Banqueting-manager, and Jones-Wyatt, the Bands-and-Cabaret-manager. And evidently the topic was the proposed special New Year's Eve fête in the grill-room.

Amadeo Ruffo had been arguing against it, and one of his reasons was that Jones-Wyatt could probably not provide a first-rate band for only one night. Jones-Wyatt, a fullbodied, youngish man well versed in the musical, music-hall, theatrical and operatic worlds, had been half-heartedly opposing the scheme. But Ruffo's sinister suggestion had in a moment changed his attitude. Of course he could provide a band, and a first-rate band. They might leave the band to him; he would answer for it. He did, however, object to the cinema proposition, because the broad, square columns which supported the ceiling of the grill-room would prevent a good twenty-five per cent. of the revellers from seeing the screen in its entirety. (Nobody else had thought of this snag.) His idea was that the entertainment should be exclusively musical, and of the highest character, with a quartet of seasonable carollers and perhaps a soprano: which artists would be fully audible if not visible.

Immerson, in his soft, earnest tones, had espoused this idea. Immerson was strongly in favour of the general scheme, partly for its exciting novelty, but more because it would spread out before him fresh vistas of piquant publicity. Cappone, the Restaurant-manager, in the secrecy of his mind, did not approve the grill-room scheme, which, he feared, might impair the glory of his own fête in the restaurant, but loyalty to his colleague deterred him from expressing himself.

Those two marvellous smilers, Cappone and Ceria, smiled upon one another at intervals in touching amity. Several men were talking at once as Miss Cass appeared. Even the disinterested burst out now and then in loud, impulsive monosyllables. Keenness and animation were the note of the polemic. All genuinely and fervently desired to increase the prestige of the Imperial Palace, but some in one way and some in another. The scene had heat without hostility. Sir Henry Savott would have been flattered and delighted could he have witnessed the various liveliness of which a casual sentence from his mouth so richly furnished with teeth was the origin.

On the whole, feeling supported the scheme. Again and again the master-argument for it had been stated: namely, first, that about two hundred would-be roysterers had received printed forms expressing regret that every table in the restaurant had been booked; and, secondly, that it would be a pity to waste these ladies and gentlemen if they could be utilised.

Mr. Cousin was calm and impartial. He certainly was not averse to the scheme; nor was Pozzi. And Mr. Cousin considered that, as the panjandrum on the telephone had vouchsafed no opinion, still less a command, he was free to come to a decision on his own responsibility. During Evelyn's absence, he had grown accustomed to making decisions without reference, and at least twice when Mr. Dacker, whose telephoning to Evelyn sometimes clashed with his--when Mr. Dacker had disagreed with him, the 'alter ego' had yielded.

As for Miss Cass, she invaded the Conference with perfect assurance. She and her notebook had attended many conferences. She came now as a sort of papal envoy--slightly irritated because she did not know what message on what subject she was carrying. She was on familiar terms with everyone in the room, but as she walked briskly round the edges of the Conference to the back of Mr. Cousin's desk, she ignored everyone except

Marian Tilton, to whom she gave the nod and feminine smile of superiority. She offered the foolscap envelope to Mr. Cousin:

"Mr. Orcham asked me to give you this."

Mr. Cousin opened the envelope, and before reading its contents murmured to Miss Cass, who was turning away:

"Better wait a moment."

Then he carefully perused the message.

"I think I will read this to you just as it is--it's from Mr. Orcham," Mr. Cousin addressed the suddenly still Conference.

And he read:

"I can think of a number of reasons both for and against the very interesting proposal for arranging for a New Year's Eve festivity in the grill-room. But there is one reason which in my opinion outweighs all others and which ought to settle the point. The grill-room has always been a place free from every rule except that of good manners. At any time of day or evening anyone can enter it in any dress, and order any meal, which will be charged either *à la carte*or at a *prix fixe* according to the judgment of the manager. No formalities are observed. The grill-room has a very large clientèle which is aware of this state of things and counts on it. It is universally known as a restaurant of relaxation, where food of the finest sort can be eaten at ease and in quietness. Thousands of customers look on it as a retreat upon which they can rely. It is open every night of the year. No holiday or fête has even been allowed to disturb its normal course. What would its habitués think if one night its character were to be altered, and a definite menu and hour imposed upon them, with various unavoidable rules affecting dress, etc., and the introduction of music and a formal entertainment? Any such alteration would be a blow to the particular reputation of the grill-room. It would cause disappointment and possibly some resentment. Confidence in the stability of the policy of the grill-room would unquestionably be undermined. Which would be, I think, a rather serious matter.--EVELYN ORCHAM."

Silence followed. The Director had spoken. He had issued no ukase. He had not employed his authority like a hammer. But he had uttered that formidable word: Policy. And he had advanced an argument which not one of his subordinates had thought of--or at any rate spoken of. Nobody in the Conference surmised in that dramatic moment that the panjandrum was as human as any of themselves. None knew that the incursion of Sir Henry Savott into the politics of the Palace had abraded Evelyn's most delicate susceptibilities, and that he had been shocked to get the first word of a proposed terrific innovation from a quite minor, if valued, person--old Perosi; and that these two things together had affected the whole trend of his thinking. The Conference could judge only of the final expression of the directorial reflections, and the final expression was so phrased as to permit of no answer.

"Thank you," said Mr. Cousin, turning for an instant to Miss Cass behind him. In the redoubtable hush Miss Cass, diminished and yet very proud of her master's moral force, and taking some share of it to herself, left the Conference chamber.

"Well, my friends--" said Mr. Cousin, reserved, detached, apparently indifferent. But he offered nothing else to the Conference save a faint bland and undecipherable smile.

The Conference saw Ceria rise from his seat and slowly and silently walk out. The young man gave one glance at Miss Powler.

"If you will excuse me," said Miss Powler to Mr. Cousin. And she too walked out. No other person in the room moved or spoke. The hush produced by the panjandrum's communication was protracted by the solemn, startling exit of Ceria; for all realised, with a sentiment akin to awe, that tragedy had been nearer than they thought. All were intimidated--and especially the emotional Italians--by the lamentable ravaged figure of the manager of the grill-room. Tears came into the eyes of the bright and worldly Marian Tilton. Miss Cass had escaped in the nick of time.

3.

Violet followed Ceria at a distance of twenty feet or so, into the great entrance-hall, across it, down the broad corridor leading to the empty grill-room, past the doors of the grill-room, into a narrow transverse corridor beyond, at the end of which was Ceria's office.

Ceria vanished into the office, leaving the door ajar. She knocked softly at the door. No answer. She went cautiously in. The room was less than small; it was tiny; but it was an office, a piece of private territory, and Ceria would now and then mention it with a certain complacency of importance: "My office." Violet, however, had never heard of it, did not know what the room was till she saw it. Ceria was seated at a tiny table-desk, elbows on the blotting-pad, chin supported by the palms of the hands, staring at a Milanese sheet-calendar hung on the wall. He heard a slight cough, and sprang up, collecting himself in order to be manly, and summoning a fairly deceptive counterfeit of his famous smile. He was pale.

"I beg your pardon. Please," he murmured weakly.

Violet did not know how to begin. Her wish was to soothe him and uplift him out of the despair which had been so alarmingly apparent on his wistful face as he walked out of Mr. Cousin's room. She had feared lest he might faint or do something silly--and no woman near to tend him! You never knew with these delicate, impressible foreigners. (As a fact she had formed an entirely wrong idea of the Latin temperament.) She could not bluntly say: "You shouldn't take it too hard." Or something like that. She said, in a tone as commonplace as she could produce:

"About the special Floors-menu for to-morrow, Mr. Ceria. Could I have a copy of it to-day? It's useful to me to know beforehand what it is...If I'm not disturbing you too much."

Ceria, with the approval of Mr. Cousin, had recently introduced a special short menu for meals in the private rooms. Upon request a special fixed price was made for it. The object of the device was to tempt visitors away from the full menus which contained dishes not easy to serve satisfactorily on the floors. Both menus were offered to the hungry, but visitors were quickly learning to choose from the special one because it simplified the plaguy task of choosing.

"Yes, certainly," Ceria answered with forced animation "Please sit down. Have this chair. I'll find it. I'll find it." He ferreted in a drawer in the table.

Violet did not sit down. Ceria failed to find the menu. Obviously he was not searching with any method in the untidiness of the drawer. After a moment he stopped, as if trying to reflect. His eye met Violet's.

"You ought to go home as early as you can this afternoon and do a bit of hard work in your beautiful garden," said Violet impulsively.

In her expression and in her voice Ceria saw and heard the benevolent purpose of her intrusion. He hesitated, fumbling for the right course to take. His eyes moistened. Violet thought "How could I suggest his going back to that empty house, with nobody but a servant there?"

At length he said:

"At this season...one cannot work in the garden. What can one do in the garden?"

"How stupid of me!" Violet exclaimed. She really felt stupid. She knew nothing of gardens.

"And it is nearly dark at four o'clock," Ceria added.

Another detail that Violet had most stupidly forgotten.

"But," said Ceria, "I will go for a drive in my little car. I adore driving in the dark. I will go a long distance." His smile became genuine, though it was forlorn, touching.

"How many days is it since you first thought of the fête in your grill-room?" Violet asked gently. "Not many."

Ceria raised his eyebrows in assent.

"No. Not many."

"Well, you are no worse off now than you were then," said Violet.

"You are a very kind philosopher," Ceria murmured. "Yes, you are very kind. I understand you. It is a lesson."

"No, no!" Violet protested. "Please excuse me. I only thought of it."

Ceria timidly extended his hand. Violet's hand advanced of its own accord. Ceria took it, and kissed it. To him the action was quite natural. But it thrilled Violet. Nobody had ever kissed her hand before, except in the make-believe of the amateur comic-opera stage.

Ceria relinquished her hand. And not a second too soon. For the face of Miss Venables appeared, as it were furtively, in the doorway. Instantly Ceria resumed control of himself.

"Come in, Miss Venables."

The older woman nodded indifferently to Violet, then ignored her for Ceria.

"I'm leaving this afternoon, Mr. Ceria," said she. "And I could not go without saying good-bye." Her heavy, prim voice was as usual charged with a martyr's melancholy; but the intense glance of her dark eyes showed that Ceria's wistful smile could make its victims anywhere and everywhere.
"Well, thank you, Mr. Ceria," Violet broke prosaically in. "Perhaps you could send that menu up to me. Or I will send down for it."
"You shall have it at once," said Ceria, in a style as prosaic as Violet's. He had nothing to learn from her or anyone about the use of vocal tone and facial muscles. None could have guessed, now, that five minutes earlier he had felt as if he were Violet's weak, clinging, passionately grateful child.

4.

Violet left quickly, without further notice of Miss Venables. Ceria took two steps to the door, and, behind Miss Venables' back, re-established intimate communication with Violet by one transient look. Violet crossed once more the entrance-hall with its ceaseless foot-traffic and quiet stir of visitors and officials and murmured colloquys and down-sittings and uprisings. And she ascended away out of all that wordliness in the lift, happy, jingling some keys and talking to the lift-man about weather, which he seldom or never had the opportunity to see in autumn and winter. And while talking she thought of Ceria as her grateful child, talented, brilliant, all-conquering--and pathetic.
Then she stepped from the lift into the withdrawn world of Eighth, where thick carpet dulled every sound of the corridor and shaded lamps gave a discreet mystery to hushed life. Afar off she saw the figures of two chambermaids--Beatrice Noakes and another--and a valet and a waiter gathered in a group. Eighth was their universe, of which each smallest phenomenon was familiar. For them the entrance-hall and the public rooms had no existence. The valet held in his hand a leaden weight attached to a long cord: apparatus by which he had just been clearing an obstruction in the letter-shoot caused by some too bulky envelope--a delicate operation more exciting to the personnel of the floor than any event in managerial offices.
At sight of the temporary head-housekeeper the group dissolved. The valet disappeared silently into his brushing-and-cleaning room, the waiter into his kitchen-and-pantry, a chambermaid, using a pass-key, into a bedroom. Only Beatrice Noakes was left. She moved towards the door of the head-housekeeper's sitting-room and confidently awaited Violet.
"There's a lamp-stand broken in 06, miss," she said earnestly.
"But you've told me about that once, Beaty," Violet answered, laughing.
"Oh! Have I? So I have, miss. Better twice than not at all, they do say. Yes, miss. I hear Miss Prentiss has gone, miss. And I know her trunks is gone. They're labelled for Gleneagles, miss."

"I wonder how you hear of all these things, Beaty," said Violet. "It's very clever of you." She smiled; but she felt disappointed and a little grieved.

Prentiss had gone without a good-bye, even a good-bye of mere ceremony. Since the scene on the night of Mac's seizure, the well-bred Prentiss had spoken with her only in the way of work. Good breeding might have prompted her to some formal alleviation of the feud. But no! She had departed for the new northern post which, thanks to Palace prestige, she had obtained without any difficulty. She would never again be seen in the Palace. And how she would try to impose her unquestioned gentility upon Gleneagles, and how, after a few days, she would tear the good name of the Palace management into fragments!

"And what's the news to-day about Miss Maclaren, miss? I suppose you'll have been hearing?"

"A bit better. She's eaten part of an omelette."

"Well, that *is* wonderful news, miss. An omelette! Do you think I might go and see her? Me and Daisy was saying last night as perhaps I might. Just to show like, if you know what I mean."

"She'd be very pleased. But you oughtn't to stay more than ten minutes."

"Oh no, miss! Such an idea wouldn't enter my head. I've got a wrist-watch and I should wear it, and I should look at it when I went in and...Miss Venables hasn't gone yet, miss

"I know," Violet interrupted the flow. She realised now that Mrs. Noakes had mentioned the broken lamp-stand only in order to start one of her grand miscellaneous gossipings, for which she lived. "I've seen Miss Venables, downstairs."

"Oh! I'm *so* glad she's seen you, miss," said Beatrice, with exaggerated relief in her voice, thereby informing Violet that the female floor-staffs had been keeping careful watch on the great housekeepers' feud, and lusciously speculating as to whether any of the parties concerned would relent at the last moment either from human kindliness or from a sense of social decency.

"Let me come past," said Violet quickly. "I've got plenty to do, if you haven't."

Beatrice stood aside from the doorway and Violet entered her sitting-room and shut the door and sat down, but not to any task. She was pleased that Beatrice, misinterpreting her words, had assumed a reconciliation between Venables and herself. But she felt disturbed. Would Venables come and say goodbye, or would she not? The question filled her mind, so that she could not settle to desk-work, nor even to a round of room inspections, nor even to telephoning. She was entirely innocent, and yet she had a sensation of guilt.

Little secretary Agatha burst schoolgirlishly into the room, a question on her lips: "Anything urgent you want me to do?" Violet shook her head.

"Better go and get your lunch, if it isn't too early," said Violet.

Agatha glanced at the clock.

"Five minutes," said she, and went away again.

Violet rose and moved to the window, and stared at the lofty roofs of the ugliest building in London. Why couldn't people be friends? Why was the lovable Ceria lonely and sad? Why did Prentiss harden her heart? Would Venables harden her heart? Why was the world what it was, when it might so easily be different?...Violet looked at the clock. Nearly one hour had amazingly slipped by since she had come into her room; and a score of jobs remained undone. She must go down to lunch. She hoped that by this time Venables would have lunched and left the housekeepers' refectory. She could not have borne to meet Venables in the presence of others. She had been through that experience too often.

5.

There was a knock at the door. Venables primly entered. Violet was both relieved and affrighted. Her heart asserted its beat. She waited, cautious.

Venables said:

"I thought I'd tell you. They've just telephoned up that Mrs. Oulsnam has come."

"Oh, thank you very much for letting me know, Venables. I suppose she'll come to see me. I was just going down to lunch."

Mrs. Oulsnam had left the Majestic in order to come to the Palace, and Venables was replacing her at the Majestic. This was another of Evelyn's ingenious changes. Through the intermediation of Mr. Dacker the transaction had been carried out with the nicest regard for the pride of Miss Venables, who had received a letter from the Majestic management to the effect that it had heard that she was leaving the Imperial Palace, and that if she cared to call, etc. Evelyn now of course in fact if not in theory controlled the Majestic. But no one referred to the reality of the situation existing between the two hotels. Everyone pretended--and Venables more convincingly than anyone--that the Majestic had sought for Venables on her notorious housekeeping merits. As for the interests of the Palace, Mrs. Oulsnam produced an excellent reference. Miss Prentiss's post was not to be refilled; for Violet had worked out Miss Maclaren's plan for the reduction of the Palace Floors staff.

"Not at all," said Venables.

"I do hope you'll be happy at the Majestic," Violet exclaimed, with a sudden outpouring of goodwill which surprised even herself. Her features relaxed and her mood was lightened by the mysterious lifting of an obscure oppression.

"Oh, thank you, Powler. I feel sure I shall. You know the Majestic is going to be very much livened up. I heard yesterday they are to make a new carpet for the restaurant there at our works. But I expect you know all about that already."

"No, I don't," said Violet, fibbing in order to flatter Venables' superior knowledge.

"And here's my keys," said Venables. Violet accepted the bunch.

A pause.

"Well," said Venables, "I suppose I must be saying goodbye."

She held out her hand. Violet gave it one little squeeze. In doing so she squeezed some tears out of Venables' eyes.

"I know it wasn't your fault. You couldn't help it," said Venables in a broken voice.

Violet might have replied: "Couldn't help what?" But instead she replied: "I knew you knew. It's all right."

Venables said:

"But I've never been treated like that before. Never. And you must admit it was very humiliating, dear."

"I'm sure it was," Violet agreed. "But it was for such a short time. It wasn't worth while appointing you head-housekeeper for such a short time as that. And you haven't been humiliated for long, have you?"

Not a word about Prentiss.

Venables brought her head forward and kissed Violet, and Violet returned the kiss and saw Venables' face very close. What a ruin, that complexion! Without doubt the old thing was feeling deeply her severance from the Palace, where she had served for so many years. And the poor old thing had now to face a new career in strange surroundings! "And," thought Violet, "she'll go on being a hotel-housekeeper until she's old. And what then? And so shall I go on being a hotel-housekeeper till I'm old. One of these days I shall be as old as she is; and what then, for me too?" She could hardly prevent herself from crying, though she did not really believe that she would ever be as old and withered and desiccated as Venables. She was mournful. But she was happy. Venables went off with the subdued self-contemplating smile of one who has righteously performed his duty to society, recognising virtue in a junior colleague, increasing the sum of kindness, and with resigned courage fronting a hard world.

Chapter 47 NEW YEAR'S EVE

A quarter to nine on New Year's Eve. Although the festive dinner in the restaurant of the Palace was scheduled to begin at 8.30, a continuous procession of automobiles and taxi-cabs was entering the courtyard of the hotel, hooting to stimulate the dilatory in front, curving under the vast marquise, setting down bright women and sombre men, and curving away again back into Birdcage Walk, whose breadth was narrowed by double lines of parked cars. And high above the building, unseen from the region of the marquise, rose the flood-lit tower of the Palace, informing the West End by an admixture of red rays in its customary white that the occasion was special. Mowlem, the head-day-hall-porter, was himself active on the steps outside the portals with a corps of janissaries larger than usual, directing and speeding traffic, bowing to his numerous acquaintances among the visitors, and disseminating goodwill and good wishes in the keen air. The crowded scene in the entrance-hall, viewed from without, was brilliantly appetising, and an unanswerable proof that Britain was not yet quite the impecunious back-number which newspapers of all political parties had got into the habit of proclaiming her to be.

A car stopped, and Mowlem gave to the chauffeur a special word of dignified intimacy. And when the occupant descended from the car Mowlem saluted him with a special bow of courtly benevolence.

"A Happy New Year, sir, if not too early."

"Thanks. Same to you."

The arrival was Evelyn. He had chosen the main entrance, preferably to the Queen Anne entrance, because on grand occasions such as the present he enjoyed seeing his organization in the full press of work. He was still young enough in hotel management to be thrilled by the long lines of automobiles and by the whizzing of the doors and by the restless glitter of the thronged hall, down which he quickly passed, unrecognised, towards his private office. He beheld the display and saw that it was good.

Now the Imperial Palace dinner was not the only New Year's Eve hotel-banquet on that night. There were of course dozens, hundreds, of others up and down the land. But for Evelyn there was only one other: that of the Wey Hotel, Evelyn's first love and charge. Every year he saw the soup served at the Wey banquet. The Wey being a residential hotel, and almost in the provinces, its meals took place much earlier than those at the Palace. Evelyn had duly seen the soup served, and even the fish; and he had given to Mr. Plott, the Wey manager, the impression that really he would have liked better to usher in the New Year at the Wey, but that the more complex organism of the Palace was in urgent need of his watchful supervision, and so he must regretfully leave the Wey celebration to Mr. Plott's very adequate sole control. And the exigent Mr. Plott had been quite satisfied. Evelyn would say to old Dennis Dover that it would have been more than his place was worth not to make an appearance at the Wey on New Year's Eve.

Having titivated himself anew in his office, he travelled by devious service-corridors to the service-door of the grill-room; for he had a quarter of an hour in hand. He had received full reports of the Conference at which his communication to Cousin had had the effect of causing a stricken Ceria so dramatically to leave the room, and he felt therefore that he owed a state visit to Ceria,

As for Ceria, his kingdom was a grand sight to him that evening; for, surprisingly, every table was occupied or had been booked. The clothes of the diners exhibited all varieties of taste, from pull-overs and plus-fours to silken low-cuts, pearls, orchids and white ties. No sign of the seasonal fête except crackers and bits of holly (no mistletoe). Plenty of gaiety, plenty of champagne, and no music at all. A large number of celebrities and notorieties who demonstrated by their presence that they preferred a decent, simple Bohemianism to the elaborate formalities of the great affair in Cappone's restaurant. Ceria felt very flattered, and happiness radiated from his wistful, smiling face as he walked from table to table bowing and greeting. Indeed Ceria would not have exchanged places with the more important Cappone. He would have liked Cappone to see his array of the famous; for he was sure that for every 'somebody' that Cappone could show, he could show half a dozen.

At a table laid for three persons, half-hidden by a column, sat a young woman alone, in morning frock. She was reading a newspaper as she drank soup. Ceria stopped in front of her.

"Is everything as you wish, Miss Savott?" he earnestly enquired. The girl glanced up from the paper and nodded, smiling; and Ceria bowed and withdrew. The next moment he descried the panjandrum and went deferentially to meet him.

"Well, Ceria," Evelyn murmured with much content and approval in his voice, "I congratulate you. You couldn't have done better than this if you'd had a dozen bands and the whole New Year rigmarole. You couldn't have done as well, because a band takes up a deuce of a lot of valuable room. Now could you?"

"No, sir. You are quite right."

"You'll beat your record to-night."

"I shall, sir," agreed the delighted Ceria.

Evelyn thought:

"He's just like a child."

The pair made a leisurely tour of the room, talking together and ignoring guests. They passed close by the table where the young woman sat so strangely alone. Her eyes did not leave the paper, and Evelyn did not glance aside, and Ceria was too obsessed by the general glorious aspect of his grill-room to give a thought to the interest which his chief might be expected to feel in any individual customer, however eminent the name. A minute later Evelyn left, by the service-door. Ceria then noticed a page-boy in converse with the solitary girl. As he arrived again at the table the girl was rising to go.

"You can have this table now," she said to Ceria. "My friends evidently aren't coming." He did not know that she had not been expecting friends, having naughtily secured a table for three in order to get ample space for herself. She dropped a form on the table for the waiter.

2.

In the foyer, which was now steadily losing more people to the restaurant than it was receiving from the entrance-hall, Evelyn could see nothing of Sir Henry Savott, who (as it had been finally arranged) was to be his guest for the evening. But the man could not yet be accused of unpunctuality; it still wanted one minute to nine o'clock, the hour of their rendezvous. What Evelyn did see was Cappone, the Restaurant-manager, talking with a rather troubled expression to Lord Watlington, and Mrs. Penkethman standing a foot or two away and carefully not listening. Evelyn divined at once from Mrs. Penkethman's dissociation of herself from the masculine colloquy that some difficulty had arisen, and he accordingly moved away, preferring to leave the conduct of Cappone's business entirely to Cappone. But Lord Watlington, still more familiarly known to his friends and the world as Harry Matcham--though two years had passed since his 'public services' had lifted him into the peerage--had caught sight of Evelyn, and totally ignoring both his lovely partner and Cappone, walked up to him, followed at a little distance by Mrs. Penkethman, while the astute Cappone descended abruptly into the restaurant.

His lordship was a man of forty-eight, of average height, but somewhat more than average girth, exceedingly dark, with coal-black hair and eyes. He bore some resemblance to his friend Sir Henry Savott. Indeed the imperfectly informed now and then confused the one with the other. Savott was dark, but Lord Watlington was darker. Savott's face was very broad between the ears, but Lord Watlington's was broader. Savott's gaze was piercing, but Lord Watlington's was more piercing. And further, Savott was a triumphant financier, but Lord Watlington was a man of wealth, wealth absolute, wealth realisable, not potential wealth dependent upon the turn of markets or the success of flotations.

Lord Watlington never touched enterprises which gambled upon the capricious tastes of the public. Thus he had a few days earlier rejected a wonderful offer from Savott to go into the cinema business. He had refused many temptations to acquire controlling interests in newspapers because (he argued) they were at the mercy of the big advertisers and the big advertisers were at the mercy of the uncertainties of trade and international politics. Instead of owning newspapers he owned mills which sold paper to newspapers. Instead of buying or building architectural structures, he bought ground-rents, that is, freeholds, and gave the risks of building to others. He was the largest shareholder in a large insurance company; ditto in a British subsidiary of a foreign bank; he was chairman of a very important Investment Trust Company. He was nothing if not gilt-edged. He had made his fortune and his position by the exercise of judgment, by his necromantic vision of the future, which after all was not vision but only an accurate weighing of probabilities, by his instinctive regard for essentials and his instinctive contempt for inessentials; and by nothing else.

Among various gifts Lord Watlington had the gift of creation. When a transatlantic liner was fully booked up he could create a suite in it for himself. When a fashionable first-night was sold out, he could create a box in it for himself within two hours of the rise of the curtain. From pride and on principle he never asked for accommodation in advance anywhere. Similarly he never carried money. Often he would borrow money for munificent tips--it was always repaid by cheque with a secretarial letter of thanks the next day.

In the previous week a slight coolness had supervened between him and Savott, who had playfully said to him: "Now, Harry, don't behave like a spoiled beauty." He did not like the remark, which had enlightened him as to the secret attitude of his friends towards his idiosyncrasies.

On the afternoon of this New Year's Eve, Mrs. Penkethman had expressed a desire to attend the fête at the Palace. Harry had shown unwillingness, but when Mrs. Penkethman had added darkly and with resignation that no table could be had, Harry had immediately promised to take her. He had telephoned on the instant to Cappone, who had replied hopefully that, while no table was presently available, some table was almost sure to be cancelled, and he would have the greatest pleasure in reserving it for his lordship. His lordship had arrived with the beautiful Nancy, and lo! not a table had been cancelled. He, Harry Matcham Lord Watlington, could not be accommodated! He had not quite contrived to mask his sentiments. Incredulity was succeeded by indignation, and indignation by anger. He saw himself publicly humiliated in the eyes of Nancy. He was furious. To save his repute he would willingly have burnt down the Imperial Palace (which was amply insured in his own company, which had reinsured a large part of the huge risk in New York). Nevertheless in his frightful and unique quandary Lord Watlington accosted Evelyn with the airiest seductive nonchalance; for he was an actor of genius.

"Let me make you acquainted with the most beautiful woman in London," he said, introducing Mrs. Penkethman. And then he explained his trouble, and said that he and Mrs. Penkethman must go elsewhere, and looked at Evelyn as though he confidently expected him to work a miracle. Evelyn enjoyed the spectacle for a few moments; it was as exquisitely agreeable to him as the flavour of a fine cigar. He knew by hearsay the fable of Lord Watlington. He cared naught for the presumed financial relations between Lord Watlington and Savott, author of the great hotel-merger. To inflict a horrible suspense upon Lord Watlington delighted the unchristian, too human panjandrum. Then he said:

"Nothing is simpler. I have a table, and if Mrs. Penkethman and you will dine with me I shall be charmed."

Lord Watlington protested, and accepted. He had won. He was still Lord Watlington. He could still support the glance of Mrs. Penkethman.

Then Sir Henry Savott appeared on the stairs leading down from the entrance-hall, and handed his hat and coat with studied negligence to a powdered, silk-calved footman.

"Don't tell me," Savott exclaimed. "I know I'm late. Three minutes. It's your traffic outside that did it"

"You aren't late, my dear fellow," said Evelyn. "Every clock in the hotel is wrong. Lord Watlington and Mrs. Penkethman are joining us. Shall we go in?"

Both Harry Matcham and Henry Savott, behaving with nobility, utterly forgot the coolness which had been somewhat marring their business alliance.

Vast curtains had been drawn between the foyer and the restaurant, leaving room for only two persons at a time to pass down the six steps to the restaurant floor. An attendant was taking tickets from the entrants, but of course no tickets were demanded from Evelyn and his guests, who descended with sovereign freedom into the noisy, crowded, multi-coloured arena of the banquet. Few noticed the appearance of the three celebrities and of the panjandrum of the tremendous scene; for in the main the revellers were merely the well-to-do, who could afford three guineas a head for dinner (exclusive of wines). The exclusive smart were hardly represented on that night at the Imperial Palace, and the merely well-to-do are not familiar with the faces of celebrities; it needs the smart to recognise the smart.

3.

Lord Watlington comprehended, as in the wake of Evelyn the party wound its way to a table in a corner, why Cappone's attitude to him had been so immovably *non possumus.* The tables were packed so close together that not another could have been inserted among them. The waiters performed marvels of self-insinuation, though with all their skill they were continually kicking against chair-legs and thus annoying scores of diners, who looked round offended at the falsely-unconscious disturbers. The whole of the space usually reserved for dancing was filled with serried tables, and an annex of the restaurant, usually separated by a glazed partition which had been removed for this night only, was filled with serried tables.

On the site of part of the partition a gorgeous bandstand had been upraised. The band was playing fortissimo, but its majestic strains had to fight a battle against the din of shouted small-talk from one thousand pairs of lips; neither the music nor the small-talk could be heard sufficiently well to enable umpires to have reached a clear decision as to the result of the contest. Moreover the sense of hearing was impaired by the appeal to the eyes of flowers, silken decorations, Chinese lanterns, variegated frocks, glinting jewels, coiffures, vermilion mouths, shining eyes, suspended bunches of tinted balloons, and a huge clock with illuminated hands and roman figures.

Disorder seemed to rule; but beneath disorder was order, and the secret sign of it was the intent, absorbed faces of the industrious waiters who grimly toiled on in the one sure hope that the moment of surcease would come when the last course had been served, and the last bottle opened, and the last tip collected. Some of them already saw in a prophetic vision the restaurant dark and empty, the tables turned from white tops to green and the chairs piled in a series of scraggy heaps.

And round and round, bowing, smiling, placating, flattering, moved the young Cappone, apparently unaware of the heavy load of supreme responsibility which lay on his shoulders.

At the directorial table, for which Evelyn had ordered two extra covers before leaving the foyer, Mrs. Penkethman was put into the best seat, with her back to the corner and a full view of the panorama of the restaurant; Evelyn was on her left, Henry Savott on her right, while Lord Watlington had to be content with a view of Nancy and the two converging walls which framed her. The beautiful creature wore a very simple dark frock, to show that she did not take the fête very seriously, was indeed condescending to it. (On the popular night of New Year's Eve the world of the Imperial Palace was not her world; the majority of her friends were away either in country-houses or on the Continent.) But she carried a few trinkets, a bag, and a cigarette case whose richness would have suited the smartest entertainment that any expert (such as herself) in smartness could devise. She alone in the group was completely at ease and happy, her appetite for pleasure being unappeasable. She lived for pleasure; the pursuit of pleasure was her vocation, and the diversions which she called pleasures never cloyed on that robust palate. Also she had three men, and every important men, to herself.

Evelyn felt a little nervous; for the origin of the dinner was his desire to justify his boast to Savott that the Palace could and would serve a thousand absolutely first-rate meals simultaneously; his ridiculous conscience had prevented him from giving special orders in regard to his own table; and in spite of his Palatial confidence he was visited by qualms of fear lest something, some detail, might fail in perfection. Withal, he would accept the risk. Savott was slightly displeased because he had been anticipating the thoroughly intimate *tête-à-tête* to which Evelyn had invited him. Lord Watlington was disappointed partly because he had won a table only by favour and not by force, and partly because he had been anticipating a thoroughly intimate *tête-à-tête* with Nancy, who had remained in town to solace Harry's compulsory loneliness. All these three males had to be soothed, smoothed, enlivened, sweetened, guided into a mood of self-complacency, freed from cares and corroding worm-preoccupations.

Nancy was the queen, and the queen knew her business. Harry Matcham, who was not facile in sincere praise, though he would fling insincere praise about in trowelfuls, always said that she was the soothingest woman in London--he did not really believe that she was the most beautiful woman in London. Nancy knew that a bad first quarter of an hour might easily discompose a party for a whole evening; she knew that great and successful men were apt to be conscienceless in the matter of social amenities, and that in particular they chatted or kept glumly silent according to their caprice of the moment: she knew that any conversation is better than muteness or reluctant, sparse monosyllables; and she knew that in the game of small-talk personalities are always trumps. Therefore, no sooner were the four chairs occupied than she softly burst out in her soothing voice, to Sir Henry:

"And where is my darling Gracie to-night? Do you know, she's very naughty. I haven't heard from her for weeks, and she writes such amusing letters--when she does write."

"Do you think I've heard from her, any more than you?" said Sir Henry, with an ironic smile. "I suppose she's in Paris. On the other hand she may be somewhere all by herself in the country near Paris. Last news I had she was writing a book."

"A novel of course," said Lord Watlington, also with irony.

"No," said Evelyn, "I don't think it's a novel. She did say 5ornething to me about it, but I forget what. Sort of journal of impressions, I fancy."

"Yes, you're right," Savott agreed, startled by this inside knowledge of Evelyn's.

"Well, anyway it won't be like anything else," said Lord Watlington. "She has more brains than any other woman I ever met--yes, my dear" (to Nancy) --"and you may rely on her to write down absolutely anything that comes into her head. You'd better see the proofs, Henry."

"I should have to bribe the printers then, Harry. Gracie would die before she'd show them."

"I always see Nancy's," said Lord Watlington. "I've kept her out of trouble more than once. I can't imagine why she keeps on writing."

"Who? Me?" asked Mrs. Penkethman plaintively.

"Yes, you!" Lord Watlington repeated with emphasis.

"Yes, you!" repeated Savott with emphasis.

Nancy divined that the two men were a little jealous of one another in regard to her. Alone with her, each of them was gentle enough as a rule. But both together, each seemed anxious to demonstrate to the other that his status with her entitled him to be rough.

"But I must write. I have to," she said still more plaintively, enveloping both of them in the same tender, appealing, wistfully smiling glance. "You're my friend, aren't you, Mr. Orcham?"

"Count on me, Mrs. Penkethman."

Nancy contributed, and sometimes she actually wrote, a weekly column of society gossip to the "Sunday Mercury." The newspaper paid not for the column but for the signature, than which none could be smarter. Nancy got nearly all her meals free and half her frocks and hats; she had the run of at least a dozen country-houses; she had further an allowance of five thousand a year (not from her divorced husband). So that, being thus in a chronic condition of penury, she 'simply had' as she said, to write. Moreover, it was the correct smart thing to write a column of society gossip in a Sunday paper. If a smart young woman did not write such a column, the sole reason must be that she lacked the wits to write it. And Nancy, for all her sweet tenderness of demeanour, had wits.

4.

Sir Henry Savott changed the subject with the abruptness of a waiter changing one plate for another. The soup interested him, being a novelty and a very delicate novelty. At the first spoonful he stopped, impressed, thoughtful, curious, as to its ingredients. He praised the soup. It was entitled on the menu-card 'Potage Gracieux.' Nobody at the table, not even Evelyn, was aware that the name was Maître Planquet's subtle tribute to the charm exercised by Miss Savott during her visit to the kitchens many weeks earlier. Maître Planquet had made enquiries about the identity and station of Gracie.

"Gracie ought by rights to try this," said Sir Henry, all unknowing, after his brief laudation addressed to Evelyn. Already he was beginning to be confident that Evelyn's boast as to the quality of the dinner which the Palace could serve to a thousand people at once would be justified. Already the gourmand in him was gaining ground; and, the soup finished, he anticipated the fish with eager hope.

Evelyn was thinking of Gracie, who had not been in his mind for a long time, thinking of her with appreciation. She had said that she would write a book, and she was writing, had written it. She was not of those who dream of authorship, start a book, drop it and relapse into futility. She had character. Yes, he was as much impressed by the news of Gracie as her father had been impressed by the 'Potage Gracieux.'

"That, I venture to think, is a unique hock," Evelyn remarked as the wine-waiter filled the glasses. "Anyone who prefers champagne will kindly say the word. But *that*--isa hock."

Sir Henry tasted.

"It is," said he, after a moment's cerebration.

Evelyn felt sympathetic towards Sir Henry's gourmandise. There was satisfaction in feeding a man who, though he somewhat deteriorated into grossness at a fine meal, could passionately distinguish between a first-rate dish and a second-rate. Evelyn had long since quite forgiven Savott for attempting to interfere in the policy of the grill-room.

Lord Watlington had left half his soup. Also he had asked for a whisky-and-soda. Mrs. Penkethman had refused soup. Instead of soup she had taken a cigarette. "Barbarians," thought Evelyn, of the peer and the lady. He was glad that he had not offered to the barbarians the barbarism of cocktails. And he was glad to think that Nancy had probably been (what she would have called) dying for a cocktail, while too well-bred and modest to demand one.

At the end of the fish the sight and taste of food and the quaffing of wine had accomplished their effect of stimulating the goodwill proper to the grandiose occasion. Not only Evelyn's table, but all the tables as far as the eye could reach across the vistas of white circles and squares, had loosed themselves into loquacity and open joyousness. The noise of the band was yielding ground to the human din. Tongues had been reinforced against the band by gifts from the management of whistles, rattles, and other instruments of music, crackers, and toy-balloons susceptible to explosion by puncture. Coloured balls were being thrown about between tables. Coloured streamers were being cast like long fishing-lines, coiling round the bodies of dignified men and elegant women, who in their gaiety found no offence in such entanglements. Perfect strangers merrily saluted and teased and slanged one another. Adults and the minds of adults diminished into children and child-minds. Dignity gave way to impudence.

And Sir Henry Savott continued steadily to eat and drink, and Nancy to smoke, while Lord Watlington was so far affected by his surroundings as to accept a second whisky-and-soda. Evelyn ate and drank little. His was the ultimate responsibility for the success of the fête; he was above Cappone, who perambulated watchfully to and fro, and above Cousin, who appeared first in one corner and then in another, also watchful. Maitre Planquet himself, in white cap and suit, peeped forth slily from the end of the corridor which led to the kitchens, to observe the sweet influences of his rich viands.

The hands of the great illuminated clock moved lazily on towards the minute which would mark the solemn inception of the New Year with its good resolutions and its bills. And despite the unseen labours of engineers deep down below in the subterranean halls tending the machinery which changed and washed and warmed and cooled the air of the glittering restaurant, the restaurant grew hotter and hotter. And no one cared. And as the crackers cracked, producing jewellery, wise mottoes, prophecies of destiny, and paper caps, the last supplemented by splendid caps, genuine caps, distributed by girls from baskets, there supervened the crisis which always arises at such a juncture. Elegant women donned the splendid caps without the least hesitation or self-consciousness. Would the men, even after having parted with their dignity? The men could not. The terrible fear of looking asinine prevented them from putting on caps. Then a V.C. of a man put on a cap, and felt himself an ass for no more than a moment. Another man put on a cap, and he was cheered by his shouting companions. Male craniums surmounted by caps soon dotted the room. Evelyn's table was encumbered with caps, as the floor was littered with knotted streamers and little balls and the wreckage of toy-balloons and crackers. Nancy Penkethman, capped, motioned to Evelyn to assume a cap. Smiling, he shook his head. Sir Henry Savott was invited similarly and refused.

"Harry!" said Nancy. Lord Watlington shook his head.

"Harry!" Nancy repeated. She was the queen, and the time had arrived for her to prove the reality of her power, which hitherto out of the instinct to acquiesce she had forborne to use.

Lord Watlington sheepishly put on a cap, and immediately he had done so his sheepishness left him. It was a magnificent cap, solidly constructed in the shape of a helmet, with an authentic blue feather in it. And Sir Henry Savott donned a cap. The fête was a success.

Nancy Penkethman relinquished her queenliness and her momentarily shrewish tone, and resumed the role of trustful acquiescence and subtle flattery.

"You look like winning--over this meal," said Sir Henry to Evelyn, in reference to Evelyn's old claim.

"I hope you'll think so after the savoury," Evelyn replied.

He alone at the table was capless. With him, Nancy had not insisted. She guessed that he was dreaming, preoccupied, absorbed by his dream. He felt sure, now, that the festivity could not fail. Nay, he felt sure that somehow in his gossip columns Immerson would make it the most marvellous New Year's Eve in all the history of London luxury hotels. But he was dreaming of more than the triumph of the festivity. He was dreaming of the future triumph of the gigantic merger of luxury hotels, of which he was the autocrat and the godfather. Both Sir Henry and Lord Watlington were indulging in the sweetness of the same dream.

Sir Henry was thinking, as he surveyed the riotous scene and digested the sumptuous food, and as he glanced furtively at the quiet, unassuming, laconic man who in his fancy rode the whirlwind and directed the storm:

"This fellow is the goods. He can't possibly let us down."

And the brain of Lord Watlington, who had never before condescended to a New Year's Eve public fête, was busily at work reconstructing for himself the intricate and immense organisation which underlay the glowing surface of the show. And he was thinking

"There's a damn sight more in this fellow than some people might suppose, to look at him."

In 'some people' Lord Watlington in fact included himself. He too had visions of a sensational triumph for the Merger, and thereby was made glad, for he was the chief of the plutocrats who in secret were lending their financial prestige and credit to Savott's scheme; and though he had ten times as much wealth as he could spend, he would have regarded the loss of a single penny of it as a heartrending and humiliating calamity.

The speech of none of the three men gave the slightest clue to his reflections. The table was talking incessantly, but the talk had no subject, scarcely a topic, unless it were the oddities of other revellers.

Evelyn was awakened from his reverie by the sight of a human being wandering, staring, searching with his eyes, among the tables. He knew from the human being's uniform that he was a telephone-man. There should have been nothing surprising in the sight of a telephone-man searching the restaurant. But this man's face was tragic in its alarm and apprehension. His face was enough to ruin the mirth of any festivity. Evelyn thought "This simply won't do." Abruptly he rose from the table, and as the man happened to come nearer he peremptorily beckoned, and the man saw the gesture.

"What is it?" Evelyn murmured as the man bent respectfully towards him.

"There's a young lady very ill upstairs, sir, and I was looking for Dr. Constam. They said he was here, but I can't see him. And I can't see Mr. Cousin either."

"Very ill, you say?"

"Yes, sir. Very ill."

"What number?"

"365, sir."

"What?"

"365, sir," the man repeated louder.

The table was of course listening.

"I'll attend to it," said Evelyn.

"365. That's one of my old numbers," said Sir Henry Savott, who had overheard the number.

"Are you staying here, Henry?" Lord Watlington asked.

"No, Harry. I'm in my new house."

"Will you kind people excuse me for a minute?" Evelyn asked. "I'm sorry, but--"

They excused him. He left the table, thinking: "Though why the devil I *should* attend to it I don't know." On his way out he had to pass by the band, the volume of whose sound shook his poise as the weight of a cyclonic wind might have shaken it.

Chapter 48 TESSA

On his way to the third floor Evelyn in reply to a question learnt from the liftman that Dr. Constam had after all preceded him to No. 365. Evidently the doctor had been told by someone other than the telephone-man that his presence was urgently required up there; and the probability was that he had left the restaurant before the excited and confused searcher had begun to look for him. But the liftman could not say who were the occupants of No. 365; he was a stranger to that particular lift; on New Year's Eve many individuals were doing other individuals' work.

Evelyn knocked at the door of No. 365, one of the six or eight finest suites in the Palace. No answer. He entered. There seemed to be no sign at all of very grave illness in No. 365: no sound, no stir. The door of the lighted sitting-room was open. He went in.

Violet Powler was standing in the embrasure of one of the windows, apparently absorbed in the contemplation of an invisible St. James's Park. Neither curtains nor blinds had been drawn. The temporary head-housekeeper turned and saw Evelyn.

"Good evening, sir," she greeted him, with placid formality. She was no longer the young woman who had smoked a cigarette in his castle on the night of his homecoming from the Continent. Indeed in the interval he had not seen her, though he had several times thought of her with satisfaction, approval, and confidence. He was about to demand somewhat abruptly by what remissness of a chambermaid the blinds had been left up and the curtains open, but Violet's steady glance moved him to control the hasty impulse.

"Someone very ill here, I understand. I looked in myself because both Mr. Cousin and Mr. Pozzi have their hands full."

"Yes, sir. The doctor is in there, and I'm waiting to see if I can do anything else." She pointed to a bedroom-door.

"Who's staying here?"

"Miss Savott."

"Miss Savott--not Sir Henry Savott's--"

"Yes, sir...It's a miscarriage, sir," she added, laconic.

The situation called for further exercise of self-control. The introductory tidings were in themselves astounding. Gracie in the hotel, and her father unaware! Why had the talk at the dinner-table turned at once on Gracie? And why had he himself taken the extraordinary course of enquiring into the affair personally? Could these questions be convincingly answered with the word 'coincidence'? Or were there in the universe forces, mysterious correspondences, telepathies, whose existence he had hitherto always rather disdainfully refused to credit? He still refused to credit their existence with his reason; but now, primeval instincts, powerful and authentic, fought within him against the scepticism of reason, and he was as perturbed as though he had seen a ghost.

"You don't mean to say that Miss Savott's here and she's--" Even as he uttered these words he charged himself with clumsy phrasing; but really for a moment he was somewhat overset: first an astonishing announcement, and then, right on the top of it, a staggering announcement! And on New Year's Eve! With what affrighting suddenness had he not been swept from the world of light pleasure into a world whose fundamentals were crude pain and disaster!

"Oh no, sir," said Violet calmly, unsmiling. "It's a--friend of hers that she brought with her. I don't know the name."

He had a tremendous sensation of relief, tempered by a dreadful private admission that he had made an unspeakable ass of himself.

Sound of pass-key in the outer door. Glimpse of a chamber-maid outside A lady advanced very quickly into the sitting-room. She wore a scanty evening frock, lilac-coloured, and a conspicuous, gleaming necklace of large crimson stones. Clearly she had come straight from the world of light pleasure.

"Yes?" Evelyn murmured.

"I'm dining in the same party as Dr. Constam," said the reveller, authoritatively, but in no accent of the West End or Oxford. "He asked me to follow him as soon as I could. I'm a nurse. Where is the patient?"

Violet made a step towards the bedroom-door; but the reveller reached it first, opened it, shut it, vanished into the sinister unknown of the bedroom: all in a few seconds.

"You don't expect to see them in party frocks, do you?' said Evelyn with a short laugh to cover his nervous diffidence. "But I suppose they're entitled to wear them just as much as other women."

Violet gave a transient, reserved smile.

"When did this thing begin?" he enquired.

The head-housekeeper related that she had been summoned on the telephone by Miss Savott herself about half an hour earlier; but she suspected that the 'thing' had begun some little time before the summons. She had come downstairs instantly. She had felt helpless, and Miss Savott too. Of course Miss Savott and herself knew each other of old. The difficulty had been to get hold of the doctor. Miss Savott was much disturbed at first, but later she had grown perfectly calm and clear-headed. She knew something about nursing; and so did Violet; but what could they do till the doctor arrived? When he did arrive he said that there was no need for the head-housekeeper to remain in the bedroom. The head-housekeeper had gathered that the two ladies had had a bad crossing, and that that was perhaps the cause of the terrible trouble.

"It's amazing what pranks women will play with themselves," said Evelyn, scandalised and sardonic. "Fancy a woman--! When was the birth expected, do you know?"

"I think the lady is over six months gone."

"And them crossing the Channel on a rough day in the middle of winter!"

A silence.

The head-housekeeper noticed that the Director's eye was on the windows She said:

"The chambermaid told me she had drawn the curtains as usual, but Miss Savott had undrawn them again. Said she liked to see the lights. That must have been before the trouble started."

Another silence. Then Evelyn said benevolently:

"I'm surprised to find you on duty to-night, Miss Powler. How is it?"

"Well," said Violet, "it's not one of my evenings, and Miss Ducker--she's the newest, sir: Sixth--really did want to go to a party at Hammersmith, so I let her go. I'm easier in my mind if I'm here on the spot."

"You shouldn't be. You must get over that."

Evelyn offered this advice in a somewhat peremptory tone. He remembered the time in his experience when he was continuously uneasy during any absence from whatever organisation he happened to be in control of. He had conquered the weakness. She must conquer it. As head-housekeeper she had the right of priority over all her staff to a night off on New Year's Eve, and for the sake of discipline she ought to have exercised it. What about her lonely old parents with nobody to let the New Year in for them? And he would have preferred her not to address him as 'sir.' He had thought that the joint cigarette-smoking had ended that. Perhaps in the presence of other members of the staff it might be well for her to say 'sir'; but when they were by themselves...How could he give her the hint? Then he said, more gently:

"I think we might sit down." And he sat down. Violet hesitated. "Sit down," he repeated, but still gently. She sat.

She had shocked his masculine sensitiveness by the calmness of the use of the words 'miscarriage' and 'six months gone.' What could or should she, unmarried, know of such things? Her sister had not been married either. Absurd! As manageress of a big laundry staff, as head-housekeeper of a big place like the Palace with its very mixed assortment of humanity, she must be familiar with all manner of strange and dubious phenomena. Indeed nothing could be hid from her. The contents of the minds of such women simply would not bear investigation. What could such women have to learn about the secret nature of mankind? He would bet that she knew far more than he did: she knew appalling things. And not a sign of the knowledge of them on her tranquil, virtuous face!

"I don't know a lot about miscarriages," he said, after a long silence (thinking audaciously: "I may as well talk to her in her own language"), "but it seems to me that that doctor of ours can't get on with his work without some--er--apparatus that he hasn't got in there. He didn't bring anything with him, I suppose?"

"No, sir. When he came I don't think he even knew what was the matter."

"Well, it's all very odd to an amateur like me." And he thought: "Why am I staying here? I can't be of any help. It must be just sheer curiosity that's keeping me here."

Young Dr. Constam burst into the sitting-room.

"Oh, good evening!" he exclaimed, startled to see Evelyn. He was laughing. He said nothing else until he had carefully shut the door. Then he looked at Violet.

"It's no more a miscarriage than my boot. Everything's absolutely normal so far as *that* goes. Nothing but an attack of indigestion. I thought you ladies could never surprise me any more, but I was wrong. The creature puts out to sea, feels queer, fills herself up with champagne and God knows what. Train journey and so on. She gets here all right, and then as soon as the tension is loosed and she has time to think about herself she has rather acute indigestion. Pains in the tummy. Must be a miscarriage! Miscarriage be blowed! I tell you I told her I couldn't help laughing at her. That did her good." He laughed unfeelingly, almost harshly. "Here I am eating my New Year's dinner, and I have to rush upstairs because a girl's got the collywobbles. The biscuit is hers, and I hope she'll have twins. I'm just going to find something to soothe her precious alimentary tract. Shan't be two minutes. No earthly need for you to stay, Miss Powler. Nurse is undressing her properly."

"I say," Evelyn stopped the young man as he was going out.

"Yes?"

"Who is she?"

"Ask me another, sir." He was gone.

Violet had obediently risen to leave. Like Evelyn, she was more relieved than she could show. But, also like Evelyn, she had a sense of disappointment, of having been shamefully cheated of an anti-climax. Comedy had replaced tragedy; and in spite of themselves, in spite of their relief, they both instinctively regretted the change. There was something magnificent in dire tragedy, in the terror of it, in the necessity which it laid upon everybody to behave nobly and efficiently. But comedy demanded naught from their higher selves. All they had to do now was to fade ingloriously away.

"I'm so glad," said Violet feebly.

"Yes."

"Good night, sir."

"Good night."

Violet went. Evelyn stayed. He was determined to see Gracie Savott. He was there, and he would remain. He cared not a fig for his party below. Dr. Constam returned, hurrying into the bedroom with a bottle and a spoon. The stylish nurse appeared and departed quickly, ignoring the presence of the panjandrum.

Then Evelyn heard faint rumours of an argument in the next room. The doctor's voice. Another voice, no doubt Gracie's, though he did not surely recognise it. Then the doctor reappeared, smiling grimly to himself. He glanced at his watch and at the clock over the mantelpiece.

"Au revoir," he said to Evelyn, in the masonic tone of one man to another when the vagaries of women are concerned.

Evelyn waved a hand, as if it were holding his stick.

"I must look a bit odd, sitting here," he thought. But he stayed.

2.

The length of the eventless interval tried his patience. But he would not budge. He could hear automobiles hooting in Birdcage Walk. Till then his preoccupied ear had not caught a single exterior sound. The bedroom-door began to open. At last! The door remained half open for several seconds. Then it opened farther. He heard Gracie's voice, now quite recognisable, talking to her friend. He prepared a smile to receive her. Gracie appeared. She was now untidy, almost unkempt, in her traveling pull-over and short tweed skirt. As soon as he saw the expression on her face he dismissed the smile from his own. Gracie was still sternly excited. She did not in the first instant perceive Evelyn. Evidently she had been expecting the room to be empty.

"Oh!" she gasped, taken aback.

"I just came up to see how things were," he said, rising.

"That was very kind of you," she said absently, and she shook hands absently. "I wish that doctor of yours had been as kind--I suppose he's told you what's happened."

"Why!" Evelyn said, nodding an affirmative to the question. He spoke soothingly, cautiously, as he shut the bedroom-door, which she had forgotten. "He hasn't been unkind, has he?"

"Yes, he has been unkind, very unkind," Gracie answered with emphasis. And while she spoke Evelyn recalled from the past the rich, changing tones of that voice. "He laughed. That's what your doctor did. Laughed. That was all he could do. Doctors are awful, especially when they're young. Cruel. They don't seem to have any imagination."

"But everything's all right, isn't it?" Evelyn said, even more cautiously. He thought: "She'll want some handling."

And he contrasted her impetuous, agitated vehemence with what Violet's demeanour would have been in Gracie's place. He wished for one moment that he had not stayed. Nevertheless he was admiring Gracie, her exuberant vitality, her passion--one might almost say her exaltation. She showed no restraint in his presence. The freedom of her behaviour could only be explained on the assumption that they were intimate. Evelyn accepted the assumption. It was based not on their excursion to Smithfield together, nor on their incursion into the Prince of Wales's Feathers. To Evelyn at any rate it was based on the angry resentment in her voice at their last parting, when he had offered to escort her from his office to the lift, and she had suddenly turned on him like an infuriated tigress, saying, "No, Please! I couldn't bear that!" She could not possibly have forgotten her rudeness in that encounter. Yet she was now behaving as though nothing unpleasant had happened between them.

"Everything's all right," she agreed impatiently. "But that's not the point. That poor girl's going to have a baby. Which is something, I hope, in a girl's life. She thought she was in for a horrible mess. I thought so too. How could she tell it wasn't that, much less me?...Last May it was--she'd been making love. She's been carrying that baby for over six months. Fancy what it means, all that. Night and day. Well, of course you can't. But I can. I've seen it all the time. I tell you it's simply terrific. And then she thinks she's going to lose the baby. All that trouble for nothing! Wasted in a most frightful mess! Can't you feel it? Can't you feel the awfulness of it? Couldn't the doctor feel it? She was mistaken. She wasn't going to lose the baby. But her agony--yes, agony--was just as real to her as though she *had* been going to lose it. And this doctor of yours merely laughs at her! Jokes! What does he think a woman is? He doesn't know the first thing about being a doctor. Any fool who's passed his examinations can tell the difference between a miscarriage and a bad attack of tummy-ache. But it takes a man to *feel.* And that doctor can't. He isn't a man. He's a--there's no word for him...Teases her about some champagne she'd had, on the top of some peaches and some seasickness medicine! Well, if you want to know, it was I who gave her the champagne, and I gave her the peaches. It isn't as if I hadn't had her examined before we started. My French doctor saw her. He said she was in splendid health. Never seen anyone better, he said, and it was perfectly safe for her to travel, and if she did have a bit of a shaking up it wouldn't do her any harm. And the voyage wasn't really so bad. It wasn't good, but it wasn't bad, though it was rather worse than we expected, I admit. And she was quite all right till she had the champagne on the train. Even here she walked by herself to the lift. She was so much all right that I went down to the grill-room to eat something. But as soon as I'd gone her nerves went queer and the pains began. She rang and I was fetched. I can understand it well enough."

"Yes, yes," Evelyn agreed, appeasingly. He felt as guilty as if he had been Dr. Constam. "Who is this young lady?"

Gracie hesitated.

"Tessa," she answered in a low tone.

"Tessa?"

"Yes, Tessa Tye, my maid."

"I don't think I've seen her."

"Of course you've seen her. She came into the hotel with me that morning when you were standing in the hall. Very pretty. And rather smart too. Don't you remember. She's pretty enough for any man to remember."

"Oh yes," Evelyn did remember. A lackadaisical and self-conscious creature. Pretty? Yes. But he wouldn't have said very pretty. He was thunderstruck. He said: "Married?...Or not?"

"Why do you say 'or not'? Why shouldn't she be married? Can't maids be married? Can't they have their own lives like other people? However, she isn't married, as it happens. That's why I made up my mind to look after her. It may interest you to know--I haven't told anyone else--to know that when we got here that first morning she tried to commit suicide. Opening a vein with a pair of scissors. Yes, that was how she felt then. That was why I kept you waiting before you took me to Smithfield. Oh, I didn't find out till later what it was she'd been up to. I thought it was an accident with the scissors. But I got it out of her in the end, when I noticed her body and it was staring me in the face! I couldn't believe it at first--you never do...Some half-English, half-Belgian rotter she'd fallen in love with in Paris. She fell for him and then he ran away. She didn't know his address. I doubt if she knew his real name. She carried that baby to New York with me and back again. And I hadn't guessed--it wasn't till after we'd gone to Paris again from here that she confessed. I wasn't going to throw her over then. No! What I had to do was to put some self-respect into her. I took her to St. Cloud. It suited me, because I wanted to be quiet to write my book. A little hotel there. Only one bathroom for the two of us. I called her a friend of mine, Mrs. Tye. I could see her growing before my eyes. We made no bones about it. We went around for walks just as if it was the most ordinary thing in the world. And so it is. When we left St. Cloud you could see how she was half a mile off. Some of them must have noticed it in the hall downstairs this afternoon, though she was wearing a big cloak. She's been maiding me just the same. It wouldn't have done for her to be idle. And the doctor, I mean the French one, said it would do her all the good in the world to work--stoop, run about--you know. And she's a different girl. It's set her up. She used to be anæmic and namby-pamby. All that's gone. It'll be the making of her."

"But why have you brought her here to London?"

"I brought her because I had to come about my book. And I thought we should be as safe here in a big hotel as anywhere." Gracie paused on a self-conscious half-smile. "I couldn't leave her behind. She'd have fretted to death by herself. And I don't quite see why my business should be held up because she's going to have a baby. She's got to take the rough with the smooth, the same as the rest of us. Don't think I coddle her. I shall be coddling her in about ten weeks' time, I expect. But not yet. We shall only be here for a few days. I've made all the arrangements at St. Cloud." Gracie tossed her head as it were defiantly, and sat down.

Evelyn, agitated, astounded, admiring, very respectful, walked to and fro in the room. He could not express his sensations. "Not now. Not yet," he kept saying to himself.

"Does your father know?" he asked, in a voice artificially negligent.

"No. Of course he doesn't know. Why?"

"Well, he's dining with me at this moment. That's all."

"Here? In the hotel?"

"In the restaurant. Him, and your friend Mrs. Penkethman and Lord Watlington."

"But I heard from him at Christmas. I thought he was going to the Bahamas for a holiday."

"He may be. But he's dining with me to-night. I left them to come up here."

"Does he know I'm here?"

"He does not."

"Is he staying here in the hotel?" She seemed to be really apprehensive.

"No, he's in the new house, so he told me."

"And I haven't seen it." Genuine relief in her tone. "Well, he must be frightfully taken with the new house. This is the first New Year he's spent in London for years. If I'd known he was to be in London I shouldn't have--"

The bedroom-door opened--was pulled open from the other side. Evelyn was near the window, and Gracie's face, as she looked at him, was turned a little away from the door. Tessa entered. Evelyn saw her first, and before Tessa saw him. She was wearing a peignoir, splendid enough to be one of Gracie's. It was boldly tied above the waist. No concealment of her condition. But a shameless display of it. The central character of the piece was indeed superbly enormous. Pale, worn, pretty face. Tousled bright hair. Thin bust. And then the swelling curves of approaching motherhood. Evelyn was thrilled. Tears came suddenly into his eyes. He blushed. "'Interesting' is the right word for it," he thought, thrilled again and again. He exulted in the girl's appearance; at the same time it put a deep solemnity into him. All this in a fraction of a second.

"Tessa!" cried Gracie, outraged. She had followed the direction of Evelyn's acutely perturbed glance. "What in God's name are you doing? Go back to bed this instant and keep warm."

Tessa had now seen Evelyn. She gave a faint cry of alarm and vanished. Gracie jumped up and shut the door with a bang. The large room with its plenteous and ornate furniture, and its dozen electric lights, was emptied of a capital presence, impressive, foolish and pitiful.

"Fools girls are!" Gracie exclaimed, and went on quickly: "Well, I think you'd better go back to your dinner now. And mind, don't say a word to father. He'd go in right off at the deep end. You don't know father."

"Very well. I don't," said Evelyn. He thought: "What separate lives they lead! And her mother--somewhere in the background." They shook hands. "Good night. I think you're wonderful. This is the greatest story I ever heard." What he appreciated as much as anything else in her recital was its breathtaking matter-of-factness.

She said:

"Everyone's wonderful when it comes to the point."

Chapter 49 NEW YEAR'S MORNING

As, in the restaurant, Evelyn with difficulty made his way back towards the table of which he was the host, he saw from the intent faces of Lord Watlington and Sir Henry Savott that these two were engaged in some sort of recriminatory argument, while Nancy Penkethman was glancing aside as if trying to dissociate herself from the affray. The rather simple-minded Nancy, however, was not a very good actress. Her expression betrayed a certain constraint. Yet it betrayed also a certain satisfaction, which sprang from her intuitional knowledge of the pleasing fact that she herself was the prime cause, though of course not the occasion, of the discord.

"So glad to see you again!" she greeted Evelyn charmingly, and at the same time bestowed upon Harry and Henry in equal proportions a charmingly mischievous smile.

"I'm extremely sorry to have been so long," said Evelyn, feeling that he had not arrived a moment too soon. "I really couldn't help it. You know, you never do know what will happen next in a hotel."

The demeanour of the other two men changed instantly from the bellicose to the perfectly peaceful. And indeed their material interests and their prestige were too closely interwoven to permit of anything worse than a tiff occurring between them; assuredly no woman on earth could have estranged them, for each of them had a hard realistic sense of the relative unimportance of women, beautiful or plain, in the world of their ideals.

"We were beginning to suspect a fire had broken out somewhere upstairs, and you were keeping it dark for the sake of business," said Lord Watlington with a laugh; and Evelyn laughed.

"No," he said shortly. "It wasn't a fire." He perceived now the risks which he ran in concealing from Savott the presence of Gracie in the hotel. Savott and he were working together in the enormous enterprise of the Merger and on a basis of the utmost candour. Sometimes they even used their Christian names to one another. Supposing that Savott were to discover Evelyn's uncandid reticence concerning Gracie, and their cards-on-the-table friendship were to be imperilled! Pooh! Savott could discover nothing. Gracie would be off again in a day or two. Moreover, it was no part of Evelyn's duty to be aware of the identity of every visitor in the largest luxury hotel on earth. Withal, Gracie evidently suffered from a characteristic girlish deficiency in the sense of danger. Pooh! Dissension between father and daughter could not conceivably bring about dissension between Savott and himself...Why, if Gracie seriously wished to avoid her father, had she chosen to come to just the Imperial Palace? Her stated reason for doing so was not very credible.

Evelyn's thoughts ran on in this vein. But absolutely no clue to them could be seen in his bearing. He was a master of duplicity when circumstances demanded it.

The restaurant, if as noisy as ever, was less crowded. A ceaseless procession of revellers was passing out in obedience to a large, painted, pointing hand and a notice which said: *"Ballroom. Attractions."*

"I think now is the moment for us to go and see these mysterious 'attractions'," Evelyn suggested. "It will be midnight before we know where we are, and by midnight we simply must be here again."

"But your dinner, darling!" said Nancy Penkethman, all of whose acquaintances were her darlings. "You haven't eaten a mouthful."

"No, I haven't," Evelyn concurred. "Unless soup, fish, and entrée are worthy to be called a mouthful. But there'll be some supper after Auld Lang Syne."

Nancy having lighted a new cigarette, they rose and went, Nancy and Evelyn in front. The high financiers behind were now fondly Henrying and Harrying. Henry's flushed organism was engaged in the true business of a gourmand at the end of a good luscious meal. Harry, as usual with him, had eaten little, but he had honoured the approach of the New Year with a fair number of whiskies.

The broad corridor leading to the ballroom section of the public apartments was full of jostling people, men and women, in the same condition as Harry and Henry: relaxed, released into a careless and quasi-shameless jollity, with neckties somewhat disarranged, frocks somewhat disarranged, splendid comic hats awry, ill-controlled mouths, loose smiles and laughs, loud tongues. Evelyn could feel their bodies, male and female, against his, see their faces very close: humanity in the mass, odorous, multitudinous, flippant, saucy, brazen, free of social discipline. The too populous corridor was like a suffocating tunnel made light and brilliant by pale toilettes, rouge, exposed flesh, and jewels.

The party reached a large ante-room, round whose walls had been ranged a series of concave and convex mirrors which, distorting everything, changed beauty into the horribly grotesque, dignity into ridicule, decency into the obscene. The reflections excited high mirth and salvos of hysterical shrieks. This, the first of the attractions, was an immense success of humour.

Next, the ballroom, which, with space for two hundred couples to dance, contained only seventy or eighty persons, who watched a stage-spectacle of three youths throwing crimson, glittering Indian clubs at one another apparently with intent to kill. But the flying, revolving clubs seemed to have a magic life and volition of their own; they flew into hands, criss-crossed in parabolic curves, lodged themselves incredibly between arms and torsos, dropped unerringly into pockets. They could make no mistakes; they were tireless on their unending shuttle journeys to and fro; the youths alone gave signs of effort and strain beneath their stage-smiles. The spectacle was a dazzling exhibition of dexterity on the part of the clubs, assisted by the three youths. But the sparse audience, while applauding at intervals, did not increase.

The third and greatest attraction was in a third room beyond. This room was so jammed with spectators that Evelyn's foursome could not get into it at all. They had difficulty even in maintaining a position at the wide doors. Guffaws, giggles, shouts rose out of the dense floor of heads like invisible raucous birds. The heat was tropic. At the end of the room, on a dais, Punch, popping up and down in a small oblong of a proscenium, was exhibiting his domestic and conjugal existence with Judy, policemen, maids, and executioners. Murders were being committed at express speed; the law was derided; and Toby watched the farcical tragedies with canine indifference.

Nancy, pouting, complained that she could see nothing. Suddenly Lord Watlington picked her up by her slim waist, and perched her on his shoulders--a feat which persons in the vicinity warmly applauded with cheers. Nancy laughed like a schoolgirl. The drama went on and on; and still on; repeating itself. Nobody was bored for a moment: everybody was passionately interested in the fate of wooden puppets.

Then, just behind the foursome, a matchless organ-voice, triumphing easily over the din, cried solemnly, warningly, imperatively: "Ladies and gentlemen. A quarter to midnight." It was the voice of the renowned chief toast-master of the Imperial Palace, in a red coat and knee-breeches. Lord Watlington deposited Nancy on the parquet; otherwise the admonition was ignored. But in a moment the curtain fell on the career of Punch, and at once the room began to empty. The foursome were shoved backwards with violence.

"What are you laughing at?" Nancy asked Evelyn as she smoothed down her skirts; she feared that something was amiss with her attire or her face.

"Punch and Judy of course," Evelyn reassured her.

It was not the truth. He was laughing, quietly to himself, at the thought of the mistake of Tessa and Gracie about Tessa's condition. Suddenly it had struck him as extraordinarily funny. He sympathised with Dr. Constam's unrepressed mirth. It was the funniest thing he had ever come across. And Gracie might say what she chose in protest. It was *really* funny. But to savour its funniness your sense of humour had to be robust. The pilgrimage back to the restaurant was a retreat from Moscow; people fell by the way; insecure possessions were torn off in the mêlée and some of them never seen again.

2.

In the restaurant as, breathless, the party struggled to their table and dropped into chairs, the great clock showed five minutes to midnight. Theatre chorus-girls dressed as ballet-dancers were entering; they carried clusters of balloons high on the ends of long sticks, and men stood on chairs to take balloons; explosions resounded. Processions of trumpeters trumpeting, and of beef-eaters not eating beef, entered the restaurant with excessive pomp. The band played "Tipperary." The colour, the noise, the heat were all increased. Every light went out, except the festooned Chinese lanterns and the illuminated dial of the great clock. In the dusk the last loiterers scrambled to their places.

The minute-hand of the great clock crept up to the hour-hand until the two joined on XII. The band was stilled. The chief toast-master, in front of the lower storeys of the clock, raised his mighty arm. The revellers obediently stood to their feet. The band resumed, in a new strain. Nancy crossed her thin bare arms. The three men hesitated, shamefaced. Then Nancy's right hand took Evelyn's left, and then eight hands were clasped in the traditional fashion. And every revelling hand at every table was joined to another, and soon arms were moving up and down to the rhythm of the music. The three men hated the ceremony. Only Nancy in her simplicity enjoyed it. She sang first; Sir Henry Savott then sang loudly; Evelyn hummed; Lord Watlington remained obstinately mum in the sheltering dusk. Gradually the revellers lost their shamed self-consciousness, and sang and wagged their arms with a will.

The waiters around the room, and the two black-robed girls behind a control desk in a corner, had no share in the grave rite. Serious, preoccupied by their duties, they were cut off from revelling humanity. The advent of New Years was naught to them.

The ageless song ended. The lights blindingly went up. The band jumped gloriously into the feverish waltz from "The Meistersingers." The waiters started into life. The revellers shook hands and exchanged fervent good wishes. Seven minutes had passed, but the hands of the great clock had not budged. They marked an everlasting midnight. They would not venture into the New Year. Time stood still.

A young man in a wondrous white waistcoat advanced smiling and victorious towards Evelyn's table. He bowed indiscriminately to the party.

"Well, sir?" he addressed Evelyn.

"All my congratulations. Not a single hitch. A Happy New Year," said Evelyn.

It was the Bands-and-Cabaret-manager, Jones-Wyatt, who had been responsible for all the complex arrangements except those connected with food and drink.

"Thank you, sir. Same to you." He bowed and retired, content.

A little later Lord Watlington made an abrupt sign to Nancy Penkethman, who submissively rose.

"Well, my dear host," said Lord Watlington very urbanely and smilingly expansive. "It's all been extremely impressive. I admire your organisation as much as I like your hospitality. Ever so many thanks. You'll excuse me if I go. I can't stand up against late hours."

"So sweet of you, Mr. Orcham," said Nancy, clinging to Evelyn's hand. "I've simply loved it. I never had such a New Year's Eve before. Thank you ten million times."

"Very good of you to come," said Evelyn lamely.

"Bye-bye, Henry."

"Bye-bye, Harry."

Henry put a chaste kiss on Nancy's cheek. The departing pair were gone. When Harry decided to go he always acted on the decision with ruthless promptitude.

Then Henry went, offering the same excuse as Harry.

Evelyn was alone in the renewed multitudinous champagne orgy of the restaurant. But within less than a minute Sir Henry Savott returned, rather bustling. He would have passed as perfectly sober had he not been a trifle too sure that he was perfectly sober.

"I say, Evelyn," he said brusquely, "what day are you going back to Paris? You are going, aren't you?"

"Yes. But I can't settle the date till I hear that the Concorde manager-- what's the name, Laugier?-- has got over his attack of flu and can answer questions."

"I can tell you that now," said Sir Henry. "He was back at work to-day. A fellow told me before I came here to-night, who'd seen him this morning at the Concorde."

"Oh! Well, then, I may go as soon as I've wired him and got his answer. I'll telephone you."

"I'll see you before you start?"

"Certainly."

Sir Henry departed for the second time that New Year's morning. Evelyn could explain his return only on the supposition that he had preferred to keep out of the entrance-hall until Nancy and Harry were clear away.

Cappone, as fresh as dawn, arrived at the table and suggested that the panjandrum had insufficiently eaten. Cappone could watch over the eating of a thousand guests, and not least of the panjandrum's. Evelyn agreed to consider a couple of kidneys, which Cappone, having received congratulations from his chief on the complete smoothness of the jollity of the grand revel, went off into the kitchen to order personally from Maître Planquet.

The revel could not die. It was now more vivacious than ever. With the kind consent of the Licensing Authority, champagne and other alcohol was still being generously served and quaffed. And a fair proportion of guests, having convinced themselves that the New Year's Eve dinner was finished, were starting the New Year well with a New Year's morning supper. When the kidneys were eaten, however, a few craven roysterers were already leaving, and a deserted table here and there showed plain white. The great clock was now more than an hour late...

She was a unique young woman, was Gracie. Her phrase, 'I had to put some self-respect into her,' stuck in Evelyn's mind. She evidently had a sense of fundamentals. She had done, was doing, a marvellous work with the silly, tragic Tessa. He thought of the two of them up there in suite 365-- and the unborn. He pictured the luxuriant embossed figure of the foolish Tessa, one instant in the bedroom-doorway. If it could suddenly appear in the midst of the hot, wild-fire revel presided over by Bacchus, Pan, Venus, and all the gods of luxury--what a sensation, what a menacing reminder of the inexorableness of life!

Why had Gracie chosen the Imperial Palace? She had a sense of fundamentals, yes; but there were streaks of folly in her wisdom. He felt obscurely that she was a girl capable of enormities which might be magnificent, but they would be enormities all the same. She frightened his deep prudence.

He rose and strolled through the deafening chatter and clatter and tinkling towards the kitchen, still in full-heated activity, there to bestow upon Maître Planquet and three important sub-chefs a reward which could not be measured in money. When he slowly re-entered the restaurant a refreshed orchestra had just replaced an orchestra which had blown and scraped and drummed itself dry. The orchestras--he had been forgetting them! After a moment he went downstairs to the band-lounge, a nondescript, large room where a score of aristocratic, exhausted toilers in evening dress, whose earnest efforts were requited with five hundred pounds a week from the Imperial Palace treasury, lounged in easy-chairs and on sofas, and languidly smoked cigarettes and imbibed drinks served to them by their own waiter and valet. None but the conductor seemed to recognise Evelyn in the haze.

"Boys, here's the boss!" said the conductor succinctly, after he had condescended to the panjandrum's hand. "Wish him a Happy New Year." The musicians lifted themselves reluctantly from the chairs and sofas, and in turn condescended to the panjandrum's outstretched hand, and drank in eagerly the sweetness of his prepared phrases...Duty done! The panjandrum thought of the grill-room and wistful Ceria. To the grillroom then, via a couple of service-bars, a glass and cutlery reserve, down more stone steps--and there his accustomed ear could catch the faint whir of a dynamo deep in the earth's entrails--up steps, up more steps, along a narrow stone corridor, bang into the mirrored resplendence of the great entrance-hall, across which a stream of coated and cloaked and subdued revellers had by this time set outwards. In the grill-room corridor he met Ceria himself. Exchange of good wishes.

"You finished?"

"Nearly, sir." Ceria pointed through the glazed wall. The interior of the grill-room was an expanse of plain white tables; only three or four tables were occupied; there were twice as many waiters as guests.

"Well, you've had a good evening."

"Wonderful, sir."

"Going to have a look at the restaurant, eh?"

Ceria unwillingly admitted that this was so. They went back together to the foyer and glanced through the curtains. A pallid and fatigued page-boy accosted Ceria with a message. Ceria's appreciation of the rich, variegated, intemperate scene was indifferent.

"Noisy," said he with his wistful smile, and dismissed it.

The great clock was now nearly two hours late: it seemed to dwell with serene self-approval in the eternal stillness of divine perfection. The pair had to move aside from the opening between the curtains to give room for a group of departing roysterers.

Evelyn thought of Violet Powler, nun-like and secluded far aloft in her bedroom on Eighth, probably asleep. Ceria bade him good night. Yet another ten minutes and the panjandrum was standing behind the Reception counter in the hall, talking to Reyer. He talked to the deferential Reyer for a long time. They watched the brilliant outgoing stream dwindle and dwindle, then increase in a sudden spate, and dwindle again. Now was the harvest of the cloak-rooms. Evelyn heard, from beyond the ever-revolving doors, the hooting of cars; he could see their lights flashing.

He thought:

"Why the devil did that girl choose this place to come to? It couldn't have been because she had a notion she might perhaps come across me again here, could it? She never apologised to me for her damnable rudeness about her party."

As for himself, he wished to see her again, but not his should be the first move towards a meeting. Never! He would die rather. More and more revellers carried forth their uneasy consciences into the chill night air to confront the New Year and imagine good resolutions and the turning over of new leaves. The fête was done.

Chapter 50 IN THE RAIN

"You remember you promised to go one night to that Shaftesbury Express lunch-and-supper-counter place. Have you been?"

Rather an abrupt stand-and-deliver sort of an opening for a telephone conversation at 10 p.m., thought Evelyn, startled. He was alone in his office, smoking a cigar and drinking mineral water.

"What on earth place do you mean?" he parried, quite intimately responding to Gracie's tone. The talk between them on the previous evening had somehow re-established their intimacy of Smithfield and the Prince of Wales's Feathers. But he knew very well what place she meant. He had forgotten Charlie Jebson's proud announcement of his position as a restaurateur. She had not forgotten it. Nor, probably, he said to himself sardonically, had she forgotten the fine masculine figure of young Charlie Jebson.

"Oh, dear! What a memory!" came the reply, and Evelyn heard her light laugh. She recalled the incident to him.

"Oh yes!" he said. "I do remember something of the kind."

"Well, have you been?"

"No. It's never crossed my mind from that day to this." He thought: "I bet anything she wants me to take her there tonight!"

"Well, don't you think you ought to go? A promise is a promise."

"But surely it was *you* that promised to go," he fibbed.

"Now don't pretend!" came the rich voice, very firmly. It might have been a kindly reproof from an elder sister! To her he was evidently no panjandrum; and he enjoyed not being a panjandrum. "You know as well as I do it was you who promised."

"Well, one of these days I will go," he said vaguely.

"That's just the same as saying you haven't the slightest intention of ever going. I should like to go to-night. Let's go." Cajolery in the tone. "Are you in evening dress?"

"I am not," he said. "I was in evening dress till pretty nearly three o'clock this morning, and I'm taking a night off, if you've no objection."

"That's splendid," came the voice, eagerness in it. "It *will* be a night off. If you'd been in your glad rags, we could hardly have gone. An Express counter isn't quite a suitable atmosphere for a boiled shirt. Shall I come down?"

"But listen--"

"No, I won't listen," came the voice. "Because I know exactly what you'd say if I let you. That's perfectly all right. You and daddy are so thick in these days, it's perfectly all right for your highness to be seen with me anywhere at any hour. And you needn't worry about not telling daddy that last night you knew I was here. If he gets to hear you can easily say you only found out to-day. Be a man. And don't be so damned dignified."

The young voice was allaying all his unspoken qualms and fears. The exhortation to shed his damned dignity was a challenge to him which his courage was bound to accept.

"It would be a bit of a lark," he said, with a laugh.

"I'm coming down this minute," the voice answered. "Where are you?"

"In my office. But look here. Is your car handy? Mine is not."

"Car!" the voice exclaimed. "We can't arrive at an Express counter in Shaftesbury Avenue in a car. It simply isn't done. We'll go in a taxi, of course."

"I'll be in the entrance-hall. Try not to keep me waiting more than a couple of hours."

Evelyn picked up his hat, muffler, and overcoat from the chair where he had thrown them. He tied the muffler twice round his neck, raised the collar of his overcoat, stuck his hat on one side, shoved his ungloved hands into his deep pockets, and went forth for the bit of a lark. He felt uplifted, and found the hall by contrast more than half dead after the late strain of the New Year's Eve fête. A sparse attendance in the restaurant. Even the distant band sounded as if it might shortly expire in a sigh. At the doors Long Sam, the head night-porter, was yawning in the lax ennui of the day after.

"Taxi please, Sam."

"Yes, sir," said Sam Butcher, quickened. "Taxi," he repeated to a janissary. "Lively."

The doors spun, the janissary dashed out, stumbling on the steps.

"If I'm wanted, Sam," said Evelyn to Sam. "I'm going out with Miss Savott to Jebson's restaurant in Shaftesbury Avenue. I don't expect to be more than an hour at the outside."

After all, why attempt to conceal the lark? The name of Savott was now illustrious in the hotel. Why not be grandly, audaciously open about the lark? At the same moment Gracie appeared, uplifted too, and hurrying. All in three or four minutes the lark had been conceived and brought to birth. Astonishing. Frightening. But jolly. You never knew what would happen next with that incalculable girl.

"D'ye mean that little place close by the cinema?" the taxidriver asked, and when told by Evelyn that that little place was indeed the place meant he gave an "Oh!" whose tone indicated that as a man of the world he had ceased to be startled at the vagaries of people of fashion. At the same time he lifted his eyebrows to indicate a mild, weary criticism of people of fashion who would leave an Imperial Palace in order to visit an Express counter near a cinema in Shaftesbury Avenue.

The conversation in the bumping, danger-affronting taxi was constrained, did not flow easily. Gracie said that Tessa was perfectly well again, and was packing for departure the next morning.

"It does her good to bestir herself a bit," said Gracie.

"I believe that is the theory," said Evelyn.

"It's the practice--with Tessa," said Gracie.

The Express Counter was very small: a long high counter running down one side of a narrow room, ending with a partition at the farther extremity; on the other side of the room three or four tiny tables, with a couple of chairs apiece. A profusion of electricity. Not a soul visible, except a blonde lady of thirty odd, dressed in black, with a thin gold necklet and a gold wrist-watch. She might have passed for a floor-housekeeper of the Imperial Palace.

"C'est très sympathique," said Gracie at once. "I love the lampshades."

"Yes," Evelyn said, accepting her verdict cheerfully. "Shall we sit here?" He put his hand on a chair at one of the tiny tables.

"No," said Gracie. "We must sit at the bar. I adore a bar." They took high chairs at the bar, and lodged their feet comfortably on a brass rail provided for customers of stature less than two yards and a half. Gracie loosed her leather coat. Evelyn did not even take off his hat; there was no accommodation for it.

"Now," said Evelyn to the bar-woman. "What do you serve here, please?"

"Well, sir. We serve the finest sandwiches in London. Salads. Oysters. And the finest chops and steaks in London--but only at lunch-time--I mean the chops and steaks. And cheeses of course--any hour." Having examined and assessed and placed her customers, she waved a bare forearm towards a range of sandwiches imprisoned in glass on a shelf behind her.

"I doubt if I've ever had the finest sandwiches in London," said Evelyn, putting his hat on the counter.

"I think oysters," said Gracie, "and stout."

"Stout? At night? Disturb my sleep," said Evelyn.

"And what if it does?" Gracie murmured, lighting a cigarette. "Stout is such fun, and all fun has to be paid for."

"Two dozen oysters and two stouts, please," said Evelyn, acquiescent. And in that instant of abandonment to adventure, it seemed to him that he really did not care whether his sleep would be disturbed or not.

"Two dozen Whits and two draught stouts," the bar-woman called to someone hidden beyond the partition. "Very mild to-night," she added, to her customers.

"Ye-es," Evelyn said. He was not an expert in the art of small-talk across counters.

"Windy," said Gracie. "Gusty."

"Well," said the bar-woman, glancing at the leather coat, "if you're motoring that doesn't matter--unless of course it's a touring car."

"I was thinking of the sea."

"Oh! Channel to-morrow morning. Yes, I suppose so. I've never been over myself, that is, I mean since I was a baby-in-arms. I began my travelling early, I did, and left it off early too." All three laughed. "They do say there's nothing like travelling for sharpening your wits. But what I say is a bar's pretty good in that line." They all laughed again.

'Express' was a fit adjective for the Shaftesbury. The bar-woman disappeared and returned immediately with two foamy stouts. And the next minute a well-dressed man appeared with two plates of oysters and the proper accompaniments thereto. He thanked the customers for accepting them, then vanished, and the bar-woman retired to sit on a stool at the end of the counter nearest the noisy Avenue. Peace and pleasantness within the bright Shaftesbury. Evelyn was happy and excited, as he might have been in a foreign town. He thought, and not for the first time: "What a rut I live in!"

"I'm not hungry," he murmured confidentially.

"Neither am I," Gracie murmured. "But not one of these oysters is going to be left. If you'd only ordered a dozen between us I should have asked for more."

She blew away some of the foam from her stout, exposing the deep, dark liquid beneath, and drank, and wiped her mouth gingerly with a coloured paper napkin taken from a pile of napkins laid handy. They went on murmuring confidentially. Anybody out of hearing might have thought that they were exchanging emotional secrets charged with terrific importance, instead of remarks about the excellence of the oysters, the freshness of the brown bread-and-butter, and the sweet velvet of the stout. The adventure was delicious, bizarre, romantic. Evelyn so felt it, and he knew that the incalculable Gracie so felt it.

He thought: "I wish I could get past her defences. There's no getting near her"--though their knees almost touched in front of the counter. "She must have a sort of a liking for me, otherwise she wouldn't run after me the way she does. She's very curt and domineering. She's infernally independent. She's an egotist, can't be anything else. And yet--Tessa! She isn't being very egotistical over Tessa. She's taking risks there. But that may be egotism too. Wants to flatter herself she's making a grand gesture, defying convention, *being herself,* going around with a maid as big as a barrel, and so on and so on. 'Maid': that's good."

He was telling himself that his estimate of Gracie was absolutely impartial, realistic, perhaps cynical. As she was not looking at him--she seemed determined not to meet his eyes--he could look at her. Benevolent expression, or the reverse? Who could say? All he could be sure of was that she had distinction and pride. Her clothes were distinguished; her untidiness was distinguished; she ate, and she drank stout, with distinction. And with distinction in her curved fingers she raised an oyster off its shell, slipped it into her mouth. Whence this distinction? Was it from the curves of the fingers, the hands, the arms, the body--the slow, reflective movements of the jaws as she munched? No, he was no nearer the core of her mystery. He was checked by her barricades. Nobody ever comprehended anybody; and certainly he refused the ridiculous notion that women were more mysterious than men. She was cogitating about something--God knew what! Why in heaven's name had she lured him out? To eat oysters and drink stout, covering her cogitations with a thin layer of murmurous banalities? It would serve her tantalising beauty right if he abducted her, seduced her by force, and then said casually: "There now! You can go back to your cogitations again. You've got something to think about now."

He murmured: "I suppose as you're leaving to-morrow you've finished the business with your publisher to-day?"

"Yes," she said. "That's all right."

"Well," he said, "there's one thing. With your name on the title-page the book's bound to make a stir in the world."

She raised her face and looked him solemnly in the eyes.

"My name won't be on the title-page."

"No? Why not?"

"Surely you don't imagine," she murmured. "Surely you don't imagine for a moment I'd let my book be helped by the name of a racing motorist and my father's name and the name of a girl who knows all the smart people in London! Because if you do you're wrong. My book will have to stand by itself--or fall. I shall take a pseudonym. That's what I came over about. My publisher was making a fuss over that very point...He's given in. So it's all right." Her tone had more than solemnity; it was religious; it vibrated with the formidableness of mystical passion.

Evelyn was daunted, apologetic, admiring; he had a thrill. "You're perfectly right!" he murmured gravely, and in his tone too there was emotion.

Gracie smiled; a divine warm stillness in her smile, and a magic power in it lifting him up. For an instant he held the key to the enigma...It slipped from him.

"I knew you'd know what I mean," she said. "Some people simply don't know the language you're talking. It's just jabber to them." Then she turned towards the distant bar-worn who was reading a paper-bound novel, and asked loudly "Can you tell us what time Mr. Jebson will be here night?"

The bar-woman rose and walked half-way along the length of the counter before calling out:

"Jim, what time will Mr. Jebson come in to-night, d'y know?"

And the answering baritone voice from beyond the partition; "The governor won't be along to-night. He telephoned."

"Can my husband or me do anything?" the bar-woman amiably enquired.

"No, thanks," said Gracie. "It's nothing. Only we know Jebson, and we thought if he happened to be here--"

Evelyn was glad that Charlie Jebson had telephoned. He did not desire the presence of the imposingly masculine Charles complicating the situation. And how could Gracie swing so abruptly from her book to Charlie Jebson? There was a lamenting disappointment, rather desolate, in her 'No, thanks,' to the bar-woman. No wonder the key had slipped from him! True, they had come to the Shaftesbury to see Mr. Charles Jebson.

Nevertheless Gracie's transition from her book to Charlie was too swift not to irk Evelyn's sensitiveness.

"Well," said she after a few moments. "I've finished my oysters, and"--she stopped to drink the remainder of the stout--"I've finished my stout."

"You'd like to go?"

"We may as well. But you've not finished yours."

"Can't," said Evelyn.

The bar-woman approached them, novel in hand this time, and Evelyn paid the bill, which was very modest compared with the scale of charges for no better oysters and no better stout at the Imperial Palace.

"Thank you," said the bar-woman indifferently. As the bell of the cash-register rang she added: "What name shall I say to Mr. Jebson?"

Evelyn shook his head with a faint deprecating smile:

"Doesn't matter."

"Oh, darling!" Gracie protested benevolently. "I'm sure Mr. Jebson would be delighted to know you've called." And to the woman: "Mr. Orcham, of the Imperial Palace Hotel." The bar-woman, suddenly excited, had a sharp, simpering attack of self-consciousness. She was no longer the experience-worn, life-weary, detached, disdainful spectator of life. Ten or fifteen years dropped from her age in an instant. She became an ingenuous schoolgirl, bridling, smirking from innocent pride in the august identity of her customer. Evidently she had heard of Mr. Orcham, and of his importance in the meat-trade, from the proprietor of the Shaftesbury Express Counter. Her husband peeped out from behind the partition.

"Mr. Jebson will be very proud, and very sorry to have missed you, sir. Good night. Good night, madam."

2.

Evelyn felt foolish as they left the room. He also felt rather resentful against Gracie for having called him 'darling' in front of the bar-woman. In Gracie's world 'darling' had no meaning, except in so far as it constituted some sort of assurance that the user of it did not regard the person addressed as absolutely repulsive and hateful. But the bar-woman was certain to misunderstand it. However, Evelyn would not argue the matter critically. The society, at a bar, of girls such as Gracie had its obvious disadvantages, which the fatalistic philosopher would accept in a lofty spirit of resignation. And at worst 'darling,' considered as an epithet, was less offensive than the 'sweetie' which on a previous occasion she had applied to him. He silently swallowed the rising poison of his resentment.

As they emerged on to the pavement two taxis drew up, and nine strong, full-bodied men miraculously emerged from them, occupying the pavement with their hearty, free masculinity unencumbered by women.

"We'll take one of these," said Evelyn.

"Can't we walk?"

"Of course, darling." That was his sole comment on her improper use of a word. Gracie ignored it.

The squad of men one by one entered Mr. Charles Jebson's establishment. The dead hour between nine-thirty and ten-thirty was ending. The bar-woman would need all her high faculties of domination, diplomatic retort, and express serving; for the nine were every one of them evidently experts in bars--not simple, diffident amateurs like Evelyn.

"It's going to snow," said Evelyn. "Oh no!"

"It is snowing," said Evelyn.

"Is it? Well, never mind. I love walking in a snow-storm. Don't you?"

"Yes. But you'll get your feet wet."

"I can change."

"So can I."

They walked briskly side by side. At short intervals down the Avenue taxis were waiting in long lines for the emptying of theatres, and in the cross streets waited files of motor-cars. Small snowflakes dallied and gambolled with one another in the dark air, reluctant to reach the ground. Gracie's hat began to whiten. At Piccadilly Circus Evelyn led Gracie down steps into the vast warm roundness of the populous Underground station, and then led her up steps again into bleak Lower Regent Street.

"It's raining," said Evelyn.

"Let it," said Gracie, cautiously unwilling this time to contradict him. "It's magnificent." She quickened her pace. "Think of a hot bath."

Then silence. Evelyn agreed with Gracie that to walk in the blusterous weather was indeed magnificent; in the wind and the rain driven against his face by the wind he experienced sensations of triumphant vitality such as perhaps he had not had for years; but he said nothing, and his silence was grim. He felt cruel towards Gracie, striding along, her leather coat now and then grazing his thick winter tweed. Well, she could indeed stride along--even in her silly fragile high heels, which no doubt she would never wear again after this soaking. At last he could tolerate the silence no more.

"You were disappointed at our Mr. Jebson not being on view, weren't you?" He was openly sardonic.

"I think I was," Gracie answered with acquiescent candour.

"You've remembered him ever since Smithfield, haven't you?"

"I certainly have." Some resistance in her tone.

"Just tell me. What was there in him that was so interesting to you? I must say I didn't find him terribly interesting. Just a well-set-up sort of a--brute." Evelyn chose the last word to annoy her; he who never quarrelled, who maintained always that social friction was unanswerable proof that somebody had been clumsy--he was aware of a desire to force her into an ugly and perhaps violent altercation. Not because she ordered him about and imposed her caprices upon him. Nor because she had called him 'darling' at the counter and all Smithfield would soon know that she had called him 'darling.' But solely because she had actively shown interest in the young butcher: phenomenon of sentiment which seriously offended him--while he sneered at it. She, beautiful, elegant, intelligent, intellectual, civilised, a masterpiece of an age of decadence--she to keep fondly in her mind for many weeks the image of a tall, powerful, coarsely handsome, self-complacent dandy of a tradesman whom she had seen for not more than a couple of minutes! And so brazen about her interest too!

She said calmly:

"Well-set-up 'brutes' aren't so terrifically plentiful, you know. And a brute is so soothing to the nerves. And this particular brute is a worker. He's getting something done, like we are. I loved his Express Counter. I could see his individuality all over it. Wholesome. And him getting up at 3 a.m. to go to Smithfield, and then looking after his lovely Express Counter last thing at night. She was funny, that starchy, wrinkled creature behind the counter! It makes me smile, how jealous all men are. Anyhow, I've never met one that wasn't."

Devilish girl! With that single word 'jealous' she had rendered a quarrel impossible. He had his dignity to take care of. He acted a pleasant, easy laugh.

"I was only asking," he said, acting gentleness.

"And I was only answering," she said, very amiably.

And she turned her head and looked up at him through the rain with a charming glance that he felt rather than clearly saw in the murk. Danger was past, resentment dissipated. He was happy; his spirit was lifted; and for no logical reason.

"Oh!" she cried, pointing. "That's marvellous, especially on a night like this. I do admire you for that. You're a poet." She pointed.

They had come out on the top of the Duke of York's Steps, into the full force of the south-west rain-bearing wind. Not a soul on the Steps. Automobiles flitting in both directions along the Mall below them. Lamps on both sides of the Mall obscured at moments by the swishing branches of trees. Beyond, the dark forest of St. James's Park, with a gleam of the lake. And beyond the forest, high in the invisible firmament, the flood-lit tower of the Imperial Palace poking itself brilliantly up to the skies. There was nothing in all London, then, but that commanding great column of white light.

The emotional accents of Gracie's rich voice moved Evelyn. If she was thrilled by the tower, he was thrilled by her thrill as well as by the tower. The rain on their cheeks came straight from heaven.

As, after skirting St. James's Park, they reached Birdcage Walk, Evelyn's damnable habit of foresight asserted itself. He foresaw that, all dripping wet as they were, they could not stop talking in the hall of the Palace. It would be too absurd, and too conspicuous. Therefore everything that had to be said must be said before entering the hotel.

'You're really leaving to-morrow morning?"

"Yes."

"There'll be some rough going in the Channel."

"Oh no! It must have been blowing up for this when we came over. It will blow itself out to-night. Besides, who cares?"

"I may possibly be down to see you off," he said. "What time?"

"Please don't!" she said firmly. "I loathe being seen off. Monsieur Adolphe seeing me off is just as much as I can do with."

"I understand. I should be the same myself," Evelyn concurred.

Within the next few days he too would be going to Paris; but she did not know this, and he did not tell her. To meet her in Paris might, assuredly would, complicate his existence, and he could not tolerate that. The Hotel de la Concorde, not young tyrannic women, was his business in Paris.

With what a sense of triumph, of tingling warm health, they entered the great, still, mirrored hall. Long Sam glanced at them.

"Wet, sir," said he. But he was too discreet to show any curiosity as to their reason for arriving on foot and not in a taxi, on a night so wild.

Crossing the hall they left a trail of drops of water behind them. And in the lift they made little pools. As the lift climbed up towards Third, the liftman looked enquiringly at Evelyn, who nodded. The lift stopped.

"Well, *au revoir,"* said Evelyn. "You mentioned a hot bath." He smiled. She smiled. They stood together for a moment at the lift-door. They were parting. He did not know her address at St. Cloud. He might not see her again for months, years, if ever. It was not he himself, but some volition not his, that said:

"I should rather like to hear how Tessa goes on. You might send me a line."

She nodded, suddenly pulling off her hat, which was sodden; so was much of her hair. She had quite the air of a child, then--delicious. They shook hands. She walked off to her rooms. Evelyn re-entered the lift to go up to Seventh and a hot bath.

"Well, I'm damned!" he breathed. He felt relief.

Chapter 51 AFTER THE STORM

A few days later, on the special "Golden Arrow" steamer, Evelyn experienced a surprise and a thrill. The New Year gale had nearly but not quite blown itself out, and after an average comfortable voyage the ship was nosing cautiously through the narrows of Calais port, past flags and marine signals and quidnuncs and amateur fishermen whose skirts were lifted at times by a gusty breeze. Although the boat was not crowded, a large group of travellers had packed themselves tightly round the spot where the gangway was to be, apparently lest the boat might start back for Dover with themselves still on board.

Evelyn sat reading in a sheltered deck-chair. He had a fine sense of freedom. He was alone. He had nobody to look after, because he had nobody to look after him. For Oldham had been left behind. Oldham and the Continent were mutually antipathetic. Oldham feared the sea and despised foreign tongues, and so far as he was concerned the recent tour in France and Italy had not been wholly successful. A holiday being overdue to him, he was exiled for a week or more to Berkshire and the society of his wife. The good-bye to Evelyn at Victoria had been wistful rather than buoyant. As for Evelyn, it seemed to him, in those moments which Oldham's presence would have rendered so anxious with a hundred cares, that he had not a care in the world. His debarkation was already organised; and for passengers by the "Golden Arrow" service the Calais custom-house did not exist. When he felt the very faint bump which indicated that the vessel was alongside the quay, he rose slowly, surveyed his three suit-cases ranged together on the deck, dropped the pocket 'Eothen' into his pocket, and surveyed superiorly, with a deplorable spiritual pride, the mass of his fellow-sinners who from mere stupidity were inconveniencing themselves for no reason whatever.

Having duly confided his baggage to an instructed porter, he strolled to the rail, aft, and from there watched the foolish urgency of travellers down the sloping gangway to the quay.

He said to himself, boyish:

"I have my seat in the train, like all the rest of us; there are no customs; the ship is on time; I will be the last passenger to leave this ship." Yes, he felt boyish.

Had it not been for this infantile resolution, he might have missed the surprise and the thrill. The stream of descending passengers had thinned; the hand of the official at the bottom of the gangway was full of landing tickets; and Evelyn was on the point of leaving the rail when the surprise and the thrill happened to him. He saw Gracie on the gangway. Her face was half-turned towards the ship, and she held by the hand big Tessa Tye, leading her with every precaution down the steep slope. The two of them safe at length on the quay, Gracie took Tessa's arm, solicitously, even tenderly, and the slim girl and the spreading, ungainly expectant mother walked slowly towards the train, whose engine was sending up a thin wisp of steam in the far distance. He was thrilled. The expression of watchful motherliness on the face of the girl, the expression of trust on the pinched pale face of the expectant mother, offered a contrast and a harmony which made the most touching sight that Evelyn had ever seen. "That girl is magnificent," he said to himself, and not for the first time. He knew that he had witnessed something unforgettable. Withal, he had lost the sense of freedom.

He had sworn to be the last passenger to leave the ship, and he was. His seat chanced to be in the nearest coach of the train. The young women were not in that coach. He superintended the stowing of his baggage, tipped the porter, and then, scarcely witting, jumped down to the platform and walked along the endless train, glancing at every window. He reached the last coach, the coach at the head of the train. There was Gracie at the end of the last passenger coach, talking to an attendant, who by much physical force was closing a case for her.

"Good afternoon," Evelyn called.

She turned, standing high above him in the doorway. "Well, well! How nice!" she smiled.

"Can I do anything?"

"Not a thing. Thanks frightfully!" She laughed easily.

"Everything's all right?"

"Perfect. We waited four days at the Lord Warden for the weather. *I* shouldn't have waited. But Tessa was really a bit alarmed at the look of the sea. Dover's a very interesting place. I'd no idea!...And you?"

"Hotel business in Paris. Your esteemed father's business. You staying in Paris to-night?"

"Oh no! Straight on to St. Cloud. I wouldn't have to begin all over again to-morrow for anything on earth. I suppose you'll honour the Concorde?"

"No. The Montaigne. And if it isn't one of the two best hotels in Paris it soon will be." They both smiled.

Officials on the platform were becoming restless, and the windy air was very bleak.

"I'd better be getting back to my seat," said Evelyn. *"Au revoir."*

2.

Gracie leaned her head out of the doorway, smiled again, waved a hand as he hurried away. Enchanting spectacle: young, beautiful, graceful, distinguished, mother to a mother! Enchanting! Faultless! In the warmth of his corner at the other end of the train, a table all to himself, he disposed his chilled limbs and his minor belongings for the journey. Not a word had been said about meeting again. Every passenger on the "Golden Arrow" is served with lunch where he sits. Evelyn did not move. He might have stumbled through the length of the shaking train to pay a visit to Gracie en route, but he refrained because of the intimidating prospect of having to talk to the expectant mother as well as to Gracie. He read little; he did not doze. He did not think. He just existed in a haze of vague meditation. Coffee. Cigar. Dusk. Darkness. Bill-paying. The industrial lamps and flares of Creil. Swift-sliding twinkles of squalid suburban stations. Weariness. A tunnel. Gare du Nord. He looked at his watch. The train was punctual. Confusion on the echoing platform of the Gare du Nord. Everyone for himself. *Sauve qui peut.* Hostile and greedy glances of porters.

Evelyn had one glimpse of a known face: that of one of the Cheddar brothers. Tall, physically as splendid an animal as Charlie Jebson, and with features more refined; indeed aristocratic. Sort of Renaissance prince. Evelyn envied him, and despised himself for envying him. Of course he was at the station to meet Gracie, to take charge of her. Of course she had telegraphed to him. In the jostling crowd a uniformed man, with "Montaigne" gilded on his forehead, discovered Evelyn, and Evelyn yielded himself up like a parcel to the ceremonious care of the uniform. As he trudged along the stone-cold platform, miles of it, he looked out for Gracie. She had gone, vanished into France.

Chapter 52 TELEPHONE

Two afternoons later Evelyn was scrutinising sheets of figures in the private office of Monsieur Laugier, *directeur* of the Hotel de la Concorde, Place de la Concorde. Although his chief business was the Concorde, he had chosen to stay at the Montaigne, partly because in London he had quite sufficient of the disadvantages of sleeping where he worked, and partly because on his previous visit to Paris he had stayed at the Concorde, and he now wished to get the general atmosphere night and morning of the Montaigne.

The directorial apartment was on the mezzanine floor of the courtyard of the magnificent old building which only thirty-five years earlier had begun its rise from the status of a lovely but chilly palace or ministry to that of a luxury hotel with steam-heating, lifts, electric bells, and baths numerous enough to lave the limbs of the General Staff of a whole army.

The luxury, however, had not extended itself to the directorial room, which was small, low-ceilinged, lighted by two bulbs only, and warmed by an anthracite stove of excessive power. The narrow window was shut tight and curtained. The sole ventilation was obtained by means of a draught under the heavy gilded door. The temperature was torrid. In strange contrast with the antique, sombre, soiled, ornately panelled walls, the elaborate cornice, and the curious parquet of blackened oak, was an assemblage of office furniture of the very newest style; last mechanical, practical ingenuity of Chicago gadgets refashioned in the last chic of Parisian design, wilfully audacious in shape, insolently flouting every tradition, rioting in the unexpected, steely, glassy, flimsy. M. Laugier's desk was as large as Evelyn's in Birdcage Walk, and far more glittering; it had apparently about a thousand drawers, and one turn of a handle, as M. Laugier had shown to Evelyn, would simultaneously lock every drawer. The slope of the easy-chairs could be modified without sound or effort, to suit the idiosyncrasy of any sitter. The cabinets had the intricacy of Chinese puzzles. The files would snap and cling to documents with the ferocity of tigers.

And in the midst, at the end of the desk, sat Henri Laugier, fat as an operatic soprano, with the abdomen of a self-contemplating Buddha, dressed, in black, as loosely as the ease-loving landlord of a country inn; black hair, seamed slack face, intensely black eyes, long black moustache, black beardlet, low collar, flowing black tie, podgy hands and short fingers stained by the nicotine of countless cigarettes; the latest of the cigarettes drooped precarious from a corner of the directorial pallid lips. Laugier had the reputation of being a unique 'figure' in the continental hotel-world; and perhaps he presumed upon his reputation, part of which resided in the pliocene, immortal black straw hat, which he wore day and evening, summer and winter; this straw hat now lay on a chair exclusively allotted to it as a chair is allotted to a privileged cat. M. Laugier came from Carcassone, and was proud of his origin. His eyes were said to be absolutely fatal to women, even at long range, and none who had fallen to him ever forgot him. A stout old lady still at intervals arrived with a grandchild or so to see him at the hour of the aperitif; her boast, not clearly established, was that she had been his first mistress.

Evelyn and M. Laugier conversed now in French now in English as they pored over the serried columns whose nines were like fives, fives like nines, and sevens like nothing in the history of British arithmetic. Evelyn thought: "Is this man really my subordinate, and am I really supposed to be in control of all his slippery and enigmatic foreignness?" M. Laugier certainly treated him as a superior, but with an exquisite, soft, forbearance such as he might have used to a noble and powerful savage. The Orcham Merger seemed a less simple enterprise here than when it was under discussion with Sir Henry Savott at the Imperial Palace.

2.

The telephone faintly rang. M. Laugier clasped the oddly shaped French instrument in his lazy, caressing fingers.

"Allo! Allo!" He listened with an intent yet dreamy smile. "It is for you, *mon cher directeur,"* he said, and pushed the instrument across the corner of the desk towards Evelyn, who said to himself:

"It's that girl!"

"Allo! Allo!" Evelyn addressed the transmitter. "Excuse me, *mon cher directeur,"* he apologised to M. Laugier.

"I beg you, please," said M. Laugier, spreading his arms in deprecation of Evelyn's apology.

"Mr. Orcham?" the voice from the telephone enquired.

It was that girl.

"Yes," he replied, with primness--for he had no intention of allowing Laugier to suspect from either tone or phrase that it was a woman who had rung him up.

"I've had a deuce of time getting you. You told me you would be staying at the Montaigne."

"That is quite correct," said Evelyn.

"But you're at the Concorde."

"Yes. And very busy," said Evelyn.

"Shall you be busy to-night?"

"Yes, I shall," said Evelyn.

"How late?"

"Afraid I can't say."

"Couldn't you get out of it?"

"I could not," said Evelyn with careful coldness, more than ever determined that M. Laugier should gather nothing as to the nature of the conversation from the side of it to which he was listening. Conceive the old man (not that he was really old) aware that his grave but younger superior, in the midst of a highly technical interview, was arguing with a young woman about a proposed rendezvous! The notion horrified sedate Evelyn.

"Couldn't you manage to be free by ten o'clock?"

"Sorry. Impossible," said Evelyn with dignity.

"Then ten-thirty."

"I might try," said Evelyn calmly, after a pause.

"Why are you so cross with me?"

"I'm not at all cross," said Evelyn.

"You're very stiff."

"Where are you?" he asked in a new tone, apparently ignoring the criticism.

"In a call-box."

"Well, you see, I'm not. Do you understand?" said Evelyn grimly, and he heard Gracie's quick, rich laugh of comprehension.

"You mean you aren't alone?"

"Yes," said Evelyn.

"Well now, what about to-night? Ten-thirty? I must see you. It's rather urgent. I had to come in to Paris to-day, and I must go back to St. Cloud some time to-night, but it doesn't matter much what time. Where can we meet?"

She had throughout been assuming his readiness to meet her provided only the hour could be arranged. The impudent assumption both amazed and pleased him. She looked like being a serious nuisance. But her voice in the telephone was so attractive, even seductive, alluring. And she knew it was, curse her! She was using it unscrupulously. (He enjoyed thinking this against her.) Then he remembered her expression, her gestures, her walk, as she had convoyed Tessa up the platform of the marine station at Calais on the previous day. She was a magnificent girl, and often had he privately admitted her grand quality. He felt proud as he listened to her cajoling, wonderful voice. She--she so *chic,* intelligent, magnificent--was running after him! Oh yes! He fancied himself!...Coxcomb! And worse names than coxcomb did he apply to himself. But there it was. She was running after him! "It's rather urgent." What was rather urgent? An excuse. She was running after him. Rather marvellous, say what you choose!

"Well," she questioned again, impatient. "Where?"

"The Montaigne," he suggested.

"Oh no! That won't do. I loathe your Montaigne. It's just something chipped off Park Avenue. Listen! You know the rue Scribe?"

"I do," he answered impassively.

"I'll be there in a car, on the Opera side."

"Very well," he agreed.

"Ten-thirty, mind!"

"Yes. Good-bye."

"Who's with you?" She was adding the feminine postscript. Impertinent enquiry!

"The director," said Evelyn, more coldly. He would not utter Laugier's name in Laugier's presence.

"Of the Concorde?"

"Precisely."

"Oh! Laugier. Isn't he a dear? Give him my love."

"I will. Good-bye!" He replaced the telephone in front of M. Laugier.

Assignation with a woman hidden in a car in the rue Scribe, Opera side. It was a bit astounding, after all! A bit romantic! The impulse to vaunt came over him, irresistible. Laugier should be made to appreciate with what tranquil severity he, Evelyn, could talk to a beautiful, wealthy, and headstrong young girl.

"She sends you her love," he said, with a casual smile. "Miss--"

"Mademoiselle Gracie?" Laugier interrupted eagerly.

Evelyn nodded, taken aback and forlorn.

"I imagined to myself that it was her voice when she spoke first." M. Laugier gazed meditatively at the glassy desk. "Ah! *La belle creature! La belle creature!"* It was as if he saw her mirrored in the desk-top. Then he gazed at Evelyn long, a thousand flattering, mischievous implications in his deathdealing dark eyes which no illness and no slow convalescence could quench.

"Eh bien, mon cher directeur," said Evelyn, fingering a sheet of paper.

"Eh bien, mon cher directeur," said Laugier. *"Revenons à nos moutons."* A wisp of a glistening black lock had fallen over the pale forehead.

In the airless soporific warmth of the little room Evelyn the man of business inexorably resumed his investigation.

Chapter 53 ELECTRONS

When Evelyn reached the rue Scribe at one minute before half-past ten, having left too early a very friendly dinner with the manager of the Hotel Montaigne, there was no car waiting on the Opera side of the broad rue Scribe, and comparatively little traffic to confuse a watcher for a car containing a particular person. No stream of vehicles. No policeman. Cars passed at intervals of a few seconds. In the near distance motor-buses rumbled and great trams screeched and rattled over points. The huge edifice of the Opera, dwarfing all the houses, piled itself up into the velvet starlit sky; a few windows gleamed yellow in the hinder parts of the building. Evelyn stood waiting opposite the entrance to one of the courtyards, in or out of which walked occasionally some vague human being on some mysterious errand. An operatic performance was going forward somewhere in the complex immensity of the Opera; but it was hidden, soundless, immeasurably far off, like a secret and esoteric ceremonial, attended by adepts and withdrawn from the profane city into another world. Evelyn was alone. He felt alone. Waiting for a woman in a foreign capital! He thought:

"Is this dignified? Something furtive and illicit about it." What could it mean? What did it presage? Still, it was certainly romantic, at his age--and hers. *La belle creature,* Laugier had called her, with enthusiasm. What did that signify in the mouth of a Laugier? One objective only could be applied to the *belle creature,* and Evelyn had several times applied it: incalculable. He anticipated her arrival with the excited interest of a reader awaiting the next instalment of a sensational serial.

But she did not arrive. One minute after the half-hour. Two minutes. Three minutes. And every second of them had been a minute. The man of passionate punctuality glanced at a dim clock affixed to a lamp-post. He unbuttoned his long overcoat to glance at his watch in the gloom. He walked nearer to the lamp-post and glanced again. He was cold, and rebuttoned his overcoat. Was he in the right street? He crossed the street to examine the street-sign, though he had already examined it once. Then he recrossed, quickly, lest the car might come while he was absent from the arranged side. He grew more and more nervous. He was humiliated. Twenty-five minutes to eleven. She was capable of being half an hour late. 'They' did it on purpose: at least such was the masculine theory, and there was a lot in it. At that moment, in Paris itself, hundreds of men might be waiting, waiting, and saying to themselves bitterly:

"She is doing it on purpose."

A car slackened speed, swerving towards the pavement. No. It could not be hers. It stopped, with the saloon-door exactly opposite to him: pretty feat of brake-manipulation. He saw a figure in the dark interior of the saloon. No resemblance to Gracie. Then a light was switched on within, and Gracie sat suddenly revealed to him, radiant, opulent in a low evening frock which a loosened, effulgent cloak hardly concealed. 'They' were insensitive to cold, especially on a cold night.

The chauffeur had descended and was holding the saloon-door open for him.

"I'm frightfully punctual," said Gracie, leaning forward.

Her lovely face was serious, unsmiling.

"You are indeed," said Evelyn, raising his gibus.

"Do get in."

He got in, crushing his hat against the top of the door. Nervousness. The chauffeur shut the door, and then stationed himself attendant with his back to the car. Evelyn subsided into soft cushions, straightened his hat; he could detect her perfume, feel the richness of the stuff of her cloak on his hand. Out went the light. The next instalment of the sensational serial had apparently started. But not with words. Gracie said nothing, and Evelyn could think of nothing to say, so constrained was he--and no doubt she too. The interior of the car was the most private, the most secure room in all Paris.

"And now?" said he at length. After all he was a man, and the older, and for the sake of his own opinion of himself he must assume an air of taking charge of the situation.

"Well, darling," said Gracie. "You haven't shaken hands." He groped for her hand and held it, without squeezing it. "It's much too early to do anything yet. What about going into the Opera for an hour? They're doing 'Le Chevalier à la Rose."

"So I noticed," said Evelyn. "But we shall never be able to get seats, at this time of night, shall we?"

"Don't let that trouble you," she replied. "You leave it to me, and you'll see."

"I should love it," he said, insincerely but rather convincingly.

"It's the best of all the modern operas," she said. "Of course you've seen it."

"Yes. I saw it in Naples. The boy chevalier, what's-his-name, was played by an aged dame with bow-legs. It finished at two in the morning."

Laughing nervously, Gracie leaned across Evelyn and knocked at the window.

"Front of the Opera," she instructed the chauffeur, in French.

Fifteen seconds, and Evelyn was handing her out of the car. She gave a brief order to the chauffeur. She was carrying a book as well as her bag. They climbed the steps of the façade and through gilded gates entered the vast marmoreal and gilded vestibule. At the Control, she drew a ticket from her bag and presented it. She had bought a box in advance.

"You've won," said Evelyn.

She lowered the corners of her mouth and half closed her eyes as she laughed in mild, sardonic enjoyment of her trick on him. Constraint was suddenly gone, intimacy established, the old intimacy of Smithfield.

At sight of the ticket, and of Gracie's frock and cloak, functionaries on the cyclopean marble and onyx staircase of honour took on the demeanour of chamberlains of Louis Quatorze, and the pair were wafted onward from smile to servile smile. Furlongs of unyielding marble to walk! An old, cringing, importunate woman, with hair ribboned like a young girl's, introduced them into the box, and her harpy-fingers closed rapaciously and ungratefully on a ten-franc note from Evelyn.

The box was like a drawing-room of the 'seventies, not refurbished nor cleaned since the 'seventies. The folds of its brocaded curtains seemed to be stiff with the dust of Napoleon III. Loud, elaborate, concealed music was heard, but the drawing-room had apparently no connection with any phenomena external to it. It was sufficient to itself. Glimpse of a fraction of a distant stage with small, moving, singing figures.

2.

The pair strolled indifferently across the drawing-room, at the end of which a gilt and velveted parapet protected the unwary from the risk of falling into the stalls. They sat down in ornate armchairs of gold and white; in front of them, below them and around them was the auditorium, with a side view of the stage; and deep down a den of crowded musicians fiddling and blowing away for life under an excited and ardent conductor. After the spendthrift spaciousness of the approach the auditorium appeared small and inconsiderable. But it was built of solid gold, and its tiers were supported by golden Herculean naked women, carved in the fearful symmetry of Titan's daughters, with breasts that might have nonchalantly suckled monsters of insatiable voracity; scores of these ageless brazen nymphs, smiling fixedly as they had smiled for half a century and more.

And everywhere, amid the stupendous gold sculptures and ornamentations, covering the floor, crowding the tiers to the topmost, sat midgets: the audience, inelegant, shabby, sombre, assisting at the secret and esoteric ceremonial hidden within the heart of the huge encircling opera-house. And of the ceremonial the stage-spectacle was scarcely the most important part. Those of the midgets who watched it did so with indifference. Which indifference was repeated on the stage by the performers whom custom had withered and use staled. Only when some disaster threatened did one or other of them glance in momentary anxiety at the conductor for help. The affair was less an opera than part of a rite.

And by no means all the audience of midgets watched the stage-spectacle. For a time Gracie's box and its two inhabitants divided with the stage the popular interest. It was one of the two best boxes, and perhaps Gracie was the smartest woman in the theatre; but in no metropolitan theatre which had not sunk to the level of a tourist-resort would the box have been a cynosure.

"Why are we here?" thought Evelyn, fascinated by the slatternliness of the stalls, where there were men in morning dress and women in three-piece raiment.

Gracie put her head closer to his.

"This and Napoleon's tomb and the Folies-Bergêre and the Louvre are the sights of Paris," she murmured.

Evelyn smiled vaguely, thinking: "Is she a mind-reader?" He murmured in response: "That's what makes the thing interesting. But is that why you came here?"

"Don't you love being a tourist sometimes?" she said. "I get so tired of being superior I simply must have a change. Sometimes I feel like going into a shop in the rue de Rivoli and buying a Baedeker just to carry about with me. Don't you understand what I mean?"

"Certainly," said Evelyn. "But then I never do feel superior."

"No. I believe you never do," she agreed, as if suddenly impressed by a hitherto unnoticed truth.

"Except now, in this box," he added mischievously.

"You *are* in a mood to-day," she said with strange meekness.

"Isn't that one of the Cheddars down there? Fourth row? Near the middle?" Evelyn asked, having perceived a very stylish young man islanded among the slatternliness.

"Where? Oh yes. I see," she calmly answered. "Yes, it is. That's Leo. I wonder what he's doing here?"

"He's taking a rest from being superior," said Evelyn. "Look at the Baedeker on his knee."

"Not a--" Gracie checked herself. "You're teasing me!" she protested cheerfully. Then she gave attention to the stage, and Evelyn also.

He was at last beginning to surrender himself to the make-believe of the story when something happened. The curtain slowly hid the stage. The musicians ceased to play. The conductor laid down his baton. A mechanical, rhythmic, professional applause sounded from two separate parts of the auditorium, persistent and formal: an incident of the great rite. The curtain rose again. The beat of the applause was now irregular. A few persons in the stalls were clapping. The curtain fell a second time. Then a row of the principal singers appeared in front of the curtain, with the conductor, who had been magically transported from the orchestra, in the midst of them. They held hands like children, bowing, smirking, smiling, with formal, insincere gestures. The applause grew to be more general, but even now the large majority of the audience was not clapping. The artists disappeared in a seeming ecstasy of gratitude for favour received. Hundreds of lamps glowed together, changing twilight into dazzling day. Silence. The next moment the auditorium was half empty. Tedium, futility, disillusion descended in an invisible vapour upon the scene.

"Why are we here?" Evelyn demanded again, in the terrible secrecy of his heart. But, such was the ennui distilled from the vapour, he might well have propounded questions still more desolating: Why are we anywhere? Why is anything? Is there after all a key to the preposterous enigma of the universe? But Gracie was smiling happily, meditative, as if to herself, as if she possessed the key in her soul. Evelyn thought: "How robust, how coarse, is a woman's taste in pleasure!"

A tap on the door of the box, so discreet, so dubious. The door opened with caution, and the ribboned harpy was seen furtively accepting money. Leo Cheddar entered. Gracie rose and went to meet him. Evelyn stood. He picked up the programme which lay on the broad upholstered rail of the parapet. Under the programme had been hidden Gracie's book. He looked down at it curiously. It was called, "The Nature of the Physical World." He had read it in his castle at home and had found it very disturbing, awakening, exciting. If the universe held an enigma, surely she was the enigma.

"Evelyn!" She was softly calling him to the other end of the box.

He turned to join the other two, and was introduced. The tall, slim, beautifully clad, aristocratic young man overtopped Evelyn by six or seven inches. His voice was deep and agreeable, his deportment faultlessly urbane.

"We were wondering why *you* are in this galley," said Gracie, mockingly.

"But you know wherever I am I never miss a performance of the 'Rosenkavalier'if I can possibly help. I'm hearing it here for the first time."

"And what do you think of it?" Evelyn asked.

"The performance? The worst I have ever seen. Ignoble in every detail, except the oboe playing." He smiled sadly. "But the opera. The most enchanting thing since 'Figaro'."

"Enchanting," said Gracie. "That is always Leo's adjective for the 'Rosenkavalier'." Mockery again in her tone and glance.

"Give me a better one, and I'll never use 'enchanting' any more," said Cheddar evenly.

Gracie went on. "I've always told you there's a bit too much slapstick in this opera for my refined taste." She was still quizzing him.

"I prefer to call it realism," said Cheddar amiably. "One must remember the period it portrays."

"'Period'--'portrays.' What an artist in alliteration he is!" She looked at Evelyn.

"'Portrays.' Noble word."

"It's in the dictionary," said Cheddar. "I don't believe in letting noble words rust there. I take them out--"

"And give them a rub up."

"Yes," said Cheddar.

His politeness was impeccable. But Evelyn thought:

"They've got across one another...Am I the cause?" His sympathy was with the man. Why did women rejoice in setting up discomfort, men never? He said aloud, to ease the discomfort:

"I heard it at Naples last. In fact, the only time I have heard it."

"Ah!" murmured Cheddar. "The San Carlo. That must have been wormwood." He passed his hand over a pained forehead.

"Gall," said Evelyn shortly, and grinned.

"Now take what you call the 'slapstick' in the last act." Cheddar returned to the defence of himself against Gracie.

He talked earnestly and ingeniously about the last act and its 'slapstick' stuff. The reputation of the 'Rosenkavalier' was evidently to him a matter of some moment. Though he lived a life of unmitigated self-indulgence, though in every detail of material existence he demanded and accepted as of right the services of others, though he toiled not nor span, though he had never known what it was to be overdrawn at the bank, though he spent his life in savouring his own reactions to works of art, in all the arts--including.the culinary and the sartorial--he was a serious youth; and admitting that he neither wrote nor painted nor composed music, his manners at any rate were an example to the world of the perfection which sustained honest effort might reach in one of the applied arts.

Evelyn liked and admired him, and supported him against the naughty malice of Gracie, and regretted that she did not invite him to stay in the box for the remainder of the performance. When the musicians crept back with lowered heads into their cave, the two men shook hands sympathetically. Evelyn never saw Leo Cheddar again, for the serious youth did not even reappear in his stall.

3.

"Shall we sit more back for this act? In this place it's better to hear than to see," Gracie suggested when she and Evelyn were alone again. All mischief had suddenly gone out of her changing, shot-silk voice, and her face had an expression of angelic sweetness. (Not a syllable about Leo Cheddar.) Evelyn agreed. They sat down. There were chairs enough in the box to accommodate a Board of Directors. A very long time seemed to pass before the lights of the auditorium were lowered. While they were waiting Evelyn said: "I see you've got 'The Nature of the Physical World' with you."

"You've read it?"

"Oh yes."

"Don't you think it's perfectly thrilling?"

"I do," said Evelyn, with emphasis, responding to the vibrations of her tone.

"Only," she went on, "these scientists don't really understand, or they pretend not to. I wonder whether any of them have condescended to read Troward."

"Troward?"

"There you are! Of course you've never heard of him! I'm quite used to that. You ought to read his Edinburgh Lectures on Mental Science. I really mean you *ought.* They're more exciting than Eddington's book there."

"And what's Troward's line?" Evelyn asked, carefully serious to suit her new mood.

"God's his line," she answered, with a sort of fierceness. "The divine creative mind. That's his line. If the divine creative mind is infinite, we are *it.* You and me, and all those people there. And these chairs and the lights from the chandelier. Everything. No getting away from it. You know the electrons, whirling around. Of course they aren't the purest form of the divine mind, I mean the first original form. But some finer kind of electrons are--that our electrons are made of. Must be. And they're everywhere and they're all the same and all perfect and all working together, doing evolution. God isn't imperfect. If you try hard and keep on trying you realise them. I can realise them now and then for half a minute. Then I can't, and then I have to begin and try again. But that half minute!...No, it isn't as much as half a minute. Two seconds, half a second. I tell you--well, I want you to read that book of Troward's. You'll be glad afterwards. I know you will. And there's something else--"

As she turned her eager, radiant face to look into his, the chandelier extinguished itself, and her features became a vague oval to him in the obscurity of the back of the box. The orchestra sounded warm, mellow, benevolent. They listened, intent. Evelyn felt the nearness of her presence, her frock, the bodily organism within the frock--she had cast her brilliant cloak on one of the empty chairs. This was another instalment of the serial, and it was indeed sensational. She stirred, restless as usual. She rose.

"I think I must watch," she whispered, bending over him, and walked to the front of the box and sat down there. Evelyn followed her.

The music had now asserted its importance over the importance of the audience and even of the musicians. The auditorium, lit as before only by the radiating brightness of the stage, was a blur of faces less distinct than in the previous act. The music mounted swiftly to a *forte,* fervid, imposing, exciting. The music was an enveloping atmosphere, intoxicant. As it were involuntarily, Gracie's fingers for an instant touched Evelyn's knee. He could feel her hand shaking. The fine shock of momentary contact was electric.

"Perhaps *this* is why we are here," he thought, intimidated, almost fearful of mysterious forces unloosed.

Now the music sank to a *piano.* The glimpsed danger receded...Later, much later, after an unmeasured passage of time, after a period in which time was not and the senses were satisfied beyond any anticipation of the future or memory of the past, existing content and entranced in the present as the music unrolled itself bar by bar of the score--three singers conspired to sing together in concert. Gracie sat moveless, upright in her chair, gazing rightwards at the stage. Evelyn, on her left, leaned his left elbow on Gracie's book on the rail of the parapet, his left hand upholding his chin, and he too gazed, across her bosom, rightwards at the stage. With her left hand Gracie touched his shoulder warningly as if to still him into a more rapt attention to the music. Slapstick, horse-play, farce there had been in the antic movement of the comedy, but it was finished, and it had never distracted him from the music, through which exquisite fragments of Viennese waltzes had tantalisingly filtered.

Now the mood was serious, lovely, sublime. Beauty was born from beauty. Impossible that the next beauty could exceed the last; but it did. The interwoven voices of the singers wavered in patterns above the mighty changing sea of instrumental harmony ascending from the pit, flames curling and uncurling over a white glow of fire. Sound louder, sound softer, in a steady, solemn rhythm. Ravishment of the soul through the delicate receiving ear. Evelyn did not look at Gracie. The ray of his glance passed by her straight to the three figures on the stage, the conductor's tyrannic stick, the swaying mass of scraping and blowing humanity down in the pit. But he was exactly aware of the expression on her set face, and therefrom of the emotions in her heart. And he was aware also of the two thousand blurred faces of the audience, distant and nearer, high in the upper tiers, low on the floor of the stalls.

And the whole vast concourse of material flesh in infinite gradations began to melt, to refine itself, to rarefy itself, into those spiritual electrons of which Gracie had spoken, glistening, scintillating, coruscating, as they whirled, immaterial at last, on their unfathomable errands in pursuance of the divine supreme plan. Individuality ceased; he was not he, Gracie was not she; nobody in the auditorium was anybody. All were merged into a single impersonal, shining, shimmering integrity of primal mind. Evolution had reversed, and at incredible speed swung back through æons into the causal eternity before the Word moved upon the waters and before even the waters were. .

The trio ended. Time resumed. Material flesh was formed. Individualities separated themselves. Evelyn was Evelyn again, and Gracie Gracie, and the audience became tourists, bourgeois, concierges, husbands, wives, mistresses, young girls.

The story of the comic opera went on its earthly way. Evelyn and Gracie looked at each other. He saw that her beautiful face was very stern. She rose, beckoning to him. He picked up the book and her bag, both of which she was forgetting, and followed her out. She offered no explanation of the sudden departure. Neither of them spoke. In the cold street, she wrapped tight in her cloak and Evelyn in his long, thick overcoat, Gracie went unhesitating to the left and up the rue Halèvy, ignoring persistent touts. Scores of waiting cars and lounging chauffeurs. She walked straight to her own car. The chauffeur saluted.

"Could I make that young man understand the last half-hour?" Evelyn asked himself, glancing at the chauffeur. "No. Not if all our lives depended on it. But according to her that cap of his isn't a cap. It's a mass of whirling electrons."

They stepped into the car. The chauffeur, unaware of his own composition, shut the door on them. Intimacy once more in the solitude of the saloon. Gracie switched the light on.

"It was the only right moment to leave, wasn't it?" she said. "Thanks awfully for not forgetting my things. Give me my bag, will you?" She pulled a mirror from the bag and powdered her face. "I'm simply frightfully hungry. Do you know the Caligula?"

"Not at all," said Evelyn.

"I'm told it's rather good. In the rue des Trois Frères, near the Place Pigalle. Shall we go there?"

"Anywhere," said Evelyn dreamily.

The chauffeur, hired by the week with the grandiose car and all their electrons, knew the Caligula. He manœuvred the vehicle backwards and forwards out of the line of cars. And soon they were shooting up the curve of the rue Pigalle, with illuminated signs of night-cafés on either side. They crossed the blazing, multi-coloured Place, and in a dark wilderness of streets beyond they found the Caligula burning red, all alone.

Chapter 54 CALIGULA

"I've never been here before," said Gracie as they passed by a negro dwarf-commissionaire out of the dark street into the strangely-lit interior of the Caligula. "But I've heard a good deal about it from French painters and Argentines and things, and--" The first glance at the walls of the first room made her pause. "Well, yes. It's just about what I expected it to be."

She looked at Evelyn and laughed. And Evelyn laughed a little, and said:

"I suppose everything ought to be seen."

The first room of the establishment was separated from the street door by only three feet and a rattling curtain of strings of red beads. The largest of three rooms in a suite that formed a vista, it seemed rather small. It had a tiny bar with a very high counter, and next to the bar an orchestra of three instruments: a fiddle, a sort of inlaid accordion, and a kettle-drum with cymbals. The music floated discreetly faint; the drummer caressed his drum instead of hitting it, and the cymbals had a muffled sound. Round the room were ranged tiny tables. In the middle, on a space hardly bigger than the area of a dray, writhed a packed mass of animals: human beings, dancing; they were closer to one another than bees in a swarm, but they danced and appeared to delight in the jam and in their asphyxiation. True the heat of the room was tempered by an icy draught from the street at each fresh arrival of visitors. The lighting was a reddish amber, achieved by a number of pendant lamps each enclosed in a very small globe of paper; it was as discreet as the music; it disclosed, even if it did not fully reveal, the existence of the room and the revellers.

The walls were frescoed with barbaric scenes--aphrodisiac, orgiastic, murderous--from the short but merry life of the Roman emperor nicknamed Caligula, the man-god who had dared everything in licence, and whose audacity the painter had successfully emulated. The fact that in the twilight of the room the frescoes had to be scanned with care in order to be completely appreciated added much to their interest.

The second room was smaller than the first and the third smaller than the second. The third was divided at the end into three alcoves, in each a table. Evelyn demanded a table in the third room. A beautiful young man raised his arms to signify that, although no table therein was as yet occupied, all were reserved. Evelyn murmured that he was director of the Hotels de la Concorde and Montaigne. The young man bowed, appreciative.

"In that case, monsieur, one will arrange oneself at once." And he did, and personally accompanied his clients to the central alcove, on whose sides were depicted with considerable ardour the loves of Caligula and his sister Drusilla (named by name on her coiffure), with a priest-horse and a massacre in the background.

Evelyn sat alone for a few minutes while Gracie was titivating in some far retreat. Then the beautiful young manager reappeared. He had vaguely heard of the Orcham Hotel-merger, though not by name. He talked to Evelyn as to a confrère, and told him that ten of the chief night-resorts in Montmartre, including the Caligula, were under one powerful control, and that the Caligula was the fashionable baby of the bunch. With pride he indicated that the wall-paintings were the true origin of its vogue. He then departed and a head-waiter came up.

"As we are here," thought Evelyn, "we may as well *be* here." And said to the waiter:

"Champagne."

"Bien, monsieur."

He named the brand and the year.

"Bien, monsieur."

"Caviare."

"Bien, monsieur."

"With chopped onions."

"Bien, monsieur."

"Ham sandwiches."

"Bien, monsieur."

"Fresh fruit."

"Bien, monsieur."

"Pears, let us say."

"Bien, monsieur."

The waiter wrote and vanished.

When Gracie returned, Evelyn said:

"I've ordered."

She said, submissively:

"I'm so glad. I hate being asked what I want. Because I never know."

"I guessed what you would like," he said. They regarded the scene.

"It's very amusing," said Gracie.

"Very," Evelyn agreed.

"You're in one of your distant moods," said Gracie.

Smiling sympathetically, he shook his head.

"Aren't you?"

"Not in the least," said Evelyn. "But I want you to know that I don't live in a universe of superlatives."

"I like you for that," she said, looking up at him.

Never had she seemed so virginal to him, so ingenuous, so receptive, as she did then. The innocence of her air ravished him. It was indeed a heavenly phenomenon. He thought:

"She lives alone. No one to protect her with common sense. Apparently she knows all manner of strange people; some of them must have told her to come here, for instance. It's all wrong. Her father ought to look after her better."

A man and two young women, all expensively smart, and French, walked up the vista under escort of the beautiful manager, and took one of the side alcoves. The young women had the melting, bold, fatigued eyes, the glance, the swaying hips of debauchery; as shameless as monkeys, as elegant as mannequins of a first-class couturière. When they had disappeared into the alcove Gracie raised her eyebrows to Evelyn.

"Yes," he murmured. "It's a nice question whether they ought to be on the floor or on the walls."

Gracie, however, ignored the sally. Already her mind had flitted away from the two Cyprians.

"You don't know," she said gently, "what I was thinking while they were singing that trio at the Opera." Her expression was very serious, and as if imploring comprehension of what she was about to say.

"I think I do," Evelyn answered, his tone and expression suddenly responding to hers. "You were thinking that everybody and everything in the theatre was kind of dissolving into those elemental electrons of yours. I can't explain quite, but it was somehow like that."

She turned pale. Beneath her powder and rouge he could see that she had paled.

"How did you know?" she breathed, in a disconcerted whisper.

"I was feeling the same," he said.

"There you are!" breathed Gracie, solemn, deeply impressed, as if she had just found the full explanation of a whole series of mysterious phenomena and the confirmation of her secret ideas as to their origin. She showed emotion, which communicated itself to Evelyn, who felt apprehensive, even dismayed, though somehow agreeably.

But the materials of the repast arrived, and the topic was momentarily suspended. Gracie drank three-quarters of a glass of champagne. Evelyn watched new visitors, their demeanour, the service of the tables, the writhing crowded mass of dancers in the distant first room. The discreet lilt of the music and the low hum of talk mingled together in his ear. Now and then a loud laugh, a thin shriek, disturbed the general rhythm. He judged that the majority of the men were American, some of whom were with their wives, others with Frenchwomen who probably had chosen the Caligula for them. He noticed how the English visitors looked at the storied walls as if surreptitiously, as if fearful of being caught in the act of looking at them. And in a corner of his mind, meanwhile, played fragmentary thoughts about the growing prevalence of mergers and the rationalisation of dubious delights. Somewhere, in some office, to-morrow, clerks would be checking the nightly returns of the ten resorts of carousal, and adding them up, and preparing statistics for the "Orcham" of the great pleasure-merger. Two waiters buzzed like flies in front of the table, officious and fussily deferential. Evelyn guessed that they must have been apprised of his important identity by the beautiful young manager. When they had at last gone, Gracie said:

"Do you know, Evelyn--I want to tell you--I knew when I first met you that morning we were bound to have the same ideas about things. I just knew it. Did you?"

He gave the expected answer, sorry that he could not contrive to put a more joyous conviction into his tone. His regret was due to the simple, girlish earnestness of her glance and voice. He had misjudged her. She was not really spoilt by sophistication. Her sensibilities had not been dulled by experience. She had the fresh, ingenuous gusts of happy emotion proper to a maiden. And she was so wise and serious too. Her interests in life were noble.

"This is marvellous! She is marvellous!" he thought, suddenly uplifted. "We are by ourselves here. Free! What a night! I've never been through anything like it. It is marvellous!"

And he in turn had a gust of happy emotion. Was it not exquisitely strange that in the opera-house they should have had the same illusion, if illusion it could be called? Call it hallucination if you chose--no matter! And was it not strange that, guessing half-playfully at first, he should have divined that what had happened to him had happened to her also? Of course the book had been the cause of it all, but the result was none the less impressive. Easy to laugh--especially for an Englishman! Nevertheless--

"And there's something else I want to tell you," Gracie went on, earnestly, confidingly, after a mouthful of caviare: "I was frightfully rude to you when you wouldn't come to my party that night at the Palace. I simply couldn't bear you not coming. But all the same I liked you for not coming. Yes, I did. I should have been disappointed if you had come. And I didn't fly off the next morning because I was in a temper with you--you thought that was the reason, didn't you?"

"I'm not so conceited," Evelyn smiled.

"Do let's be frank," she appealed. "I feel so near to you. You're always drawing away from me. Remember our dance? Now honestly, didn't you think I'd left the Palace because I was vexed?"

"Yes," said Evelyn bravely, and felt as though he had snapped a chain which was holding him.

"Well, that wasn't the reason. I went off because I was afraid of you...I know it sounds very odd, but truly that was the reason." Gracie continued without a pause: "I told you a lie the other day. I didn't come to London on account of my book. I could have fixed that by post. I came because I'd been thinking about you for weeks and weeks. I felt I was missing you, and it was silly of me to go on missing you. I'm saying all this because it's easier for a girl to talk than a man. People think it isn't, but that's nonsense. I know how men feel--how you feel, I mean. And I went away again because I was afraid of you again. It comes over me. But to-night I'm not afraid of you. I'm very close to you. And I need to be close to someone. I'm a beast. Yes. I am. You can guess lots of things, but you'll never guess why I was so keen on going with you to that Shaftesbury Express Counter of Mr. Jebson's. It was because I wanted to see if I could make you jealous."

"Me! Jealous!"

"Oh! I know I didn't make you jealous, darling, though I said all men were. I knew you weren't, without being told. But wasn't that walk to the hotel in the rain heavenly? I got specially frightened of you on that walk. I felt like nobody when I saw your lighted tower from the Duke of York's Steps. You're so wonderful with your hotels. Father's said so again and again. You know, daddy and I don't see much of each other, but we're great friends, really. He always says you're wonderful. I don't know *how* you're so wonderful, but I can feel it. You make me feel it. And I was walking with you in the rain, all wet, and I was nothing. I knew I was nothing. If I hadn't known I was nothing I might have stayed on at the Palace for a bit. So I just faded out. I know you think I'm brilliant, and so I am in a way. But right down in me I'm nothing. Why should I want to feel near you when I'm nothing?...Now don't speak. Don't answer. I'm only telling you all this because I should hate to deceive you any more. I'm not going to make any excuses for myself...'Girls don't talk as I'm talking.' And all that. To hell with girls! I'm not girls. I'm me. That's all. Pour me out some more champagne, will you? A girl likes to be looked after. I suppose I *am* girls. But I'm me too. Wasn't that trio too lovely to bear?"

Evelyn said:

"You told me not to speak. But I shall speak if I like." He smiled. "And I shall say what I like. You're miraculous. I say no more."

Instinct warned him to say no more. His eyes were speaking for him, telling her his admiration, telling her that he was 'near' to her, and that when he said 'miraculous' he meant it. He was convinced, then, that there had never been a girl like this girl. She was wise in her ingenuousness, in her direct simplicity. She understood. She had said, "It's easier for a girl to talk than a man." And she was so honest: and so humble: telling him with such sincerity that she was "nothing." She thought that she really was nothing. He was more than touched; he was shaken by the force of his own wondering admiration of her courage. Of course he thought: "Is she in love with me?" He would not answer the tremendous question. He would only say to himself that she was pathetically lonely in the world, and that she comprehended him and trusted him. It was the need to confess this fact that in her opinion had made a meeting between them urgent for this very night. The meeting had happened, and she had confessed. He desired, he yearned, to protect her, to assuage her loneliness. Her eyes met his, and he saw happiness in hers as the result of what she had seen in his. And in her happiness he was happier than he had ever been. Happiness surged through him. Life itself, the essence of life, throbbed serenely in his veins. There was no sensual image in his mind, and no wish for anything but her happiness. He was content. Hotels, a victorious career, autocracy had no significance for him. The poor little lamp was extinguished in a general blaze of glory.

She said:

"I think I ought to go home."

"Now?"

Her trusting eyes implored him.

"Very well," he said.

The sandwiches had been served. He picked up the plate.

"Just one."

"Well, one," she acquiesced with the sweetest submission.

2.

Evelyn discharged a bill which, even after a deduction of twenty per cent. voluntarily conceded to him as a member of the great catering profession, demonstrated that the pleasure-merger was meant to yield large dividends. The pair rose and passed down the rooms, wafted along by deferential bows and smirks; Evelyn went so far as to shake hands with the beautiful manager. He was wondering why, for so short a stay, Gracie had put herself and him to the trouble of visiting the Caligula, when she suddenly stopped.

"Shall we have just one drink before we go?" she suggested, with bright persuasiveness.

Since she was irresistible, he yielded. But he thought:

"What next? And what an anti-climax! When we've had the drink we shall have to begin the departure business all over afresh. Nuisance!"

The man who was holding Evelyn's hat and overcoat moved away with an unconvincing smile. They climbed on to the very high chairs at the bar.

"And the drink?" Evelyn questioned, disappointed in his miraculous girl.

"Oh! Your favourite," said Gracie.

"What's that?"

"Orange juice." She laughed quizzically. How did she know that he affected orange juice? Still, he was relieved. The choice at any rate showed that the miraculous girl had some sense. She went up again in his esteem.

"Deux jus d'orange nature," she gave the order herself.

The barman disguised his stupefaction.

Gracie turned round to gaze at the dense mass of dancers contorted, gyrating, swaying, perspiring within six feet of the high chairs. What a crew (thought Evelyn)! Foolish faces, lascivious, abandoned, inane. How grotesquely indecent the faces of the old men in the sweltering crowd! How hard, insincere, grasping, or sentimental and sensually loving, the faces of the girls! All pretending joy, in the hope of satisfactions to come! All utterly despicable! He was ashamed to be there, ashamed to have Gracie by his side, ashamed that she was not ashamed. Only the orchestral trio were worthy of a mild respect. They were earning a living, making money--not squandering it. Calmly, efficiently, indefatigably doing their job, they plodded on from measure to measure, hundreds of measures, thousands of measures, ruling the fatuous dancers; and they would conscientiously plod on and on until five o'clock, when the Caligula closed. The entire spectacle was incomprehensible, frightening. And was the spectacle of the dance-floor at the Imperial Palace less incomprehensible? Evelyn's mind ran back to Volivia, now dancing at the Casino de Paris.

Two glasses clinked on the counter. Gracie twisted her body, picked them up both at once, and handed one to Evelyn. He said, after a sip:

"You might tell me just why you've come to an affair like this. Is it amusing, or is it silly?"

"It's both," she answered. "And didn't you say yourself that everything ought to be seen? I love it because it shows what people really are. I'm always wanting to know that. I've enjoyed it. And so have you--so you needn't say you haven't."

"Then I won't," he said grimly.

"But it is interesting, isn't it?" she cajoled, ignoring his grimness.

"Oh! It's *interesting,"* he agreed, rather condescendingly.

"It teaches you, doesn't it?" She was still cajoling.

"Teaches you what?"

"About--well, human nature."

"Some sorts of human nature."

"Aren't we all God's creatures?" she said gravely.

He gave in with a sympathetic smiling nod. He was beaten. Gracie's eyes ranged round the exciting walls; but while she gazed she seemed to be absorbed in reflection.

Then two girls extricated themselves from the thronged floor and approached the bar. One was tall and slim, in a closefitting, high-necked gown which rendered the wearer conspicuous by its long trailing skirts. The other was short and plump in the scantiest possible flimsy frock. The demeanour of the tall girl was protective. They settled themselves at the bar, next to Evelyn and Gracie. The tall girl furtively, delicately, fondled her friend, with whom she had been dancing.

"Shall we go?" said Gracie, very abruptly. And in the doorway, as Evelyn held aside the bead-curtain for her, she murmured harshly: "I can't stand that kind."

"Why not?" Evelyn demanded. "Aren't we all God's creatures?" After being defeated, he had won.

In the chill, dank winter night of the street, Gracie's car was waiting with other cars, and her chauffeur with other chauffeurs, nonchalantly patient. How these chauffeurs ate, drank, kept warm, passed the interminable time, was their affair. Gracie's chauffeur saluted very amiably; he might have had to wait till 5 a.m.

"I'll drop you," said Gracie.

"Oh no! It's out of your way. I'll get a taxi."

"It isn't out of my way." A pause. "And I don't care if it is. I'll drop you. 1 can be home in twenty minutes at the most."

"Thank you."

The chauffeur whisked them away. In the darkness of the saloon they did not speak. When the car swerved swiftly round a corner and Gracie was thrown against Evelyn, she did not immediately straighten herself. They were entering the Champs Elysées before she said:

"You're quite right."

He knew that she was referring to her attitude towards the two girls at the bar.

"Well, well! Who knows?" said he quietly. He was asking himself when they were to meet again. He wanted to suggest a rendezvous, but his unconquerable reserve prevented him from doing so. "It's my place to do it," he thought, impartially. Yet he could not do it. The car drew up at the Montaigne. He looked at her. She looked at him. Something expectant in her dimly seen eyes. He kissed her. The kiss fraternal, friendly, companionable. Naught in such a kiss! Such a kiss was a duty. They had been very 'near' to one another. The kiss gave him pleasure, too. And as for her, it seemed to comfort her.

The chauffeur had hardly descended from the wheel.

"I say," she said, as Evelyn stepped down on to the kerb. "Where shall you be to-morrow, about lunch-time?"

"Concorde," he replied.

"I'll telephone you," she said, and yawned.

"That's fine," he said. *"Au revoir."*

He thought:

"I was a perfect boor not to make the first move. However, it's all right..."

The car was gone, and she in it. He stood on the pavement for a few seconds, recalling the taste and touch of her soft girlish lips. "I am an idiot," he murmured. A functionary emerged from the hotel to welcome him.

Chapter 55 ON THE BOULEVARD

The next morning (a Saturday), after a very short and very restless night, Evelyn was again working with M. Laugier in the latter's room in the Concorde. But, at work, he had the appearance rather than the reality of earnest application. And, when the Louis Philippe clock struck noon, he began to grow anxious lest Gracie should telephone to him once more while he was with M. Laugier, because M. Laugier would certainly himself answer the ring, and he had no desire to see a quizzical look on the southerner's face. Noon was the customary lunch-hour for M. Laugier, and Evelyn made a polite remark to this effect. M. Laugier replied that the clock was ten minutes fast. It was. They laboured until the clock struck the half-hour. There had been no ring. Evelyn was not surprised. He said to himself grimly that with Gracie lunch-time meant any time between noon and three o'clock, or even four. They went down into a little basement room, where M. Laugier entertained his dear director to an admirable, plenteous meal.

Evelyn was now more at ease. When Gracie summoned him he would be told merely that he was wanted on the telephone, and thus he could talk comfortably to the girl from a telephone-cabin, with nobody to listen. Of course she was a wonderful girl, but this admitted fact did not prevent him from manfully and superiorly cursing her. She was really too much of a mixture to appeal to a serious man. Her earnest moods frightened him, and her moods of levity pained him. Yes, she had nobility, impressive nobility. She had given him to think. Nevertheless with a girl like that you never knew where you were. The disorderliness of her mind was fantastic. She had no daily common sense and no sense of danger. To be connected with her was to be a kettle tied to the tail of a magnificent mad thoroughbred dog. Was she in love with him? Who could say? Probably even she herself could not say. She was a girl who might ruin the careers of twenty men out of sheer impulse and caprice, and then be startled twenty times to learn what she had done. He had best bring the affair, courteously, to an abrupt conclusion. He would have no tampering with his career, which had now reached a new and more splendid period. He hoped that she would not ring him up. He would have finished with Laugier by five o'clock, and if he did not hear from her, damned if he would not depart for London on Sunday morning! He would have a sound excuse for doing so, as she had omitted to give him her address at St. Cloud. She could communicate with him, but he could not communicate with her.

Well, she did not ring him up. The lunch was eaten without hurry, and the after-lunch cigars were smoked as cigars ought to be smoked. At a quarter to three the mutually dear directors returned to the study of statistics and other documents. And now she would assuredly ring up. Women were always confoundedly inconvenient. She would ring up, and he would be compelled to go through again his tight-rope telephone performance of the previous day. But there was no call. Once the telephone-bell did tinkle, exciting alarm--also a not unpleasant expectancy--but the call was for M. Laugier. Four o'clock. Dusk. Lights. Five o'clock. Endless afternoon. She had not rung. Good. Excellent. Hang it all! He was twice her age, and had an objection to rendering himself ridiculous in the sight of men. The task of the dear directors was finished, and satisfactorily. The Englishman, having congratulated the Frenchman on the final result of the exhaustive inquisition, announced that he should leave for London on the morrow. The Frenchman, charmed by the congratulations, invited the Englishman to yet another meal--dinner. Evelyn said regretfully that he had an engagement. "Ah!" twinkled M. Laugier. They parted in the grand manner, providing a spectacle to inspirit circumambient functionaries in the hall.

Evelyn came back a minute later, and said to the concierge:

"I suppose there's been no telephone message for me?" There had not. He walked to the Hotel Montaigne, and to the concierge of the Montaigne he said:

"Any telephone message for me?"

None. He was on the point of asking for a corner seat to be reserved on the "Golden Arrow"; but he did not ask. Better wait a while. She might yet ring. He must give her every chance. At seven o'clock the frightful, desolating vista of an empty evening stretched out before him. The director of the Montaigne was out, and not expected home till midnight. He had an impulse to ring up Laugier and say that, through a misunderstanding, he was free after all; but he checked it. Too proud! Instead, he got London, twice: first for the Palace and then for the Wey, and at both hotels kept important members of the staffs engaged too long in quite unimportant conversations. To Cousin at the Palace he said everything except that he should return the next day. Besides, Oldham would be still with his wife in the country. Not that Oldham was indispensable. He could manage, was managing, very well without Oldham. Still--He dined alone, reading French newspapers. Then he strolled about the hotel, chatting beautifully with the flattered staff. Then he walked to the Etoile--a constitutional. Then it rained, and he returned in a taxi. Then he went to bed. Only five minutes past ten. Clocks and watches would not move. He stared at them for hours, and the hands budged not. Yet they had not stopped, for he could hear his watch ticking plainly enough.

The moment he was in bed and the light out, his thoughts began to whirl round and round, and round and round. Why the hell had he not taken her address? She might be ill. Or the Tessa girl might be ill. Gracie would be extremely conscientious where Tessa was concerned. By the calendar he was indubitably twice her age. But not by any other measurement. While he was with her he had absolutely no feeling of seniority. They were equals. He realised more and more in the darkness how wonderful she was. He saw her image in the darkness. He had kissed her. Damn it! She had invited his kiss, or at least she had warmly accepted it. Was this an adventure to be clicked off as by hanging up a telephone-receiver? She was miraculous--he had told her so--and because she was miraculous the adventure was miraculous. Paris! The freedom of Paris! Marriage. Had she been thinking of marriage? No. Anyhow, he would never marry. And never would he allow his career to be fooled about with. But she was miraculous. She said astounding things. She had a unique intelligence. Why had he not taken her address? He was miserable, he the eponymous hero of the greatest hotel-merger in all the annals of luxury. He knew he would have no sleep that night...He awoke. Four o'clock. He had slept four hours. At the Palace he could have telephoned for some tea; but the Montaigne was not the Palace--though it would be. He dozed at intervals. Six o'clock. Seven o'clock. The electric timepiece on the wall made a disturbing little noise every minute, as its finger was pushed on. Exasperating. He had heard it ten million times. But the Montaigne was not the Palace...A faint, pale discoloration on the blind. Dawn. Eight o'clock. He would ring for tea, and also he would give orders for a seat in the train. What an inferno of a night! He felt like a towel flung into a corner of a bathroom.

2.

Just as he was about to ring, he heard the telephone-bell delicately murmuring on the floor, and he grasped the instrument. It could not be she. But it was, and this was the most incredible, solacing thing that ever befell any Englishman in Paris.

"Is that you, Evelyn?" Her rich voice, changing at nearly every word, again like the sheen of shifting shot-silk.

"Speaking. Can't you tell my voice? I can tell yours." When he had spoken he thought: "This won't do. I mustn't use that excited tone." Then he waited. She did not continue immediately. It was a delightful experience to be on his back in the wide bed and in the ease of pyjamas, holding the mouthpiece to his lips and the receiver to his ear, and wait for her next exciting sentence. All fatigue had gone from him. He understood, afresh, that fatigue was a nervous sensation, an illusion which another nervous sensation could obliterate as a sponge wipes pencil-marks from a slate.

"I hope I haven't disturbed you too early." Her voice was now tense with that terrible earnestness which on the previous evening had affrighted him. He recalled her manner of saying in the Caligula, "I need to be close to someone," and her manner of confessing that she had missed him and that she had tried to make him jealous. A man would naturally, inevitably, think that a girl who talked in that style was in love with him, or fancied she was. But Evelyn could not honestly believe it. In the first place, he could not see in himself anything for her to fall in love with. And in the second place, it appeared to him that her accents were too grave for mere love.

"Are you there? Can you hear? I said I hope I haven't disturbed you too early."

His mind had been wandering--as hers too often would wander.

"I beg pardon. No, you certainly haven't disturbed me too early. In fact, you're about twenty hours late in disturbing me. Didn't you say you'd ring me up yesterday at lunch-time, or was I dreaming?" He meant to put some affectionate banter into his tone, but the attempt was somehow not very convincing.

"Yes. I know," she said. "But I couldn't."

"Why not?"

"Well. I couldn't. And I've rung you so early this morning because I knew when I awoke I never *should* ring you if I didn't do it instantly--instantly. So I did."

"And you've just caught me in time. I'm leaving by the 'Golden Arrow,'and I have to pack and do all sorts of things. And I'm not up yet." Still the same unsuccessful effort towards cheerful banter.

"Evelyn, you aren't! You can't go to-day!" she protested solemnly.

"Why not?"

"I must see you."

It appeared to him that she was repeating the telephone conversation in Laugier's office.

"Anything wrong?" he questioned, dropping the banter.

"I--I don't know." A hint of desperation in her voice. "We must have lunch together. If you *must* go back home to-night you can take the four o'clock. Surely you can do that for me, Evelyn." She was pleading, irresistibly.

"All right, my dear," he soothed her.

"Listen!" she went on, more vivaciously. "You can pack up your things and bring them along with you, and then you can stay with me till it's time for you to go to the station. You can have my car. Listen! I'll come with you to the Gare du Nord and see you off."

"It's ideal," he answered. "But I wouldn't agree to being seen off by anybody else." (Why had he gone out of his way to say a thing like that?)

"You're teasing me," she said, as it were plaintively.

"I'm not! Now what time lunch?"

"I'll expect you at twelve o'clock. Noon. Listen. I'll send the car for you to the Montaigne. Five to twelve. I know I shan't be fit to be seen till twelve."

"But I can't get to St. Cloud in five minutes, can I?"

"Oh! I'm not at St. Cloud. I'm in the Boulevard des Italiens." She gave a number.

"You must have got up frightfully early."

"No. I came here yesterday."

"Is it a hotel?"

"No."

"You're with friends, eh?"

"N-no. It's rooms. I had to be in Paris."

Evelyn was considerably startled, as much by her tone as by the news; but he made no comment.

"I'll count on you then," she said.

"You may, my dear."

The talk ended there. Evelyn felt bewildered, perturbed; yet happy--and excited enough in his expectancy. He rang for tea, and he rang for the valet.

Gracie's car arrived at the hotel ten minutes before time, and Evelyn's suit-cases were downstairs ten minutes before the hour. Therefore he had to wait, chatting with the concierge. Ridden by his mania for punctuality, he objected as much to being one minute early as to being one minute late. Yet he was quite hungrily anxious to set eyes on Gracie again. He could not recall every detail of her features and bearing, and he was impatient to refresh his memory. Also he was impatient to know the reason of her formidable earnestness on the telephone; though he kept saying to himself: "It's nothing. It's nothing. She's a child, after all."

Rain began to fall, not unexpectedly. The boulevard had the desolating aspect proper to a wet Parisian Sunday. Little traffic. Few wayfarers. Imperfect umbrellas sailing horizontally along over glistening dirty pavements, each umbrella the canopy of a mysterious, undecipherable soul. All the shops shuttered in grey steel, except the tobacco-bureaux, which were open. The kiosks, which offered for sale every newspaper and periodical decent and indecent in Europe, had no customers.

The Morris Columns, with their advertisements of the stages of Paris, shone somehow morbidly in the rain. The cafés did no business to speak of. All was depressing, but not for Evelyn, whose age had gradually diminished to twenty-five.

The car halted opposite a large but inconspicuous portico between two big shuttered shops. Evelyn jumped out. His heart was perceptibly beating. He was now only twenty-two. On one side of the portico was a small, discreet brass-plate: *"Appartements meublés."* The entrance seemed very dubious indeed. But within the entrance, against a pair of glazed doors, stood Gracie, waiting for him, a figure of perfect, serious respectability. She wore a mackintosh and carried a red Baedeker in addition to her handbag. Close by her stood a sad, pale houseman, in slippers, striped sleeves, and a long white apron.

"Well?" said Gracie, and shook hands.

The houseman silently went to the car, seized the suit-cases and disappeared with them into the building.

3.

"C'est ça," said Gracie to the chauffeur, who touched his cap and drove away.

"Now we're here!" she said to Evelyn, and at last smiled.

"What's the object of that Baedeker?" he enquired, with a quasi-sardonic blandness.

She replied: "I went out specially to buy it yesterday, and I shall carry it with me everywhere. Just for a sign to myself that I've climbed out of the rut of being always so correct and rich and knowing the best places, and being superior to common people. That's why I bought the mackintosh too. I want to be common. I'm sick of being in the swim--in everything. It's come over me. I simply had to have a change. If I hadn't I do believe I should have--well, I don't know what! I think it's rather romantic to carry a mackintosh and a Baedeker and walk in the rain. Don't you?"

"I see what you mean," Evelyn said negligently. "You aren't feeling unwell, are you?"

"No. A bit tired, that's all. Why?"

"Oh, nothing. I had an idea you looked pale...Well, what's the next move?"

"The next move is lunch. We must have it early."

"Where?"

"Anywhere. The first rotten little place we see. There's lots of 'em about. Places you and I have never heard of. I'm sure they're great fun. Come along. Quick! Quick!"

She crossed the boulevard in front of him, and they turned westwards towards the Madeleine; then into the rue Tronchet; half-way up the rue Tronchet she took a side-street to the right. They did not speak.

"Now here's one, for instance," she said, pleased, stopping suddenly at the first corner in the side-street. Yes, lo! A little restaurant and wineshop, situated like a minor public-house in London. An untidy zinc bar on the ground-floor, not as yet very busy. A narrow staircase hardly visible in a corner.

"It must be up here," she murmured, and up she went, Evelyn following.

The dirty bare staircase, which in its middle part was dangerously dark, ended in a restaurant of the same dimensions as the bar-room. A buffet. A number of extremely small tables, covered with coarse grey-white linen. Clumsy black-handled knives and black-handled three-pronged forks. Salt in lumps. Bread in yards. Glass cruets, twin receptacles containing vinegar and oil. Odours. Warmth. No air.

A plump, pleasant young woman in soiled blue dress and still more soiled white apron was serving some dozen Sundayed customers of the small bourgeois class. They were all absorbed in eating, and they were nearly all talking; and while they masticated and talked they ledged the extremities of their tools on either side of their plates. The napkins, which a few men wore as bibs, were of the same material as the table-cloths, but apparently larger. The scene was squalid enough, until you regarded it as romantic, when it ceased to be anything else but romantic.

The plump woman, lively without haste or flurry, pointed to an empty table, with a friendly yet commanding gesture which said:

"You aren't absolutely compelled to take that table, but on the whole you will be well advised to take it."

They took it. The waitress then ignored them; she attended to customers in what she deemed to be the right order of precedence.

Evelyn removed his big overcoat, which was damp. Gracie loosed her new mackintosh and disposed her bag and the Baedeker on a corner of the table. They settled themselves on insecure cane-bottomed chairs. Nothing more to do till the waitress should occupy herself with them.

Constraint and self-consciousness separated them. And they were marked customers. Everybody in the room knew, and showed by curious glances that they were different from the ordinary clientèle. Evelyn felt incapable of making conversation. Gracie appeared not to care whether they conversed or were silent. The waitress at last arrived at their table, and at once displayed an amiable and genuine interest in their individual desires. Gracie altered her mind twice about dishes, but the waitress was not to be ruffled by indecision.

"And to drink?" said she, when the menu was definitely fixed.

"Beer," said Gracie suddenly, not consulting Evelyn.

Then they had to be idle until the first dish and hot plates were planted before them. Eating for a time obviated the social necessity for talk.

The waitress popped her tousled head between them and asked:

"That pleases you?"

"Much," said Gracie.

"So much the better," said the waitress, and left them. They were still separated by a constraint which, instead of diminishing, grew in intensity. As for Evelyn, he feared to meet Gracie's eyes. Why? He did not know. Honestly, he could not imagine why. All he knew was that he felt ridiculously self-conscious, and that she too was self-conscious. He could not even think consecutively. He did not try to understand Gracie's motive in this extraordinary caprice. He tried neither to examine the immediate past nor to foresee the immediate future. He had to be content with mere existence in an uncomfortable and interminable present.

"You've never been in a place like this before?" said Gracie.

"Oh! Haven't I!" said Evelyn, who was reminded of his first frugal visit to Paris a quarter of a century earlier.

Islet of talk in a vast heaving ocean of taciturnity!

The meal did come to an end. Coffee was drunk, thick, out of thick overflowing cups. Evelyn paid the bill, whose total was the equivalent of five-and-sixpence. All the tables were filled. Two more customers rose into the room from the stairway.

"We're interfering with business," said Evelyn, getting up. The waitress warned Gracie of the peril of the dark stairs. They reached the street, and took deep breaths.

"I loved it!" Gracie said with emphasis.

"Yes," Evelyn reluctantly agreed. "And now what next?" Gracie glanced at him, half tenderly, half slyly.

"I'm still tired," she said. "I expect I've eaten too much. I did love it. Suppose we go back to my rooms? It isn't raining."

Chapter 56 DECLARATION

"Isn't it all lovely and vulgar?" Gracie exclaimed, looking at Evelyn for some expression of morbid delight to match her own.

"No exaggeration to call it vulgar," said Evelyn with a humouring smile.

They had climbed some fusty, dusty, ill-carpeted stairs to what was marked as the first floor, though it was really the second, the first being a mezzanine. Gracie had produced a latch-key to open the double-doors leading into her rented flat; they had gone through a small ante-chamber or hall, and were now at the open double-doors leading therefrom into the drawing-room.

A large and lofty apartment: carved and partly gilded cornice, discoloured ceiling, heavily patterned wall-paper torn in one or two places, heavily framed oil-paintings of landscapes and of richly breasted girls whose flimsy draperies were on the very point of slipping off to disclose the root of all evil, a life-sized white statue of a woman whose modesty was similarly imperilled, a stuffed black bear close by it, heavy and cumbrous imitation Louis Quatorze furniture, all shabby gilt, on the mantelpiece a vast ormolu and gilt clock (not going) with vast candelabra to correspond, and a stained crimson carpet which covered the entire floor. Seen on a stage from the pit such an interior might have passed for luxury. Seen from within itself it was as hatefully spurious as a false coin. It shocked Evelyn.

"I adore it because it *is* so awful," said Gracie, as they gazed around.

"Why?"

"Well, I don't know. I told you I wanted a change from all that expensive respectability that I've been imprisoned in all my life. I like to be vulgar and low sometimes. That's me, you know, and we may as well be honest about it."

"Expensive!" said Evelyn. "You aren't getting this show for two francs a night, I'm sure."

"No, it isn't cheap," she changed her ground. "But I don't mind that. It's what I wanted. And I found it all by myself. Come and see my bedroom."

She led him through a masked door in a corner of the drawing-room along a short passage, and so into a bedroom of the same dimensions and in the same style as the drawing-room: enormous bed, two night-tables, enormous cheval-glass, enormous sofa, enormous dressing-table, and enormous wardrobe. The room was in a state of extreme disorder: open trunk, open toilet-case, open door of the wardrobe, white fabric protruding from a shut drawer in the wardrobe, garments thrown on several chairs and on the floor. The garments, however, tended to civilise the room. Evelyn noted the costly splendour of Gracie's brushes and other toilet utensils spread higgledypiggledy over the dusty glassy surface of the dressing-table.

"The bed's very comfortable," Gracie remarked, apologetic despite herself.

"Well, that's a good mark, anyway," said Evelyn. "Then you stayed here last night, I see."

"Considering I rang you from here at eight o'clock this morning, you might have guessed I hadn't just got here. Besides, didn't I tell you I'd only that moment wakened up?"

"Of course you did," he agreed. "But I thought you said Tessa couldn't be left."

"Oh! Tessa!" she answered lightly. "Tessa must stick it for a day or two, like other people...And you haven't even shaken hands with me yet," she finished, as if adding one final item to a series of grievances.

They were standing side by side. Gracie had pitched her hat and her handbag and the Baedeker on to the bed, and she was taking off her mackintosh. She stopped and looked sternly at him, one arm out of and the other in the mackintosh. But though her glance was stern, the forward, upward poise of the head and a tremor of the vermilion lips seemed to draw him to her. He kissed her. A formal kiss, a kiss of ceremony. Little more than a peck. No significance in it, even less significance than there had been in the kiss of the previous night in the car. He knew that between many men and women kissing was a habit, like handshaking. And what could a kiss mean when the kisser was wearing a big overcoat and the kissed entangled in a mackintosh? And they were separated now, if not by constraint, by an obscure hostility.

Gracie, having got rid of the mackintosh, turned back towards the passage. In the passage was a door.

"That's the bathroom and so on," she said. "You can hang your overcoat in there--and powder your nose."

When he re-entered the drawing-room she was reclining with her feet tucked under her on an easy-chair. Her eyes were closed.

"Sit down," she said weakly, not opening her eyes.

As he came in Evelyn touched a large gilded radiator; it was very hot.

"Oh, dear!" she said. "I do feel so tired."

"I thought you were never tired," he responded, with surprise, but sympathetically.

"Well," she said, glancing at him covertly, "I do get tired sometimes in the afternoon, and then I rest a bit, and then I'm perfectly all right again. We're all ups and downs. Women, I mean. I say, would you mind if I went and lay on the bed for a tiny weeny minute?"

"Do," said he.

"I think I will." She rose from the horrible easy-chair "Here! You can read this." She handed him "The Nature of the Physical World," which had been insecurely perched on a console.

He accepted it in silence. She left the room, turning her head at the door to give him a doleful smile. She forgot to shut the door, as she forgot to shut all doors.

Evelyn, dropping the book, thought:

"This is rotten."

He felt exceedingly gloomy. Still, some intimacy had been reached. She was treating him as an intimate. And he was less ill at ease. There was something rather piquant, interesting, provocative, in the situation, and in her strange demeanour. And at worst they could not be interrupted. They had themselves to themselves.

He strolled to one of the big windows and looked forth at the boulevard. Rain, persistent and ruthless. The road and the pavements were mirrors reflecting the melancholy of the universe. He thought he heard a voice, distant, thin, shrill, lacking its customary richness.

"Evelyn! Evelyn! Evelyn!"

"Coming."

He went to the bedroom, of which the door was wide open. He halted at the door.

"Yes?"

She was not on the bed; she was in the bed. Under her head was her own pillow. He saw her frock on a chair. Other garments, which had previously disfigured and civilised the room, were now hidden somewhere, and the baggage was stacked in a corner.

"I think I must have some tea," she murmured, eyes directed towards the ceiling.

"Well, there's some attendance here, I suppose. I'll ring, shall I?"

"Oh yes, there's attendance of a sort," she answered, shifting her head to look at him. "Come in. Come in. I shan't explode." She was fretful. He advanced into the room. "But they'll never be able to make my kind of tea. I'm going to get up and make it myself. The things are in the bathroom. I never travel without my tea-gadgets. Will you have some too?"

"You stay where you are," he said firmly, feeling sorry for her. "I'll make the tea."

"But you can't make tea."

"Can't I? You'll see in a minute. I've shown more than one person at the Palace exactly how tea ought to be made."

"No. I can't have you making tea for me. It's not decent."

"Please do as I tell you," he said sharply.

She yielded with meekness.

"You are a darling."

2.

In the bathroom he discovered the tea-gadgets complete on a tray on the floor, concealed beyond the end of the bath. Everything was there: saucepan, teapot, hot-water jug, cups and saucers (two), spoons, sugar, white dry "metra" fuel, a lemon, a monogrammed fruit knife, a box of matches, and a small canister of tea. It was true that he could make tea. And indeed one of his theories, perhaps sex-biased, was that men could make tea better than women. While the water was boiling he sliced the lemon, warmed the pot, and dropped four spoonfuls of tea into it. No hitch. No slip. Perfection. The watched saucepan did boil, with startling alacrity. As he carefully carried the loaded tray into the bedroom, he was aware of an even higher degree of intimacy. Strange vocation for him, being a chambermaid! But he enjoyed it, and was proud. Gracie smiled at him celestial thanks.

"You might stick it down here on the bed. There's plenty of room. And will you mind shutting the door?"

"Lady," said he, depositing the tray on the soiled crimson satin eiderdown, which must have had vast and varied experience in keeping human bodies warm, "I was about to do so. But having both hands full of tray--the rest is silence." He thought, carefully shutting the door, that a request to shut doors came in from the greatest leaver-open of doors that ever lived.

"I like you when you're sprightly," she said. "And I like your new suit."

"It's an old suit," he corrected her.

"Yes, of course. That's what father always says."

"And while I'm about it," he said, "I'll shut a few more doors."

And having shut the door of the room he shut the doors of the wardrobe, opened a drawer, straightened some linen that had been sticking out of it, and pushed it to again. Gracie smiled at the operation, lowering her eyelids.

"Will you pour?" she asked.

"I shall pour," he answered, drawing a heavy gilt chair up to the bedside.

"I'm so grateful," said she, relapsing into fatigue after her few sentences of liveliness.

He poured out the tea. She turned and lay on her side, facing him, and, her head propped on her right hand, took the cup without the saucer in her left hand and sipped.

"You were quite right, darling," she said. "You can make tea. It's a gift."

They each drank two cups.

"Another."

"No, thanks," she said. "You might put the tray on the floor. It's only in the way."

"On the table will be better," he said, and moved the tray.

"Won't you sit on the bed?" she suggested.

He sat on the bed.

"Now do you feel better?"

"I just want you to listen," she said, ignoring his question. "I've got to tell you something, and I swore to myself I'd tell you instantly we'd had tea. All day yesterday I was dying to tell you, but I couldn't make up my mind to it. I kept putting it off and putting it off. That's why I didn't telephone you. And it's why I was so stiff and awkward with you at lunch.

Nervousness. You know--it stops you from being natural. You can't be natural and easy when you know you have something awful to do and can't bring yourself up to the scratch. It sort of weighs you down. And I'm so tired. I couldn't sleep last night."

"Nor could I," said Evelyn.

She glanced at him sharply.

"Oh, couldn't you sleep either?" She seemed pleased. "I'm in a most terrible mess. Terrible. I don't expect you can help me. But if you can't no one else can. I know I oughtn't to worry you. Still, when one's desperate"--she paused--"as I am. Evelyn, my dear--" She was silent.

He thought, anxious:

"What now? What's the scrape she's in? It's an infernal shame the way her father leaves her to take care of herself. She's incapable of taking care of herself. Look at her now in this place, and me sitting on her bed, and her father not giving a damn where she is!"

Her face was pathetic to him. The sight of it roused his protective instinct, his instinct for solving problems and for setting people in the right path and seeing that they kept to it. Whatever foolishness she had committed, his wisdom must save her somehow from the consequences of it. And he was convinced in his pride that there was no difficulty that he could not vanquish, no trouble that he could not conjure away. A nuisance, of course; but nuisances had to be squarely confronted. The image of the four o'clock train shot surprisingly through his brain. He had forgotten it.

"Well?" he encouraged her.

"I'm too fond of you, my dear."

As the full significance of those first five words penetrated into his mind--a matter not instantaneous but occupying a few seconds--his first reflection was: "This is what comes of having anything to do with a hotel-merger!" And his second: "But what *is* there in me to attract her?" He had had this thought before, but not so puzzlingly. He opened his lips to speak, though he did not know what he would say. She raised her arm for silence, gazing at him with a long, woebegone, martyrised, mercy-imploring look. He was not genuinely startled by her confession. He had only been misled for a moment by the phrase, 'most terrible mess,' and the word 'desperate': which had appeared to him to indicate a calamity more material than unrequited passion. Now her soul was newly lit for him, and he began to discern a little more plainly the deeps of her character. He understood, as by revelation, that different people may have different estimates of the importance of passion. The question was one which he had seldom pondered, and never exhaustively.

She proceeded:

"When I told you how I'd been thinking of you for weeks, and how I'd come to London just to see you, and all that, I was putting it much too mildly. It was far worse than that. One reason why I've been so keen on taking charge of Tessa was to keep my mind off *you.* Yes. I may as well admit it. If you hadn't happened to catch sight of me at Calais, I should have tried never to see you again. Because I was frightfully depressed in London--I mean about you. The walk in the rain was lovely, and we *were* near--weren't we?--only somehow things were very chilly, very chilly. But when we met at Calais like that, I thought that couldn't be just accident. I don't believe in chance, but I do believe in providence--God. Yes, I do. I believe God's in everything. I couldn't get over that meeting. So I rang you up. I had to. And you were so sweet on Friday night--though you weren't a bit sweet on the telephone on Friday afternoon--and then your knowing what I'd been thinking while they sang that trio, and your thinking the very same--well, that was too much for me, that was! I might have got over the meeting at Calais, but I couldn't get over *that.* I thought, surely it must mean something. So yesterday I took this flat, and I hadn't the pluck to ring you up until this morning. You know, my dear, I've been rather in hell, still am. I'm not the tiniest morsel conventional. No! But there's something deep in me that says to me a woman ought never to say the things to a man that I'm saying to you now. It's against nature; and nature isn't conventional; it's against my nature--part of my nature. Only, however deep you dig into your nature, there's always a layer that's deeper. And it was that deeper layer, when I half got down to it, that decided me I *ought* to speak to you. Must speak, in fact. And--and--then you--"

He foresaw that she was going to remind him that he had kissed her. But he was wrong. She definitely stopped. He liked her for not referring to the kisses. She was too magnanimous to refer to them; and she had too just a sense of proportion to give any real importance to such social trifles. How far they had progressed in intimacy, and at what speed, since her first telephone call only two days earlier! And it was all due to her initiative alone! He felt once again, and more strongly, the impulse to protect her, to save her from the consequences of her headlong, capricious temperament. He admired her gift of self-analysis; as for him, he was always very reluctant even to try to analyse himself; he accepted himself as he was, and indeed he regarded self-analysis as a rather morbid exercise. Nevertheless it suited some people, and it suited her, and she could do it. That bit about her not being conventional but feeling all the same how it was against nature for a woman to say to a man what she'd said to him--that was good; it showed a masculine breadth of mind. And then deliberately to go against her own axiom of conduct--that showed a still greater breadth of mind, super-masculine. But of course she did possess a mind; her conversation continually proved it. And she could be so formidably, so disturbingly serious. With all her disadvantages, she was a creature to respect. Impossible, even in one's most secret soul, to condescend to her. And how marvellous her mere voice! It enriched everything she said.

But for him a woman was either an asset or a liability, and she would be an everlasting liability. Long ago he had decided that to live with her would be to live in an inferno mitigated by transient glimpses of paradise. Leave her for your work in the morning, and you could never be sure what would not happen to her while she was out of your sight; you would be on pins until you saw her again in the evening, and after that you would have no peace of mind until she was asleep. To live with such a woman would be a career in itself. All these thoughts ran through his mind in a moment.

She had put him in a perfect hell of an awkward position. But that was a point which would not have occurred to her, naturally! She was egregiously self-centred. What in the name of God could he answer to her? Withal, he was happy as well as distracted. The situation was terrible, but it was terribly flattering, and there was beauty in it, and the beauty communicated itself to the whole environment.

The rain rained harder than ever; through the interstices of the once-white curtains he could distinguish raindrops slipping down the window-pane; but now the rain, the sadness of the implacable winter rain, was beautiful. Her toilet-gadgets, offspring of wealth and taste, were beautiful; the eye could gaze on them with a voluptuous satisfaction. And her blue *négligé,* or whatever it was--wondrous. And how well it became her hair and her pale face. And they were together in an inviolable solitude. They were on the boulevard, but as safe from prying interruption as in a boat by themselves at sea. For nobody knew where he was, and he was sure that nobody knew where she was. They were lost and undiscoverable in Paris. Something beautiful in that piquant, provocative security.

She said, in a lower tone:

"Don't say anything. Don't answer. I know I've put you in a frightfully awkward position. I know. I know." Her voice sank. Then louder: "Will you draw the curtains, please? It's getting dark. I hate these winter afternoons, but I love winter evenings...Yes, I know I've made it awkward for you. I know."

Her voice died quite away. She was not so self-centred after all; he had been unjust to her. 'They' had an extraordinary faculty for putting a man in the wrong.

3.

He drew the heavy curtains. He saw a light behind him. She was sitting up and had switched on one of the bed-lamps. He switched on the other lamp, the one nearer the window. In the soft shaded light the room grew quite presentable, and its false luxury authentic. She patted the surface of the bed at the spot where he had been sitting, to indicate that he must resume his seat. He obeyed. It was all a marvellous experience, unique. She had not uttered a word.

"Don't say anything until to-morrow," she said. "Say nothing. Nothing...You're very dignified. But then you always are. I do admire your dignity."

He thought:

"To-morrow!' And my train this afternoon?"

His train, however, seemed to have lost every shred of its importance. It was not his train; it was no train in particular: it was a train that left Paris monotonously every afternoon at four o'clock.

She was now sitting up, and therefore nearer to him. She looked away from him, staring with a stern, mournful expression at the expanse of the window-curtains. She turned and looked not at his face, but at his right hand, which was resting on his right thigh as he sat half-turned towards her on the side of the bed. She leaned forward a little more to pat his hand, maternally to soothe him, girlishly to excuse herself for having put him in a position so intensely difficult. The folds of the blue wrap slipped aside. He observed for the first time that under it she was not wearing a camisole; she was wearing pyjamas, unbuttoned at the neck. She had undressed completely and put herself to bed in earnest. As she leaned forward he could not fail to see her sumptuous breasts, mysterious within the shadow of the loosened, thin-spun garment.

What elemental force, raising his left hand, drew it to her shoulder and laid his fingers gently on her velvet-covered shoulder? Madness perhaps, but a divine madness. There was something tremendously exciting in the fact that whereas he was fully clad and might have walked out into the street without causing remark, she was unseemly for any eye but his. Her expression changed slowly from sternness to soft, timid bliss. She was very beautiful: her face, her hair, her eyes, her lips, her bosom--all were intolerably beautiful. Their beauty redeemed the entire room from its horrid vulgarity. The lamps had somewhat changed the room, and now her beauty, trembling, changed it completely. Bliss awaited him, a dozen inches off. There were no liabilities, only assets. He ceased to reason. He felt that reason was an absurdity. Reason was dissolved in emotion. Anxieties, apprehensions, careers, worldly considerations were cast away and forgotten. His hand still on her shoulder, he pushed her backwards on to the pillow, pushed her violently; and she yielded in ravished acquiescence to his violent gesture. And waited, resigned, humble, ecstatic in bliss.

He leaned over her, and kissed her open mouth. She closed her eyes. Suddenly she lifted her head an inch from the pillow and repaid his kiss. And he too, having given happiness to her, was happy beyond measuring. No matter what the price, the happiness outvalued it.

She whispered:

"And did you really not sleep last night?" He nodded.

She whispered:

"So we were both lying awake." He nodded.

"Were you glad when I rang you up on Friday?" she asked, whispering.

He nodded. He could distinguish every detail of her eyes as he gazed at her, the down on her cheeks.

"How pale you are!" he whispered: the first words he had spoken!

"I didn't put any rouge on this morning," she whispered. "I didn't want to look well. I wanted to look pale. Was it wrong of me?"

He shook his head.

"Sure?"

He nodded, in his heart justifying what he imagined to be her motive.

She said: "I don't mean I did it to make *you* think I looked pale--"

"But I did think you looked pale," he murmured. (Once more he had been misjudging her.)

"I did it because I wanted to look pale for myself," she finished her sentence. "And so you noticed I looked pale?"

He nodded.

"Very pale?" She was smiling.

"Rather pale."

"And did you feel sorry for me?"

He nodded.

"Were you sorry for me because you thought I was sort of pining away for you?"

"No."

"I'm so glad. That would have been awful. I couldn't have borne it. Then why?"

"I thought you were unwell. And you looked so tired."

"Did I? Well. I was tired. But I'm not tired now. Are you?"

"Not a bit."

"How lovely!...Darling, tell me all you ever thought about me. I want to know all you ever thought about me. I know I'm an egotist, so you needn't tell me that. Tell me all the nice things."

She was a child, he reflected, answering her smile with a smile. Fancy being curious about what people thought of you, about the impression you were making! It never occurred to him to wonder what impression be himself was making. He just went blandly on his way. Perhaps it was he who was the egotist, with his instinctive indifference to outside opinion.

He said, louder:

"You haven't been very egotistic with Tessa."

"Ah! But that's a special kind of thing. That was showing off--to myself. Tell me some more."

"I'll tell you the finest thing I know about you. I've never forgotten it and I never shall."

"What?" she whispered, eager. "Whisper it."

He whispered:

"Be still and know that I am God."

"But I never said that to you. Quoted it, I mean. I can remember everything I ever said to you--or you said to me. Everything."

"No. But you said it to your father, and he told me. It puzzled your father, but it did impress him." He thought for a moment of her neglectful father.

"But it didn't puzzle you."

"It's the greatest saying ever said," he replied. She raised her head and gave him a delicious warm kiss; then, contemplating, slowly stroked his cheek.

"How well you shave!" she murmured. "Much better than father. Tell me, you weren't annoyed that morning when I had the nerve to ask you to take me with you to Smithfield?"

"A bit. For a moment."

"Oh! How honest you are, darling! I adore you for that. I'd sooner hear that than something smooth. But did you enjoy the visit--me being with you?"

"Yes I did, as soon as I'd given myself up to it."

"Wouldn't you like to read what I wrote about it, in my book. I've got a carbon of it here. It's in the middle drawer of the dressing-table."

"Shall I get it now?"

She nodded. He stirred.

"It must be very uncomfortable for you, on your elbows like this, and your legs all twisted."

Yet she had called herself an egotist!

He found the typescript half-buried in gloves and handkerchiefs. He held it in his hand, without opening it. No title on the limp green paper cover. No name. No clue. Nothing. He fingered the dark green silk which bound the sheets together. Her book would certainly show what she thought of him, her reactions to him; and for this reason alone he was acutely impatient to read it. How wrong he had been: superiorly crediting himself with indifference to outside opinion about himself! He was quite as curious concerning her estimate of him as she had been concerning his estimate of her. Through the curtains he could hear the drumming of the raindrops on the pane.

"I'm to read this thing now, eh? At once?"

"Of *course!"*

"Shall I go into the other room to read it?"

"No. Stay here. I should be so lonely."

"I can't read by those bed-lights, I'm afraid."

She sprang like a leopard suddenly out of the bed, rushed to the door, and turned on the chandelier-lights, then to the dressing-table and turned on the two toilet-lights.

"Now can you see to read?" She was standing close by him. The blue *négligé* was a lovely flimsy thing. Below its curving hem showed her blue trousers, and below the ends of the trousers her feet, bare. Her eyes flashed with joy and pride. He recalled the soft assent of her shoulder under his hand, and thought: "What an ass I was to hesitate for a single second!" Did one hesitate to enter heaven? And the pure intimacy--exquisite almost past enduring! He sat down in the sole easy chair, and opened the typescript. She moved to and fro restlessly. He glanced at her with a benevolent reproving frown.

"Look here," he said. "If you want something to do, you might take away that tea-tray. I'm sure you're like me--you hate to see things out of place, especially on the floor. In fact while you're about it you might do a bit of washing-up." His tone was lightly teasing.

She smiled enigmatically. "But there's nothing in there to wipe with."

"There's a million towels or so. I saw them."

"Very well."

She stooped and picked up the tray, and off she went, lodging the rim of the tray against the door-jamb while she turned the knob.

"And leave the door open," he said. "Leave both doors open."

"But why?"

"I want to hear the sound of you washing-up."

His false sternness enchanted her.

"I shall spoil my beautiful dressing-gown," she objected. "Take it off then." She vanished, and came back in a moment in her pyjamas and threw the peignoir into the middle of the bedroom floor, where it lay--furnishing the room afresh. She was gone. He could feel her ardent happiness like a heat ray. Soon he could hear, faintly, the sound of crockery under the hands of the new kitchen-maid. He was ineffably happy. Out of what strange material could felicity build itself!

In such felicity he would have been unable to concentrate on any other book, but he found that on this book he could concentrate without the least difficulty. It began with her sensations in Smithfield Market. It was frank, wholly shameless. Was it fit for print in England? Well, it must be, since a publisher had agreed to publish it. He read on the second page that her companion and escort was masterful without quite knowing it. She knew in herself that he was masterful, and she knew it too from the demeanour of others towards him. He expected to find a lot more about her companion. But he was disappointed. The book was about her, not about him. Was he masterful? He supposed he must be. Because she could not be wrong. Everything else in the chapter was so convincing. He marvelled at the total picture of her reactions to Smithfield. He had to admit that he had been blind to some of the secret essence of Smithfield. She was more fully revealing it to him. Her reference to the nun was shocking. But beautiful too. On each page she unveiled beauty whose existence he had not suspected.

He thought:

"She has a lovely mind...Of course. I knew that before. The girl's a genius! But is she? Can I judge? She may be able to write this, and nothing else. Anyway, she's a genius in herself, even if she sits idle and doesn't do a thing. I'm a conceited idiot. I've been condescending to her."

After a short time she reappeared in the bedroom.

"Have you read it--about the meat-markets?"

"I've just this moment finished that part, and I'm going on."

"Well?"

"I think it's simply wonderful. That's all--for the present."

"You really mean that? Be careful of your words. Because I shall believe you."

"I really mean it."

"Oh, my dear!" She breathed. "I'm so relieved. You can't tell how happy you make me. I had a sort of idea it mightn't be anything after all."

"Well, it is something after all."

"You're a great reader, aren't you?"

"I've read a fair amount. But I've never read anything like this--since Marie Bashkirtseff."

"Who was she?"

"Never heard of her? No. Of course you wouldn't have heard of her. She was before your time. But in *her* time she made a devil of a stir in the world."

She approached the chair where he was reclining.

"Thank you," she said, with extraordinary modesty, and kissed him.

He calmly turned a page.

"I'll tell you some more later." He bent his eyes to the new page.

"But you can leave it now," she suggested.

"Why?"

"Why! I want to talk."

"I will not leave it," he said positively.

"But don't you want us to talk?"

"I want to listen to you. And this is you." He raised the typescript. "Haven't you got anything to do?"

"Yes. Plenty."

"Well, go and do it then. But not here."

"Why not here?"

"Because you're too exciting."

"Very well, darling," she acquiesced, looked for and snatched up her handbag and departed, shutting the door.

His attention was now distracted from the page. What would an impartial observer say? There he was, at his ease in her bedroom. And she in pyjamas! Pooh! There was not and could not be an observer, impartial or otherwise. Neither he nor she had anybody to consider. They were their own convention-makers. And what was wrong with pyjamas? He was ridden by outworn social prejudices. In these days did not both sexes go to cocktail-parties in pyjamas. And her suit, in addition to being at least as decent as an evening frock, was very handsome and very elaborate: obviously intended to be seen and admired. The fact was he was being scared by the word 'pyjamas' and its associations. Silly! And if anyone was entitled to see and admire pyjamas, and her in them, was not he the man? Had she not welcomed his kisses as she lay in bed in those very pyjamas? If so, why in the name of reason should he not watch her as she walked to and fro in the pyjamas? Yes, utterly silly! And more--was she not the writer of the astonishing pages which had thrilled him? She, the actual author, somewhere outside, probably in the bathroom, obedient to him, submitting meekly to his command! That was what was so marvelous--marvellous enough to be hardly credible. Had not such a girl the right to wear what she chose? And still more--he was happy. And she was happy.

He repeated to himself that they were their own convention-makers. And why not?

She returned again, but not soon. He was half-way through the typescript.

"How do I look?" she asked, as she stood close by him. Her cheeks had become delicately rose. She no longer wanted to be pale for herself. She wanted to signalise her happiness, her perfect content.

"You're an artist," he answered.

"Say you're happy," she appealed to him, finger on lip, rather childlike.

"I am." His tone was gay. "Well, I see I mustn't read any more just now." She took the manuscript from him. "But I shan't be properly happy till I've read every word of it. And that's your fault. I expect you know I've missed my train."

"You *haven't!*"

"Let's guess what time it is."

"Three o'clock," she guessed.

"I guess five to four."

His watch said five o'clock. They were both astounded. He had always maintained that he had the hour continuously at the back of his mind, to ten minutes or so. And now he was sixty-five minutes out. His happiness was mysteriously increased, his spirits heightened.

"What does it matter?" he exclaimed joyously. "I'd telephoned to London, but I can call them up again--"

"And say you've missed the train."

"Not a bit of it. I've got my reputation to think of. I never miss trains. I'll say I've been kept."

"And so you have!" she said. "But you're glad, aren't you?"

He nodded. She put her arms round him.

"I'd better telephone to the hotel for a room," he added.

"Not yet," she appealed.

"All right. Plenty of time. But oughtn't you to be getting dressed?"

"Dressed? I don't want to waste my time dressing. Shan't I do as I am?"

"But we shall have to eat, shan't we? And I gather we can't eat here."

"Of course we can eat here," she said. "You don't know your Paris, darling. All we have to do is to telephone, to Larue's--say. And order what we like. They'll deliver it here, complete; and they'll take away the ruins and remains. I'll do it now, shall I?"

"'Do it now' is a pretty sound motto."

"What would you like?"

"What you'd like."

"May I order anything I want?"

"You must."

She ran off into the drawing-room, where the telephone was. Alone, he smiled to himself.

She came running back.

"Tell me what champagne," she said, as it were breathless.

"Krug 1919."

She vanished.

He thought:

"Now where do I stand with her? I've kissed her. That kind of a kiss must mean something. What? What does it mean to *her?* Marriage? I don't care whether it means marriage or not. No, I don't care!" He had been starved of women for long. The fast was at an end now.

She reappeared, and lay down like an animal on the hearth-rug, shaking her head at the suggestion of the sofa.

A little before half-past six he had finished reading the account of her reactions to life in London and Paris: fragmentary impressions connected only by her individuality; a series of Very lights that shot up into the sky, dazzlingly illuminated the dark landscape with a strange, perhaps sinister revealing splendour, faded, and left the landscape in darkness again. Not all the flashes were equally vivid; the later were not as brilliant as the earlier; but on the whole the book was to him what he had called it: wonderful, simply wonderful. It had fascinated and somewhat dismayed him. Some minutes elapsed before he could think himself back into the accustomed three dimensions of daily existence. He reflected: "But this girl is staggering." It was scarcely to be credited that there she lay enveloped in the blue *néglígé,* on the hearthrug at his feet, her slippers kicked off and her narrow feet bare, poring over "The Nature of the Physical World," which apparently, from the look of the volume, she had by no means yet finished. Twice, with an exclamation, she had sprung up and run into the drawing-room, and through two open doorways he could hear her loud, clear, telephone-voice, altering in French her order for the dinner.

Then they talked, she on the floor and he in the easy-chair, her fingers occasionally stroking his ankles. The intimacy of their seclusion! The intimacy was exquisite to him! And plainly so to her too! The old question: What could she see in him? Then a bell rang, and startled him.

"Don't move!" she smiled. "It's our dinner. I'll see to it."

Her tone and radiant glance thrilled him. He had never seen anybody as rapturously beatified as she was. And he the sole cause! If he had repelled her, what would have been her state at that moment? She passed quickly into the drawing-room and closed the door. He dashed on tiptoe, stealthily, into the bathroom to prepare himself for the enchanting meal.

"Oh! There you are!" she said as he emerged.

She was coming out of the drawing-room. She clasped his hand and without a word they went to dinner. The round centre table was laid for two; and she must have laid it herself, for the two places were set close together.

"It's what's called a cold collation, except for the soup. Do you know how to open champagne?" She laughed.

It was all miraculous. At moments she sat on his knee, and they ate from one plate.

He thought: "This cannot last. It's bound to end. It's too good to last."

Hardly had they finished when the bell rang, and startled him again.

"They've come for the things. I told them nine o'clock. Can it be nine o'clock already? Now you go back into the bedroom, that's a good boy. I'll attend to all this."

He obeyed. She ran after him into the bedroom, snatched at her handbag, kissed him--a touch only.

"Here!" he said. "I'll--"

"I'm the hostess, if you don't mind," she said, giving him another kiss. And was gone. Both doors closed.

His heart was thumping in nervousness. The thing was bound to end; and the duty to end it was his. She returned.

"Coast clear!" she said. "How stuffy this central heating is!" She threw down the *néglígé.*

"Well," he said, extremely self-conscious, "I shall have to be off soon." He had said it. He had no feeling at all of having eaten and drunk.

"But surely, darling," she murmured, facing him with a candid, artless look of pure amazement. "Surely you aren't thinking of leaving me here all by myself to-night." Her eyes moistened.

Chapter 57 THE GLOVE

Next morning at about ten o'clock Evelyn, in his big overcoat, was sitting on the *terrasse* of a large café on the north side of the boulevard. The January air was sharp enough, but Evelyn sat in full sunshine under the glass roofing, and an absolutely clear pale-blue sky above. Not a trace of mud or dampness on the boulevard and its broad pavements. You could no more believe that the Parisian climate was capable of serious rain than you could believe that a pretty and charming woman seen at a party was capable of a scowl or a tantrum.

The staff was attending to two huge stoves whose warmth enabled customers to persist in the open-air habit characteristic of Paris. Evelyn had before him on a tiny round table a tray containing chocolate, rolls, butter, and a glass of cold water. Boulevard coffee he had reason to distrust. Tea, which might have been excellent, would have suited his alimentary tract better than the chocolate; but he had ordered chocolate for the novelty of it, for the joy of the first sip, and because he knew that he could rely on its quality. The rolls nearly equalled the rolls of the Imperial Palace; the butter was delicious. He revelled in anticipation of the light meal; he would be sorry when the last morsel was eaten, the last drop drunk, and the palate. cleansing water had to be tasted. He revelled in the generous sunshine. He revelled in the incessant traffic, the tooting of horns, the moving spectacle of wayfarers brushing past his table, a little shabby and hurried, not a single smart girl and hardly a man whose face did not show the Latin melancholy, exacting, covetous, implacable, and preoccupied by desires; hundreds of those pallid faces in the great motor-buses and in the taxis; sardonic faces of the taxi-drivers; occasionally a magnificent auto; occasionally a tourist-crowded charabanc; a small policeman with a big white baton; shops, other cafés right and left and opposite; enormous gilt signs on the monotonously similar façades, and signs black against the pale-blue sky; Morris Columns advertising the performances at the Opéra, the Opéra Comique, the Francais, the Odéon, the Variétés; the Palais Royal, the Trianon, the Casino de Paris, etc., etc.:

Paris. He had a sensation of vigorous well-being, of adventure, of an unplanned idle day awaiting him. And he had a sensation of freedom. Who would have foreseen that he could share a bed with a fellow-creature and yet would sleep moveless for more than six hours, awaking at nine o'clock, fatigued, but agreeably fatigued, and refreshed?

Gracie, on being asked at 2 a.m. about the hour of breakfast had said that she would sleep till called, and that if she was not called she would sleep for ever--noon, 2 p.m.! She was like that. She had told him to call her. He had refused; she must have her sleep out. She had repeated with a yawn that she must be called--she could not bear the thought of losing in sleep the consciousness of bliss. A slightly peremptory note in her rich, tired voice. Silence. Sleep.

At nine o'clock, by the twilight of a bed-lamp, he had gazed at her asleep. Unique vision: relaxed, the lips parted, the eyes hidden, quiet, regular breathing, youth, beauty. He had gazed, and then risen. If she wakened, so much the better for her satisfaction. If she did not waken, so much the better for her health, and for his satisfaction in adhering to his refusal to wake her. He had left the room to bathe; returned; she still slept. He had transferred his studs to a clean shirt, opened and shut drawers, found another suit and pair of shoes, every operation making a noise. She had not stirred. The project of a solitary breakfast on the boulevard had irresistibly enticed him. He had discovered her latch-key, and crept away, like a thief in danger of being caught. Then the sunshine had smitten him. Yes, he was aware of a sensation of masculine freedom.

As he luxuriated in the breakfast he kept muttering, or perhaps only thinking, to himself: "By God! By God!" Meaning that he had done it, had voyaged to Cythera. He muttered

"She is mine! Incredible! She is mine! What about her father? Curse her father!" And thinking of the smooth organisation of the admirable dinner, he muttered: "By God! She knows how to make a man comfortable!" This had rather surprised him. Nevertheless, on reflection it was not so surprising. Had she not presided over her father's household! He thought: "Lucky I had my luggage with me!" Then a shaft pricked him: "Had she schemed that luggage business beforehand?" No matter! He drew out the shaft and threw it down. She was marvellous, she was miraculous, and she was his. A virgin? He shook his head. No matter! These notions about the importance of virginity were obsolete. What was her sexual history? He had no right to enquire. Her experiments were her own business. One must be fair. Beyond doubt she was passionately in love with him. He thought of her with extreme tenderness. He could have forgiven her anything. A woman of her extraordinary qualities was entitled to a code of her own. He exulted in her.

A waiter having emerged from the interior of the café, to serve another customer who had rapped impatiently on the window, Evelyn asked for a newspaper--any newspaper. Two very well-dressed English tourists strolled past the *terrasse.* He had a vague memory of having once seen them, the woman assuredly, dining in the restaurant of the Imperial Palace. They did not notice him.

"By Jove!" he thought, "I might be recognised here at any moment!"

He had a spasm of apprehension. Absurd. Supposing he was recognized--what of it? The boulevard was a free country. And at any moment he could disappear beyond the possibility of tracing into the apartment of his mistress. Still, he had the spasm, and he admitted to himself that he would not have had it if he had been staying, a bachelor, at a hotel.

The waiter brought the newspaper. Of course it was a continental Anglo-Saxon newspaper. But it was uncrumpled, fresh as newly gathered fruit, and almost as appetising. He spread it out. The first thing he saw on the front page was a little inconspicuous couple of paragraphs, to the effect that the governmentally appointed Commission to examine and report on the Licensing Laws and make recommendations thereupon was to hold its first meeting on the Wednesday, and that a number of leading provincial and Scottish hotel-proprietors were coming to London to give evidence. He was thunderstruck. He would have to return to England on the morrow, Tuesday. Was he not the leader of the great national agitation for the reform of the Licensing Laws? And he remembered that he had not telephoned to London on the previous night. He who never forgot anything had forgotten the nightly telephoning. Stranger still: he had not once thought of it till that very moment! His exultation died out like a finished candle. He became perturbed and gloomy, full of forebodings and of disconsolate dejection. Probably, as he had failed to arrive home on the previous night, Cousin or somebody would have called him up at the Concorde or the Montaigne, or both, and would have been told that he had left Paris. Be sure your sin will find you out...He had had no expectation that the meetings of the Licensing Commission would start so soon.

He must go and break the news to Gracie instantly. He in his turn rapped on the window. A waiter emerged. He paid the bill and set off. Forebodings! Forebodings! Gracie's flat was within two hundred yards of the café. He wished it had been further away. He had crept out of the flat like a thief, and like a thief he re-entered it. Curious that, though he was completely innocent in the affair of the Licensing Commission, he had a sense of guilt, as if he was conspiring against Gracie; and he could not shake it off!

He began minutely to plan his procedure in order to minimise both the shock of the news to her and the inevitable resulting friction. She would no longer be the author of the wonderful book; she would be a girl in whom emotion would supplant reason: he knew it for certain. Should he take off his big overcoat before going into the bedroom? Or not? He would not take it off. The sight of the overcoat would at once convey to her the awkward fact that he had been out; she would be faced with it, and no word said. The fewer words the better, until she had accustomed herself to the new situation.

2.

The bed-lamp was burning. She had wakened, then. No, she was peacefully, touchingly, asleep. He had merely forgotten to extinguish the light on departing. Where had been his wits? What had come over him? He purposely shut the bedroom door with a bang. The bang disturbed her. She stirred, opened her eyes, saw him. She smiled all her love. Love for him was her first thought. The overcoat apparently did not disconcert her in the least.

"Darling!" She stretched her arms to welcome him. He advanced, bent down, kissed her, tenderly fondled her, kissed her again. She held him close to her, his thick, rough, overcoat pressed against her thin delicate pyjamas. "Darling! Were you going out? I'm so glad you didn't go out without me. Why didn't you wake me when you got up? I asked you to wake me, didn't I?" Her lips were under his; she was murmuring into his mouth. Her rich voice was soft with sleep.

"Did you?" he murmured vaguely. By a single misconception she had deranged all his plan. He would be compelled to speak his confession.

"I thought I did."

"I shouldn't have dreamt of waking you," he said. "You looked too lovely asleep."

She went on:

"I've just this second had a most heavenly idea. Of course we *could* have *petit déjeuner* here. It's not bad either. But let's go out and have it on the boulevard. At some café."

"Fine!" he agreed. "It's a beautiful morning."

He perceived the utter impossibility of confessing that he had already breakfasted on the boulevard. To do so would break her heart, child that she was. He perceived too that in breakfasting alone he had committed an outrage. No! Despite the taste of chocolate on his tongue he had assuredly not breakfasted.

"Well," he said gently, "I'm not going out. I've been out."

'Oh! Darling!" she protested, but very lovingly. "And I did want to lie here and watch you dress. I had a delicious dream of watching you dress yourself. Why did you go out?"

"Only to buy a paper. Must keep an eye on the world, you know."

"Darling, you are funny. Of course you must keep an eye on your funny world," she assented, with ravishing humurous charm.

Yes, she was unique. He would do anything for her, anythingwithin reason and perhaps a bit beyond reason. But he was troubled. He foresaw terrible complications from the momentshe was made to realise that he must leave her the next morning. While he was removing his overcoat, she slipped from under the bedclothes and silently took the overcoat from him and put it on, and laughed at her image in the cheval glass. Evelyn laughed too. She seemed not a great deal shorter than himself, and she could hardly be called thin; yet the overcoat was immensely too big for her; it covered half her hands, reached to her ankles; and as she wrapped it round her body it doubly enveloped her, like a cloak.

"How enormous you creatures are!" she said. "Still, it shall be my dressing-gown. Don't you love it on me, dearest?" She glanced at him for admiration, and turned up the deep collar. "How's that?"

"I suppose you're somewhere inside the thing," he answered. "But I don't quite know where. Oh! Is that your head peeping out of it? What a morsel!"

She went to the window, and drew the curtains apart and raised the blind. Bright light rushed like an inundation into the room, filling it to the ceiling and transforming it. The bed-lamp, which to the eye had been the most important object, was now scarcely visible; it went on burning unseen and neglected. She gazed forth at the blue sky.

"The morning has repented," she murmured. Then she examined her features close in the dressing-table mirror. "Oh! My God!" She set to work on them. She roamed around, did forty things.

"Bath!" she said; and vanished.

Evelyn sat down to wait. He wanted to read again the fatal paragraphs, but the newspaper was in the pocket of his overcoat. How the devil was he to tell her? Nothing had been said between them as to his departure, but he was deeply aware that she would resent being left less than two days after she had seduced him. (Thus did he too realistically phrase the event to himself.) He heard faintly the water pouring into the bath. He observed the details of the bedroom. She had passed through it like an invading army; the havoc and the litter she had made in two minutes were unbelievable.

"Darling!" He heard her distant voice. "Help! Help!"

He hurried into the bathroom. She lay in the steaming bath, white and pale pink, idly splashing: amphibious; a marvellous, shameless, indecorous vision; but from the door he could not see her face.

"Darling! Do give me that dark soap from the lavatory-basin. Is it there, or have I--"

"It's there."

He gave her the soap. Her wet fingers touched his.

"Let me see you," she said.

He advanced obediently towards the window, and her eyes met his.

"What are you hiding from me?" she asked, as it were casually, but with complete assurance.

They were necromancers, women; they possessed the mysterious senses of animals. His guilt overpowered him. Well, the moment had come. He bent down and drew the newspaper from the overcoat, which she had thrown on the tiled floor, with her pyjamas on the top of it. He folded the newspaper and handed it to her, indicating the paragraphs. She began by letting it drop into the bath-water.

"That's what I was hiding from you, Mrs. Clever." He tried to make his tone airy, amusing; but failed. She retrieved the newspaper, and read the paragraphs.

"Well?" she demanded. Her eyes were very wide open as she looked at him innocently, candidly, a puzzled child.

Explaining to her why it was essential that he should be in London for the first sitting of the Commission in order to marshal the evidence for reform, and telling her that it had long since been arranged for the visiting hotel-potentates to stay at the Imperial Palace, where they would count on his presence and guidance, he said:

"The odious fact is, that I must leave Paris to-morrow morning. And I'm most frightfully sick about it. I'd no idea that the sittings would start so soon. And nobody else had, either."

Gracie laughed, still with assurance, but a less complete assurance.

"You needn't worry about the first day, darling, or the first three or four days," she said, with a confident air that had in it a trace of something akin to condescension. "You probably don't know much about Parliamentary Commissions. I do. Daddy has had to give evidence before them lots of times--well, two or three times--and I've often heard him furious at their goings-on. He says they generally waste at least a week before they get down to work, and they'll even adjourn for a week or a fortnight or a month at the first meeting. Believe me, darling, I know! I've not lived with daddy for nothing. No!" She was calmly quite peremptory, as one who has settled a question once for all. Inexperienced in Evelyn, she did not even suspect that her technique was very badly conceived.

"That may be so," he said quietly, benevolently; "but all the same I shall have to leave to-morrow morning."

He saw her face change into a tragic discomposure. She had continued to splash the bath-water. She ceased. She had looked at him innocently, candidly, like a child. Now she wept like a child--a child that simply cannot comprehend some cruel decree of a malevolent providence. Her grief desolated Evelyn. He was ashamed of that unspoken sardonic thought of his which had defined their coming together as a seduction by her, not by him. She was ingenuousness itself. Stricken, she needed protection, defence, everything that he could give her. She was entitled to the satisfaction of her young instincts. And withal, what a woman! He recalled her phrase: 'The morning has repented.' How exquisite! How easily it had come out! Doubtless she had lovely fancies like that endlessly, all day, every day. The mind in the delicious, forlorn, suffering child was amazing. To see her suffer was intolerable. All had been happiness. Now all was woe. He must soothe her, succour her in her irrational weakness. No. There was no 'must' about it. He most ardently desired and yearned to soothe and succour her. He moved near her, bent down, and took her soft cheeks in his hands, and raised her face to his. She was still crying.

"Would you leave me alone here for a Commission?" she bubbled.

"Darling!" he murmured. "You don't know how I hate to do it. Listen. I'll run along to the Concorde at once."

"What for?"

"To telephone to London. I shall get the communication quicker there than here. I ought to have telephoned to the Palace last night that I wasn't coming. But I absolutely forgot. They'll be thinking I died en route." He smiled.

"Don't joke about dying," she said, loud. The joke had frightened her, "And as for getting the communication, I'll get that for you better than any hotel. I know a man at the Quai d'Orsay--"

She freed her cheeks and climbed impulsively out of the bath, wetting him. And, all wet, she put on his overcoat, and ran into the drawing-room, leaving a trail of wet footmarks. He followed. What decision, what resource she had! She was no more the defenceless child. She was a woman engaging in battle to retain possession of a treasure to her priceless.

"What's your number at the Palace?" she demanded sharply over her shoulder. He gave the number and waited. In three minutes she had used her influence at the French Foreign Office. She rang off.

"You'll see how soon you'll get London!" she said triumphantly.

Evelyn had somehow temporarily dwindled into a nonentity. She padded back into the bath and he after her.

"You'll see it's bound to be all right," she said. Her self-deception was touching. She believed what she wished to believe. 'They' all did. He knew that there was no hope whatever of it being all right. But he did not say so.

"You might turn on some more hot water," she said. "This bath's nearly cold."

Nevertheless the water was still giving off steam. She lay passive, all her enchanting body immersed except the head. She lay for a long time. At intervals she burst into a sob, and tears fell. Evelyn hung up the damp overcoat, inside out. No sooner had he done so than she said, brokenly:

"Let me have that, will you?" and got out of the bath, wiped herself, got into the overcoat once more, and passed into the bedroom.

"I shall lie down for a while," she said.

And down she lay in the overcoat. Comical sight. Evelyn attentively covered her with the eiderdown. Then the telephone-bell rang.

"What did I tell you, darling!" she exclaimed. He was relieved that she had resumed the use of that last word, though he was well aware that ordinarily it meant nothing in her vocabulary. Since their union, however, he had decided that it had begun to mean all that he could have wished it to mean. And in fact it had.

Voice of Mr. Cousin in the telephone in the drawing-room. It explained that as he had not rung up, Oldham, recalled upon his holiday, had gone to Victoria to meet his master on Sunday night, and that on the man's report that his master had not arrived vain attempts had been made to communicate with Evelyn at both the Concorde and the Montaigne, in which places it was understood that he had left Paris for London. In answer to this Evelyn stated with careful vagueness that he had decided to take a brief holiday from his hotels, but had been prevented from telephoning news of the change of plan. He enquired about the sittings of the Licensing Commission. The answer surprised and intensely relieved him. And then Cousin began to talk generally of Imperial Palace affairs.

Evelyn resisted the onset of business; he preferred to reserve his mind exclusively for the affair of Gracie; but the force of habit overcame his resistance. He wanted not to enjoy the familiar sensation of dealing with the problems and difficulties of the hotel organism; but he enjoyed it, and he could not deny this to himself. Such sensations had constituted almost the whole of his emotional life, until the last two days. Gracie had brought about a revolution in his mind, overturning a throne; but now the deposed monarch resumed dominion in a moment. Strange! Disconcerting! Yet somehow reassuring, comforting! His thoughts were far too complex for analysis, especially by one who was temperamentally hostile to the process of analysis.

3.

Gracie was enveloped in his overcoat on the bed in the next room, incalculable, exacting, an exquisite, adored, brilliant, childlike monopolist..."Concerning the arrangements for lodging the northern hotel-managers. Yes. No. Yes. No. Sixth. Nothing should be higher than Sixth..." Gracie was lying in his overcoat..."Leave all that to Miss Powler..." Gracie was unhappy...The telephone time-allowance had to be renewed twice. God! And an hour or so earlier he had been visualising the day as a day of idle dalliance without a programme!..No, he could not give a telephone number to Cousin; he did not know quite where he would be. But he would telephone to the hotel for news. *"Au revoir. Au revoir."* He replaced the receiver, sighing as much in apprehension as in relief. Before returning to the bedroom he reflected, unfruitfully.

He was amazed, and a little hurt, to find Gracie lying on her stomach, absorbed, scribbling fast with a pencil on a block of manuscript-paper. She must have got out of bed, for the eiderdown was on the floor. Had she forgotten her woe and her suspense?

"Well, darling?" She did not look up; indeed she continued to write.

"It's all right," he said.

"I knew it would be," she said.

"Yes. But not in the way you think. The Chairman of the Commission has caught a chill, and he doesn't want them to start without him. It's all postponed for a week. The journalists didn't hear the news yesterday, so to-day's papers are a bit behind the times."

Tenderly he restored the eiderdown. She now looked up at him, offering her lips. He kissed her. He clasped her. If she had the whim to write, was she not her own lord? He felt no hurt. What were hotels, mergers, organisations, careers? Naught. He was as variable as a woman. His ideals, his desires, changed from one minute to the next. His mental processes (he admitted) were, then, as crude as a woman's. What alone was certain was that the sight and feel of her affected him overwhelmingly. His instinct to protect her, to please her, to delight her, to produce the smile of bliss on her beautiful face, shot up resistlessly and ruled his being.

"Darling," she said, still half absorbed in the dream of her composition. "Breakfast. You must be terribly hungry."

"Not very," he said, with truth.

The chocolate reproached him, in the French sense of the word as well as in the English.

"Will you order something?" she suggested.

"Oh! Hadn't you better order it yourself?" he countered. The Englishman in him was intimidated by the prospect of demanding breakfast for two in the apartment of a young woman!

Gracie replied:

"Oughtn't a hotel-keeper to be capable of ordering a breakfast?" She said the words with a delicious, roguish, and loving smile. And he was undoubtedly a hotel-keeper. Nevertheless his sensitive pride felt a prick, as if from her disdain of his calling. Moreover, could the managing director of the world's greatest luxury hotel-merger fitly be described as a hotel-keeper? Childish vanity! Still, the dart stuck in the wound.

"He certainly ought," he agreed manfully. "What will you have, my dear?"

"Oh! Anything. Tea?"

He nodded and left the bedroom. His hat lay on the centre table of the drawing-room, where he had dropped it. He put it on, ridiculously, idiotically arguing to himself that a hat on his head might persuade the waiter that he had merely dropped in for breakfast with the young woman. He rang the bell, and then, ashamed, he went into the little entrance-hall and hung the hat on the hatstand there. The waiter arrived in long white apron, sleeved waistcoat and noiseless slippers, and accepted the order with a bland and totally indifferent: *"Deux thés complets. Bien, monsieur."* The folly and futility of pretending to a waiter in such an apartment that things were not what they were became humiliatingly clear to Evelyn. Nothing was or could be hid from the waiter. The service was very rapid.

Gracie, having heard the front-door close a second time, called out from the bedroom: "Is it there? You go on with yours, will you, darling? I'll be there in half a minute."

In less than half a minute she indeed was there, in knickers and camisole, frockless. She said, lightly:

"You think I shall be two hours over dressing. You'll see. I can dress as quick as any woman you ever knew." She sipped the tea, tore a roll into two halves. "I think I'll get my frock on, if you don't mind, dearest." And she ran off, cup in hand and her mouth full of buttered roll.

Evelyn sat miserably alone, sipped tea, ate nothing. Gracie returned for a second cup and another mouthful; she was still frockless, but she had exchanged her bedroom *mules* for shoes. This time she sat close to Evelyn.

"Of course," she said, "if it hadn't been for that lucky chill, you'd have simply had to go to London to-morrow morning."

"I should," he answered, and added with a sigh: "Duty before--love."

"Yes," she said.

She was charming in her sweet acquiescence. She had seen reason. Tears gone, resentment gone. Happy as a child. Throwing a kiss to him, she vanished once more. Evelyn was still not happy. Her demeanour was exquisite, but was it not perhaps mysteriously deceptive? His own was deceptive. At last she returned fully accoutred, bag in one hand, gloves in the other.

"Now I must fly," she said brightly. "The car's been waiting I don't know how long."

"Where to?"

"To see poor Tessa, of course. I daren't neglect her. Oh! damn these gloves!" She crunched the gloves into a ball in her hand.

"What's the matter with them?'

"They're the wrong ones."

"Give me one of them," he said.

"What for?"

"Because you've worn it." And the fact was that in that moment he did feel a real desire for one of her gloves as a keepsake. A very odd desire, for him, but it existed.

"Oh! Darling! Isn't that morbid?" She put her arms lovingly round his neck, but she was reproving him. "I couldn't do *that."*

"No," he agreed, forcing a pleasant smile. "Of course you couldn't. Excuse me one second."

He went into the bathroom, merely in order to hide from her.

'Morbid,' was it? He would not deny that it was morbid. And what then? She ought to have felt tremendously flattered by such morbidity. He was hurt for the second time that morning. He waited to recover from being so incomprehensibly an ass. Then he heard her run back to the bedroom, and he emerged. In the drawing-room he saw the gloves conspicuously placed on the breakfast-tray. He thought, querulously:

"She should know better than that. One glove is a keepsake. But two are only a pair of gloves. No man ever kept a pair of gloves for a souvenir." And he left the gloves where they lay, and sat down in front of them, harshly ignoring the fact that she had yielded to his morbid caprice. He thought, shamed but obstinate: "My character is changing. Why is it changing?"

Gracie reappeared with another pair of gloves. She glanced for the fifth of a second at the pair on the tray, and at him.

"Well," she exclaimed with self-possessed, affectionate cheerfulness. "I must be off."

"Am I to come with you?"

"Oh *no,* darling! That wouldn't quite do, would it?"

"Why must you go just now?" He forced a new smile. If she could still be self-possessed and affectionately cheerful, he could.

She said:

"Duty before--love, dearest."

This was her unkindest blow, for it silenced and paralysed him. He glanced about the room while she put on the gloves. When they were on she came to him and kissed him many times. And her clothes were so exceedingly smart, and so fresh and cool, and her smile so perfect, loving and unvirginal! But, though his bearing was as admirable as hers, his heart would not be comforted.

"And when shall I see you?" he asked.

"When I come back."

She was maddening, but he refused to be maddened.

"And when will that be?"

"Oh! Not long."

"Two hours?"

"At the most, my lion."

"And supposing I want to go out, how shall I get in again?"

"Sweetest. Here's the key. Stick it under the mat. If you don't find it there, ring. I shall be in. If I don't find it there, I'll ring--"

She departed. Solitary in the flat, he felt more miserable than ever. He was beloved--yes, perhaps; nay, surely!--but he was miserable. Everything had gone wrong. The suddenly announced excursion to St. Cloud was mere feminine vindictiveness. Must be!..Her 'lion' indeed!

Then he happened to look at the breakfast-tray. Only one glove on it among the crockery! She had needed no telling. She had understood. While he was looking about the room, she had surreptitiously snatched a glove away. She was astounding. There could not be another like her. Strange, strange indeed, that this trifle should comfort his difficult heart, exhilarate his mood into joy. But it was so. He picked up the glove, examined it, turned it over and over, smelt its perfume. The glove was a precious morsel of herself; she had left herself in the glove. He put it into his pocket, and he could feel it there, an authentic treasure.

Chapter 58 THE LOVELY MILKMAID

Evelyn was in the drawing-room when he heard voices in the hall. Voices of Gracie and a man--doubtless her chauffeur. Closing of the front-door. Gracie peeped into the room. At last! She had evidently changed her clothes while at St. Cloud. She ran into the room, smiling in happy anticipation of the reunion. He rose. She kissed him and kissed him, and her embraces gave him acute pleasure, pleasure whose intensity surprised him. He thought: "Yes, I am really in love." This thought itself gave him pleasure. She seemed not to be able to cease from kissing him. Impossible to disbelieve that she too was passionately in love.

"You poor thing!" she said, in eager commiseration. "Have you been sitting here ever since I left?"

"Not quite all the time," he answered. "The man came in to do the rooms, so I went out for a walk. I left the key under the mat. When I came back it was still under the mat. The man hadn't absolutely removed the dust, but he'd shifted it about a bit. I waited till you'd been gone two hours and a half or more, and then I thought I'd better be getting something to eat. So I stepped over to Larue's. I had a cold snack there. And I've just come in again. The key was still under the mat. How's Tessa?"

"She's quite all right. But she had to be soothed, and I decided to stay and see her eat--"

"You haven't eaten anything?"

"Oh yes. I ate with her. Then I had to collect some clothes I simply hadn't a rag here."

"No. Only a wardrobe full," he interjected.

"And here I am. Sit down, because I want to sit on your knee."

"Well, then, take your coat off, *and* your hat. If you keep them on it'll make me feel as if you were sitting on my knee in the street."

"How right you are! I was going to."

She obeyed and she sat on his knee and secured her position by putting one arm round his neck. "You aren't cross with me for being so late?"

"Do I look cross?"

She gazed at him. "No. You look heavenly."

"Well, I know I don't look heavenly, but I'm not the tiniest trifle in the world cross, my dear."

This was true. He had forgiven and forgotten her vindictiveness in leaving him, if indeed vindictive she had been. But he still felt a physical weight of oppression in the chest, such as one feels at the announcement of the possibility of a grave misfortune. She was not acting; she was too young and too candid to act convincingly for long together. But he was acting. She was 'near' him (her phrase), but he, despite love, was not near to her. He was afraid. He feared that a disaster had only been postponed. One day, and soon, he would have to leave her. And then--what? More tears? More ruthless tears? Yes, her tears were ruthless. She had used tears without regard for the cost of them to himself. Passionate love was ruthless. It could not argue. It could not see reason. Serious trouble had been averted by an accident, but he had had a glimpse of it. And the imminent menace of it was bound to recur. Their situation was not defined. It continued from hour to hour. Undefined, it could not continue for ever. They had loved, but they had not spoken, save to assert that they loved.

And Evelyn could not bring himself to attempt to define the situation to her. To do so would appear too practical, too prosaic. And the situation between them was too delicate in its beauty to bear such rough treatment. How could he say to her:

"Look here, darling! All this is lovely, but where are we?" He must obviously await his opportunity. And to be forced to wait exasperated his nerves. Such was his character: he had a horror of an undefined situation. He must have his programme clearly before him if he was to be at peace within. No matter what the programme! He preferred a harassing programme to no programme. Marriage? He was entirely ready for marriage and all its risks. But she was just the kind of girl to laugh at the notion of marriage. Liaison? He was entirely ready for that too, with all its ecstasies and frightful trammels of deceit. But was it to be understood to be permanent? Or merely a charming, transient episode in their lives? No. The latter alternative was absurd, for she was passionately in love with him. He thought of her all the time, of her wishes and her happiness. He did not think of himself, except in so far as he wanted an answer to the question, "Where are we?" The question could not be put. It was too crude...He felt the weight on the chest. But her kisses were surpassingly sweet, her companionship quite marvellous. She was utterly his. And he loved her unselfishly.

"Shall we start out?" she whispered. "I vote for the Louvre. It isn't three o'clock."

"The Louvre!" he objected.

"Not to see the Titian Venus?"

"But the Louvre's so hackneyed."

"That's why we must go there." She kissed him. "Have you forgotten we're going to be tourists? What fun!"

"The Louvre then!" he yielded, and this time it was he who kissed her.

She slipped from his knee, passed into the bedroom, and returned, laughing, in the mackintosh, and the Baedeker in her hand. Entrancing child!

As they descended the frowsy, dubious stairs he asked:

"Got the car here?"

"Oh no! Tourists in mackintoshes don't have cars. They take taxis."

"Of course. What was I thinking of?" he agreed, joining in the make-believe.

Outside she glanced up at the sky and said:

"I'm so glad it looks like rain, for the sake of my mackintosh."

The taxi was rolling along the rue de Rivoli, and the Louvre well in sight, and their hands comfortably clasped, when Evelyn suddenly signalled to the driver to stop.

"What is it?" Gracie's face changed from joy to alarm.

"We shan't go to the Louvre," he said firmly, masterfully. "Very well, darling," she instantly acquiesced. "Anywhere you please." Her submissiveness made him ashamed, for his tone had been a trick.

"It's closed on Mondays," he said with casualness. "We'd both forgotten that."

"I believe you remembered it all the time," said Gracie, accusing him with a laugh; but when she saw on Evelyn's face the beginning of a half-serious rebuttal of the charge, she ceased laughing and put a soothing hand on his knee. "No, I didn't really believe that. What a tease I am!"

He had never noticed in her any tendency to tease.

"Well now, what is to be the next move?"

"I'll tell you," she replied at once. "But you can turn it down if you don't like it. I want to buy a frock at Jolie Laitière. Of course, darling, you hate shopping."

"I love it," he said. "When I get the chance. Especially in a big shop."

The fact was that he was always strongly attracted by the spectacle of the organisation of any large commercial establishment, and he considered that in this respect department stores were the nearest rivals of the big hotels.

Gracie popped her blithe touristic head out of the taxi-window and reinstructed the driver, and the taxi swerved into the rue des Pyrénées. She was gleeful; the Louvre, demolished in one second, no longer existed for her. Her mood communicated itself to Evelyn; her girlishness and the intimacy of the taxi had lightened the weight on his chest; life was joyous. Now they were going up the Avenue de l'Opéra. Just south of the Place de l'Opéra there was the customary block of traffic, and scores of vehicles were chafing against the white baton on a pigmy policeman.

"Arrêtez/" cried Gracie, though the taxi was stationary at the kerb. She opened the door and jumped down. "That's a car that daddy always hires, in front! I remember the number on its tail."

She ran ahead a few steps and tattooed on the window of the car. Evelyn thought: "Is she mad? What will she do next?" He too got out, judging that the safest course was to stick to her. The door of the car swung open. Sir Henry Savott's head appeared. Gracie eagerly kissed her father. Already the girl was innocently chattering.

"Here's Mr. Orcham. I waited three days for weather at Dover; it was simply frightful, and when I got on the boat *he* came on board. He looked after me on the train. And now he's finished his work and I've made him take an afternoon off. We were going to the Louvre, only it's closed on Mondays; so I'm dragging him off to do some shopping with me, and he has to buy some cigars. You off to London by the four o'clock, daddy?"

Sir Henry nodded.

"I thought so from the luggage."

It all sounded impeccably proper and natural, and Gracie's demeanour had the perfect grace of easy innocence. But what was the significance of that touch about cigars?

"And where are you picnicking, child?" asked Sir Henry.

"Oh! At St. Cloud as usual."

The two men shook hands. Sir Henry said that he had had one night in Paris. He did not pursue the enquiry concerning Gracie. He accepted her statements with bland and kindly indifference. It was no affair of his where she might be picnicking, or whom she might have inveigled into an afternoon off. The block was loosened; vehicles began to move; there was some impatient hooting of horns because Sir Henry's car and Evelyn's taxi were impeding the outer line of traffic; car and taxi stood their ground, and the taxis and cars behind swerved past them.

"I say, Evelyn," said Sir Henry. "I suppose you're at the Montaigne. I shall probably be telephoning to you early tomorrow morning. Say nine o'clock?"

Evelyn collected his wits. If Gracie could invent misleading but persuasive detail on the instant, he reckoned that he could do as much. He answered nonchalantly:

"Well, I'm not quite sure about to-night and to-morrow. I've nothing else to do here..."

"Everything all right with old Laugier?" Sir Henry interrupted.

"Quite. Quite. And I had an idea of running up to Brussels to-night. I've heard of a proposition there that might possibly suit us."

"Really?"

"Yes," said Evelyn, and thought: "If he asks me the name of the hotel I'm done. Ah! The Splendide would serve." He said aloud, but in a semi-confidential murmur: "The Splendide."

"Really! But you'll be back in London to-morrow evening, Evelyn?"

"I might or I might not. It depends."

"But the Licensing Commission business. I saw it in the paper to-day."

Evelyn explained.

"Oh well, if that's so, I shan't trouble to telephone you to-morrow. It was about the evidence." Sir Henry glanced at his watch, and then proceeded to demonstrate that he had been studying Licensing Reform with some care. He raised, briefly, several points. Evelyn's mind had been void of Licensing Reform for days, and he had feared that his erudition on the subject had left him for ever. But Sir Henry's questions brought it all back complete, absolutely complete. He welcomed its return with satisfaction, and answered the questions with satisfaction--and fully. Sir Henry might have studied the matter with some care, but he, Evelyn, would prove to him that he was an amateur talking to an expert. And Evelyn did prove it. As for Gracie, she amiably and modestly listened to the panjandrums, without the slightest impatience. Sir Henry glanced at his watch again.

"I must be off. I'm not quite sure about my seat in the train. I'm going to Berlin to-morrow."

"Films, daddy?"

Sir Henry nodded. He kissed his daughter, shook hands with Evelyn, and was gone at once, a second traffic block having been by this time freed.

2.

Ensconced again in the intimacy of the taxi, Gracie and Evelyn broadly smiled to one another.

"Fancy seeing daddy like that! I couldn't not have two words with him, could I?" Gracie justified herself.

"Of course not," Evelyn agreed. "And you're very clever. But what's this about me wanting cigars?"

"Oh!" she exclaimed, and popped her head out and told the driver to go to the tobacco-bureau under the Grand Hotel. The driver complained that, according to the police rules, he would have to make the circuit of the Opera in order to reach the bureau.

"Deux fois si vous voulez," Gracie laughed. Then she turned to Evelyn. "I noticed yesterday you hadn't any cigars. A man must have cigars. I intend to buy you some. It's a good bureau, the one under the Grand Hotel is. If it isn't under the Grand Hotel it's next door. Anyhow he knows where I mean." She indicated the driver.

"This is the height of hospitality," said Evelyn, and comically raised his hat.

"And you're pretty clever too!" she went on. "What was the bit about Brussels?"

"Nothing," he said. "It just occurred to me and I brought it in."

They both laughed again. Nevertheless Evelyn was somewhat perturbed by the brilliant glibness of the perversions of truth with which she had fed her deceived father. Not a word about Tessa. (Well, of course not.) If she could hoodwink one man she could hoodwink another. Hers was a rich, wondrous individuality; but could she be called a reliable helpmeet? And she had been so light-hearted and prettily shameless in the bravura performance.

Arrived at the tobacco-bureau, Evelyn was requested to choose cigars, and Gracie insisted on paying for a box of fifty and on carrying the box--in addition to the red Baedeker.

He was perturbed anew. Was it her dream that they two would live together in the dubious apartment for ever?

Evelyn paid off the taxi, and they walked side by side in the thronged, noisy, gay streets round the back of the Opéra to Jolie Laitière. At the foot of the wide and high stone-faced façade were a series of al fresco counters, covered with an apparent confusion of stuffs, feminine garments and fal-lals of a hundred varieties, all of them fingered, handled, and turned over and over by crowds of besieging, appraising women. Behind the counters, against the immense windows of the store, a row of men stood in the dying light and in the cold, hatless but overcoated, who with chilled, bluish hands served the women while protecting the goods as well as they could from the rapacious female assault.

More business was transacted at those counters than had been transacted in the whole establishment during its early days. The Lovely Milkmaid had started a long career as a small shop whose dimensions were not unsuited to its sentimental title. It had been burnt down once, and rebuilt three times, larger and larger, growing incessantly until it was now one of the wonders of the retail world. But it was still called the Lovely Milkmaid, and no Parisian perceived any incongruity in the name. Indeed the good will of the mere name was probably worth some millions of francs.

Gracie and Evelyn went in by one of the ten grand entrances. Heat smote them; light smote them. The winter day died much earlier in the store than in the street. Electricity was festooned everywhere. Dozens of counters, hundreds of saleswomen and salesmen in black, multitudes of women customers and a few men. Incalculable heaps of commodities in all tints. Lifts on every side ascending and descending. Huge as the place appeared from the street, it appeared much more huge within. It was measureless, infinite. In the centre a monumental stairway, all balustraded with lamps, rose in curves from storey to storey till it ended at the sixth. Above the stairway, in the roof, an incredible chandelier of a thousand lamps! Gracie pushed forward through the throngs, between the counters,straight to the stairway.

"I want the first floor," she said. "It's more amusing to walk up..."

"You seem to know the geography here," Evelyn observed.

"No. I've only been here once--for Tessa. She came with me."

On the first floor they were in another universe, the universe of frocks, coats, cloaks, peignoirs. All seemed to be disorder; every individual was preoccupied, busy. Yet Gracie had not gazed for ten seconds at a long straight range of hung frocks before a plump little black-robed woman of thirty-five or so materialised magically at her elbow.

"Madame desires?"

The plump little woman's tone, speciously urbane, conveyed the great truth that the one object of her existence was to devote herself solely to the satisfaction of the wishes, however exacting or capricious, of Gracie. Soon the saleswoman had three day-frocks on her arm, and was leading Gracie towards a trying-on cubicle in a street of cubicles.

"Don't leave me, darling," Gracie murmured.

All three entered a cubicle full of mirrors and lamps, and glistening with polished woodwork. The door was shut.

"No, not that one," said Gracie. "My husband loves not green."

"A pink then," said the saleswoman. "Monsieur loves pink?" She turned deferentially to Evelyn, as to one whose preferences were a law. "I have a ravishing pink." She left the cubicle, hurrying.

"What's the idea of all this?" Evelyn asked, but he said nothing about having been made a husband. "Is it for Tessa?"

"Certainly not. It's for me."

"But--"

"You are *sweet*" Gracie laughed, and kissed him. "Don't you see I want to be a tourist? These things I have on don't go at all with a mackintosh and a Baedeker."

The saleswoman came back with the ravishing pink. Gracie took off her mackintosh, and then her frock. Evelyn, abashed, caught the saleswoman's eye with alarm, but the saleswoman's eye gave no sign that she was shocked. Gracie put on the ravishing pink.

"That suits madame to a marvel. Is it not so, monsieur?"

Gracie surveyed herself in a mirror.

"I think it will do," said she. "I am pressed for time."

"But madame," the saleswoman protested against this rapidity of decision. "These others--they are worth the trouble of essaying."

So Gracie essayed the others. But she held to her first ideal--the ravishing pink, and put it on again.

"I will take it."

"It needs a quite little touch on the shoulder."

"That is nothing," said Gracie. "I do not wish that it should fit too well. I will wear it at once. You can send my old frock to my address."

"But certainly, madame," said the saleswoman, as suspicious now as she was astounded. She seized the old frock, held it up and examined it. "That," said she, "that is high dressmaking."

"Now can I try on some cloaks--in here?" Gracie asked.

"But with pleasure, madame."

Another saleswoman was fetched, with an assortment of coats. The first saleswoman remained; the cubicle seemed to be full of women. Twenty minutes passed on the choosing of a coat.

"And now a hat," said Gracie.

"Here, madame?"

"Yes."

"Ah! madame, that will be more difficult. The department of hats--"

"I supplicate you."

"It is well, madame."

The first saleswoman vanished once more. The second saleswoman was studying Gracie's old hat. A third saleswoman appeared, followed by a young girl bearing a shallow basket of hats. With five women in the cubicle Evelyn deemed himself extinguished. But as soon as a new hat was established on Gracie's head, all four assistants brought him back to life and importance by one combined glance of appeal for approval. A hat was selected from a dozen. Gracie resumed the mackintosh, strapped it at the waist, took the Baedeker, her bag, the box of cigars. And the first saleswoman, price-tickets in hand, escorted the lovers to a cash-desk, and complex arrangements were concluded for the delivery of Gracie's cast-offs.

"Madame can count on it," said the first saleswoman. *"Au revoir, madame. Au revoir, monsieur.* Many thanks. To the pleasure of seeing you again."

As soon as they were free of the assistants, Gracie laughed with abandonment.

"Isn't it too lovely? Don't you adore me like this? Shall we have tea now?"

"Where, my dear?"

"Why! Here, of course. Upstairs."

They regained the vast curving stairway. He took her arm, and she pressed his forearm between her arm and body, and leaned slightly against him.

"Trying-on's great fun," she said. "But it's frightfully exhausting." Because he was supporting her she wanted to feel fatigue, and she did feel it.

He reflected:

"Supposing I was seen by someone I knew arming a young woman up these stairs! They'd instantly think I'd brought her to Paris for the week-end--a typist or some girl of that sort, they'd think--with those clothes she's wearing now. Whereas if she'd looked really smart they wouldn't have thought that, and what's more, if she'd been wearing her own *très chic* things, I doubt whether I should have taken her arm. Extraordinary how people always think that girls of a lower class than themselves, or a higher, are less moral than they are!" He wondered what Miss Cass would say and do if he tried to abduct her to Paris for a week-end. The mere notion made him smile. Miss Cass would assuredly give notice--and with haughtiness too. But at that moment he didn't care who might see him with Gracie on his arm. He abandoned himself without a qualm to her capturing love, recalling sardonically the line of Racine:

"Venus all clinging to her helpless prey."

He savoured the sensation of being a prey--especially a prey which could when it chose turn on its captor and tear her to pieces.

"What are you laughing at?" Gracie asked in a low voice charged with her love.

"Smiling," he corrected her.

"Well, smiling."

"Your clothes, my dear."

"I'm so glad you like them, darling!" she breathed. (Not that he did like them!)

"How do you know there's a restaurant in this place?" he questioned, mischievous in his happiness.

"Well, there must be."

"I'll bet anything there isn't," he said.

"And how do you know?"

"I know because I haven't seen a single notice about it," he said. "They think here that customers come to buy--not to drink tea. And I beg to state that your acquaintance with these big shops is still very imperfect."

"Perhaps it is," she assented.

She questioned a liftman on the third floor. No. So far as the liftman knew there was no restaurant in the Lovely Milkmaid.

"You are clever!" she said to Evelyn admiringly. She would lose no pretext for admiring him. "I'm tired," she murmured. "Let's sit down."

They were now in the household furniture department. Gracie glanced around for chairs.

"Not a chair," she said.

"Scores of chairs," he corrected her, and moved two chairs from a dining-room suite close by, and put them near the balustrade.

"I meant chairs for customers," she said. "They'll come and complain"

"When they do, we'll deal with the new situation," said Evelyn

"Oh, darling! I'm so happy you're happy." They sat.

"There's one good thing," said Evelyn. "Anglo-Saxons may come here for frocks, but they certainly won't come here for furniture."

" What do you mean, darling?"

"I mean we're safe."

Gracie made no answer.

They both looked over the brass-ornamented steel railing down, down, into the deep well of the vast shop. The string of electric lamps beneath the railing confused and dazzled their eyes; but they had a general vision of the spectacle of the glittering mart; the bottom of the well seemed to be packed with a struggling mob of women's hats, among which a few masculine hats moved strangely--hats of intruders, of Paul Prys, who had no right to insinuate themselves into this illimitable, esoteric purdah. The intermediate floors, of which the lovers from their vantage could see only the half on the opposite side of the well, were almost equally crowded; the stairway was as busy with women as a street, and at short intervals crowded lifts could be glimpsed, sliding mysterious and silent up or down. And everywhere, except in the lifts, half the women, bareheaded and in black, helping the other half, hatted and in colours, to adorn their persons for the allurement of absent males: while at broad, sloping desks men were writing out bills and receiving cash, cash, endless cash, and in the parcels-enclosures girls and boys were tying up parcels, parcels, parcels.

"It's rather wonderful, I must say," Evelyn remarked.

"It makes me feel sad," Gracie answered.

"Sad! Why? Half a minute ago you seemed to have so much happiness in you you didn't know what to do with it all." Evelyn's tone was benevolently bantering.

"There are too many of us. Women, I mean. And we have to fight. It reminds me of the world, this shop does: too many women, and all fighting for a niche and trying to stretch ten francs into twenty to make the best of themselves. I can see them all naked. I can see into their naked minds, and all their minds are the same. But I haven't seen a happy face. Every face I've seen is anxious. Do you know what this place is--it's the Western Front."

"What do you know of the Western Front, my dear? You aren't old enough to have been a Waac."

"Don't I know! I've read 'All Quiet,' and I've read 'Not so Quiet.' Not know the Western Front! Why! In a few years, ten, twenty, it'll be only people as young as I am, and younger, who *will* know what the Western Front was. And I tell you this is the real Western Front to-day."

She had suddenly fallen into a new mood, and Evelyn could feel that she wanted to envelop him also in the mood. He resisted.

"Anyway," he said, turning to her and smiling. "Anyway, you haven't been trying to make the best of yourself this afternoon. You've been trying to make the worst of yourself. Only you haven't succeeded. You simply can't wear bad clothes as they ought to be worn. You give the show away all the time. You told me the other day--yesterday, was it?--you wanted to be common. Well, you just can't be common. And you've only half-done the job even this afternoon. Look at your five-guinea shoes, and your stockings, and your gloves, and your bag. And think of your undies. This noble effort of yours to look common is merely pathetic. I'd give something to have heard what those *vendeuses* said about it all, after we'd gone. They must have wondered what on earth you were up to." He patted her knee--one touch--affectionately, reassuringly.

3.

A silence. She was gazing straight in front of her.

She said, in an even voice, as though she were asking the time:

"Would you like us to get married?"

He was discomposed. There was no end to the girl's incalculableness. Fancy starting such a subject in the public promiscuity of the Lovely Milkmaid! And what a misinterpretation she had put upon the spectacle of the interior of the Lovely Milkmaid! He controlled himself.

"Of course I should like us to marry. You know I should."

"You know, you don't love me."

"Liar!" he gently smiled.

"You don't know what love is, real love."

"My dear! My dear! I undertake to say my ignorance isn't quite as complete as you imagine to yourself you think it is. I'm a very learned man."

"Evelyn! Listen! You see this well. There's a--a chasm as deep as that between us. Deeper. You think I left you all alone this morning because I was angry with you. It wasn't that. I left you so that I could look down that awful big hole by myself. And I couldn't bear to look down it. I pretended it wasn't there. And I've been pretending all the afternoon. Because I did want to be nice to you, and I do. But it's been all pretending. I mean pretending about *you,* not about me. You're everything to me, and I haven't tried to hide it. Now have I?" Evelyn did not speak. "But I'm not everything to you. You're only trying to make yourself think I'm everything to you. Because you're a heavenly kind man. D'you know why I kept you in my flat last night? D'you think it was because I was so terribly hungry for you? It wasn't that. It was because I just had to find out whether you loved me. I could wait--but I couldn't wait to know that--"

"But--"

"No. Please. Don't stop me. Let me empty my mind now; I've begun. I've told you before I'm nothing, nothing at all. And I've told you I'm a beast. And so I am. It was only half true what I told you about Saturday. I kept you waiting all day on Saturday partly because I wanted to see how you'd stand it. And I chose those rooms so that they'd frighten you off, if you could be frightened off. And I asked you to bring your luggage along so that it should be there all ready if you stayed. And I had the tea-things all ready as well. You noticed there were two cups. And I've told you about leaving off my rouge. Somehow I couldn't help telling you about that, and I wasn't really tired yesterday afternoon. But I am to-day. And I didn't ask you to stay the night until the very last thing because I knew how nice and shy you are, and I didn't intend to give you time to hesitate. You had to decide one way or the other at once. And--Oh! It all sounds frightfully mixed up. But motives *are* mixed up--especially women's. Now and then yesterday afternoon and evening I felt like sticking at nothing to keep you. I won't go into details--you can think of them without me helping you. But at other times now and then I tried to do nothing that would help you. I tried to play the game, and I did play it. And I went to sleep absolutely sure you did love me. I was happy. And I dreamt happy dreams of you. And I was happy when I woke up this morning, until I saw you in your big overcoat. It was the overcoat that began it. You couldn't lie in bed and wait for me to wake up. You were too restless for something outside me. And then the newspaper. Those paragraphs. And what you said then...I've been happy today too. But I've been happy in *my* love, not yours. It is happiness to be in love. But it's misery as well, if you're the only one who's in love. Now you've heard. I'm a beast. But I'm honest. At any rate I've been honest with you. And I'm not going to cry, or whine, or anything of the sort. I'm going to be terribly nice, because it isn't a bit your fault. You deserve I should be nice. No, no! I shall play the game all the time now."

At this moment a middle-aged and bearded floor-walker appeared from behind them.

"One occupies oneself with you, monsieur, madame?" he asked with a ceremonious bow, looking more at Evelyn than at Gracie.

Gracie replied at once:

"While essaying your chairs, my husband and I are discussing the matter, monsieur." She smiled urbanely.

"Perfectly, madame. At your service, madame." With another bow the man went away.

Gracie made a humorous face at Evelyn, who was startled, even a little shocked by her extraordinary aplomb. He himself was incapable of changing his mood with her lightning rapidity. He said gravely:

"My dear! You can only play the game by marrying me." He was determined that she should marry him. He foresaw marvellous hours with such a wife. Her mind alone would be a continual refreshment and inspiration. She would be an intellectual equal. He ignored the incalculable flightiness of her mind. Nevertheless the thought ran through his whole being:

"Her liabilities will exceed her assets." And was gone. She said:

"When you said we were safe here, did you mean you don't want to be seen with me like this by anybody who knows us?" He was about to prevaricate, but he decided not to do so.

"I did, my dear."

"But why?"

"Well, it's natural, isn't it--in the circumstances? Don't you think we have an air?..People do talk, you know."

She went on:

"Darling, if you were in love with me as you fancy you are--oh, quite sincerely!--you simply wouldn't think of a thing like that. It wouldn't occur to you, and even if it did, you'd laugh at it. No, you wouldn't. You'd glory in it. I do glory in it. I'd deliberately go out to be seen by people we know. It would be magnificent, like walking in the wind and rain." Her voice took on its full richness. "Darling, that's the chasm between us. You're afraid of the consequences of love. I'm not. I want every consequence, and I don't care, because I'm in love. You do care. Darling, when you said you must go to London tomorrow--and leave me all by myself--" She broke off. "You're an artist in *your* way. I admire you for being an artist--and a great artist. I know women are supposed to be the enemies of art, when they're in love with the artist. It's been said hundreds of times."

"And aren't they? I'm being frank with you."

"A man ought never to be frank with a woman. Not one woman in a thousand can stand it, unless he's in a temper. And you aren't in a temper. You're too damnably self-possessed. But I happen to be the one woman. I can stand it. To me your frankness is like eating an olive. It's the sharp taste of it I adore. You know, astringent. Well, go on being frank."

"You haven't answered my question: aren't women the enemies of art?" Evelyn murmured, with an appearance of complete calm. But he was excited by the flattery of the word 'artist,' which she had so stimulatingly pronounced. She understood him: that was it. Yes, he was a creative artist, in *his* way, as she had said.

She answered:

"Of course women are the enemies of art, when they're in love with the artist. It's their business to be the enemies of art and of everything else that makes men egotists. Both sexes can't be egotistic. If they were, it would be the end of the world, and the death of society. Men are only amateur egotists. Women are professional. It's their nature, and so it's right, because the divine mind did it. When you see a woman has got hold of a man, firm, and she's forcing him to fight for his art, and beating him--it's the finest, most gorgeous thing you ever could see! It's supreme! It's God himself, working out his plan, that is! And when she's clasping him tight, and he struggles, and he gives up struggling and the artist in him sighs terribly and dies happy in her inflexible arms, and she smiles, that's God's smile. It's a tremendous moment. I'm telling you; but I might just as well not tell you. You won't understand. Can't. No man can. Only women can understand what is the greatest thing in the world. When I hear people say a man has ruined himself for a woman, I laugh. I hug myself. I know of three. There were General Boulanger and Parnell. I've read nearly everything that's been written about those two. They thrill me whenever I think of them. They sacrificed everything for women, and the women took it as a matter of course. That's the spirit. What lives! What ruin! It was so lovely, and majestic, and awful, I could cry. But God *is* awful."

She turned and looked at him, and Evelyn faced her. She had not raised her voice; her tranquillity was as awful as God; but Evelyn was determined to meet her eyes. He thought:

"And she's clasped me tight," and, recalling her embrace, quivered as one quivers at a peril past. He said:

"And the third one?" She dropped her voice:

"Leo."

"Leo?"

"Cheddar."

"Oh! Him."

"Yes. Him. One of God's errors. Leo chose wrong. Not his fault, I expect. But he did. And he can't undo it. But *he* understands. He's sacrificed everything for me. Even his greatness. He might have been great, if he hadn't met me. He preferred being my victim to being great. Wherever I go he goes. He's quarrelled with his brother because of me. His character is as splendid as his mind. But I couldn't love him. I tell you I could kneel down and crouch on my breasts before him, and wash his feet with my tears, and absolutely implore him to forgive me. But he knows there's nothing to forgive. He knows it's no more my fault than it's his."

She stood up.

"But we haven't finished," said Evelyn. They gazed at one another.

"Yes, we have, and I can't bear this place any longer. It's full of vibrations that scare me."

"That's the central heating," said Evelyn grimly, half closing his eyes.

"You can call it by that name if you like, darling." Her tone was softened.

The floorwalker lay in wait for them, ready to pounce. Carrying the chairs back to the rest of the dining-room suite, Evelyn made no attempt to evade him; nor Gracie either.

"Eh bien, monsieur," she said to the man. *"Pour cette salle-à-manger?"*

"Monsieur and madame have decided themselves?"

Another member of the selling staff of the Lovely Milkmaid came to assist the floorwalker in the sale of the suite. Then the floorwalker departed, leaving the second man to the job.

"What's she going to do now?" thought Evelyn, as he watched Gracie minutely examining the suite.

It was a very ugly suite, very banal, the suite of large-scale rationalised commerce; thousands of precisely similar suites were the pride of modest, comfortable homes up and down France.

"There are naturally leaves for the table?" Gracie demanded.

"Yes, madame. Two."

"One can buy supplementary chairs?"

"But there are six, madame."

"But one can buy more?"

"But yes, madame."

"And another sideboard?"

"But yes, madame. But perhaps it would be more simple to buy two suites, madame, if madame's dining-room is very large, if madame has many guests."

"That is an idea!" said Gracie.

"What *is* she going to do now?" thought Evelyn.

She bought two suites, and six extra chairs--eighteen chairs in all. The salesman made a calculation: something over twenty-thousand francs.

"Payment on delivery," said Gracie. "To-morrow?"

"Ah, madame!" said the dark Latin male with prodigious apologetic deference, "if madame would give me two more days! It will be necessary for me to communicate with the factory as to the supplementary chairs."

"Very well, Thursday."

She gave the St. Cloud address. The salesman bowed almost orientally. Twice in less than an hour had Gracie confounded the Lovely Milkmaid.

When the formalities were finished, Evelyn enquired:

"And the answer to all this furniture riddle, please?"

She lifted her shoulders negligently.

"A surprise for the landlady of my little hotel. She's been incredibly kind about Tessa. She's an angel. And her dining-room furniture is all falling to pieces."

They descended the stairway in silence, and on the ground-floor made a difficult path for themselves through the ruthless egotistic throng of priestesses of the martyrdom of men. Evelyn noticed a counter placarded: *"Chemises de nuit. Occasions."* Without consulting Gracie he bought the most expensive, paid for it, stuck the tiny parcel into his overcoat pocket.

"I don't very much care for pyjamas for the instruments of God," he said.

"Perhaps we might have a few flowers," she suggested, ignoring his purchase.

He enquired for the flower-department and bought flowers of his own choosing.

Outside in the dark populous street, where the sack of the alfresco counters was still proceeding, he raised his arm for a passing taxi.

"See. What's your number?"

"But we aren't going home yet!" Gracie protested.

"Yes, we are--with all these parcels!"

She told him the number. He told the chauffeur. He opened the door of the little, low taxi. She got in, bowing her head to avoid the lintel. Just before turning into the boulevard he halted the taxi in front of a confectioner's illuminated window which displayed an irresistible assortment of éclairs, madeleines, babas, brioches, tartelettes, millefeuilles, and petits fours.

"Wait for me one moment, will you?" he appealed, getting out of the vehicle, and presently came back with a quite sizeable fragile parcel. They drove on.

Chapter 59 TEMPER

Parcel-laden, they entered the deteriorated, dubious, garishly-lit drawing-room, and saw again the statue of the almost-nude woman, the paintings of almost-nude women in the heavy tarnished gilt frames, the tiger-skin, and the clock which one day in the past had slipped into timeless eternity at seven minutes to three. The red Baedeker was dropped on to the centre-table, together with sundry items--the cigars, the cakes, the flowers, Gracie's bag, and the slim parcel drawn by Evelyn from his overcoat pocket.

"Now I wonder whether it would be asking you too much to make the tea," said Evelyn. The formula was ceremonious, but the tone commanding.

"Hadn't I better do the flowers first?" Gracie suggested.

"Men before flowers," said Evelyn. "Organise your energy, my dear. You can see to the flowers while the water is boiling for the tea. And give me your mackintosh, will you?"

"Yes, darling!"

She went away mysteriously smiling into the bathroom with the flowers and the cakes. He hung up her mackintosh and his overcoat and hat in the ante-chamber. He unpacked the box of cigars and put it on a side-table with the Baedeker. He took her bag and the slim parcel into the bedroom; and then he stood idle, wondering what he could do next. He thought of his yesterday's suit and pulled it from the wardrobe. After a minute or two she called out from the bathroom: "What are you doing?"

"Attending to my clothes."

She appeared in the bedroom. She had tied round her waist a bath-towel for an apron. In the apron and the cheap reach-me-down frock and hat she looked, to Evelyn, perfectly delicious, not to say exciting.

"I thought I heard brushing," she laughed. "It's like home. Not my home at home. A nice little home."

He was brushing his trousers laid carefully along the length of the bed. He glanced up.

"Why the towel, my dear?"

"Flowers, darling. They're rather messy. I want two vases--three. The water's on." Her eye roved about the room. She snatched a vase from the mantelpiece, and disappeared into the drawing-room.

As he finished brushing the suit and restored it to the wardrobe, Evelyn reflected:

"And that's the girl who made that frightening speech to me in the Jolie Laitière?..Like a home, is it, a nice little home! A disreputable *appartement* on the boulevard! And I bet it isn't costing her a penny less than five pounds a night!"

He would not admit, even to himself, that it was like a home. But he felt that it was, and that he was the master in it. He was ingenuously happy and tyrannic in it. He loved the towel-apron. He heard the rattle of crockery. He heard her passing busily to and fro between the bathroom and the drawing-room. He said to himself that she was doing his will. But the menace of her speech in the furniture department of the Jolie Laitière shot lancinating darts into his mind. As he was drawing the curtains together she came, apronless now, into the bedroom with a vase of flowers and deposited it on a table.

"Tea's all ready," she said in a quiet tone falsely casual, and threw her hat on to the bed.

Then she took his hand and led him, a male child-tyrant, towards the tea. Was it symbolic, that act? Was he the victimised captive of her ideal? "I'll teach her!" he thought grandly.

He felt a condescending pity for Leo Cheddar, the hopeless prisoner. He was bound to despise Leo for a weakling. And yet, on the previous afternoon, as he sat on the professional egotist's bed, had not he, Evelyn, in a single moment become utterly weak at the sight of her beauty? Was she his, or was he hers? He had strange fears in the midst of his masterfulness.

The tea was indeed all ready, very neatly arranged on the centre-table, the cakes on two plates, and a vase of resplendent flowers between them. She had been very quick, and very efficient too. He could not deny that she had the capacity to make a man comfortable.

"It's delicious having tea together like this," said Gracie, as, having filled the cups, she bit into the first cake. "You're a terrible sultan, but you do have ideas. When I think of you lunching all alone and me lunching all alone to-day I feel as if I could weep real tears. I'm frightfully sorry, darling. I*was* a beast. Call me a beast."

He smiled magnanimously.

"Now don't be forgiving. I couldn't stand it. Call me a beast."

"Beast!" said he obediently.

Her mouth half full, she stopped eating the cake, as if a new thought had occurred to her.

"And you've got more than ideas--you've got taste. Anyhow in confectionery. This brioche is the finest ever! Oh! And I must make quite sure what your taste's like in something else."

She jumped up and ran into the bedroom and came back with the slim parcel, which she undid. She shook out the folds of the nightdress, and, close at Evelyn's side, held it against her figure.

"It goes with the frock," he said.

She moved away, and examined herself as well as she could in the overmantel mirror. Not satisfied, she pulled a chair on to the tiger-skin and perched tiptoe on it, so as to have an entire view of the garment in the glass. And then laughed quite loudly.

"Isn't it too comic?" she giggled. "And when you think there are millions of girls who would really adore it--and men too!"

"It's exactly what you deserve," said Evelyn. "And I should like some more tea, please."

"Oh!" she protested, stepping down. "Don't imagine *I* don't adore it! Because I do. So do you. We're both a bit morbid in our liking for ugliness--when it's ugly enough. Yes, I admire your morbid taste. Poor Tessa would drop dead if she saw me in this affair...Your tea! Your tea!" She threw the nightdress across his knees, and poured out another cup for him. He calmly folded the garment in its original folds, and pitched it with accurate aim on to an easy-chair.

"Now we'll continue," said Evelyn.

"Oh! You needn't be afraid," she exclaimed. "I shall continue till every one of these cakes is eaten."

"I didn't mean tea," he said. "I meant we'd continue about that chasm of yours." Gracie's face changed. "I always like to have everything clear and straight; and the sooner the better. You've been upset because I told you I should have to go to London to-morrow morning."

"And leave me here all alone."

"Yes. And leave you here all alone. Well, you know, I couldn't help it happening like that. Just a chance--"

"Haven't I said before that I don't believe in chance?" she interrupted him. "And there isn't any chance. How could there be? It was a sign. Fate meant it, so that I should see what your real feelings were--in time. If it hadn't happened like that I might never have known what your real feelings were until it was too late. Now I do know. It makes no difference that you haven't had to go to London after all. I *know.* And it wasn't chance. I'm not blaming you, darling! You are you, and you can't alter yourself." She was sweet, but grave.

"But can't you see?" he reasoned. "Can't you see I shouldn't have gone because I wanted to go? I should have hated to go. The very thought of going was awful. But I should have had to go. There wouldn't have been any alternative. It's best to look facts in the face."

"No alternative?"

"No." Evelyn was almost curt. He added, to placate her:

"Of course if I'd been ill--But so long as I could physically go, I should just have had to go."

"What about morally?" she asked.

"Morally?"

"Yes. You said 'physically.' Is physically more important than morally? In your opinion?"

He hesitated.

"No," he agreed. "Instead of 'physically' I ought to have said 'physically and morally.'"

"So you think you were morally able to go?"

"I think I should have been morally compelled to go, Mrs. Counsel-for-the-Prosecution."

"Well," she said. "If this is cross-examining, it's only because I'm trying to get. everything 'absolutely clear and straight'--for you and for me too. That was what you said you wanted."

"Quite!" he admitted.

"This licensing business is the most important thing on earth for you."

"Not at all," he cheerfully contradicted her. "The most important thing on earth to me is to keep my word, my engagements. You see, I'm indispensable to the case for Reform. I put the case together. And I'm the engine that drives it forward."

"So that if you did happen to be in for a serious illness, the campaign would fail. There's nobody to take your place. You've taught no one else the job. You've deliberately kept yourself indispensable. You're the director of the finest hotel in the world, it runs perfectly so long as you're in charge, but you don't believe in the maxim that a director ought as quickly as he can to teach the people he directs how to carry on without him."

2.

"See here!" said Evelyn. "Where did you pick up these notions about organisation?"

"Daddy," she answered. "Daddy always says that a boss who is indispensable is a rotten organiser and a rotten boss. He used to take that line sometimes about my housekeeping. Darling!" she proceeded with no pause. "You needn't answer. I don't want to catch you out. I'll admit that now and then a man may really be indispensable, and if he doesn't stay on the spot everything falls to pieces. Here, for instance. Here you *are* indispensable. No one can take your place here. You're so indispensable that nobody could possibly be more indispensable. All this hotel and licensing business and so on is only machinery *for* living. Here it's a question of living itself. It's more vital than any machinery could ever even begin to be. I daresay it's most frightfully important that customers in your restaurants should be able to get champagne and whisky every night till 2a.m. instead of 11 p.m. Still, champagne and whisky are only helps to living. Sort of preliminaries to being properly alive. But here, you and I have got past preliminaries. We're living. Or we were living, until you came in this morning and told me while I was in my bath that you must stop living--and me too--because you had to rush off to London to argue with M.P.'s and things about whisky and champagne."

"Is that quite the way to put it?"

"It's the only way I can put it, darling. And any other way would be merely the voice of common sense. You won't tell me that you don't know that common sense is not the law of laws. If you tell me that, I tell you you just don't know the first word about living. Jesus Christ never said anything about common sense...Darling! Please don't fidget your legs." She left her chair and with one bound planted herself on his knees, and curved her arms loosely round his neck. "Darling!" Her voice softened into a dreamy tenderness. "We were divine last night, darling. God was pleased with us. But this morning...to-day--"

"Yes," said Evelyn, and his tone was hard because he hated her, he was afraid of her, in that moment. "And you're being the professional egotist and doing all you can to cure my egotism. You're trying to make me ruin myself, and you call it working out God's plan."

"No, no."

"You said so yourself this afternoon."

"But surely you can see I was exaggerating, then!" she exclaimed. "I'm always ready to compromise...If only you'd given us a few days, a week. You could easily have arranged that, with all your cleverness. But no! We were in heaven last night. And this morning, the very next day, when I'm lying in my bath in front of you, you smash our heaven to pieces. You couldn't keep your whisky and champagne waiting. Not an hour! As I said, I don't blame you. It's myself I blame. I was mistaken, not you. I laid a bet, and my stake was everything I had. And I've lost. You understand love in one way, and I understand it in another. But I can only *live* with a man who understands love in my way. I don't say my way's right. But it's my way. Darling!" She kissed him. "I do love you. You can't guess how much. And you love me--in your way. But your way would kill me. No. That's not fair. I should be killing myself." She kissed him again. "That's a good-bye kiss."

And Evelyn thought bitterly and tenderly:

"And I suppose that's what she calls playing the game!" He said aloud: "My way! My way! But that first night at the Palace, when I refused to go to your party because I had work to do and you got angry, you told me afterwards you liked me for refusing."

She reflected a moment before answering:

"That was different. You weren't in love with me then."

3.

He was about to make a retort, when the door-bell rang. He had not quite settled the nature of the retort; what he chiefly felt was that he must hide his irritation better than he had hidden it in his previous remark; you could not, decently, be cross with a young woman who was still sitting on your knee and kissing you, even though she had used the word 'goodbye'; moreover, she did not, could not, mean it. She sprang from his knee.

"I'll answer the door," he said, standing up.

"You'll do nothing of the kind, thanks," said she, faintly showing irritation.

"What reason has she to be irritated?" he asked himself. His attitude to her had not changed. Hers to him was changing from moment to moment, in a manner totally incomprehensible, not to say inexcusable.

She returned from a parley in the ante-chamber bearing a large cardboard box.

"Hello!" he exclaimed brightly. "What's that?"

"My old things, from the Jolie Laitière," said Gracie. "They're pretty quick, aren't they?" The second half of her reply was evidently meant to mitigate the perhaps excessive curtness of the first.

She went straight by him, through the masked door, along the corridor into the bedroom; and her chin was raised. His instinct and desire were not to let her out of his sight. But he sat down again, because he disliked to think of himself as running after her. All his thoughts were resentful. Good-bye, indeed! What damned nonsense! And dangerous nonsense! Women, however, had no sense of danger. They were all--women. Within a few minutes the desire to see her had become irresistible. He strolled into the bedroom, grandly, masculinely casual. The Jolie Laitière frock had been flung on the bed, and Gracie, in her knickers, was bending over the open cardboard box.

"What are you doing?" he asked in a kind tone; but the words 'my dear' refused to add themselves to the question.

"I'm putting on my own things," she said, not looking up, and drew forth the frock which had won praise from the saleswoman at the Jolie Laitière.

"But why?"

"That game is finished," she said. "I don't feel like being dowdy any more. It's no fun." She slipped on the frock, and as her head emerged from the neck of the frock she turned and faced him, shaking down the skirt impatiently. Her glance, defiant, and rather hard, displeased him. Still, he could control himself, being a man.

"I think I'll try one of your cigars," he said, in a neutral tone, and left her, and after some trouble opened the box of cigars. "This situation has got to be handled," he said firmly to himself as he lit the cigar and walked back into the bedroom.

"What a heavenly smell!" she murmured agreeably. She was perfuming herself.

"Your scent or my cigar?" he asked, with equal mildness.

"Your cigar."

"Yes, it's what I call a pretty good cigar. Now, my child, I want you to--"

"I'm not so much of a child as you think I am," she stopped him.

"Now, my dear girl," he began again. "I'm going to ask you to do something for me. I want you to do it to please me. Take that frock off and put on the other one. I love to see you in it. You invented a most amusing game. Do keep it up. It's great and original fun. Do oblige me. I should feel frightfully gloomy if you wouldn't play any more. It would spoil everything." He smiled, varied the tones of his voice, did all he could, by employing a semblance of airy, affectionate humour, to be persuasive.

She shook her head.

"No, thanks. I've changed now, and I'm not going to waste this scent either." Her tone was challenging; her features were beginning to be contorted into a vindictive ugliness.

Evelyn, amazed and hurt, thought: "Only a few minutes since she was sitting on my knee, and hanging round my neck, and kissing me, and saying how she loved me. And now she's all altered! And I'll swear I haven't said a word, not one word to upset her. On the contrary. What sort of a creature is she?" Still controlling himself, he continued aloud: "I always thought women liked to dress to please men, and--"

"You thought wrong then," she stopped him once more. "Everybody who knows anything at all knows that women dress to please women. I mean, they mind what women think far more than what men think. Men aren't judges. Women are. And if a woman has to choose between pleasing a man she's fond of and pleasing a woman who hates her, she'd please the woman every time--in her clothes."

"But even if that's true..."

"Even if it's true! It is true!"

"Well, let it be true. You knew it before you started the game, and you didn't care. Why have you altered?"

"Listen to me," she answered. It struck him that she was now using the same tone as when she had flared up at him at the Palace on the night of his refusal to go to her party; also, the vindictiveness of her expression was candid and intense. "Do you imagine I can't read you like the front page of a newspaper? If you do you're mistaken. You just made up your mind to come the grand over me. You said to yourself you'd force me to keep on wearing that dowdy thing. You thought you'd show me who was the master here. Just because I've been fool enough to tell you and show you how I've gone crazy about you."

"Not at all," he protested unconvincingly.

"I say yes!" she cried.

He saw that she was inexplicably losing her temper. "Oh, very well!" he thought superiorly, and waited.

"The truth is," she cried, louder and louder, "and you may as well know it, you're conceited. You were always conceited, and I've made you more conceited. You show it the whole time! You simply can't move without showing it. You're taking advantage of me every minute, that's what you're doing!"

He sat down, near the door, thinking what a brilliant idea it was to sit down.

"Now, come here! Please!" he begged her. If only she would obey, he could restore her to his knee, and soothe and fondle her into being rational.

"There you are again!" she cried. "I'm in love with you. So I'm to be your slave. Finger up, I come. Finger down, I go."

He shook his head, with a gesture of fatigue.

"You say you're in love with me," he resumed, very low and careful. "I believe you are. And I'm quite sure I'm in love with you."

"You're more sure than I am, then."

"But I am!"

"So you say! But I'll just ask you one question. This morning, the very next day after you'd made love to me, you were ready to leave me because of something you'd seen in a newspaper."

"Well?"

"Supposing they telephoned to you to-night that you were wanted in London to-morrow, should you go?"

He replied uncompromisingly:

"Yes."

"Of course!" she sneered. "And after all that explanation I gave you this afternoon! Of course you'd go. And glad to. Men soon get tired of a girl who's been fool enough to let out that she's in love with them! I've heard that from lots of girls, and mothers too. But you just don't know what love is. You take everything for granted. Men generally do. And you're worse than most. I'm an idiot, but I'd sooner be an idiot than a conceited ass like you are!" Her eyes were radiant with fury, her fine nostrils twitching, and she leaned forward in her defiance of him.

"Oh, if that's it!" Evelyn exploded. "If that's it, I'd better be off." He threw his cigar fiercely into the fireplace.

"Yes, you had!" she provoked him further.

"But before I do go, I'll tell you what I think of those explanations of yours. How they struck me. Silly. Absolutely silly. There you were, choosing your words, and thinking you were being so damned eloquent, and feeling conceited about your book because I'd praised it. And your explanations were perfect bosh. All over the place! All over the damn place!" He had not yet quite realised that he too had lost his temper; but he was distinctly aware of a sensation of voluptuous happiness in his outbreak. "Not an argument in the whole blooming performance that couldn't be riddled to pieces by any man who took the trouble to argue. Not that anything you said was worth an argument! You the author of that book! You must be if you say so. But don't you forget that I read it under your influence. You looked after that all right, didn't you? You managed to lie on the floor and watch me read it, didn't you? But I wonder what I should think of it if I were to read it a second time." He had stood up.

"And now you *can* go!" she shouted. "I've listened to you. Most women would have shut you up. But I'm different. Off you go." Her hands were clenched.

4.

He did go. In the ante-chamber he threw his overcoat on anyhow, seized his hat and went, and banged the door. He felt hot and he was breathing hard. He turned westward down the boulevard, but he knew not whether he had turned westward or eastward. He merely moved on, rather quickly.

"She's absolutely awful," he exclaimed, half-aloud. And, "Of all the" And, "She must be mad." And, "What excuse *can* there be?" And, "I'm jolly glad I let her have it." And, "What an escape! My God!"

He repeated all these remarks several times. One or two passers-by glanced at him apprehensively. When he had cooled a little, he looked round, and discovered with surprise that he was in the rue du Faubourg St.

Honoré. How he had arrived in it he could not remember, for he had no recollection whatever of going down the rue Royale, as he must have done.

The night was sharp, with a clear starry sky. He began to notice the crowds of wayfarers, the noise of traffic, and the January night-frost. He buttoned his big overcoat, whose front had been flying loose. He thought: "Seems to me my coat-collar is higher than my overcoat!" In other men he was very scornful of this negligence. He put his hand to his nape Yes, the coat-collar was half an inch higher than the collar of the overcoat! He halted, set it right, with an angry tug at the coat behind, and walked on. He decided that he would send for his belongings. She was dreadful, dreadful! The utter lack of reason! The injustice! He hated injustice. The same thoughts ran round and round in his brain.

Was it what they termed a lovers' quarrel? No, by Heaven! He said: "My character's changing. I noticed that not long since. I can't remember ever losing my temper before. Well, anyway not for ages." He passed the Hôtel Bristol. What sort of a new-fangled noisy place was that? He turned down the avenue Matignon. He was in the avenue des Champs Elysées, majestic and vast and beautiful in the night. An illuminated shop on the south side appeared to be miles away, and full of mysterious magic. He thought: "It was childish of me to lose my temper, if I *did* lose it. But there are limits to patience." Then he felt humiliated because he had lost his temper. He, at his age! He was no better than she was. Yes, he was better, because she'd begun it, but he was not enough better. She was magnificent in her defiance. Her nostrils! Her burning eyes! Her stance! Nevertheless an impossible Tartar. She might be a genius, but she was hellish. Imagine her as a wife. You couldn't.

About sending for his things. How could he? He couldn't. He might go to a strange hotel; but he would have to give his right name, and then the hotel would know that he had had to send for his luggage to a dubious flat on the boulevard; and that a young woman had opened the door of the flat. Besides, his things weren't packed.

No! He had his dignity to think of. He must jump into a taxi at once, and go and get his luggage himself. And he must be very calm and cold and dignified. No alternative! None. He had blundered. He must repair the blunder. He could; and he would. And the incident would be a lesson to him. By God! It would be a lesson to him!...What injustice! What infernal foolishness and cheek! A conceited ass, was he? Ah! And she--what was she? he would like to know. No doubt she was magnificent in her madness. But--He hesitated, and then raised his hand to a taxi-driver, and gave the address. The taxi had wings, for it flew. No trafficblocks, no slackenings. In five seconds, so it seemed to him, the taxi had pulled up at the portico of the house of furnished flats. Should he keep the taxi, or pay it off? Easy to get a fresh one on the boulevard. He paid off the taxi. He climbed the stairs very slowly; yet he was at her door in an instant. He paused, because he was afraid, so afraid that his hand shook on the bell push, and he touched it before he had definitely decided whether or not to touch it. Hours passed.

Then the door was opened. She was wearing the Jolie Laitière dowdy ravishing pink frock. She was smiling. He entered. She slammed the door. She burst into tears. He put his arms round her. Not a word was said.

Chapter 60 THE CASH-GIRL

"Now you mustn't cry," said Evelyn, in a voice low and tender. "I don't like to see you crying." He charged his voice to the full with tenderness, thinking: "I have never been as tender as this before to anybody." Then he added, on a note of humour equally tender: "Well, you may cry for three minutes--not more. And I won't look at my watch."

He peeped down, to glance at her averted face, and saw a plaintive, weak smile. There they stood, uncomfortably, near the door in the drawing-room, Evelyn not daring to move her towards a chair, or not having the wit to do so. She murmured something inarticulate.

"What? What did you say?"

"Hanky. My bag. Handkerchief," she snivelled.

"Bag be blowed!" said Evelyn, and took out his own handkerchief.

He tried to raise her face, but she resisted; he felt delicately for her eyes and with extreme care wiped them. Then he tried again to raise her face, and she no longer resisted. His hand pressing on the top of her forehead, he pushed her head backwards, until her face was in full view beneath his. Her eyes met his eyes, and she smiled. Her shoulders rested softly upon his left arm. All her body was limp, lax, acquiescent, utterly yielding to his will and strong muscles. It confessed its weakness and the weakness of her spirit. He lightly brushed away the last trace of moisture from her shining eyes and a stray tear from her soft ripe cheek; the handkerchief fell to the carpet. Her smile died as if from exhaustion, returned to life, died, returned, stayed. Moment agitating and exquisite. The women painted in their gilt frames, and the sculptured woman on her pedestal, regarded the human scene with the callous indifference of goddesses; the clock stirred not a finger: the room was a phantasm. Only the two bodies, held together by their invisible mysterious souls, were alive under the garish downpour of light from the chandelier, whose pendants faintly tinkled now and then in response to vibrations set up by footsteps overhead in another abode of human beings invisible and mysterious. No recriminations, no explanations even, nor justifications. Silence. Words were unnecessary, because there was absolutely nothing that needed to be said. In the quarrel words had lost all meaning, and perhaps were now discredited. As for the quarrel, it merely did not exist; more strange, it never had existed; that which is annihilated has never existed.

"You'd better sit down," Evelyn murmured, and led her to an easy-chair. She sat, reclining in the abandonment of emotional fatigue. Evelyn had an impulse to kneel at her knees. He checked it. He could not persuade himself to kneel; the posture would have been sentimental, ridiculous. He had won the battle; conquerors do not kneel. Still less could he have knelt if he had lost the battle. He leaned against the side of the back of the chair and stroked her cheek, endlessly, and so compassionately that sometimes he did not touch it.

When he thought of the annihilated past, as he did, he thought of it as something which, even had it had existence, would have been entirely negligible. Its sole importance lay in the fact that out of its nothingness it had engendered this marvellous bliss. And he had not won; neither of them had won; he would have hated to win. His desire was to preserve her equality with himself. Self-complacency? Perhaps.

Absorbed in contemplation of Gracie, he yet could detect in the far distance of his mind, faint as the rumour of boulevard traffic through the closed windows, fragmentary rumours of the unreal quarrel. Was it true that women dress for women, not for men? It was not true. Women submitted themselves to the judgment of women only in so far as concerned the efficiency of their effort to please men. Women did not think in criticism of a woman: "That frock does not please me." They thought: "That frock does not achieve its aim, which is not directed at me at all." Example of the girl's inability to think straight, or, in the alternative, of her instinct to think dishonestly...No. The quarrel was not growing real to him. Even when he recalled her phrase, 'conceited ass,' he smiled; he could have laughed. It had no significance. Nothing of the quarrel had significance. The memory of the quarrel did not humiliate him now. He had not been wrong, nor had he been right. They were both of them beyond good and evil. They had ascended, for a while, to the plane of pure, unconditioned existence. She lifted her hand and gently seized his, and looked up at him.

"I suppose I ought to be getting ready," she said, in quite a prosaic tone.

But how enchantingly! It seemed to him that all the prose of their life would for ever be poetry, that within the dailiness of life their joint existence would always be pure and unconditioned. Unresolved problems? Pooh! Trifles of less than no importance! She rose slowly; he held her against falling; they passed silently into the bedroom, where she had left the lights burning.

On the bed, the Lovely Milkmaid nightdress was laid out in all its graceless attractiveness for the morbid. At any rate her repentances and surrenders seemed to Evelyn to be thorough. He was pleased. She hated to be his 'slave'--with what scorn she had uttered that word!--but she loved to be his slave. He was more than pleased, he was more than content. He felt that he could be wondrously kind to a slave. She put her hand on his shoulder, and said with apologetic timidity:

"What time is it? I think I shall soon be hungry." The admission had the instant effect of lowering the plane of their mood to the normal, the humdrum, the safe. And they both became cheerful.

"Oh! It's not late," he said. He too was aware of the onset of hunger. But he would not admit it. Slaves might confess hunger, not masters.

"What about dinner, darling?"

"Where would you like to eat? Here, same as last night?"

"If you prefer it, darling," she answered, submissive but reluctant.

"Not at all," he said. "Anywhere you please, my dear. I want you to choose."

"A Durand?" she suggested.

"Have you ever been in a Durand? I haven't."

"No. But I'm dying to try one. It ought to suit this frock." She smiled. Her childlike fancy had returned to the idea of the game of mackintosh, Baedeker, and Jolie Laitière frock and hat.

"They're awful, aren't they?"

"I hope so," said she.

"You are a funny little thing!" He patted her.

"Shall we go now?" she cajoled, less humbly.

"Isn't it frightfully early?"

"Not for cheap tourists like us," she said. "They always dine early."

Yes, she was a child.

"Right then! But aren't your lips a shade too brilliant for a Restaurant Durand?" He would show her that he also could act the child.

"I was just thinking of that," she said eagerly. "Wait two minutes. Wait here." She ran laughing into the bathroom.

He was quite youthfully happy. When she emerged, she presented her face for his inspection.

"Will it do?" she asked.

"I love it."

She had removed every trace of rouge and powder. Her cheeks were pale, her lips a pale, imperfect crimson. She looked unwell. The artlessness of her complexion appealed to him as the nightdress appealed to him.

"I haven't washed my face with water for years and years," she said. "But I couldn't do anything with my nails. The stuff wouldn't come off without too much trouble." She displayed her elaborately manicured hands.

"Hide them! Hide them! Shocking!" said he. "Even if you did forget to buy proper gloves."

She had noticed a Durand in the avenue de l'Opéra, near the Café de Paris. In less than another minute they were on the way. How different was the bliss of the walk from his miserable, tragical, solitary promenade to the Champs Elysées! Were they walking, or floating?

2.

"There are thirty-two Durands in Paris," said Gracie, as they stood a moment hesitant at the door of the restaurant. (No welcoming official at the doors.)

"Who told you that?"

"Uncle Laugier."

"You seem to know the old rascal pretty well."

"No. But daddy and I have stayed several times at the Concorde, and Laugier is rather a dear."

The large interior, like the exterior, of the Durand had the sedateness of panelled brown wood which might have been mahogany, or rosewood, or even synthetic wood. The mirrors and the small window-panes were bevelled, and the bevelling split the light of the lamps into glints of all the colours of the spectrum. Many small tables arranged in rows strictly rectilinear. Waitresses in black and white. One man, short and fat and shabby in morning dress, overseeing the entire place. Two enormous sideboards bearing fruit that appeared to be artificial but was not. A brass-protected service-door, which the waitresses kicked open as they entered with hands occupied by trays of food. A broad staircase, with indiarubber treads, showed that there was another room upstairs. The restaurant was nearly full of dowdy, staid people of all ages from twenty-five to that of Methuselah, eating seriously. No sound, or hardly a sound, save the faint clatter of knives and forks on earthenware. Paris!

The overseer advanced to meet the new arrivals.

"Two?" he asked in English, imperceptibly bowing, with a slight smile. He directed them to a distant table, still encumbered with the debris of a recently finished meal. Then he left them. After a time a stout, very deliberate, middle-aged waitress came up and restored to the table its virginity.

"Do let me order," said Gracie mischievously when at last the waitress drew a menu from the bib of her apron and presented it, first to Evelyn, who indicated that she was presenting it to the wrong person. The waitress shut her lips together, and stood patiently impatient while Gracie scanned the card. Evelyn heard the order: vermicelli soup, skate, cutlets, fried potatoes, crême caramel, carafe of red vin ordinaire. The waitress wrote nothing, remembered everything.

"This place is a million times worse than where we had lunch yesterday," said Evelyn.

"I should just hope so!" said Gracie. "I should have been very disappointed if it hadn't been. But haven't I chosen the perfect Durand dinner for you?"

"You're the kind of girl that gets murdered and nobody can guess the motive," Evelyn replied. He felt gaily sardonic.

"You'll have to eat it," she enjoined him.

"Oh! I shall eat it," said he. "If I die for it."

"I think it's all heavenly," she said, glancing round. "It was nice of you to let me come here. I shall bring Tessa here now, for a treat. It's the very place for expectant mothers--I bought Tessa a wedding ring."

He gazed at her pale, virginal face, thinking: "Well, there's one good thing about her--she's depraved!" Her morbidity strongly attracted him. There was no end to it, no end to her unpredictable caprices. He was absolutely determined to marry her. 'Good-bye kiss!' Nonsense!

The wine appeared first. Then, after an interval, the soup. She took a spoonful of the soup, swallowed it with a noise, and looked at him for approval of this realistic touch.

"When you think," said she, "that in thirty-two Durands at this moment respectable people are eating vermicelli soup! You know, it's exactly the same menu in all these places." The soup was hot and wet, and as interesting as a uniformly overcast sky.

"What was that you were writing this morning, in my big coat?" he demanded.

"I think I'll take my mackintosh off," she said, and did so and Evelyn hung it up on the rack behind him where he had hung the big coat and the hat. Then he repeated the question.

"I tore it up," she said.

"But what was it about?"

"Oh, nothing! I'm not going to write any more."

"It was something about me," he said.

"It wasn't. You flatter yourself. It was about me. I've only got one subject. That's why I'm not going to write any more." Disillusion and sudden melancholy in her rich voice. "I want to work."

"But isn't writing work?"

"Mine isn't. It's fun."

He thought: "She's like all the rest of 'em. Flirting about all over the place. Can't stick to anything. She gave up motor-racing. Now she's giving up writing. But when she's my wife I'll put the fear of God into her." He was absolutely confident of his power to form her.

"What sort of work?"

"You see that girl there at the cash-desk," she said, and without moving her eyes from him went on: "Look at her. See those black wristlets to keep her cuffs clean? You may be sure they're white linen cuffs to match her open-work collar. See her hair? She's not like any other girl in this place--I mean on the staff. See the expression of her face? No, you can't get it from here."

"No. I can't," said Evelyn as he looked, scrutinising.

"I noticed her as we came in," said Gracie.

"I didn't. Well, what about her?"

"See how she can't move so long as she's at that desk. Rather like an A.B.C. or a Lyons cash-desk, isn't it?"

"Do you patronise those places?"

"Yes, sometimes. They're far more interesting than your Palace restaurants, darling. And the tea's just as good...And she has to sit on a stool--it isn't a chair. And she has to sit there behind that grill until the last customer has gone. Same for lunch. I expect. She never speaks to anyone unless a customer asks her something. She isn't quite as solitary as a bus-driver in the Strand, but she nearly is. She just sits behind that grill and looks at bills and takes money and gives change. Now that's the sort of work I want to do. No, you needn't smile. Please don't smile. It is. I should love the monotony. It would be so restful. She loves it; I could tell from her face. She can be herself. She has time to be herself. I want to be myself, only I never have time as I live now. That girl's job is better even than being a nun. It's nearly as good as being in the grave."

The solemn sincerity of Gracie's tone as she spoke those last words dismayed him.

"I should like to do that girl's work for years and years," Gracie continued. "Nothing would happen to me. I'm tired of things happening to me. She's meek. She has to be. Blessed are the meek. It's a blessing I've never had, and I need it. You don't know how much I need it. I don't know how much I need it. I don't know who I am. And I simply must know who I am. Couldn't I have a job like that, in one of your hotels? Not in London. On the Continent. I can talk both French and Italian frightfully well. Do you understand how I feel?"

"Yes, I understand, my dear," said Evelyn. "But are you ready to what I call talk straight?"

"Yes. I adore straight talking."

"Truly now?" His voice and an upturned finger warned her.

"Truly. Neither you or anyone else can be too straight for me."

3.

"Well, listen, my dear. In the first place, the girl hasn't only got to look at bills and take money and give change. She has to enter every bill on a sheet. And when the last customer's gone she has to add up the sheet, probably several sheets, and wait while somebody else checks the total. And she has to count her cash, and the cash has to agree with the total, and she can't go home till it does agree with the total, and if it's more than the total she doesn't pocket the difference--oh no! But if it's less than the total she has to find the difference out of her wages. And all the time while she's taking money and paying it out, that's what she's thinking about. She isn't thinking about herself and the mystic beauty of being meek and the virtue of monotony and so on."

"Darling, you're laughing at me," Grace interrupted him with sweet plaintiveness.

"I'm not!" He rapped the table in emphasis. "I'm perfectly serious and I'm just talking straight. However, I'll stop, if you can't stand it."

"You go on. I'm sorry. But do you imagine I couldn't do the adding-up business and the counting? Of course I could. I'm very good at it. As if I hadn't kept the house-books at home for daddy. And they're no joke either."

"I don't say you aren't good at it," he replied, soothingly. "But you couldn't *do* it. I mean you couldn't keep on doing it. You say you've kept your father's house-books. But who's keeping your father's house-books now? Not you. You kept them as long as you felt like keeping them, and then you turned them over to someone else to keep, someone who had to keep them whether she felt like it or not. The moment you didn't feel like it you chucked it. And quite right too!"

"But I *could* keep books whether I felt like it or not."

"You're wrong. You couldn't. That's the whole point. It isn't your fault. You weren't brought up to it. That cash-girl there was brought up to it.

She's always been used to being in a certain place at a certain time, whatever the weather, and whatever she feels like. If she can move her feet, she's *got* to arrive on time and stay until she's finished. She's been disciplined. It takes years to learn discipline, and you must begin early. You have to begin to learn discipline before you can talk. There's no other way--that is, if you are to be happy under discipline. That cash-girl has learnt one accomplishment that you've never learnt and never will, and she took years to learn it."

"What's that?"

"She's learnt to stick it. You've never learnt that--you've never had the chance to. You could no more stick it as she sticks it than you could learn to play Beethoven sonatas in public without being laughed off the platform. You think that that girl's work is easy and you could do it on your head. It isn't, and you couldn't. It requires gifts that are beyond you. You're young, God knows, but if you wanted her qualities you ought to have started out after them twenty years ago."

He added, in silence to himself:

"I might twit you about throwing up motor-racing and wanting now to throw up writing; but I won't. I'll spare you that. You've had all you can swallow. And all this talk is a pure waste of time. I've got something else in store for you, and right down in your heart you know it."

"Aren't you being a little hard on me, darling?"

"Hard, my dear? No. Only straight. A straight line is the nearest way between two points. A line isn't hard. And I'll tell you another thing. You couldn't get a responsible place like that girl has. You just apply, and you'll see. They'd ask you quick enough what experience you'd had, and they'd ask for your testimonials. And then when you couldn't deliver the goods they'd laugh at you."

"But everyone has to begin."

"Not at your age, and with your money. Sell all that you have and give to the poor. And make your father do the same, so that he couldn't help you when you didn't feel like sticking it; and you might have a chance. You'd probably die of the experience, or do something worse, but you'd have a chance. Oh yes, you could get a place. I could push you into some kind of place, just as you are, if I was an unscrupulous scoundrel. But you'd only be playing at it, and everybody would know you were only playing at it. I can hear the other girls talking among themselves about you. 'Oh, her! She's a scream! And keeps girls that want a job out of it!' You'd like that, wouldn't you, my dear!"

A considerable silence. The buxom matron removed the remains of the *raie au beurre noir*. Gracie's plate was empty except for the spine of the fish, but Evelyn had eaten little. The matron with placid indifference set down tiny cutlets, and minute quantities of vegetables which had apparently been weighed to the nearest dram in chemists' scales, accurately according to a doctor's prescription. The matron made no enquiry as to the reactions of her customers to the Durand diet. Evelyn thought, of Gracie:

"Have I driven any of the mysticism out of her? When was it she was talking about secret Signs with a capital S, and Fate with a capital F? Oh yes, my seeing the paragraphs in the paper was a mystical sign--that I didn't really love her. 'No such thing as chance!' What a world the witch lives in! And what a sardonic devil I am! Still, she asked for it. It's ask and ye shall receive--when I'm the person that's asked."

Nevertheless, beneath all this sharp irony his tenderness was flowing into her. He divined from her glance that she was as aware of the one mood in him as of the other.

"Darling, how can I argue with you? I can't. You're too strong for me. You're ruthless. I don't say you aren't right. Haven't I told you I'm nothing--nothing?"

"I'm not ruthless," said he, with love. "It's common sense that's ruthless."

"It doesn't seem to help me," she murmured. "What I always want is encouragement."

"Not encouragement on the wrong path," he said. He was startled to hear that she always wanted encouragement--she so independent, so full of initiative, so adventurous (as in the affair of Tessa). Was he getting down to the deeps of her individuality?

"Then the right path--what is it?" she asked gently.

"You're rich," he answered. "And you can't not be rich. You've got to go on being rich and spectacular and all that. It's not a bad thing, really. Has its uses in what political journalists call the fabric of society. We others are entitled to have something to look at. Of course I know you'll say I'm talking like a manager of luxury hotels. But I mean it. If I didn't I shouldn't be what I am. In any case it's not the slightest use selling all you have and giving to the poor, or trying to do jobs that plain ordinary girls can do ten times better than you ever could. That would only show that you're afraid of your responsibilities and want to shirk them. That would show you were a coward, and you aren't. We're all discouraged and discontented and crying out for the moon at times."

"But I must *do* something!" she pleaded. "And I wasn't brought up to do anything."

"That's the sins of the fathers. The fathers have eaten what-ever-it-was--sour grapes--and the children's teeth are set on edge. That's what you've got to stick--not sitting at a desk and counting thirty thousand francs a day for a hundred francs a week and your food...Well, you've seen through motor-racing and you've seen through writing" (he failed after all to leave out the jibe), "but there's Tessa. You've taken on that responsibility. The baby isn't born yet, and your responsibility there won't be done with until either you or both mother and baby are dead. And it'll need a lot of thinking about. And I shall rely on you not to do anything that will set the child's teeth on edge. And you'll have to marry, you know. And your husband will be all you can manage for years. And if you have children you'll have twenty pretty busy years setting them a good example.

The fact is, you won't have a moment to spare. And if you do happen to find you have some leisure on your hands, it'll be up to you to think out some schemes. Nobody else can do that for you. The preacher will now step down from the pulpit. This cutlet ought to be put in the British Museum. Egyptian antiquities. No. Elgin marbles."

"Darling! I've never heard you like this before."

"No. You've thought I was just an ordinary man. You see how mistaken you've been."

"And so you think I must marry."

"You can't avoid it."

"But who?"

She smiled at him weakly; he could not interpret her smile, which somewhat troubled him.

"I'm nothing," she breathed.

"That's exactly as it ought to be," he said. "I've always sworn to myself I'd never marry" (he might have added "again"; but he was sure that if he did she would question him closely about his first wife, and such questions would have irked him); "but if you're nothing and I marry you, I shan't be marrying. See?"

She continued to look at him with her loving, disquieting, undecipherable smile.

He thought:

"Her money may be a regular curse to me. On the other hand it may not. Also, her father might go bankrupt, over the films."

The crême caramel followed the cutlets.

"Well," he said, having tasted it. "I propose we go."

"Where?"

"Any place where we can dine."

"Sweetie!" she protested. "I'm so sorry you haven't enjoyed it. I've enjoyed it all. But we can't eat another dinner."

"Then I must have some cheese. Let's order two portions, and I'll eat both."

When at last he demanded the bill, she said: "I'll pay it."

"No."

"But I want to. It's my dinner."

"No."

"Well then, give me the bill and the money, and let me pay at the desk."

He gave her a hundred-franc note, and a tip to the impassive matron.

"It isn't good and it isn't cheap," he muttered to Gracie. "And women don't understand food."

He followed her to the cash-desk, putting on his overcoat as he walked between the emptying tables. Standing by Gracie at the desk, he examined the face of the cash-girl, and in spite of his wish not to do so he seemed to see in the face all that Gracie had seen. Something significant ought to have happened, but nothing did. Gracie, tendering the money, smiled at the cash-girl, who handed her the change and stamped the bill.

"Merci, madame," said Gracie,

The cash-girl appeared to be a little startled, but did not respond, even with a smile. No doubt Gracie would say that she was dreaming her private dream of meekness behind that casual, insensitive glance.

"There's one good thing about this restaurant," said Evelyn in the street, as Gracie bestowed on him the change. "No music."

Then, to atone for his persistent irony, he took her arm possessively, and made her happy. Her smile was modest enough; but Evelyn, impressed, thought that her general demeanour had a certain grandeur, and he was proud of it.

Chapter 61 THE HELPMEET

"Evelyn, you haven't forgotten to telephone to London, have you?"

Gracie, who had changed the reach-me-down frock for her peignoir, came as far as the door of the drawing-room, where Evelyn was smoking the second of her cigars. She had asked him to sit in the drawing-room for a while. Her tone now was serious. 'Evelyn,' she had begun, not 'Darling.' And she spoke as if she realised, in the way a wife should, that communication with the Imperial Palace was a duty not to be neglected.

"Oh! It doesn't matter. There won't be anything," he answered very casually. He was in an easy-chair, with his back to the masked door. The next moment she was perched on the arm of his chair, and bending towards him.

"Darling, you know you ought to. You know they haven't got your number and they'll be expecting you to ring them up. Do be a good boy."

Yes, she had taken the role of thoughtful wife, gently determined that her husband's interests should be protected, even against himself. After pretending not to notice her nearness, he glanced at her, happily; for he enjoyed the unusual sensation of being looked after. True, Miss Cass was devoted to his highest welfare, but her methods were less delectable than Gracie's.

"Woman!" he exclaimed. "What in God's name have you been doing to yourself?"

She had made up her face again with the utmost elaboration of artifice.

"I felt positively indecent in that restaurant," she laughed.

"You hid your feelings pretty well then!"

"Of course I did! It was my own fault I went out naked, and I had to stand for it, without making you uncomfortable too. Besides, you were so interesting. Now, darling, you must do your little bit of telephoning."

"Shan't!" he said, playing the recalcitrant child. All his sensations were novel and delicious.

"I'll get the hotel for you," she whispered, and went to the telephone.

He puffed voluptuously at the cigar, and in a sultanic style watched her do the chore. She was a serious girl. He had always known that at heart she was a serious girl. And in the restaurant he had beaten her and silenced her. She was marvellously his to command. Not another word from her about her infantile scheme for finding herself. She had accepted the ultimatum.

"They'll ring you when you're through," she said, rising from the instrument, on which she was certainly a very accomplished virtuoso.

He expected her to stop on her way out of the room and kiss and caress him. But all she gave him was a trifle of a satisfied, warning nod. He solaced his disappointment by the reflection that there was a time for everything and that in her opinion the present was a time for seriousness. How changed she was, the explanation doubtless being that he had been forming her: the man's business! He pondered dreamily upon her. She was not a woman, and hers was not a love, to be lightly lost. What a helpmeet! What a comfort! And her nerves were all pacified now, after the storm. 'They' needed a storm at intervals. A quarrel, a scene, a wild expenditure of nervous force, was a physical necessity for them. Emotional instability: that was their weakness, poor exquisite things! .

The telephone bell rang. He smiled and sat still. It rang more than once. Gracie came running into the room; she must have dropped her peignoir en route. He continued to smile, mischievously.

"Evelyn! What *are* you thinking of?" She pulled him out of his chair.

"All right! All right! Mind my cigar! I'm coming. But I won't touch the damned telephone until you've kissed me with your sticky vermilion lips!"

She kissed him, wifely. As soon as she had seen him safe with the instrument to his ear, she disappeared again. His eye caught her in the act of vanishing, and it winked at her. It laughed because of the comicality of her evident notion that without her moral spurring he would have been feckless in a difficult world. He chatted gravely with Cousin for two periods of three minutes. At the close he said: "Very well. I'll give you a ring about ten in the morning." He replaced the instrument. Gracie was standing at the door. She had assumed the Lovely Milkmaid nightdress; she was indeed more or less loyally playing the game.

In the bedroom he put his hands on her half-bare shoulders, and surveyed her and shook her, and laughed loudly, as if unable to contain his joy.

"You *are* uproarious!" she said. "Or are you pretending? Anything exciting at the Palace?"

He shook his head, and turned suddenly to empty his pockets into the smallest of the drawers which Gracie, out of her riches, had bestowed upon him for his exclusive use. (Home!) In his hip-pocket he felt a soft protuberance. It was her glove. He slipped it into the drawer surreptitiously. Then, happening to glance at the bed, he observed that she had laid out thereon, with a scrupulosity of balanced line that Oldham could not have equalled, his pyjamas. Final touch of conscientious, forethoughtful wifeliness.

And yet, later, though nothing lacked in the responsiveness of her loving ardour to his, there seemed to be always a veil over her wide-open eyes when she looked at him, peering and probing in silence into the secrecies of his mind. The veil foiled not her vision but his. Having given apparently everything of herself, still she was withholding something: so he surmised, subtly disconsolate in joy, baffled.

The bed-lamps were extinguished. Darkness. The intimate warmth of her invisible body. The faint, faint sound of her delicate breathing. Relaxation of limbs. Tiny frictions of apprehension in the confused, vague activity of his sympathetically fatigued brain. Checked stirrings of the limbs. A crumpled rose-leaf in the pillow. Subdued yawns. Intense wakefulness. Uncontrollable racing of the machine of thought.

"You can't sleep, darling!"

"I shall, soon," he answered, startled but reassuring, in a tone to imitate sleepiness.

Blinding light. With her feminine instinct for drama, she had switched on the lamp at her side of the bed. She raised herself on one elbow.

"Something's gone wrong at the Palace," she asserted sadly. He shook his head lazily, and noticed again the coarse ecru lace at the top of her nightdress.

"Nothing to speak of. Nothing. What makes you think there's anything wrong, my dear?"

"You said you'd ring them up again in the morning. I heard you. And as you do all your hotel-telephoning at night--at least that's what I understood--"

"Now just to show you how mistaken you are, I'll tell you exactly what I did hear to-night. Ceria--the Grill-room-manager--hasn't been seen for two days. And our head-housekeeper is ill--but not seriously. That's all, and if we never had anything worse--"

He smiled, but ceased to smile when he saw tears in her eyes. One of them reached the prominence of her cheek-bone and then dropped on to his shoulder.

"Believe me," he said, caressing her. "It's nothing serious."

"But why didn't you tell me?" she murmured. "I asked you if there was anything at the hotel, and you shook your head."

"'Anything exciting,' you said. Well, there wasn't. And I didn't want to spoil your evening with any of those things. Why should I?"

"But *I* want my evenings to be spoilt by those things. I don't care whether they're serious or not. It's just those things that would make everything so lovely between us. If you keep things from me it means you don't believe in me being able to take them just right--not too seriously and not too unseriously. Oh, darling!"

The grieved, dignified, affectionate expression on her face made him contrite.

"My dear, it wasn't that at all."

"Really?"

"Really!" He asseverated the word with a calm emphasis, but she continued to gaze down at him seemingly unconvinced. However, the tears were quenched.

"That housekeeper," she asked. "Is that the one that came to me when Tessa had the attack?"

"Yes. Miss Powler. Violet Powler."

"Oh! I know her! I was only wondering if it was she who was your head-housekeeper at the Palace. You know, her sister used to be daddy's housekeeper."

"And Violet was too, for a time."

"Yes, but I wasn't at home much then. She's splendid. Susan was fine too, but I think I should admire Violet Powler more than Susan if I knew her. I wish I'd got some of her qualities." Gracie sighed. She showed no curiosity as to Ceria. "Darling, put your arms round me. We aren't a bit near. And shall we ever be?"

He enfolded her. She was weeping again. She wept on his face.

"There, there!" he murmured. "You're only tired." He held her close. How long? He could not guess. At length, kissing him, she gently freed herself, put the light out, and went immediately to sleep.

It was a wondrous, enlarging experience. But disturbing, disconcerting. Yes, he had to admit that inexplicably they were not 'near.' But it was she who was far away.

2.

The next morning, when he opened his eyes and grunted--first sign, grunting, that conscious cerebration was about to be resumed--the room was dark, but the door was open, and there seemed to be a faint light in the passage; and in this light he seemed to see, vaguely, the figure of Gracie, which immediately vanished. He felt for her in the bed; she was not in the bed. He closed his eyes again and yawned, wondering--not without apprehension--what she could be about. He thought: "I must have gone to sleep after all." Yet he could hardly believe it, because he had made up his mind in the night that he would not and could not sleep and had reconciled himself to the situation.

Then the chandelier light was switched on from the door, and Gracie came into the room bearing a tray. She appeared to be dressed, except for a frock...She put the tray on the side of the bed where she had lain. The tray contained breakfast for two. Her smile as she leaned across the bed, over the tray, was angelic; it expressed joy, pride, and devotion, all in a high degree.

She said:

"I do like your funny old front teeth. Oh! How rough your complicated chin is!"

"Here!" he said. "What's the meaning of this miracle? I wake up, and breakfast walks in by magic."

"Well," she said, drawing a chair to the bed and sitting down. "I got the rolls and butter from the house, but I made the tea myself. I've been up for ages, and I'm frightfully well, and I didn't wake you up, did I? You woke all by your little self. Well, I had the water ready just off the boil, and the tray ready, and as soon as you began to be a bit restless, I made the tea, and here we are. My poor darling, I know you've had a bad night. I could feel it all the time while I was asleep. I can, you know. But when I woke up you were asleep, and so I simply *crept* out of bed. I didn't turn on the light. I just took your watch into the bathroom and it was a quarter-past eight. So I got busy then. I dressed in the bathroom. And I must have come in here about ten million times for things, and you never heard me! But I could hear your breathing. You sleep like a child. If you snored I don't think I could have borne it. I did want to see you asleep, but of course I couldn't in the dark. Now, you comic child, sit up and drink some tea." He sat up. "Wait a moment. He must have his mummy's dressing-gown over his shoulders." She arranged her peignoir on him.

"Oh! He does look funny!" Then she passed him the cup. "I've stirred it."

"But I don't take sugar."

"You will, this morning. Makes a change for you."

Her tone was most exquisitely loving and tender. To listen to it, to watch her eyes, was worth a month of bad nights. And his sincere conviction was that he had never tasted such tea. He thought: "I haven't half appreciated my girl. She's astounding. I'll lie in bed for hours and let her do what she likes with me, looking after me. Only women can look after men. They have a way...No man could do it a quarter as well." Another of his sincere convictions was that he had never been so happy as he was then. The sensation of bliss was acute.

"*She* made his night worse than it would have been--she knows that," said Gracie, "and she's so sorry. But he knows what she is. How's the tea?"

"Perfect."

"I should have given you chocolate, but I couldn't be sure of it here."

"Why chocolate?" he asked.

"You like chocolate for breakfast when you're in Paris, don't you?" She looked at him with a sort of loving, teasing, mischievous shrewdness.

"Sometimes," he murmured. He guessed that she must have tasted chocolate on his lips on the previous morning, and knew that he had fibbed, then, in pretending to her that he had not breakfasted. And she had known it ever since yesterday morning and said not a word. Duplicity! No doubt she could surpass him in duplicity. He drank three cups of tea, and finished the last roll regretfully. She picked up the tray in a very business-like manner.

"Now he can lie down again. Wait a second, though." She freed him from the peignoir and went off with the tray.

"What time is it?" he asked, when she was at the door.

"I'll get your watch."

In a moment she returned with the watch. "A quarter to ten," she said. "I must get London for you, dearest, now."

"London?"

"You told them you'd telephone them this morning at ten."

"Yes, perhaps I did. But I needn't bother about it until to-night as usual."

He was full of delicious sloth.

She bent over him and gazed at him with an indulgent smile. "I love to see you putting off things," she said. "With all that common sense of yours that always makes me feel so small and silly. It's such a relief." She kissed him, and her lips lingered on his cheek. "All right. We'll attend to London later...You're in a heavenly mood this morning." She left him and sharply drew back the thick curtains with a metallic swish of brass rings on the brass pole. Then she tripped towards the door, and switched off the electric light.

"You aren't going, are you?" he demanded as she opened the door.

"Only for a minute, darling." She went away, shutting the door.

Daylight had deprived the bedroom of some of its romantic intimacy. The morning had a neutral colour; so far as he could judge from a glimpse of a bit of sky through the window, it was overcast: large clouds, and they were stationary. He was a little disturbed by what she had said. 'In a heavenly mood *this morning.'* Was he not generally in a heavenly mood? And could it be true that his common sense about things made her feel small and silly? Undoubtedly, whatever his own moods, he had grown hypersensitive to hers. He would hate to think that her appreciation of him had any reserves, that his demeanour fretted her in the very least. He ardently desired that their relationship should be without flaw. He was impatient for her to return. His eyes needed her. He would not lose a moment of her. Yes, she was managing him, thinking for him, regardful of his interests, with her prim, girlish, ravishing assumption of superior wisdom. Even the moments of her absence were divine.

She came back, mysteriously smiling, and slipped on a frock--not the reach-me-down. She had been undressed; in five seconds she was dressed, fit to receive ambassadors, radiating energy and efficiency!

"Shall I do?" she sought his approval.

He nodded, content. Indeed, she was exceedingly beautiful, and her chic matched her beauty. And she was his. He was continually surprised, and rather incredulous, in spite of all evidence, that she was his, anxious to please him. What astounding good fortune! How proud of her he would be when the time arrived to exhibit her as his wife? The contrast between the tired, weeping--you might almost say deliquescent--girl of the later night, between the racing-motorist, between the author of her amazing book, between the fiery fierce fury, and this prim adorable feminine wife, this clever wise housewife, this helpmeet! She was five girls in one. Bewildering! There she stood, chattering in a manner original and charming about the weather, and about his shirts. She seemed to be learned in the lore of his shirts. She must have been exploring them in secret while at some time or other he was out of the room.

"I think you might wear the black and white stripe," she said. Naturally her choice was his law. "Do let me change the studs. Anyhow I will." She laughed, hummed a tune.

Why worry about getting to heaven, when you were there already? Damn the Palace! And the Orcham Merger! And every hotel *in* the Merger!

Dropping the black and white striped shirt, she ran out of the room. What next? She was very 'near' to him, surely. But was she? Even in the early night there had been the veil--tenuous, nearly diaphanous, but a veil--baffling him, though possibly it had added to her allurement. Was the veil now torn away, or did it still delicately separate them? When first she had mentioned 'nearness,' he had privately smiled at the fancy. But now 'nearness' preoccupied his mind before everything else. Was she near, or was she withdrawn? He wished she had never put the fancy into his head, for he could not put it out again.

She reappeared, in a hurry.

"I've got London for you, darling!" she announced casually, in a submissive tone.

"But--" He was dumbfounded.

"I thought I'd better," she said. "When you've 'phoned we shall know where we are."

He wanted to be cross with her; but he could not. She had deceived him, cheated him, taken far too much on herself, forced his hand; but he could not be cross with her. After all, it amused her girlishness to manage him, gave her a sense of power (quite illusory). And why should he not telephone at once? He would have to talk to Cousin sooner or later.

She seized his dressing-gown, and by her serious glance drew him from the security of the bed. She held the gown for him.

"Your slippers, darling."

She propelled him towards the drawing-room by an affectionate wifely pat between the shoulders. The sensuousness and the sensuality of the night were their own justification (he thought as he hastened), but even so this wifeliness, this housewifeliness, seemed to purify them. One of his old-fathioned puritanical notions!

"Well?" she questioned anxiously, when he returned.

"It's really nothing," he replied falsely.

"But how is your Miss Powler?"

"She doesn't seem any better."

"Is she worse?"

"He didn't say," Evelyn said equivocally.

"Who didn't say?"

"Cousin."

"And the Grill-room-manager--Ceria, is it?"

"No news."

"Darling, don't you think you ought to go back?"

"Certainly not. Why should I? It's all in Cousin's department. It's nothing to do with me. Is the hotel to stop because one person's ill and another missing? It's up to Cousin to deal with the thing. That's what he's paid for, isn't it?"

"What did you tell him?"

"Nothing. I only said I'd call him up again to-night."

"Darling, you aren't easy in your mind about it all."

"I'm perfectly easy in my mind. Here one day you're terribly hurt because I think I ought to leave you, and the next day you're positively urging me to go. Do you *want* me to go?"

"Yes."

"Why?"

"Because I'm sure if it wasn't for me you wouldn't dream of not going."

He knew she was right there. He looked away from her. His conscience was siding with her against him. Cousin was undoubtedly perturbed, and had undoubtedly transmitted his perturbation to his superior. But Evelyn would not face the prospect of leaving her; he merely could not.

"Well, there's plenty of time," he said glumly. "I couldn't catch the 'Golden Arrow' now."

"Why not?" she said. "You've got lots of time. It's only just after half-past ten. I'll run out to the Wagons-Lits office."

"There won't be any seats." He knew that he was in full retreat. She smiled and kissed him.

"There'll be seats," she said. "Did you ever see the 'Golden Arrow' full in January? I never did. Why, when we came over it was half empty. What a good thing I've put the studs in your shirt for you! You'll catch it easily. You go and have your bath and shave off that beard, and I'll do your packing." She embraced him fondly. "Darling, I couldn't bear to think I was making you slack. I couldn't bear it. And if you don't go, I should *know* I was making you slack. It would spoil everything."

Women were devilish.

"But hang it all!" he cried. "I can't go off all in a rush in this style. It's so sudden. And I did have a rotten night."

She kissed him again.

"I'll turn on the bath-water for you."

"And I loathe being in a hurry," be added.

"You won't be in a hurry," she said, and went into the bathroom

3.

The whole episode was incredible. If he had seen any other man behaving as he was behaving--putty in the hands of a woman because he couldn't resist her--he would have scorned that man.

Sudden, by heaven! It was more sudden than an earthquake, than a street-accident. His mind was a chaos of resentment and revolt. Why was she persuading him to leave her? For the sake, not of his conscience, but of hers...The hour? Was it really only just after half-past ten? He searched for his watch and saw it on the night-table, where she had put it. Twenty-two minutes to eleven...What finally decided him to leave her was the realisation of the calamitous injury to the idyll if he should defy her. Her distress would be terrible, her brave hiding of her feelings would be still more terrible, and he himself would be sunk deep in gloomy unease.

Despite the usual obstructive conspiracy against train-catchers on the part of all Paris traffic and traffic-policemen, they reached the Gare du Nord at twelve minutes to twelve, in the automobile which Gracie had telephoned for. Gracie had done nearly everything, got the railway ticket and the seat, telegraphed to the Palace, finished the shirt-studs, achieved some packing, and generally made straight a pathway before the traveller's face. As for her packing, it seemed to Evelyn to be outrageously and ruinously comic, but he had felt obliged to temper his criticisms of it, because the earnest girl had shown herself very sensitive about it. During the drive he had been far less apprehensive than Gracie as to the chances of missing the train; partly by reason of the fact that he would have been well content to miss it, and partly by reason of the fact that his mind had quite another preoccupation, namely, his return to Paris. Gracie had not mentioned the question of his return; no single word had she said as to it. Evelyn thought that she ought to speak of it first. And he had waited and waited for her to mention it.

At the station she masterfully attended to each detail preliminary to boarding the train, just as though he had never travelled alone in his life, just as though he were a simple schoolboy departing to school. She acted and she paid; and she would have it so.

"I hate this train," she observed as they climbed up into the coach. "It's so pleased with itself."

"But you always take it."

"Yes. But I hate it all the same. I'd sooner go second-class by the ordinary train and let it be as crowded as it likes. This is so superior and conceited; it makes you feel ashamed."

There she was again, yearning to be 'common'! Except for one traveller at the other end, the coach was empty.

"Didn't I tell you, darling, there'd be plenty of room?" she said with kindly forbearance.

The suit-cases were stowed under her orders; she tipped the porters and the carriage-attendant. Seven minutes to twelve. Now she would, she must, speak of his return.

"This train is awfully stuffy," she said. "Let's go out a minute."

In the doorway of the corridor, where for an instant they were unseen, she suddenly kissed him. Her kiss and her glance had a voluptuous quality which reminded him of Volivia's performance on their first evening together, at the Palace, and of her remark, "We all know what we are." What sort of a girl was she? He said to himself that he knew nothing about her. She loved him; she thought for him; she was efficient; she had initiative. But he knew nothing about her: he could not guess what was passing in her brain. The veil separated them. She loved him, but he was disturbed and unhappy. He was almost persuaded that he had never been so unhappy. Time flying. And they were both tongue-tied, and they did not move.

"What are you going to do now, my dear?" he asked. "Shall you stay on in that queer flat?" The enquiry would give her the opportunity to reply that she would stay there for his return.

"Queer?" she said. "What do you mean, darling?"

"Well, isn't it?"

"I don't know what you mean."

"Do you call it respectable?"

"It's just as respectable as any suite in any of your hotels, darling. Do your people ask for marriage-certificates from visitors? What's the matter with the flat? The pictures? Have you ever been to the Paris Salon?"

"Oh! I suppose it's all correct," he capitulated.

"I told the waiter when I took the place that my husband might be coming to join me."

"But the ring?"

"Well, do you imagine if I bought a ring for Tessa I shouldn't remember to buy one for myself? Oh, darling! You are funny, you know!" She raised her left hand. Six rings on it, including an *alliance!* He had never noticed it. "However," she went on. "I shall leave my queer flat this afternoon. I mustn't neglect Tessa. She'll need me more and more now...Oh! I remember what you told me in the Durand last night. I remember every word of it."

She moved now to the open door of the coach, and he followed her. The platform had the quiet which presages departure of a train. The majority of its population, their heads upturned, were talking and laughing with unseen passengers in the train. A boy came along with a selection of newspapers and magazines, all English. Gracie bought a bunch of them at random and thrust them into Evelyn's hands.

"I was forgetting you'd want something to read, darling!" she said. "You'd better read. If you read you won't worry so much. I do hope you won't find things too bad at your wonderful hotel."

He resented her inflection. He resented the assumptions that he was worrying, and that his hotel could not function perfectly without him, and that he was leaving for the sake of his hotel. He was very proud of his hotel.

"My hotel will be all right," he said with a difficult smile. "I shouldn't be surprised if I came back here to-morrow." After all she had not mentioned his return; so that at the last minute he found no alternative but to mention it himself. Astounding, absolutely astounding, that she had avoided the slightest reference to it! Shocking! Monstrous! And yet, her kiss!

"But, darling, you can't do that!" Her tone was startled and very serious.

"Why not?"

"You haven't got any excuse for coming back--just yet. Even as it is, do you think your staff aren't talking about you, and wondering why you haven't given them an address, and why you've been staying on in Paris after your work's finished? Nobody ever finds any but one explanation of these things. And if you came, where should you stay? You wouldn't come to your own hotels, and you'd have to leave an address at the Palace, wouldn't you? What address then? You see, you've always been so respectable--that's your trouble. When you've started a bluff you can keep it going for a while, and your respectability helps you. But if you drop it, and then try to start it again--well you're bound to be done in. If you told them to-morrow morning you had to go back to Paris at once, what would they think? And if you went off without saying where you were going, what *would* they think? Even to explain these two or three days you'll have to invent a pretty good story. No, darling!..Isn't it strange how things turn out? Yesterday morning you were saying you positively must leave Paris to-day--and you are leaving Paris to-day! Darling, I'll write you."

The train gave the mysterious shiver which precedes movement. Gracie jumped down. Evelyn had so many things to say that he could say nothing. The situation was beyond his handling. Gracie stepped away from the edge of the platform. She stood below him, looking at him. She stood straight. She was all youth, elegance, and beauty. And her face had an expression of such proud, dignified sadness, disillusion, and despair that it intimidated Evelyn. Then he saw tears in her eyes. She made no effort to hide them. She remained quite still, crying. Imperceptibly her figure began to slide across the space framed by the doorway of the coach. The train was in motion.

Chapter 62 MELODRAMA

The distance between Victoria and the Palace was short; the early night was fine and cold. Greeting Oldham and Brench, his chauffeur, with a somewhat casual kindliness--casual because he was absorbed in a dream--Evelyn told them that he would walk home. Throughout the journey to London he had brooded upon the multiple enigma of Gracie's character, acts and demeanour, and his relations with her, with no clear result. He had postponed any reflection about the problems of the hotel, thinking: "Time enough when I get there." But when he stepped off the train he suddenly realised that postponement must go no farther. He tried to face the problems. What he did not perceive was that the man facing them was not the old Evelyn. The new Evelyn saw the hotel, and the Merger, in a mist, which no effort could disperse. Whereas Gracie would appear out of the mist with all the solid and detailed reality of life itself. His interest in the Palace was not authentic.

As he passed into the courtyard and glanced up at the dark familiar façade, he saw a window open on the second floor and a youngish woman appear, and behind her hung a bird-cage silhouetted against the brilliant electric light of the room within. Then the window was closed and the curtains drawn.

He climbed the steps under the portico rather nervously, saluting in silence an overcoated janissary who was all deferential smiles of welcome. The revolving doors swung round for him. He had the sensation of revisiting a forgotten world, and then each aspect, feature, and particularity of it returned into his memory. He pictured every floor, nearly every room; he knew what everyone was doing--or ought to be doing. His mind descended into the deep engine-hall where Ickeringway, the chief engineer, and his men were engaged in meeting the heavy winter demand for light and heat; it darted into the bill-office and into the strong-room; it saw the different sections of the staff finishing their evening meal; and the last touches being given to the tables in the restaurants; and Violet Powler in her sick-bed; and housekeepers counting linen, and the page-boy writing in a book the time-details of every ring upstairs as it was signalled in coloured lights on the indicator in the corner behind the Reception-counter; and he saw the ringing visitors and the dozing visitors; and Cousin and Pozzi and Miss Cass and old Perosi awaiting him, and many other individuals hardly less important keyed up to a hundred per cent. efficiency on the chance of a summons from him.

And the entire organism seemed phantasmal to him, bizarre, unnatural, negligible, even indefensible. Why was he in London? Why had he left Paris? Why had he allowed that astounding girl to bundle him out of Paris? He would have paid a high price to be in Paris again at that moment. He had the illusion that one embrace, the mere feel of her frock in his arms, would have mystically solved the multiple enigma of Gracie and of their relations.

He hoped that old Mowlem, the head hall-porter, would not be in his cubicle. But old Mowlem was in his cubicle, having hurried through his dinner in order to be there for the panjandrum's arrival. He shook hands with the magnificent and hoary Mowlem, as always after an absence from the hotel. He felt guilty before Mowlem, before the immense rectitude of Mowlem. His private affairs were no concern of Mowlem's; but he felt guilty. He was deceiving Mowlem. He knew now that he was another Evelyn, whereas Mowlem confidently took him for the old Evelyn. What would Mowlem think of his master's proceedings in Paris, were they revealed to him? A few conventional exchanges of greeting between them, on Mowlem's part sincere and hearty, perfunctory on Evelyn's. For Evelyn's brain had in the very instant been startlingly occupied with a new, unthought-of difficulty.

"I am an idiot. Where are my wits?" he reflected. "I ought to have cabled to her."

An omission surely easy to rectify? Not at all. For he could entrust the telegram to no one. Hundreds and hundreds of people in the place, ready to execute his demands, devoted people very many of them, and some of them on confidential terms with him, people from whom he had the habit of concealing naught. Miss Cass, for example. But could he dictate to Miss Cass: "Arrived safely. I kiss you tenderly. Writing. Your lion"? Or anything like it? Could he even write any such message and hand it even to a page-boy for despatch? Unthinkable! Of course he had always intended to cable, but inexcusably, incredibly, he had not envisaged the precautions necessary. He was committed to daily deceit. He, the panjandrum, must henceforward go forth, making a mystery of his errand, and send off his own cables! He who never did anything for himself except think and talk

"Who is it who's got that bird-cage on the second floor?' he asked Mowlem, with a smile and in a tone artificially light.

"Bird-cage, sir?"

"Yes. No. 216." Evelyn could give a number to every room seen from the outside: more than Mowlem could do.

"216. That's Lord and Lady Levering, sir."

"Not--"

"Yes, sir." Mowlem permitted himself one of his infrequent mildly humorous smiles.

"Well, I'm--! He has some courage."

The aged Lancashire peer (cotton), a zealot, a ferocious fanatic for total abstinence, was the self-constituted leader of the opposition to the movement led by Evelyn for Licensing Reform. He was a terrific fighter. He had at least a couple of millions of money, and was ready to spend a lot of it in utterly smashing Evelyn's movement. And he had chosen to make Evelyn's hotel his home for the sittings of the Licensing Commission! Characteristic of him! Evelyn admired him for a grand old belligerent. Ought Cousin to have admitted the old cock? Certainly Cousin had been right to admit him. Still--Mowlem glanced significantly and warningly at

Evelyn. Evelyn looked round and saw an aged, erect man, enveloped in a tremendous overcoat, coming towards the doors with a youngish, buxom, somewhat coarse-featured woman--the woman of the bird-cage. Evelyn recognised the man from press photographs. He was ninety-one; the woman must have been at least half a century his junior. He had married her--his fourth wife, apparently he could not exist without a young woman to handle--and she had wheedled him into allowing her to travel with a bird in a cage. But you could see at once, from his mien and hers, that he was her ruler. Not unjustifiably did he regard himself, with his long white hair, white moustache, shaggy clear eyes, and pure white complexion, as the finest living witness to the value of total abstinence.

Just as he never 'drank,' so he never swore; and yet he swore all day and every day, for his bearing said continuously in a language impossible to misunderstand:

"I don't care a damn for anybody on earth!"

He called in his loud, firm, authoritative voice to Mowlem in passing:

"My car here?"

"Yes, my lord. It's this minute come."

If Mowlem had been engaged with any person less important than the panjandrum, he would have left his cubicle to escort the splendid Methuselah to the car, but Evelyn could not be left. Lord Levering gave Evelyn one careless glance and went out, attended by a mere janissary. Lady Levering was carrying a plaid for his shoulders.

"His lordship doesn't know who you are, sir," Mowlem murmured, as if apologising for his lordship.

"He will do soon," said Evelyn.

"They've brought their little girl with them," said Mowlem. "She doesn't look more than ten or eleven. The image of his lordship."

A remark which Evelyn ignored; but it engendered in him the novel idea that he himself was perhaps not too aged to become a father.

"Anything new as to Mr. Ceria?" he was about to enquire. He did not put the question, which he decided was too delicate for any ear but Cousin's. Instead he asked: "What's the latest about Miss Powler? I hope she's better."

"Better? Oh yes, sir. I hear from Mr. Maxon she went out an hour and a half ago."

"Really!"

Evelyn hid his astonishment. Earlier in the day Cousin had told him on the telephone that the temporary head-housekeeper was not at all better. And now she had gone out!

"I shall be back in a few minutes," he said to the surprised Mowlem, and departed. In the broad thoroughfare he called a taxi off the rank and, where he could not be overheard by janissaries, instructed the driver to drive to the nearest post-office. It occurred to him that to lead the double life was a business both onerous and humiliating, and being in love an ordeal more arduous than the direction of many hotels.

2.

When he returned from his degrading excursion, the illuminated sign over Mr. Cousin's door attracted him as he was on his way to the directorial office. He went in. According to etiquette, the less important personage should have been summoned by the more important; but Evelyn disliked any formal expression of his own importance, though he could check unceremonious familiarity well enough when he chose; he even regarded the importance itself as a nuisance, if a necessary nuisance; withal his attitude towards both his importance and the expression of it was full of contradictions. In the outer room Miss Marian Tilton jumped up from her desk at the sight of the Director, warmly greeting him in her thin, vivacious, worldly voice, and asking after the Channel and his health. Yes, Mr. Cousin was in.

"Mr. Plimsing is with him," she said, with an intonation to imply that very strange matters were afoot. Her eyes, not her tongue, uttered the word 'Ceria.' "Oh! And Miss Powler is better. She went out this afternoon. We're all so glad." Her eyes, speaking again, subtly and very strangely connected the name of Ceria with the name of Powler. It was a marvellous exercise in benevolent innuendo, and characteristic of Miss Tilton.

"I'd heard she's gone out," said Evelyn drily.

"Oh! I beg pardon, Mr. Orcham. I thought you mightn't have." She opened the inner door.

"Mr. Orcham, Mr. Cousin," she announced. Evelyn entered, and she softly shut the door.

The French manager and the Nordic detective stood up. More greetings. More small-talk about the journey and about health. More manifestations of pleasure at the sight of the Director. Plimsing mechanically consulted his jewelled wristwatch. Evelyn felt that he would be relieved when he had settled down again into the daily groove.

"Well," he said. "Shall we sit? What's the latest news?"

"About Ceria?" Cousin suggested.

"About anything."

"Plimsing has just been telling me. Tell Mr. Orcham, Plimsing."

The detective cleared his throat.

"The fact is, sir," said Plimsing, "I've been rather handicapped in my investigations by the fact that Mr. Cousin thought it better not to call the police in--at any rate at present."

"Quite right," said Evelyn.

"Yes, sir. I quite agreed. Of course I did mention the disappearance at Scotland Yard, but unofficially. The car has been traced."

"The car? I never knew Ceria had a car."

"No, sir. Nor did I until yesterday. Either our friend was somewhat secretive or his colleagues here omitted to tell me of it. I heard of it as the result of discreet enquiries in his neighbourhood. The car was found several days ago on the Great North Road, having apparently been run into a milestone and bent its front axle. The accident must have occurred at night. But something went wrong in the identification of the vehicle. Notice of change of ownership had not been given, and the affair was further complicated by Ceria having recently changed his garage and not given his name at the new garage. Extraordinary negligence. His mother and two sisters went off very suddenly to Italy before Christmas; no one knows why; they are Italian subjects, sir. Scotland Yard was inclined to think there might be something in that. I reserve my opinion. A false clue may give rise to endless trouble, especially when you have no official standing. No one seemed to know the address of the ladies in Italy--if it was Italy they went to. In the neighbourhood reports were not unanimous. Some said Ceria was in the house, others said not. I must not omit to point out that the family had an Italian maid. She has disappeared. I tried a few likely places in Soho and Clerkenwell, but without result. My difficulty was to get into the house. This would have been easy for the police, but for me it was an illegal act. However, this morning at an early hour, after suitable warning at the Hampstead police-station to keep the officer on the beat out of the way, I did effect an entrance by a lavatory-window at the back of the house. Of course this is very confidential, sir. The electricity was working--I mean it had not been turned off at the main switch. Before leaving I turned it off, as a measure of precaution against unauthorised. intruders. Not that I was authorised myself, sir."

Mr. Plimsing smiled and fingered his tie-pin.

"I made an exhaustive search, sir," he continued. "Ceria was not in the house. Nothing suspicious. His bed had not been made since he slept in it. But exactly how many days had elapsed since he *did* sleep in it, I could not conjecture. The dressing-table was very dusty, but not disarranged. The tops of the brushes were as dusty as the table. The comb was missing. There were no letters in the letter-box. There was no food in the kitchen or the larder, except a tin of biscuits, half empty. All the crockery had been washed and put away. One saucepan was dirty. All the blinds and curtains were drawn."

Mr. Plimsing proceeded with his report, and Evelyn and Mr. Cousin continued to listen with seeming interest. But as for Mr. Cousin, he was listening in the slightly perfunctory manner of one who hears a story for the second time. And further, he had his Latin, sardonic, reserved air of listening with forbearance to the child which for him was in nine Anglo-Saxons out of ten. As for Evelyn, he would not interrupt, but his attention wandered. He noticed the horizontal creases in Mr. Plimsing's black waistcoat, and the evidence of strain on the lower buttons and buttonholes. Mr. Plimsing's girth was increasing; Mr. Plimsing ought to be warned to eat less, and to eat no potatoes, bread, or other starchiness; Mr. Plimsing...

Then he began to forget Plimsing and to recall his visit to the post office and the inscrutable look of the girl behind the counter as she read and counted the words of his cable. Pooh! They were accustomed to all kinds of telegrams, those girls were; they must be. The cable would now be on its way to Paris and St. Cloud. Soon Gracie would be reading it. Had he been wise, or silly, to sign the thing 'Lion'? Would she smile critically at the word, or would she be delighted, touched, that he had remembered the strange French term of endearment which she had once, only once, used to him? And about her share of the love correspondence, cabled or written! He felt apprehensive; for he was living in a glass house. He hoped that if she indulged in any odd telegraphic tendernesses, she would put them into French. Because Miss Cass knew no French, and Miss Cass of course opened all telegrams. But even so, there would be danger, owing to the inconvenient similarity of the two languages. The word *'tendresses,'* for instance. Miss Cass's lightning intelligence, upon which she somewhat naïvely prided herself, would translate such a word correctly, and with horror and sinister satisfaction, in the hundredth part of a second. Yes, he was helpless, he could not instruct Miss Cass not in future to open telegrams. Indeed, he could hardly instruct her not to open letters. She did open the majority of his letters; but he admitted that she had an uncanny power of divination which withheld her envelope-opener in doubtful cases.

Not that Evelyn had hitherto had anything to conceal! He could live, and he had lived, in a glass house with mind undisturbed. But now he had something very important to conceal, and he must persevere with his double life, amid danger, until his engagement to Gracie should be formally declared. If ever! Why did he add 'if ever'? An absurd proviso! And yet, was he sure of her? A weight of anxiety oppressed him.

The monologue of the detective had ceased. Both the detective and Cousin were awaiting some pronouncement from the panjandrum.

Evelyn said:

"We don't seem to have got very far, do we? Now, Plimsing, have you formed any theory about this disappearance?"

"Frankly, no, sir. Not yet."

"None at all?"

"Well, sir, I couldn't call it a theory. But--"

"Well? You aren't on your oath, my friend," Evelyn encouraged him.

"The whole Ceria family has disappeared," said the detective, after a short pause. "And the maid has disappeared. All Italians, I beg to point out. The Imperial Palace is a hotel with an international clientèle and an international staff. It is a very suitable and likely field for any activity, good or bad, of an international nature. According to what I hear and read in the papers, there is a lot of friction between France and Italy, and all sorts of movements are going on. Two detectives have just been over to the Yard from the Paris Surety, as they call it, and from what I am told confidentially at the Yard, the tales those two men tell--Well!"

"Do you mean to say that Ceria is mixed up in some anti-Fascist plot?" Evelyn demanded; and Cousin gave him a quizzical glance.

"No, sir. I don't mean to say any such thing. But people who *are* busy on some scheme might have reasons for wanting to shift Ceria."

"But this is melodrama," said Evelyn.

"Yes, sir, it may be. But when a whole family disappears, and a maid, melodrama is what I should call it myself. And it's along those lines that I should look for a clue There's been melodrama in this hotel before now, sir. And if you ask me, I don't know of any big hotel where there hasn't been melodrama."

'That's true," Evelyn admitted; for he remembered at least two instances, including a manslaughter suspected to be a murder, whose scene had been the Imperial Palace. And Cousin and Plimsing remembered them. (The press had been admirably reticent.) A new vista of speculation opened in Evelyn's mind. Why not melodrama? Melodrama existed.

"And there's another thing, sir."

"Yes?"

"I haven't been able to see Miss Powler. Dr. Constam wouldn't let me. Said she was too ill. Of course I didn't tell *him* why I wanted to see her. I gave him to understand it might be about some missing saltspoons."

Evelyn was really taken aback by the detective's astounding insinuation, which drove the figure of Gracie completely from his thoughts. Despite the shock, he gathered his wits together, and made an instantaneous decision to say nothing whatever: a policy whose wisdom he had proved in previous crises.

Plimsing waited vainly for a word. Both his superiors were silent.

"I know," the detective went on; "I know Ceria had been seeing the lady. And what do I find to-day? She's supposed to be so ill that I can't see her, but I find to-day that she's gone out of the hotel by herself. She went out by the Queen Anne doors and proceeded into Birdcage Walk, where she took a taxi. It was observed that she was a little lame."

Cousin, who had comprehended and enjoyed Evelyn's policy of silence, said casually:

"That is her sciatica."

"Sciatica" said Evelyn. "Is that what was the matter with her? I thought you didn't quite know."

"I didn't," said Cousin, "until to-day. Constam confessed to me this morning that he had been misleading her and all of us. She had had some symptoms in the umbilical region, and he told her that they might be very serious, and she must stay in bed and keep perfectly quiet for quite a fortnight. But now he tells me that those symptoms were without importance and he knew it. She was really suffering from overstrain, and she was in danger of a complete nervous breakdown. He argued that as women are what they are, a diagnosis of overstrain and danger of a breakdown would not be sufficient to keep her in bed and idle. That was why he put emphasis on the other symptoms. Constam believes that he has no illusions about women. The sciatica is more recent. It began only yesterday, very slightly. She told him that her mother had had sciatica as a girl." Cousin gazed meditatively at the opposite wall as he spoke.

Miss Tilton knocked and entered with a note for Evelyn. The sight of Miss Tilton reminded Evelyn of the connection which a few minutes earlier she had implied, without stating it, between Ceria and Violet Powler. He opened the note and read:

"DEAR SIR, I am confined to my bed, and should like to see you about something important. Might I ask you to come up when convenient to yourself. With apologies. Yours obediently, V. POWLER." The note was written in pencil.

"Well, Plimsing," said Evelyn calmly. "We shall hear more from you to-morrow, eh?" (He was thinking, ridiculously "How the devil did a fellow with his paunch manage to squeeze through a lavatory-window?")

"I may see you later," said Cousin to Evelyn. "Shall we dine?"

"Charmed. Nine o'clock," Evelyn decided.

As to the contents of the note, he said not a syllable. It was exceeding strange that a woman who had just been out and about should write to announce that she was confined to her bed.

Chapter 63 VIOLET AND CERIA

There was no answer when Evelyn knocked at the door of the head-housekeeper's room on Eighth. He opened the door and went cautiously in.

Except for Miss Maclaren's framed photographs on the walls, and the absence of cushions, the room had much the same appearance as on his visit to the former Mrs. O'Riordan many weeks earlier. Same sofa in the same place near the fire; same eiderdown; and same cat--the cat being one of the assets of the Imperial Palace Hotel Company Limited, and counting among landlords' fixtures. But the woman under the eiderdown was Violet Powler, instead of the betrothed of an Irish baronet; and she wore the coloured frock in which Evelyn had last seen her on the night of his previous arrival from the Continent. No alluring *negligé* for Miss Powler!

"Oh, Mr. Orcham, thank you very much for coming. I'm so sorry about the chain of authority, but--"

"'Chain of authority'?" For a moment Evelyn failed to catch the allusion.

"You remember you told me that Mr. Cousin was the next above me in the chain, not you."

"That's all right," he said, with a reassuring smile, rather pleased that she should have begun by recalling his phrase and admitting the irregularity of the request in her note.

"I couldn't have talked to anyone but you, and it isn't really about the hotel I wished to see you; and yet of course it is."

"That's all right," he repeated. "I'd better sit down, hadn't I?"

"Please do."

She had been lying on her back when he entered, and had turned only her head. Now, as if to look for a chair for him, she attempted to turn her body, and he observed a slight contraction of the facial muscles indicating pain.

"Sorry to find you ill," he said, moving the easy-chair so that he could see her as he sat in it.

"I'm not what you'd call ill," she answered, "in myself. It's only sciatica. That's what Dr. Constam says it is. But it was nothing to speak of till I went out this afternoon."

"So you've been out?"

"Yes, sir. I had to go out."

"But I hear the doctor ordered you complete rest."

"Oh, that wasn't for sciatica. The sciatica only came on two days ago. I must say going out's made it much worse. I've sent for Dr. Constam to come and see about it, but he isn't in the hotel just now. He'll be in some time this evening."

"You said you were in bed."

"In my note? Yes, I have been. And I am going back to bed, but I found I couldn't quite manage it. So I lay down here and Beatrice got the eiderdown for me and took my shoes off."

(Odd similarity between Violet Powler's case and Mrs. O'Riordan's.)

"I suppose you've been overworking."

"Oh no, sir. But when Dr. Constam told me I must stay in bed I did."

"You haven't been staying in bed much this afternoon, I'm afraid." Evelyn was benevolently ironic.

"It's like this, Mr. Orcham. I had a letter from Mr. Ceria, and I felt I ought to go and see him at once."

She made the motion of swallowing. For the first time she had given a sign of nervousness, and her nervousness communicated itself instantly to Evelyn.

"Melodrama!" he thought, very impatient for her to continue, but incapable of showing her that he was impatient. Why had Ceria chosen the head-housekeeper as the person to be written to? What was there between them? Plimsing had perhaps not been so wildly wrong, after all. Evelyn had been wrong, not the detective. And he, Evelyn, ought to have known that the utterly cautious and judicious and experienced Plimsing would not lightly have connected the names of Ceria and Miss Powler. The detective's tact and discretion in the discharge of duties demanding the most delicate wiliness had earned the admiration of all the heads of departments, every one of whom was an expert in the vagaries of human nature; and his work was appreciated by Evelyn perhaps as much as any. And here was the ex-Laundry-staff-manageress practically admitting herself to be the key to the puzzle of Ceria's disappearance! Fascist plots! Anti-Fascist plots! Vanishings of Italian individuals, families, servant-maids! And the matter-of-fact English girl from South London in the centre of the mystery, the sole recipient of Ceria's confidence! But she had ceased to be the Laundry-staff-manageress. She was changed. Her deportment, her tone, her self-confidence were all still developing--though heaven knew that in her mild way she had been confident enough before! She had indeed become the head-housekeeper of the world's chief luxury hotel. Her manner of sending for and addressing the panjandrum was alone sufficient proof of an extraordinary feminine capacity to acquire a new status and be at ease in it.

Evelyn waited, saying nothing.

"I must tell you," she continued. "Mr. Ceria asked me to marry him."

"Really!" Evelyn exclaimed quietly. But he was startled. What could an Italian see in a staid English girl? Attraction of contrast, he supposed. Love and marriage appeared to be in the air. He had left love in Paris; he had been in the hotel less than an hour, and discovered love in London. He himself had been dreaming of marriage, and Ceria had been dreaming of marriage.

He heard pride in Violet's voice.

"Yes. Of course, Mr. Orcham, this is very private. I'm only telling you because--" She stopped.

"Of course! But I'd no idea--"

"I hadn't any idea either. Not the least. You know, sir, when Mr. Ceria had that scheme for a special New Year's Eve evening in the grill-room and it couldn't be done, I felt very sorry for him and I expect he--Well!

And he'd told me all about his mother and sisters one Sunday afternoon. They were away, still are, and I expect he was feeling lonely. And he came up here to see me once or twice about the Floors meals and so on. No one could help liking Mr. Ceria, could they, Mr. Orcham?"

"No. He's certainly very likeable."

"And then one evening he suddenly broke out and--asked me."

"You were surprised."

"Yes, I was, until after he'd done it, and then I wasn't surprised. I could see it all then. Oh yes, I could see it plain enough. And really I was frightfully sorry."

"When was this?"

"The day you went to Paris, sir. And I think I'd only seen him four times--I mean to what you'd call talk to! And I did think it very strange for a man to propose to somebody after he's only talked to her four times."

"Well," said Evelyn, very judicially, "I don't know about that."

His thoughts flew over to Gracie. He could sympathise with Ceria. Not in four days but in twenty-four hours had he fallen in love, and far more than fallen in love, with Gracie. He was conscious of falseness towards Violet Powler. She was thinking of him as a man of dignity, a man of settled moral habits, a man who could and did live serenely in a glass house! If she guessed the truth, or half the truth! If she could picture him loving Gracie, Gracie sitting on his knee in a dubious Paris flat, him buying *chemises de nuit* for Gracie, quarrelling with Gracie! The thought was affrighting. And as for the rapidity of love, he knew all about that!

Violet said:

"Of course I had to disappoint him."

"Of course!" Evelyn repeated her words.

"I don't believe they sort of understand English people, Italians don't. They can't. There was a very bad scene then, when I told him I couldn't accept him. Not that he didn't believe me. He did. But he was so upset it was terrible. The poor boy quite lost his head. Somehow I managed to keep mine--I don't know how. Oh! I needn't tell you how glad I was when I got him out of the room. I didn't know where to look. I'm afraid I did rather go to pieces when I was by myself. But--excuse me troubling you with all this. I oughtn't to."

Her face twitched.

"You're in pain," said Evelyn.

"No, it's nothing, thank you."

"Sure?"

"It isn't half as bad as it was when I came in. And if you know just what a thing is, it's easier to stand it, somehow, a pain. There I am again, going on about myself! I've only told you about Mr. Ceria and me so that you can understand why he's written to *me.*"

"Quite. I quite see. It must have all been very trying for you," said Evelyn soothingly. And to himself: "And she had her worries with the excellent Purkin too!" She was in demand. Cousin's left eyelid, drooping, had once hinted to him that old Perosi was just possibly looking upon her as serious tutors do not look on their pupils.

"Yes, it was," she agreed quietly.

Her demeanour and her tone had throughout been noticeably quiet. She might have been relating some episode of Floors management, instead of the strange passion of a handsome young man with an irresistible smile for herself. She had not troubled to give her reasons for declining Ceria's offer. She had somehow assumed that Evelyn would need no explanation of the refusal, she being a sedate English girl, and he being with all his charm a foreigner as to whose individuality and ways of thought nothing could be safely predicted. She had refused him by an insular instinct, and finally. She might have shown him some kindness in his adversity, but between benevolence towards a man and marrying him there was an incalculable difference. She was not of those women whom an adventurous and thoughtless disposition flings into dangerous experiments. She had sense, and was fully conscious of it. And yet her quiet 'Yes, it was,' in response to Evelyn's remark that the affair must have been very trying for her, had an intonation which indicated that 'trying' was hardly the right adjective for the occasion. The affair might have been trying, but also it had flattered her, pleased her, quickened her existence. From Ceria's discomfiture and grief she had drawn a feminine joy. Already Evelyn had heard pride in her voice. And now her glance, subtle, subdued, momentary, was a glance of triumph.

She lay on a hotel sofa, under a hotel eiderdown, in a common South London frock; she was ill; she was in pain; she stirred with difficulty; she was a housekeeper; she was prosaic. But she was not prosaic, she was romantic. She was not a housekeeper, she was a girl desired and unconsenting. She was not ill, she was tingling with the sharp animation of essential life, and pain was less than nothing to her. She had lived, was living. The transient gleam in her eyes as she glanced at Evelyn lit her sober face, and for an instant transformed it and her frock and the eiderdown and the sofa and the whole environment as a streak of lightning bafflingly perceived on the horizon behind a forest irradiates the landscape and the firmament--and leaves darkness again.

Evelyn felt a tremor at this glimpse beyond the reticence of a soul. The cat sidled casually up to his feet, surveyed him, yawned, and strolled away.

"Tell me," said Evelyn. "I don't understand. When Ceria disappeared and the entire place was disturbed about him, why didn't you inform Mr. Cousin--at any rate give him some hint--that you might be able to throw some light on the mystery? Mr. Cousin hadn't the least notion that you were mixed up in it."

"I didn't know Mr. Ceria had disappeared," Violet answered, "until I got his letter early this afternoon. I never was so surprised in all my life. You see, it was on the same night he disappeared that I had to send for the doctor for myself."

"Do you mean to say that nobody said anything to you at all?"

"Nobody!"

"It's very odd!"

"I expect Dr. Constam gave orders to everyone that I wasn't to hear a word about hotel business. It was Beatrice who brought me the letter. I didn't want to let on to her, but I did just mention Mr. Ceria after I'd read the letter; and then she admitted he wasn't here. She looked rather awkward for a minute, I must say. But she ended by telling me the fuss there'd been. Once she's started she can't be stopped, Beatrice can't. She did enjoy telling me. One good thing--she'd no idea who the letter was from. She thought she was telling me something I simply didn't know anything about. And all the time a lot of it was in the letter I had in my hand. I sent her out of the bedroom and then I dressed as quick as I could and went off, and it was a great chance I wasn't seen on this floor. If I had been goodness knows what would have happened!" She smiled to herself.

"Did Ceria *ask* you to go and see him?"

"Yes, sir."

"Up at Hampstead?"

"Yes, sir. At his house. He said in the letter that he was in dreadful trouble about not turning up for duty here and not writing to Mr. Cousin. So I went--of course. I felt as if I was to blame."

"And then?"

"He was all alone in the house. His mother and sisters are away in France. He'd told me that long ago."

"But there was a servant--Italian."

"Yes. But she has a brother married to an English girl, and this sister-in-law wouldn't hear of her sleeping in the house while the ladies were away and only Mr. Ceria there. So she slept at her brother's--he has a café or something in Chelsea. He wrote me that after--after he'd had that scene with me he went home and took out his little car for a drive to calm himself. He likes driving at night. And he ran the car into a tree--"

"A milestone."

"Yes, I believe he did say a milestone, now I come to think of it. It's my belief the poor man didn't know what he was doing, he was in such a state. He was shaken but he wasn't hurt, because he could walk. It seems he walked a long way. I don't know where the accident happened--it couldn't have been anywhere near Hampstead. In the end he came back home to Hampstead. Middle of the night. And the next morning he felt he couldn't face the hotel. And he couldn't bring himself to telephone. But he did telephone to the maid and told her he was leaving the house until his people came back, and she could take a holiday till he sent word to her again. I don't know where he went, and I don't think he quite knows either. And he said that each day he stayed away from the hotel and didn't let them know, the harder it was for him to do as he ought, and so he didn't. He just let things drag on. You can understand it, Mr. Orcham, can't you? Anyhow, I got his letter this afternoon, saying he'd be at the house all afternoon, and would I come? He was quite quiet. That made it all the worse. I couldn't tell you half he told me, not because there was anything you oughtn't to hear. I couldn't remember it all, and it was all so mixed up. He looked ill. In fact he was rather changed. You can't imagine how he was. He's terribly afraid of you, Mr. Orcham. I never thought any man could be as upset as he was, though he's quite made up his mind to take my refusal. If he hadn't, I should have walked out of his house. I didn't know *what* to do with him. I thought I'd better put his bed straight for him. And he promised me he'd go out somewhere and have a proper meal. While he was telling me he walked all over the house and I had to follow him. That was how I saw how his bed was. Oh! You can't imagine...If I hadn't seen it I couldn't have believed it." She ceased.

Meanwhile Evelyn had gradually, in private, been resuming his role of director of the Imperial Palace Hotel. He was hardening his heart. Every shred of melodrama had been stripped from the affair, which had become a poor little pseudo-romantic tale of weak, conscienceless passion. Not love; passion; southern passion; despicable to Anglo-Saxon restraint. Nor was he uncritical of Violet Powler. It was she herself who had referred to that supreme law of the hotel's organisation, the chain of authority. She had said that she could tell to nobody else what she had told to Evelyn. But why not? Duty was duty, however unpleasant. And her duty had been to enlighten the management of the hotel without a moment's delay. Supposing that Evelyn had not, unexpectedly, returned from Paris, would she have withheld her story?

"I am an ass," thought Evelyn. "What's the good of supposing? I *have* returned...And she's ill."

The more he considered her bearing, the more he was impressed by it. She had told a very difficult story, and told it courageously and straightforwardly. No nonsense! No insinuating feminine appeal! No attempt to impress him, Evelyn! No attempt to justify the unparalleled conduct of the man whose mad worship of her must have inclined her to judge him mercifully! She had indeed accomplished a remarkable feat of truthfulness, impartiality, and self-control. How would the present Lady Milligan, or even Gracie, have behaved in similar circumstances? It disturbed him to think how either of them would have behaved. But as for Ceria, though he had ceased to criticise Violet Powler, his verdict on Ceria grew harsher. 'The poor boy,' she had commiseratingly called Ceria. 'Poor boy' be damned! Ceria had committed the sin against the Holy Ghost. He had failed the hotel. He was wonderful, perfect, in his professional capacity as Grill-room-manager; but he had failed the hotel, and from mere weakness of fundamental character! He had allowed the distracted suitor in him fatally to undo the Grill-room-manager. He was worse than Miss Brury, for Miss Brury, when she went in at the deep end, was at least engaged in protecting the interests of the hotel. Ceria's defection was utterly unrelated to the hotel. And therefore inexcusable. Men of character did not permit themselves to lose their professional heads over a love-affair. They faced the music. There was not a head of a department in the place who would not be hotly indignant if he heard what Evelyn had just heard.

A stirring on the sofa.

"It wasn't his fault! He couldn't help it!" Violet spluttered. She gave one sob. She was crying. She stopped crying, and most absurdly, most comically, most pathetically, patted her wet eyes with the edge of the eiderdown. Evelyn was abashed, daunted. He felt as though he had collided violently with something unaccountable and frightening in the dark.

He rose from his chair with a nervous movement, and walked to the window, and waited, pulling aside the curtains and staring intently at black nothing. What was Gracie doing with Tessa at that moment? Perhaps she was writing a letter to her lover. Her letters would certainly be very exciting compositions. He would have given much to be rid of the PowlerCeria situation. Why were hotel-employees so cursedly human, falling in love, and leaving motor-cars against milestones in the middle of the night, and disappearing, and getting sciatica, and lying on sofas, and sobbing, and weeping, and whimpering silly compassion for adult male cry-babies? He was fed up with it all. The ideal was robots, mechanical, bloodless, tireless, without bowels and without human ties.

He heard the door open at the end of the room and a woman's rapid, bright, vivacious voice. He would not move from the window.

2.

"Well, Miss Powler, this is a startler. Out of bed! Oh! And you're dressed too! I *am* glad. I've only a minute, but I thought I'd dash in and tell you I called at the Laundry this afternoon in my time off as you asked me last night, and I saw Mr. Purkin about those seventy-one pillow-slips. I told him exactly what you said. I assure you my modest female politeness to the great little man was just heavenly, but he was furious, perfectly furious. Some men are very funny. He said he couldn't believe his eyes when the lot of them came back to him yesterday. He said they'd been finished exactly like all the others and there couldn't be any mistake, and they weren't rough at all. And to make sure he'd put one on his own pillow last night and it was absolutely smooth, and if he hadn't slept well it wasn't because of the pillow-slip, it was because he'd been so upset. I had all I could do to keep from laughing, but of course I didn't laugh. Can you imagine the gentle creature putting the slip on his pillow himself and laying his dear little precious head on it and then not sleeping? And him telling me in the most serious way! And I'd never seen him before! Perhaps it was just as well you didn't warn me what you were letting me in for. If you had I should have been prepared and that would have spoilt it." A resonant, jolly laugh, possibly somewhat too loud for a head-housekeeper's room.

Evelyn dropped the curtains in spite of himself and turned. "Oh! *Oh!* I didn't know you were engaged. So sorry. Excuse me."

"This is Mr. Orcham," said Violet in a flat, casual voice. "This is Mrs. Oulsnam, sir."

Evelyn saw a plump, rather short girl with a quite undistinguished face, but gay, laughing eyes and lips. She might have been any age under forty. Evelyn had never seen her, knew nothing about her except that he had arranged with Cousin to have her transferred from the Majestic. Since she was Mrs. Oulsnam she must possess, or have possessed, a husband; but she had no air of being a Mrs.; she was the born Miss, even if she had had half a dozen children.

"Good evening, Mrs. Oulsnam," he greeted her.

"Good evening, sir," she replied, in an entirely new voice, subdued, murmurous, respectful. In no other respect did she betray trepidation.

"How I take the life out of them!" Evelyn thought. "I never know them as they are."

But Mrs. Oulsnam showed not a sign of discomposure, and offered no apology for her garrulous cackling. In her eagerness to tell a story to Miss Powler she merely had not observed the presence of the mighty panjandrum near the window, and at first, when he had moved, she had not guessed his identity. (He was wearing a tweed travelling suit, and had no resemblance to the formal autocrat of the largest luxury hotel.)

"She'll make a fine tale of this to some of the others," thought the panjandrum sardonically. Still, he wouldn't hear her telling the tale. And somehow his heart was momentarily lightened.

"Well, I'll leave you, Miss Powler," said Mrs. Oulsnam primly.

"But how did it all end?" Violet demanded with authority.

Was she displaying her authority for the benefit of the panjandrum; or would she have used the same tone if he had not been there? The panjandrum could not decide. He would never know. He would never, and never could, know anything worth knowing of the rock-bottom psychology of the women members of his staff. They were mysteries for him. They hid their nakedness from him in a veil of ceremony.

"I soothed him as well as I could, Miss Powler," said Mrs. Oulsnam, still prim and murmurous. "But he *says* he is coming up to see Mr. Cousin."

"Well, thank you, Mrs. Oulsnam," said Violet.

"Good night. Good night, sir...Oh! I think everything is in order for the Rajah, Miss Powler." Mrs. Oulsnam nodded and went away. You would have thought butter wouldn't melt in her mouth.

3.

Although he felt slightly perturbed at this merest suspicion of a slur on his darling, matchless Laundry, which had stricken with naïve wonder so many American hotel-panjandrums, Evelyn offered no remark on the droll incursion of Mrs. Oulsnam. Trouble between the Palace and its Laundry was Cousin's affair, not his, and Cousin must settle it and settle it satisfactorily. It was a detail not important enough for the august notice of the Director. Yet he would have liked to handle the thing himself. He was amused to think that Violet Powler was standing up to the ruler of the Laundry. Surely she would not have complained about nothing. She was not that sort. He surmised that in a real set-to she would beat Purkin. He had a vision of the serious, conscientious Purkin putting a specimen slip on to his own pillow. A less conscientious person would certainly have told Violet's emissary that he had slept excellently with his head on the pillow-slip alleged to have been roughly finished. But not Purkin.

There was a knock and the door opened again. Fluffy pink Agatha entered. At the formidable spectacle of the Director she hesitated, flushing.

"Come in. Come in," said Evelyn.

"Thank you, sir."

Agatha became as secretarial as she could in the stress of the moment.

"I've only brought the reports for Miss Powler, sir," she said.

"Well then. Only give the reports to Miss Powler," Evelyn smiled.

Agatha obeyed, adding to Violet as she did so: "And there's this about the Imperial suite." Then she quickly departed.

He thought:

"That child's working rather late." And he recalled also that according to Constam Violet Powler had narrowly escaped a breakdown through over-work. Some revision of hours or duties or both might be advisable. Violet was holding a thin sheaf of papers in her hand.

"May I look at those?" he asked formally.

"Certainly, sir." She gave him the sheaf which comprised brief notes of the day from each of the Floors. Evidently the head-housekeeper had been initiating some organisation of her own.

"But I heard from Mr. Cousin," said Evelyn, glancing at her, "I heard you'd been prescribed complete rest. And here I find you're giving battle to the Laundry and receiving reports at night from the Floors! What's the object of having a doctor?"

"Well, sir," Violet answered, "you know what women are." She did not smile. "I haven't been giving half an hour a day to my work. But I must keep an eye on things, and I like the staff to come in and see me. And then the Rajah arriving tomorrow."

"Does Dr. Constam know you're attending to business?" he demanded, ignoring the point about the Rajah.

"Not from me, sir."

"Then you're deceiving him." He smiled, and Violet smiled weakly in response.

"I suppose I am, sir. But it does me good. And besides--"

"Besides what?"

"Dr. Constam's been deceiving *me.* Does he think I don't know? I know there's nothing the matter with me except I'm a bit tired--and this sciatica now, of course. And he's been pretending I've got something wrong inside me, just to frighten me into being completely idle."

"Somebody told you that."

"No, sir. No one told me. I guessed."

"Has your mother been to see you?" he said quickly, to hide the fact that her second-sight, or second-hearing, had made an impression on him.

"Oh no, sir. I only sent her a post-card to say I was too busy to go home on my usual night. If she knew I was under the doctor she'd worry to death. But I shall tell her about the sciatica, because that doesn't matter. She knows all about sciatica."

"She may know all about sciatica, but does she know her daughter is a wicked and deceitful woman?" Evelyn laughed. Then thought, "Why this badinage? It's out of place." And as Violet did not immediately respond to the badinage he went on, altering his tone to the grave: "To return to Ceria. Why did he ask you to go and see him?" He restored the sheaf of papers to her, and began to move up and down the room.

"He didn't like to come here, and he wanted to talk to me about what he ought to do. So he asked me to go to him," Violet replied, smoothly but firmly.

"What he ought to do? Do about what?"

"About returning to his work."

"Then he had a notion of returning after all. That was something." A chill sneer in Evelyn's voice, disclosing his resentment against the young man. "If he thought he ought to return, why didn't he return and have done with it? There was no need to consult anybody."

Evelyn knew that he should have shown some consideration for Miss Powler, as the innocent cause of the trouble; but he was not perfectly master of his tone; and, having used the wrong tone and being ashamed of it, he grew a little desperate, and, to justify himself to himself, determined that the wrong tone was really the right tone, and that he ought to persist in it. The interests of the Palace demanded such a tone, and if Miss Powler suffered by it, and even if she was ill and in pain, that could not be helped. Moreover, had she not expressed a tearful sympathy for a man who merited no sympathy? Evelyn deliberately fostered his own indignation; it had been a spark, genuine enough--he blew it into a fire. And, as he waited for Miss Powler to speak, he put more coal on the fire, and blew again, and found a sombre, half-voluptuous joy in the procedure.

Violet did not speak.

"Is she being obstinate?" Evelyn thought, and continued aloud: "And so he has the nerve to send for you, though he knows you're ill!"

"No. He'd no idea I was ill. He couldn't have had, because I didn't send for the doctor until the morning after he'd--he'd disappeared." Her tone was now mild and placatory.

"She's trying to humour me, is she?" thought Evelyn. "Soft answer turning away wrath and so on! Well, it shan't turn away wrath. Does she imagine I'm a child to be deceived by those dodges?" He said aloud: "Even if he didn't know--"

"But he really didn't."

Evelyn controlled his exasperation.

"I say even if he didn't, he ought not to have appealed to you. I repeat, there was no need for him to consult anybody. But if he had to consult someone, he has experienced colleagues here, friendly colleagues too, whom he knew years before he ever heard of you. They were the proper people to consult. Mind you, I'm not blaming you." The assertion was unconvincingly made because it was untrue. He was blaming her--for her hysterical outburst, 'It isn't his fault, he couldn't help it.' He had treated that cry rather lightly at the moment of utterance; but now he very seriously objected to it, and the more so for the reason that by its revelation of her secret attitude it had frightened him, imposed itself upon him.

He said aloud, with an assumption of formidable judicial calm:

"You say he couldn't help it. I say we don't want men here who 'can't help it.' And we don't want men who, when they're in a fix solely through their own fault, send for our head-housekeeper and take her away from her duties. Remember, you yourself say he didn't know you were ill. Therefore for anything he knew to the contrary he *was* taking you away from your duties."

"I expect he sent for me because he thought I should understand," said Violet, as it were meditatively, but uncompromisingly.

"But *do* you understand?" Evelyn proceeded. "Do you appreciate that a man occupying an important position in this place can't be permitted to behave as Ceria has behaved? He asks you to marry him. You refuse--and quite right too! And then forsooth he absents himself from his job and gives no explanation and no warning even. If he'd only telephoned or wired he was ill, everything would have been all right. When a head of department says he's ill, we accept what he says. We don't hold a court of enquiry and demand doctor's certificates. But Ceria does nothing--nothing. He just leaves us in the lurch. Oh yes! The grill-room, I've no doubt, has been functioning as usual. But that's no excuse for Ceria, and no thanks to him. And think of the disturbance and all the anxiety for Mr. Cousin, and others too. A good thing we happen to have a detective of our own here. Otherwise Mr. Cousin would have had to call in the police. A nice thing, Scotland Yard making a hue and cry after a missing head of department who's only hiding himself because he's been crossed in love! Think of the effect on the hotel!..Well, Miss Powler, Ceria sent for you. You went. And he consulted you. What then? What did you advise him to do?"

"I told him he ought to come back at once, sir."

"And is he coming back?"

"He's afraid. He asked me to speak to you first."

"But he didn't know I was here."

"Yes, he knew that."

"How?"

"I told him. Beatrice told me before I left that you were expected back about seven. She'd heard. Of course everybody had heard."

"And so what he really wanted was that you should make an appeal to me on his behalf. He daren't do it himself. He shelters behind you! Nothing doing, Miss Powler! Nothing at all! Ceria was an excellent manager of the grill-room, so far as we know. But we didn't know far enough. His behaviour when I sat on his ridiculous scheme for a New Year's Eve show in his precious grill-room ought to have enlightened us. We passed it over. Mr. Cousin, I may tell you privately, did suggest to me that some notice ought to be taken of that. But I said no. I said we must excuse it because it evidently sprang out of his enthusiasm for his work. But this new affair hasn't the remotest connection with his work. And further. If he's capable of going on in this style because of a crisis in his private life, how do we know he wouldn't do something fatal if a really big crisis occurred in the grill-room? We don't know. We should never feel safe. You've heard what happened to Miss Brury and to Miss Venables when they failed us. It had to happen. We can't have these upsets. To certain rules there simply can't be any exception. Nobody is indispensable. Now honestly, don't you think I'm right?"

The last words, said in a persuasive, almost kindly tone, were a tremendous concession to Violet. Conceive the Director deigning to ask a housekeeper whether or not he was right on a fundamental question of managerial policy! Evelyn, self-approving, considered that he had shown himself a very reasonable human being.

Violet, as she gazed at the ceiling, answered resolutely, indomitably, and with a mild defiance:

"I'm sorry, sir. But as you ask me, what I say is there's an exception to every rule."

"So am I sorry!" Evelyn snapped with a great and not unsuccessful effort to keep his full dignity.

He was thunderstruck, and despite himself he had a sensation of alarm. Had the earth ceased to revolve? He was being defied, for the first time in the history of his Palace rule. He could hardly believe it. No other head of a department, not even Cousin, would have carried a defiance of opinion so far. No disobedience in her remark. If she had declined to accept an order she would either have resigned or been dismissed. But an employee could not be punished for an opinion, particularly when the opinion had been demanded. She would not resign.

She might resign. He would not, could not, dismiss her. The idea was wildly ridiculous. He certainly desired to keep her. But still more he desired her support for his opinion. He glanced at her--she did not glance at him--and he saw her as a being very challenging and very feminine. Yes, she was a human individual as she lay there on the sofa. She was all woman. She had attraction; but, very strangely, he felt a repulsion for her. In his heart he was furious against her; he hated her. That high cheek-bone underneath the curious curve of the cheek, that bosom, that soft brown hair, those flickering eyelashes. She drew him; and she repelled him horribly. Curse her! She had amazingly succeeded in her job. And she had amazingly stood up to Purkin: which in itself was a prodigious feat. And now she was standing up to the Director. He had had to do with hundreds and hundreds of employees, but never one like her. She was a girl of quite unalarming aspect; but she had undoubtedly alarmed the Director. He was very uneasy, and he did not know why. The interview was ending in a manner totally unsatisfactory.

"Well, Miss Powler," he said, grandly. "I regret you've had all this trouble while you're ill. But you wanted to see me, and I thought I ought to come. I do hope you'll have a good night and get well quickly. I'll see that Constam has a look at you this evening without fail."

"You're very kind. Thank you, sir," she said, negligently.

Evelyn left the room.

Chapter 64 HER LETTER

It was after a quarter to ten when Evelyn and Mr. Cousin finished their rather rapid *tête-à-tête* dinner in the little nondescript room where they had once entertained Miss Maclaren with a lunch and the conversation which she had so sharply criticised to her new friend Violet Powler. They had eaten the dinner quickly because Mr. Cousin wished to make his regular evening tour of the restaurant and, particularly, the grill-room; also because he had to inspect the Imperial suite, which was being very specially prepared for the august arrival on the morrow of his highness the Rajah and retinue. Further, Evelyn had an engagement of his own in his private office. At dinner he had related to his subordinate the principal facts elucidating the great Ceria mystery, and Cousin, a telephone being always on that meal-table, had at once transmitted them to Plimsing--but to nobody else. The panjandrum and the sub-panjandrum, the one apparently and the other as usual really unperturbed, had agreed that the only right policy was to await the next move from Ceria. Meanwhile the grill-room was taking no harm under the control of the very experienced French under-manager. Three times during the meal the waiter had been sent away in order that the two chiefs might talk of their secrets at ease. They had, however, reflected silently upon the strange affair at much greater length than they had spoken, Mr. Cousin being by nature rather taciturn and Evelyn having been rendered taciturn for the moment by the intensity of his musings upon the reactions to men of two entirely different women--Violet Powler and Gracie.

As the chiefs slowly crossed the hall in the direction of the grill-room, an imposing figure, with a cigar still more imposing, came magnificently up the length of the foyer.

"That's your Levering, isn't it?" Evelyn muttered.

"Oui."

"I'd better meet him."

*"Oui...*Good evening, Lord Levering. I hope you found everything to your liking to-night in the restaurant." Cousin made a beautiful obeisance.

"Can't say that I did," was the magnate's strong, loud, inexorable, but quite cheerful reply.

"Sorry to hear that, my lord," said Cousin with similar cheerfulness. "May I present Mr. Orcham? Lord Levering, sir."

Lord Levering glared inquisitorially at the panjandrum; then held out the shiny ivory hand of old age.

"So you're the foe!" said his lordship, shaking hands, and shut together his splendid teeth.

"I am the arch-foe," said Evelyn.

"Well," said his lordship, "we shall soon be over the top, eh! What!"

"The sooner the better," said Evelyn.

"Your strategy was wrong at the start," said his lordship.

"Oh! How was that?"

"You'd like to know. But you won't," said his lordship, and laughed grimly.

The laugh was the laugh of an old man, but not his handshake nor his bearing, though the bearing was extremely deliberate. Climbing the carpeted stairs up into the entrance-hall, Lord Levering had had the air of carefully considering each step in advance. He was old enough to be old Dennis Dover's father, and Evelyn's grandfather; but he could have passed for seventy, and seventy in his case seemed youth itself. Behind Evelyn might have stood the spectre of death, and Lord Levering might have been defying both death and Evelyn.

"I'm not as young as I was," he went on, "and I expect to be told I haven't moved with the times. This is my first taste of your hotel, for instance. I'll tell you what your hotel is," he glanced at Cousin. "It's a drinking den. That's what it is. At least the restaurant is. If your restaurant is the times, perhaps it's just as well I haven't moved with them. I've seen enough alcohol drunk to-night to float a company. And I hear this is what you call your extension night, and you keep it up till two o'clock. I'd like to know what your female customers look like when they wake up in the morning soaked in the poison you give them--at how much a glass? And what sort of a day's work their men do next day. And young women as brazen as strumpets painting their faces in public! Even strumpets didn't do that in my young days. And smoking like chimneys." He puffed gorgeously at his immense cigar. "And then I'm positively told you keep young men here, pay them, to dance with libidinous old women. Holding them in their arms, women they haven't been introduced to, and clasping their fat bodies, and smirking at them, and making eyes at them, and cantering round with them. That's what's not to my liking in your restaurant, you, sir, I don't know your name." He looked at Cousin again after gazing at Evelyn. "Your food's good. And so is your mineral water. But for the rest--You've heard of the fall of the Roman Empire. We used to learn at school that Waterloo was won on the playing fields of Eton--not that I went to Eton. No, I went to the mills. I don't know where Waterloo was won. I should have said myself it was won at Waterloo. But I know this. The Roman Empire was lost in circuses and orgies, and the British Empire's being lost in your restaurant. Yes, right here, and now! And yet you laugh at me if I fight your proposed arrangements for losing it quicker. Want to get it over, I suppose! You wait till Prohibition comes, as it will."

The restaurant orchestra could be distantly heard, accompanying the loss of the British Empire with a tango.

Evelyn said, laughing:

"I shall be very interested to see Prohibition at work. It's been such an unqualified success in America--"

"You laugh, Mr. Orcham. But you're laughing on the wrong side of your face. As regards America, don't forget that America isn't a law-abiding country. England is. And if England votes for Prohibition, it will obey Prohibition, sir. And then where shall you be, and where will your fancy men and your fancy women and your fancy dividends be?"

"No doubt in the soup," said Evelyn.

A plump little woman emerged from the ladies' cloak-room and walked up the stairs.

"Come along, Maria," Lord Levering addressed her sharply. "When you girls get into one of those places, God knows when you'll come out again. Ten minutes I've been waiting."

His tone, despite the words, was markedly benevolent. But Lady Levering frowned and dropped her coarse lower lip and was silent. Lord Levering did not trouble to introduce his wife, whose acquaintance he had made in the first tea-shop ever known in Rochdale.

As the pair moved away towards the lift, Lord Levering turned back to Evelyn for an instant.

"I don't mind telling you where your strategy went wrong," said he, grimly genial. "You'll never do anything with this Licensing Commission. You ought to have begun by packing it. I *did.* Good night to you. It's the rule to shake hands before a fight." He shook hands again heartily with both Evelyn and Cousin.

"It's fortunate there weren't many people about," said Evelyn, smiling vaguely, somewhat self-consciously, when he and Cousin were alone.

"Ça n'a pas d'importance," said Cousin. "This is only his second full day here, but everyone knows him and his style. Lady Levering was not really offended by him. She quarrels with him once a day on purpose."

"Why?"

"So that he shan't kiss her, I'm told. She'll come back here soon and order a liqueur brandy. She did that yesterday after lunch. So long as he doesn't kiss her she's safe."

"Well, it's a shame!" said Evelyn. "He's a great fellow."

"C'est malin, les femmes!" Cousin murmured.

Then they both laughed. Mr. Cousin directed himself towards the grill-room, and Evelyn went to his private office. Miss Cass was working at her desk in the outer room.

2.

"Hello!" said Evelyn, with no preliminary greeting. "I told them to tell you I shouldn't do anything to-night. You know I never do till next day, when I get home." And in fact he had had no time even to look in at his office. Dashing off to cable to Gracie; dashing back and being caught by Cousin and Plimsing in a most urgent crisis; being caught again by Violet Powler; long interview with Violet; then dressing for dinner while listening to Oldham's experiences in the country. Not a moment to himself.

"Good evening, Mr. Orcham." Miss Cass greeted him with pleasant indifference, as a worker might reply to a shirker. "I had a few things to do, and I thought perhaps you might just look in."

Evelyn thought: "All these girls work too hard." Violet Powler had nearly had a breakdown. He felt guilty. Was he a slave-driver?

"Any telegrams for me?" The words were uttered before he had considered them. They were a symptom of his preoccupation with Gracie; she might have cabled her love or something of the sort.

"Yes sir, one."

He was alarmed. Had Miss Cass opened it?

"Who from?"

"Sir Henry, sir."

He was relieved.

"And there's a very long letter from Sir Henry too. From Berlin. I've left them on your desk in case you did happen to come here, and I'd gone."

"Thanks. And you ought to be gone. Tuesday isn't one of your late nights. You'll be falling ill."

"I was just going," said Miss Cass with decorous but masterful dignity. She tended him like a mother; she watched over his flowers and his Malvern water; and she held that she had nothing to learn from him about the management of the human machine.

"Good night."

"Good night, sir."

Evelyn passed into his own room, where the desk-light was burning. He was glad that the interview with Miss Cass had been so short. The cable from Sir Henry Savott had to do with the Merger; also the letter, which comprised ten quarto pages on German note-paper. Sir Henry might be busy on his film scheme, but apparently he was still determined to prove to Evelyn and the world that his attention to the progress of the hotel-merger was as minute as ever. Evelyn scanned the cable and glanced through the letter, which raised a large number of complex questions. He thrust both documents into a drawer, out of his sight and out of his mind too. Then he lit a cigar and sat down and smoked very slowly, showing respect for a cigar worthy of it. Then he got out a sheet of note-paper, and his reserve fountain-pen, which was kept with the notepaper, and wrote the date on the sheet, and even the hour.

"My--" he began. "My what?" He stopped. "My everything." That was rather good.

He wanted his office to be the isle of Cythera. He wanted to yield himself, helpless prey of Venus, to drown, to expire in bliss: as when, weary of all else, one sinks with ecstasy into enfolding sleep. He wanted too many things that night. Not a single lamp, but several, burned in his brain...Lord Levering was a terrible old man, and you could not hate him. He might win the battle. Mean, deceitful, low-down creature, his wife! Disloyal. You could hate the wife. But not the venerable bruiser. Lord Levering had the legions of the Nonconformist Conscience behind him. And even if the Commission favoured Reform, vote-catching politicians in Parliament in their pusillanimous fear of the vengeance of the Conscience, might shelve the Commission's Report or even condemn it in the Lobbies.

'Drinking-den,' 'lounge-lizards,' 'libidinous old women,' 'fall of an Empire,' etc., etc. Preposterous! But something in it, something in it! He, Evelyn, might be a Spartan by temperament (Was he? What about the boulevard flat?), but he was committed to expensive luxurious hedonism...

He listened for the noises of the departure of Miss Cass. Not a sound. That woman's appetite for work was morbid; it was depraved. He would order her to go; he could not be at ease while she stayed. No, it would be a mistake to open the door and let more of the vulgar air of the world into the scented groves of Cythera. 'Scented?' He sneered at the word which had uttered itself in his sentimental mind. He rose and refreshed the fire which, tired of waiting for succour, was nearly dead.

3.

The image of Violet Powler teased him. Gracie could not think straight. He had always thought of Powler as a woman who positively could and did think straight. She couldn't. 'They' were all alike. Have anything to do with them--and your peace was gone! Damn her 'exception to every rule'! Ceria was impossible, and indispensable he was not. She was affected by Ceria's unhappiness and its consequences because she was the author of his unhappiness. Ceria worshipped her: therefore he must be saved from his own acts. Nonsense! Yet, now, Evelyn could understand Ceria's madness for Powler; for, upstairs in her room on Eighth, he had had one glimpse of her as a girl human, feminine, as a Venus, this head-housekeeper whom hitherto he had looked upon as a sexless functionary. She had behaved, as a functionary, marvellously; she had surpassed his hopes. And not the least--indeed perhaps the greatest--of her feats was to rise up from a bed of some degree of pain, and dress, unaided, and go forth, doctor-defying, at the call for help, and face the winter day and the desperate man, and counsel him, and make his bed for him, and force promises from him, and then return, too ill to put herself to bed again, but not ill enough to prevent her from sending like a queen for the Director and defying the Director as she had defied the doctor! Grit in her. She was no doll stuffed with bran. And Evelyn could not deny, in the disturbing honesty of the central core of his mind, that she had infected him with the microbe of sympathy for the poor little love-lorn Italian recreant. But he would annihilate the mischievous microbe by force of straight-thinking will.

The telephone bell! He could hear it faintly ringing in the outer room. Ring-ring, ring-ring, ring-ring, ring-ring. Miss Cass had gone, then. With an impatient savage gesture he got up and strode into the outer room. He might have ignored the ringing. But he longed for another grievance as a man longs for another whisky. It was only the conscientious Smiss, asking whether the Director desired to see him that night. The Director softened his voice. Politely and appreciatively he thanked Smiss and told him to go home. Instead of drowning in some enchanted lake in the arms of Venus hidden within the secret groves of Cythera, the Director felt himself drowning in the vast sea of the life of the hotel.

He returned to his desk.

"My dear Everything. Are you in bed? Are you wearing the nightdress I bought you?"...How the hell did you write a love-letter? Look here! He was in love. He ought to be able to write a love-letter! True, this was almost his first love-letter, for his wife before their marriage had lived so near to him that correspondence had been unnecessary. True, he was worried, preoccupied, by professional cares. No! They were naught. The chief of his worries was Gracie herself. *Was* he in love with her? He argued that he must be, but how could he be sure? He was only sure that he did not feel happy. Gracie so baffling! A grand figure--at moments! A heroic figure--at moments! But at other moments--what? A genius. Lovely always. Intoxicating in her acquiescences. Oh yes! All that. He thought of her ardours in surrender, her smile, her wifely initiative, her strong volitions...The affair was so strange. The opera, the cabaret, in one night. Two days and two nights with her; the exquisitely awful quarrel; and the last morning of violent surprises.

And the morning was the morning of this very night on which he was trying to write to her, Tuesday. On the previous Friday morning the affair had not begun. In the space of a few days he had changed his life, changed hers, bound himself for ever. And he was suffering. Affliction was his. Oh! To be free of women, with their damnable complications! To live solely for his work! Nevertheless, his yearning to be with Gracie, to caress her, to gaze close at her face, to forget everything in her--this yearning excruciated him.

"I want to share you intimately, and I want you to share me intimately. I've had a fantastic time since I got here." He scribbled hard, telling her without any reserve, and in detail, the story of Powler and Ceria, the episode of Lord Levering, Lady Levering's brazen disloyalty. He filled two sheets, front and back, at terrific speed. "Darling, I love you. Thine, Evelyn the so-called lion."

He would not read what he had written, lest he might doubt its sincerity or deride its phrasing. He addressed and stamped the envelope--penny extra. He pushed the sheets into it, stuck it down with a thump; turned off the light, left the room.

4.

At the lift he said to the liftman:

"Get a pass-key from someone, and go upstairs to my room and bring down my hat and overcoat."

He went into the empty hall. Long Sam was on duty. Reyer had just come on duty. He nodded smiling to Long Sam, and talked to Reyer. (Reyer was certainly due to get a rise in the world.) And all the time he was carrying the letter. If Reyer could read it, had the least notion of its contents! It was like a bomb in his hand. He dropped it into the vermilion letter-box. Safe. No longer a bomb.

Visitors passed through the hall. One of them, a young woman, pretty, and endowed by heaven with much self-confidence, argued at length with the attendant at the Enquiries counter about the departures of the Indian Air Mail. The liftman arrived with the hat and overcoat.

"You see," said Evelyn to Reyer, "I'm not borrowing yours to-night." And to Long Sam: "I'm just going out for a short walk, Sam."

Long Sam looked at him benevolently. A janissary swung the door. He walked towards Westminster Bridge. No distance. Cold. Not a star. The leafless trees in the park moved in the wind with scarcely a sound. The Palace tower was still illuminated. Suddenly, while he faced round to look at it, the tower went out...The Abbey loomed above him. The Clock Tower of Parliament gleamed forth the time of night...He stood on Westminster Bridge, saw the curving, twinkling, noble river; a menacing red lamp here and there in the strings and groups of white lamps. In the distance on the left bank of the river he could see the lights of two great hotels. One of them was the Majestic. His word was already law there, as at the Palace. Romance. He was thrilled. He thought of Rome, Paris, Cannes, Madrid. Romance on a tremendous scale.

Women! What were they? Toys, distractions, delectations, retreats. But, though Ceria might not be indispensable, women were. He felt their monstrous power. Gracie was in bed, wearing that nightdress with ecru lace. No! Perhaps the fear of Tessa's disdain had prevented her from putting it on after all. And Violet Powler, stern, sleepless from sciatica.

Chapter 65 CERIA'S OFFICE

The next morning Violet, in a dream, was trying to do something that Mr. Orcham did not want her to do, and the presence of his restraining hand on her arm grew stronger and stronger till it woke her up. The dream reminded her of an incident in the engine-hall on her first day in the hotel, when she had shown alarm at the unexpected sound of a suddenly-started machine, which alarm Mr. Orcham's firm hand had stilled. The reality was that Beatrice Noakes was rousing her with tea and bread-and-butter, according to order.

"Where am I?" Violet asked of the fat, smiling chambermaid. She recognised nothing in the room. The wardrobe had changed its place and increased in size, and the window could not be seen at all.

"In your new bedroom, miss. I should say Miss Maclaren's." Then Violet recalled that Dr. Constam had insisted on her sleeping in that room, because of the trouble of carrying her along the length of the corridor to her own. Yes, at last she had the head-housekeeper's bedroom as well as the head-house-keeper's sitting-room. The news of Miss Maclaren's convalescence had not been very reassuring; and it now seemed as if Violet's exalted post would in due course, and soon rather than late, be changed from the temporary to the permanent. She cautiously moved her limbs in the bed. No pain. She moved them less cautiously. No pain.

"I'm better, Beaty," she said.

"It's them violet-rays, miss. Violet to the Violet, miss." Beatrice grinned.

A nurse, by means of a portable lamp, had under Dr. Constam's direction given Violet five minutes of the ray on the previous night; and, unknown to the patient, a sedative afterwards.

"I do believe I'm quite better," said Violet.

"Well, miss," said Beatrice. "Dr. Constam did say to me--he's always very nice and friendly like with me, and to be sure I've been here a lot longer than he has--he said it might be three days or it might be three weeks, and I said, I said, with you it was more likely to be three days. There's some here as would be three months with it, not three weeks, because when they get down nothing will get 'em up again. But what I always say--"

"Beatrice. Fetch Miss Jixon for me, will you? She's bound to be about somewhere. It's frightfully late." (Miss Jixon was the secretarial Agatha.)

Violet's mind, as she drank the tea, advanced its tentacles eagerly, graspingly, towards the idea of the arrears of work that must have accumulated during the period of her repose. She finished the tea and stepped boldly out of bed, and found her slippers. She felt quite firm on her feet. Energy was forming in her, like sap in a tree. Dr. Constam would be angry with her, of course.

"Damn the doctor!" she exclaimed aloud, defiantly. "He told me he should cure me, and he's vexed because he has cured me. Well, he can *be* vexed! I'm certain I've had ten times more of his repose than was good for me."

She was half dressed when Agatha entered.

"Agatha!" said Violet, forestalling all greetings and enquiries. "Before I forget. Tell everyone I shan't want any more of those reports to-night. I'm perfectly well again, had a splendid sleep. Sciatica all gone. Have you brought the letters? No? Well, bring them to me in half an hour. And any message from Craven Street about the new carpet for 441.And find out what's happened about the leak in the radiator in 275. And telephone Mr. Cousin and see if Mr. Purkin has written to him about coming up. And--that'll do for the present. Run along. We shall have a big day to-day. Oh! If Dr. Constam rings up, say you've seen me and I'm much, much better, and there's no need for him to come and see me until he's quite free."

Agatha departed, with a scared glance.

"The little thing can't understand me getting a move on. She's fearfully slow," thought Violet. She was critical. In her private mind she was always critical and exacting, but seldom showed it: though behind her invigorating, helpful smile, the really intelligent could divine a certain condescension towards the weaknesses of other people's human nature. Agatha was really intelligent, and therefore Violet had upon her an intimidating effect at times. Just as Violet was making up her face the telephone-bell rang in the sitting-room. She looked about her for her black frock, and did not instantly discover it. At her urgent behest, all her possessions had been transported from the old bedroom to the new, but they were not yet in place. She went into the sitting-room frockless.

"Who's speaking?"

"Ceria. I've come."

She hesitated, dismayed and irresolute. Ceria's voice was abashed, foolish, guilty. She had advised him, instructed him, to resume his duties that morning, and had promised that she would 'speak' to Mr. Orcham. But she was not expecting the young man quite so early.

"Where are you?"

"In my office."

She hesitated again.

"I'll come down and see you there," she said brightly and smoothly. "That will be better than you coming up here. I'll be down in three minutes."

She found the frock, slipped it on, examined the appearance of the head-housekeeper in the wardrobe mirror, scribbled a note telling Agatha to await her return, and went forth, as on the previous afternoon but less fearsomely, into the open, dangerous country of the corridor.

Less fearsomely; yet she was aware of grave qualms. Her mood was rash rather than courageous. She frankly admitted to herself, as she descended on the lift, that she had accomplished nothing whatever with Mr. Orcham. The Director, incomprehensibly harsh, shockingly pitiless, was against her. She knew too well his attitude towards even the appearance of disloyalty to the Palace. He would allow no excuses, except physical excuses. If only Ceria had telephoned that he was ill all would have been different. She recalled, on this point, the Director's very words. But the tiresome Ceria had not telephoned, having entirely lost his head. Still, he had come. He was there. That was a *fait accompli* (she thought in French), which the Director would have to face. He surely would not send Ceria packing. No, he could not.

2.

The door of Ceria's office was shut. She tapped, and walked straight into the absurd little room. A pile of opened letters lay on the tiny desk--accumulations; and a few unopened envelopes--the morning's batch. Evidently Ceria's official mail had been dealt with in his absence. Nobody was indispensable. And there sat Ceria, bowed, limp, shamefast. He did not rise at her entrance. He had no notion that she had been what the doctor termed ill, no notion of the miracle which had made it possible for her to come down and see him and watch over him and inspire him.

"I'm so glad you're here," she began cheerfully.

"Yes, I'm here." Ceria said in a weak, half-despairing tone. "But what am I to do?"

He expected guidance from her. Without it, he was helpless. He was the very image of disastrous woe. He was a beaten child: he, the once brilliant, resourceful, successful ruler of the famous grill-room, the rival of Cappone, the darling of the Palace.

"I have brought him down to this," she thought, pricked to the centre of her soul. She wanted to cry, but if she yielded to tears she might ruin everything. She would not cry. She was the man, and he was the woman. "Poor boy! He can't help it. It isn't his fault." How often had she used that phrase to herself! And she had used it to the Director, who had thrown it on the floor and trodden on it. "It's *my* fault. I must have encouraged him without knowing it. I do like him. He's a dear."

She would have paid any price to succour him, to put him back on his pedestal, from which love of her had tragically cast him down. "If I married him, if I even gave him the least sign, he'd be a new man. I could make him the greatest man in the world. He might have a fashionable restaurant of his own. Would not this be the simplest way? I could go to Sir Henry's and Ceria could find a new place, and then when we'd saved some money--And he's such a dear! And he worships me--how funny! Me! And he'd do anything I told him. And I *do* like him. Nobody could help liking him."

She softly touched him on the shoulder, bending a little over him. He could not read her mind. He was in a trance of despair. She touched him, but he could not touch her; she was unattainable. Naturally she was unattainable, being peerless among all women.

"Now I'll tell you," she began gently. "Who have you seen?"

"No one, except Maxon. I walked quickly from the staff entrance and no one saw me; at least no one spoke to me."

"That's splendid!" she said. "I don't want you to see anybody--at first." She seemed to convey that he had been doing her will and was a good boy.

"Have you spoken to the Director?" Ceria asked timidly.

"Oh yes! I think that will be all right."

Not only the last words themselves, but her manner and tone were a deliberate lie. She lied because she could not tell him the truth. He was at a terrible crisis, in which he needed help very delicately rendered, and only she could give it. The rough truth might, would, have undone him. Moreover, she hoped, or so persuaded herself, that what was now a lie would in the immediate future be the truth. And further, he had put the question to her in nearly the same accents, tentative, timorous, certainly not sanguine, in which he had asked her to marry him a few days earlier.

That scene was permanent in her memory. It had passed in her sitting-room on one of his afternoon visits, in the slack period when he would have been at Hampstead had not his trio of women gone away and left him alone. Pathetic, it was to her, that her answer had not astonished him; it had merely destroyed him, destroyed the man he was. Despite her secret critical propensity, she did not even in secret criticise his weakness. Criticism could not live in her pity, and in her totally irrational sense of guilt, and in her self-depreciation. What, she had wondered again and again--what in her had attracted him? She was so prosaic, so matter-of-fact: while he was the mirror of romance. True, though in practice she was anti-romantic, one part of her, she could appreciate romance, foreignness, the exotic.

And now, suddenly, in his little office, she divined for the first time that he felt in her the same romance which she felt in him. What was prosaic to her was exotic to him. And did he conceive himself as exotic? She thought not. She was sure not; though here her imagination was working in unaccustomed ways, and therefore imperfectly. She could put herself in the place of a laundry-girl or a chambermaid or a housekeeper, but an Italian was extremely different. Withal, Italian or not, she had laid him low with her refusal. She had made him into a victim. And the worst was that he was an apologetic victim. She was ashamed of her strength, her self-control, her unshakable commonsense; which last, however, had not prevailed to obviate her feeling of guiltiness towards him. She had warily questioned Perosi about him--the old man had invented a method of killing two birds with one stone by imparting to her much information about the hotel and its personnel through the medium of French conversation--and she had heard measured but genuine praise of Ceria: his table-side manner, tact, charm, resource, unique skill with the clientèle, which liked him as sincerely as his own staff liked him. And now--! She was continually saying to herself that brief phrase, so heavy with disturbing implications: "And now--!"

Then the thought recurred to her powerfully: "I could make him." She meant that she could recreate him, and better than he had been before she had blighted him. And the resolve to 'make' him--quite apart from any idea of marriage between them--filled her whole mind and heart, inspired her, and inspirited her, so that she began to be cheerful and her face lightened. She spoke to him firmly but yet tenderly.

"You must go on just as if you hadn't been away at all. Everybody will be glad to see you. Don't begin explaining or finding excuses. You've no call to explain anything to the people under you. It's none of their business. You can do it all right. Of course you can. In fact it's quite easy. Whatever you usually do at this time of the morning, do it now, as if nothing had happened."

"Yes," he interrupted her. "But Mr. Cousin...and Mr. Orcham? I must tell them I've come back. I shall have to see one of them, perhaps both of them."

She smiled indulgently.

"Of course you'll have to see them. But not at once. You go on with your ordinary work and go into the grill-room at lunch-time as usual. And you'll see--you'll see how nice everyone will be. You'll feel better. They'll make you feel better. They'll make you feel more equal to things. And then this afternoon you can go and see Mr. Cousin or Mr. Orcham. They'll know you're back, then. They'll have heard. And don't you go and think you haven't been ill, because you have. That motor-accident was enough without anything else. You *are* ill; your nerves are ill; and it would have been more sensible if you'd sent for your maid back and gone to bed and had a doctor. But as you're here--well, you're here! And if you ask me I think you've been wonderful. Yes I do, really! You don't know how wonderful you are. If you'll only do as I say I'm perfectly certain there'll be no trouble. There can't be. Now I shall rely on you, dear Mr. Ceria. I'll answer for you to anybody, and I'm sure you won't let me down. Why! I should like to know how many men who'd been in a motor-accident, in the middle of the night too--" Her tone changed in an instant, became stern and hostile, and she spoke louder. "You may have been ill, Mr. Ceria. I don't say you haven't been. I'm sorry. But I can't help that, and I have to think of the Floors menus. You may say they're not in my department. But what I say is, the visitors complain just as much to me as they do to Mr. Perosi. They've been complaints about the short menus for weeks, and--"

Making an infinitesimal sign to Ceria, she turned round. In a looking-glass at the end of the room she had seen a figure atthe door, which had been left open on her entrance.

3.

"Oh! I'm so sorry," she addressed the figure. "Aren't you Mr. Fontenay? I came to see Mr. Ceria about something on the Floors. I'm the head-housekeeper. I can come another time. I know I mustn't interfere with grill-room business." While talking she moved out of the room, stopping quite close to the door and to Fontenay. But she did not shut the door.

"Yes, miss," said the Frenchman, who had heard all that Violet had intended him to hear, and no more, of her remarks to Ceria. He was a man of middle-age, well favoured, grey-haired, the second-in-command of the grill-room, of which he had been efficiently taking charge in Ceria's absence. His attitude to Violet was courteous, reserved, and receptive.

She continued, still more loudly and clearly:

"You know Mr. Ceria has had a motor-accident. He wasn't hurt, but he's been rather upset by it. I think he must have fainted, and I daresay he lost his memory. If he hadn't he'd have telephoned to you or got someone to telephone. Anyhow,he was too much upset to go home till last night. I'm afraid I haven't been going the right way to work with him. If you heard me I do hope you won't say anything. I've had some worry upstairs, but I know that's no excuse for speaking to him as I did. I believe he's come here to-day when he really wasn't well enough to come. But he told me he was quite recovered. If he hadn't I shouldn't have talked as I did talk."

"Yes, miss." The second-in-command smiled sympathetically, adding in a low voice: "It is Mr. Rocco who wishes to see Mr. Ceria. He heard that Mr. Ceria was in the hotel. Mr. Rocco--there has been a misunderstanding--it is urgent."

Violet thought:

"Fancy the poor boy hoping he hadn't been seen! As if everything wasn't seen in this place!" And she recalled something of what Perosi had told her of the terrific conferences between Rocco and Ceria about the bewildering tastes of customers. Then, dismissing all that as secondary, she made one decided step towards the interior of the office, showing Fontenay her back, and winked at Ceria and then smiled at him with enheartening tenderness. A slight vivacity in his answering glance contented her.

"I think I'd better go," she murmured, fronting Fontenay. "Least said, soonest mended. I'm sure you understand, Mr. Fontenay."

"Yes, miss." Fontenay bowed as she departed.

She was uplifted, even happy. She had instantaneously seized the situation and saved it. She had given Ceria his cue. She had changed the complexion of the affair. Her version of the explanation of his mysterious vanishing would spread through the grill-room staff and thence to the general staff of the hotel in five minutes. It would have precedence of other versions. It was plausible, and who could deny its truth? Why had she not thought of it on the previous afternoon? As for reconciling what she had told Fontenay with what she had told Mr. Orcham--well, that was a difficulty that could be met later. Was she proud of herself? She was. And she was pleased with her final smile to Ceria. At any rate he would admire her for her quick-wittedness. Of course he would be regretting all the more that he had not won her... Had he lost her? Could she keep a heart of flint towards him?

She went upstairs in a dream. She was out of the lift before she knew she had been in it. She walked along the corridor, but ithad no floor. What

Italian girl could have done what she had done? Conceited--that was what she said to herself she was.

Fluffy Agatha was obediently waiting for her in the sitting-room, documents ranged on the sofa, note-book in hand, cooing to the cat.

"Now, my dear," said Violet gaily.

Chapter 66 HER LETTER

The office of Sebastian Smiss was over the Queen Anne entrance. Of late weeks its importance in the cosmos of the Palace had greatly increased. Mowlem, the head-hall-porter, and Skinner, head Queen Anne porter, were continually being asked for its exact location by unfamiliar callers. Smiss, like other working directors and heads, had of course always had his secretary, in whose girlish yet sometimes bored eyes he was the real effective central figure of the cosmos; but now he had two secretaries, and they were both employed to the full capacity of their eager appetites for hard labour. Mr. Smiss would be at his desk till ten, eleven, twelve o'clock, night after night, and the young women took it in turns to stay with him. Thus had it happened that Evelyn, on the evening of his arrival, had been rung up by Smiss at something after ten o'clock. Smiss exulted, quietly, in his new excessive toil; hence naturally the two secretaries exulted, but not always, in theirs. The Palace indeed had little or no use for retainers who were not ready to exult in work till they dropped.

Mr. Smiss had somehow, without trying to do so, got the better of his co-director, Reggie Dacker, in the perhaps unconscious rivalry between them for a seat on the Board (not yet officially formed) of the Orcham Merger. He had won, not because of his superiority in foreign languages and in experience of the Works Department, but because of his higher power of intense, tireless application, of his voracity for detail. Evelyn had begun by favouring Dacker for the post. Facts, however, had made Evelyn gradually change his mind. And now everybody knew that Smiss had mysteriously become, under Evelyn and Sir Henry Savott, the working chief of the improvised organism which was creating an organism vaster than itself--the Orcham Merger. "Ask Smiss. See Smiss. Mr. Smiss will know." Such were the phrases the constant repetition of which was establishing the young man in his new role.

No one save Sir Henry Savott had realised the complexity, the enormity, and the difficulty of the mass of detailed manœuvring which had to be accomplished before the Merger could be floated out on to the market. Certainly Evelyn had not realised them. Everything had been settled, all the main contracts signed, and yet it appeared daily afresh to Sebastian Smiss that nothing had been settled and that no contract duly signed and sealed and stamped could withstand the warring tug of interests. Smiss was confronted each morning with whole ranges of mountains of trouble, reared by a mischievous providence during the night, which it was necessary to raze to the smooth level of a plain. The more Smiss did, the more remained to do.

And the trouble arose in utterly unexpected quarters of the compass. The Duncannon Hotel, which all had at first regarded as the most amenable item of the nine, had proved the toughest; the manager there created snags almost daily. And as for the Escurial at Madrid--often Smiss had regretted that he could speak and write Spanish. Eight or ten English solicitors (including Mr. Lewisohn and Mr. Dickingham) were deep in the affair of the Merger, besides French, Italian, and Spanish lawyers whose code of conduct and whose ingenuity in delaying answers to letters and evading the points of letters notably embittered Smiss's already sardonic estimate of human nature. And there were accountants, surveyors, valuers, financiers, sub-financiers, secretaries, secretaries' secretaries, nameless agents of all varieties to add to the grand confusion of the mêlée. And every one of them stood for a sectional interest which he fought for without the slightest apparent consideration for the general welfare.

Happily Mr. Smiss had no wife, mistress, or other hobby. Happily he lived near the hotel, ate nearly all his meals in the hotel, and maintained health by orange-juice and fifteen minutes of very scientifically devised morning exercises naked in his bathroom. Who could believe, seeing him at work, that he even ate. His meat was the Merger; his drink was the Merger and orange-juice. What he really lived on was the consciousness that he was making his reputation with Evelyn and the originator of the Merger.

2.

Sir Henry Savott, rather imperious in a shapeless lounge suit, sat by his side at the loaded desk. Sir Henry had magically arrived from Berlin, via Ostend. He could sleep on trains and in ships, and he was as energetic as though he had just risen from a feather-bed in some farm-house a league from anywhere. Sir Henry gazed upon Sebastian Smiss, so dandiacal, dapper, and quiet. And Smiss gazed upon Sir Henry's masterful face with the cruel, regular teeth. And they disliked one another. Sir Henry disliked Smiss because he could never penetrate the six-inch armour of bland reserve within which Smiss protected himself, could never exasperate Smiss into raising his meek voice. Smiss disliked Sir Henry because, at work, he had the demeanour of a bruiser rather than a gentleman. Smiss particularly objected to Sir Henry's manner of addressing Smiss's defenceless principal secretary, who was summoned by bell into the room every few minutes either to take down notes or to produce documents. For Smiss was a perfect gentleman before the Lord, and could read Cicero's wisdom without a dictionary.

But the two had a mutual respect. Sir Henry saw in Smiss a marvellous subordinate, a man whose mind was a large chest of tiny drawers all full and all in order. And Smiss saw in Sir Henry a Titan; brutal, possibly ill-bred, but a Titan.

Sir Henry glanced at his watch and compared it with the clock.

"Time's up!" said he curtly. "I have an appointment. You're safe for a week, Smiss."

"I think so, Sir Henry." Smiss gave a gentle but chill smile. "If this barbarian had been to Balliol," thought Smiss, who had been to Balliol, "he might have been a little more civilised."

At that moment Evelyn strolled in, and beheld Sir Henry with extreme astonishment. No greetings from Sir Henry--he had an appointment.

"I say, Evelyn," said he. "There's just one nuisance about the Duncannon. You'll be able to straighten the thing out for me." (Not 'For us.' 'For me.' Smiss was of no account.)

"Yes?" said Evelyn, and to Smiss, benevolently: "Good morning, my boy. How are you?"

"Good morning, Mr. Orcham," said Smiss, thinking: "Although he was never at Balliol, or even at Cambridge, the Director is a civilised being."

Sir Henry violently described the nuisance, and Evelyn could straighten it out, and did--but only by happy chance. (For Evelyn's work in the Merger was such as he alone could perform, and had to do with policy, and rearrangement of staffs, and internal reconditioning and reorganising. It did not touch the Merger itself; it assumed the existence of the Merger, which in fact did not yet legally exist and could not legally exist until the work of Sir Henry and Smiss was completed.) In two minutes Sir Henry had yet once again demonstrated that the nascent film-merger was not absorbing him in any way prejudicial to the Orcham Merger. Evelyn admired Sir Henry as much as Smiss admired him. The Titan's grasp both of essentials and of details was wondrous.

Nevertheless Evelyn considered that the Titan, having surprisingly arrived in the Palace, ought to have called first on the Director thereof instead of going straight to Smiss.

The conference adjourned. Evelyn had come to speak to Smiss about the Works Department in Craven Street, of which Smiss had had special charge until the Merger had begun to monopolise his time. But Sir Henry drew the Director out of the room.

"You're pretty friendly with Gracie, aren't you?" he said, after explaining the circumstances of his flying visit to London. His voice was subdued to the confidential.

Evelyn felt a shock.

"Yes," he answered. "I think we are very good friends." What did Gracie's father know or guess?

"Did she ever say anything to you about Leo Cheddar?"

"Nothing much. She did once tell me something about him. She's got a fairly good opinion of him. I liked him myself."

"Oh! You've met him then?"

"Quite accidentally, in Paris, one day."

"Oh! There you are! She's got a good opinion of him? I always thought she had, but she's never said so to *me.* I found a cable from her here this morning. It had followed me from Berlin. She didn't say so in so many words, very cautious she is--sometimes; but my notion is she means to marry Leo. I should rather like it. I want her to marry, and Leo's quite her sort."

"Really!" said Evelyn. "Well, if it suits both you and her I'm glad."

"I'm rather excited about it," Sir Henry added, and hurried off without even shaking hands.

Evelyn returned at once into the room, and, dragging Smiss's mind from the Merger, discussed the Works Department with him for a few minutes. The first onset of the news concerning Gracie had produced no effect at all upon Gracie's lover, except that Sir Henry's admitted excitement about it surprised him, and that the swift transition in Sir Henry from the steely financier to the somewhat naïve father had both amused and pleased him. He liked to see people betraying their humanity. He reflected that if Sir Henry approved of Leo as a son-in-law there must be qualities in Leo that he, Evelyn, had not observed at their short interview; for Leo lived wholly for the arts, whereas Sir Henry would probably have contemplated the destruction of all the arts--at any rate all the fine arts--with some equanimity.

As the talk with Smiss proceeded Evelyn began to think more and more upon the capacity of the hard-headed for self-deception. Because Sir Henry desired to be rid of every trace of paternal responsibility for Gracie, he had read a preposterous significance into some word or phrase in some wild cable of Gracie's. If the arrogant man only knew that his highly esteemed and serious Evelyn had just spent two nights in the girl's flat, and had loved her and quarrelled with her and loved her, he might have sung a different tune. However, papa would one day in due time learn the relations between them, and then--would he be glad or sorry? Evelyn was inclined to think that he would be glad; for Sir Henry at worst was not a snob and did not give tuppence for 'honourables' as such; and to have Evelyn within the fold of the family might assist the prosperity of the Merger.

Evelyn was in a kind of dream when he left Smiss. He could not decide what job among many awaiting him he would do next. He went slowly downstairs in his dream. Then he thought:

"I suppose there *is* nothing in it."

The thought startled him for one instant. No more. The idea that there might be something in the wording of the cable had not occurred to him before...No! Of course there was nothing in it. Obviously there could be nothing in it. He had not heard from Gracie, and the absence of a letter had disappointed him very much indeed. But he knew his Gracie; he knew women. A girl who would leave ends of lingerie sticking white out of imperfectly closed drawers in wardrobes was the girl who would miss mails, or while passionately meaning to write would forget to write or postpone writing until too late. Besides, the conveyance of letters from St. Cloud to Paris might be grossly inefficient, no doubt was. France was not England. The afternoon delivery would assuredly bring a letter and a wonderful disconcerting, annoying, and enchanting letter it would be...He was in Cousin's private office. Why had he gone there, how he had reached there, he could not say; because he was in a dream. Cousin sat alone.

"You have heard about Ceria?" said Cousin.

"He's returned. He's at work."

"Oh!"

"He hasn't been to see me yet."

"Oh!" Evelyn's voice was blank.

To Cousin's amazement Evelyn walked out of the room, omitting to shut the door. Cousin wanted guidance as to the treatment of Ceria; and he had received none. He thought that the attitude of the Director was very odd, very unhelpful. But how could he divine that Evelyn was in a dream?

His dream carried Evelyn away to his own office. No! There could be nothing in the cable. It was a remarkable fact that, though Gracie was continuously in his mind, though he lived again and again the marvellous hours in the boulevard flat, though he was most disturbingly in love with her, he had, for an instant only, the incredible thought: "If there *was* anything in it, what a solution it would be, what a simplifying of my life!" Which thought was as shocking to Evelyn as it would have been to anybody to whom he might have confessed it. He scorned it, scoffed at it, routed it ignominiously out of his brain.

Why a fully occupied man, such as Evelyn ought to have been, should, after spending time in apparently important but really quite purposeless wanderings into various departments of the Palace, have gone off to lunch at the Duncannon, Evelyn could not have explained, even to himself. He had nothing to learn about the food at the Duncannon, which was not quite first-rate, and would remain not quite first-rate until the well-entrenched chef and a few other culinary officers had been taken by the scruff of the neck and ejected with violence from their strongholds. After the lunch he had a plan for visiting the Laundry, but he abandoned it, deciding that he had no wish to mix himself up at that juncture in the polemics of the pillow-cases.

He might have summoned Ceria; but wherefore? He discovered in himself no symptom of interest in Ceria. Besides, Ceria was Cousin's business. He was much too inclined to relieve Cousin of responsibility in delicate situations.

3.

He entered Miss Cass's office in the afternoon. Miss Cass, with her assistant, sat sternly at her desk, and gave her chief an accusing glance which said: "You aren't taking this hotel seriously. You are in one of your rare funny moods, and you are shirking. If *I* shirked, I should soon be hearing about it."

She spoke sharply to her assistant. She had to speak sharply to somebody, and to the panjandrum she could not. Evelyn kept her in idle conversation, under the strain of which she grew restive. No more than Mr. Cousin could she guess that the panjandrum was in a dream and agitated by the dream.

The door opened and a page came in with the afternoon mail: a sizeable bundle of assorted envelopes and packets, tied up with string.

Evelyn had timed his return very well. He held out his hand, and the white-gloved page delivered the bundle.

"Now let's see," said Evelyn, undoing the bundle. It was as if he had said: "I happen to be here, so it occurs to me to amuse myself with this trifling menial task of untying a bundle."

Among the first envelopes he touched was one with a foreign stamp and the post-mark of Paris. His hand shook. A woman's writing. To make his manœuvre artistically complete, he chose a few other unbusinesslike envelopes.

"Here you are!" he said to Miss Cass, pushing across to her the rest of the mail. "I'll look at these myself," and retired quickly to his room with the selected few.

Quite a competent bit of acting; but Miss Cass, he knew, was a perfect she-devil of suspicious insight. He sat down in privacy, but not on his own monarchical chair. A fine, rather large, distinguished hand, had Gracie. He was sure it was hers, though he had never seen her handwriting before. He hesitated to open the cheap, flimsy, foreign envelope. All his body was trembling. He opened the envelope.

The letter was written on the diaphanous ruled notepaper of the Café de la Paix. That was Gracie all over. She wished to write to her lover, and so, impulsive, she had popped into the most famous or notorious café in the world and ordered a drink and said to the waiter in her rich voice: *"Donnez-moi de quoi écrire, s'il vous plait."* He could hear her saying it, imperiously, yet not ungraciously, and with a smile. He looked first at the end of the letter, to see with what phrase of hot love she had signed it. 'Your loving'? 'Your devoted'? 'Thine'? 'Thine ever'? 'Darling. I fondly kiss you'? 'Your longing'?..None of these phrases in conclusion. No phrase. Merely the initial 'G.' A chill settled on his damp skin. He read:

"DEAR EVELYN. You will understand. I am deep in grief. Don't hate me, but I don't think you will, you are so supersensible. Why say it over again? I said it all yesterday afternoon after we'd been to the Jolie Laitière. Perhaps you do love me, but not in my way. And it's too early for you to know for certain in yourself whether you love me or not, even in your way. You may think you do. I *know* you will never love me in my way; you couldn't. Your sense of proportion is too just for that. Yes, I love you, but I shall cure myself. And it's more important to me to be loved than to love. To be loved without a shred of any reserve is a necessity for me. I've felt it for years; but I've never had it--I mean I've never had it to live in, like an atmosphere day and night. If I'm not absolutely everything to a man, then I'll be nothing to him. That's how I am made, and I can't help it. I'm an egotist. Well, I can't help that either. They say there's more happiness in loving than in being loved. Not for me. I'm not the sort of woman for you. You need the other sort. And you'll find it, and sooner than you think, perhaps. You don't wish me to apologise to you, do you? I should never have been content if we hadn't tried our experiment. I should always have regretted not trying it, because if I hadn't tried it I should always have suspected that I'd missed a chance. You'll be miserable, but it was worth it, wasn't it? You'll forget it. It will fade out of your commonsensical heart. Good-bye, lion. I saw Leo this afternoon, and I told him I'd marry him. He's asked me several times. He was very happy. It was touching. I'm not happy yet, of course, but I shall be. The atmosphere of *his* love will make me happy. I've sent him away while I'm writing this. Naturally he knows nothing of *us,* and won't. Good-bye. G."

So she had composed this crucial letter, and written it--with a scratching pen, in the stir and promiscuity of the Café de la Paix! (Impulse!) So, 'deep in grief,' she had proposed to the worshipping Leo! Of course, if one man could not satisfy her instinct, and another could, she was right to forsake the first for the second. She was justified in flouting conventions for the sake of honesty. And she had done well not to delay. His 'commonsensical heart' admitted all that. Yes, he could put himself in her place. She was she; she could not change by an effort of will; and there was no more to be said.

He opened the other letters, but did not read them. Gracie's envelope he tore into little pieces and burned on the fire; the rest of the envelopes he tore vindictively into little pieces and threw on to the floor. Her letter must be answered at once. When he had answered it, he would know better where he was. He went to his own chair and wrote:

"DEAR GRACIE.. Thank you for your letter. Good-bye. Yours, E. O."

He addressed an envelope--to St. Cloud. He began to read her letter again, but he could not bear to finish it. He ripped it to fragments and dropped them carefully on the fire. No vestige left now of his love-affair.

"Here!" he said curtly to Miss Cass in the outer office. "You can deal with these."

"Give me a twopence-halfpenny stamp, will you?" he said to the man at the Enquiries counter in the entrance-hall. He did not care what the man might think of the spectacle of the panjandrum who had two secretaries asking in his own person for stamps at the Enquiries counter. The letter disappeared into the vermilion post-box. "Some contrast between this one and the one I posted last night!" he thought grimly, glancing not without an absurd self-consciousness round the hall--as if everybody in the place was not only staring at him but reading his mind. There were appreciably more people than usual about, and they had an unusual air of animation. He beckoned boldly to Mowlem.

"What's going on here?"

"His highness the Rajah has come, sir. His highness has gone upstairs, the ladies as well--veiled, sir. And we are expecting another motor-car yet. But there won't be any more ladies--people are hoping there will be." Mowlem smiled with due` dignity.

"Oh! That's it, is it?" Evelyn murmured casually.

He had had news by telephone in Paris of the suddenly decided visit of the Rajah. Cousin had talked of it, with a shade too much unction, at last night's dinner. Violet Powler had mentioned it as one of her excuses for having disobeyed doctor's orders. Her secretary had brought a special report concerning the Imperial suite. And now the rumour of it had drawn a regular collection of quidnuncs, gossipers, curiosity-mongers, journalists, and God knew what into the great entrance-hall. A lot of fuss about a mere twopenny Oriental, in a hotel which had housed European kings in the great days when kings still flourished.

Mr. John H. Harbour, the American cigarette-king, was a much more important visitor--and richer, rich though the Oriental was. Withal, the Palace was doing pretty well to have the second or third richest millionaire in the United States and a Rajah with veiled ladies, together on one floor--and in the dead season too! Immerson would make fine use of the gorgeous coincidence. And if only the Palace could have boasted of the presence of Henry Ford stuck away in an attic Immerson's cup of joy would have been run over. Thus Evelyn reflected sardonically.

But behind these light fancies, far withdrawn in the dark jungle of his mind, terrible thoughts were crouching and creeping. Monstrous, her conduct was! Monstrous! When, at precisely what moment, had she determined to jilt him? No doubt at their tea-colloquy after the Jolie Laitière escapade. And yet after that, that same night, she had...No doubt she would defend her false acquiescence by the plea that she had been loyally playing the game to the end. And the next morning, her wifeliness, her anxiety that he should return at once to London to do his duty!..She cared not a fig for his duty; she merely desired to reach the end at the earliest possible moment...

Love him, did she? That would depend on what you called love. She might be a genius--she was--she might be a miracle of a girl, but she was a wanton, for all her 'Be-still-and-know-that-I-am-God.' Well, she had not been very still...She had wept with nobility at the Gare du Nord. Yes, because she was the world's greatest histrionic performer! She had seduced him, deliberately; and thereby created a tragedy, and she knew the right spectacular gesture for the tragedy and at the Gare du Nord had executed it. Why, even as she wept, she must have been meditating upon the warning cable to her father. She had probably despatched the cable from the Gare du Nord itself, within five minutes of the departure of the train. That was the 'sort of woman' she was. True, she was not 'the sort of woman' for him! Truer than she imagined!..And the simpleton Leo! Would she ever tell him of her 'experiment'? No fear! Her duplicity would be inexhaustible. 'They' were all alike! All! The fact was notorious. And how many 'experiments' had she tried prior to the 'experiment' with himself?..Never would he have admitted it, even to his most secret soul, but the direst wound was the wound to his pride...Monstrous! Monstrous!

4.

There was a stirring in the hall. Mowlem had gone forth into the portico. The belated automobile--last of the Rajah's! Evelyn impatiently shrugged his shoulders--those strong shoulders which Gracie had admired.

He could tolerate no more fuss about the Rajah, and he walked away, bitter, ironic, sarcastic. He would allow people to guess his attitude towards the visit of the Rajah; he simply did not care; but none should get a glimpse of the thoughts hidden behind the irony and the sarcasm. He went back to his office, and his face--he convinced himself--was an effective mask, even to Miss Cass. He was proceeding straight to the inner room, but she halted him.

"Mr. Orcham."

"Well?" He answered with a deceitful blandness.

"There's just come down a message from the Royal suite--Mr. Harbour, you know, sir--for Mr. Cousin to go up there at once. Some difficulty. Miss Tilton has telephoned me that Mr. Cousin is out--she thinks he's gone to Craven Street about something urgent for the Rajah."

"What's the difficulty with the cigarette fellow?" Evelyn negligently demanded. To refer thus to a visitor--any visitor, to say nothing of the second or third biggest American millionaire--was to outrage the etiquette of the hotel; but Evelyn enjoyed committing the outrage upon Miss Cass. He felt reckless, and his recklessness wore an appearance of the gaiety of a man who had not an anxiety in the world.

"I can't say, sir."

"Can't Mr. Pozzi go?"

"Mr. Pozzi isn't in either, sir."

"Well, he ought to be."

"Yes, sir. But Mr. Harbour asked particularly for Mr. Cousin. It was *Mrs.* Harbour who telephoned, Miss Tilton says."

"Oh! *Mrs.* Harbour, was it? Well, I'll go up myself."

He used a tone to imply that if he went up himself, Mr. and Mrs. John L. Harbour would have to deal with someone who would stand no nonsense from millionaires, Rajahs, or anybody: indeed, they would have to deal with the head of the unparalleled Orcham Merger. A cynical energy was rising in him and must be employed somehow. He might have been jilted by a wanton, he might be in the deep depth of misery, but he was Evelyn Orcham.

There was considerable animation in the broad second-floor corridor. Evelyn had gone up by the east lift; the west lift had been reserved for the sole use of the Rajah and his retinue, the Imperial suite being westerly, while the Royal suite lay easterly. In the western distance Evelyn saw some piles of baggage of exotic aspect, and two attendants in rich Oriental costume standing sentinel at two doors. Other attendants, in European costume, were moving with grave deliberation to and fro. At several doors, giving on the south or inferior side of the corridor, people, apparently visitors resident in the hotel, were looking curiously forth. At ordinary prosaic times they would have been too haughty to permit themselves the role of inquisitive sightseers; but the exciting rumour of the arrival of a picturesque Rajah and his court had got the better of their sense of dignity and propriety. Lady Levering and her daughter were sightseeing. It was fortunate that the Imperial and the Royal suites between them nearly monopolised Second on this occasion, so that the number of spectators was small; otherwise the corridor might have looked like a street full of bystanders when a procession passes through it or an accident occurs.

The accommodations of the Imperial and Royal suites varied according to the demands of the occupants. Rooms could be added, or subtracted, to suit requirement. More often than not there was no Imperial suite and no Royal suite, but just suites. The Royal suite could be divided into two first-rate suites, and the Imperial into four. The Rajah, when he travelled, travelled in sovereign state, and in addition to the four suites with a northern aspect commanding the park he had taken several trifling suites, sufficiently important to gratify the taste of most visitors except film-kings and film-stars, on the inferior side.

As Evelyn knocked at the main door of Mr. Harbour's Royal suite, he saw one of the Oriental sentinels of the Imperial suite suddenly stand back and salaam. The aristocratic figure of a very dark and handsome slim young man in a lounge suit and white turban emerged from a doorway. The figure paused a moment, and then, followed by two satellites of almost equal distinction, walked down the corridor towards the west lift. The Rajah! Although a hundred or more feet away Evelyn could recognise the gait of sovereignty. So the Rajah was young. Evelyn in his simplicity had always imagined Rajahs as fat and bearded and venerable.

The main door of the Royal suite was opened by another young man, in another lounge suite similar in style to that of the Rajah, but not finished off with a turban.

"Yes, *sir.*"

An American voice and an American jaw. Neckwear recalling the advertisement pages of the Philadelphia "Saturday Evening Post."

"Mr. Harbour, or Mrs. Harbour, wants to see the manager," said Evelyn with mildness, feeling uncomfortably that in his haste he had cast himself for a too minor part.

"But say! You aren't Mr. Cousin. We asked for Mr. Cousin."

"My name is Orcham. Mr. Cousin is not in. I'm what you may call Mr. Cousin's superior officer."

"Well, I thought Mr. Cousin was the head-god here. Will you please come in, Mr. Orcham? Glad to meet you. Boss, this is Mr. Orcham."

He had turned to address a stout, middle-aged man who was coming out of a room to the left, where were congregated a miscellany of persons of both sexes, two of whom, girls, were seated and tapping at typewriters. The busy room was evidently the cigarette-king's antechamber for callers and clerks, and the stout gentleman was evidently the cigarette-king himself.

"Mr. Orcham? Mr. Orcham. This is a great pleasure, Mr. Orcham," said the cigarette-king very amiably. "Come right in."The cigarette-king heartily shook hands with Evelyn. "I was very sorry to miss meeting you when you were over on our side. Mr. Staten's an old and valued friend of mine. He told me about you. He's a lovely man. You've got *some* hotel here, Mr. Orcham. I've not stayed here before. Mrs. Harbour liked the Majestic."

"That's mine too," said Evelyn.

"Oh, I know. Been a lot of talk down town in New York about your Merger, Mr. Orcham. You've got a great thing there, sir."

Evelyn, pleased by the knowledge thus displayed, at once liked Mr. John H. Harbour, who had a firm grip, a pleasant democratic smile on his round red face, a jaw surpassing that of his young "Saturday Evening Post" secretary, a heavy, protruding, hanging lower lip, and a cigar which depended from his gold-studded teeth as lightly as a cigarette. The state of being the second or third biggest millionaire in a continent of millionaires had clearly not demoralised him. Yet he had the air of his high rank. He would have passed for what he was in any company. Indeed, it was impossible that he could have been aught else but a major millionaire; and his glance announced to the observant, without, however, a trace of self-complacency, that he manufactured twenty million cigarettes a day--and sold them.

He led Evelyn through a large drawing-room into a small one. They sat down. A cigar was offered to Evelyn.

"No, thanks," said Evelyn. "But if I may have one of your cigarettes--"

"You sure can."

Evelyn suspected that Mr. Harbour was not feeling quite at ease.

"Mrs. Harbour uses this room as her boudoir, that's why I brought you in here. It's *Mrs.* Harbour you've come to see."

Yes, Mr. Harbour was certainly nervous. He called out loudly:

"Emily!"

After a couple of minutes Emily entered, from the farther door. She was a lady of perhaps fifty-five, five years younger than her husband, and a little less stout, but not much; with a gigantic bust tightly and smoothly encased--no promontories--in a plum-coloured dress which had long sleeves and a long skirt. Her iron-grey hair surmounted a broad, set, grim, uncompromising face. No style, no distinction, no powder, no rouge. She had the stiff inelegance of shyness without the shyness. Her appearance and manner gave poor support to the widely held sexual theory that women will adapt themselves to change of class and of circumstances. She was born to be a provincial matron, and she had remained steadfastly a provincial matron throughout the astounding series of leaps in the circulation of her husband's cigarettes. She had had neither the wit to learn nor the wisdom to forget. She was immutable. And she bestowed upon herself such personal prestige that she compelled thoughtless beholders to believe that it was Mrs. Harbour, not Mr. Harbour, who had invented and was manufacturing and selling the famous Harbour cigarettes.

Evelyn detested her gaze, her voice, her handshake, and the way she received Mr. Harbour's introduction of him and brief recital of his claim to special notice. And he felt a benevolent contempt for the cigarette-king's obvious subservience and his cautious fear of her. He rose, and she did not invite him to sit down again; but he sat down.

Strange that he should immediately transfer some of his detestation of her to Gracie. 'They' were all alike, and so on, though no two women could have been more acutely dissimilar than Emily Harbour and Gracie Savott.

"Well, Mr. Orcham," Emily started, "I want you to know that I'm from Kentucky--"

The rest of her remarks were in that key. She had been informed that the new gentleman next door was a Rajah or whatever it was. And he'd come with a harem. With her own eyes she had seen the harem, or part of it, on a neighbouring balcony. And she supposed there were eunuchs too. Such a terrible outrage would never be tolerated in the Mississippi Hotel in Louisville. And she could not stay, and Mr. Harbour could not stay. It was an insult to white people, Christians, even Roman Catholics it would be an insult to. And the Harbours must leave at once. Not another night could they stay, with a harem next door.

"I am not aware of any harem, Mrs. Harbour," said Evelyn.

"Then what are all those creatures?" Mrs. Harbour demanded. "That's all I'd like to know. With their veils and gauzes and things." It might do for London and Paris, but as for her she'd made up her mind about it, and if she'd ever had the slightest idea that such things could be...

At first Evelyn suspected that a wild farce was being staged for his diversion. But of course the suspicion was ridiculous. Mrs. Harbour, though utterly incredible, was true. And you might as usefully argue with her as with a rhinoceros. He settled his policy in an instant; it was based upon the maxim: The visitor is always right. He said:

"I admire your stand, Mrs. Harbour. Of course we innkeepers are not quite our own masters. The Rajah comes from one of the oldest reigning families in the East. His forefathers have lived in what I daresay they'd think is splendid civilisation for many centuries, long before Britain was colonised or America discovered. But I admit that all that is beside the point. Yes, I fully admit it. I would ask his highness to leave, but that might lead to serious trouble, in fact to international complications, for he will be lunching with King George tomorrow."

"But not his harem, I hope."

"Certainly not. If harem there is."

"If! Then what are they? Nautch girls? I know the world, Mr. Orcham, and I know that there must be immorality, but to flaunt it openly, and in a respectable hotel where respectable people stay never thinking, never expecting--"

"Mrs. Harbour," Evelyn ventured deferentially to interrupt her, "I agree. I agree. And let me say that you have taught me a lesson which I shall always remember. And I do hope you'll accept my sincere apologies." He said to himself: "If it's to be a farce, I'll be farcical." And he went on to be still more farcical, until he feared lest Mrs. Harbour would rise in fury and strike him for an impudent clown. Groundless apprehension! The hide of the rhinoceros was undamaged. Mrs. Harbour grandiosely accepted his humble apologies and the hint that she had deflected the dangerous curve of his life. Could she have smiled, she would have smiled.

"Now as regards leaving," he said. "I fully understand your scruples about staying here. I sympathise with them. You wish to leave at once. We shall be exceedingly sorry to lose you, for visitors like you and Mr. Harbour mean a very great deal to us. We don't get them every day, no, nor every year. Still, we have brought your leaving us on ourselves. Now I have two other hotels, the Majestic and the Duncannon. I think you'd rather approve the Majestic, and I may say that it is even better now than it used to be. I will personally guarantee...I will see to everything myself...I will telephone myself and give instructions--"

In five minutes it was arranged that the Harbour ménage with its retinue should be transferred to the Majestic.

"I think Mr. Orcham has met us very fairly, my dear," said Mr. Harbour. These were his first words in the interview. His relief was touching. He lit a new cigar; its predecessor, scarcely half-smoked, was extinguished and cold.

Mrs. Harbour nodded assent to her husband's remark. At the outer door the two men, alone together for a moment, contrived to maintain an admirable seriousness.

"This Merger of yours is a very interesting proposition, Mr. Orcham," said the cigarette-king.

They chatted. And at last Evelyn said:

"I've really nothing to do with that side of it; but I'll speak to Sir Henry Savott. I'm sure he would feel flattered."

Outside in the corridor, which was still busily astir and now had added the watchful old Perosi to its floating populace, Evelyn's thoughts followed one another thus:

"This hasn't really happened, because it couldn't have happened. That Rajah, with two thousand years of civilisation in his way of walking and holding his head as he walks, shovelled up and thrown into a corner by the Kentucky squaw from Louisville. Nobody will believe it. Who could? The cigarette-king's in fear of his life of her. Why make twenty million cigarettes a day when this is all you get for it? A good stroke--it will divide the publicity between the Palace and the Majestic. Palace doesn't need publicity, Majestic does. Must find a good picturesque reason for the flitting. Immerson will think of one. Immerson will simply go off his head with joy. He's never had anything to touch it. Monstrous! Monstrous! They're all alike. She was so damned attentive and efficient yesterday only because she'd positively made up her mind to get rid of me. No! Well, perhaps she wanted to make me regret her all the more with her thoughtfulness and her smart organising; make me realise afterwards what a complete all-round sort of a creature I'd lost. 'Be still and know that I am God.' How does she make that square with what she's done? I suppose she thinks that it means being still and being herself and letting everything else go, and God created her as she is, and so it's all right, and it doesn't matter what happens to other people so long as she's herself and acts herself. Doesn't matter about me, for instance, so long as she's herself. It's enough to make you laugh. I'm miserable, and what a fool I am to be miserable! She's ruined me. No, she hasn't. I won't let her. I'll show her. But they're all alike. Monstrous! I'm miserable. Idiot!

"I hope she'll appreciate my letter. My letter was a masterpiece. There's something tremendous about that girl. There never was another girl like her. What a mind! What breasts! I'm miserable. She could make a mackintosh and a sixty-franc *chemise de nuit* look stylish and expensive. Says she's in love with me. Well, I believe she is too. And I hope to God she won't be able to sleep for thinking of me. No. She's only in love with herself. Didn't she say she was an egotist and they all were? She'll ruin her Leo Cheddar, though. I've escaped. Not his money. No, she's not mean. She's magnificent, curse her! She'll draw the soul out of him, and eat it and drink it, till there's nothing left. What breasts! And what a voice! She's glorious. I've escaped. What kind of a mess would she have made of me? And I've escaped and I'm miserable. And nobody knows, except her. I'll send her a wedding present. Six nightgowns from the Stores. Chaste Anglo-Indian taste. Then she'll have to explain them to her Leo. 'The Nature of the Universe'! The Nature of Women! They're all alike. She's terrific, but the Kentucky squaw is more terrific, because she's got nothing but her self-conceit to do it with. She's ugly and stupid and old, but she can do it. She's done it, and she'll keep on doing it until she drops. She ought to be abandoned to a brutal and licentious soldiery, that squaw ought. Teach her a thing or two. But it'd be no use. They wouldn't touch her if you bribed them. She's safe. She's safe even from the cigarette-king. If he doesn't amuse himself with something less like a female rhinoceros he's the biggest ass that God ever made.

"If she was the mother of the Rajah she'd rule the Rajah and all Java and Morocco and Cambodia or wherever it is he comes from. She'd stick behind the purdah, and she'd be the boss of all the Orient. And nobody could tell how in hell she did it. And wouldn't the odalisques have a thin time! Like hell they would. But I've beaten her, if she's never been beaten before. She didn't see I was laughing at her. What a woman! She'd swallow anything. The top of her bent's higher than the Himalaya. I'm miserable. Fancy her taking that boulevard flat all on her own! And buying the Baedeker. An artist! Female Don Juan. Donna Juana. That's it. Donna Juana! Always running around and making out to herself that she's searching for the ideal. And I believe she really believes it. A whip might keep her in order. It's the only thing that would. And I never thought of it. What I ought to do is to go back with a cane and rip everything off her, and give her a hiding until she fainted away, and then when she came to make her kneel down and beg my pardon for being thrashed. That's one argument we always have, muscles, the muscular argument. Oh! What a rogue and peasant slave am I! And it's the one argument they understand.

I'm dashed if my stomach isn't all cold lead. Curious the connection between mind and body. It's all imagination, but my stomach's like lead."

5.

As Evelyn strolled along the corridor and walked downstairs--he would not take the lift because he wanted to luxuriate in his sinister thoughts--a lamp burned vividly incandescent in his brain; another lamp, not either of the old ones; the lamp of destruction, not of creation. But like the others it was magically invisible. Those who saw him at the end of a corridor, or on the unfrequented stairs, saw the panjandrum of the hotel and the Orcham of the Orcham Merger, calm, urbane, reserved, mysterious as became the acknowledged monarch of the world of luxury hotels.

At the very moment when he was crossing a corner of the entrance-hall towards his own retreat, he saw Cousin enter in haste through the revolving doors. And Cousin saw him and hurried to him. Cousin clearly had something of importance to communicate. But Evelyn had something of greater importance to communicate, and by right of precedence Evelyn began. He was in a state to explode with the Kentucky squaw story; there are stories which cannot be restrained; and this was one, and no one in the hotel would more finely savour it than Cousin. They turned their faces a little to one of the pillars of the entrance-hall, and Evelyn narrated the tale.

"Yes," Cousin answered with his aloof smile, "I could believe anything of these Anglo-Saxon ladies. But it is necessary that this affair should be arranged."

"At once. I leave all the details to you, *mon cher."*

"Hm!" said Cousin musingly, as if saying: "It's all very well for you to give the order, but it will want some doing."

"Send up Pozzi or someone to offer any help they need about packing, and then get busy on the Majestic."

"I've just come from Craven Street," said Cousin inconsequently. "I wanted to see you. Collifant is on strike."

Collifant was the manager of the Works Department.

"On strike? What do you mean?"

"About a *lit de repos* that the Rajah has asked for."

"What on earth's a *lit de repos?* A day-bed?"

"Yes, that's what you call it. He says he can't supply it today *or* to-morrow. He says the Rajah's visit has exhausted him already, and exhausted the carpenters too, and it can't be done until the day after to-morrow. He will not listen to the suggestion of overtime. He says the carpenters were working all last night, and there would be an insurrection. The Rajah objects to a sofa, or at least they say he objects. It must be a day-bed. I thought it would be well to buy one. That man Harris in Oxford Street might have one, and in any case he would know where to find one."

"Not on your life!" Evelyn exclaimed. (The old lamp was burning afresh.) "What's the point of having a Works Department, I should like to know!"

"Well, I have done all I could."

"But I haven't," said Evelyn. "I'll go over to Craven Street myself, and I'll see whether Master Collifant will strike or not. I never heard of such a thing. If we want a day-bed we'll have it, and we will have it from Craven Street."

"Thank you," said Cousin drily, half maliciously. He was conscious of a relief profound and unexpected. He added:

"Ceria came to see me."

"Well, you gave him notice?"

"No. I received no instructions from you. It seemed to me you had decided nothing--when I spoke to you."

Then what did you say?"

"I listened. He told me that he had not been in a state to telephone or write. I said to him that he should carry on--for the present."

"But last night I gave you--Never mind now. I'm off to Craven Street."

The panjandrum turned sharply away. His head was full of the Craven Street situation. The Ceria situation could wait. All his resentment against Gracie, all his blighting contempt for the Kentucky squaw, were transferred to the preposterous Collifant. He would show Collifant what was what. Collifant should contrive a day-bed, perhaps out of nothing; but he should contrive it. And instantaneously. The panjandrum could be as implacable and as imperious as any rajah.

He passed with careful consideration through Miss Cass's room. She was alone now. Rajahs. Seraglios. Veiled women. Ancient Oriental civilisations. Aristocracies of the East. All those things flowed together and formed--a visitor to the Imperial Palace! The visitor was always right. What the visitor desired he must and should have. The absurd Collifant was outraging the cardinal principle of the Palace, of the entire Orcham Merger. Gracie was naught, curse her! In his private office Miss Cass's meek assistant was on her knees on the carpet laboriously picking up one by one tiny fragments of envelopes, lest the disdainer of opulent squaws and the purveyor to Oriental civilisations functioning only two floors above her head might on his return be offended by the sight of them.

"Sorry, sir," she apologised for her conscientiousness.

Chapter 67 WORKS

It was Mrs. Oulsnam who told Violet of the Rajah's imperious demands for a day-bed in the more intimate of his drawing-rooms. Mrs. Oulsnam flew up to Eighth full of the news and of fun. She gave her opinion that a nicely covered mattress on the floor would have suited his highness's reclining habits better than any day-bed. She laughed at his objections to a mere English sofa, seeing that, like most Oriental potentates, he evidently had a desire to be as Western as possible while in the West. She laughed also at the total absence of day-beds in the furniture of a hotel with the international pretentions of the Palace. Agreeably giggling, she surmised that the Rajah's fancy for the day-bed must be due to the fact that he had only quite recently heard of the existence of day-beds as a Western institution, and was determined to be in the movement.

Violet, who had been conversing on the telephone with Ceria, said at once that she should attend to the matter personally. Whereat Mrs. Oulsnam was much relieved; for, as the brightest among the floor-housekeepers, she had been charged with the delicate responsibility of satisfying the Rajah's eccentric requirements in the way of furniture, and for all her gaiety of spirit was beginning to feel the strain.

A certain incoördination of effort, due to Violet having been laid aside, vitiated the activities of the Floors. Mrs. Oulsnam was not aware that the power of Mr. Cousin himself had been directly invoked by the Rajah's French secretary. And Mr. Cousin did not know that Violet had resumed duty. He would have known, had not her subordinates and others, secretly from Violet, conspired to conceal her dangerous defiance of Dr. Constam from the superior authorities. Violet had impulsively taken the day-bed job to herself, because in a flash, even as Mrs. Oulsnam was speaking, she had an idea. She had never before heard of a day-bed, but she recalled having seen, amid the litter of the carpenter's shop on Eighth, an article which now seemed to her to correspond with Mrs. Oulsnam's description of what a day-bed was.

Off she hurried to the carpenter's shop, and there it was, with a pile of old chairs and light occasional tables stacked on the top of it. The only carpenter present in the shop first told her that it was nothing, then that it was junk, then that he had heard years earlier that it was supposed to be a bit of 'old Empire.' Anyhow, it was broken, and the part missing had long since utterly vanished.

It was in truth a two-ended *lit de repos,* not Empire but Louis Philippe; lacking one of its ends; with bronzes on its mahogany sides; upholstered in worn and faded green and gold silk; a pitiable object. The carpenter said that to restore it properly would involve very expert labour and a fortnight's time. Violet's reply was to request him to extricate it and get it down to the goods-entrance instantly. She explained that she was going to take it herself to Craven Street in a taxi. The carpenter said that it would not hold in a taxi. Violet said that it would hold in a taxi if the taxi was open.

Pleased with her own initiative, she ran off to prepare for the street. She descended in the goods-lift with the day-bed and the carpenter. A brilliant Laundry motor-van was unloading baskets in the dark tunnel of the goods-entrance. Violet had some acquaintance with the driver. Knowing that he must have to wait there for an hour or more for his cargo of afternoon soiled linen, she instructed him in a friendly, firm tone of assured confidence to drive her and the day-bed to Craven Street, and to help the carpenter to stow the day-bed into his van. The driver hesitated and yielded. Violet felt triumphant. Heaven was aiding her enterprise. She admitted privately that to travel through West End streets in winter in an open taxi with the end of a French day-bed protruding backwards beyond the hood would have been rather ridiculous.

The porter hoisted her into the van after the day-bed, upon which she had the happy notion of sitting down. Then the porter banged the doors of the van, and Violet found herself in a darkness blacker than that of the tunnel. The darkness was total save for slits of very faint light at the jointure of the double doors and below them. A jerk, and she was thrown violently against the remaining arm of the day-bed, to which thenceforth she clung for her life. The voyage began thus stormily, and the storm increased; now and then it attained the rank of a tempest. The day-bed crawled to and fro in the vast, mysterious interior of the van. While the van was in motion she could hear nothing but its tremendous roar and the rattle of its vibration. When it stopped she was frightened by the menacing thunder of circumambient traffic.

"It's worse than being on the blasted ocean," she muttered. Not till that memorable journey had she realised the awfulness of the perils of the central thoroughfares of London. And the van was infested with icy draughts. And less than twenty-four hours earlier she had been a bedridden invalid. And trouble might be awaiting her at Craven Street, for Mr. Collifant, the new Works-manager, was notoriously a pernickety fellow. But she was content, and she felt equal to anything. Mr. Ceria had informed her by telephone that he had paid a formal visit to Mr. Cousin, and that Mr. Cousin had not pitched him out of the hotel. She felt sure that the worst of the Ceria affair was over. She had saved Ceria. His voice on the telephone was as beautiful and as wistful and as grateful as the meek smile he had given her in his little office. He was her victim, and she had rescued him from ignominy and ruin. Never could she desert him.

The distance from Birdcage Walk to Craven Street appeared to be about a hundred miles. Either that, or the driver was abducting her. Then the van came to a definite halt. She tried to open the doors, but they were fastened on the outside. She shook them, and tore a glove. She called aloud. No answer. At last the doors opened to the rattle of a chain and pin. Blessed were the gleams of electricity after the black darkness. The driver stood below her. She put her hands on his uniformed shoulders and jumped down.

"Well," she laughed, looking at her damaged glove. "I've arrived--what's left of me!"

2.

The Works Department of the Imperial Palace was reallynot in Craven Street at all, but in Craven Place, beneath the immemorial shadow of Charing Cross Station, which rose above it like some gigantic relic of an extinct race of Titans. The van had come to rest under another archway cut out of two storeys of what had once been a modern town residence. No one came to greet the van.

"Can we get it down?" Violet asked.

"I can't, miss."

"You can if I help you."

They got the day-bed down.

"That's all, thank you," she said. "Good night."

The driver backed into the Place, and was gone. Solitude with the forlorn day-bed. Not a sound except the low hum of the motor, within, which worked the sewing-machines, and fitful booming echoes from the heights of Charing Cross Station. She began to climb up the flight of stone steps leading to the offices on the first floor. Luck favoured her once again. The junior carpenter from the workshop on Eighth, who had come on a professional errand to the Works Department, appeared at the top of the steps on his way back to the hotel.

"Frank," she cried, "just get someone. Tell them I want the lift for a piece of furniture to go to the Upholstery."

Frank touched his cap. It took nearly ten minutes to transport the day-bed to the Upholstery on the second-floor, but the operation was at last successfully achieved.

"Mr. Collifant about?" Violet asked a girl who, with some dozen others, men and girls, was busy in the large, bare room, covering the nakedness of assorted chairs.

"I think he's in his office seeing someone, Miss Powler," said the girl.

"Then run and find Mrs. Rowbotham for me, will you? Iwant her this minute." Violet spoke with authority because she had authority. The head-housekeeper of the Palace herself bought all materials for the Upholstery, and gave her own orders for the fashioning of it. And Mrs. Rowbotham, forewoman of the Upholstery, was her washpot.

Thin, anxious Mrs. Rowbotham, whose ambition was to resemble an under-housekeeper of the Palace as closely as possible, appeared with a face of apprehension. She quite unconsciously loved difficulties, therefore created them if they did not exist. She beheld the forlorn and ancient piece of cumbrous furniture with alarm. *That,* for the Rajah's suite? Which room of the suite was it meant for? Violet having given her the number, Mrs. Rowbotham opened a shallow drawer in a huge chest of such drawers, and produced the plan of the room, accurate and full of minute detail, scale half an inch to a foot. And she measured the dimensions of the sofa. Where was it to be in the room? In what spot could it be placed without a general disturbance of the rest of the furniture? Yes, well, it *might* do on the south wall. But of course everything had to be thought of--Miss Powler would admit that.

Miss Powler admitted that; but she would not be fussed. The fantastically elaborate organisation of the Works Department, while it always impressed her, was apt to make her impatient, especially in a crisis of haste; but now she was not to be made impatient. She felt the blandness of an assured conqueror. She had found the day-bed, brought it to Craven Street in a Laundry van; there it was, and it was going to be upholstered immediately and in accordance with her own ideas. The material--she described it to Mrs. Rowbotham, who was afraid that not enough of it remained in stock. A girl fetched the material, and there was enough of it. But what about the broken wood at the damaged end of the day-bed? Did Miss Powler really mean that the stuff must be flounced at the end to hide those old scars? Miss Powler did. And then the polishing of the visible wood?

And so on. And then finally Mrs. Rowbotham's great question:

"What about Mr. Collifant? I take my orders from Mr. Collifant. And you know, Miss Powler, he's--"

"Mr. Collifant's engaged just now, and the day-bed's very urgent. It must be started at once, and finished somehow in one hour. I shall stay here till it's done, and I shall take it back with me. I'll settle with Mr. Collifant. If Mr. Collifant isn't available, I can't help that. I've got my own responsibilities as head-housekeeper, and if I say a thing's wanted it *is:* and Mr. Collifant knows that as well as anybody. It's not as if the Rajah was an ordinary visitor."

Mrs. Rowbotham was hemmed in on both flanks. She yielded with a sigh, but she yielded. A man and a girl were drawn away from other work; a table was cleared for cutting out the material. Furniture-paste was brought for the summary polishing of exposed wood. Not a moment to be wasted, not a second.

Violet was uplifted by the sense of dominance. She was not in the least ill, could not credit that she had ever been ill. Why was she so eager and so arbitrary in her resolution to get the day-bed restored? If she had not happened to recall the existence of the day-bed, if she had not been a girl of unusual character and resource, the Rajah might have had to do without his day-bed, were he ten times a rajah. But because she was she, the Rajah should have his day-bed, and with astounding promptitude. She could perform miracles by mere volition, and she was performing one now, and everyone of importance in the Palace would hear of it.

Then a man of thirty-five or so, with a dark face and a heavy dark moustache and rough dark hair and a thick defiant figure appeared in the doorway. Mr. Collifant himself. He was scowling. Violet marshalled her nerves for another conflict. David against Goliath.

Mr. Collifant perceived at once that something out of the ordinary was afoot. He saw a piece of furniture that he had never seen before; and he had had no official notice of its arrival. He saw employees engaged on a task which was obviously not in the schedule of the day. Was he no longer master in the Works Department? Every employee in the room had a guilty or a constrained look. He turned on agitated Mrs. Rowbotham like a tiger. Mrs. Rowbotham glanced at Violet for help.

"I'm afraid it's all my doing, Mr. Collifant," said Violet, placatory, and briefly explained the situation. She did not know that Mr. Collifant had just emerged from a very trying interview with his superior, Mr. Cousin, nor even that Mr. Cousin had been to Craven Street or had interested himself in the affair of the day-bed. She thought that she alone had the grave matter in hand. She did not know that Mr. Collifant had told Mr. Cousin that the creation of a day-bed was absolutely impossible. Mr. Collifant turned on Violet, and in doing so he threw a curt, savage order to the man and the girl to stop the new work and go back to their scheduled jobs. Mr. Collifant did not usually behave thus; he usually controlled himself to correspond with the Imperial Palace tradition of a quiet courtesy under all provocations. But under a provocation quite unparalleled and quite inexcusable, the real Mr. Collifant was coming out.

"Can I speak to you a moment?" said Violet, and left the room.

Mr. Collifant murderously followed her. Beyond the door, unheard by the staff, Violet explained further. Mr. Collifant shook his head angrily. Violet continued:

"I'm very sorry I couldn't consult you. But I couldn't. This day-bed job is really urgent. I tell you so as head-housekeeper. I've come here on purpose. If you stop it I shall hold you responsible and I shall go at once to Mr. Cousin and report." And she thought: "And a nice mess I'm getting myself into! It'll be war between him and me now for ever and ever."

"I shall report to Mr. Cousin too," said Mr. Collifant, but he went back into the room and growled: "Here! You! You'd better get ahead with this thing."

Violet having heard him thus announce his own defeat, set out on a stroll through the other rooms; for she could not stay with Mrs. Rowbotham and the day-bed; to watch the processes of upholstering would have been as exasperating as to wait, watching, for a kettle to boil. And she could not stand still. She was too excited to stand still, and too happily excited. She had an attack of moral pride, and her individuality was extended so that the entire Works establishment could hardly contain it. If there were to be endless altercations with Mr. Collifant, let there be endless altercations. She had stronger weapons than he had...She was in the largest room of the department, on the first floor--the carpet-room. A large carpet (for No. 141 at the Palace), having been sewn, was being finally pared at the edges, prior to the definite hemming. Women were on their knees all around it.

Violet observed, and said not a word. How romantic was everything! The day-bed was thrillingly romantic...She was in the mattress-room, where a man was arranging ten thousand springs within a small oblong...She was in the eiderdown-room, where eiderdowns were being filled and stitched in patterns with the initials "I. P. H." in the centre. One girl bending upon a table had her mouth protected by a pad...She was in the sewing-machine-room, where a dozen women were loosing and withholding the power of electricity in needles upon all manner of stuffs...She was in the window-blind-room, and in the furniture-repairing-room. She spoke to none.

Then she saw a mirror, and examined herself, her face. She deemed it a plain sort of a face, but the eyes were very bright indeed, flashing, challenging eyes. She smiled, in order to judge whether or not her smile had winning charm. She decided that it had. Victory seemed to enhance her appearance. She fancied that she looked younger. She was excessively conscious of herself. It was not the meek who were blessed...

Ceria! She must cure Ceria of his present meekness. She would endow him with a supply of confidence from her own private overwhelming store. Of course Mr. Orcham had been quite right *in a way.* She could realise that now, in her serene triumph. Mr. Orcham cared only for his hotel, and he was right. The hotel must come first and come last. Loyalty to the hotel! Terrible retribution for disloyalty, even if you couldn't avoid it! Same as in war, if you lost your head and deserted, you had to be shot, and it would be silly to say you didn't know what you were doing when you deserted...What shocking wicked nonsense! In another way Mr. Orcham was most frightfully wrong, and well he must know it. As if a hotel counted for more than a human being!

However, she had got Ceria back at his post, and all difficulties would settle themselves. They always did. It was not in her character to exaggerate difficulties. Her tendency was to minimise them. Some employees were continually worrying about frictions between members of the staff. Others worried about their work and its value to the hotel. She belonged to the second class. Frictions were easiest lubricated by ignoring them.

Unexpectedly arriving at a door, she opened it and saw the day-bed. She was re-entering the upholstery-room from the other end. Mr. Orcham, of all people, was conversing with Mr. Collifant. Both men were very serious. Mr. Orcham glanced at her and glanced away. The mantle of moral pride slipped from her shoulders; it did not fall to the floor; it was annihilated; there was no mantle. Kind of conjuror's trick.

Chapter 68 THE SCENE

"I think you and I can go now," said Evelyn, calling across the room to Violet, who came forward at the words.

He had already decided exactly what he would do and how he would do it. Violet could not decipher even his general mood, so reserved was his voice in its urbanity. But she felt sure that he would support her in the attitude which she had adopted towards Mr. Collifant, who after all was only an executive officer whose principal duty was to carry out the instructions of, among others, the head-housekeeper.

Mr. Collifant said nothing, and looked at nobody, but he glared resentfully at senseless objects such as the window.

"I thought I would stay, sir, and take it back myself." Violet glanced at the day-bed, which under the hands of three workers was already losing its appearance of incurable antiquity.

"I've arranged all about that," said Evelyn, with decision. "You quite understand, don't you, Collifant?"

"Yes, sir," Mr. Collifant reluctantly mumbled.

"You can come with me in my car, Miss Powler. I left word for it to follow me. I came here in a taxi."

"Yes, sir," said Violet, feeling herself now under the sway of a higher power.

Evelyn, who was in hat and overcoat, walked quickly out of the room. Violet followed submissively. She had no idea why the panjandrum had paid a visit to the Works Department at just that crisis, nor could she guess what had passed between him and Mr. Collifant--except in so far as the manager's appearance gave a clue. The car was waiting.

Evelyn stood aside and asked her courteously to get in. When Brench had shut the door, Evelyn bent down and extinguished the interior light in the car, which drove off.

Violet said:

"I see the house next door is to let. You'll have four hotels now to deal with, and perhaps the Works Department will have to be enlarged."

She thought that this suggestion was rather bright, had value. Evelyn thought the same; he had not been aware that the next house was to let, nor had he considered the probable necessity of enlarging the Works Department to cope with the needs of the Merger. But he concealed his appreciation of the girl's brightness. He was in no state to award any good marks to her. Moreover, he was in Paris driving in another semi-dark car through other winter streets, with another young woman by his side. The sensation of the nearness of a girl in a car had delivered him into the past and into Gracie's treacherous, delicious arms. He thought grimly, of Miss Powler: "If she knew!..

He said aloud, with negligence: "Yes. We've got it in view." One of his daily allowance of fibs. He thought: "I'll mention that to old Dennis. She has a head on her, no mistake! Curse her!"

The conversation, after an interval, shifted to the damnable weather, then lapsed.

2.

In the entrance-hall of the Palace, Violet, content to have been seen arriving with the panjandrum in the panjandrum's car, had a surprise.

"I'd like you to come to my office if you can spare a minute," said Evelyn to her.

"Certainly, sir. Now?" She was mystified by his tone, which was unexceptionably polite, even amiable, but somehow blank, like a windowless and doorless high wall. She had a qualm: anything might be on the other side of that wall; anything! Still, she could accuse herself of no sin in her professional work. On the contrary her notion was that she merited a little commendation for enterprise and despatch.

As they went through Miss Cass's room, Evelyn said coldly to his chief secretary:

"I'm engaged, and I don't want to be disturbed."

Miss Cass thought:

"Hello! What's this?" And, silent, she gave him a slow,stern nod; and a tiny quick nod to Violet. Through the secret channels of the vast organism of the hotel she had already learnt something of the day-bed business and had heard of the strange impending departure of the cigarette-king for the Majestic.

"Sit down, will you?" said Evelyn in the inner room, removing his hat and overcoat and lighting a cigarette.

Violet knew then--what she had known before while refusing to admit it to herself--that trouble existed, and that she was concerned in it. She took off her gloves, and loosed the black coat which she had bought to wear with her housekeeper's dress when she went out on hotel errands. But *really,* instead of divesting herself, she was putting on the invisible armour of defence. She had an uncomfortable feeling of perplexity and pique. She was still worried about her protégé Ceria and resentful of Evelyn's attitude to him. According to Dr. Constam, who stood officially for the hotel, she was ill, and therefore deserved the treatment due to an invalid and an invalid who in the interests of the hotel was displaying all the activity of perfect health. (Incidentally she now began to be fatigued.) And finally she had done a wonder for the hotel, and the hotel ought to be grateful to her, for really she need not have--etc., etc. And the panjandrum was evidently preparing himself to be unpleasant. She had no grounds for this assumption. She simply directed her feminine X-ray apparatus into the Director's brain by way of his glance and his gestures and his tone (all irreproachable), and knew with absolute knowledge that things were so! Ah! The last time they had been together it was midnight and she wore her green frock, not this prim black affair, and he had given her a cigarette and their clouds of smoke had mingled. Her X-ray apparatus, however, furnished no information as to the condition of her own nerves. She believed that they were normal and in excellent order.

Evelyn was regretting that he had given her the cigarette that night. He was painfully absorbed in thoughts of Gracie and her wickedness. Or rather, he wanted to be painfully absorbed, but the hotel would not let him. He was much exercised about Ceria. He blamed himself for not having instructed Mr. Cousin that Ceria must leave. Ceria might go to the Majestic or wherever else Cousin chose to send him. Evelyn had been weak, irresolute. And to allow Ceria to stay at the Palace as though nothing had happened would show further weakness. What on earth did Ceria mean by his pranks of an operatic tenor? Monstrous! Monstrous! That girl was larking around in Paris, smiling at Leo Cheddar and returning his kisses. And only yesterday--or was it the day before?--she had...He, Evelyn, had dashed off to the Works Department to put the fear of God into Collifant, and to command that a day-bed should be created in a moment out of nothing. And he had found that another person had had the infernal cheek to put the fear of God into Collifant and to cause a day-bed to be created out of nothing--well, you might say almost nothing! Without saying one word to anybody! And there were other matters. Enough to make a man lose his temper! Not that Evelyn would lose his temper. No. His nerves, thank heaven, were in ideal order.

He took the seat of authority behind his desk, and made some notes on a pad of the topics which he had to discuss with the head-housekeeper. He wrote with deliberation. Let the woman wait!

Suddenly he looked up and began:

"You were ill last night, Miss Powler, in the doctor's hands. But to-day you are up and about. I was amazed to see you at Craven Street. Was it wise? We don't keep a doctor here for him to be defied." He smiled, to soften his words. Weakness again. But he was so absurdly good-natured. "You might easily have a relapse. Serious. And then where should we be? Where would the Palace be? The first duty of everyone on my staff is to keep healthy. There's such a thing as too much zeal, especially with you women."

Was his tone right--the proper mixture of urbanity and severity? He really must watch over his tongue. That playful phrase which he had used to her last night, about whether her mother knew that her daughter was a wicked and deceitful woman--that phrase was silly; it was mischievous; it made a wrong atmosphere between employer and employed; familiarity was a mistake, even with the best of 'em. She hears a phrase like that, in his accursed nice tone, and naturally she thinks she can go and do what she likes!

Violet answered mildly:

"I quite see what you mean sir. But perhaps you don't know that Dr. Constam sent a nurse last night to give me violet rays for my sciatica. And they made me sleep as well, and really when I woke up this morning the sciatica was quite gone and I haven't felt it since, not one bit." She smiled, with correct submissiveness, thinking: "Well, what's come over him? He brought me into his precious hotel, and I'm sure I've worked for *him.* And now he..! I'm the best one to tell whether I'm well enough to work or not. Does he take me for one of those hysterical creatures who'll go on till they drop, simply because they haven't any sense and they think it's grand? If he does, he's mistaken. Still, he isn't going to make *me* lose my head. And my tone's perfect. Last night he was charming, and to-day he's all nerves. Something else has upset him, and I'm to bear the brunt of it. All right! All right! He'll recover. But if he thinks he can put me in the wrong and make me play the idiot--"

"At any rate," Evelyn went on, after a judicial pause, "there's one thing you ought to have done. You ought to have seen the doctor before you got up this morning, and obtained his permission. If you have a doctor in, you must show some respect for him. There's a code, and all sensible people obey it. I wonder what Dr. Constam would have thought if he'd seen you out of bed--again. I know what he thought when he heard you'd been out of doors yesterday. A doctor *is* somebody. You know what *savoir vivre* means. You haven't been practising it." But he smiled once more.

"Dr. Constam mightn't have been able to come," Violet argued.

"Did you ask?"

"No, I didn't."

"Well then!"

"I did send him a message," she said, thinking: "What's all this about codes and things? And *savoir vivre?* He's making a fuss over nothing. I'm well, and here I am!..He's trying to be nice. And he's worth working for. I do wish he'd stop his lecturing. If this is all he has to say, I might as well go and get on with my business. That day-bed ought to be here soon. He looks at you in a nice way. His smile's nice. Every now and then he looks a bit like a boy--just for a second. And yet he's so hard about Mr. Ceria!" She smiled, and she felt as if she was knowing the panjandrum better.

Evelyn pored over his notes: a formality quite unnecessary, indeed a somewhat puerile showing-off by the man of affairs; for he knew perfectly what his next topic was.

"Now about Ceria." He paused.

"Yes, sir?"

At the mere name of Ceria the restive animal in Violet's mind jibbed and reared. She controlled it masterfully, and with a calm, superior inward smile. She had come to a very definite decision about Ceria. She had a duty to Ceria, and it was the most important of all her duties. She realised again, almost exultantly, her power over him. She could *make* Ceria: her relation to him was that of a creative goddess...Unguided, unaided by her, he might well sink into ruin. With her moral help there was hardly any limit to the potentialities of his achievement. He possessed all the qualities necessary for brilliant success, except one, and that she could and would supply. She would stop at nothing to supply it.

She thought of him tenderly. She recalled all his words, tones, glances hopeful and despairing, smiles, gestures, attitudes, when he and she had been together. He was innocent of evil, and she would not see him crushed. He was in her heart. Not that she loved him as a woman is supposed to love a man. And yet, so very tender were her thoughts of him, she did love him, with the softest affection, as a goddess can love a mortal martyrised by fate. He was more to her than anybody or anything in the world. If she could not save and recreate him otherwise she would marry him and take the risks of life with a mysterious and incalculable foreigner, who would not understand her and whom her reason would not understand. But her heart would understand and enfold him. And, for him, she would abandon the dream of a thoroughly English home ruled by English habits and customs and ideals, and submit herself to one of those uncomfortable compromises which were an unavoidable consequence of the mixed marriage. She would exist for ever with an essential stranger. She would have hybrid children by him, children who also at moments would be strangers to her, and incomprehensible by her Englishness. She had had glimpses of mixed marriages: there was one in Renshaw Street, on which her fretful mother had often made carping comments; it was the wife there who was foreign, a serious and economical woman; but the whole street sympathised with the English husband, to whom it attributed a special virtue because he was English. Well, a whole street might sympathise with *her* if circumstances rendered marriage the only method of carrying out her duty to Ceria--she didn't care. And she looked at the panjandrum's maleficent face, and secretly defied him.

"I'm bound to tell you," said Evelyn, "I think you were wrong yesterday afternoon. As soon as you got Ceria's letter you ought to have gone straight to Mr. Cousin and told him you knew Ceria was back at home. Your first duty was to the hotel. It isn't even as if you were engaged to Ceria. Personally I don't think that even that should have made any difference, but I admit the thing might be argued. However, you weren't engaged to him. You refused him, and he was nothing to you. So there was no excuse. I'm sure you'll agree with me that it's best for me to speak plainly."

"Oh yes, sir," she said with coldness. "I much prefer that. Then we know where we are."

"And I must tell you something else. You remember what I said to you last night about Mr. Ceria when you were lying onthat sofa in your room. I abide by it. My opinion hasn't changed in the least." He was about to add: "And I intend to act on what I said." But a new expression on Violet's features stopped him from finishing. A dangerous expression; it intimidated him; he feared, not her, but a scene. And he would not have a scene.

"But Mr. Ceria is there to-day, working as usual. And he's seen Mr. Cousin," said Violet firmly.

"Who told you?" Sharply, like a cross-examining barrister.

"He did. On the telephone."

"I am aware that he has seen Mr. Cousin," said Evelyn. "But what's that got to do with it? Naturally if Ceria comes back he comes back to work. Did you expect Mr. Cousin to prevent him from working? This hotel has to go on functioning." Evelyn very much wanted to say more and to say it with sarcasm; but again he was intimidated. He proceeded, not pausing: "And now about Mr. Collifant. Before you gave orders to the people under his control, did you make any attempt to see him?"

"No, sir. I was told he was engaged, and as my business was very urgent--"

"But was it very urgent? Even if you'd been kept half an hour, would that have mattered? This hotel wouldn't come to a standstill because of half an hour's delay in supplying an article that nobody had ever heard of before. And you wouldn't have been kept. Mr. Collifant was only engaged with Mr. Cousin, and if Mr. Cousin had had the slightest idea that Mr. Collifant was wanted on urgent business he would have understood at once, and perhaps helped too. It isn't as if you didn't know all about the chain of authority. The chain of authority works upwards as well as down. Suppose someone came along and gave orders to one of your floor-housekeepers without a word to you, what would you think? As a result of your interference Mr. Collifant has given me notice. I haven't accepted his notice, but I may have to. Now Mr. Collifant is a very good man." Evelyn was thinking: "It's true I went to Craven Street intending to have a row with Collifant myself, but she doesn't know that and it's got nothing to do with her. It isn't true that he's a very good man, and I don't care so much if he does leave; but he's good in some ways, and anyhow I'm not going to have a lot of women spreading themselves and upsetting men so that they give notice. I'm being very effective with her because I'm talking to her so quietly and reasonably; but I'm being firm too, and I shall go on being firm. I can see she's calming down a bit. Now with a girl like Gracie you *never* knew. It's quite on the cards she'll treat Cheddar as she's treated me, and write to me and ask me to forgive her. But I shan't. What is off is off--with me. No, I wouldn't make it up. And if she came over here to vamp me--she might--well, I don't know. She has points. It's possible I could tame her. Oh, damn!" He said to Violet: "You see my point, Miss Powler?"

"Yes, sir," Violet answered perfunctorily. She thought:

"But he doesn't give me a word of thanks for what I did. I have got the day-bed for them, and nobody else would have got it. I *do* get things done. But he says nothing about that. Oh no! No encouragement to do your best in this place. It's all codes and rules--red tape. Why did he edge away from the subject of Ceria so quick? I must have Ceria cleared up. I told Ceria positively I'd spoken to Mr. Orcham and everything would be all right. Positively. He *must* let Ceria alone now he's come back. Ceria's seen Mr. Cousin and he's working and I told him everything would be all right. Can't the Director see reason? He simply must see reason. If he doesn't--"

She was filled with a passionate protectiveness for Ceria. She thought of nothing else. There was nothing else, for her, but the salvation of Ceria. Her heart and her brain were aflame. She actually felt hot. Her hands were dry and hot, and then clammy and hot. But she thought: "I'll be calm and cool. He's excited himself. You can hear it in his voice. *He's* only trying to be collected. He's pretending, with his nine hotels. But I don't care if he's boss of nine hundred hotels--he must see reason."

3.

Evelyn said:

"You know, more tact, more discretion is needed in your work than you appear to realise, Miss Powler. For instance, there's your trouble with Mr. Purkin. However, I'll leave that for the present. But I must remind you, though I've never mentioned it before, that you didn't succeed in keeping the peace with either Miss Venables or Miss Prentiss. Both very good in their way. You were put over them, and you couldn't keep the peace. I don't say you didn't try. All I say is you didn't succeed." He was thinking: "I always thought she had plenty of tact. That was why I brought her here. And now I'm accusing her of no tact. Well, there it is!"

Violet was shocked to the point of utter amazement by the man's injustice. She thought: "Never mind. All this is nothing. Ceria's the only thing that matters. I won't let him upset me." And when she did speak, her tone was almost a cooing. She said:

"But, really, sir, the trouble with Miss Venables and Miss Prentiss began with Miss Maclaren. They were jealous. And anyone could understand their being jealous."

"Yes, of course," said Evelyn. "But Miss Maclaren was sickening for her illness. And as for their being jealous--"

"And they were still more jealous of *me,"* she interjected quietly.

"As I was saying, of course they were jealous. It was natural. But don't you know that jealousy is a very common thing indeed in this place? I'm always meeting with it and having to deal with it. And Mr. Cousin too. When we choose a head-housekeeper, even temporarily, we choose her partly because we believe she'll be capable of dealing satisfactorily with such ordinary little things as jealousy. We don't imagine there won't be any jealousy and the machine will always run smoothly. We know it won't. If it did there wouldn't be any need for tact and so on. Anyone can be tactful when there's nothing to be tactful about. That is so, isn't it?" He thought:

"And hang it! Am I being tactful now? Or not? This ought surely to be a lesson to the girl."

"Yes, sir," Violet replied, still perfunctorily. "I'm sorry." She thought: "But you haven't lost Venables--you've got her at the Majestic. And as for Prentiss, she's a good riddance, and well you know it!" In the same instant she said aloud:

"And what about Mr. Ceria, sir?"

"Why? *What* about Ceria?" He thought: "What the devil has Ceria to do with her?"

"What are you going to do about him, sir? You'll excuse me asking, but I feel rather responsible."

Evelyn thought:

"Well, I'm dashed! Does she think she ought to take a hand in running this hotel? However, I've calmed her down. Now's the time to be firm." He said aloud, with emphasis, and a condescending smile: "I've told you I haven't changed since last night. And I don't see that you're responsible--in the least. And even if you were--the managerial policy of this hotel remains." He thought: "Yes, I'm being hard on Ceria, and all the grill-room staff will be against me. Perhaps I oughtn't to sack him; but I've said it, and I shall stick to it. Must!"

Some people would say that the panjandrum was not now behaving very well. But some people are super-human, whereas Evelyn was only human; and possibly also his character had been somewhat impaired, under the years-long ordeal of being an autocrat.

"Well, I think it's very unfair," Violet exclaimed with bitterness unmasked.

And her thoughts corresponded exactly with her words. She had no thought of the advisability of restraining herself and keeping calm and employing tact or any other such paltry device. She had forgotten all that; forgotten all about prudence and discretion; she was high above these meannesses; lifted to a new plane, the plane of indignant emotion, and heedless of all consequences. She thought furiously that the Director was very unfair.

As for Evelyn, he was tremendously startled. He admitted to himself with disgust that her previous demeanour had deceived him into a misjudgment.

"Now please," he began. "Please don't--"

Violet jumped up from her chair, and her coat fell a little away from one shoulder, and her bag and gloves fell to the floor. Her eyes were on fire, her neck flushed; her mouth was half open for an explosion.

"She's not so bad looking. She's magnificent. She's beautiful." The thought flashed through one part of Evelyn's mind and was gone. But in another part of his mind glowed dully and steadily the thought: "Damn these women! They're all alike. All. I had an idea she wasn't like the rest. But she is. She isn't the girl I took her for. She's somebody else. Damn her!"

He looked at her and looked away, smiling awkwardly.

Violet said, her voice rising till Evelyn began to be afraid that Miss Cass would overhear from next door:

"Last night I spoke the truth, Mr. Orcham. I don't know why, except that I wanted to be honest with you. It was wasted. I might have told you the tale that I told to Mr. Fontenay to-day, and you'd have believed it. And I wish to God I had! Everything would have been all right then. But I told *you* the truth. And you've taken advantage of it. I say it's very unfair, but it's worse than that. It's simply frightful. *Frightful!"*

Her voice resounded in the hard, masculine room. Evelyn was dumbfounded, and more than a little overwhelmed. She wasn't like the rest of them. She was like a Fury. She was transformed from a head-housekeeper into a Fury. She moved towards his desk and stood above him, shooting angry darts down on him from her blazing eyes. Mr. Cyril Purkin had never seen her in such a state, nor her sister Susan. But a couple of recalcitrant laundry-maids had seen her in such a state once; and her mother once, after a whole Sunday of complainings, and the spectacle had cured Mrs. Powler of public lamentations for quite a month.

Evelyn was shaken by the exposure of the woman in her. Sex will out. But he was not daunted for more than a few seconds. The exposure of the woman in her suddenly excited him, and led to the exposure of the man. He had just been preaching in his offensive male way that anyone could be tactful when there was nothing to be tactful about. And now--he cared no more for tact than Violet did.

"Miss Powler," he angrily exclaimed, "will you oblige me by leaving the room?"

"Yes," she answered. "I will. And please take my notice to leave, Mr. Orcham. You wouldn't take *Mr.* Collifant's, but you'll take mine. It won't matter to you. I'm only 'temporary'." She laughed.

He sank slowly into his chair, thinking, aghast:

"This won't do. This is absurd. Tact! Tact! I'm cleverer than she is. I brought her into the hotel, and it would never do for me to let her go after a row. There'd be too much talk. Besides, she's a first-rate housekeeper, and they're rare. She's rather marvellous in a temper. I hadn't a notion of it. Though she *is* awful! Mrs. O'Riordan was nothing compared to her. No, nor Gracie. She's kissing Leo Cheddar before dinner. Tact!" But his interest in Gracie had suddenly diminished. He recalled a phrase in her letter--something about it being too early for him to judge yet whether he was in love with her or not.

He said:

"Please sit down." And, as she hesitated, "Sit *down."*

Authority. The man dominating the girl, bringing her to her senses.

Violet sat down. In her obedience he felt a glow of masculine conceit. He was happy. She was a woman, was she? Well, he was a man. Why didn't she burst into tears? He hated women to cry. But now he wanted her to cry. He would have been happier if she had cried. She did not cry.

"Miss Powler," he said very quietly, "people like you and me can't behave in this style. It's not worthy of us. And really you can't give me notice all in a minute because I don't manage my hotel as you think I ought to. It's not right. Now I want to suggest to you that you withdraw your notice, and let's forget this. You may think quite differently to-morrow. And perhaps I shall."

A silence.

"Very well," said Violet. "I withdraw my notice."

"Thank you. I admire you for doing that. It's what I expected from you."

Violet picked up her bag and gloves.

"But," she said, gazing at him with face averted, "when you say *you* may think differently to-morrow, do you mean about Mr. Ceria?"

"I make no promise. I can promise nothing," Evelyn answered firmly.

Violet said:

"I'll stay on. I'll do my best for the hotel. But things can never be the same between us again. Good afternoon."

Chapter 69 EASY-CHAIR

In three months much happens. Though each event taken by itself may seem small enough, the totality of events always amounts to a considerable change in the world. It was forenoon on an early day in April. In the world of the Imperial Palace much had happened since the early day in January when Evelyn had returned from Paris to London to discover the true domestic explanation of the mystery of Ceria's disappearance and to quarrel with Violet Powler.

Dr. Constam's vindictive hope was realised: Tessa had had twins, thus exceeding the arrangements made for her delivery by Gracie. Miss Maclaren had surprisingly reached full convalescence, and had left the St. James's Hospital. But she would never resume duty at the Palace, for the reason that, the origin of all her troubles having been fashionably diagnosed as dental, she had caught the fancy of her dentist, a middle-aged Scotsman and a widower, and was engaged to marry him. Old Mowlem had retired from the revolving doors of the great entrance-hall, and in some remote spot secret and withdrawn was holding converse with a spirit in the form of a literary 'ghost,' who had undertaken the job of putting his invaluable reminiscences into bright journalistic English; the work was about to appear serially in a morning paper, and popular success had been predicted for it on its appearance in book-form. Skinner had been promoted from the Queen Anne entrance to the main entrance in Birdcage Walk, and was now head hall-porter of the Palace. And already there were page-boys in the Palace who had never heard of old Mowlem. Reyer, no longer night-manager, had been promoted to a higher position in the Minerva at Cannes. Mr. Cyril Purkin had effected a love-match with a superior nurse-maid just young enough to be his daughter, and was spending himself and his substance, but not neglecting the Laundry, in a vivacious attempt to satisfy her appetite for pleasure.

And as if these things did not suffice to prove that the earth revolves, the Craven Street premises, not under the dominion of Mr. Collifant, were being enlarged to thrice their former size, and were supplying some hundreds of new carpets to the Majestic, which needed them.

But perhaps the most sentimentally interesting occurrence of the three months was the death of a housekeeper who had had charge of old Dennis Dover's home and whom father Dennis had quite gratuitously assumed to be immortal. A very severe blow for father Dennis. Deciding that he could never risk a new, unfamiliar housekeeper, he had installed himself in a small suite at the Palace, where he had lived as a child. The suite was not the suite of his infancy, but it bore the same number, and for its number he had chosen it. On the other hand, among the moveless permanencies, Violet remained at her post; Ceria, smiling again, remained at his post; and Perosi at his; and Beatrice Noakes at hers.

Father Dennis, much more than three months older, was now sitting uneasily in an easy-chair in his suite on Fourth. With him were Sir Henry

Savott, Lord Watlington, and Mr. John H. Harbour. These four men--not excluding even father Dennis--recked little or nothing of the events above enumerated. Their thoughts were centred upon an affair which they regarded as surpassingly momentous. The joint work of Sir Henry Savott and Sebastien Smiss had been completed; every minor, as well as every major, contract had been signed; a prospectus had been drafted, re-drafted and finally settled; the prospectus had become a chief ornament of the financial advertising columns of the principal newspapers; the Orcham International Hotels Company was before the public; the List of applications for shares had been opened that morning, and the four men in father Dennis's sitting-room had just had telephonic information that the List had been closed at noon, the shares having been applied for several times over in about a couple of hours. Success! Brilliant success! Success surpassing all hopes! Three of the men were happy and showed their happiness. Sir Henry Savott displayed his teeth with glee because he had unloaded vast responsibilities on to the investing public, and still more because he had received a cable from Paris to say that his daughter Gracie expected to be a mother. Mr. Harbour--unaware that to an anxious Sir Henry he had appeared with his financial backing like an unexpected angel from heaven--Mr. Harbour carried his abdomen joyously to and fro in the room because, for a sum trifling to him, he was destined to be a notable figure in the Europe of luxury hotels, and still more because he was free for at least a month of Mrs. Harbour--to whose uncompromising puritanism nevertheless he owed his personal introduction to Evelyn Orcham and to the Europe of luxury hotels. Lord Watlington, perched nervously restless on a piano-stool, was happy because he was once again intimately connected with a triumphant flotation, and still more because he too had grown financially intimate with the titanic Harbour, and perceived in this friendship prospects of new and larger fortunes and an increased hidden influence upon the stock-markets of two hemispheres; Lord Watlington had not invented a cigarette, but he knew himself to be a cleverer man than the stout, democratic cigarette-king.

Father Dennis, on the score of the Orcham Merger, was neither happy nor unhappy; he was indifferent, for he suspected that at a pace ever quicker he was steadily nearing the frontier beyond which mergers lose all their exciting interest. And he was definitely unhappy on the score of his easy-chair. It was the easiest chair in the room, but for old Dennis it was not easy. He had frequently complained of the uneasiness of the Palace easy-chairs. He had gone so far as to assert that there was not a single truly easy-chair in the whole hotel. The ground for this criticism lay in the peculiar conformation of the lower part of old Dennis's backbone. He now sat and grunted and grumbled and squeaked, trying rather ineffectually to be cheerful and benevolent, trying to pretend to himself that the Orcham flotation, not the easy-chair question, was the major question of the day.

The four men were waiting the arrival of Evelyn, who was strangely absenting himself. After all, he was the head of the Merger, and ought surely to have been with his colleagues on this sublime occasion. They thought more than they spoke, and the talk was spasmodic. Sir Henry Savott was thinking about his unborn grandchild, who would carry on the family if not the name, and about his profits, actual and potential, from his own child, the Orcham Merger. And both Lord Watlington and Mr. Harbour were thinking about the Savott profits. Everything had been made clear, all the cards had been put on the table again and again. Yet Lord Watlington and Mr. Harbour could conceive ways in which the astute Sir Henry might have gotten gains which no enquiry could ever disclose; and that possibly the capital of the Orcham International Hotels Company was greater than it ought to have been. But also Lord Watlington and Mr. Harbour had doubts as to this, and at moments secretly admitted that peradventure they were being unjust to the sole parent of the Merger.

Father Dennis, suddenly ceasing pretence, interrupted the various reflections of the trio of chams with a hoarse, whispered:

"I'm damned if I don't try a gridiron!" And with a frown of exasperation he hoisted himself to his feet.

Everybody assumed a pained expression of sympathy, and everyone thought: "The old man's getting past it. He won't be Chairman of the new Board for long."

"But, my dear Dover!" Sir Henry almost cooed. "Let me find you another easy-chair. Let me telephone to Miss Powler. She'll discover one."

"You may be able to sell pink for blue, my lad," said old Dennis with enigmatic, kindly grimness, "but you won't find what I call an easy-chair in this hotel. I ought to know. Who's Miss Powler?"

"Head-housekeeper." Savott showed a lenient surprise at the question.

"Oh! Her! Never set eyes on her. Don't know her."

"But I do," said Sir Henry gently. "May I use your telephone, my dear Chairman?" That morning, so persuaded was he of the goodness of God, he felt ready to obey all the precepts of the Sermon on the Mount, even the simplest.

2.

Violet was eating her lunch alone, with "The Hotel-keeper" propped before her, in the housekeepers' section of the staff restaurants below stairs, when in dashed young Agatha, who was only convinced that she was doing her duty if she was doing it in a hurry.

"Please, they've telephoned for you to go up to Mr. Dennis Dover's room at once. It was Sir Henry Savott who 'phoned."

The head-housekeeper, now not 'temporary,' dropped her spoon and fork into the vestiges of a sweet and, picking up "The Hotel-keeper," left the table.

This, she thought, must be truly important business, for on a day so important only important business would be allowed to arise for discussion. The whole staff of the hotel was more or less excited by the flotation of the Merger. Some were uplifted, they knew not why; others went about murmuring that things would never be the same again in the Palace, and their excitement took the form of qualms concerning the future, qualms which were sharpened rather than allayed by a vague report that wealthy investing people were tumbling over one another in a fierce struggle to get hold of shares. Many members of the staff had applied for shares, with a promise from that influential gentleman Mr. Smiss of preferential treatment. Among them was Oldham, who still retained possession of a little more than half of his thousand pounds.

Violet, whose business it was to know everything on the Floors, knew that several of the very highest personages were with Mr. Dennis Dover in his sitting-room. No doubt Mr. Orcham among them. Why had not Mr. Orcham himself telephoned, instead of leaving Sir Henry to summon her? The answer seemed obvious to Violet. For three months she had had no contact with Mr. Orcham. Only twice had she even seen him, by chance in the corridors, on which occasions they had exchanged non-committal salutations. Once she had been on the point of entering Mr. Dover's suite to enquire after his comfort, but the news that Mr. Orcham was with him had altered her purpose, and she had deputed the official mission to Mrs. Oulsnam.

All her dealings had been with Mr. Cousin, next upwards in the chain of authority. Her relations with Mr. Cousin were admirably perfect. His demeanour, like her own, was always reserved, and yet friendly. He spoke sense, and he listened to sense; and when he had decided he had decided. Why therefore should she ever have had speech with Mr. Orcham? Mr. Orcham was beyond her in the firmament. Everybody was aware that Mr. Orcham had been more and more withdrawing from the actual daily overseeing of the Palace. Mr. Cousin had told her that Mr. Orcham now had other and greater matters to attend to, and the fact was evident.

Nevertheless Violet, with her realistic feminine unreason, was convinced that, but for their calamitous affray, Mr. Orcham would have continued to meet her, despite his new preoccupations with eight other hotels. She appreciated Mr. Cousin's adroitness in making excuses for Mr. Orcham's aloofness without seeming to make excuses. A man who would gratuitously smooth the rough face of things was the man to please her; for she too had the instinct thus to smooth. But she saw through the adroitness. She had at length definitely relinquished the hope of contact with Mr. Orcham, who had introduced her into the Palace, and whose protégée she had once been!

Her private meditations had often been sombre, especially in the night. But she was seldom uncheerful, even to herself, for long. The figure of Mr. Orcham, with his irregular teeth and his sudden funny movements and tone and phrases, had been her original inspiration to work hard for the hotel. The inspiration was weakened; but not her ardour. She had developed a passion for the welfare and the efficiency of the Palace. She studied its organisation day and evening. She maintained a bright acquaintance with heads of departments. She was ready to be of use to anybody and everybody. She knew everybody by name. Out of the Palace she was like a fish out of water, and her parents noticed this, critically. Mr. Powler had permitted himself to suggest that she was 'getting morbid' about the Palace, with her late arrivals in Renshaw Street and her early departures therefrom.

She had quietly ignored the cautious complaints. And sometimes she would relate with pride how her hints for the betterment of the working of the hotel had been sooner or later acted upon. For instance, as to the hours of the housekeepers. After several floor-housekeepers had been eliminated, in accordance with Mac's plan, an extra one had been engaged, and a completely new system of housekeeping surveillance devised. (She saw the hidden, active hand of Mr. Orcham guiding the revolutionary change. Or at least he had approved, while giving no overt sign.) To have mentioned this at Renshaw Street was one of her mistakes. Naturally her parents had asked how it came about, if hours were shorter, that she was never free of the hotel. Question which she answered but lamely.

On the way to obey the summons, she called in at her rooms to titivate. Mac's photographs had vanished, and the walls of the parlour had a forlorn air. She must buy some pictures, and deliberately make the place a home. For it was to be her home for ever and ever. But was it? Why had she been summoned? Did the high personages intend to transfer her to some other hotel more in need than the Palace of her service? Probably. She felt flattered, but sad. Still, if she was invited to leave the Palace she would leave it; she was a soldier in the army, and an invitation was a command; she was in the hotel-world for life.

There was one satisfaction: she knew that Ceria was secure. Mr. Orcham had yielded there. Not that she was sentimentally interested in Ceria. She had consistently kept Ceria at a proper distance. She had sworn to save Ceria, and she had saved him. The Ceria-Violet accounts were balanced and closed and her role of creative goddess to him was done. If he continued to sigh for her--well, it couldn't be helped. She would marry no foreigner, nor any man whom she was not gloriously in love with. She had seen love glorious on the faces of couples in Battersea Park on Sunday evenings in the summer. Her conception of love was more negative than positive; she conceived it as an emotion utterly unlike the tepid excitement which during a few weeks she had experienced in the society of Mr. Cyril Purkin.

She entered the lobby of father Dennis's suite without knocking, and then knocked at the sitting-room door. No sound of talking within. Well accustomed to introducing herself to all manner of celebrities and notorieties, male and female, titled and untitled, plain and picturesque, haughty and genial, in the factitious privacy of their temporary homes, she had lost such trifling nervousness as had ever troubled her. But she was nervous now, not because of the prestige of the personages to be interviewed, not even because of the supposed gravity of the interview; rather because Mr. Orcham would be one of the high personages. She knocked again.

"Come in."

She opened the door, and the next instant was in the midst of great men.But Mr. Orcham was not among them. Mr. Dover she had seen once at a distance, Mr. Harbour she had once long ago spoken to while placating the hardly placable Mrs. Harbour. Lord Watlington she recognised from his photographs in the papers. Sir Henry of course she knew. Father Dennis gave her the benevolent smile of an old fellow who has finished with women except as a spectacle agreeable to behold. Lord Watlington ignored her, looking out of the window with boredom on his face. Mr. Harbour was ready to be sympathetic. Sir Henry surprisingly stepped forward and shook hands, saying that he was glad to see her. She smiled and bowed.

"Miss Powler," said Sir Henry, taking charge, "you know the suite my daughter had here last year--I forget the number."

"365," she informed him.

Neither of them knew that whereas Sir Henry was referring to Gracie's first visit, Violet was referring to her second, of which Sir Henry had no knowledge. But on each occasion she had had the same suite.

"By the way, you'll be interested to hear that my daughter is expecting a baby." Sir Henry could not contain the great news of his approaching grandfatherhood; it came forth with a rush, of its own volition.

"I'm so glad!" said Violet. Her eyes said far more than the words. She really was glad, if only because of Sir Henry's ingenuous delight.

Lord Watlington's boredom seemed to be intensified.

"Yes, I shall tell her I've told you and how pleased you are! Well, in the bedroom there was a peculiar sort of easy-chair."

"I know the one you mean."

"Could you get it for us? This one here"--he indicated the empty chair--"doesn't suit Mr. Dover, and I think that that one would. Could you get it for us?" Sir Henry's attitude was the attitude of an owner of the Palace: at any rate he was the creator of the Merger!

"Certainly, Sir Henry."

"Now?"

"Certainly."

"Thank you."

Violet made a quick exit. In the lobby she laughed, partly from relief at the absence of Mr. Orcham, and partly at the comical difference between what she had been anticipating and what had happened. Steeled to listen to a proposition unpalatable but epoch-making for her, she had been asked to supply an easy-chair! Withal, she felt some twinge of disappointment. The spirited heroine in her would have preferred Mr. Orcham to be in the room (so that their relations might be defined after a long period of indefiniteness), even had the result been unpleasant. She always did like to know where she stood with anybody. And the ambitious, adventurous heroine in her regretted that no fresh adventure awaited her. Why had they sent for the head-housekeeper to procure a mere easy-chair? Clearly because despatch was desired. She slipped downstairs to Third, and abruptly enlisted a valet en route. The suite comprising rooms 365, 6, 7, and 8 was, she knew, occupied but the visitors might not be in. She knocked at the bedroom door. No answer. She entered. The room was empty.

"Here!" she said to the valet. "Pull that easy-chair out, will you, and take it upstairs in the lift to Mr. Dover's sitting-room. Get Fred to help you. I'll be up there before you."

While the chair was leaving, the door between the bedroom and the bathroom opened, and a magnificent dame in full street attire began a vexed enquiry.

"Excuse me, my lady. This chair has to be repaired. I will see that you have another one at once. I thought there was nobody in."

Violet followed the chair. In Mr. Dover's lobby, in front of the shut door of his drawing-room, she waited for the easy-chair and the valets.

"This is the chair you meant, isn't it, Sir Henry?" she said, having opened the door.

3.

Evelyn had a rendezvous with the others in father Dennis's room--chosen because the old man had now reduced the fatiguing transport of his large and heavy frame to the least possible--but he had been delayed, by an encounter with a man much older than father Dennis--Lord Levering.

The panjandrum ought to have been cheerfully happy. He was not. The flotation of the Merger was obviously a triumph of finance. Savott, Smiss, and--on the purely publicity side--Immerson had employed the finest technique. The name of Orcham resounded everywhere in the press. Miss Cass spent much of her time in declining for her chief the specious allurements of interviewers and photographers. The chief's salary would have been considered high even in the United States, where according to report no official worth his salt receives for his salt less than fifty thousand dollars a year. And his commission on profits might well double his salary. But he was uneasy about the profits, and he faltered before the immensity of his responsibilities. *He,* not Sir Henry Savott, was the Merger. Without him, nothing! Without that mysterious little contrivance which he carried in his head and called his brain, the structure of the tremendous Merger would almost certainly tumble to pieces. Frightening thought! The prospectus of the new Company was a work of art, the figures in it dazzling, the list of Directors majestically impressive. But Evelyn whispered to himself:

"What has all that to do with managing hotels? There isn't a soul on the Board who knows the first thing about hotels, except Smiss and me. I wouldn't put sixpence on any of the foreign directors. Except Smiss and me all of them are manipulators of finance, parasites on the industry, perhaps necessary parasites, but parasites."

And he had recently visited the Escurial at Madrid, the management of which had engendered apprehensions in his Anglo-Saxon mind.

Apparently the Director of the Escurial believed that if he rose at midday he was applying himself seriously to business.

Further, the panjandrum had just received from John Crump, secretary of the Imperial Palace Hotel Company, the draft of the agenda of a meeting of I.P.H. shareholders, at which was to be passed a resolution for the winding-up of the Company! To initial the draft agenda was like ordering a funeral. The I. P. H. Company would cease to exist, and the Imperial Palace, once a unique individuality, would sink to be a mere unit in a motley herd of hotels. Not to speak of the little Wey Hotel, which in his late youth had been all that Evelyn ruled in the world.

Grave matters; grave happenings! And yet they disturbed him less than another development which had hit him in the face that same morning. He had seen Savott early and received the news about Gracie from the excited grandfather-to-be. Savott had proudly shown him the cable: "Darling daddy, I'm going to have a baby. Gracie." There must be a genuine attachment between these two, despite the strange separateness of their lives. Evelyn pictured Gracie in the swelling condition of Tessa, whom he had twice glimpsed. She would be a handful for a man, especially for a dilettante such as Leo Cheddar. And Sir Henry would be buzzing around the pair like a whole swarm of wasps. Sir Henry had already announced his firm resolve that that invaluable baby should be born on English soil. Evelyn envied Leo. Not that he was in love with Gracie or had any regrets concerning his loss of her. He had no regrets, and he was not in love. The conflagration in his heart had died out as rapidly as it had flared up: like a fire of old newspapers. But it had left him with a black and empty grate; the great conception of marriage, companionship, quarrels, domestic anxieties, procreation, parturition had been implanted in him, and then sterilised so that it could not grow. He was solitary, continuously dissatisfied. He was the busiest man in London, and he, really, had nothing to *do.* He wanted comforting, and none could comfort him. His secret was still his secret, and Gracie's. Of course he had confided in nobody. He had a few friends, including particularly father Dennis; but he could not bring himself to confide in any of them. He was living on dust-sandwiches, and the dust was his extraordinary material and vocational success.

This was Evelyn when by chance he met Lord Levering in the bill-office, where the venerable, lusty millionaire was discharging his last bill, to an accompaniment of forthright remarks on everything. The sessions of the Licensing Commission were finished, but no date had been promised for the Report. Both the antagonists had worked hard and tirelessly, and in the course of months had become superficially quite intimate. Also they had learnt to admire each other.

"Well, my friend," the teetotal millionaire accosted Evelyn. "You've made the profit--you've skinned me alive with these damned bills of yours--but I've won."

He spoke gleefully and loudly, never caring who might overhear. The correctly dressed bill-clerks, leaning over mahogany and brass, were thrilled to hear, but they knew their duty of feigned deafness and practised it.

"Well," said Evelyn. "I have my shareholders to think of...So you think you'll win?"

"I don't think. I know. And so do you, sir," insisted the snowy, shaggy, cold-eyed disputant. "I've been reading reports of Parliamentary Commissions for sixty years, and they're always sitting on fences and weighing pros and cons in a balance. The present gang of hair-splitters will make a lot of recommendations with a lot of reserves, and the result won't be worth a fig to you. And even if they gave you everything you'd get nothing, because nobody will read the Report, and no party will touch it. Too dangerous for vote-catchers to meddle with. It will be postponed again and again until it falls to bits. It will be in every King's Speech for half a century, and then it just won't be. I'll tell you something--you'll soon be old enough to learn things. They say that what England stands for is justice. Infernal nonsense! English justice be hanged. What England stands for is the *status quo.* And that's what I stand for, and that's what you've been up against. But you've put up a good fight, Orcham. I've smashed you to smithereens, but I like ye. I'm leaving this afternoon. Come in and say good-bye to Lady Levering. Women love good-byes."

Evelyn laughed gaily. Lord Levering radiated gaiety at all times, save when he radiated terror. But the panjandrum was thinking:

"He said I knew he would win. And I daresay I did."

The admission did not depress him. What was Licensing Reform to a man without personal interests? And yet a few months ago, when his personal interests were as negligible as now, he had been capable of passion about Licensing Reform, and could violently curse D.O.R.A. to hell.

Upstairs he saw two valets manœuvring an easy-chair out of Mr. Dover's small lobby into the corridor, and he heard a woman's voice: "Don't forget to put that in the bedroom you took the other one from--at once." Violet Powler's voice!

"What's all this?" he demanded.

"Miss Powler, sir," replied one of the valets, and explained what was being done.

Violet had stooped to smooth out a crease in the lobby carpet, which had been deranged by the passage of the chair. She straightened herself and beheld Evelyn.

"Oh, good morning, Mr. Orcham," she greeted him in a light, friendly tone, just as though there had been no sort of estrangement between them during the whole of the past three months.

The tone startled Violet as much as it startled Evelyn. The fact was that she had used it without thinking and before she knew what she had done. The unexpected sight of him had somehow drawn it out of her subconscious being. Abashed, she hesitated one instant and then went into the room, from which she had just come.

Evelyn, who was in the outer doorway, hesitated more than an instant. To him she seemed to be wonderfully at ease. Her habit of speech to him had always been deferential but never humble. There was perhaps more of the equalitarian in her attitude towards authority than in that of any other member of the staff, except Mr. Cousin and the redoubtable Rocco. Evelyn liked this demeanour, which she had exaggerated only on the unique occasion of their brief quarrel. He liked to think that she was incapable of the kowtow, and that she regarded the difference between them as purely official, not in the least a human difference. If he was democratic by reasoned conviction, she was democratic by instinct.

What did her tone imply? It must imply, he reflected, that whereas he had been nourishing a grievance and some resentment, she had not. She had forgotten; women could forget. He would forget. His mood was changed; he felt happier, or less unhappy. He had had a glimpse of her expression--that characteristic air of being ready to consider benevolently and sympathetically any proposition that was put to her. In her rather high cheek-bones there was a suggestion of self-reliance and individual power. Her official frock was conspicuously smart, and she carried it, and herself, with dignity. Of her methods and deeds as head-housekeeper he had full knowledge from Cousin, who, while never actually praising her, subtly disclosed his opinion that she was an improvement on Miss Maclaren in style, and on Mrs. O'Riordan in tranquil temper. Evelyn had never said anything to Cousin about the quarrel. As his relations with Gracie were hidden, so was his brawl with Miss Powler.

Well, the estrangement was apparently ended. He loathed estrangements either outside or inside the hotel. Yes, he was relieved, and admitted his relief. He did not think of Miss Powler as a miracle of enterprising efficiency in hotel-housekeeping, as the woman who had learnt her job more quickly than any woman ever did in all the history of the Palace. Not at all. He thought of her as the girl to whom one midnight he had impulsively offered a cigarette, and whose mere demeanour or way of existing had comforted and soothed him when his nerves were on edge. Several times he had regretted offering her a cigarette. Now he was glad that he had offered the cigarette. He passed into father Dennis's sitting-room.

4.

The old man was testing the chair. Violet bent over it from behind, and was apparently trying to peer between the sitter's back and the back of the chair. Mr. Harbour and Sir Henry stood near, spectators absorbed in the operation of fitting the chair to the man. Lord Watlington was still perched on the stool, restless and impatient.

"Is that any better, do you think, Mr. Dover?" Violet asked.

Father Dennis whispered hoarsely:

"I'll say this. It's not worse than the other torture-rack. Yes, I believe it is better."

"It seems better for the small of your back. But if it isn't I'll have the back re-stuffed for you to-day. I'll have it done in the workshop here, Mr. Dover."

"Yes. You're very kind," Mr. Dover squeaked and growled. "And while it's being done I am to lie on the floor, I suppose." He twisted his head round and smiled at the head-housekeeper.

"Oh! Mr. Dover. I'll promise to find you something softer than the floor."

Violet laughed. The other two smiled, but not Lord Watlington. Evelyn smiled. No one gave attention to him. Violet might have glanced at him for confirmation of her offer. She did not.

"I think it'll do," father Dennis whispered.

Violet, unaware of the permanent trouble in his vocal chords, assumed that he had a very sore throat.

"It isn't easy to tell right away," she said. "If it isn't just what it ought to be, will you get someone to telephone me, and I'll come up."

"A cushion would do, anyhow," Lord Watlington remarked, staccato.

"Only women like cushions," said Violet, with a new variety of smile, half humorous and half propitiatory.

Sir Henry Savott laughed; he was pleased at his success in suggesting a particular chair.

"Good morning then, Mr. Dover," said Violet. "If I don't hear I shall take it it's all right."

"Thank you, my dear," father Dennis grunted. Violet embraced the rest of the party in one bow, and, passing close by Evelyn, left the room.

"Evelyn," father Dennis demanded, "is that the young woman you took from the Laundry?"

"Yes. Why?"

"Nothing. Only she's so damned like a lady, nobody could tell the difference. I couldn't."

"Her father's a town-traveller--in proprietary foods," said Evelyn drily.

"Married above him, I expect."

"No. I've seen them both."

Father Dennis said:

"Then he may be one of those nature's gentlemen you hear so much about. I've never met one myself."

"Why!" said Mr. Harbour. "I said to my wife when she came in to see us before we left for the Majestic last time--you remember--" the cigarette-king grinned privately to Evelyn--"I said to Mrs. Harbour that she'd be an asset anywhere."

"Yes," Evelyn concurred negligently.

Lord Watlington jumped up, unable to wait longer, and burst out:

"I can buy the Splendide at Brussels for a million francs. I stayed there two nights last week. What about it?"

"But it was sold," said Sir Henry.

"I know that. It's for sale again. That's all."

"Isn't that enough to make us not want it?" said Evelyn, controlling his astonishment.

He had casually improvised the possibility of including the Splendide in the Merger months ago in Paris to give colour to his story of a projected journey to Brussels. And in the meantime nobody had even mentioned the Splendide to him. Savott must have perfunctorily mentioned it to Lord Watlington and then forgotten it.

Lord Watlington gave a little gesture of dissatisfaction; but he checked it, and said very quietly:

"But listen here, Evelyn. It was you who spoke to Henry about it."

"Yes. But I heard things afterwards that put me off."

Lord Watlington threw up his hands.

Strange how fibs returned to the fibber after many days!

"We've just had a 'phone message to say that the lists have been closed, Evelyn," said Sir Henry.

"I had one too," Evelyn answered lightly, as though such news was naught, as though the absence of such news would have surprised him. He added: "And I am told that letters of allotment will open at a premium of one and a half."

"Who's the prophet?"

"Immerson. Not that he'd agree he's a prophet. He says he *knows.* And I bet he does. He's very much in with one or two Stock Exchange clerks."

The conversation drooped. The fact was that the news, the large, the enormous general success, rendered all embroidering comment otiose. There it was! The five men fell into an anticlimax of contented exhaustion. Evelyn's sense of happiness increased. The prospect of the immense labours which lay before him was now far less intimidating than half an hour ago, even a quarter of an hour ago. He did not examine himself to discover why. He had always been averse to self-examination. And as he sat there with his lounging companions in the triumph he was more averse to it than ever. He, and all of them--except old Dover--had many urgent calls and tasks, but that day was to be celebrated in lethargy.

"Say, Evelyn!" Lord Watlington, who had been walking to and fro, suddenly woke from a reverie and broke the silence. "What did you hear about the Splendide to put you off it?"

Fibs breed fibs. The fibber had to improvise again. Evelyn improvised with a very careless disregard for convincingness. Lord Watlington scowled.

"Let us go down and have some lunch," whispered father Dennis.

Issuing from the lips of the venerable Chairman of the Orcham International Hotels Company, the suggestion amounted to a command. The party rose, some hungry, some welcoming the meal as a distraction to pass the time. But Lord Watlington said:

"Can't lunch. I've got to go."

Savott winked at Evelyn. They both guessed that his lordship's refusal to lunch was merely the sign of a vexation which would disappear before the day was out. The peer had taken a fancy for the Splendide, and Evelyn's negligent dismissal of the fancy irked his haughty pride as a great creative financier.

5.

The other four lunched in a corner, but a prominent corner, of the restaurant, under the most assiduous vigilance of Cappone himself. Evelyn had now become a recognised figure in the public rooms of the Palace; and the other three men were current celebrities, the cigarette-king not least. As the restaurant gradually filled, the table of panjandrums grew to be more and more the target of inquisitive eyes. Visitors nudged one another, leaned together, whispered, and in the game of chatter and small-talk he won who had the largest supply of secret information, authentic or invented, concerning the unexampled success of the flotation of the Merger. The flotation indeed had enlivened the sedate restaurant in such a degree that it began to rival the free convivialities of Ceria's grill-room. And the observed table, being human, was not ill-pleased by the shameless curiosity which it excited.

Evelyn was the first to depart, excusing himself on the plea of multitudinous, pressing correspondence. The correspondence was a fact, but the excuse was a white fib. He went straight to the bookstall in the entrance-hall. This now openly acknowledged prince of the hotel-world was in a reality a child. He wanted to see what prominence the early editions of the evening papers gave to the flotation of the Merger in their financial columns. He bought, and paid for, the three papers which monopolise the nightly allowance of printed information for seven million people, and put them under his arm to examine in his office. Then he saw, well displayed, a slim volume in a green and yellow jacket cubistically designed, with the title: "Sensations and Ideas."

"Hello!" said he to the clerk in charge of the stall. "What's this?"

The clerk murmured confidentially:

"There's no name to it, Mr. Orcham. But it's by Sir Henry Savott's daughter, Mrs. Cheddar. That's why I've got a few copies."

"Oh!" said Evelyn, with a sardonic inflection. "Who told you it's by Mrs. Cheddar?"

"The publisher's traveller, sir. He called here on purpose."

"And do you tell everyone?"

"Well, not everyone, sir."

"Any demand for it?"

"Some, sir. Miss Powler bought a copy yesterday."

"Did she! I may as well tell you you can't sell a copy to me--I've read it. Have you?"

"Yes, sir."

"And what do you think of it?"

"Well, sir, between ourselves I don't really believe there's much chance for it. It's rather queer. Some people won't quite like it. I have to be very careful in recommending it."

"That's right," said Evelyn, and walked away.

He felt a desire to possess himself of Gracie's book, but was mysteriously inhibited from doing so. At any rate he would not buy it in the hotel. He had known for several days that it was out, from somewhat sensational newspaper advertisements. But he had thought: "I've read it. I don't want to buy it." The last statement was still another of his fibs.

So Violet had bought a copy! Well, why not? Possibly she had learnt at second-hand through gossip of the hotel bookstall-clerk that Gracie had published a book. And had she not served in Sir Henry's house and been acquainted with Gracie as a big girl? And had she not met Gracie again in the affair of Tessa? Her purchase of the volume might be a proof only of curiosity. Nevertheless Evelyn found pleasure in the alternative theory that Miss Powler had a taste for literature.

He entered his office quite gaily, refusing--so eager was he to scan the three newspapers--to be delayed by a Miss Cass exuding questions about correspondence. He saw on his desk a solitary letter, unstamped. At the top of the envelope he read:

"Private. From Miss Violet Powler." As regards Miss Violet Powler, two things had definitely lodged themselves in his mind: father Dennis's remark that you couldn't tell the difference between Violet and a lady. And the cigarette-king's single word 'Asset.' Asset, asset, asset, he kept repeating. He had always divided women into assets and liabilities, and for him, as for most men, the second category contained many more names than the first.

He tore the envelope, thinking: "It must have cost the excellent Cass something pretty stiff not to open this!"

"DEAR MR. ORCHAM. I feel I should apologise to you for my behaviour in your office last January. I ought to have apologised before. Please accept my sincere excuses. Yours respectfully, V. M. POWLER."

"Dash the girl!" he thought. "I didn't *want* her to apologise! I hate being apologised to! Who'd take any notice of anything said by a woman in a temper? Dash the girl! And why the devil does she sign 'Yours respectfully'?" He was delighted with the letter.

Chapter 70 THE DUNCANNON AFFAIR

"Is that Malpass? The Director speaking." Evelyn was in pyjamas and dressing-gown, in his castle. The time was 3 a.m.

"Yes, sir," was the answer from Malpass down in the entrance-hall. He was the new Night-manager, who had replaced Mr. Reyer; a former reception-clerk, he owed his rise to a suggestion to Mr. Cousin from Adolphe, the Reception-manager

"Have you got the key of the bookstall cupboard?"

"Yes, sir."

"Just open it. You'll see a book with a funny cover called 'Sensations and Ideas.' Send it up to my room by the liftman, will you? And be sure to put a check-slip for it in the cupboard."

"Certainly, sir."

Evelyn glanced at the clock and lit a cigarette. In four minutes there was a tap on the door of the sitting-room, and he received a copy of Gracie's book from the liftman. Proof of the efficiency of the living organism of the hotel, which boasted that you could obtain any food, any drink, any flower, any book or magazine in stock, at any hour of the night in the Palace. Evelyn was pleased. His heavy heart lightened somewhat for an instant.

He returned to his sleepless bed and, scientifically arranged in every detail for perfect comfort, he began to read Gracie for the second time--a certain chapter which had been recalled to his memory by the great sinister event of the earlier night at the Duncannon. Yes, the book was good, better even than he had deemed it when he read it in typescript in Gracie's boulevard flat, with Gracie lying at his feet. The bookstall-clerk--he could not remember the youth's name--was clearly an unlettered idiot, and could not distinguish between a real book and a Bath-bun.

But he, Evelyn, might have known what would happen. Instead of sending him to sleep, Gracie completely woke him up. Still, he could not have rested until he had re-read that particular chapter; so that in fact he was no worse off than before. He shut the book and put the light out...A terrible chapter, that chapter.

At a quarter to five o'clock, when he could detect the first pale tinges of dawn through the blind, he resolutely arose and selected a suit from the wardrobe-cubicle, and a shirt, and a pair of shoes, without the aid of Oldham. A surprise for Oldham, it would be! And Evelyn himself, not for the first time, was rather surprised at the number of trifling necessary things that Oldham must have to do every morning in order that his employer should be correctly attired. He revelled in the huge expanse of leisure that stretched in front of him. No hurry, no haste. Each operation of the toilet could be conducted at ease. He shaved with meticulous care. He stayed rather longer than usual in the bath. Nevertheless he shirked his physical exercises; he was too weary, too discouraged by life, to perform them. He knotted his necktie as conscientiously as a Beau Brummel. He surveyed himself in the long mirror and saw that he was perfect. The day had come; the planet was punctually revolving. He drew back the curtains, lifted the blind, opened wide the window, and beheld the early, ghostly, half-leafless St. James's Park, whose gates had not yet been unlocked.

He was dying for some tea, but he would not test again the efficiency of the organism. Had he done so, the entire Palace would have known that the panjandrum had rung for tea before six o'clock, and there would have been gossip. He wrote a short letter, and sat reflective for a few minutes until he heard Big Ben strike six; and then, picking up the letter and nerving himself to affront the corridor and the whole world of success, he emerged from his castle. He was too tired to feel tired. He had no purpose as to where he was going or as to what he would do. He felt only that he was in a torment of restlessness, and that if anybody spoke to him the top of his head might blow off. He said to himself:

"Then why am I out here? I'll go back."

But he was too proud or too cowardly to go back. The corridor had all the aspects of night. The two electric lamps, one near either end, burned with their maddening, patient endurance!..(At that season of the year they ran through their allotted span of a thousand hours in six weeks). He could hear a snore; it penetrated two doors.

"My God!" he thought. "If that man has a wife!"

No member of the staff astir yet on Seventh. None on the stairs. None on Sixth. None on the stairs. On Fifth he glimpsed the disappearing skirt of the night-chambermaid far away. In the service-room on Fourth he saw the night-waiter uncomfortably dozing, and an orderly row of boots and shoes through the open door of the valets' lair. Everything seemed normal, and life was duly suspended according to schedule.

At the end of Third a large screen, removed from some suite, hid the herd of round meal-tables which in a couple of hours the day-waiters would be wheeling into the rooms laden with bacon and fish and newly baked rolls and coffee and tea. He must get some tea somehow. Idly inquisitive, he peeped right behind the screen. An easy-chair behind it, no doubt from the same suite as the screen. He gave way to the sudden impulse to sit down for a minute in that tempting chair, and watch some sea-gulls from the water of St. James's Park, circling against grey cloud beyond the window which lit the corridor of Third. He was safe there for a good hour or more. He knew that nothing would send him to sleep.

When he awoke, alarmed, his watch showed five minutes to seven, and he could hear the movement of workers in the corridor. His head ached now, and he felt very much worse than before. Tea. He must have tea. But it seemed to him that in an enormous building, where hundreds of teapots were marshalled to be filled with the sovereign restorer, he could not get a single cup because he could not ask for one without appearing ridiculous in the eyes of the person asked. He, the Director, abroad on the floors at 7 a.m. and asking like a lost stranger for tea, when he could have rung for it in his own rooms! Not to be conceived! Well, he was certainly in a strange state. The masses of the personnel might live and die and never suspect what fantastic moods fluster the heads of august and unapproachable panjandrums.

He put his nose round the edge of the screen--thief in mortal danger!--chose his opportunity, and got away down the stairs unseen. Narrow escape!

No activity in the vast lugubrious entrance-hall, where the chandeliers were still obstinately struggling against the light of the sun. No boat-train that morning. The gang of blue and brown charwomen had not yet arrived. Malpass was clearing up behind his counter, Sam Butcher was apparently not on duty, but a janissary stood at the revolving doors. Taking care not to catch the eye of Malpass, Evelyn descended the steps into the empty foyer twilit by one lamp. The ladies' cloakroom was brightly illuminated. Then its lights were extinguished one after another, and a figure emerged: Violet Powler. She was the last person he wished to see: of course it would be so: but he had been asking for trouble.

2.

"Good morning, Miss Powler."

"Oh, good morning, sir." She was frighteningly alert, active, spick-and-span.

"You're up very early."

"No, sir. This is one of my early mornings, and once a week I come and take a look at the ground-floor, before the cleaners arrive--it would be too late afterwards."

"I have a letter for you," said Evelyn, and gave her the letter from his pocket; at last he was rid of it.

"Am I to read it now?"

He had not foreseen this question.

"Why not?" he said, without thinking, and then added:

"Any time," trying to save himself.

Violet gazed at him for a moment, and opened the envelope. The solitary lamp in the foyer gave hardly sufficient light for reading. She went to the corner where the switches were and turned on two more lamps and gazed at Evelyn again. Then she read the letter:

"DEAR MISS POWLER. Thank you for your note. I appreciate it. Sincerely yours, EVELYN ORCHAM."

Evelyn had the idea of leaving her, but he could not move.

"Thank you so much," said Violet, with a warm smile. "You're very kind, Mr. Orcham." And then very quietly:

"Will you excuse me one second?" She disappeared into the ladies' cloakroom, switching on a light as she entered. Now he was bound to stay until she came back. He could see her using the telephone within. When she reappeared she no longer held the letter in her hand.

"If you can possibly wait a few minutes I've ordered some tea for you from the grill-room."

"But why?" he smiled; but behind the smile was resentment at her managingness. As if he could not direct his own bodily affairs. Still, the prospect of tea was irresistible. And he had not had to ask for tea. Did he then look so pale, so ill? She must have pushed the letter down the neck of her frock. Naturally she had no bag, and her key-girdle was too loose to hold anything.

"It struck me you look a little tired, sir," she said firmly, ceasing to smile. "And I thought some tea--if you hadn't had any--"

"I am a bit tired," he admitted. He lacked the strength to oppose her. He dropped on to a wall-sofa.

"Perhaps you didn't sleep very well, sir?"

There she was, relapsing into 'sir'!

"I didn't. I suppose you've heard the news?"

"No, sir. I've only just come down."

"Willingford shot himself last night--or rather early this morning."

"Willingford?"

"Manager of the Duncannon. On the very day of our flotation." He need not have said the last words; but he said them; they disclosed his train of thought. Where now was the glory of the Merger flotation?

"What a pity!" Violet murmured, her tone showing that she felt deep pity.

"Yes," said Evelyn. "Of course I'm very sorry for him, because he was a very decent fellow, and he'd had a lot to put up with. But that he should have been driven to do it just now...Most unfortunate. Makes a bad impression. It oughtn't to, but it will."

"Had it anything to do with the new big Company?"

"No." Then Evelyn modified his negative. "Well, it had and it hadn't. You see it was like this." He could not resist the impulse to confide in her; he had no real desire to resist it. "Willingford was manager, but he had a pretty big block of shares in the old Duncannon Company. His wife was head-housekeeper there. Not a satisfactory arrangement. A manager isn't able to control his wife as well as he could someone not connected with him. It can't be done. Still, I believe she used to be rather good. *She* didn't want the Duncannon to be sold. I daresay Willingford would have given in to her, but he hadn't got a controlling interest, so he couldn't have stopped the sale anyhow. But I gathered from Willingford himself that she always maintained he could. They'd had rows, great rows, at intervals all through their married life. She's a terrific talker--I had to listen to her last night--this morning. And ever since the sale was decided upon their quarrels have been very frequent, and the housekeeping has suffered. I knew that from Willingford--only the day before yesterday. You see she interfered at every step of the business side of our deal. I heard that from Sir Henry Savott and from Mr. Smiss too. Willingford couldn't hide it. I thought he looked a bit queer in the eyes last time I saw him, but I'd no idea--"

"Excuse me, here's your tea, Mr. Orcham," said Violet, seeing a waiter with a loaded tray coming down the steps into the foyer. She put a dusty cocktail table into position in front of Evelyn, and she signed the check for the order: tea, toast,and butter.

"May I pour out for you?"

"Yes, do, please. But you'd better bring a chair and sit down. I've begun to tell you, and I may as well finish."

He looked at her as she poured out the tea, watched that benevolent, receptive expression of hers, her quick, efficient movements, the faint shadows below the prominence of her cheeks, the faint, reassuring smile on her shut lips. Interrogatively she held up the sugar-tongs with a piece of sugar between them. Her mouth opened slightly: the smile increased.

"Yes, please. This morning. One," he said, as it were yielding himself to her care completely.

She stirred the tea and passed it across the tray. He sipped nectar, tonic. She buttered some toast. He felt that never before in all his life had he been softly tended. Gracie had tended him once, and well, but Gracie had been too conscious of the perfect excellence of her ministration. He wanted to yield more and more to Miss Powler's care. It was like eiderdown between him and the stony world; it soothed his positive fatigue into a comfortable negative quiescence. The difference between her care and the care of Gracie was as notable as the difference between that of Gracie and that of the devoted, untidy Oldham.

"When did it happen?" Violet asked.

"They got me out of bed at ten minutes to one. I went over to the Royal London as quick as I could."

"The Royal London?"

"Yes. I must tell you he didn't do it at the Duncannon. He went to the Royal London to do it. All that's very strange. Very strange. But I can understand it. It was the poor fellow's last thought for the Duncannon. He knew well enough how bad a suicide is for a hotel. So he went to the Royal London. He always had his knife into the Royal London--I don't know why." Evelyn smiled sardonically. "Of course it's quite bad enough for the Duncannon as it is, but it would have been much worse if he'd shot himself *there.* It won't do the Royal London any good. That must be why he chose the Royal London. Very strange. You never know what is in the mind of a man who has decided to commit suicide. But he meant well by the Duncannon. He did it in the London lounge. Nobody was there. The night-porter heard the shot. I saw him lying on the carpet. There was a policeman there by that time, and the night-porter and the manager. They wouldn't let anyone else in. The doctor hadn't come. They couldn't get hold of one. So I telephoned for Constam. But the man was dead all right. Blood on his face. He was all crumpled up. The most forlorn thing you ever saw. It was so pathetic you could hardly bear to look at it. I was awfully glad you couldn't hear their orchestra playing, though it was playing. I could hear it from the hall plain enough. Of course they couldn't stop the orchestra. That wouldn't have done at all. And there he was, lying there. He looked very small, all shrunk up."

Tears were in Violet's eyes. She said:

"It reminds you of that piece in Mrs. Cheddar's book. The motor accident."

"Oh! You've been reading that?"

"I was reading it last night in bed."

Gracie had described how, motoring in France, she had seen a young woman lying by the side of the road, dead, and blood all over her. Terribly injured. The woman had been driving her car too quickly down a hill and must have put the brakes on too suddenly, and the car had turned right over and thrown her out.

"I've read it too. A pretty good description, isn't it?"

"It is," Violet agreed. "And her thoughts about it afterwards."

"Yes. You like the book then?"

"I don't think I've ever read anything as wonderful. It's all so *new.* But then of course I haven't done a great deal of reading. I only got the book because it was by her. But she was always wonderful, Miss Gracie was--Mrs. Cheddar."

"Yes," said Evelyn sincerely. All his rancour against Gracie had died out.

A pause.

"When Mrs. Willingford came, not long after me, they tried to keep her out of the lounge, but they couldn't do it. She made such a noise she'd have brought everyone in the hotel down to the lounge to see what was the matter. So they let her in. Naturally I was her dear husband's murderer and so on. But she knew well enough who it was had driven him to suicide; you could see that from the self-conscious look in her face. So I had to be the murderer. She must be about fifty, but she turned on me like a prize-fighter out of his senses, and the policeman and the manager had all they could do to keep her off me. It was a simply awful scene. I won't go into details. And him lying there under her feet all the time! Still, I must say I felt sorry for her. You couldn't help feeling sorry for her."

Violet made a commiserating sound with her tongue against her upper teeth.

"It was frightful for you. Frightful! May I give you another cup?"

"It was fairly bad. However, when Constam arrived, and just after him the other doctor they'd been trying to get, the two of them had her taken off to a nursing-home somewhere, and they'll see she doesn't get out of there in a hurry. Anyhow not till she's calmed down. She'll have to attend the inquest, if she's fit. And I expect I shall too. But she'll behave herself at the inquest. They always do, for their own sakes. As soon as I could leave I went to the Duncannon and gave a few orders. I said she wasn't on any account to be admitted. Perhaps you don't know what sort of a place the Duncannon is. It isn't at all like the Palace, I can tell you that. Here they'd treat a suicide case as rather interesting and picturesque. They'd be shocked, some of 'em, but not too much. But the Duncannon is very English--you know, official, services, lieutenant-governors, and that kind of thing. The waiters are English. It isn't a bit cosmopolitan. And they want quiet decorum before everything. Doesn't matter so much about the food. Curries and things. It isn't very smart to look at; but it's dignified. You understand. No band except during dinner. If there was dancing they'd do the lancers and the polka. Anything in the nature of a scandal would horrify them. They'll all pretend to themselves that the trouble had something to do with the Royal London, which they think's a bit fast. Not that it is, really. There isn't a fast hotel in London outside Jermyn Street, and even there--"

A troop of blue and brown charwomen equipped with utensils appeared from the dusk of the restaurant and passed in a file through the foyer. Violet rose and stopped one of them and, pointing to the ladies' cloakroom, gave her a few instructions. All the charwomen turned their heads to see the unique spectacle, at that hour of the morning, of a tea served in the foyer. Few of them recognised Evelyn for the panjandrum. Violet sat down. The next moment the foyer was empty again.

Evelyn was thinking:

"She's a better judge of a book than that ass of a bookstall clerk." He said aloud: "I've decided to put Pozzi in charge of the Duncannon for the present. He isn't English, but he needn't show himself much. I must speak to Mr. Cousin. He'll have seen it in the papers before I see him. At least I hope he will. I don't precisely feel like beginning the story all over again. That's the worst of it. There's about ten people in this place who'll consider themselves entitled to hear the whole story first hand from me."

"Perhaps you could put Dr. Constam on to telling them," Violet suggested.

Evelyn thought:

"She understands my nerves."

"But what about the housekeeping?" Violet asked. "If Mrs. Willingford isn't there? And of course everyone will be in a dreadful state and nobody will know quite what they're doing."

"Yes," said Evelyn. "What about the housekeeping? There's only one under-housekeeper. And if I know anything about Mrs. Willingford's ways, that under-housekeeper has never been allowed one ounce of responsibility. That's just it: what about the housekeeping?"

"I suppose you wouldn't care for me to go over?" said Violet.

"What! And leave us to go to rack and ruin here!" He frowned, holding a last fragment of toast near to his mouth without putting it in. But he knew that there was nothing he would like more than for Violet to go over to the Duncannon.

"I only mean for an hour or two a day until things settle down a little and you know where you are."

"But you couldn't leave here. You couldn't do both."

"Why not?" Violet smiled sedately. "The Palace can run by itself for a little while." (Gracie's notion!) "And besides, Mrs. Oulsnam is very good. And I could be here at any rate in the evenings, and a bit in the afternoons."

"But you don't know anything about the Duncannon!"

"I should know a lot more about it than I knew about the Palace when you put me in charge here," said Violet, drily.

"How soon could you go?" Evelyn demanded hesitantly.

"I could go now."

"Now? Do you mean *now*?"

"Yes. Before visitors are up. And if you could get Mr. Pozzi as well. And if you could come with us, just to introduce us. You needn't stay long. I'm sure the doctor would say you ought to have a sedative and go to bed, Mr. Orcham." Violet stood up.

"Well," thought Evelyn, "this young woman is the goods. She's too managing with her sedatives, but she's the goods." He said aloud: "D'you know what you are, Miss Powler? You're the willing horse. You know what happens to the willing horse. You'd better look out for yourself."

"That will be all right," she said, serenely confident.

The horrible situation was losing much of its horror for him. He saw it in a new light. And their relations were absolutely ideal, far better than they had ever been: complete mutual comprehension. He was still very tired; but comfortably tired. The casque of steel round his head had been magically loosened. How marvellously right he had been! What astonishing instinctive insight into character he had shown (astonishing even to himself) in carrying her away from the Laundry. He had a conviction, a religious faith; that nothing serious could happen to the Duncannon while she was there. Yet what had she said, what had she offered? Nothing but the obvious. It was her way of existing that affected him, something deeper than either words or acts.

"It's all so awful it seems as if it would go on being awful for ever. But these awful things are soon forgotten. I've often noticed it," said Violet.

He thought she was reluctant to leave him unprotected. "Yes. That's true," he said musingly. Then louder, in a new tone: "And supposing that woman, the widow, manages to get into the Duncannon after all, and she comes across you?"

"Oh! I think I could deal with her," she answered.

The quietude of her perfect confidence reassured but to a certain extent daunted him.

Chapter 71 NIGHT-WORK

Five days later, and Sunday night. Violet's sitting-room still lacked pictures, but it had a larger desk, which Violet, exercising her rights as head-housekeeper, had chosen for herself from store. She was sitting at it. She needed a larger desk, at any rate temporarily, because she had taken to doing some of the Duncannon work at the Palace.

The time was about half-past eleven--nearing the end of a full day. She had toiled for five hours in the Palace--but nothing was toil for her--and after lunch, and a French lesson from the assiduous Perosi, she had paid a visit to Renshaw Street and spent several interminable hours with her parents, who had a parental fore-vision of their daughter as the star housekeeper of the whole European world of hotels. Then swiftly by a pre-ordered taxi from Renshaw Street to the Duncannon; and finally to her boudoir-parlour-office in the Palace.

She was perfectly happy, loving her work, and aware that she was doing it pretty well. She never felt fatigue, nor boredom, nor any of the qualms which trouble those who are not fairly sure of themselves. She went to bed with reluctance, and arose joyous and eager to start the new, long day. She found a grim satisfaction in overworking both the loyal Mrs. Oulsnam and the equally loyal Agatha. She argued with herself that Mrs. Oulsnam's gaiety of mind and Agatha's youth could withstand a few weeks' overwork without the least harm to their constitutions.

She had established relations with Pozzi, the new temporary manager of the Duncannon, had indeed almost entered into a league with the young man for the total reform of the Duncannon organisation on Palace lines. She liked the Englishness of the Duncannon. She knew where she was with the members of the staff, and comprehended their cerebral processes; at the Palace, where nine out of ten of the males with whom she had contact were foreigners, she was still disturbed by the thought that while they spoke in English they were thinking in French or Italian or Czecho-Slovakian.

Mrs. Willingford had attempted no invasion of her former realm, and Mrs. Willingford's possessions had been despatched to a boarding-house in Cornwall. On the day following the night of the suicide the afternoon papers had intemperately jubilated in an orgy of sensations concerning the affair, and the streets of Central London had fluttered with the white, scarlet, and yellow of their contents-bills announcing horrid mystery. But the next morning--naught! Not even the shortest paragraph on the front pages; for a famous and lovely daughter of the peerage had married her chauffeur and nothing else mattered on earth. The inquest had passed off quietly. The jury had viewed Willingford's body, cleansed of its red stains, and Willingford had been buried with more secrecy than had hidden the honeymoon of the daughter of the peerage; and Willingford was as though he had never existed, loved, suffered. Sometimes the planet revolves with incredible rapidity. As for the flotation of the Merger, it continued to be a triumph untarnished.

Violet's evening at the Duncannon had been protracted by a very agreeable episode: a personal call from Mr. Cyril Purkin, who was in the finest benevolent mood, benevolent not only to Violet but to himself. He had sought Violet first at the Palace, and then had done her the honour of seeking her at the Duncannon. He had greeted her with such warmth that the critical Violet had reflected: "Am I such a pleasant change from his wife?"

But there was good foundation for Mr. Purkin's mood. It had been decided that the linen of the Majestic and the Duncannon should go to the Imperial Palace Laundry, and that the Laundry should be enlarged, like the Works Department. Soon Mr. Purkin would be unable to boast of the garden of the Laundry in which laundry-girls drank tea *al fresco* on suitable afternoons. The garden would be built upon. But Mr. Purkin did not in the least regret that. He would have new and better boasts than the old one. Although the existing Laundry premises had hitherto been the acme of perfection, the additional premises, according to Mr. Purkin, were in some mysterious way to surpass them, to leave them out of sight as venerable relics of an inefficient age. Mr. Purkin swelled with pride and importance, but not offensively--blandly. He had discussed at length with Violet the question of immediately arranging for deliveries to and by the Laundry from and to the Majestic and the Duncannon. He was cheerfully convinced that, terribly antiquated and inadequate though the old premises were, he could easily cope with the linen of both the Duncannon and the Majestic. Violet had offered him some ginger-ale, had joined him in drinking ginger-ale, and they had parted on more friendly terms than had obtained between them at any time since before he kissed her. Not a reference to pillow-slips!

2.

Agatha Jixon came into the sitting-room, and saw her principal earnestly bent over the large desk covered with papers and books of figures, under the light of a green-shaded lamp which illuminated the desk only, and not even all the desk. The desk and its contents looked very important, and the head-housekeeper also.

Violet turned to the girl in severe reproof.

"Why aren't you in bed? You know you ought to be. You know you can't possibly be in trim for to-morrow--and tomorrow's Monday too!"

"I was in bed, Miss Powler. But I had to get up again because I'd forgotten to tell you something. Mr. Orcham was asking for you to-night. He came up here, and he told me to tell you."

"And couldn't that have waited till to-morrow morning? Run along back to bed now." Then in her felicity Violet relented, adding: "That's rather a nice dressing-gown you've got."

"Is it?...Your fire's out. Did you know?"

"Run *along!*"

"Good night, miss."

Violet, feigning absorption in her very important work, did not reply. The girl fled.

The news of the panjandrum's call considerably excited the young woman of whom the younger stood in affectionate awe. She had been very happy before. She was now happier. She had not set eyes on Evelyn for several days. The panjandrum had been busy at the Majestic and elsewhere. And it was the gossip of the Palace on this Sunday that the cigarette-king had insisted on taking him out for a day's golf. Evelyn had introduced Violet with marked ceremony into the Duncannon organism; but after two days he had left her to do as she chose with the housekeeping department of the place. Without guiding her, he flatteringly trusted her. And he had not concealed his gratitude to her for so zealously relieving him of an anxiety. The spectacle of his fatigue on that morning when she poured out tea for him in the foyer had touched and saddened her; but the talk with him at the small table had filled her with bliss. 'Bliss' was the sole proper word for her sensations. She had felt, then, as if his life were in danger and she was saving it by her strong maternal care of him. No cloud between them!

And, ever since, an old, extinguished lamp had burned anew in her brain, steadily, brightly, inspiringly: the lamp of loyalty to Evelyn as an individual. She had worked for the hotels; she was devoted to the Palace; but she had worked more for him, and to him she was more devoted. She expected nothing from him in return, except his approbation. He had discovered her, and lifted her up, and in fact created her; and that richly sufficed. She desired nothing better than to prove her value. As for the deplorable quarrel, the reconciliation, hardly perceived, was worth it. She would have been ready to go through another quarrel for another reconciliation...Was it not marvellous that he respected her, admired her qualities, chatted with her so freely?

Her thoughts grew quite sentimental. She pretended to be proceeding with her very important work. A pretence merely! How could she check calculations while thinking endlessly the thought of her calm happiness, under such an employer, in the romantic career of head-housekeeper of the Imperial Palace? She breathed in a dream of beatitude. She might just as well have gone to bed for all the good she was doing at the new large desk; but she hated to go to bed. Then, several seconds after it occurred, she realised that there had been a tap on the door.

"Come in," she stammered.

She knew that the intruder could not conceivably be Evelyn; but she knew also that it was Evelyn: hence the hesitant timidity in her voice. And it was Evelyn. Idyll, with no sex in it! Nothing but work and loyalty in it!

The panjandrum was no fit sight for a fashionable hotel on Sunday evening. He wore a thick loose tweed suit, not specially designed, but not wholly unsuitable, for the game of golf; with thick brown boots; and he had a rural air. Violet rose at once from her busy desk to receive him. She smiled to see him so arrayed, thinking maternally that a day in the country was just what he had needed.

"So you've been down to your mother's and came back late, and now you're working, and it's after half-past eleven and you ought to have been in bed long since. How do you expect to be in form for your work to-morrow morning if you sit up like this? You know you ought never to work on Sunday nights." He had begun with no sort of greeting, and his tone was very curt, even harsh.

Violet laughed.

"Yes, you laugh," he went on. "Don't you remember what I said about the willing horse? I might as well talk to a post. You're all alike. Miss Cass is just the same. And Miss Tilton too--from what Mr. Cousin tells me. Why are you laughing?"

"I don't know," Violet answered. But she did know. She laughed because she was reduced to the role of Agatha, and the panjandrum had been repeating her own criticism of Agatha in the same dissatisfied querulous tone. Not that she was disturbed by his tone. She knew with the certainty of omniscience from which nothing can be hid that he was using that tone in order to hide constraint arising out of the self-consciousness due to the lateness and the strangeness of the visit. His tone gave her pleasure; she delighted in it. She wanted to seem intimidated by it, and could not. She had never been so happy. The obscurity of the room (except in the region of the sinful desk), the fact of his presence, the informal rusticity of his clothes--all this struck her as exquisitely romantic.

She thought, puffed up: "*He* is in *my* room." And she thought:

"I can't help showing how pleased I am. Well, I don't care. It's rather dark. Perhaps he can't see."

"Well," said Evelyn, walking uneasily about. "I've been after you all the evening. I shouldn't have come in now, but I happened to be up here and I saw the light under your door."

"Happened to be up here!" thought Violet. "I wonder what it is he wants."

"Hello!" exclaimed Evelyn; he had reached the desk and was glancing at the papers on it. "But this is Duncannon stuff!"

"Yes, sir."

"That's all wrong, bringing Duncannon stuff over here. If you can't attend to it in the time you spend over there, you ought to leave it. Now I won't have it."

"Sometimes it's easier to do things here. I like to be on the spot in case I'm asked for."

"Oh indeed!" He was sardonic. Then he changed his tone suddenly. "Mr. Cousin was suggesting you might go to the Duncannon altogether for six months, and get it all absolutely smooth and oiled. He says Mrs. Oulsnam and he between them could carry on here. What do you say?"

So this was what he had come for! Her expression altered with the swift candour of a child's. The suggestion of leaving the Palace for six months desolated her. She had been very sympathetic towards the Duncannon. Now she hated the place. It would be a place of exile. The Duncannon was dead compared to the Palace. The Palace was her home, far more so than Renshaw Street. No! The suggestion very seriously alarmed her. Perhaps her theory in explanation of his tone when he entered the room had been entirely wrong. Perhaps...

"Of course it's for you to say, sir," she muttered cautiously, glumly.

"It isn't for me to say. It's for you to say," he snapped.

"Well, if you ask me, I don't think it's at all necessary for me to live at the Duncannon and leave here. But Mrs. Oulsnam might go. She's very capable. And she's so cheerful. The Duncannon does need cheerfulness. She might quite enjoy it. And it would be a step up for her."

"That's enough!" said Evelyn. "If you don't want to go, you don't. As for Mrs. Oulsnam, we'll see."

The question was settled. Her spirit lightened instantly. She hoped he was not vexed. No, he could not be. But she felt more puzzled than ever. It surely could not be about the Duncannon that he had come to see her in her room at getting on for midnight. He had not troubled to argue; he had dropped the proposal instantly.

"Look here!" he said brusquely, almost bullyingly. "If you'll kindly sit down I might sit down. I detest standing for long."

"Oh, please do! I'm so sorry."

She sat down near the dead fire. This was the second occasion on which he had had to suggest sitting down when he came to see her. She was clumsy, no mistake! He was treating her as an equal, and she was not being equal to the part. He sat down opposite to her.

"Your fire's out," he observed. Violet smiled again, to herself. "Still, with the radiator the room's quite warm."

"May I give you a cigarette?" said Violet.

Evelyn shook his head. "But please smoke if you want to." Violet shook her head; his permission was too perfunctory to encourage her. "I scarcely ever smoke," she said, inexactly. She felt disappointed. To smoke with him, to offer him a match, to light her cigarette from a match held by him, would have been delicious. However, she put the notion resolutely aside. What could it matter, really, whether they smoked or not?

"They're determined to arrange a supper for me. The upper staff, I mean," Evelyn began. "That's what I've come to see you about. I must have your opinion." He was talking now in an ordinary social, friendly tone, man to comprehending woman.

"Oh yes?" she said with bright interest.

"Yes. To-night fortnight it's supposed to be. It's a supper of the hotel, to celebrate the success of the Merger. I don't know why people want to do these things, but they do. And I can't say no. Directors and heads of departments--that will be the company. Nobody else--except the manager of the Majestic. Mr. Cousin thought they couldn't decently leave him out. Pozzi will come, not so much as manager of the Duncannon as because he's still in theory assistant-manager here. Old Mr. Dover probably won't come down; he may, but I shall be surprised if he does. Says he feels too old. Of course there'll be Sir Henry Savot--the supper ought properly to be for him--and Lord Watlington, and Mr. Harbour. And then there'll be the Directors of the old Company, Mr. Dacker and Mr. Lingmell and Mr. Smiss--Mr. Smiss is a director of the Merger too. And then the heads of departments: Mr. Adolphe, Mr. Immerson, Mr. Jones-Wyatt, Mr. Crump, Mr. Cappone, Mr. Ceria, Commendatore Rocco, Mr. Planquet, Mr. Ruffo, Dr. Constam, Major Linklater, Mr. Exshaw, Mr. Ickeringway, Mr. Stairforth, Mr. Semple, Mr. Pipple--Bills Department, he's really cashier. Perhaps that isn't all, but it's nearly all. There's about a couple of dozen there anyhow. I've agreed the list with Mr. Cousin. But do you know what I said? I said: 'What about ladies?' Mr. Cousin said it wouldn't do to ask the wives. He said we know what the men are like, but if we ask one wife we must ask all, and some of 'em wouldn't do. You know, people are apt to think the staff of a hotel is all alike. Well, of course it isn't. Class distinctions are as sharp in a hotel-staff as they are elsewhere--sharper perhaps. So Mr. Cousin said his idea was to have men only. Now I don't think that's right. If a woman happens to be head of a department she's just as much entitled to be asked to take part in that supper as any other head of a department. Women work as hard as men, and as a rule they're nicer to look at, and they have the vote and they sit on juries and even in Parliament, and so why shouldn't they sit at supper? I'm not a fanatical feminist, but I do believe in playing fair. What do you say?"

Violet trembled. She knew she was the sole woman head of a department in the hotel. Was she to be invited to share in the supper? And if so was she to be the one girl among twenty or thirty men, including millionaires? Or was she to refuse--refuse to be at a supper given in the honour of the panjandrum? His masculine logic was putting her in a fix. To refuse would be cowardice. And yet--"I think the principle's quite right," she said nervously.

"Well, then!"

"Let me see, who are the women heads?"

"There's you."

"But who else?"

"There isn't anybody else," Evelyn smiled with humour.

"I should love to come, but not by myself," said the head-housekeeper, whose common sense was after all stronger than any masculine logic.

"But why not? Would you be afraid to?"

"I couldn't come by myself, Mr. Orcham. But are you sure there isn't anybody else? What about Mrs. Rowbotham?"

"Works? Certainly not. By the way, I was forgetting the new head at Craven Street. No, Mrs. Rowbotham isn't a head. And what's more, she isn't presentable. We might as well ask Skinner; he considers himself now the greatest man in the entire show. No. Everyone must be presentable--that's cast-iron."

"Lady Milligan. She'd adore to come."

"I daresay she would. But she doesn't happen to be on the staff," said Evelyn drily.

"But for the sake of old times? No?"

"The old times when her ladyship ran off and left us. No, thanks."

There he was again, the panjandrum, with his tone all hardened by the mere thought of a disloyalty to the Palace. He was surely the strangest man!

"Well, Mrs. Oulsnam?"

"She isn't head of a department. If we had her we should either have to ask about twenty more second-in-commands or there'd be such a flare-up of jealousies as never was seen."

"But if you made her head-housekeeper at the Duncannon, and she sort of belongs here and Mr. Pozzi is coming, couldn't you squeeze her in?"

"That's an idea," the panjandrum admitted. And to Violet's astonishment he added: "And there'd be four of you if we roped in Miss Cass and Marian Tilton. Both those two are perfectly convinced that they run the hotel. Yes, four wouldn't be so bad, would it? Might even have some dancing."

"Four would be lovely," said Violet.

"I'll see Mr. Cousin first thing to-morrow," said Evelyn; and stood up.

3.

"It's awfully nice of you to come and ask me," said Violet, scarcely audible.

And she too rose. The affair was finished, and he was going. She wanted him to stay for ever in her room. But also she wanted him to leave her, because it was urgently necessary for her to indulge in her sensations, and to find answers to certain questions. Had this man who was not a fanatical feminist come up to her solely from an abstract sense of fairness? If another than Violet Powler had been head-housekeeper would he have spent the evening in trying to get hold of that other, just in order to satisfy his desire to play fair? It was plain that he was pleased with her, that he thought rather well of her, that her work had earned his approval. She returned to her theory that the harsh curtness of tone at the beginning of the interview was affected in order to cover his self-consciousness--say his nervousness. He was capable of being very boy-like. She must buy a new frock for the supper; there was that new place in Shaftesbury Avenue that Mrs. Oulsnam had told her of.

The panjandrum leaned against the mantelpiece.

"Isn't it about time you had some pictures here?" he demanded, as it were casually.

Violet was ashamed of her bare walls with their oblong marks of vanished pictures that had belonged to her predecessors.

"It is," said she. "I've been intending to get some, but I've been so busy."

"We have some good etchings somewhere," said the panjandrum. "I'll give you a few. I mean they're the hotel's, but that needn't worry us. I'll ask Miss Cass where they are. I'll have them sent up to you. And I think these rooms of yours ought to be done up. I suppose visitors come in here sometimes to see you, don't they?"

His tone was still casual; he had started by grumbling at her; the constitution of the supper was a hotel matter; the furnishing of her rooms was another hotel matter. But Violet had not been talking about, nor listening to, any of these subjects. She was, without quite knowing it, in the groves of the isle of Cythera. Her eyes saw the groves of the isle; her vague shining smile confirmed her eyes. Her sensations frightened her to the point of speechlessness.

"Thank you," she said at last, coldly.

"Don't mention it," he said with the most casual negligence of manner.

Their hands wavered, hand approaching hand. She felt the pressure of his. She glanced shyly up at his funny, kindly face. Her hand was limp. But she thought: "If he presses mine it's only right for me to press his." And she pressed it. And by the channel of their hands her whole body seemed to her to flow into his. He nodded. She smiled steadily. Not another word. He went.

She was alone. She had meant to think clearly as soon as she was alone. But she could not think clearly, or think at all. She was too happy to think, and too profoundly unhappy to think. She obscurely realised that the man who had gone was set apart from all other men in her sight. The conception of his existence filled her mind until there was no room for anything else. But he was the panjandrum, the head and heart of the great Merger, the monarch of the hotel world. And she was a daughter of Renshaw Street. (An old story, though she did not identify it as an old story.) Still, he had been to see her in her own room. And their relations were, to her, idyllic.

She looked at the reproachful desk.

"Not to-night," she said to the desk. "To-morrow morning, early. I really couldn't to-night. Shall I even be able to take my things off and get into bed? I'm done in for ever. And I shall never have a moment's peace again." But she was saturated with a hardly tolerable bliss. Through the terrifying felicity shot the thought: "I must find time to go up to Shaftesbury Avenue--to-morrow. Something's bound to want altering, and you never know how long they'll take over it."

Chapter 72 QUEEN ANNE

One morning, nearly a week later, it happened to Evelyn while at breakfast under the care of Oldham, to perceive a small round hole prominently situated in the middle of his waistcoat. Oldham suffered, not because of the hole, which had been made by incandescent tobacco from a cigarette, and which even a more perfect valet than Oldham might have missed, but because Evelyn had slept ill (having youthfully lain awake thinking about the precise nature of his feelings towards Violet Powler). Oldham, who ought to have suffered in silence, committed the vain error of trying to defend himself by quite preposterous excuses. Evelyn had to change his suit, which involved changing his necktie, and he went downstairs to his office in a state of mind unworthy of a philosopher and a gentleman.

Nevertheless he hid his mood, as effectively as he could, from Miss Cass, until Miss Cass, confessing that she had omitted to obtain an order to view a certain Queen Anne house close to the hotel, gave her opinion that there was no hurry and that Mr. Orcham could just as well view the Queen Anne house on Saturday or even Monday. It was perhaps the 'even Monday' that broke the back of Evelyn's self-control. Miss Cass was icily requested to go forth and obtain the order to view from the agents, and not to return without it.

Miss Cass, who feared neither God nor Evelyn, answered icily:

"Yes, Mr. Orcham. I'll go at once. By the way, there's some trouble about that staff-supper."

"Never mind the staff-supper. Run off and get that orderto view."

"Certainly, Mr. Orcham," said the indomitable Miss Cass, continuing: "But several secretaries, especially Mr. Smiss's senior secretary, are complaining because they haven't been asked to join in, and Mr. Smiss thinks--"

"Will you oblige me very much by going instantly for that order to view? I really cannot be bothered with all these ridiculous jealousies when I'm as busy as I am now. You've been asked to the supper, and Miss Tilton has been asked, and Mr. Cousin has decided that no other secretaries shall be asked."

"Yes, Mr. Orcham. I only thought you'd like to know."

"Well, I don't like to know. It's not I who am giving the supper."

"Quite, Mr. Orcham." The frigid and inimical calmness of the woman's tone was a blighting commentary on the panjandrum's tone.

"I'm sick to death of all these women!" Evelyn exclaimed aloud when Miss Cass had triumphantly departed and he was alone with the morning's documents on his great desk. "Let 'em go to the devil!..That supper isn't beginning very auspiciously."

Then he dismissed the piffling matter from his thoughts, and turned to the charts of business at the Palace, which were still from old-established custom brought daily to his notice, though as head of the Orcham

Company he was now supposed to see them only weekly and as part of a more comprehensive tabular conspectus embracing the business of all the Orcham hotels. The fact was that his activities were still in transition. He was Managing Director of the vast Orcham Company, without, somehow, having ceased to be Managing Director of the old, smaller, dissolving Imperial Palace Company.

Largely if not exclusively as the result of unique indirect advertisement due to the flotation of the Orcham Company, business at the Palace had considerably increased, and business at the Majestic had increased a little also. Excellent! Very encouraging! But something had to be done to define with exactitude the panjandrum's actual position as between the Orcham group and the unit of the Palace within the group. And Evelyn himself was the only person to do it. And he was determined to do it. After all, was he not the supreme and unchallengeable autocrat? Of course there was the Orcham Board of Directors; but he was used to imposing his will on Boards. Hence the idea of the Queen Anne house whose back-garden abutted on Birdcage Walk. The Orcham Company must clearly have offices of its own. It clearly could not continue for ever to watch over and direct the careers of nine important hotels in a scattered makeshift lot of rooms in the Imperial Palace. The notion was grotesque.

Only on the previous day had Evelyn heard of the beautiful spacious mansion to let on long lease within a hundred yards or so of the Palace. He had beheld its exteriors, and had immediately decided, with all the impulsiveness of a creative artist, that that building and no other would suit the purposes of the Orcham Company. Damn it! A company with a capital of more than five millions was entitled to be housed in dignity. So ran his grandiose thoughts.

At this juncture the door of his private room opened, and Sir Henry Savott imperiously walked in, unannounced. Outrage! Who did the fellow think he was? What would he have said if Evelyn had stamped into *his* private office unannounced? Of course the invasion was one consequence of Miss Cass's absence on a job which she had inexcusably forgotten to execute yesterday. Her subaltern could not arrest the arrogant Sir Henry on his way. But Miss Cass would have arrested him. Yes, she would!

"Morning, Evelyn."

"Morning, Henry." Evelyn deceitfully smoothed his forehead and softened his voice. "Sit down. Glad to see you. What's up? How are the talkies?"

"Talkies are going some," answered Sir Henry, in a voice to indicate that naturally the talkies were going some and that even to ask about their welfare was to cast a slur. "I say. I've been seeing Smiss. He tells me you're thinking of taking new offices for Orcham." ('Orcham' was now Sir Henry's habitual abbreviation of the Orcham International Hotels Company Limited.)

"The idea has crossed my mind," said Evelyn, an ironical tinge in the colour of his tone. "I expect to submit a proposal at the next Board Meeting."

"Do you think it's quite necessary?"

"I certainly wouldn't dream of doing anything without submitting it to the Board," said Evelyn, naughtily misunderstanding the Titan.

"I mean, to take special offices," Sir Henry explained with impatience. Evelyn tranquillised himself, as always when an opponent began to show excitement.

"How else do you expect Orcham is to carry on business?" he enquired, in a drawl.

"Well, in a big place like the Palace I should have thought you might have found room--"

"Just listen to me, my dear Henry. The Palace is big because it's doing a big business. And it isn't too big for its business. And a big place isn't any more elastic than a little place. If you can't pour a quart into a pint pot, it's just as true that you can't pour fifteen hundred gallons into a thousand-gallon cistern. Even as it is, the Palace is being very seriously cramped by Orcham work. Why should the Palace be inconvenienced for the advantage of all the other hotels in the group? I don't know of any other business that's run without offices. Proper offices make for efficiency--or ought to."

"I was thinking of the expense. Someone has to think of it," said Sir Henry, not without resentment.

"Quite, my dear chap!" Evelyn answered soothingly. "And I'm much obliged for the hint. But I'm doing a certain amount of cerebration over the expense myself. That's part of my job. Only I feel sure you'll agree with my maxim that one can't have something for nothing. The Orcham staff isn't fully organised yet: the sooner it's organised the better, and it can't be organised until definite offices are organised. Anyhow the decisions will be with the Board. Have a cigar, old man." Evelyn was perfectly at ease, because he was well aware that he had a majority of the working Board in his pocket.

"Not now, thanks, Evelyn. I'm in a hurry. I just looked in--that's all." Sir Henry refused with slight vexation.

Evelyn did not know that the Titan had been embroiled in intimate dissensions with the beautiful and stylish Nancy Penkethman, and was not satisfactorily himself.

"Well, thanks very much." Evelyn gave him God-speed. "I shall bear in mind what you say. *Au revoir."*

Sir Henry departed.

Evelyn reflected:

"He's gone off with a flick in his ear. If anybody thinks I'm not the real Simon Pure boss of this show, he's wrong. And I don't care who he is."

The panjandrum forced himself to work. After something like half an hour Miss Cass's assistant--not Miss Cass--came in with the order to view and the keys of the Queen Anne house. Evidently Miss Cass was indicating to her employer who she was.

"Oh! Here they are at last!" said Evelyn mildly to the girl. He put on his hat and picked up his stick and twirled the same in an airy manner.

"You'd better come over with me," he said curtly to Miss Cass in her office.

Miss Cass was affecting to be monstrously busy. She infinitesimally tossed her head. But she obeyed the order. She left her hat behind, however, and Evelyn had the experience of accompanying a hatless girl in Birdcage Walk and in an April wind. (You could never get the better of them.) Fortunately the distance was very short.

"There surely ought to be a caretaker here," observed Evelyn, after they had contrived between them to open the front door of the mansion.

"It's Crown property," Miss Cass retorted.

Evelyn led the way into the first room.

"Excuse me, Mr. Orcham. But you told me that Report on the Escurial must be finished in triplicate by twelve o'clock."

She might have made this unemotional announcement in the office. But she had delayed it in order to serve him right. Evelyn had forgotten. He thought with exceeding rapidity.

"Very well, go and get it done. And see you have fresh carbons. Send--er--Miss Powler to me, and ask her to bring a tape-measure with her. I must have someone. And she may be more useful than you."

Either Miss Cass or the April wind banged the front door. At the end of five minutes, when Evelyn had made a complete tour of the mansion and left one cigarette to expire on the marble staircase, he began seriously to expect the arrival of his head-housekeeper. At the end of another five minutes a new grievance had taken possession of him. Surely it could not take her nearly a quarter of an hour (his grievance had turned ten minutes into nearly a quarter of an hour) to run across from the hotel. Nothing had gone well with him that morning. First the gross negligence of the ass Oldham. Then Miss Cass, in one of her moods of severity. Then Henry Savott with his interfering impudence. Then Miss Cass in a still severer mood, but of course as usual exasperatingly correct in her stiffness. And now his ideal head-housekeeper dallying! The mansion, too, had a damp chill in its unoccupied air, and Evelyn was without overcoat. He lit a third cigarette. He had peered into every corner of the mansion, and now could only stare through the windows of the main drawing-room, and fidget and fume. If the telephone had not been removed he might have passed the time in worrying the hotel by captious enquiries. But in the absence of the telephone he must either resign himself to tedium or go back to the Palace and demand caustically whether all the members of the directorial staff thought perchance that he had nothing on earth to do but kick his heels in a cold and empty house. Such was his philosophic condition.

2.

Then a taxi drove into Old Queen Street, on which the drawing-room fronted, and his head-housekeeper descended from the taxi. She seemed a bit hurried and breathless, and (said Evelyn to himself) well she might be! He went cautiously down the slippery marble stairs to open the door for her.

"I was at the Duncannon," she greeted him.

That she might be at the Duncannon had not entered his tired, harassed head.

"Can you pay the taxi?" she asked. "I came away without my bag."

At any rate she was properly dressed for the street--not like Miss Cass.

"Certainly," he answered, and crossed the pavement and paid her taxi. Strange that women never had the price of a taxi-fare. They were all the same. They would forget their bags. It was not as if she would be expected to pay the taxi out of her own money; she would have charged it to petty cash. But there you were! He was paying her taxi, just as though he had invited her to lunch or something!

He said in a colourless business voice, as soon as they were secure within the mansion:

"I wanted you to look over this place from the practical point of view and tell me what you think of it." He might have added that the notion of sending for her had only occurred to him when Miss Cass became restive and unanswerable. But he refrained from his explanation. To have betrayed that he had acted impulsively would have been unwise. The meeting was to be purely technical, official; therefore it had been planned.

He described to her the use to which he proposed to put the place. She said 'Yes' and 'Yes.' They started their visitation with the basement, for the reason that it was scientific to start with the basement.

Violet, although she had wasted not a minute in obeying the summons, had not hurried herself, nor was she breathless, nor had she forgotten her bag through any haste. She had forgotten her bag because the sudden summons had put her into an emotional turmoil. Since the Sunday night *tête-à-tête* she had seen Evelyn but once, and for a few moments and by chance. Each day she had wakened with the hope and with the fear that she would encounter him, and each night (save one) she had gone to bed disappointed and relieved that she had not encountered him. Each hour of each day she had been happy and she had been unhappy. She had blamed herself and she had held herself innocent. She had interpreted his demeanour towards her in a dozen mutually quite contradictory ways. The summons to join him at the Queen Anne house was like a thunderclap in her ear at the telephone-receiver. It had the intensity of violent drama.

She had hoped and she had feared that others would be present in the house in Little Queen Street. Nobody else was present, and she was delighted and she was frightened--equally. No! More delighted than frightened. No! More frightened than delighted. She studied every inflection of his voice as he spoke. But he said nothing that was not banal, and she could read no significance whatever in his tones. Except that his nerves were in a sensitive state. She divined positively that something had happened to vex him.

She thought:

"I ought to soothe him; he needs soothing. I know I can soothe him, because I've done it before." Yet how should she soothe him? To soothe, one must be calm oneself, one must be in full possession of oneself. And she was not calm nor self-possessed.

Their voices uttering banalities resounded and reverberated as the pair ascended the broad, marmoreal stairs. Their voices hit the hard walls and were flung back. Now they were on the first floor. A vast drawing-room at the front, a smaller but still large drawing-room giving on Birdcage Walk and the Park, with the Palace obstructing a considerable section of the view. Large folding-doors between the two saloons.

"Just look at that ceiling!" said Evelyn enthusiastically in the front room.

"Yes," she said. "Beautiful." She was thinking: "But you couldn't always be craning your neck to look at a ceiling, however beautiful it was."

"This would be the Board Room," said Evelyn.

"Yes?" she queried. "What about the double doors? Anyone in the back room would hear everything you were saying at the Board meetings."

"Oh no!" he protested. "Besides, we could do away with those things and continue the wall all across. Quite simple. Lovely fireplaces, aren't they?"

"Lovely," she agreed. "But they'd never warm these rooms enough in winter. I don't know how people managed in these old houses in winter. They must have been starved to death sometimes."

"Well," he said impatiently, "we could soon fix that. Central heating. Of course. Or electric radiators."

"There aren't enough switches. You'd have to re-wire it all."

She really did desire to soothe him, humour him, yield to him. But what could she say? She had to be honest. Although she tried to soften her tone she somehow could not soften it sufficiently. Nervousness. Self-consciousness. Withal, there was one heavenly advantage. They were all alone together in the immense mansion. Wander as they pleased, they would be in privacy. Which was pleasant, even delicious, thrilling to her. And if she vexed him it would still be thrilling.

"Obviously a lot of re-wiring would have to be done," said Evelyn stiffly. What the deuce was the matter with the girl, with everybody? She seemed determined not to be pleased. She was not genuinely pleased even with the marvellous ceilings. She was in a queer mood. He regretted having sent for her. Still, he would have regretted not having sent for her. So it was as broad as it was long. No luck! But if she kept on with her carping he would tick her off. He would rather enjoy ticking her off, for the fun of seeing her hot and upset. Exciting, to see her upset. Something fine came out that you'd never see otherwise. And they were all alone together. They were free, beyond the rule of social laws and usages.

"Well," he said, sinisterly, "we'll go a bit higher." And they climbed to the next storey.

"I thought I might live myself on this floor," he said; but he felt as he spoke that he was very daring. "There's a splendid bathroom. Come and see it...How's that for a bathroom?"

"But the kitchen's in the basement," she objected, amazed at his scheme. "And the service-stairs are frightfully narrow and twisty."

"Oh!" Staccato. Yes, he was annoyed. He was allowing himself to be annoyed. "Where's your tape-measure?"

"Tape-measure? I haven't got one."

"I told Miss Cass to tell you to bring one."

"I'm sorry. I didn't hear anything about any tape-measure."

A pause.

"Well, we may as well see the top floor." Tone weary and disgusted.

On the top floor were apparently numberless small rooms.

"These would make excellent offices," Evelyn said with brightness.

"But you'll want a room for Oldham. To say nothing of a caretaker and a cook and a maid."

"Now look here!" he addressed her harshly, defiantly. "I've got you here to have your opinion. Well, let me have it, straight out. I don't want all these 'buts.' You've said nothing but 'buts' up to now. Say something positive. You simply don't like the house."

He would break down her guard. And he didn't give a damn. They'd had one row, and if she couldn't behave decently, show some sympathy, be less cursedly stiff, she'd be letting herself in for another row. She was as bad as Miss Cass. He admitted that his character had changed since the adventure with Gracie. Never mind. He was sick of all women.

"Yes, I do *like* the house," said Violet, in darkest despair. wondering how she might have avoided this imminent catastrophe. "But it isn't *offices.* It would be as if you were trying to make a thing do--for something else. If I was in your place and I wanted offices I should *build* offices. And fancy the kitchen in the basement and you living up here! And *I* don't think it'd be a good thing for you to live where you work. I know you *do,* at the Palace--but--but--" She gave it up. Disaster was upon her and she was helpless. There he stood in front of her on the landing in the great bare, empty, echoing house--there he stood as hard and stony as Satan.

Evelyn was touched by her solicitude for his welfare. Which solicitude, however, struck him as rather comical. What could she know about what was good and what was bad for a mature single man? He was at least fifteen years her senior, and she was treating him as an inexperienced youth without sense. He was touched, too, by the mysterious emergence of the girl in her; not the protesting girl, but the weak, perplexed, defenceless creature, this time. Not efficient, not 'commonsensical.' Her embarrassment brought out her beauty and gave a strange glistening transparency to her brown eyes...Dressed primly in black. But the black was romantic; it suited her and the moment. He felt all his steely armour melting. "What am I going to do next?" he asked his soul, and then abandoned himself.

"'But'--'but'--'but,'" he quoted her, in a gentle, teasing, yet tremulous, voice. "You *are* a dear!"

And he advanced two steps, smiling and masterful, smiling at her delicious but comical solicitude, and just kissed her. Instead of resisting him with all her sturdy maidenliness, she began softly to cry.

None could say whether he or she was the more astounded by this remarkable example of emotional instability in the male.

Chapter 73 THE SUPPER

On Sunday nights both the restaurant and the grill-room closed, theoretically, at midnight. The restaurant in fact did close at midnight, because the restaurant had its orchestra, and the orchestra played "God Save the King" on the stroke of the hour, and though the National Anthem may mean different things at different times, people always know exactly what it does mean and they obey it exactly. The patrons of the grill-room, having no Nunc Dimittis to scatter them, were sent away home only by their consciences and the significant demeanour and activities of the waiters; and some of them had been known to stay as late as one o'clock. Neither Cappone nor Ceria appeared in his realm on Sunday nights. On this particular Sunday night, however, Ceria in a black tie surprisingly did appear in the grill-room at a quarter to twelve, the reason being that he had arrived too early at the hotel, and having nothing better to do, thought it well to give a glance at the directive attitudes of his lieutenant, Mr. Fontenay. He came, smiled, and vanished.

Still more surprisingly the panjandrum himself came into the grill-room for a moment, smiled diffidently, and vanished. Similarly he honoured the restaurant for a moment. The reason for this singular performance on the part of the panjandrum was merely that he did not know what he was doing. The hands of his watch would not move, and he had to do something.

There were three very nervous individuals in the Palace at a quarter to twelve: Amadeo Ruffo, the Banqueting-manager, who had charge of the great staff-supper and who knew that his arrangements would be subjected to the criticism, silent but ruthless, of sundry supreme experts; Violet Marian Powler; and Evelyn Orcham.

Evelyn and Violet shared a unique secret, and it really was a secret--by the decision of Violet. Violet simply could not contemplate the announcement of the betrothal in marriage of the Managing Director of the Orcham Company and the head-housekeeper of the Imperial Palace. The event was too enormous, too upheaving. It would have had the effect of an earthquake in the Palace. The staff might have swooned and visitors been shaken out of their beds. How could she go about her housekeeping work as the acknowledged fiancée of the panjandrum? She could not. She would have blushed through a quarter of an inch of powder, and all her underlings would have behaved to her as unnaturally as she to them. The excellent Beatrice Noakes would have been completely intolerable. Hence Violet's decree.

Evelyn had smiled masculinely at the decree. He had told her that she was childish, or at best school-girlish. He had teased her to death. He had attacked her position with unanswerable arguments. But he was glad to fall in taking it; for in reality he thought as she did, and shared all her trepidations. Of course one day the secret must cease to be a secret. When? How soon?

She had said:

"Not yet, not yet. We'll see."

In other respects Violet showed admirable sense and dignity. In her bearing towards Evelyn she was a woman with a man. She did not look up to him, or no more than any woman except a reigning princess or a film-star would look up to her betrothed. Her engagement was not more wonderful to her than any engagement is to the woman engaged. She did not regard herself as the favoured of heaven, nor Evelyn as a silver Lohengrin disembarking from a swan-drawn boat. She was just Violet, and Evelyn was just Evelyn (though the perfect man).

As for Evelyn, he had admired her deportment intensely during the tremendous nine days. It had convinced him, if he needed convincing--and every man in his circumstances does--that he was making no mistake. They had seen each other only twice in the tremendous nine days. How should they see each other? Could he run upstairs to her room when they had a couple of minutes of leisure and kiss her and ask her how she was getting on? They both lived in the most transparent glass-house that ever was. True, they wrote to one another--Evelyn had not the slightest difficulty in composing his letters--but surreptitiously and by means of the post. Evelyn used a disguised hand on his envelopes and slipped them into the pillar-box at the end of Birdcage Walk in Storey's Gate. Violet dropped hers into the letter-shoot flap on Eighth when no one was looking.

The first occasion of their meeting was in Victoria Street on a dark Sunday evening. A woman in a taxi stopped the vehicle at a certain lamp-post. A man who had obviously been waiting jumped in. A plot, sinister, suspicious! The driver had his ideas about the pair. The driver had never before heard of Renshaw Street, and when he at length discovered the street it seemed to him precisely the kind of street where anarchistic conspiracies or even burglaries and assassinations might well be hatched. Also he misinterpreted the munificence of his tip. It was Evelyn who had suggested the trip to Renshaw Street. Violet did not warn her parents. Her father had opened the door. Violet had said: "Oh, dad, this is Mr. Orcham," as casually as if Evelyn had been Mr. Smith from next door hut one. Her father and mother--but especially her father--had received the news with a praiseworthy imitation of calm. And in fact they were not minded to be overcome. After all, Violet was Violet, and they had always known that she stood in a class absolutely by herself. Witness her rise in the hierarchy of the fabled sumptuous Palace. They gave their consent and blessing to the pair. And they were much relieved at the departure of the pair. So was Violet. Odious little snob, she had had social qualms about the introduction of the panjandrum to the humilities of her home and the lowermiddle-class manners of her parents! Evelyn had conducted himself like the angel he was. They had refused supper, but Evelyn had eagerly joined the old man in a bottle of beer.

On the journey to Shepherds Bush Evelyn had tactfully, and with exaggeration, recounted to Violet the simplicity of his own early days.

Shepherds Bush does not lie between Renshaw Street and Birdcage Walk; but such was the route they chose. At Shepherds Bush Evelyn paid off the taxi; they walked arm-in-arm amid the crowd emptying from the big cinema; and then Evelyn called another taxi. Which taxi did not draw up under the marquise of the Imperial Palace; nor did the twain re-enter the Palace by the same door nor at the same moment. It was all superbly exciting, and had the piquant air of an immoral intrigue.

The second occasion of their meeting had been at the Duncannon on the evening of the following Wednesday--Pozzi's night off. Evelyn, carrying a bundle of documents, had been at his curtest with the Duncannon hall-porter: "I suppose Miss Powler isn't here, by any chance?..Oh, she is! Well, tell her to come down and see me in Mr. Pozzi's room at once. And to bring those charts that she was showing me this morning at the Palace. She'll know which I mean. At once." The hall-porter had concluded that Miss Powler was in trouble with the panjandrum. Miss Powler did know the charts that the panjandrum meant. The study of them lasted about an hour and a half and Miss Powler had emerged therefrom in a somewhat nervous and ruffled condition. So much so that she had departed immediately home to the Palace, whereas the panjandrum had remained to work in Pozzi's room till after midnight. Since the second occasion--nothing but a chance public encounter, and exchanges of letters. An insufficient diet.

And now Evelyn was waiting for midnight and the ordeal of the sight of her at the grand staff-supper, and having fluttered into the grill-room and out again, and into the restaurant and out again, he decided to walk upstairs, because watches and clocks were still moveless. Not to walk up to Eighth. No! It was not for him to wander into Violet's sitting-room and have a private view of her new frock from Shaftesbury Avenue! He went no higher than Seventh, where he stuck totally and foolishly inactive in his castle, and then walked down again, floor by floor, from corridor to dimly lit corridor, staring at the blank faces of the doors of uncounted temporary homes inhabited by persons who probably had their own estimates of the importance and unimportance and bliss and misery of love in human life.

He stood in the foyer. Guests were now leaving in a thin steady stream. He glimpsed the restaurant, and saw that it was nearly deserted. The orchestra began to play "God Save the King." Midnight, by God! He was due at the supper. The hands of watches did move.

2.

The Queen Anne room, the largest of the private dining-rooms at the Palace, was panelled in unpolished wood in what a celebrated decorative artist stated to be the Queen Anne style. Its lighting, however, brilliant and yet delicately soft, had none of the characteristics of the antique. Indeed the lighting was so modern that, going beyond the present, it foretold the future. The Palace continually rejuvenated its interiors; and the Queen Anne had just been so treated.

The magnificently floral supper-table was narrow for its length. And with a purpose. Mr. Cousin, Mr. Ruffo, and Mr. Jones-Wyatt (the heads of the restaurant and the grill knew better than to poke their noses into any affair of the banqueting department) had been confronted with one of the most terrible problems that ever puzzled a majordomo: how to distribute four girls among a couple of dozen men without causing a riot of grievances. Mr. Immerson, who was responsible for the illustrated menu-cards, ultimately solved the problem and prepared the plan of the table. Mr. Cousin (in the Chair), with Evelyn on his right and Mr. Harbour on his left, sat in the middle of one side of the board. Opposite Mr. Cousin sat Mr. Stairforth (Stock Department) and Lord Watlington, flanked by Mrs. Oulsnam and Miss Marian Tilton. The graver young women, Miss Cass and Violet, were each next but one to opposite ends of the table, on the same side as the Chair. By this masterpiece of ingenuity, no girl had to waste herself on a girl opposite, and every man was at worst either within one man of a girl on his own side or had a girl opposite or nearly opposite to whom he could talk or listen or on whom he could gaze: the Chair and its supporters had the pick of the chatterers; but no girl was monopolised by Directors to the detriment of the staff, each girl having a Director on one hand and a member of the staff on the other. Cappone sat at one end of the table and Ceria at the other, and Amadeo Ruffo next to Cappone facing Violet. Enough of the arrangement of seating; the beauty of its skilfulness could not be fully set forth in five pages.

The men wore dinner-jackets, symbol of informality, and a unique sight was seen: Maître Planquet and the Commendatore Rocco, not in white with white caps, but in evening dress. All the girls had new frocks. Everybody had foreseen that the dashing Marian Tilton would be the smartest and daringest of the four; she was. Mrs. Oulsnam made a radiant close second. Miss Cass and Violet, while smart, were less dashingly effective.

Mr. Ruffo was the last to sit down. He lowered himself into a chair with the mien of one committing himself to the deep and trusting in God. He had done everything possible to ensure for the feast an unparalleled perfection, and he could do no more. He at once began talking to Violet. Mr. Stairforth and Marian Tilton could utter more words in less time than Ruffo; but at intervals they paused to take breath. Mr. Ruffo, talking slowly, could breathe while he talked, and be never paused, save occasionally from Italian politeness.

Talking, he surveyed his *chefs de rang* and his waiters: all was in order. Caviare on miniature crumpets, and vodka. Abstinence was contrary to the code. All had to drink the vodka. Mr. Ruffo had a calm, sure belief in the virtue of vodka on an empty stomach as an inspirer of gay backchat and broad-minded conviviality. The vodka was the best in London, and had run into money, for Ruffo had not boggled at expense. The bill for a similar supper to mere visitors would have sufficed to buy a small hotel in the country. But Ruffo had received instructions from Mr. Cousin that everything was to be charged at bare cost, so that all the staff, proud girls included, could pay their scot without inconvenience. This generous precaution on the part of the Palace authorities proved to be otiose, for the next day Mr. Harbour got hold of Ruffo, and discharged the entire liability out of his privy purse. A final gesture. On the following Wednesday the cigarette-king was to rejoin Mrs. Harbour at Cherbourg.

The waiters were watchful and rapid as if for their lives; the sub-chefs and lower cooks in Maître Planquet's kitchens were even more assiduous than if the master's eye had been upon them; and through the partially opened sliding partition dividing the Queen Anne room from the Queen Victoria room next door, a diminutive orchestra sent music dreamy and low, accompanying and not drowning the conversation. All these people, from first violin to dishwasher, laboured as joyously as though they were present at the eating itself of the supper. And above, floor after floor of visitors, unaware of the romantic affair below, prosaically and ignorantly slept.

"Monsieur le Directeur, j'ai l'honneur de boire à votre santé." The gruff booming voice of Commendatore Rocco suddenly dominated the table, silencing all conversation. The Commendatore raised his glass of hock, bowed and drank; and Evelyn ceremoniously responded. Trust Rocco to impose himself! He had got ahead of his rival, Maître Planquet.

Evelyn, only a moment ago a nervous wanderer over the carpeted furlongs of the Palace, was now the super-panjandrum. He hated it; but he had to be, and he succeeded in being, the super-panjandrum, the mighty guest, mightier than three millionaires. He could act, and he was helped by the accident that he was not able to catch Violet's eye, nor she his. Had their eyes met the result would have been to humble them both into a bottomless deep of self-consciousness. He teased Mrs. Oulsnam and Marian Tilton.

Both girls were a shining success. They did in truth grace the feast, which would not have been half so festive without them. See on the table in the midst of the flowers the handbag of Mrs. Oulsnam, the handbag of Marian Tilton, the cloisonné cigarette-case of Mrs. Oulsnam, the gold cigarette-case of Marian Tilton! These matters changed the aspect of the board. See Marian Tilton using her lipstick and showing her teeth, while dangerously flirting with Lord Watlington (who was a bit jealous of Evelyn's teasing)!

The effect on male spirits was irresistible. Pan and Bacchus were abroad in the Queen Anne room. The cigarette-king emitted jolly expletives in the American language. And Evelyn was moved to oblivious mirth. He had been counting the courses: "That's one finished." "That's two." "That's three." In his longing for the end of the ordeal--he missed the passage of one course; and was the more pleased when he discovered this carelessness...

Coffee, cigars, cigarettes, liqueurs, repletion. Mr. Ruffo gave a subtle sign and the staff of waiters faded away.

"Ladies and gentlemen," said Mr. Cousin, rising. "There will be no speeches. You ought to applaud that." (Uncertain laughter.) "But I give you the health of our guest." The revellers stood up. The health was drunk. The revellers sat down.

"Ladies and gentlemen," said Evelyn, rising to applause whose formidable and prolonged uproar of appreciation frightened him; many seconds which were hours elapsed before he could continue, his voice shaking a little: "I thank you. I'm not going to forget this supper. Before I sit down I want to propose the health of our Chairman, Mr. Dennis Dover, who would have liked to be here, but isn't well enough to join us. The health of Mr. Dennis Dover." Very loud applause, during which Evelyn sat down as relieved as a man who has had an aching tooth out.

"C'était chic, ça!" Mr. Cousin murmured to him.

Now Mr. Jones-Wyatt had his moment of glory. Saying not a word to anyone, he had arranged for the appearance of the cabaret performers in new turns--turns not shown in the restaurant: a lady-conjurer, and a French imitator who could imitate a crease in a rug or a woman silently wondering what shoes would best match her frock, or anything like that. These turns were more applauded than enjoyed. Bacchus and the wraith of Venus diverted from them the attention which they merited. Then the music resumed, and the sliding partition was opened wide into the Queen Victoria room, which had been cleared for dancing.

3.

"You will dance," Mr. Cousin enjoined Evelyn.

"Oh, hang it! Well, if I must." He knew that he must. "Who ought I to dance with first?"

"Miss Powler of course, *mon cher.* She is the most important. *Les autres--ça ne compte pas.*"

Mr. Cousin was wrong there. The others did count. Voices had been heard against the inclusion of secretaries. But both secretaries, like Mrs. Oulsnam, had indeed definitely triumphed; even Miss Cass--to-night the mirror of sweet softness--had had her triumph. Not merely was every man present fully aware of the real importance of these secretarial girls, of their secret influence and power in the politics of the hotels; but they were girls among a couple of score men, rare, courted, flattered, splendid. None of the usual competition of girls for men! The boot was spectacularly on the other leg this evening. All, girls and men, agreed that the evening was simply terrific--and it was not yet by any means over!

On the parquet of the Queen Victoria room there were only four couples, because there were only four girls in the party. But they fairly well filled the floor. Everything had been thought of. By a palisade of chairs the space for dancing was limited to suit the maximum number of dancers. Beyond the palisade were tables equipped for bridge, and one table labelled in large letters: "Maniglia"--a compliment to the Commendatore Rocco. Lord Watlington had seized Miss Marian Tilton and was swirling around with her; Sir Henry Savott was vitalising Miss Cass; Mrs. Oulsnam was vitalising Mr. Cousin; and Evelyn held Violet, it being right, proper, expected, and unavoidable that the panjandrum should open the dancing with the head-housekeeper.

Those two were alone together in the Queen Victoria room. They spoke low, and none could overhear them; besides, the other three couples were absorbed in themselves.

"I felt awful while I was on my legs waiting for the acclamations to stop," said Evelyn, who had been profoundly impressed, and was still preoccupied, by the reception of the toast of his health. The furious outburst and din had done more than anything else ever did do to persuade him that after all he was somebody of some importance in the world. And now he wanted to hear a word or two from Violet on the subject.

"You looked so sweet I could scarcely bear to look at you. If it had gone on any longer I should have had to cry," she said, murmuringly, and not glancing at him. The reply, which be could not in the least have predicted, entranced him: that is to say, it put him into a trance. His right hand on her back, his left hand in her right, he could feel Violet's emotion. Her sober tones were charged with emotion. He just danced.

"Fine little orchestra, Evelyn!" Sir Henry threw at him in passing. He nodded and smiled in his trance.

So that was how he had struck her in his ordeal! Well, her reaction was the ideal reaction. It seemed to him to typify their future existence together. She the efficient, resourceful, hard-working housekeeper, so moved by the sight of him in his ordeal that she nearly burst into tears! Not that she ever would have burst into tears: he knew that: in any circumstances she would be mistress of herself. He had a sense of all the faculties, capabilities, reserves of strength within that new bright blue frock. And she was his, and the fact that she was his was the most marvellous and incredible thing on earth, past, present or to come. And yet it was not incredible--it was quite natural. He knew his worth as well as he knew hers. He knew he could give as richly as he received. She could rely on him. And she would always be there for him to rely on. And she was so excitingly and so subtly feminine. She radiated femininity, and her femininity was, for him, her most important attribute. She was far more feminine than those terrific flirts, Marian Tilton and Mrs. Oulsnam, who were charmingly exploiting what superficial femininity they had the whole time. She was more feminine, and more dangerously feminine, than the siren Gracie. What responsive sensibility and what wise understanding and what mother-wit she would display on the honeymoon! He would be able to set out on that delicate enterprise with a mind at ease. He recalled the trials of his first honeymoon.

"Tell me what you're thinking about, my dear," he whispered under the shelter of the music, slightly squeezing her hand.

Violet was thinking that this protective male who held her and guided her about the floor was a great man, really great, far greater than the assembled millionaires, and that he was a child who needed protection, and that she could give the protection and would, and that he was immeasurably her superior in everything except daily commonsense, and that she was intolerably in love with him, intolerably happy, and that things always did work out right in the end, and that she wanted to dance with him till she dropped, and that she wanted to leave the publicity of the dance and the noise and the chatter and go upstairs by herself and think and think and think about him and her bliss. She said:

"I had an awful thought that all these sharp-eyes here are bound to guess there's something between us two."

He pooh-poohed the notion, while admitting to himself that it might have some basis.

"And what if they do? There *is!*" he said, defiantly.

From that moment, however, both of them suffered under the delusion that the entire company was looking at them in a rather peculiar way.

The music paused. But they might not dance the next dance. No couple on the floor might dance the next dance. Justice reigned. At least sixteen men had to dance with four girls; and as regards the panjandrum, having danced with Violet he was compelled by the fundamental laws which hold society together to dance with Miss Cass, Mrs. Oulsnam, and Miss Tilton. And as regards the two latter, each of them was determined so to manœuvre as to be in a position to boast on the morrow and for the rest of her life that she had danced with three millionaires; but the cigarette-king did not dance. The millionairedom of Sir Henry Savott was doubtful, but not on that night.

After a very long period, during which the four girls performed miracles of joyous endurance, the pardonable thirst of the orchestra brought about an interval, and everyone sat down. There were two bridge-tables in action, and at another table the Commendatore was playing manila with Ceria and a few more. The relations between the Grill-chef and the Grill-manager were now as smooth as a pane of glass.

Mr. Harbour, Evelyn, Sir Henry, and Mr. Immerson were discussing, not too seriously, a new project for an office-building with two frontages and two entrances, one for the offices of the cigarette-king's new European headquarters, and the other for the offices of the Orcham International Hotels Company Limited. Mr. Harbour had mentioned his scheme for the complete exploitation of Europe, and Evelyn had suggested a joint building--of which the cigarette-king would take about eighty per cent. of the space. Mr. Harbour talked in fabulous numbers of dollars. In all his existence he had had one idea--for the treatment of tobacco, and he had never loosed it and never had another idea and never would have another idea. His idea had put him second or third in the majestic catalogue of American millionaires. He had swollen his idea to the extent of twenty million cigarettes a day in the United States, and his ambition was to sell a minimum of ten million cigarettes a day in Europe. And his share in Orcham was a trifle to him, and he was calmly prepared to come down with a million dollars for an office building which would make London stare. But otherwise he was an ordinary decent fellow, and never said anything, save in figures, that you couldn't forget in five minutes.

Violet, having quitted the whirlwind Stairforth, approached the table vaguely.

"Do sit here with us," said Evelyn impulsively. All the men rose. Immerson discreetly departed, and Violet took his place.

"It's a lovely party, Miss Powler," said Mr. Harbour in the way of small-talk.

"You must have some champagne," said Sir Henry. "Here, waiter."

The waiters had reappeared, and were generously dispensing drinks.

"I really couldn't, Sir Henry."

"Oh, but you must," he insisted. "This evening is an occasion. Champagne won't do you any harm. As an indulgence it will do you good. It's only when it becomes a habit that it harms you."

Violet glanced at Evelyn for help, received none, and sipped at champagne poured out by Sir Henry himself.

"I hear you've read my daughter's book," said Sir Henry. "And like it. I'm glad. But I should have left out bits here and there if I'd been consulted. Only I wasn't. These modern daughters are very secretive, Miss Powler. However, now she's married and going to have a baby I suppose it doesn't matter how modem the book is." And thus he went on.

Lord Watlington came to the table.

"Good night, Evelyn. Good night, everybody. I'm off. Just had a telephone message." He grinned, and in ten seconds was gone. He was the first to leave. He knew how to leave a party.

When the orchestra returned, Sir Henry asked Violet for another dance.

"You're the finest dancer in this room," said he. "And I'm not flattering you."

Violet shook her head. But she probably was the finest dancer in the room, thanks to her stage study and experience in connection with the Laundry Amateur Dramatic Society. She would not dance; said she really must go to bed. The example of Lord Watlington had encouraged her resolve. Sir Henry, realising that he would fail to cajole her, instantly resumed the subject of the office-building with Mr. Harbour.

"I must go," Violet repeated to Evelyn.

"You're very tired," he agreed. And added gallantly: "I'll see you to the lift."

Mr. Harbour shook Violet's hand with warmth, and Sir Henry absent-mindedly.

4.

The corridor of the private dining-room was empty and dim and miles long.

"Who put them on to that office-building idea?" Violet asked.

"Well," said Evelyn. "So far as we're concerned, you did--via me."

She smiled weakly.

"Yes!" said Evelyn positively.

"Darling!" she said as they strolled up the corridor. "This really can't go on."

"What?"

"Our engagement being a secret. It's too trying, and it's certain to come out."

"I quite agree."

"But," Violet continued, "it hasn't got to come out while I'm here as head-housekeeper. I couldn't face it."

"Yes, you could," said Evelyn. "But you needn't. Why should you?"

"But what shall you do for someone to take my place?"

"I neither know nor care," Evelyn laughed grandly. "It's Cousin's affair, all that is. I'm not the manager of the Palace."

"Then as soon as I can I'll go back to Renshaw Street," said Violet.

"I've got a better plan than that," said Evelyn the great organiser.

He outlined his plan. He would disclose the secret to Cousin, who could be trusted to keep it, and trusted to make the necessary arrangements as to staff-appointments. The Orcham Company had several staffs to choose from, and a considerable list of applicants for minor posts which would fall vacant when their present occupants went up in the world. In less than a month he would be going to Paris, Rome, Madrid. They could be married at a registry office on the morning of his departure, and the trip should be their honeymoon.

"And," he said, "you could give me a lot of good advice about those hotels."

"Only when we're by ourselves," Violet said quickly. "I shouldn't be a housekeeper then, darling."

"No, of course not," he concurred. "Of course not."

Still, he was just the least bit surprised when he saw that she intended her future role to be solely that of wife. Then he saw that he was a simpleton to have been surprised. Even the most earnest of 'them' threw away their business careers for marriage, and without a pang! But what a career she would make of marriage! She was serious; she knew what work was. And he too. She was his sort; he hers. Gracie was not his sort and never would have been, because she was not serious and did not know what sustained work was. He had learnt one supreme lesson from the brief, violent affair with Gracie: namely, that Gracie was not his sort. Yes, Violet was indeed his sort, and as his mind flitted back over the history of their relations, he saw mystically that from the first he had been destined for her, and she for him.

"And when we come back to London?" she asked.

"Oh! We'll fix that later. Plenty of time. Heaps of time." The lift was up above. He rang for it. She suddenly kissed him with the abandonment of exhaustion, clung to him, clutched him, kissed him again. As if she were saying: "You are all I have in the world now! I haven't even myself now!"

He watched her ascend away from him in the lift. Marvellous sensations he had, as he returned slowly to the party in his honour. Heavenly girl; and so touching in her feminine fatigue! Was it for these ecstasies that he had climbed to his particular pinnacle? Was Violet, or the perfecting of luxury hotels throughout Europe, his life-work? If both, which was the more important? Were luxury hotels sociologically justifiable? He didn't know. He couldn't decide. He knew merely that he was going straight on. He said to himself: "There's a lot of things in this world you'll never get the hang of. And only idiots try to."

THE END

Printed in Great Britain
by Amazon